Sippican

Also by the author

The Mists of Manittoo
Torn Covenants
The Painter

Sippicon

LOIS SWANN

authorHOUSE®

AuthorHouse™
1663 Liberty Drive
Bloomington, IN 47403
www.authorhouse.com
Phone: 1 (800) 839-8640

© 2015 Lois Swann. All rights reserved.

No part of this book may be reproduced, stored in a retrieval system, or transmitted by any means without the written permission of the author.

This is a work of fiction. All of the characters, names, incidents, organizations, and dialogue in this novel are either the products of the author's imagination or are used fictitiously.

Published by AuthorHouse 07/30/2015

ISBN: 978-1-5049-1722-3 (sc)
ISBN: 978-1-5049-1725-4 (hc)
ISBN: 978-1-5049-1726-1 (e)

Library of Congress Control Number: 2015909454

Print information available on the last page.

Any people depicted in stock imagery provided by Thinkstock are models, and such images are being used for illustrative purposes only.
Certain stock imagery © Thinkstock.

This book is printed on acid-free paper.

Because of the dynamic nature of the Internet, any web addresses or links contained in this book may have changed since publication and may no longer be valid. The views expressed in this work are solely those of the author and do not necessarily reflect the views of the publisher, and the publisher hereby disclaims any responsibility for them.

For the First Nations of Massachusetts

You Endure

Acknowledgments

For the forty-two years of carrying in my heart the characters of *Sippicon* and those of its two preceding novels, *The Mists of Manittoo* and *Torn Covenants*, my family and friends have by their loyalty to my passion emboldened the course of my writing. Because of the blessing and sacrifices especially of my husband, Nicholas L. Eden, my parents, Peter and Edith Riso, late, my children, Peter B. Swann and Polly Swann May, my granddaughters, Margo Swann and Zoe Swann, and the late Robert Tolan Ph.D., and Stephanie S. Tolan, my heart and pen never wearied.

I expresss special gratitude to the late Howard B. Gotlieb founder of The Howard Gotlieb Archival and Research Center, Mugar Memorial Library, Boston University, for honoring the theme of the trilogy and his inclusion of my body of work in the collection and to his successor, Executive Director, Vita Paladino, for her sustaining interest and artful support.

I am indebted to Sonia Caus Gleason for her sensitive rendering of phrases in Italian that augmented the chapters set in Venice and to Alysa Iafrate for her patient and precise notation in the exquisite hour of perfecting the format of the novel.

Without the validating acceptance of my first novel by then chief editor of Charles Scribners Sons, Burroughs Mitchell, my work and my life would have been differently written.

After all, it is not given to many to start a nation.

Winston S. Churchill

A HISTORY OF THE ENGLISH SPEAKING PEOPLES, VOL. II, THE NEW WORLD

FOX

CHAPTER ONE

March 1749

He slipped out of the Massachuseuck hideout. Four days later he stood on the steps of a clapboard house perched above the roaring Atlantic.

He had bled on and off since his dream. His head ached all the time. He quaked in his light clothing, common trapper's clothes, which disguised who and what he was. He knocked. English manners came easily to him since his own more complex ones were the stuff of tribal survival. Grace made him welcome among the foreigners. He spoke their language better than most of them, and read, and, since his marriage to the New-English woman, he had added writing to his skills. As recently as the year before, his finesse and his influence among other tribes and among the traders allowed him the use of Boston's great homes as if they were his club. Right now all he wanted was a corner out of the wind. Wakwa, Silent Fox, as the English said, knocked a second time.

"Renard!" An immense, black-robed Frenchman opened and stuck his face out.

Wakwa dropped to his knees.

The Jesuit looked down the path for signs of companions or pursuers while his hands capped the Indian's head. Then the priest's beefy arms scooped Wakwa inside.

Wakwa gained balance almost smoothly, fighting a ripping of skin. Another man appeared in the hall and the two stood and stared.

The priest talked above their silence. "There was somezing in ze knock. Somezing that move me. And so, I come running like a gatekeeper before ze housemaid. So! Ze Fox is 'ere!"

The native man looked as long as a beam of moonlight and was as quiet. His flesh and bones, face and body, had been drawn by the elegant hand of a different god than the English knew. Wakwa watched the other man who spun down the vestibule at him like slow shot.

"Let me see," came the nasal voice of Dire Locke, agent for the great merchant house of V.T. Kirke, Ltd. He stepped in a semi-circle testing the lights in the Indian's eyes. "You're a man still. No one's taken that." Then with pique, "Fledgling sachim still. Clear as a bell. Clear as hell. For a man thirty-five you make a poor fifty. The sap seems frozen in you. I've had only silence from you for over a year. Some rascal robbed your tongue? You've got the look of a fast-stepping foot soldier. Have you been fighting? In what war? And then again, what war could you not win?"

Wakwa swallowed hard.

The spindly, dun-coated man looked the full foot upward to the Indian's face. The shadows made by its structure seemed deep and dark. Locke, quite his senior probed, "Fox?"

The visitor gingerly undid the lacing of his doeskin shirt. He dropped it to the runner of the hall. Against the papered walls, a disfigurement of his torso looked ugly, shocked more than in the woods. "I should have come to you long before this," Wakwa said. "May we talk somewhere?"

Dire Locke's left hand searched for the support of the hallway mantel. The calmness of the Indian's voice and the grossness of his wounds left Locke dumb.

It was the priest who wrapped his shoulder cape around the Massachuseuck with the naturalness of a mother covering her child from the rain. "Venez."

Without knowing the word, Wakwa went after the Jesuit into the heart of Thomas Kirke's Pemaquid house. The room they found was something like the hold of a ship, its greens and blacks darkly gleaming like wet wood, glittering like seaweed or slime or resin under the oil lights. It was the perfect place for confidences or confessions, a place to hatch plots, and Wakwa sat there gratefully.

He looked at Locke. Locke eyed him. The priest padding to and fro, a considerate bear, did quiet service bringing them little cups of black coffee.

Convulsing as his body warmed, Wakwa said, "I have been living in a cave, Dire."

"Whatever for?" Locke, a Welshman and an English Jew with no creed and little use for anybody but his Indians, his French Canadian wife who was now far away, and Thomas Kirke, listened from a hard square chair at perfect point to the room's darkest corner. He recrossed his legs, his bony fingers travelling the chair frame.

"We came to Agiocochook, or, as you would say, the White Mountains, before Nickommo. That was the worst feast time I have had to live through."

"Apparently. Are your stripes the new style in torsos among the Massachuseuck? I don't worry, though. Fashion is fickle. Next year they'll carve marks on you in a downward pattern and you'll have plaid."

"Dire...."

"What the hell are you doing to yourself?!"

"Four days ago I woke from a dream...."

"Should we be glad?"

"It was the pleasantest dream I remember since we came to Agiocochook."

"The White Mountains." Now, Locke knew how to be polite, to perform the verbal calisthenics pertinent to successful discussion with the natives. Yet, the younger man's victimized sincerity made Locke impatient, incautious, inconsiderate, and downright tart. "Don't tell me you were dreaming of a third wife. Looks like two are more than you can handle."

"How can I contemplate a third, wetomp, when I have but one wife left me?"

"Not Qunneke! Not in childbirth?"

"Dire, each woman is in fine health."

Locke twitched and sweated slightly. He wanted to wallop the man for letting himself get into some desperate condition.

"Dire, I woke from a dream so pleasant that I knew it was a day to draw blood."

"Obviously."

"This may seem strange to you."

"Not at all." Locke waved a bird claw of a hand in nonchalance. "Four open and bloody gashes across each of your sides look very smart."

"I woke from my dream. It was cold. I was shivering but between the rocks red flowers were blowing."

"On Agiocochook?" Locke broke in, giving the Indian some of his own medicine.

But Wakwa's honey voice proved unequal to some reminiscence. The brass clock ticked a minute away. Then - "I made a light for myself and went back into the cave to find my knife."

"The old obsidian?"

"None other!"

They savored it until Locke concluded, "One thing constant, praise Abraham, Isaac, and Jacob."

"I beheld a narrow thing slide across my foot."

"Eh?"

"I stepped backward and a muscle, one outside myself, free of any body, rose up the back of my leg."

"What?"

Wakwa's tiny cup rattled in its saucer. "I must have lain next to them the whole night. In the belly of the mountain. The cave had been clean in winter but spring had come without my seeing it, I am so distracted, and eggs must have been all about. I had been dreaming such pleasant dreams, all the while making warmth for nests of snakes' eggs. Caressed, perhaps, by the mother snake. Caressing her curling babies. Mayhap I broke open the shells as I slept."

"Stop! This is horrible! I will not watch you in this condition!"

"All night I had been feeling...she was there."

"She?"

"I stood among the snakes in the early morning watching them weave in an out, and I wondered why it is my life has become one of bursting open beds of serpents."

"Has it?"

"Dire! I let them take her."

"What are you talking about?"

"I gave her away. Gave her back."

"Back? Back! You gave back...? You don't mean the land heiress? Dowland's daughter? I can't believe it! What for? This was ideal love, I'd heard."

"I deserve everything you say to me."

"I say good riddance to her! I told you when it began it were no good for you. Never work. So much for the power of Eros. You are well shed, should be dancing in the streets not habitating caves!"

"Dire! I am a fugitive. An outlaw."

"No. No." Dire's nervous hands baffled the air in front of his face. "I won't hear it. I won't have it!"

"Dire!" The priest came out of the dark and claimed those hands. "Listen to him! He is telling you!"

Wakwa leaned toward them. "My journey from Sweetwood to the tribes near here two winters past, fourteen moons ago, but a year and two months before today, was laid bare before the court at Boston."

"No!" Dire and the Jesuit rejected it together.

"Every man who walked with me to talk to the northern tribes is as good as dead. All their families are listed as enemies of King George."

The priest took to the walls.

Locke said, "You didn't do a damned thing but chit chat. Where's Beckett, your famous solicitor?"

"Dire, "chit chat" with any Indians about the state of things is not allowed in the Treaty of Submission. You know that."

"You knew it too!"

"Then what could Michaelbeckett do?"

"How much is he paid? For the last couple of years, Sachim, you have been hell-bent on being a hero."

"I was a man then."

"And now the Crown has got you by the loin cloth. No protection due from His Most Canny, Most Thrifty Highness now that you've passed the time of day with some northern cousins over a French and English fence. There's the Treaty. Very neat."

"I shall change all this."

"I find you a flawed character much to my surprise. Integrity seeping right out of the stripes on your sides. What reason or right had you to be a Messiah with a beauty like Qunneke to vanquish all your life!"

St. Aubin, the priest, lashed out at Locke. "Merchant! Moron! Shithead!"

"Pipe down, Your Excellency." Dire was at no loss. "Of anybody I know on this bloodthirsty coastline you have the most to gain from spilling Fox's bowl of beans. You and your puppety, Popish Indians. Watch your tongue, for I'm watching your turf."

They were unlikely housemates. The Jesuit headed the local French fur trade; Locke dealt with the trappers on the English side. More than an anomaly in the political tide of 1749, sharing Kirke's house was a complicity that could have gotten Claude de St. Aubin and Dire Locke hanged. But who was around to see to it? The unruly times helped their breach to go practically unnoticed and certainly unattended. In Claude's and Dire's way of thinking, a man had to have some basic rights. And it was clearly better to keep Kirke's house in full use than not, to indulge harmlessly their mutual appetite for intrigue, to supply each other with a competent whist opponent when and for as long as they were in the same vicinity. Locke picked up a little pocket money besides on courtesies having to do with the Trade, packing, portages, and the like. Moreover, as Wakwa proved, they had friends in common.

"Do not quarrel, Pereclaude and Dire. I know who gave the names."

"Then let's go get him!" Dire howled.

"Too late!"

Dire Locke watched Silent Fox with a certain distaste. He did not like to consider that this Wakwa, Wakwa Manunnappu, literally, Black Fox Who-waits, son of Pequawus, the Gray Fox, the wisest man Locke had ever known, nephew of Waban, the Wind, the eagle-souled strongman of the Massachuseuck, was mortal, subject to error, weakness, or naïveté, and not to be relied on absolutely. Locke traced the tip of his thin nose, his lips, his chin with his forefinger. "Why did you not contact me?" And then he had all he could do to hide his pleasure in the Indian's answer.

"And dirty you and Thomas Kirke with my troubles after all the years you and he have fed my tribe?"

To be considered more important to a man's way of life than his wife was the supreme flattery. It was also correct in a factor's way of thinking. Locke did not preen. He saw Wakwa examining his own words.

Pain crossed Wakwa's face and he confessed, "These sides of mine show where she held me as she was ripped from my arms." He bent to look and he touched the open flesh and shuddered. "She...she...."

"You are all about the bush! Why can't you come out and say a thing anymore?"

"I must not."

"What!"

"I am never to pronounce her name again."

"What horse shit is that?"

"The holyman forbids her and her name to me."

"You are suddenly religious."

"I walk through the camp and the people whisper after me."

"I don't wonder."

"They see her hand on me because I keep these wounds open where she held me when they pulled her away. They know I am in pain and I continue in their service. Her name I do not say burns in me like a salt. The longer I am silent with it the better the tribe holds together."

Locke shot out of his chair and faced the wall.

The priest lumbered over. "Renard! Do you blame the little English lady for your debacle? And do they?"

"Priest, I have killed two men over all this since last we met. And so has her uncle, Gilbert Worth."

"Zheelbert!" Claude rocked back.

Locke twisted around from the waist. "Who are the dead men?"

With a satin voice Wakwa answered, "Gilbert's two were Indians who were on my trail.

Mine were an Indian and Annanias Hudson."

Turning away again, Locke said, "Wasn't that the Sweetwood preacher? The man she was to marry before she ran across you? You had her. What did you bother with him for?"

"Friend, it was he gave our names away to the English."

"Ahhh! Then you did all right."

"I did not kill him for that!" Wakwa came to his feet. "My heart may be turned into a swamp but of this I never lose sight - I ended him not because he betrayed me and mine, not for what he did to my life with her!"

"What the hell else could he have done?"

"What is the worst thing a man can do to a woman?"

Locke had handy a barrelful of glib retorts but he did not dare to ridicule this friend. He gave it a minute. Turning, he said, "Stick her for his proving ground?"

"Most brutally."

"How did he get to her?"

"After I gave her up."

"Oh, ho." Locke did not even blink. "Did you make a good show of him?"

"I did."

They linked arms.

"I promised her father that life among us would never injure her. My promise was forfeit with that Information to the court. The truth is, I have ceased to be. I am barely alive. I watch out for my children's sakes. I live in them. I do not see her family. I must never see...again."

Claude softly separated Silent Fox from Dire. "Shhh. You and I must talk! You have all zeese matters mixed up together. What is past is past. You cannot deny so pure a love as you 'ave. Be 'appy! The future belongs to the constant heart."

Evening came to the Maine coast wrapped in fog. The cold, bright air gently turned gray and was company for the fishermen closed off from the world until dawn. The near-night bestowed grace through silence, its silver shoulders pressed close up to everything.

The three men in Thomas Kirke's house did not notice the change outside, yet they lowered their voices. Violent emotion slipped. Their wit sparked from nearness to one another like the kindling in the grate.

Wakwa sat in a big chair taking small bites of the dinner Locke had arranged. The agent drank wine poker-faced. St. Aubin watched his creamed cod and chewed his Vespers over.

Locke matched fingertip to fingertip. "Fox, why did *you* say you should have come to me much sooner?"

The Indian put down his dish and said, "We are friends. You help me to think."

"Claude, are you getting through there?" Locke looked uneasy.

"I 'ave 'ad enough!" Claude snapped his Breviary shut.

"You are a bad priest." The imp in Dire said.

With sour solemnity, the Frenchman took up the black book again.

Dire lifted the brush of conversation and began to paint Indian-style. "You cut me to the quick, Sachim."

"How is that, old friend?" Wakwa's newfound serenity was sullied.

"You may think it selfish in me, but the fact is, Silent Fox, you are a supplier of mine. I represent you and your labors to V.T. Kirke Company, Ltd., ergo you merit my attention, time, and advice for the amount and quality of the furs you bring to trade, or, as in our last agreement, the ginseng you carry to Wareham. On the basis of some trade or other one amasses experiences, which if friendly, constitute friendship. Take Claude and me. For a terrifying sum of money I provide him with certain of his requirements - a decent house, wonderful food, if only he would eat instead of pray, my own packers for his peltry, not to mention my occasional and sparkling company. As for me, I receive the money, yes, but also his amicable abuse, he chasing me up and down the halls with a chastity belt, for one example, and in general being laudably obnoxious within the realm of his Frenchness. Thus we relate to one another in trust and understanding.

"You, my Silent Fox, I have not seen in a year. From you I have received no communication. There has not been a shred of fur or a measly man root presented to me by you personally, or through any henchman of yours. I have been left holding the bag, empty, as it were, of fur as it is of friendship. What have we got between us anymore?"

Wakwa was as still as if he had been chiselled out of marble.

"Just what do you offer me to renew ties?"

There was the opening bid. Wakwa did not let it pass. But before he could frame his reply, the priest intervened.

"He is like an old woman, Renard. Sharp-tongued and correct. This fish is cold!"

Pitted against them both, Wakwa defended his position. "Must not things be even between friends? One must not be too much in debt to the other, nor must the other create too large a debt for the one."

"That is the coldest philosophy I have ever heard. Obligating no one to anything," Locke said. "Demanding no commitment. You see how far it has taken you."

Barely blinking under his hurt, Wakwa countered, "Then, there is a favor I shall ask of you."

If he were not so good at this sort of thing, Locke would have broken into applause at the smoothness of Wakwa's change of tactic. All he said was, "That's more like it. Put up the ante."

Wakwa was wondering if Kirke's house were furnished with feather beds, if the pitchers were kept filled, if all the fireplaces were in good working order, and if the sun understood it must hold off and not waken him until mid-day. He rested his head against the back of his chair, his throat exposed to the light of the lively embers. "Myself. And a faithful supply of man root. Ginseng in handsome quantity each year. At fall-of-leaf. Will that suit you, Dire Locke?"

"Even half-conscious, half-crucified, you remain the supreme negotiator. This is our bargain of two winters ago warmed over. Do better."

Claude fretted, "Dire! Look out! The poor fellow!"

"Claude, you know very well that Silent Fox is neither poor nor any mere fellow. He is the master of a noble spread of territory and quite a number of people. He is important enough to be condemned to a self-inflicted stigmata over a love affair so he doesn't need assistance from the Roman Catholic Church in a simple trade. What's your next offer, kid?"

"Information."

"Of what kind?"

"Any you do not have."

Locke pursed his lips as at the taste of lemon. He crossed his legs. "That comes close to being a clumsy remark."

"You know it is not." Wakwa put backbone into his end of the exchange. "I did not say you have lack. Or that I have held back important news from you. You have hundreds of suppliers bringing you news of anything that affects... our business."

"Then what damned good is your bargain?!"

"I mean to say that I shall bring profit to Kirke Company by finding the truth in all the stories, that you can tie together the ends of two differing tales."

"Isn't it a pleasure?" Locke exclaimed to the Jesuit over Wakwa's turn of phrase. "Since the day I first had the honor to trade with his father I have not heard more sagacious and sombre offers of next to nothing. How wonderful to feel the old Massachuseuck rope settling about me once again. Promises or no, he and his always brought me the most gorgeous furs."

And for the first time on this visit, Wakwa smiled.

St. Aubin, held to his chair and thought of the woman doing without that spectacular light. Then he was up and about like a mammoth in a stall. "Dire, you 'ave a most perverted mind."

"You are not my confessor! If you intend to be let in on delicate matters, do be quiet. The point is that the man before us has ever brought me the truth of situations potentially harmful to the Trade. He's even created some. He has yet to make me an offer."

In other days Wakwa would have begun to talk and jest and have gotten his way by sheer charm. Tonight he said, "I offer you a new kind of news. From afar."

"How far?"

"As far as the river that flows upward."

"I think I should step out." Claude tiptoed toward the door.

"If the young chieftain doesn't mind baring his soul to my arch enemy in the Trade, why should I?" Distinctly glowing from excitement, Locke said just short of deferentially, "Wakwa, it is up to you if the Frenchman stays."

"Dire, if I am anything anymore, as much as even the most common hunter, I should do what I have been freed from...her... to do. And that is to make peace. The French and the English are at each other's throats for what? It does not matter! Over these months I have come to see. It matters only that there be peace. In peace trade grows like a happy child. And where there is trade there will come agreement over lands and rights to lands. That is why the Trade must be *between* the English and the French, and then even Indians shall profit. Just as he lives here, Pereclaude should know the news I will bring from the West. He must be prepared to help make the peace."

The Jesuit breathed, "He is brilliant!"

"It would appear so. And he is not through."

"You know me well, Dire."

"So I think."

Wakwa's black-tinctured eyes took in Locke only. "I bring one last thing on top of this, like flowers upon fruit. Protection. We will follow your steps, Dire, openly or in secret, how you choose, always. The times are full of horrors. War cries in every wind. You need someone at your left side and at your right."

"Guardian angels by the pair!" Locke clucked. "He offers to put me under surveillance! Never a private moment. What a fabulous appeal. What have I done to deserve it?" Blue from Locke's eyes twinkled over his face.

Wakwa was intent and shadowed for a moment, and he nearly spoke to explain the gravity of his plan. But he brightened instead and bowed slightly. "You have been a good friend."

"Full circle!" Locke cried. "Sophistry sublime! And off the cuff. Without a shirt on! Silent Fox, I accept your dark and gossamer proposals. You disappoint me not."

Wasting no time, Wakwa produced an object from his pouch. He gave it over to Claude. After a look, Claude transferred it to Dire.

The agent examined the piece. "What a weight! Astounding. I've never seen a buckle so ornate. You didn't buy it?"

"No, Dire. Yet, I paid dearly. This is off Annanias Hudson's shoes."

"Well, well. Where's the other?"

"You are a great trader."

"Yes?" Dire licked his chops over this bone. "You are really saying I've got this thing from you and there is another somewhere else in the world," Locke turned the buckle over in his hand, "and it is not with you. Since you're not giving anything away easily today, I'd better keep this as long as I've got it, wouldn't you say? Like a pass-key or a calling card. The other one will turn up. I sense. It will turn up at a pivotal moment. I am sure." He slipped the silver buckle into the big pocket of his dull, rich coat. "Now. What is it, Silent Fox, that I can do for you?"

Wakwa's head snapped to the side as if Dire had hit him on the jaw. "I want nothing for myself from you. Forever."

Locke sputtered.

Wakwa pleaded. "But for someone else. Forever."

Interested keenly but on his guard, Locke said low, "For whom?"

"For her."

"Her? Which her!?"

"You know."

"I can only conjecture."

"I have told you! Our holyman says I must not say."

"You'd better or you'll get nothing!"

Wakwa twisted again. The red crystals of his cuts glittered as the skin stretched. "Dire, why cannot you understand?"

"I do! I don't buy into questionable enterprises is all. If your medicine man wants to wind your soul publicly around a pole in the middle of your camp, that's his business. Mine is a lot cleaner, I am surprised to find. I advise you to play into hands that have never hurt you." Locke reached him and held his arms and unabashedly examined him.

The long neck bore a long, shiny scar. Wakwa bowed his head toward the factor. By grace of the gesture, Locke let his hand slide around to the spine at back, his forefinger finding what he feared, a matching mark a hairsbreadth from the vital column of nerves as on the neck of a murdered deer. Dire forced his eyes away from this marring of the Indian's perfections to the stripes on his sides. They were red, wide, showing meat, but they were clean. Magic herbs. Magic words. Locke gripped the redman by his waist.

Wakwa descended onto Dire like a giant axed at the spine. "Elizabeth." Wakwa's voice rang it softly, brokenly. "Elizabeth!" He started yet again and a wetness came over the sound, but he battered on through her name caring less if he were caught at tears than if he failed to give Locke what was wanted. "Elizabeth." And then he was lost in the name. "Elizabeth! Elizabeth! Elizabeth!"

"Enough!" Locke took one side of him and St. Aubin the other, kicking open the door to the hall.

The odd trio toiled up the stairway. They passed the absent Kirke's room, and Locke's, all plunging for the same objective, Claude's chamber, for sanctuary, altar and all.

The priest and the factor pushed Wakwa down onto a cot and piled blankets on. Wakwa blurted his thoughts in thrusts, English serving him more like a fist than a language. Locke huddled close, as if glued to him; St. Aubin swept around preparing Communion.

"I thought...know...she...I...she and I were...she was...is...greater than human! Save her from me for I saw to it the love would never die." His arm wound around Locke's skinny neck. "I put a mark on her, inside, do you know? A mark a man dreams his whole life to put on a woman."

Dire stayed suspended like a hawk transfixed.

"It is not a thing that will pass. Her soul that I have eaten is all that keeps me alive without her. Relieve her of me!"

"What are you asking?" Dire tried to loosen Wakwa's hold on him.

"A little at a time it could be done. This woman must have her life!"

"For God's sake, go down there and scoop her up yourself!"

Wakwa lay back with an older face. "I am not alone like a god to do as I please. A long time ago when you thought me in trouble you said you knew every blackguard and gentleman on this coast. You said you would be hurt if I did not let you use them to help me."

"Trade or no trade."

"Kirke is one of these?"

"He is both."

"Tell him about her."

"A marked woman? He'd set sail for America in five minutes and then what chance would we have to patch this all up?"

"It would take longer but he would come."

"You want...? Oh, I think I see. Listen here. Marriage brokering is not in my line." Again Locke struggled to be rid of Wakwa's embrace.

Wakwa turned his eyes on Dire. "Did you not do the selfsame thing for the woman that you love?"

Dire swung away, stood. He folded his arms across his chest and he looked down at the trembling, big man. "There's not one thing the same about it. Establishing a household with Jeanette would have been the solution to our lovers' woes not the converse. Claude changed her name so suddenly to Mrs. Locke for the town would have had her on the rack otherwise. And she was not torn from my side but sent away, for though I care for her, I worship myself."

"You settled her with a man who would take care of her."

"No. I settled her with a lawyer. Your lawyer. Devil take him! And she eats by governessing his son." And after a pause, "And whatever else is implied by that domestic posture."

Wakwa struggled to his feet in the welter of blankets. "Look at me! Look at what I am! What white man besides yourself and Gilbert Worth would not kick Elizabeth Dowland to death for having coupled with an Indian?"

Dire did look at him but not to give in. "There must be some sophisticated men in the world. Some freethinking, some right-headed men."

"That is not a thing to be left to chance."

The buckle was heavy in Dire's pocket.

"Wetomp, my dearest friend, Thomas Kirke who is old and not wholly English and who enjoys power without killing those in its sway is the only choice."

Locke retrenched. "What if she doesn't want it?"

"That is your trial. You must see that she does."

Locke was disgusted with himself for faltering in debate with the Indian. "You may change your mind; you may be sorry!"

"Never."

Dire paused, then, "Fox, will it make you happy if I do this business?"

"No, Dire. It is for her to be happy."

"What d'ya think, Padre? Is he going to die of those rows he's been ploughing into his sides?" Locke asked later as he and Claude went down the hall.

"His advisors are not idiots, Dire. All zis agony is loaded upon Renard so that they 'ave 'im alive and to themselves. The cuts are clean. You saw. The Indians 'ave remedies for everything. Almost."

"Truly their medicine is amazing."

"Oh, I don't know." The Frenchman cocked his head. "These people 'av little else to do but explore the woods and what she offers. If they did not come up with cures they would be a race of stupids. I am amazed at you. You, little Dire, turn out to be a doctor of the mind better than ten medicine men."

"I don't hold a candle to a Jesuit, yet the issue of self-preservation seems to be won. But it's going to be a fascinating time selling him on love."

CHAPTER TWO

April 1749

Locke had a wonderful nose for ramification; it made him sure that the success or failure of his trust would spread like rings on water. And so he travelled not two weeks later to Sandwich by that means to find Elizabeth.

Serious about business, Dire had declined to conduct any of Kirke's until his mind was at ease about the matter brought to him by Silent Fox. He scheduled his visit to Elizabeth Dowland for the most vulnerable time of day, teatime. At three in the afternoon, anchored well off shore in Cape Cod Bay, and having pressed a tender boat into service, Locke entered the surfless aqua cove fronting the farm where Dowland's daughter was living.

It was the witching hour of the tide, too shallow for him to be rowed the whole distance. Several sand bars revealed themselves as golden whales in the April light. Locke pointed out the central one to his oarsmen, took off his shoes and stockings as an Indian would have, and jumped down onto one of the temporary islands. He waved his aquatic carriage off and curled his lip at the chill water between him and true land. There was a figure on the shore.

Locke stood in contemplation and grew numb to the ankles. The figure paced the beach. How he wished that he could wing over the Bay like a parrot to settle on that shoulder. The friendly sun put a hot cheek to his cloak influencing him to remain where he was.

Dire had given no exact shape to this unfamiliar errand. He simply had brought with him a sturdy bag containing a change of linen, two China and two metal cups for tea and liquor, the tinned tea, a full flask, some unfinished correspondence, sufficient quills, paper, and ink for thrashing through any sort of time. The silver buckle was in his pocket. "Back! Back!" He snarled at the salt puddles. After a while they shrank measurably and Dire Locke began his soggy march.

The person on the sand, dressed in some flying stuff of white, threw off sunshine like the skin of a trumpet. Dire saw that it was a female who moved before the wind and then into it, straight of spine, a sloop adrift in high seas and uncaptained. Dire held back, hoping hard that this spirit was not the party he had pre-labeled, Elizabeth D.

It was obvious to him that the woman became aware of him first hearing, then seeing. He fancied that she had gained much practice in listening at Stirling's quiet coastal farm. She must have listened for one sound in particular since coming there in the frigid New Year - light feet in soft shoes running to her over the snow-covered sand. Bearing the weight of a wish that must have built to breaking her, she at least appeared to acknowledge the sounds that were really there: the moves of the sea, its imminent advance and pulling back, duck's eggs cracking in the commotion of whipping reeds, buds quaking in cold April. From her tense, concentrated stance, Dire could tell it had become her lot to see by ear like an animal then to raise her head to look.

Elizabeth Dowland stood her ground. The change in the ripple of the tide of sleepy Stirling's Bay stole her attention. She heard, then, verified with her eyes that a man had come from nowhere and was moving through the water toward her as if over a bed of nails.

At water's edge, Locke swept his hat off in a French sort of greeting and then held it athwart his naked shins. "Afternoon!" Hose of silken purple waved from the shoes in his pockets.

There was time for her to ease away to the house and to watch the intruder from the safety of the Stirlings' dining room. Instead, she guarded the doctor's beach with a question. "Are you a guest?"

Locke remained entrenched in the shallows. "Are you?"

She did not know she smiled. "Yes!"

Instantly, Locke was sure she was his object. He regretted it not at all anymore. She seemed like a fine and young man. Better than worldly, she seemed beyond the reach of the world. She was only about twenty and made the heart swell at her considerable and still gathering beauty. She inspired his imagination like the ruin of some marble city. Why should her grace lack the polish of contentment? Why the restraint that was the token of her eyes? Her smile enchanted him so that Dire thought Wakwa a damned fool to crush her and then to cast her away.

"With your permission, Mistress, I'll take a seat on that green rock and put my shoes back on."

"Please!" Condemning herself for a sparseness of speech, which the gentleman might mistake as rudeness or welcome, she added, "Have you come to see the doctor?"

He thought, "Lamb! She needs taking care of, handing me my lines like that." And aloud, "I have."

She curtseyed. He bowed. Then he churned out of the tide pool to dry his feet.

Elizabeth looked out to sea and made many white boats of the far breakers. She remembered how the small man had materialized in the bay like a lobster. Yet, she did not think badly of him.

He crunched over to her across the tepid sand. "Mistress, I am not a pirate. But I have had some dis-ease or other for at least a week and, hearing good things about Doctor Stirling, got myself rowed over in this inauspicious fashion from anchor, expecting to startle only a gull or two," he paused, "not such as yourself."

She stiffened when he threw a name of hers out like a slur however innocently. *Herring Gull*, or in the ancient native language, *Kayaskwa*, had been her name in her marriage. She managed to say, "The doctor is quite in retirement. But you have gone to such trouble to visit him...."

"No trouble!" He turned another card. "It is much pleasanter to go by water. No roads or ruts, no fences or detours, no dust and sweat, no rattling about, no...mess!"

The smile again. "I agree."

"Ah! A rarity! A woman who loves the sea." Kirke would need that. "Long voyages? Tall ships?"

"Short excursions only."

"Picnics off the shore in a yacht?"

"It was a large canoe."

Locke stood transfixed by her stamp of pride. He saw that the Indian was right about something - he had done a job of work on her, had scored her properly. Her voice was raw from pining for the redman's hands wrapped about the paddle, clear water running his arms and throwing a mist across her eyes through which she saw the world differently than before she knew him. Although she did not bitch or belittle herself or the Massachuseuck, her thinness of mood made a quicksand Locke noted.

"I beg your pardon." Locke's apology was more complex than she knew. "I detain you. Could you only tell me, is that the doctor's house?"

"It is." She turned and walked in that direction.

Although he felt that she had clammed upon him for good, he hurried to keep pace with her. As they ground up the incline, he observed her brown hair fraught with the colors of fire, her eyes the same but steady and as engrossing as candle flame. Her skin attracted like certain silks. He found her face to be iconic, the sort of face one would find engraved on a coin. He thought her face merged the comely with the ideal. The bones compelled, the eyes consoled, the flesh inspired - a Sophia's face. A nature confounded.

Dire tore his attention away from the woman to what she was saying. Stirling's carriage was out and his son, Israel, was either with his father or off in the fields.

"I've outwitted myself, Mistress. Is there a guest house in the town?"

"There may be one, I don't know." The flame wavered. "You can wait here. The housekeeper can make up a room for you."

"That would be an extraordinary imposition...." Dire speedily computed advantage versus disadvantage. "I only need a word with him. May I wait on his beach?"

"You won't be comfortable at all, sir. The wind will be up."

"And the tide in. And I can get my lift back to my ship."

Her mouth opened around a possibility. "Sir...if you will tell me about your ship, I could make tea for both of us at the pond."

Dire thought this a very interesting female. She had the wisdom to protect them both from breaches of convention by naming her terms straight out. It stung him sweetly that she was and took him to be numb to any male - female pull. He was encouraged, nevertheless, that she was neither the prude nor the romantic imbecile he had imagined her to be years before. Wakwa's wounds were not so reprehensible now that Dire had met the woman who had opened them.

Locke insisted that they use his cups, donated his tea to her larder, and added some of his biscuits to the tray of oatcakes which she put down between them. He did not follow her into the vaulted black mouth of the barn where she obviously kept a pantry. He waited on its skirt of salt-bitten grass and looked into blue eternity above the rim of a dune.

He kept this posture on her return but held her in his vision well enough to observe privately the way she moved. She arranged things with a frank dignity unimpeached by finishing school fussiness. "My God!" Locke thought. "If her trays were silver instead of wood, she'd cowe a queen." He saw her pull open an Indian punk shell and touch the smouldering matter to her kindling. Her copper kettle was on. Locke concluded that if she continued this woods-wise existence on the verge of civilization she would be fully lunatic before the summer was over.

He kept silence until she spoke, then cut her off, testing and teasing. "Anything I say will seem inquisitive, but shouldn't a lady of your graces be taking her holiday in more conventional ways? A yacht to the Carolinas? A round of fittings in Boston?"

"I am not on holiday, sir. This is how I live." Again the civil pride. "I do not know or love the South and I have no need to be fitted with clothes as I can make anything I want with my own hands."

"This suit?" He showed the sleeve.

She examined it as one would a rose. "Better. Respectfully."

Locke stared at his coat, horrified. "What's wrong with it?!"

"One day, sir, though the fabric is grand, it will tear at the seams. The stitching is neat but done without tenderness. It divides warp from weft instead of binding them."

"Terrifying!" He said of her and recovered with, "And my father was a tailor! How shall I wear it anymore? I must throw away my whole wardrobe!" He made her laugh. And when she laughed, her head thrown back, the joke consumed her and she Dire.

She stopped herself, purposely dashing her high spirits and said in a voice that smoked of dead delight, "If it tears, bring it to me. I'll mend it."

"Mend? If you are that good, Missus, you ought to be 'broidering vestments for the Pope."

She brightened on this kindling. "Does he need new? I lack for work right now."

"Well, aren't you something!" He thought her easy to handle after all and that he could be back to Kirke's daybooks by eventide. He held the company hand out to her. It would not be long before he would offer Kirke's hand delicately. "Suppose I told you, my esteemed, salt-air hostess, that I could get you such work?"

She said, "I should welcome it." Then she drank her hot tea steadily enough to burn.

Seeing her willful injury of self, Locke's poise slipped. "Why?!"

She looked out of eyes rich with messages.

"Why should such as you welcome tedium?"

"Sir, if I do not settle that within myself, I am condemned to it."

"And you do not want to be?"

"I think that I do."

He panted, confronting this unexpected thing, a full and complex personality surviving on its own woe. Wakwa was right about something else - this was to be Dire's trial indeed. And Dire girded himself as if to wrestle with a sage. He grew wretched as he prepared to rake the ashes of her soul.

His hands in his lap, he enquired, "Do you mind if I pour?"

"Oh! I am sorry."

"For you?"

Her glance fell. "Not for me."

Only then did Dire lift the kettle.

"I mean, yes! Thank you."

"Just a simple question." Locke lied, working up a grin.

"Sir, my manners have gotten very bad living like a hermit."

"You could be calling mine into question. I won't ask another thing."

She looked at the little man and liked him for being so artful with his interest. "I shall tell you." Her face took on a gleam. "I was greatly loved."

Dire thought her either demented or superior to common discourse. "Was."

"Am."

This statement netted him like a flounder. It dragged his heart up the coast to Pemaquid. His questions and her answers would be important now because Locke had a mind to tell her who he was, whom he represented, and to solve her tragedy by depositing her at the redman's doorstep in a basket tied with ribbons.

"Then you are the happiest of women."

"I was. I had a child, too. Have. I think."

"Yes." He told her nothing.

The need to cry turned the rims of her eyes orange. Tears forbidden to fall collected there magnifying the discoloration so that she seemed to be rusting away from sorrow. "The man let me go."

"The man," Locke hissed, believing it just then, "is mad."

"He may be!" Her hands trowelled her forehead and her face.

"You say this seriously?"

"I wish I could! I wish I knew! I do not think so though." Her lips began to jar and pull. "Could it be that a man gifted with every good thing must squander some just to continue to breathe?"

Locke hobbled over, stiff, he told himself, from the damp ground. He stood directly above her. "Then, do you hate him?"

"I cannot!" Her voice was no voice but the cry of an ancient hinge.

"Why don't you let him go!"

"No!"

"This is not good treatment! It is dangerous for you."

"He is in danger."

"From what source? The law? Your family? From you?"

Some jaundiced mood changed her as a sky is stained by eerie light. "I am not smart that way like other women."

"Then he is in the clear!"

"Please, see, you see, he and I...he was...with me he was what he believed himself to be."

"Pray tell, what was that?"

With no hesitation she pronounced, "He was a god."

The sight of her face brought Locke down on one knee. "Are you sure? Suppose he doesn't think so! Be sure!"

"You do not know him!"

"Sure? Sure? He is not a man? Is just a man?"

"Not like other men!"

"But a man? Not a god. Did he get empty and need food? Did he sweat? Did he hurt? Did he bleed?"

"Yes!"

"Did he not laugh or weep? Did he not have muscles and labor with them?"

She raged, "He had greatness!" Her body collapsed about itself as if she were a bird wrapped in her own wings. "Forgive me!"

Dire was very near. "I do! You describe a Messiah. Let him prove himself Divine. But alack! As you said, without you he is likely not."

She fled him for the darkness of the barn and took shelter against the raw wooden wall.

Locke said sharply through it, "And you mend for your supper to keep the dream alive?" He did not hear a female's weeping or whimpering. He saw the siding throb as she beat against it, it seemed with iron, blows of iron on wood that could have cracked a skull.

He ran around to the doorway disbelieving such strength from her, tearing inside from the sound of her bondage, shaking like the boards from the power of her frustration. He blinked away sun-blindness and stood appalled at the sight of her pressed against the ungiving wall like a dead thing hung to dry.

He used his eyes like torches, flashing them from spot to spot to learn something of her so that he could help her. There was nothing of human comfort inside. The old barn had not been converted to suit as a house yet he knew as sure as his sex that she lived there.

Forked clean, it still smelled of cow dung and hay dust. The ghosts of the departed cattle filled its lower region. The gentle, hopeless specters gave even the driving businessman condolence. He rubbed shoulders with the herd of idiot animals with long, long memories. He walked toward two dusky hulks. Her wheel and her loom became plain. A cloth batted a whorl of wind as daintily as a spider's web. It caught his coat sleeve like a burr and took some trouble to detach. He could see that she slept in the loft on a miser's allotment of straw. So! She was afraid of rats.

The agent picked his teeth, calculating how long it would be before Elizabeth Dowland would forget she was the daughter of a rich man. "Isn't there a better way to keep it alive? Something more valuable to others? More suitable to yourself?"

She gave him silence.

"Are you afraid to think it?"

"Yes!" She slipped and held, slipped and held her way down the splinter-ridden wall to the dirt floor.

"Afraid you would desert the dream for something comfortable?"

Her voice wandered in shame, "It might happen."

He came close but she would not raise her head to look at him. And so Dire took her by the arms and lifted her. He breathed very quickly, finding she was flesh. He led her into the open air. "Why worry then? Mend or spin or dance or love another. It's all the same if you don't stop loving him. And pain enough."

They stood dumb near the pond until Dire made up his mind that he had done a good thing. Holding to a tree trunk, he skipped a stone across the water's green skin. "Do you have a sample of your work? I'll study it and see what we can do for you. I shall go now, but I'll be back. To see the doctor. And to talk to you."

He watched her quite far into the recess. It was as if she illumined her own way. She came out holding something to her chest.

"Here is linen which I wove springs ago, sir."

It was the first moment since Locke had set eyes on her that she seemed free of her trouble. "May I?" He took the white square.

"I have stitched the trapunto and the appliqué since. It was a study for a pocket."

He loved her as a friend for her exquisite statement. He looked at the scrap. "How rich you are!" Extravagance of materials, of labor, of purpose had yielded up art as permanent as a tapestry. And it was a discard. He winked at her and walked toward the water.

CHAPTER THREE

April 1749

Doctor J. Macmillan Stirling was in Sweetwood. His large, square person could be seen through the north window of the study in Elizabeth's father's house. The doctor dominated although he faced the interior and his companion sat in a shaft of captured sun. Stirling's wild, white hair, ruddy face, and clothes of black gave him the mentor's air.

The blond man across from him sat the corner of the late Charles Dowland's desk in a posture of listening that belied his forty-nine years. Gilbert Worth was, so far, enjoying the Scot's scolding.

"Gil, I'm takin' you t'task for holin' up in this echoin' place instead of conductin' your business at home as usual."

"Nothing is as usual, Mac."

"An' what's usual in this family?"

"You brought it up."

"You're behavin' the same way as Bonnie Beth!"

"You tolerate her escape."

"She has not a mate pinin' in the bedroom window waitin' for her."

"We don't know that for a surety and my own mate can't possibly be pining."

"And the reason for that?" The Scotsman stuck out a pugnacious chin.

"Is the reason I asked you here except for your company. You're a physician. You may know why...." Gil hesitated.

"Lad, gi'me somethin' to go on."

"Dammit, it's not easy to say."

"Then don't. Give i' a bit. What I want to know is whose tack and horses 's in your barn?"

"The east barn, you mean? The guest barn? You know, Mac, with Elizabeth living in one of yours, and Beckett commandeering one of mine for...."

"Michael Beckett!"

"For his private equerry, we ought to consider what's so attractive about them. Do our fugitives and beasts of burden live better in barns than we in our houses? Should we develop them? Create a town of them? Barnton. Barnville. No. Too French. Barnford! That's it! Or should we be Puritan and raze all barns for being voluptuary hotels?"

"Gil?"

"Why shouldn't I allow his heavy-flanked, brown, tall and mighty horses to perfume my white barn? Hanna Worth is profitted something by this. I, certainly, am no use to her at stud."

"I'm not talkin' of fatherhood, lad."

"Neither am I."

"Oh?"

"Oh, yes. Or shall I say, oh, no. It's a hell of a thing." Gil's face twisted. But even struggling against the man within, his features were delightful to view. They were delicate and brave without arrogance; the nose fine, the eyes chartreuse, the mouth thin-lipped and quick, a gift to his happy moments since it looked so good in laughter. His gold hair cast not the angel's but the tiger's spell over him. His fair skin was burnished with the rush of life. "How can it be? How can I be near her and never be drawn to her? I'm talking around it, I know, but I worry, it seems, all the time. And I've gotten afraid, O God, of something. There's art enough left in me that I could pump something up, I could look at that form, remember every blessing she has let fall to me, and slide home for one moment more turgid than the empty opera glove I've turned into - do something - anything to make her feel a woman, but that seems awful. Not good enough for her perhaps. Or is it insufficient for me? And why is it this way? Mac! I'm all right when HE flits across my mind. I think of...the Sachim...of Wakwa...and the elixir comes flooding back. Then I am a man and not a truffle. I could go after Beckett's mares! Mac, it shouldn't happen when I think of Silent Fox! Was my friendship with him tainted? Or something I knew not I was capable of? It was always man and man. I'm nobody's fag. But I can't come to a woman thinking of him - just to get it done!"

"So you dandle a tall and handsome widower in front of your wife because you can't have an erection, laddie?"

"Jesus! I struggle through the labyrinth of my slimy soul and you just rip the roof off it like that?"

"I'm a doctor, Gil."

"I'm glad one of us is. I wish you'd cut it off."

"I know."

"Damn you!"

"You need a whiskey."

"Oh, no. I won't be a sot like Beckett. And not in my brother-in-law's house. This is my holy of holies. I'll figure this out for myself, if you won't help."

"I think you're fine."

"God!" Gil broke. He cried without sniveling or blubbering. His flood of sorrow was as clean as a crow's call. Some of the sound he reembraced in his throat and it took the breath of the listener.

"Gil. The matter wants time."

"I'm scared, Mac!"

"Gilbert Worth, think of it this way if you can, that Silent Fox and you WERE man and man. So much so that you admired the juices in him and, as far as I saw, he never ground his heel into you because you gave him credit. He treated you fine and you him. And so, of course, when he withdraws from the scene like a dead man an' you are left alone juggling nearly a world full of silly persons, you're tired before you begin. An' you do not hate him for leavin' your niece-by-marriage because he HAD to. An' so you hate yourself for her sake."

"How neat."

"Not in my book!" Stirling shifted on tired feet. "Does it add up that you deny yourself the pleasure of pretty Hanna? Tha' you throw her to the wolf if not the wind? Tha' you expose her to a dark-eyed, dark-haired, social-climbing, womanizing, son-of-a-..., son-of-a-Cambridge lawyer with no title to his pretensions?"

"Being a little harsh on Beckett are we?"

"I don't give two hoots about him!"

"Ha!" Gil scraped humor from somewhere. "You're just angry with him because he didn't like you on the stand last June in Beth's land conveyance."

Stirling gripped the back of his chair. "I'm mad a' you for no' seein' your malady began without his being involved. Or Silent Fox! It lies with you! Though Beckett can be a stupid man sometimes."

"But he gets it up no matter what!" Gil shouted.

Mac shouted back. "How do you know that?!"

"Give Hanna the benefit!" Gil lowered his head. "What's wrong with me, Mac? I've lost a friend and the luxury of some family happiness not a wife to the pox as Beckett has."

The Scot ran his thick, old hand through his white hair and turned toward the window. There was a smile on his lips as he said, "Gil, it is so painful to be wha' you are." Stirling ambled over to see the green and purple countryside.

"It's painful all right, Mac, but what am I?"

"You are a noble man."

Gilbert Worth pushed himself away from the desk and staggered this way and that. He knocked mindlessly against the clavier he had abandoned for conversation. It did not fall. He slunk about the square study where Wakwa had sued for Charles Dowland's approval of his exotic match with Elizabeth and won it. Worth growled, "Fine thing to say to a friend. 'Friend, your hell on earth's decreed by Fate - everyone else was born to guzzle honey.'"

"That's the way of it." Mac's hands were in his britches pockets. Their wide seat held a shine from too much pressing and too much sitting.

"Oh, is it! I won't believe it. Not even a 'patient, cure thyself!'"

The doctor's neck went stiff and red and he became irritably attached to the view. "That's a secondary matter!"

"Damned if it is!"

"Damned if it isn't. Look a' that, lad."

Gil could see nothing with Stirling in his way. "What is it?" He heard it. It was awful. Ugly.

Mac let him by not politely but resolutely.

"No!" Gil's hands shot out to stop what he saw. Hoofbeats, as dark and irrevocable as a cavalry charge obliterated reason. Gil stood there and screamed, his hands splayed against the glass. He saw his wife pushing her Gray too fast toward a stone fence marking a drop too severe for jumping.

Mac was out of the room battering his way down through the kitchen and out.

Hanna was astride, her narrow brown boots jammed into short stirrups. Her veil was her filly's and the filly's mane streamed as Hanna's hair. And all Hanna's skirts did not begin to hide the impertinence of the jumping posture.

Galloping behind was Beckett, riding her down efficiently with his taller, stronger Brown. He whipped past Dowland House, tearing up the lawn. Beckett's spine so perfect in attitude in spite of his rocking rush revealed his nature to Gil. The solicitor's back told of anger and not enough of the correct concern. There was an unearned possessiveness in Michael Beckett's sternness that swelled Gil's tongue into the back of his throat.

Stirling hopped into the way screaming. Beckett cursed and swerved and lost momentum and time. The doctor bellowed, "Hanna Dowland Worth!"

Gil doubted that she heard over her mount and Beckett's, over her thoughts, whatever they were. Yet, as the filly's flanks started to muscle to gather to jump, Hanna held up. Somehow she kept her stirrups, coming down hard on her tailbone on the Gray's rump as the horse reared and writhed. The filly's head snapped hard to the right from the rein and her mouth tore. "God." Gil said.

The struggle for balance went on in a flying spiral of foam and blood. Beckett drove his horse's shoulder just hard enough against the Gray's side to keep her upright. Hanna freed her foot just in time, landing on her belly on the saddle during the dance of horse against horse. Hanna tore her right foot loose of the other stirrup to try to roll clear as the spinning slowed. But the skirt of her habit hooked over the saddle horn and Hanna Worth dangled above the grass her arms shielding her cranium from the hoofs. Stitch by stitch gave. In instants that were endless she fell to the ground. Mac reached her.

Hanna ducked the Scot's waiting arms and scrambled across the lawn to the house of her childhood. Gil was in the open doorway. She passed him by for the steps and the room where she had slept before Gil had come to Sweetwood.

Worth stood outside the second floor room, his hand firmly over the latch. "Ana!" He called her in his voice almost too deep and strong for his modest height.

Downstairs, Beckett knocked at the wide-flung door.

Gil muttered, "Stupid ass."

Beckett came shyly in, a misfit in the ascetic main room but, when he saw Gil on the gallery, he crossed the rag rugs swiftly and sped up the stairs. "I don't understand why she did it!" Beckett's sparklessly handsome face was mapped with dust and sweat.

"I should thank you for what you did, Michael."

"For God's sake, let me pass!" With a look from his unemotional brown eyes, he lunged against the panel much like his horse against the Gray, Gil thought.

Hanna opened the door. Beckett fell past her into the room and she escaped both men.

Gil watched her limp down the shady staircase. He turned away from her loveliness.

Hanna hid her face from Doctor Mac just at the front step.

Beckett went quickly to the top stair. "I guess she's all right."

"Do you think, Michael?"

Beckett flaunted a conspiratorial smile. "Just capricious."

Gil's eyes went as hard as slate. "I have never known her so."

Beckett fluttered stiff black lashes.

And then, the pounding again, but this time without frenzy - incessant although fading. The men rushed outside.

"She's taken mine!" Beckett struck his thigh in frustration.

"She will get tired of him and give him back."

Beckett glared at Gil.

Gil merely handed Michael the lead of the suffering filly. "If you'll be good enough to have the stable patch this one up, I'll join you for a drink at my house after your bath.

Dowland House was tall and lean, its shoulders squared to the southeastern sun. Its back staunchly ignored the blast that sailed snow across the country in some winters transforming the fields into the face of the moon.

Worth Farm was conceived on a different plan. The house of low-slung wings embraced with walls of windows a wide sky and high grounds overlooking the faraway sea. In admitting so much light, so many views of a flowering countryside, so many sights of the pines of the tract bordering it, the house's inside was grand although possessing only half a flight of stairs.

A hill prevented sight of the bottomland and the manse where the town's minister, Annanias Hudson, had lived for more than a decade before his bizarre demise. But any barrier was inconsequential in shielding Worth Farm from the upheaval that had caused and had followed the clergyman's murder or, as the family understood matters, his summary execution.

In the simplest ways the Worths' place was not the same. Its old cherry bloomed profusely this spring to no applause. The sitting room window it graced was blinded by a drape; since their recent break with the Indians, Gil and Hanna could not face the whispers of past joy in their favorite room. They had taken to their kitchen like their simpler neighbors. When more pomp was called for, they used the couches in one or the other of the dining rooms.

This night, Doctor Stirling hunched sourly over some reading in the northeast one. Gil was there too, glowing inadvertently in the traces of a sunset filtered through Hanna's glass collection. His wife was still in the sheep pasture and her lover was singing in his tub.

Worth, healthy, small, possessing cat's quickness, dressed for country life in a way that directed the eye toward his physical blessings not to his clothes. His evening grays finished with black hose and a waistcoat and queue-ribbon of watery blue affirmed his attractiveness without overawing or overdisplaying. Only his green eyes were dressed with his passions.

"Qunneke should have had her baby by now." Gil threw out.

Mac's forefinger continued to progress across a line of prose.

"Mac?"

Stirling twisted around. "Why do you trouble yourself over it?"

Gil's hair bristled like gold wire. "No particular reason."

Mac leaned back. "Due the twenty-fifth of last month. March, the twenty-fifth."

"New Year's Day."

"Keep up wi' the times, lad. That's in January now."

"In France."

Stirling sank back into his essay. Then without looking around, "Why ask about the Indian wife? Why not ask about Beth? Bonnie-Beth's the one you're related to."

"By marriage only. Don't raise the Hebridean brow. It's Beth who doesn't want to own me. She turns me away. She refuses every offer of help I make. In person. Through you. Through letters. Through Hanna, through Israel. She won't open her lips to give a polite no." And after a wait, "Much less a graceful yes. You would think I am a criminal." Gil amended, "I withdraw that. I am. But considering the Reverend Annanias Hudson's betrayal of Wakwa to the Crown, could I have done less than strike down Hudson's accomplices, trespassers, about to make their third attempt on Wakwa's life? Could I have done more to keep her marriage with him together? With all due respect, would her own father have done as much?"

"We have history to educate us on tha' point, Gil."

"Well, then, she should be here! At tea with us. Letting us hold her up a bit. Is there something wrong in my offering to make at least one part of her life a little easy? I am haunted by Charles wrestling with the shackles of the grave, boring holes through my head with his empty sockets. 'Help her!' he pleads."

"Maybe he doesn't like your idea of helping her."

"I look for new ideas every moment of the day. But how many ways are there to crawl?"

"Oh?"

"I can't stand her look anymore. Is she insane or just cruel? When did she develop that knack? And what good is your fostering her wild mood? Her martyr's half-starvation. Living by her needles for paltry pay."

"Those needles were your gift to her, Gil, and precious."

Worth covered his eyes. "Thank God her family are far flung! They would gossip us to death."

Stirling turned his bulk fully toward the speaker. He heard Beckett down the hall and up the stairs.

"In moments, Mac, the only ones of mine truly enjoyable anymore, I sense how it would be to be free. To be myself, once again. To be alone. Ah! Even lonely. To rely on that at least. To take a day's miseries and ecstasies by the hand, goddammit, without a wife to cast that wifely eye, without any woman reaching up for me, without the least notion to greet a man who might by chance wave an innocent hello. I am crushed under obligation! My heart is so heavy I am surprised it can still beat." During the long wait, they listened to the slight creaks of Beckett's strides to and fro as he performed the rituals of his toilette in the chamber above. "But I sorely want it to beat!" Gil faced Mac's crackling blue eyes.

"Ah, Gil! Can you no' think these same wants pass through Beth like a knife since her husband and his People shoved her out? And for no particular fault of her own?"

Gil took out his handkerchief and blew his nose.

"And that she can survive in no other way than what you've described as your ideal state? She canno' do any better. And considering you and her man never let her in on the problem as it developed or let her think it through with you or gave her the chance to act to save her place according to her lights, she could behave worse. She loves the feelin' of her heart pumpin' too!"

"I am glad you break my solitude tonight. It is a privilege when you come to us."

"Don't be flowery!" Beckett barged into the room in a gorgeous suit of brown. His lace and linen, the color of old cream, bobbed and bounced as he laughed, "Have me anytime! I always have a spree in your palace, m'friend. Now, what may I get you gentlemen to drink?"

"Your blood." The doctor.

"Are Scots always like that, Squire Worth? I have none as friends so cannot pass judgment." Beckett clacked away with decanters and glasses and measures, concocting a pitcher of flip along with small talk.

Hanna heard his pleasantries as Matthew Freeman, the African houseman, carried her silently to her bed.

"Too bad you don't open the sitting room anymore, Worth, old champ. A south exposure's a little kindlier than this on a chilly spring night."

"We could open the summer dining room if you would be more comfortable, Michael. As you see, this table's not been laid yet. It's all the same to me."

"Rambling are we? Distracted? You can't afford to be. I haven't told Hanna, and I will the first minute she stands in place, but I'm just bursting with news. Not one piece but two! Which do you want first?"

"How would I know, Michael?"

"Quite. I'll decide. First things first. The decision has been handed down by Duhmmer's court."

"Decision?"

"You must recall. You've been paying the fees. I've studied it upside down and backwards for a flaw for the past two days only interrupted by Hanna's runaway this afternoon. I read it over again in my bath...."

"Ye sang in your tub!"

Beckett gave Mac a lacquery look. "Was I good?"

Worth held to his chair arms. "Tell me!"

"Here's the gist. That Bible which Hudson's replacement, The Reverend Mayhew Low, found in the manse library did its job. Justice Duhmmer matched Hudson's infamous pasted letter to the court, character-by-character with the Good Book, to wit, the eyelet Isaiah. That is, the evidence entered. You know? That careful preacher did not let one letter go to waste. Tiny, tiny letters, too. Each one cut to a T. He had eyes."

"Oh, he had an eye!"

"The case turned on our proving that the minister himself pasted up the message after seizing on gossip to get revenge. Revenge for what? For being done out of his betrothed wife, Elizabeth, and his *promised land* by none other than a bloody red Indian. Love was the key. Two men rivals for one woman. And the loser racking his brains how to assuage his humiliation. Up he sits all night in his study with sticky fingertips, composing anonymously, cravenly, a saga of treason. Man against man, the defeated against the victorious, white against red, ousted, unemployed parson against reigning Indian prince. Here, under my instruction, our barrister lays upon the canvas like a painter with a palette knife, the reminder that the beloved, your niece...."

"His niece-by-marriage." Mac stuck in.

Beckett clicked his heels. "That your niece-by-marriage, Elizabeth Dowland, went with a mighty parcel of choice land which, last June, by judgment of Judge Duhmmer himself, was conveyed into Indian hands. Not incidentally, another case in which love was the key. It has been like dominoes. My, it was grand watching His Honor from the risers knocking another case of ours into the victory pile. The first victory is always the most important. You see, Duhmmer will never cease being reminded by me that if Westminster Hall gets hold of his decision against the Royal coffers in favor of a half-breed infant, that is, the conveyance of Dowland's fat lands to Moses Bluehill, Elizabeth's spawn, your great-nephew-*by-marriage*, Duhmmer'd be out of a job and probably his head. Old Duhmmer is acutely aware that in the instance of a decision against Silent Fox, my appeal to a higher court would parade that costly conveyance before His Majesty's reviewing stand brasses blowing and drums a' beating." Beckett hoisted his great glass. "To quiet revolutions!"

Worth sat mute, weight descending on his soul instead of lifting. Elizabeth's pain visited him. The waste of her marriage had lost all justification. She was no drawback to the survival of the tribe: she and her lost son and Dowland's estate had just saved it from annihilation. What would Wakwa say when he knew? Gil rifled his imagination for ways to get word to the Sachim.

"Well, Gilbert, your thanks are greatly appreciated and eloquently bestowed. I'll take them out of your pocket, thank you all the same. And I know where you can find a highly qualified solicitor if Voluble Fox's and your sundry murders surface some day. With the charge of treason dismissed, His Royal Red Highness can come home with his retinue, however many concubines he's got now, and his clan, pardon me, Stirling, his tribe. Oh, it's sweet as candy for every word that Hudson glued on is true! The Fox DID go up there to the Maine, DID bitch about your cousin, King George...."

Stirling reacted. "George is a Hanover. No' English. And Gilbert Worth is no German! He's no' even a Scot!"

"Those would be weaknesses in him, I agree. Worth is indeed English as he has the courtesy to let me finish my statements... where was I...although bitching, as you know, *oughtn't* to be treasonable. I refrained from making that argument to the Court lest my most lucrative clients be hanged, drawn, and quartered. I leave making history to the Indian."

Gil stood. He granted a soldierly kiss to each of Beckett's cheeks. "You're a miracle man, Michael. I hate your gut but you do get the job done."

Mac said only, "When did you get word about this, Mr. Beckett?"

"About six weeks ago, about the time I came here, Doc. I had to make up my mind about the timing of the announcement."

Gil glared ahead of him seeing the destruction wreaked by this gap in his information.

Stirling declared, "So! You were definitely not reading in your tub."

"Your tenacity, Doctor Stirling, is an attribute I am just recently considering worthy of perfection. It has to do with my other bit of news. You see, I had a son-of-a-bitch of a father who was tenacious too. Too tenacious. He finally let go life last spring. I got the news late November. His English house has become mine. It is made of stone, I despise it, but the grounds are nice and it's free, better yet, and there's money in the cellar, as it were, although it's never enough. I am quitting America, how do you like that?" Not cut out for it. Too much work. I am retiring to the shire and my horses with me."

"I wish you well!" Gil took the words out of Stirling's mouth.

"Well, I'm asking Hanna if she'll come. I love her to within an inch of her life and my baby, Ho, does too. She's got a family ready-made if she comes with me, Worth. You know that. I could represent both of you and have the worst part of divorce over in a flash. What do you have to say?"

The evening and the firelight caught on Gil's features as onto cut crystal. "I say, sir, if she goes with you it will be because she wants to. If she stays, it will be because she chooses me. She is a Dowland and will not lack for conclusive opinion."

Beckett's sleek self dimmed for an instant. But his confidence swept back and he took Gil's hand in a sportsman's gesture. "Stoutly said. More courageous of you than a duel. I'm sorry you and I never played roulette. You've a damned cool head when you want to. I wish...I wish I will come up with the same brave phrase in your circumstances."

Gil gave his head a minor toss and said, "Your compliment is not kindly to my wife."

In the morning, Beckett accosted Gil at his porridge in the kitchen. He looked at the gold fringe of Worth's caftan etching the slate floor. Gil observed Michael's travelling clothes.

Beckett commanded, "Come away from the help."

Mrs. Cooke, the housekeeper, a widow, and Matthew Freeman, bought out of slavery by Worth, stood at attention, silent, ready to respond to any demand of their easy master.

Gil came to his feet knowing his life was about to change. "Say please, please Michael, or feel free to speak among the household."

Beckett turned down the short hall for his whip. Gil touched his mouth with his napkin and, without hurry, found his houseguest.

"Worth, I think I like you better than I like her. She is so American. Look me up when you are abroad." Beckett opened the front door for himself. "She's yours. You've won. I suppose."

Gil flooded with Beckett's loss. "Michael!"

"What?" Beckett, half down the path, confronted Worth.

Seeing the cut of him, Gil wondered how Hanna might have suffered his kiss. "I don't like roulette with you."

Matthew Freeman went into a state carrying and ordering trunks and boxes out to Beckett's coach. And Gil stood against his house wondering in the light.

Almost before Beckett's dust had settled, Mac came up behind him. "Gil. I'm going, too."

"Mac? Must you? How is she?"

"I peeked in. She was asleep. So, I woke her up. No bones broken, no sprains. She's a bit tender 'though she insists everything's normal no matter how many times I asked or in how many ways I tried to learn some facts. She had a hard ride yesterday. She's pale. She's tired. Keep her in bed and feed her honey, don't y' know. She is peculiarly tired. I leave her to you for Bonnie's been without me nearly four days. I want to see wha' improvements have taken place while I've been gone."

Gil walked next to him, his hand on Mac's ledge of a shoulder. "You're modest, thinking your patients wax better in your absence."

"Healthy patients are the secret of my medical fame!"

CHAPTER FOUR

April 1749

Gil looked into the lucid morning long after the Scot's coach had left the grounds. He sat on his stone step admiring the day as if it were a saucer of Champagne. He could not leave the foretaste of New England summer for other pleasure or for his routine. Even the momentous question of how to tell Elizabeth that Wakwa was unencumbered by the law and could come back was left to tomorrow's logic. His world was sound again.

It was April, not warm, and noon. Reason enough to go indoors.

Matthew hovered discreetly and finally could announce, "The lunch is laid in the summer dining room, Master Worth. We've opened it for you."

"Perfect day, old Matthew." Gil thanked the black-skinned man who was at least a decade his junior. "But I thought I would take lunch on a tray upstairs to eat with Mistress Worth."

"Before you decide, sir, there is a note at your place."

Gil ate alone. He was not unwelcome in his servants' quarters but they had set him a master's place and the note from Hanna asked for her privacy. Gil ate by himself, considering her.

She had the sheen of girlhood. Thirty-nine years of life had not eaten the ripeness of her flesh. Neither her character nor her body had ever been inundated by conception.

Unaltered opinions of herself and appetite for life kept youth in her step. Yet she was not giddy. Gil thought that because she was from the Bay Colony her soul had been spared the vice of sentimentality. Her heart responded to good fortune and to bad by expanding. Better than that, she evinced an assiduous reason. She was a rounder, dispassionate Elizabeth who moved as gently as lake water and, as peacefully, slaked thirst.

Two o'clock chimed and Gilbert Worth was still at the table straightening the silk tassels of his robe. One by one, he drew them out between his slender fingertips and laid them against the back of his hand. Some, of course, had to hang like combed hair from the cuff at the underside of his wrist. He straightened the glimmering threads if they got tangled in the golden hair on his hand. Just when he had half the strands gathered and had started to braid them, Matthew knocked and came in.

"Master, all is well?"

"Just dandy."

The freedman studied his master's uncustomary idleness. "Shall I lay out clothes, sir, while Mistress is trying to eat?"

"She is better then? Eating!"

"Broth Cooke has forced on her. Cooke says, all day Mistress has pretended to sleep."

Gil twisted the tassels as absently as a country girl might twist her pigtails. "We are naughty children today, your mistress and I, eh, Mr. Freeman?"

"Not children. Master."

Gil laughed harshly. "You are never wrong, Matthew."

"I hope I am this time. Clothes, sir?"

"No. Thank you."

Gil satisfied himself plaiting the strings into little clumps since they were too short for doing up grandly. In an hour he had created a weird bracelet standing out from his wrist. He wanted to rip the sleeve of his robe right off but kicked his chair back instead and went out not shutting the door after himself. He unknotted the fringe as he walked over the grass to Dowland House, planning to clean Charles' study after the excitement of the day before. Matthew had done it already. Even the clavier was dismantled, ready to be toted home.

Gil did what he had never done before, sat in the chair behind Dowland's desk. Charles' chair, stuffed and leather-covered in some places, carved of hardwood in others so that Dowland could be both propped and strapped into working posture during his crippled years, impressed Gil better than a sermon.

The chair, an outer skeleton, had supplied Elizabeth's father some of what lacked in him physically; it also had supported the man's mind. Ensconced there, Dowland had decided to let the marriage of his daughter to an Indian stand. Dowland, sitting in judgment, had set that marriage on its feet for what it was - a new, a foreign thing, disassociated from his life. It followed that he disassociate himself from Elizabeth. But he anchored her to his heart by the weight of his land left to her issue, never altering his well-made Will. The wisdom of his sacrifice, of his curse, perceived, allowed love to survive between the man and the daughter he denied in the fabric of his days. Straight against the chair's stern back, Gil contemplated such difficult kindness. He found it possible to accept that loyalty was not love, and loyal love no wellspring of passion.

He strained to see into the blackness he - life - had lowered over Hanna. For his pains he was nearly blinded by the light wrought by Hanna's embracing a stranger. This to be clean of the foul secrets of marriage, free of the weariness of the fight for right, to be simply the desired of another, to burn from touch and burn back, to be taught by flesh, the engine of innocence, of ascendance, of goodness, of a beautiful nature mad for its own salvation.

The onset of evening inspired Worth to move out onto the ridges of the hills, his robe flapping like a beggar's tatters in the fickle wind. With a careful step, he kept on up his stairs to see what salvage there was from the wife he had known.

All was covered in a violet-gray haze admitted by windows not facing the dusk. The fragile stream of the post curtains hinted at the four corners of the bed. The vacant fireplace was lost in the dark hulk of the wall.

"Ana!" He moved toward the center of the cold floor, his hand out, his fingers spread because the dark and the quiet made him feel as if he would fall. He brought his knees up against the soft mattress and held to one bedpost with both hands. There was a small mass on the bed. "Ana?" He called her, sounding like snow. His hands crept toward her.

A scream shot out of the rounded heap. Gil clutched the sheet and gritted his teeth not to jump away a mile.

Again, he edged near and he turned the sheet down to see her face. It was lavender and hollows like a scorched spot in the woods.

"Please!" She begged.

"What? What is it?"

"Leave it alone. I will be better."

"How? I'm getting Cooke and Priscilla. Where is Matthew? He's got to go for the doctor close by because Mac is gone. I'll be back. I'm going for some light."

"Don't dare!"

Gil stopped short near the door. He almost ignored her.

"Gil, please!"

He closed them in so she could speak freely. He found the bed again.

"No one must come. I sent them all off to the Spinneys' so Priscilla could visit her Sam!"

"You are alone here? Why wasn't I called? Matthew knew just where I was. He should have come for me!"

"He wanted to. I told him no."

"It will not go lightly with him for obeying you in this condition."

"No condition!" She uttered.

"How can I leave you to go get someone?! Have you left me a stable boy for an errand?!" He was incensed with her.

"Help me!"

Her plea astounded him. She never depended on him. The sound of his fingers snapping for servants rang in his memory.

He neared her gingerly. He sat on the down and stretched toward her and wrapped her in his arms. She was deathly still with something. He let her go. He stood, twisting this way and that, wiping the sudden sweat off his face and up through his hair.

She groaned and swivelled onto her back, stiff as a log.

Gil listened, poised, waiting for thunder. The silence shattered at a wavering, wet call. Gil stayed put like a rivet.

"Cloth of diaper!" Hanna waved her arm without direction. "Lowboy!"

Gil stumbled into it. Stacks of ghastly white rectangles stood waiting in order. He pulled half of one away steadying the soft pile under his chin while he fumbled with her coverlet. All he saw in the colorless room was the whiteness of linen and the blackness of spreading blood.

"Hanna, my God!" It was too late for cloths. The sheet was mired already. Her legs were aswim in her blood. The down had matted and it stank like a battleground.

Her hands would come down to seal her off and then by her will fly up to clutch the pillows.

Gil stood like a footman balancing the diapers.

With a grunt she gave up blood fruit.

His heart broke free and he moved as if knowing what to do. He laid cloth over her and wrapped her legs in white. He lifted her hips and wadded clean cloth under as he would to stop a spill from a keg. He gripped her obedient hands in his slippery, stained ones. "Is it all right?"

"Now it is right."

Gil slumped in the dressing chair watching her until there was no trace of light to see her by. He toyed with matchsticks and striker to get up a spark to light the candlewick.

"More, dear!"

He took the tiny flame with him to gather another armful. "I must get you off that bed."

"Not yet."

"Go to the manse? Get the Lows?"

"Oh, no!"

"Hanna." Gil fetched again, then sat, his red hands meshed nearly in prayer. "This is not normal."

"No."

"Then why not have a physician in here!"

"Just peace."

He let her rest until an idea struck. "Did Beckett...?"

Of the Dowland line, she looked straight at her husband. "This is not from that, Gillie."

He turned his face aside. There it was. He had been brave about it for months. Feckless about it. But it was hard to hear from her.

"Poor man." She moaned.

Each held the other in unrelenting view.

"Yes." Gil said of himself, not of Beckett. "What was that ride? Did he...bungle? Did he force you?"

"Oh, Gil! How can you!"

He yelled at her. "A thousand pardons, you are bleeding half to death!"

"Not I."

Like the first sprinkle of spring rain, the two words broke over him. Pinpoints. If not she - a child. He knew all about himself now. Nothing wrong with that. Hanna had conceived. Gil had not seeded her. She had taught him through Beckett that he could not. He had come home to discover who this Hanna was. He looked at her as if into a mirror.

Gil began to fold the gore into the hot, soaked cloths. With his bare hands he massed the evidence of fertility not his. Kindly, he cleaned away the traces of the miscarriage. He took the purpled gown off her and knew shame at how long it had been since he had looked at her naked body. Now she was not the same. The flesh had changed with her soul. The breasts coming into blossom to give milk would relax, true, but they would lie lower always, pulled down by Beckett's hand. "When I'd got used to it, I'd have given him a name. I do think."

"I was sure you would!"

Another proportion of the woman changed for him. Even sure that she could have it all settled in her favor, she had made that rough ride. It was that which had uprooted a sprout of life - a germ of humanity she had longed all her life to nurture and deliver whole into her husband's arms.

Never mind that, Hanna had seen to it consciously or not that there would be no rival to Elizabeth's child for the Dowland estate or for Worth's own. And bearing the name of Worth, her son by Beckett would have been in contest for both.

Was her reckless ride a headstrong race back to herself? Summary murder? The tortured admission that the cheat of her womb was the creation of two quite different men?

Gil would not ask. He saw in blood that Hanna was a woman faithful to the Dowland line. Gil's lips trembled at an idea that she had stayed with him only because of this. How he wanted her to make him disbelieve it. He held her.

His plea, "Will you be well?", did not fool her. She could not lift her chalken arms to him but enfolded his throat with her throat. His joy at her mute answer pierced him as a woman is pierced.

He placed her in the side chair so that he could finish the work. Gil fought with the terrible mattress, doubling it, then, standing on it, he savaged the post curtains to use for tying bands. A powder from the ripped cloth floated on the fouled air and the tester nearly fell.

"Goddamn!" He had forgotten to include his smeared robe with the burden in the cylinder of ruined down. He sacrificed it and the tenderly worked pillowcases and any gory thing in the room.

They were both naked but numb to the April cold. Neither hated the sight of the other's bloody self.

"You will feel safe enough in that chair?" Gil wiped the soles of his feet so he would not leave a record of that night in plain view.

"Must you leave me?"

"Only to heat water, dearest. We want a sudsing."

Her eyes sparkled as if set with precious stones.

"You are better?"

"I am fine."

"You are!" Gil adored the Dowland will in her.

When they were clean, combed, and robed, he lifted her and started for the stairs.

"Where are we going, Gil?"

"Together."

"Down? This room?"

He struggled holding her at the same time that he opened the wide, white doors of the sitting room. He crossed the disused threshold with her and pulled back the window hanging. The tree they had planted before the house was built offered its blossoms to the dark sky.

He carried her toward the settee.

"Gil! No! I am covered the best I can be but I'll bleed again. I am sure."

"Finish off the upholstery! Fine with me. Not a thing's gone right since we had this couch done over in yellow."

He lighted a fire with the candle flame but would not tolerate any other illumination. He settled his wife looking out toward the land. Her allure was magnified for him with the family mud under her nails. She was not soiled grasping for territory but for the native claim. A noble effort.

Gilbert Worth took his harp between his legs and when it warmed he closed his eyes and began to play.

CHAPTER FIVE

June 1749

According to the Scot there was change in Beth if not improvement. Gil rode out to the Cape to see. Too impatient to bear with coach travel he went on horseback trespassing at a gallop the pastures of distant neighbors and negotiating efficiently the rotting bridges over the wetlands joining the mainland with Cape Cod.

It was brilliant June. He arrived at the hamlet of Sandwich hardly dusty. Nothing and no one ever seemed soiled in the Cape Cod air.

Gil hated, or, more precisely, was jealous of Elizabeth's surroundings. Not that he wanted them for his own. He wanted her to give them up for the beauties of Sweetwood. That was where she was from - inland and uphill, a place affected by the sea, bright with it, but not doltishly staring at it.

Sweetwood in the region of Sippicon had strong forests still and got its name from its trees: white pine, balsam, juniper, maple, birch, chestnut, cedar and more, and a variety of fruitwood - plum, pear, apple, cherry - growing wild, in profusion, and above all, fragrantly. In good weather the sun heated the past night's dew into an ascending mist that no incense of the Church of Rome could replicate. To Gil, these perfumes were God's. Or the gods'. That debate was of less consequence than that on golden days or gray,

Sweetwood threw good smells into the air instilling a confidence in the Earth that was basic to life if one chose not to live in London, Paris, or Italy.

Whereas, Sandwich was a hallucination, pristine as glass, a lost village built on sand. Sun touched the salt that glazed everything from the beach to the population like bakery cakes. A glow as precious as babies' sweat perseverved in the air, day and night.

Riding up to Stirling's block, Gil said venomously, "Walking to the outhouse around here must be a regular Transfiguration." He caught Israel Stirling with this remark, the doctor's carrot-haired son, an apprentice physician and no mean trumpeter, who Gil knew to be terrified of him. So, he said more sociably as he swung down from his six-year-old Bay, "I see you've painted, Little Stirling. The house looks pretty now. The Irish all right with the planting? I hope so. What does your father say about the farm taking too much time from your studies? I worry about him. He is lonely for your mother, rest her. Is he home? Let's find him!"

The walk to the silver-shingled barn was always a walk to the scaffold for Gil. The barn stood on a green hip of earth overlooking the water. Gil had had the roof fixed before Elizabeth got there. In her mood he knew she would have fought to let it leak. He had also gotten some panes of glass put in the loft to give her a square of light. But Elizabeth had allowed no one to take so much as a broom to the cobwebs. She had transacted with Stirling for the place. She rented it with money she earned by sewing. Every time Gil passed down the sand path that brought him to the ridiculous dwelling he could be nothing but ashamed of his lights and wary of his instincts that had assisted her steps thither.

Worth saw Mac in his shirtsleeves, half in the sun. The harsh music of the Scot's voice played over the expanse outside although he looked into the dark belly of the barn. Occasionally, he would jerk his thumb in the direction of the pond that fronted it.

Gil could tell the moment he had been seen by his niece. The doctor looked his way then hurried into the barn as if chasing a butterfly.

"This is as far as I go." Worth said sadly to his young host. "I will not introduce myself just to invite her shouting or waving some lately-woven monstrosity in my face. Do the people in town know what else she produces in there besides socks with no holes? Your father must agree on a date for her definite improvement for beyond it I am determined to try another cure. I am the executor of Dowland's estate, as you know, and her legal guardian. I'd rather drop her into a pit of snakes than witness her rotting away into a witch."

"Yes, sir."

"What the hell are you saying yes for?"

"Because, I agree."

"I see."

"She's better than she was. We don't know why. She hasn't worked on the web lately. I haven't noticed it getting any bigger."

"Israel, how can you look at it at all?"

"Well, sir, people who like to be doctors have to look at the inside. Looking at that web is looking into her heart."

"If I were not so fond of your father, sonny, I would hurl some abuse your way."

Israel gasped, "I go to look at the web when she is out at the water. It sits on the loom in the blackest corner. It is quite black. And perfect. Thin as a spider's would be."

"I know. I know."

"I've always thought it a healthy sign that it is so like a real web. It means she is weaving with her eyes closed."

"What nonsense!" Gil resented Israel's collegial tone. "Nobody weaves with eyes closed. And what difference?"

Israel stammered, "A great deal, Mister...Mister Worth. If she wove with black in blackness, night after night for so many nights, with her eyes open, she would be going blind."

"Are you sure?"

"Father thinks so. She couldn't come out in the sun if her eyes were going bad. But she does!"

Gil passed his wrist across his forehead as Israel helped him to sit. "This is frightening. If what you say is true, and I've seen how exact a thing that web is, think of those hands. There is light in their skill." Gil stared at his own. "It is Lucifer's genius. Oh, do not mention it to anyone from the town. Hide it from the Irish! They'll have her out and burn her. A skill like that...." Tears came and went. "Israel, couldn't she be weaving in the day?"

"In the days she walks out. Every day. Regardless of the weather. I watch her sit at her wheel at night. Regardless of the weather."

"You do?"

"Aye, sir."

"Every night?"

"About, sir."

"Does your father want you spying on her?"

"Into her private snake pit, as it were."

"Well! Well then, how can you see her weaving if she cannot?"

"I see her at her loom through the glass you put in the roof. Until I cannot see her anymore."

"That's a hell of an occupation."

"She is a fascinating study."

"I can imagine."

"I think she is the bravest woman yet to live."

"Do you? How old are you?"

"Mr. Worth, have you ever sat with your eyes closed in a room twenty times as tall as you, an hundred times your breadth, more, with little noises here and there? And waiting for someone besides? A leaf skids - drips of water slip from beams when there has been no rain - air moves against your neck though the barn doors are closed - your eyes softly shut, not squeezed shut, but softly, and your hands involved in a thousand threads so that you could not get free to defend yourself if some intruder brushed your elbow?"

Gil shot to his feet. "How dare you! How dare you!"

Israel looked up at him a blade of long grass between his teeth. "And we know she is ashamed of being lonely the while."

"Do you think this is play? You are painting the nightmare end of a fine spirit."

"I think she has a great heart, if somewhat unusual, and that she is still sane because she is so brave. But...."

"But what!?"

Israel rose for his diagnosis. "If, as you said, by a certain date she does not abandon things that give her fear, then she may no longer feel fear."

"And then?"

"She will be mad." The young man flushed. Dressed like a farmer in denim and clogs, he watched with attention ants on their hill.

"Young doctor," Gil gave respect when he thought it was due, "what is your suggestion?"

"That we watch her carefully to the bottom of the pit, and then strongly, even harshly, pull her out."

"Bravo! And your papa?"

"My father?" Israel sounded in despair of him. "He thinks she is climbing out now on her own."

Gil looked at the younger Stirling and found a smile for him. "We can pray he is correct."

"Judge for yourself. I'll invite her outside." Abruptly, Israel strode away.

Gil began to pull himself to order, ruff to cuff.

"An' how're you?"

"Mac!" Gil sought his hand and shook it. "Quite well. Grown up some since last we met."

"Sounds bad."

"It's splendid, thank you."

"Sounds bad."

"Ask Hanna if it is. She wants to speak to you, anyway."

"Where is she then?"

"She's cautious about riding or sitting in a carriage just now."

"Sounds good and bad."

Gil smiled. He wore soft skin breeches and black riding boots. His shirt was white linen and his coat and waistcoat a raw silk. His straw hat was crushed happily against his side.

"If there were only two of you." Mac shrugged and walked toward the barn.

"Beth's husband did not need to be two."

"Wha' are you saying?"

"Not what you think, though more than one person has insinuated I might like to do double duty. Why don't we tell her Fox is a free man."

"You're daft."

Gil switched his tack. "I agree we shouldn't. If he's going to come, he'll come."

64

"Oh, she's well out of that situation. I was thinking some person more conventional."

"Conventional is the word! Why can't we men let her be? All her woes were born out of her run from the altar. Maybe we should help her to be alone."

"If you can make her laugh by it," the old man's neck was stuck out like a turkey's, "see to it!" He left Gil and trudged up to the house with Israel.

Not overanxious to rush to Elizabeth's doorstep, Worth sat at the edge of the pond. The water was brown or green depending on the force of the sun through passing clouds or densities of leaves. Now it was packed with something and had no color at all. Straw? Flax! So there was a change. Making linen was a long task. A year's work for little yield. These thin bundles of sticks were the beginning of a major undertaking. Gil hardly hoped something so constructive could come from his desolate niece. He saw a vision of her on the water. Even on the green mirror her face was white, of clay as luscious as memory. Cruel memory. The vision dipped its arm in the pond up to a green sleeve. Real drops of water pebbled his boots and a cool, wet hand touched his wrist.

"Beth!" Gil gasped. He looked at her touching him. "I was thinking of you, and you are here!"

"I was calling you."

"Were you?" His voice became tenor.

"I am glad to see you."

"You are?" He wished he could have hidden his amazement.

She withdrew. She stepped backwards. She knew some untoward behavior of hers must be uppermost in his recollection. "You seem well."

Gil could not help feeling reprimanded about his absence since the end of March. Humbly he offered, "Better all the time. Are you - well?"

"I wonder about Aunt Hanna." Elizabeth said in a voice so thick that Gil wondered if by craft of magic she knew. Elizabeth picked up a branch and proceeding around its circumference stirred the dark pool.

Gil walked at her side. He took her arm. It was straight and thin and cold - a limb of silver. He let it go. "This is linen?" He remarked rather stupidly, he thought.

But his struggle moved her to talk. "Of course!"

Her voice was as deep and soft as he remembered. But today her words were all mistakes.

Gil started them over. "This is Stirling's flax?"

"I paid him for it."

"By simple sewing?"

"I have been lucky getting some fine work."

"I didn't mean - you know this is not necessary."

"It is - what I want."

"Right now."

"It is what I wanted to begin with." Her eyes turned toward the sea. "A long time ago."

It vexed Gil that she did not look west and inland to Wakwa's woods. And her fragmented phrases bore no resemblance to the sluice for thought and feeling her speech had once been. But at least they were talking.

He chanced leading her. "What do you want now?"

She shocked him. "Sleep."

"You are uncomfortable!"

She smiled. Her thought made sense to her. She talked aslant of it, "It is just that it is too carefree now that it is growing warm."

Carefree? Was that the right word? She was still hollowed by the Indian. Still rang inside like a bell. Gil grabbed for her imagination. "Next year, your aunt and I will travel. We count on your coming with us. No one knows what will happen on the seas as politics are running, so we should all go abroad soon and be back."

"Will you come inside?"

"Elizabeth, yes, but...."

"Just once."

He stopped.

She pulled him on. "You are always welcome. When you are down this way." At his distraught expression she added, "At any time!"

"Good." He pecked her cheek and took her hand and caused her to look at this link, although she had not yet pronounced his name or title of relation. "Let's go see."

It was brown and gold inside, much richer than the bland sunscape.

"You've swept up."

"Noticeably so?"

Gil passed a quaking hand across his mouth. "I only mean it seems pleasant in here. Not a lot of stuff about. Tools all hung. Very clean. Not a shred of soiled hay on the floor. I'd be disappointed were I a cow."

She smiled as at a memory of humor.

Gil forged on. "Your loft looks tidy. Fresh stuff for your bed. I like the effect of those flowers heads down. Roof still tight?"

She turned on him, all suspicion. "It has always been fine."

"Everything needs care, Bethy. You know that."

She bit her lip.

He wished she would cry - fall into his arms and cry. "I see some weaving folded away. That black business?"

"I stopped work on it."

Gil trod on eggshells now. He even tried to soften his diction. "That so?"

"I suppose it was all a waste."

Obligated to pay it attention, he went to the platform where her wheel and her baskets of stuffs stood. He touched the web and was surprised to find it nice to the hand. "Beth, it feels the way..." he searched for something complementary and not encouraging, "the mane of a unicorn would."

"You think I should continue then!"

"No!" He damned his outburst but saved them with cunning. "You have the linen now."

"I do want to do the linen."

"Make that your course then. This other seems complete as it is. Your aim was not to catch flies."

Her lip curled at the corner. Then she hid behind the query, "Does it seem dirty in here?"

He sighed and spoke the truth. "I have to say it does not. The floor is definitely dirt but packed and hard and healthy. You've worked it with a rake. You've got the edges tight. Not creeping. It is rather pleasant. As I said. You have made an attractive place for the space and the quiet. It's part cathedral, part cloister. Very restful. Almost Mediaeval if the floor were some sort of stone. You know, dear, if you take the fancy, you can, next time you rake, cut some lines into your packed floor for a border or design. Then sprinkle a little water on it and watch it harden. You could have a new design every week!"

Elizabeth regarded Gil with fascination, as if she were meeting him for the first time.

Unnerved, his voice shook. "Like this. Do you mind?" He began to draw on the earthen floor with the point of a garden plough. A line grew like a vine. He wound it around her foot.

She seemed delighted. "A trapunto underfoot!"

"You can do it better than I, dear, your lines are always right." And to himself he said, "Small steps." Gil swore himself to them. He polished the point and rehung the tool.

"And Aunt is fine?"

He took hold of her arms. "Your aunt loves you and yours more than you could know."

"Mine?"

Gil blinked away the horror of her confusion. "Do you think you could visit her? Come along with Mac?"

"Oh!" She quaked like an aspen.

He had overstepped but finished boldly, "Try to see to it." He backed away toward the sun. "Hanna has nothing but your wishes in mind." He left her hiding her face in her apron.

CHAPTER SIX

Summer 1749

Dire saw a great public trust in the success of the affair of the tall, straight, good-looking man with russet skin and the queenly girl of English parentage (count in grandfather Dowland's diversion to a Corsican wife before his emigration to America, pixilating the bloodline). In Locke's estimation, the prosperity of growing numbers of people, issues of war and peace, the death and birth of moralities dangled from the smiles or tears of the red man and the white woman.

And as long as he had been asked to do it, Dire considered himself equal to the gigantic manipulation of events yet to be. Ridiculing himself as, "Shachtan!" the Matchmaker, when he looked in the mirror to shave, Locke became absorbed by the project because he saw it as more than mere personal business. It was business itself.

In a quandary about how to proceed in bringing Wakwa to his senses and Elizabeth back into his sachimmaacommock, Dire, directly after meeting Elizabeth, went to Boston to visit Jeanette, his onetime mistress, now wife.

Governess to Beckett's infant son, Horace, the French-Canadian woman would have a gospel to tell. She might, put in the right mood, do so in a way comforting to him, a hectic factor of fifty.

Dire justified any personal indulgence on company time by striving as well to pick up some loose business from the solicitor, not that Beckett was a spender of money. But the man at law was in Locke's debt for the survival of his offspring and was about to move his household, lock, stock, and barrel to Cambridgeshire in England, not inconvenient to Kirke Company's London headquarters.

Whatever the demands of Dire's lightning excursion to Boston, he considered precious any insight he could gain into the management of the great schism - the breach of faith between Wakwa and Elizabeth.

Dire Locke calculated that the Dowland girl, but in her early twenties, had thirty good years of marriageability in her. Maybe more. Kirke had to be sixty, a clean, good-smelling sixty. But he was not immortal. Elizabeth would, barring mishaps with children or her emotions, emerge the survivor of a union with Kirke and be widowed at the helm, as it were, of Kirke Company's commercial empire. Not even Kirke managed the vast enterprise alone.

Locke's agenda clarified. They were in business together, the Fox and the factor. Big business. The love would take care of itself - if love it was - and Dire saw it as such. Elizabeth's marriage to Kirke would not only put her in business with the tribe, it would be the extension of Dire's lifeline.

He set himself to find what talent the Dowland girl might have for business. As for Silent Fox, Dire would grant him what he wanted - nothing. No approval, no special treatment, no easy road back. This would give the Indian time to suffer and to broaden his mind.

Locke rapped at the barn door one evening in July. He saw what he had hoped for. Surprises.

The first was Elizabeth who looked like an independent sun in the blue hour. The last time she appeared to be a flickering flame. Now she was metal in the forge. Her eyes were the human touch in her burnished face. Her hair poured back like a spit of copper. Her figure draped in thin summer cloth stunned like a spare, bronze statue. One thing was the same. She smiled and his arteries went into a frenzy.

"Sight of you works toward the shame of women everywhere who cower from the sun."

She invited him inside. This was another surprising thing; she had shed her guard.

"Are you so trusting of a stranger, a man sporting a not very well-hidden pistol, that you risk yourself and your possessions to him?"

"Do you intend to murder me?"

So! She had humor and she was hard. Rather, could be hard. "You're quite right to scold me for that. I see your wit is not impaired by your living alone."

Her eyes took a varnish of black tears. "I live not alone."

"People are going to say clumsy things. You must be easy on them." Locke bowed.

With courtesan's art she made curtsey. "Sir, you are kind to care. And kinder still to have kept your promise to return. I counted on it. And welcome you. How rare in our time to find a man as good as his word." She turned shy and glanced away but asked him to enter with a motion of her hand not inept.

Dire's understanding was whipped this way and that by her inconstant moods. He grappled for her personality and for his next phrase. Conventional conversational lines were waste with the woman.

"My father was such a man." She relieved her visitor of the responsibility to reply and poured him water from a pitcher of ice.

Dire drank, of course, and the liquid tasted as rich as wine.

"And my aunt's husband is."

"Your uncle."

"My uncle-by-marriage."

He gave her a widened eye.

"My uncle and my true friend."

Locke had anticipated that if she came near to revealing her identity he must set her back with his first. She would recognize his name from the Indian Trade. To take the lead with her would keep her guessing not thinking. He set down his wooden cup and stood as handsome as a bird in his navy silks. "Mistress, I do myself the honor of placing myself in that category with you, though newly. Dire Locke is my name."

Another odd turn. She did not seem shocked by his stunning announcement. Instead, recognition beamed from her. But as the complexity of his visiting struck, she swayed. Locke hurried over, full of concern, never dropping his charade. "You are not unwell? Please sit! Do drink!"

Elizabeth broke from him and dragged herself to the narrow ladder that led to her loft. She hung her arms through the rungs. "Oh, my God!"

Locke watched her for disaster. She turned to him, bloodless, looking burnt, treated, cooked and dried, tanned as with chemicals and time. Locke could see her stacked in his heaps of pelts stamped for the backs of the rich.

"Do you know who I am?" She came toward him.

"Should I?" He slipped out of a lie.

"I am the wife of Wakwa."

"The wife...?" Locke struggled.

"One of his wives."

"He has two."

"No! He let me go. It was he! Your greatest supplier."

Locke smarted at this impersonal association, as he had never done before. He began to teach her. "But who *are* you?"

"I? Oh. I am the second wife. I am the late Charles Dowland's daughter."

"Have you a name?"

"My name is Elizabeth."

"Yes. Elizabeth."

"Dire Locke." Her voice seemed to chime from various places inside her. "Mr. Locke!"

"How out of the ordinary." He commented.

"You are just as I thought."

He nearly laughed. "Dear lady, sit down." He pointed her to her bench. "And what did you think about me? What did you think of the Trade the years you were involved with it? How did it treat you? What do you know of it?"

"Mr. Locke?"

"What are you doing here? Was the Trade, or Thomas Kirke... Limited...in any degree responsible for the Indian's breaking off with you?"

She seemed to leaf through some text about it compiled in her memory. Slowly she admitted, "No. Your House was never a trouble. It was the only support. Aside from my aunt and uncle. Ever a support. Let me thank you now. And apologize. I rather disliked you."

"Did you?"

"Or distrusted...his...trust of you."

Locke found her sabre-sharp. "And now?"

"He was right to love you."

Locke cleared an untimely mist from his throat. "Whatever he thinks, you are here. Well known we are, one to the other. You and I, Mistress Elizabeth, have been partners for a long time. Set up in business. You and I."

She gazed, feeling and seeing her losses.

Locke put a stop to that. "I knew of you from the beginning. I supplied him the woolens and linens and cottons for your clothes. That cutting board was my idea! My answer to his request for something special for you. My gift to you. I worried over you from the beginning. And over him. Yes, over him. And what I predicted has come to pass. Well. Well. Wouldn't be the first time. Your work is singular. You know it; I know it. They are all masters' pieces. Even to the clay, here, underfoot. I would be a pale agent for Kirke if I left such a source untapped. I see no reason why our relationship should not continue in full force, your marital status notwithstanding."

"Mr. Locke!" She stepped toward him, her anxiety for word about Wakwa pitiable to see.

Dire heard it coming. "You must understand, if we are to do business, you cannot presume on my commercial relation with him."

"Is he alive?"

"Yes."

"Is it he cannot find me?"

"I do not see why he could not."

Her eyes seemed to grow and she backed away not wanting to hear bad opinions of her hopes.

"I don't understand the man. He must have his reasons. I think him outright wrong to have taken you to wife in the first place.

And having done it, he is, now that I know you better, I feel I can say, plain wrong to have put you out. And out you are, for the Fox is a man of his word too."

She tore this spear from her heart. "Will you see him?"

"I may. I never know. But it would be unethical for me to philosophize about one to the other. Bad form. Bad business. I'll cut him out if you push me. Don't push me. His reasons have to be good to do what he did to you. Good to him, anyway. If you badger me ever, Madam, I'll starve him to death."

Elizabeth stared in horror. "Be fair!"

Locke's face was stone. It would not change.

She backed away from his coldness. She shut out his impassivity, her hands over her eyes. After time she looked at him again, the skin of her face switching as if bothered by poisonous insects. "Do you know, at least, where he is? Say nothing but that."

"I am not without a heart." Dire came close to deliberately throwing his bargain with Wakwa. The thought of ultimate resolution steadied him. "I can understand what you feel...."

"Can you?!"

"My dear lady, you are not the only one living with love gone awry. All I can say honestly is that I have not seen him for some time and am constantly worried about him. He may turn up."

"Do you think? Do you?" She gleamed.

"I have no way of knowing. No more do you."

At this levelling she remarked, "And so I stay here."

"Ill advised. What would my life be if I never did a trade with another hunter on the chance that Silent Fox would show with a shipload of furs or ginseng? I would have no work and no reason. I deal with those who will deal with me. Will you?"

"Yes!"

"Good girl! With what?"

"Linen?"

"Are you asking?"

"Linen." She faced him like a bulldog.

"When will it be ready?"

"In a year. It is soaked and hulled. I am at the boiling stage and it does not take me as long as others to spin...there is little to interrupt my distaff."

"Who will weave?"

"I shall weave."

"You! Where?"

"Right here."

"But how much can you get in a year?"

"I aim for twelve yards."

"An overestimate."

"I did half that when I was half my age."

"You'll kill yourself. A yard a month. Twelve long yards. Even at five pounds per, sixty pound, you've got tax and expenses. How much for the flax?"

"Seven Spanish dollars."

"Got it from the Scot, I suppose."

"It is a good price!"

"It is. But it is not cheap."

"It is good flax."

Dire gave her a cheer.

"Can you use what I will produce?"

"Oh, I can." Locke clucked for Kirke. "Raw or bleached?"

"Bleached, if there is time."

"Bleached how?"

"On grass."

"Hmmn. It might be pretty fine in this air. I advance you thirty pounds now." He doled it onto the potting table between them. "The rest on completion."

"I have never seen such money spread upon a table!"

"I don't imagine a Presbyterian has."

She looked up quickly. "Will you make a profit?"

"I expect."

They looked at each other across the money. Her brown eyes and his brilliant blues gave off the same glint.

"Mistress Elizabeth, your sell is a good hard one, but not ruinously direct." Dire seated himself lightly, comfortably in a dilapidated chair which was deemed unfit for the house. The bad mend in its left leg gave him a place to hook his thumb. "You would do very well on the buyer's end. You understand already that the skilled can never do as well as those who sell his skills and meet his costs. An agent must sell above to meet them and his own and yet stock the warehouse under market costs. The merchant must be cleverer than everybody. He and his fellow merchants must judge the times and set the ultimate price to keep the whole jig going. For, if he is great, the merchant knows that to let down the agent is to let down the supplier, such an one as you, who is his beating heart. And suppliers let down, the hunters and craftsmen, the artists whose hearts beat for their works, grumble until they roar, and there is rebellion, and kingdoms topple."

It was then he came to where she sat. He put one trim foot up on her bench. "Commerce is a mighty work. My part must be done very quick so I will not starve. If I do, you do. And, as for you, you must set aside everything else. The world is now your slave for it labors under a yoke of desire and credit and it has just extended some to you."

Her color was back and she looked up at him, the pace of her breath altered forever. It was the difference between existing in the womb and the world; the slip from maidenhood into experience. Uneasily, with the fingers of her mind, she touched the net of tyranny and independence, the net Wakwa was caught in. It made her happy, somehow, to think of herself in that coil. Trapped she was not lost - struggling not discarded.

She heard the voice. Wakwa's voice came as Dire Locke took her head against his thin hip. It was the same voice that had said she was not his wife anymore but woman. *"Wenygh! You are woman!"* Wakwa had said it, and she heard it now and believed him.

Locke said, "Believe me, my dear, nothing of moment is created in this world in any other way." He gathered his papers and purse and tucked them into particular compartments in his coat. "The word is, the bane is lifted. The treason charge is dropped."

"No!"

He hacked away at her at her high moment. "We will see what comes of it. Mayhap nothing."

She rose as if against a stone press. "Will you tell him? Tell him!"

"Of course, I will. I make you a bet I hope I'll lose, that he will not come for you." Locke reached the doors.

"Don't go!" She was there in a second.

"This in my stead." He rummaged in the coat again and came up with a letter of stiff, folded paper. "Almost forgot." He clucked his tongue. "Getting old. You'll appreciate it. From Kirke. About the sample." He made for the torches blazing on each side of his carriage.

"But the doctor! Won't you see Doctor Mac?"

"Next time! Thank you! It's gotten very late."
"But when will you come again?"
"I'll send a line ahead."

15 May 1749

My dear Dire,

For God's sake do not send me magic parcels anymore! This patch of cloth I am staring at is alive! My eyes tell me the cursed thing is linen but I touch and feel an angel's wing. Is there an American fibre I know not? It is mixed with silk, thought I, and ran to the weavers who frayed a bit and said, "Linen," with the most jealous looks. To calm them down, I told them "twas made by a nun doing a penance.'

Lord, it's only linen and I thought I'd felt the finest but this speaks! It speaks genius - the taking of a simple task and embellishing its secret steps to make that which sustains the spirit in all ways. For instance, a thousand pelts we get from most cannot match in beauty or value one of the prize kind your Indian, Silent Fox, sends over here from time to time.

The design of the sample I will not comment on. Gave me a headache. I thought only Sicilians wild enough to risk their health to such sewing - white on white with patterns raised - that plus such linen - linen on linen is not known at the Vatican. What the hell is the thing? I bet you any money it is an Indian charm and once touched a man is bewitched.

It's a spell, isn't it? You are too little employed if you have time for such departures.

Is there more of it? My mouth waters over this scrap. Do you want to market it? Who makes it? Not a man. His blood would boil, not to mention...Jesus! It is fine. A woman, I say. Crazy. Not quite. Obsessed? Religious? Same thing. In love. With what man? What a man! Poor she is, or poor in spirit because a party-goer has no time. Old Locker! Is this your Jeanette's? How nice to be young. But if it were your wife's you wouldn't be so coy. With all I have to do and think about without any help, how dare you send me witches patches! You've been on that foreign rock too long. Why don't you come? It is hard as hell to convince the Parliament of anything to do with the Trade without your advice.

I said to them the other day, 'She'll dry up on us in no time, if Parliament don't raise import duties on the right items. Then what'll England do? The suppliers will laugh in our faces or worse.'

Have you got any plans in your pocket for after the deer? Pocket? You don't mean the pocket? You old sly. You might have written me two sentences for a clue. I stare at it. I carry it around. Pocket in pocket. It is swallowing me. Pretty soon I'll be in its pay!

You've sent it as a sign. Something in America we don't give her credit for. Is that it? Damn you! Write to me immediately and explain it away. Can you be saying there is a civilization in the New World? Does it bode good or ill for the Trade? The artist whosoe'r she is has lights for many things imprisoned in a woman's form. Or is it man's work? Come home! Idler! I shall have you found. I'll do it myself." V.T. Kirke

Much of Elizabeth's lantern burned before she put this letter safely in the leather trunk where she kept her clothes. She stretched out on her straw and occasionally touched the hard, dark chest as if to tell it that she knew a guest was there. KIRKE. The name of him was as familiar to her childhood as words like TEA and THREAD and CHINA.

She was moved that a man like Thomas Kirke, a man who had seen all that was beautiful in the world, who had been in the East, could rhapsodize upon an effort of hers. She was glad that she had not signed it. Her artful pieces were her poems, not her bread or her card. She did like that she existed for him in some measure, though. It made her feel that she existed at all to be guessed at by a stranger.

Her hours before light were entirely pleasurable. Her confidence built like the tissues of her body in her sleep. She dreamt of her son without pain. She felt the nearing of his father.

Dire did not stop for night. In spite of the provincial curfew, his coach went flaming along. He managed survival on the velvet seat cushion with not quite the ease of travel by sea, but after necessary pauses on the road and laying over at company headquarters in Wareham, he pulled up to Gilbert Worth's door by mid-afternoon of the next day fresh as a daisy.

He was too seasoned a wanderer to take slow impressions of an alien locale. He caught the soul of Worth's place while winding his watch. The sprawling white buildings studding the green and fluctuating meadows were Anglo-Saxon manna. The lack of gates and guards and pillars and pretensions showed predilections to simplicity, to faith, and to joy. A crystal dome sitting the north meadow like an Olympian bauble revealed the courage of Worth's dreams.

These assessments were borne out when Locke sent in his card and was able to exchange the confines of his coach for the splendors of Worth's sitting room in one hundred seconds flat.

Hanna and Gil each knew or knew of Locke from different vantages of time and circumstance. Each estimated his character the same. His range of ability and consistency of performance assured their trust of him. His omniscience attracted them to him like a Beelzebub.

Greetings were hasty, frothy as beer. They watched Locke make his way around them, fascinated to see his gentle playing with their anxiety. Worth knew Locke never relaxed. Hanna was glad. Out of gaiety grew a moment in which Gil asked Dire if he knew what had happened to the family.

"I know everything." Locke's typical response.

Husband and wife looked at each other, doubting this. Just then Locke exhibited great interest in their denuded couch.

"It was another beautiful thing you procured for our house," Hanna said. "We had it reupholstered locally while we were both away the winter before last. It was not a success."

Locke passed up the opportunity to cite what a magnificent understatement this was of a season that had broken his leg and the back of Wakwa's and Elizabeth's marriage. He concentrated on the swatches laid liberally over the wooden frame.

Hanna prompted, "What would you think of the odd green?"

Locke looked from the silk to the rug to her face. "Elegant. Soft but not weak. I'll get it for you right away. Accept with it, won't you, a piece of Celadon that I'll find. That way your settee will have a friend in the room."

Prettily, in return, Hanna asked him to stay.

Adroitly, he refused, planning to extract dearer payment.

From the window recess, Locke proclaimed the sweetness of the glass of orange juice squeezed from Worth's hothouse fruit at the same time observing a bitterness in Worth, a new trait. Locke heard volumes in Hanna's babying of her husband. That was his springboard.

"Your ideas, Worth, are too big to be squandered on this small hamlet." Dire was up, into the room, walking among the tables, the flowers, the desk, and the harp.

"You and I have had this discussion before." Gil was annoyed. "I chose this place over all of Europe. I married here and here I'll stay."

"At any cost?"

"I believe I've paid up my mortgage in this year's agony alone. And it is yet young. Now the place must start paying me."

"Exactly."

"Imagine! I have a commission from the local Presbyters to write a hymn for the church! Poor Doctor Low will do anything to try to cheer me up. Can you see me writing a hymn? And for a church in which the minister is the lamb and the congregation the wolf pack?"

Locke swivelled toward him. "That is the way it is supposed to be."

"Nevertheless!"

"Gilbert." Dire fingered the fiddles and scratched the backbones of the books with his nails. "Throw over these small activities. The only thing you cannot consider in this life is to stand for public office. This is not in your line of risks anymore."

"How did you know? How much do you know?"

"I am well informed. You know that. Well informed enough to warn you to cut the chain from your leg attaching you to this twin estate. Burst forth from this bog and make mountains to move!"

"Oh?" Gil increased in caution. "What mountains are those, Dire?"

"Why not let Elizabeth Dowland and Silent Fox lead you to them."

"What?"

"They did once before. By simply falling in love they made two ages of man converge in the palms of their hardworking hands."

"Is this you, Locke? You have hated the idea of them."

"I did not want them to come to harm. And you see they have. No one asked my advice when all this was slipping through their fingers. But I see spectacular opportunity in the ashes of this affair which I would not have believed last New Year's Day in March."

"You have seen him! He wants her back!" Gil came to his feet. "I have both feared and hoped it was behind us."

Hanna's hands crossed her bosom. "How could they renew?" Caught by her own diary she modified her question. "Do you think they could? Is it to do with their baby? Dire! Have you seen Moses?"

Gil went to his wife and she put her arm around his waist. "I cannot believe the moment is here!"

All Locke said was, "Those two will found an empire."

"What do you want from us?" Gil demanded.

"That you put nothing in the way of Elizabeth Dowland meeting and marrying Vaughan Thomas Kirke."

Gil's head bobbed like an old man's from the top of his spine or like a prisoner's beaten once too often.

Hanna watched him, one hand covering her mouth.

Worth pulled open the drawer of a nearby table to find something to blot the pearls of sweat forming under his eyes.

Looking down naturally, not inquisitively, Dire glimpsed the buckle that matched the one he had carried in his pocket for a long time. He reached for it with no hesitation. Quickly there were two in his hand.

They became the seal of his mission. All his persuasions after that had Wakwa's stamp, unquestionably in silver.

In the mountains the change of light had advanced so far that the cooling air was steeped in purple. Two men sat talking although the sky told them it was time to go.

Wakwa was one, as withdrawn as the departing day. Awepu was the other, Wakwa's cousin on his father's side. They stayed talking, avoiding going down the slopes to their incommodious mountain-town.

As if they already stood there, Wakwa and Awepu could see the roundhouses built in desperate imitation of the style in

Massachusetts. At home, outside Sweetwood, with materials at hand, the buildings were as neat as overturned cups. Large or small, they were smoothly formed of bent saplings and bark shingles. Here, on Agiocochook, were different weather and growth of wood. The huts stood squat and shapeless forming alleys of deadwood walls. The People and their leaders thought of it as a squalid works, the achievement of demented beaver.

The thin summer air was a womb for sound. At night, from far away, one could hear wildcats snore. And when it was silent the peace was profound. To the Massachuseuck exiles it was the quiet of bereavement. And much had been lost.

Tonight's silence had a singing voice as when they watched a great bird fly and from their distance knew he was screaming out some victory or joy although the sound did not reach them, only the sight of wings cutting the face of the sun.

"Have you ever seen such stars?" Awepu whispered as they appeared.

Wakwa hurt from appreciation. "Awepu we must all go home. Life continues here. It should not. My father could die here! The children feel the mountain in their bones. I do not want them to."

"The time is coming. I know."

"How do you know?"

"By looking at the stars."

"Awepu! I look inside myself, and I see nothing. I am as I used to be. It hurts me."

"You can never be what you were before she came. That story is not ended."

"It should not have begun!"

"How can you say your unhappiness and then say that? Who forced you two together?"

"She had such a manner of speech."

Awepu rolled his eyes. "And you the spokesman for us all. All I say is, if you do not want her, you shall keep hurting."

"How can you say such a thing to me, old friend, with such silence and such stars above?"

One wiry arm of Awepu's found a home on Wakwa's shoulders. "Sequan, your daughter, your firstborn, runs with the boys and calls herself woman-king. The little one, your second son, Lightfoot, throws his first smiles at me. And the other one, your firstborn son, Wolf-of-the-mist He-hopes, is not yet two and asked me yesterday why he has no father. He does not even know who his mother is. Can you see to your nest? Change your mind and have...her...back. I have no idea what your wife, Tame Deer, thinks of you but things were better for her when Elizabeth was by your fire."

"Do not say her name to me!"

"I do forget." Awepu's head moved as gently as a lily's in a breeze.

"When will I forget?"

"We should go down." Awepu took punk to their torch.

"I do like to go down after climbing up here, Awepu. I always feel while we were gone there may have come some news.

Wakwa saw his wife at her fire. She turned to him, full, smooth, polished as an apple. She pinned her upper lip with her tiny, white teeth when she saw him. She stood without flutter or rush, much like her name, and took the firelight. The children's chatter stopped. The helping girls scuttled away with them.

"Dire!" Wakwa saw him then.

Their moment was not awkward - it was slow. The wish to rush toward each other out of warmth yielded to the courtesy of host to guest and guest to host, and these to issues of power, practical and natural, the whiteman in the redman's sphere, and the redman in his own, bringing them to the precipice of their partnership. Neither man moved.

Wakwa rasped. "It is accomplished. So soon?"

Dire came then, picking his way among the people. "Can you know how I wish I were in Paris now?" His voice was pudding thick.

It was fine. The men embraced, sore heart to sore heart. They left the crowded quarters for the cover of night. Guards were motioned away. Awepu did not offer to join them.

Their torch singed itself to slow death as they climbed to the cliffs, the small animals darting in all directions, confused by illumination. The drumming, the humming, the screeching, the chittering exploded the strange peace and made it hard for them to hear one another as at large assemblies.

The men fought the terror of not saying well enough things deeply felt. Dire sat folded in a nook of rock. Wakwa lay belly down against the trunk of a listing tree: one man, a bug, the other, a leopard.

Again, the agent made the first move. He left the ledges for the tree. He pressed two cold things against Wakwa's palm. "These are your trophies. Bury them or hoard them. Whatever you do - do not sell them. Never show them except to Elizabeth."

Hudson's shoe buckles weighed Wakwa's hand. One might say - stayed it.

"I produced mine smooth as a trump card at whist in your English uncle's house, capturing his. They treated your inspiration as any announcement from Zion. In trembling obedience. You are their prophet. I do not know how you do it, after all else you have done to them. But you were right not to tell me the match to the buckle was sitting in the corner of the drawer of Worth's handkerchief table. I might have gone there first."

Wakwa knew then that Locke had seen Elizabeth. He moved no part of his body. He closed his eyes. Locke's words poured into him, swelling him.

"This is your moment, man! You can yet call it off! I am convinced she would put this episode behind her. And now you can. She loves you mightily and you are free!"

"Free?" Wakwa turned to the beloved voice.

"Free as the breeze. Free as the proverbial Indian. The charges are dropped. Move like the black fox you are and you can have your way in all things. I will help you. What do you say?"

"Awepu is safe? And all the men? And the families?"

"Your son has his wealth again. Has it because of it. But never mind. What is it to be, for the die is cast and there will be no moment for Elizabeth like this again."

It was then that Wakwa moved, stood clear of the woods and went out under the spangled ceiling of the sky. Locke stayed with him, tight at his side.

"The treason is no more? How did you do this?"

"The lawyer has had his way with the law. Your position is stronger now than it ever may be again. It is time to move!"

"Move? Go back?"

"Go anywhere, but go to her! Everyone's trying their damndest for you."

"Free!"

"As the saying goes. Free to do your duty by those you love."

Wakwa looked far down to the lake gleaming as if the morning sun were sleeping in its sandy bed. "I know. Now, my part with you. Now I go West."

"Let it go! Let it pass. You owe me nothing. Some day, if you like, toss me a lion's skin, but do not trudge away from happiness on my account. And do not think to trifle interminably with that gentle heart."

Wakwa waited for this speech to settle. It hung in the rare mountain air. It cloaked his skin in miniscule droplets then sank beneath and joined the marrow of his bones. He felt an influx of strength in his hands. "The People will stay here while I am away."

Locke gave up. "You will come an extremist in politics, Wakwa. Beware one thing that will bar your success. Never again act against your nature and be hasty as you have in this instance."

"If that advice is good, Dire, it is good even for now."

Locke stood with the torch and clutched Wakwa's shoulder by way of encouragement. "Don't worry about her. Even if Kirke fails you, she has her liberty. The woman is weaving for me. She owes me thirty pounds."

Wakwa Manunnappu kept watch that night. He never went home or slept. He stayed above the lake with no desire for comfort. He sat tall, his head scraping the starry sky, knowing at last what it meant to be the chiefmost man - this petrifaction, this feeling of rock in the chest.

He heard the mountain crickets sawing away at the tendons of his desires. If he closed his eyes, he could see the wants of his soul hanging in strings from his groin.

With an executioner's hand he had severed the last cord between himself and Elizabeth. It was as clear as the air that there would be no more dreams. He would not dream of her. He would die at night and be reborn in the mornings because he had made himself not free to dream. But he could think. He was free to think about her and for her.

He had freed himself. His hair lapped the gusts like tongues telling him about his freedom. The male of the species. He had cut himself loose of the seasons and satisfactions of life.

When he was born, his mother and father called him Manunnappu, He-who-waits, more, Who-waits in a wise way. Free of the woman who was different from his kind, who consumed him, he could be himself, could forbear to move, or could move with judgment. In the forest, in his very young days, he had found another name. It was Wakwa, the ancients' name for fox - a fox of a special kind, black and seen in dawns, and so dazzling in the light that it was never captured. Free.

Now, on this mountain, although he saw no ropes, no stones to pin him, he felt a tightness, as if his skin had shrunk. It squeezed all that he was so tight, he could not feel his limbs, his neck, his feet, his manly parts. All the power of his body and soul were constricted by his skin so that if he desired to move he must like a serpent spring or ripple to his objective inch-by-inch low and out of sight.

In a terrible dawn, he beheld this new vision of himself, askug, the snake, the character he had given the true owner of the buckles. He recognized the prophesy of the serpents in his cave.

Southeast of his mountain, Elizabeth came awake on her knees. Her cheek was down against her rough mattress and she was on her knees. Coming from sleep into the dark night of the barn, she was aware of nothing but the pull of her flesh. She was as open as a shell upon the beach.

Her flesh, the hidden parts of her, and her bones, told her she was on her knees and in a barn, as frank a construction as a wheelbarrow. She had no decent bond with any surface. She was on her knees feeling the pull of the varying fashions of her flesh. Truer than in a beam of sun she could see her breasts against the covered straw, the white weight of her thighs, her buttocks, on high, made taut and round.

No sorrow, no desire moved her left hand behind to the hole. Bone and flesh only were the forces and she worked them, delving the flesh-covered bones of her fingers into the tight place that received her hand, sucked, a place that could be widened, that beckoned because it was not made to take in.

The deeper she visited this reluctant hole, the truer it seemed that she was kneeling in a barn. Her hand was her mind and the more it was devoured by the worried hole the more it was a sage. Up on her knees, out of sleep, the flesh was fiercely curious about itself. By means of her hand she pushed into her earliest region like a conch wound around itself. The hand snaked against the buoyant walls of flesh in this base hole until it was accommodated.

With no sense to please, sense jumped like lights with the dilation, welcome invasion. Innocent as a fish swimming from its jelly, she worked until she learned there was no difference between out and in. She pounded this lesson home in the hellhole of her body, rewarded by the aromas of waste.

This friendship with snails, with herself as a mass, did not deny her woman's flesh. Her heart burst over it and that she had embraced the black hole happily. She folded down on her belly prostrate before the truth of how utterly she was alone.

CHAPTER SEVEN

July and August 1750

In a rash moment the following summer, Thomas Kirke wrote his name on the manifest of his largest merchant ship bound for Boston. The hand that held the pen was as yellow as a sheepskin and decorated with brown spots. A big gray pearl shaped into an enormous tear by some troubled oyster held the shirtsleeve closed.

The captain pressed encouragements on The Company, as Kirke was called, in his search for his missing factor, Dire Locke.

"Yah!" Was all Kirke replied, although his fingers tucked briefly under Captain Dray's broad lapels in thanks.

With so much of the corporation in the hands of a man on protracted and mysterious leave of absence, Kirke, the President and Chairman of the Board, had vital reasons to book passage to America to find him. Yet, his sailing was not strictly a matter of business, for the business rolled along well enough under Locke's sub-factors. Neither had their friendship nor the keeping of a brother made old man Kirke stand out of his chair, hurl shirts and breeches and stockings and shoes into a trunk and catch *The Psyche* as she prepared to leave her berth.

Kirke never did reflect but there were reasons he did things even if he did not trace their genesis explicitly. Locke had given him silence. Vaughan Thomas Kirke was an exquisite listener and a happy cry was in his ear.

The great sails got round with wind. With ecstatic sighs they filled to tearing. The sheets and shrouds creaked against the mast and thudded against decks alerting Kirke to the eternal force that drove the ship. Shrugging off wind, blue sky, and the clouds which were losing the race due west, he made for the chartroom and remained there. For most of the voyage, a remarkable six weeks considering the headwinds, he gazed at land- masses in print, leaving the nautical stuff alone.

Kirke had so many places to scour for Locke that he decided to set up a command post in Boston, well located for darting letters to the out-towns and for acting upon replies. His inspiration was to find the Indian, Silent Fox, sure that the mystery of Locke would be revealed in that tall shadow.

By the third week in August, he was dressing for dinner in front of a twelve-foot mirror in Crosswhite's house, a fellow merchant's on Beacon Hill. Every night at Crosswhite's seemed to turn into a Ball because so many of his friends and connections used his place for a hotel. Kirke did not see how Crosswhite could get any work done, let alone clear a profit, with his constant round of luxe distractions.

Kirke watched himself bathe. At sixty, he laid no claim to youth. Many of his circle had died already of things like pneumonia and pox and bladder and prostate. On account of these absurd losses of otherwise healthy men whose sicknesses, he was convinced, should have been curable, Kirke drank nothing but hot water and lemon, and tea with milk. Yet, some friends Kirke's age appeared to be young. They were the ones who rode or fenced or undertook the other athletic pastime, the search for the perfect woman. Kirke had no pastimes. He lived to master time, and, accordingly, had attained a great age in his mere sixty years. His existence activated his brain and his blood but it crumpled his flesh.

He was six feet tall, or six feet bent, although only slightly. His good-sized bones and respectable volume of muscle were evident and not unpleasantly sagging inside his paper skin. The skin had the Celtic wash, not completely pale or pure. It looked splashed with whiskey, more likely Sherry, the Spanish in Ireland. His face was like better paintings of the Christ gone old: precisely jawed, deprived around the cheek area, not lewd or poignant in the eyes but confidently burning. His eyes were stone blue or whitish-green, depending on his coat, but he called them gray. They appeared to be lashless. He had forgotten what color his hair used to be. Now it was as white as a tablecloth and straight where it grew head and body. He drew on his underclothes conscious that he remained handsome where it counted although it did not matter to his kind of life. The suit he wore of costly cloth looked indifferent on him, as if it would rather hang on a hook. Women never failed to gather around and admire him when he stopped at some party, irrespective of the fact that he did not know particularly what to say to them.

He was getting ready for a bevy of them. Kirke reached the middle of the curving stairs on his way down to the festivities and remembered something, another night years before, although not too many years before, when he had met Silent Fox and Dire at this particular spot. They had been coming up as he had been going down. Later, they introduced him to a lady, a Mrs. Gilbert Worth, who danced finely, especially considering she was from Puritan stock.

For some reason she had been in Boston spending a lot of money on the Indian's second wedding. Kirke had never been clear about it.

But their joy moved him to dig around personally for nimble-fingered furriers and specially bred horses and even for the latest in operatic scores. Such was the charm of that trio. Spenders all. Excellent dancers. Now he thought, "Might not they be together still?" On that same step, he consulted his book to see if he had kept the Worths' address. There it was. Worth Farm, Sweetwood in Sippicon, Massachusetts Bay. Kirke could hardly stand Crosswhite's evening in his anxiety to repack his stuff and follow this golden thread.

～

Like desire, work builds. It is like salt. Hard work, in the countless muscle-movements it takes, in the brain-heat it engenders, catches on itself like crystals and builds. Work lavish enough becomes a whole and happy creation - a pastry, a painting, a fugue, a child. Elizabeth was sure she would complete her contract with Locke in the stipulated time because she knew work.

The linen would be lying there in breadths overlapping like whitewater. This vision depended on victories over her appetites, over the elements, over her body. Combatting their drain on her, their lure, was work of another kind. She wrestled fatigue to which she submitted at first as if to the devil, finally holding it at armslength by strength of soul blown out of all proportion to the sane.

The warp and weft crossed without whisper. An inch a day grew on the loom. Each inch egged her on to more each day until the loom could not hold them and the inches slipped to the floor in yards. Twelve.

Twelve months after making her contract with Locke, Elizabeth Dowland received a note for thirty pounds from him, with instructions that she should hold the fabric there for he continued in perfect trust that she had met their bargain. Elizabeth could only lie with the money on her bed listening to its many messages. But by the fifteenth of August, she wrote to her aunt and uncle that nothing could please her more than to see them at their house.

Gilbert Worth held her letter in his hand, which held another saying almost the identical thing. "Hanna, why do you suppose that Nebuchadnezzar constructed the seventh wonder of the world when marvels like this occur on their own? Thomas Kirke and Elizabeth Dowland would descend upon us. I don't know how I like it." He sat with his wife in their shuttered sitting room, hiding from the unusual heat.

"Stop, Matthew! Please!" Elizabeth twisted to see Dowland House as they trotted by.

Matthew nudged the horses on. "It's a hard grade for them to stop on, Mistress, and in such a sun. But we can pull around if you want to look in." Matthew kept his eyes straight ahead.

"No, no. It would be a strain. You are right."

"Heigh!" Freeman sped them away.

"But let me out! I want to walk to my uncle's door."

The sounds special to summer grass inland, sizzling and hissing, rose with her step. Matthew walked the chaise far behind her on the gravel coach lane to let her hear her footsteps home, recalling that he had heard her steps running away to the woods four years before and that he had done nothing to stop her.

There was a telling first look. The three standing in the airy vestibule were not visibly marred by their histories. Degrees of beauty had developed from pain.

Hanna had surmounted prettiness. She was at the peak of her beauty. Elizabeth wrapped her arms around the woman who must then softly, slowly slide from this pinnacle to age. A grave grace now tethered Gil's impetuosity and his gold was darkened, was of greater karat, purer, softer, the product not so much of years as of soldier's secrets, unspeakable service to humanity. Elizabeth shyly sought answers with her embrace of him.

The Worths' tenderness toward one another leaped at her with bared claws. The symbol of bliss in the polished floors, the grace of the furnishings, the luxe of the rugs, the many choice objects, the musical instruments, the books, lodged in her like a bullet.

Gil brought the women of his family in. The extent to which Elizabeth had become a stranger astounded him and Hanna. Elizabeth stood alone, wrought up by the household refinements. "It is so beautiful." She stated. "No! You have changed it."

Hanna steered them around trouble. "It is as it was. You are simply as sensitive as ever to light. The white walls got dingy with the smoke and so we toned them down this year to cream."

"A daub of pigment!" Gil made excuse, covering Hanna's reference conjuring roundhouses and center-floor fires. "No change."

"It softens the glare." Hanna volunteered.

"I do like it." Elizabeth crossed and recrossed the room. "I do." She stood in the unfettered window.

"I don't know." Hanna said.

"Too creamy, perhaps." Gil agreed with his wife.

"It is nice with the settee." Hanna retrenched.

"What a silk! May I sit there?" Elizabeth turned to them with imploring eyes.

"Sit!" Gil and Hanna were stricken by her timorousness.

Everyone, including Elizabeth, worked to render the perfect house more perfect for the guest on his way. Master and maid took turns stirring the berries in their fevered pots to calm Cooke, the housekeeper, who was frantic with the labor of guests just at jam-making time. Elizabeth ran to assist one and then the other, cooking, adding columns of figures, polishing the window panes, pruning the roses. By noon of the third day, everything looked only a trifle more delightful than before and just in time for the final effort at beautification - the entrance of the hairdresser.

It was an expensive thing to import him from Boston but the Worths made their extravagance acceptable to the thrifty community by inviting the neighbors to come for a cut and to donate to his fee according to their means.

With no compunction, Elizabeth gave her undisciplined growth over to the shears and emerged with a corolla of waves. She felt that her life would change.

She had sewn a dress out of wilted linen that had been in her inventory for several years. It looked like a beige flower on her, petals down. The loose sleeves fell to just below her elbows. The torso skimmed her body more gently than the prevailing fashion. It ended in an arrow-point between her hips. The skirt rushed down from there.

Hanna gave it a look as she set her rouge. "The neckline's a little high on that, Elizabeth!"

Its wheat-sheaf color accentuated the pallor Elizabeth had acquired by absorption in activities indoors. "Should I do something for my face?"

Hanna, luscious as jam in cotton so purple it was nearly black, turned from her mirror to daub her niece with colored powder. "It makes me happy that you want to be with us. I am going down to sew and your uncle will jot at his clefs. If you wanted to bring some work down, or read, or just sit with us and wait, it would be fine." She was exquisitely careful but even care seemed insulting.

"Aunt, are you sure this is only an acquaintance you are expecting? Everything on the farm is holding its breath for him. Even the rose buds suspend their blooming. Who are we having here?"

"An acquaintance only. But an important one. Not even your uncle has met him. You'll meet him together." She hastened to say, "But you don't have to!"

"I will just rest until he is here." Elizabeth lay down in the blue and lion-colored afternoon. She hardly felt her scars of unhappiness and rottenness on the soft, sweet, bed. Corrupted by solitude, darkened by discipline, hardened by principle, she was ruined for gaiety and judged herself poor material to entertain acquaintances, particularly, important ones.

She gathered her skirts and rose from the bed. She watched herself as she passed the mirror. She admitted frankly that she wanted Wakwa to see her as she looked in this gown - not to punish him, but to save him from his private quicksand of denial and discipline and principle, and hardest to admit, his impotence. She wandered into the hall longing to walk out of the house and down the back path into the woods to see if she could stand under the greenery and not drop dead of memory.

Voices woke her and in reality she struggled up, smoothed her gown, and ran her comb through her hair. There was a new voice in the house. It was not a Massachusetts voice. Red or white. Its accent was not English as her uncle's was English. The new voice had a tautness and sheen like the sails of a ship bursting with the power behind them. The man's voice wrapped around the ear as she had seen a dancer's in a reel wrap his partner around his shadow, as her uncle had explained a toreador winds the cape about the bull. The voice was English with a flourish. It was proud, high Irish.

Elizabeth passed the open sitting room doors heading for the kitchen and the meadow beyond. She could not resist turning toward the voice as she swept by and she saw the speaker for the first time. She continued to look at him as she walked on.

"Gold, pure gold...." Thomas Kirke left off what he was saying to watch her. He resumed, "Alas, it is the future of the Earth...."

Elizabeth eased into the kitchen and shut the door. She leaned against it looking at Cooke's perspiring face. The housekeeper held out a pair of floury hands. Elizabeth went like a child to be enfolded by them.

"Miss Bethie, why don't you go in and sit with your aunt and uncle? I'm about to bring in lemonade."

"You are doing everything by yourself, Cooke. Let me help you bring the tray and then I'll go walk."

"That is all you do. It is no good. It is too hot."

"I'll go up for a hat."

"Dearie, don't." Cooke's ageing face sweetened with sympathy. "I know." She drew her former charge tighter against her. "I know what this time of year means to you." She could not talk for sorrow but patted Elizabeth's back. White flour marked the exposed skin like talc. "Stay in, Beth. Weather like this brews storms."

"I must not be susceptible to storms anymore."

"I don't want you out watching for one."

"What difference?"

"A great deal. You are beginning to look well."

"What difference?"

"If there be no difference, Miss Beth, you may as well stay in."

Elizabeth left her to look out the open top portion of the door. She gazed past the farm to the trees. "There are no woods like this in Sandwich."

"Aye, it's nice there."

"How I loved the woods!"

"You and I will go berrying with Matthew in the forest in the autumn as we used to do when you were a child."

Elizabeth flitted from the sight of the forest and opened the door to the main hall.

"...In the next thirty years it will become the marrow of civilization, not just its bones. It is already the stuff by which invention comes to be. It is the glistening heart of everything. Gold is a state of mind. On it our dreams turn...."

Elizabeth whirled from this malediction onto the sight of Cooke skewering the meat and shoving the brace over the fire. "Cooke, the ice is melting in the pitcher. Let me bring the lemonade."

"I'll spank Priscilla Marley when I find her!" Cooke wiped her face with a square of white cloth pinned to her apron. And wherever Matthew is...!"

Elizabeth picked up the tray. She started toward the sitting room, the ice chiming with her walk.

"Gold is more than I've said. It is not only the means of the flowering of ideas - it is to *be* the idea."

A hum of disagreement from Worth.

"Dizzy as that may sound to you, the seas and the rivers are already populated with golden nuggets not fish. The ground grows it. It is the only commodity. Human creation is mere truck in its brokerage. Unforeseen thought will one day flourish to feed it. It will be the only value and its possession mean more than power - it will mean Supreme Power - divinity itself, and man will serve a tangible god once again."

"God!" Worth gasped. He gasped again at Elizabeth laden in the doorway. "God!" He went over quickly and swept the tray out of her hands. "Do meet our company, Elizabeth. Mr. Thomas Kirke."

Her brain and heart stopped together.

Gil turned toward the merchant who was on his feet, alert. "Our dear niece, Mistress Elizabeth Dowland."

"How are you?" Kirke's hand was out.

In amazement, Elizabeth offered hers, wondering if he would shake it like a man's. But he dropped his to his side leaving her hand stretched in front of her like a forsaken olive branch.

"I know you by your name." She said wondering, wondering.

"Young lady," Kirke brayed, "are you a Bess, or an Elise, or a Liza?"

"Beth, some say." Elizabeth felt Hanna's arms around her.

"They do that to you? I'd think you no less than a Liz! Mistress What?"

"Dowland."

"Of course. How do you do?"

"And you?"

"I won't say till I get your answer!"

Elizabeth found herself sitting next to Hanna on the settee staring at the uncluttered space between her and the white-haired man with lustrous eyes.

Hanna came to their rescue. "Elizabeth and I were raised at the house you must have seen coming in. Dowland House."

"It is quite like many others on the way although they all seem to lead up to that one. The summit of that design." Kirke gave one Dowland woman his look and then the other.

Gil tried to assist. "It is still a working farm."

Kirke snapped, "Permanence!" Having shattered the conversational pattern, he picked up the pieces on his own. "A nice thing. I am more a person of habits than of permanence myself. What do you think of habits versus permanence, Mistress Beth Dowland?"

Gil and Hanna suffered to see her on this rack.

"I would say, habits are chosen, perennial activities. Permanence is a condition of living that endures. Indefinitely."

"Marvelous!" Gil crossed his legs and leaned back in his chair, smiling at the ceiling.

"You are clear on the difference?" Kirke made a verbal charge.

"I am." Elizabeth said.

"I am not!" Hanna fretted.

Thomas Kirke and Elizabeth shared a first smile.

Elizabeth poured from the pitcher.

"How do you pass your time, Mistress Dowland?" Kirke boldly enquired.

The Worths went stiff at their joints. Elizabeth was caught at room center holding two sweating glasses. She offered one to her aunt and brought the other to Kirke.

"Sir, I live in a barn at Sandwich."

"You do?"

"Yes."

"Then that is WHERE you do whatever you do. WHAT do you do there?"

"I walk."

"Habit."

"I sew."

"Inculcated habit."

"I weave."

"A pastime."

"No. It is what I do, Mr. Kirke."

Kirke appeared troubled. "A dedication."

"More than that, sir, I live by it in spite of my family." Elizabeth colored on more than one count.

"She has turned art to gold, Kirke." Gil bit out.

"This is a permanent condition?"

Elizabeth cried out softly.

Gil gallantly threw in, "You are interested in dancing, Kirke. I know. After dinner I'll play some music for you."

"Oh. How very nice." Kirke drank his drink away and joined Elizabeth. "Might I see your weaving sometime?" His accent poured cream. "I am interested in American linen."

"I'll be off to Mrs. Cooke!" Hanna carolled back to her niece, "You are welcome to join me, Beth!"

"Mr. Kirke, I am a great trial to my family."

"That I cannot imagine."

"I should not have been here to meet you in this way."

"Why not?"

Elizabeth stepped back. "Mr. Kirke, I have woven for your House."

"I won't believe it."

Hanna went down the hall. "What a disaster!"

"You have seen my work."

"I won't believe it."

Gil mistook him. "You'll get over it, Kirke."

Elizabeth explained. "Dire Locke sent a sample of mine to you in the form of a pocket."

"I won't believe it! MY pocket? THE pocket?" Kirke began to search his coat. "I meant to bring it on this crossing but I didn't take my everyday coat and so I left the most important thing behind. You know the pocket I am talking of?"

"I made it, Mr. Kirke!"

"I won't believe my search ends so soon!" He cried out.

Her attention was acute. "What is it?"

"I don't express myself very well. I counted on that bit o' cloth to lead me to a secret - an answer!"

"El Dorado?" Gil defended.

"To the mystery of that Indian, the Fox, if you must know."

"God almighty." Gil murmured.

"Uncle Gil!" Elizabeth pleaded.

Gil was blanched and breathless.

"To the Indian. Beyond the Indian. To Locke. Beyond Locke. To something. I'm not at all crazy. The pocket was my compass! YOU are the answer, Miss! The promise of my crossing. Can you see my trouble?"

"Help me, Uncle Gil!"

"Whatever you need, Beth." His hand slipped from her shoulder. Then dourly, "But you are doing fine on your own. Why don't you walk outside with Mr. Kirke. Otherwise the room will burst." Curtly, Gil left them.

Kirke took strides into the hall, came back for Elizabeth, placed a hand of hers on an arm of his, grabbed a parasol from the stand and led her at a good clip across the fields. He had her entire biography firmly in his grasp by the time they stood in front of Dowland House.

Under the mighty sun he said, "Now you have given me that dose to swallow, would you grant me a favor?"

"What, Mr. Kirke?"

"That! Do not call me, 'Mr. Kirke.' I won't have Tom, and most cannot get their chops around Thomas. Vaughan is a lost cause, I don't even like it, not much anyway, though I'll take almost anything for a name that isn't a slur. Show me no deference for my age or any for your having received money from Kirke Company. It would be unkind to remind me that I outclass you only by virtue of my purse."

"Sir," she said almost vacantly after her pouring out, "it is a common mark of respect. You are not a yeoman."

"I am not a sir, either! I think it stupid in this world to call a man mister or not as the shades of his closeness to the King allow. The very idea of kings leaves me uneasy now that I am old."

"You are not old."

"I am." He insisted.

"I, more than you."

"Well, you shouldn't be at twenty."

"Twenty-two."

"That's all right then!" He laughed about her. He looked down upon her. "You did right to make the conveyance."

"Do you think so?"

"I said it! At the time you could not have done better. Now you must not leave the house to itself. It'll go to seed and that must not happen. You see what I mean? It will get old."

"My uncle cares for it."

"It is you must give its heart something to beat for, Liz. The house is you."

They sat her across from him at supper. The shining mahogany board was an ellipse, planned to put guests at close range leaving master and mistress flung far at the table-ends to observe the needs of their company.

In high expectation of dessert to come, Kirke said over the peaches, "All I can say is, if you've got gold, keep it. If you haven't any, get some. Sell land to get it and then store it up." Kirke's voice curled like ivy over Gil's objections. "I'm telling you that gold is the only asset worth anything to a man for at least the next fifty years. Lands and houses are swamps that'll swallow him. But he who has a store of gold will pull through the muddy times ahead. He or she with a skill will survive but not so well as the possessor and, of course, the lender of gold."

Worth got very hot. "We cannot all be Rothschilds or Venetians!"

Kirke narrowed his eyes to take Worth's measure. "Venice is exactly where I am about to rent a house."

Gil was silenced briefly. It had happened in the past when he had touched a nerve in conversation that quiet took him. He proceeded carefully, although curious. "That seems a lonely prospect unless you've got warm friends there. It can't be for the carrying trade anymore, not on the scale you'd need. It's a place for music schools and elaborate dinner parties and the finest painting in the world and diplomats. Why Venice? Is it her banking? Her gold?"

"Mr. Worth! Venice is a Republic."

Inundated by Kirke's tidal-wave mind, Gil swam for any convenient shore. "Renting, though! That'd be a foolish expenditure. You'd pour your capital into a bottomless pit."

"Never! As a renter I am a liberated man. When I want to quit the place, I just pack a trunk and leave. If I owned and wanted to sell, there would be no one to buy me out if people are hoarding gold. And what good to me a house in Italy should I want my bones somewhere else? I am no spendthrift but a conserver of gold, pure gold. If I were not, I would be sitting here with a long face telling you I am about to be a poor man and a ruined one!"

"Nonsense!"

"It is true! I am trying, I have been trying for years and desperate hard to avoid the end of the Trade. And so was Dire Locke when I had him. But the crash is coming and when the Trade breaks, she will never be in once piece again."

"This is not in our lifetimes." Gil denied him.

"This is next year, sir!"

"No!" Elizabeth almost leapt onto the table. Her arms spread across it embracing tiers of candles and a cornucopia of fruit.

"I see you have a head on your shoulders. You've got a stake in this sort of commerce, considering the Indian and your child." Kirke spoke plainly with no attempt to hurt or comfort. "It's deader than a door nail right now, my dear. We're all only eating from the carcass and pretending there'll be enough meat on the bones to feed us, but it's over."

"So bad, already?" Elizabeth was wounded but keen.

"Yes, without a coherent trade law from the Parliament, from the King. Every merchant is pouring money into it - there's a bottomless pit for you - funding and funding and bribing and bribing to keep the fur flowing in and scraping by for our reward. The Crown is not so interested in having the Trade work at all. They patch, they paste if they are dragged into a meeting on the subject, do the peers, but notice that the rulings on trade are never the law of the Kingdom. Policies. Only policies. Insufficient policies." Kirke fell from his pearly inspiration into a murky mood. "Depend on gold only, not on the Trade, and certainly not on land."

Hanna's eyes turned to the verdure beyond Elizabeth. "Not on a place like ours?"

"Dear hostess, the land has importance not because the King desires to tax, if not raise your potatoes and raspberries, 'though that's also in his mind's long eye. And may your husband's relations excuse me, King George II wants the land to hit the King of France over the head with."

Gil stopped Kirke there. "No need to excuse you, Mr. Kirke. There's not a drop of Hanoverian blood in me."

Kirke blinked at Worth not seeing advantage either way. He pressed on with his theme. "King George wants it because he feels this heavy club slipping out of his hands. There is no reason for him to protect the Trade from the French. Better let the French bungle it to death and then to get the French out of here. That's what he's got on his Royal Mind. And after that do you think His Far-Flung Majesty's going to keep sufferin' you sitting pretty on these fat lands? No tax will satisfy him. But your heads in a basket. Then it's raspberry and potato time."

Gil remarked with some respect, "These are mighty thoughts. You have made this assessment in the course of your business over the years?"

"I got it on the boat over here. I'm perfectly sure of it. Have you looked at the great spaces on the map west of Appalachia? I'm sure George Hanover has. The kings of this world always turn to financiers to fund their schemes when they have made paupers out of the merchants who fill the national treasury with the tariffs. For wars, for settlements, for sustenance of their permanent and luxurious habits they borrow and at a healthy interest. And, at this pivotal juncture, I am without Dire Locke!"

Gil and Hanna sat mute and in some shame at their discretion over Dire's part in leading Kirke to Elizabeth and Kirke's total ignorance of it.

"If he had ever seen your place, Locke would have mentioned to me long ago what depth of pocket you have, Mr. Worth. You're made of gold and you ought to be exploiting your position for your future benefit."

"I don't have that kind of money, Kirke! I'm just a third son whose father was generous and made a settlement on me when I was young to avoid cheating me by his death. Considering current estate law."

"And so falls your head and the fortunes of your entail. You must have the money or be able to get your hands on it. You must first appreciate the situation, next appreciate the gold, and after that turn your assets as much as possible into the yellow, shiny stuff. This is the time to persuade your friends and neighbors to put together a fund and to buy gold so that when the King comes to market for it, gold, much gold will be at your fingertips and you will be able to protect your land, because, God save you, you will bring this King to his knees for your gold and not be seen as a philanthropist, a politician, a partisan of any kind, nor a traitor of an aristocrat. You will be Old George's banker and he will lick your boots ashine because you'll own his dreams outright. And you can whisper in gold which dreams he ought to entertain."

"My God!" Worth looked about himself for a weapon to fight Kirke's eloquence for his tongue was no good against the Irishman.

"And you will weave him dreams of ancient Greece, you lot, I finally have it! I have been groping toward this night for years, it seems, but hell, an idea can flower as truly in a dining room as in a great hall of government and that makes your room a hall of government. What do you say? I plan to surround myself with such talents as yours all over the world! Mine will be a corporation bigger than the Trade, poor old hag of a Trade. And when the time comes...."

"Thomas, excuse me and my wife momentarily. We've domestic matters to see to."

Hanna followed him, leaving the doors ajar for some semblance of politeness. She and

Gil came together in Matthew Freeman's small, striped office sectioned out of the northeast corner of the sitting room opening into the room and on the hall.

"He wants to incorporate us!" Gil clung to her. "He has outlined the rest of my life and in five minutes permanently taken away our peace of mind. He's a worse threat to civilization than Christianity, damn him! 'You lot'?!"

"Gil, he is a revolutionary!"

"What I mean!"

"Like you."

"Not a bit. All this talk about money at table!"

Hanna dashed his elitism. "Around that same table, we've talked of polygamy, insanity, and adultery. Can talk of money be so bad?"

Gil hung his head not contrite but remembering.

"Gil! Gil! Look at it another way." Her hands worked down his silky sleeves. "He's a fresh wind, all newness, albeit cold, and sharp, and sudden, but he is a visionary, obviously successful from these bouts of inspiration and like fresh blood, a tonic of a person. Tonics never go down easily."

"He's a bitter, frustrated, senile old snipe."

"He is an honest, just, brave and angered man. Again, he is like you."

"You don't like his traits in me. You never have."

"They made me love you!"

"Then why...?" He gripped the strips of white moulding. "Why did you...lose interest in me?"

"I never, never lost interest!" She might have been angry with him for warped memory but she forced herself to place her hand over his on the wood. "I never lost interest."

"Never? Not for a moment?"

She leaned against the green and white paper and showed him a terrible expression through the summer gloom. "What will it take to convince you of how I love you?"

He braced himself against the doorframe. "Forgive me."

"Be quiet."

"Not just for now. For then. For killing - them."

"It was legally justified. They were trespassers. Assassins."

"Not they! Though they were part of the other murder. If I hadn't killed to save Wakwa, would he have obeyed Waban and let her go? No! Nor would there have been the horror of my neglect of you when you were grieving too."

Hanna sank her fingers into the brilliance of his golden hair.

"You don't mind me then?"

"I mind you very much and all the time."

He drew back. "Then how will I come back to life?"

"Come back. Come."

"And have you hate me for my temper?"

"I hate to be excluded from your passions. That is all."

Then he kissed her.

The housekeeper found them in that embrace. "Master! Mistress! Excuse me! But Matthew and Priscilla cannot be found. The dinner is suffering. There is cream to whip and the shortcake to do and there is breakfast tomorrow and no help with the serving or the clearing up."

Gil walked Hanna gently past her. "Offer our excuses, Cooke. Make breakfast as late as you like. It is my wish you get some sleep."

Cooke shook off his distracted kindness and drew around her the brace of her former service at Dowland House. She went close to the dining room to see to Beth, her charge of long ago. She could only see Kirke's bowed back, his hands painting pictures of sights unknown to her. He took an interest, in Cooke's way of thinking, far beyond the norm for one day's acquaintance. After all they had been through, it was good to have Mr. Kirke in the house, taking charge, telling them all what to do, telling the truth, thinking for them. Hadn't he driven the master and the mistress up the stairs? Cooke did not care about the great subjects Kirke had on his mind. She liked him for caring about the Worths and her Beth, and for not looking down his terrific, bold nose at her for being a housekeeper. She tagged him as family.

A hand of bluish-black pulled on the knob and closed the door.

"Where have you been!?" Cooke demanded of Matthew. "You can loaf if you like, but Priscilla Marley is my responsibility!"

"I run this house, Cooke."

"When you're in it, you assist Master Worth to run it. Now you can assist me to run the dessert into the dining room."

They stood squabbling in whispers.

"I deem it not the season for a party."

"Who are you to deem or not deem that?"

"I am houseman. My charge is all these people. And they know it. My value here is not simply to obey. I am not after impressing old man Kirke."

"You?" Cooke was horrified. "Master Worth has him here. That's enough for you!"

"He's had a lot of people here, Cookey." Matthew's accents were Gil's, his teacher's, overlaid with the African lacquer. "But this is a bad time of the year for Mr. Kirke's visit. Considering Mistress Beth. And not just she. I had an hysterical Priscilla on my hands for she's through with Carpenter Spinney and told him so and refused to come home for mortification in front of Master Worth as he has put money in that turd's furniture business."

Cooke marched away for a shawl for Beth. "Where is she then?"

"Dowland House. I left Priscilla Marley there that I might come here to help you serve the dessert."

"Poor Pris, after her day, keeping a houseful of ghosts all night! You are a terrible man!"

"I'll keep the watch. Don't you worry. Marley and I will be back with fresh milk by dawn. See to it the biscuits are ready."

"I take it, I may bake Mr. Kirke his rolls then."

"You may not. But he can eat what the family eat. I like your morning rolls better than anybody else and so they are mainly baked for me. But, I share." Matthew reopened the door and followed her into the dining room, neither of them interrupting the flow of conversation, neither of them causing notice.

Cooke crossed the square of pink over Elizabeth's breast for the advancement of night and for the color. Matthew collected plates.

Kirke announced, "I had a wife once!"

"Did you?" Elizabeth tilted her head and smiled.

"She was a Greek. Daughter of a shipbuilder. A beauty. Died of a baby. It did too. Her father was upset with me after that."

"How unfair!"

"I did not understand her. I may as well have shot her as got her with child. I had very little time for marriage anyway. She mooned much. Shouted at me when I was in port. I was rather relieved, I'll tell you, when I didn't have to sleep with a pillow over my head at night. I don't know why she married me."

"Mr. Kirke!"

"Anything but that, please."

"I do not think I can say Thomas." She meant out of respect.

"Some call me V.T."

She could tell he refused to understand her. "I will try."

"Try soon."

"How long will you be in America?"

He laughed. "I don't know, Miss Liz. I must accomplish my purpose and I am not sure what it is." He gripped the tabletop. "I must find Silent Fox!"

She stared at the sputtering candles.

"And so must you." He was firm about it.

Matthew poured him cold water and splashed his hand.

"Do not...!" She implored Kirke to let the subject of her torn marriage rest.

"I am going to help you."

When Kirke said this, Matthew, with his full tray, saw Cooke out of the room and slammed the door.

Kirke delighted in the sight of Elizabeth in her buff and fragile gown wishing it were blue. This sweep of linen lengthened in the shining tabletop like an ocean wave. It stretched toward the candle-flame, doused it. Kirke was conscious of his hands on the slippery table and he kept them there so he could float.

Elizabeth watched Thomas Kirke sleep. His scalp showed through at his crown. His thin, white hair was combed into a brief, stringy queue and tied with an orange ribbon. One hand, fingertips against the slick surface, lay near the table's center. She crossed to him and settled the shawl over his dark, summer coat.

Matthew and Cooke reopened the long glass doors.

Elizabeth asked them, "What shall we do for him?" She pulled on the shawl to cover Kirke's exposed hand. "Good night, Viti."

"Come upstairs, Miss Beth. Matthew will see to him."

"The old dog would have heart failure if we woke him before morning. Better leave him."

"You can't!" Cooke protested.

Elizabeth assented. "Leave him."

"The weather has passed of itself. It has become cool without a storm." Gilbert Worth trailed Cooke down the hall to the kitchen, settling his shirtsleeves under his dressing gown. "Does Mr. Kirke forgive me for abandoning ship?"

Kirke answered. "He doesn't. Nothing to forgive you for." The merchant stood in yesterday's clothes, his head dripping water over the big washbasin.

"What has happened?" Gil rushed to him.

"You know, Mr. Worth, your kitchen reminds me of my mother's."

The Worths' kitchen was like a daisy field, white and black and yellow from paint and slate and sun.

"I am shocked!" Gil said, perturbed that Kirke had not been tended.

"I didn't mean your kitchen was old fashioned."

"Nor did I."

Cooke began her excuses.

Worth waved them back. "What countryside did your mother's kitchen grace, Mr. Kirke?"

"'Twas in London."

A laugh cracked in Gil. Like an egg. "You're funny, and before breakfast."

"Understand, the kitchen did not look like this."

"Of course not."

"You're funny too, sir. We comprehend each other uncommonly well for the difference of one Irish part between us."

"That is the Catholic in you and the catholicity in me. I imagine an Irish father with a kitchen in London and following the Pope would have to be a good humored man and a model for conversation."

"Mother was the Catholic. An English one. It was an unpeaceful house. Except for her kitchen."

"I comprehend." And Gil gave the nod to Cooke.

Kirke gravitated to the fireplace across the room from the oven and pulled his chair close to the flames. He rubbed his arms. "Change in the weather!" His nose dripped a single drop, which clung stubbornly to the tip.

Matthew pushed open the back door, Priscilla behind him. He glared at the intruder.

With an equally jaundiced eye, Worth set him to attendance on Kirke. Gil sat near Priscilla where she was hulling blackberries and asked her quietly about her wedding date. It bothered Cooke the scolding would be left to her.

"I must teach you daybooks before you tie the knot with Sam." Worth stated.

"I'll teach her." Kirke chimed in.

Matthew flashed a warning look. "My job, sir!"

Gil put in, "Really, Kirke, you are too kind. I couldn't possibly permit it. We don't offer you a bed to sleep in or a proper bath. Shall we squeeze you for a tutor too?"

"Think about what you're refusing! Who better to learn from? Sleep slumped over a desk half the time anyway."

A single tear ran each of Priscilla's cheeks.

Kirke sped to her. "Maid, I'll get down to the bottom of my trunk for a tin of a tea that'll take away your jitters." To Matthew he said, "I'll show you how to brew it, my man!"

Matthew tidied up the room with a sour face.

Not too many minutes later, Kirke poured water from the kettle into the big porcelain pot. Like a wizard, he watched the steam that rose, his wispy hair standing out. Then he grabbed the pot, dashed its contents out the door and tiptoed back. He doled his tea into the sweating vessel. He trickled water just off the boil onto the fragrant bed. The merchant whispered into the agony of the leaves. The lid was on. He jammed his back against the wall-bricks and breathed, breathed deeply in. At his signal the tea-pageant ended. Matthew poured.

Gil said as they entered the sitting room, "You've domestic skill. A pity to waste it alone."

"Worse for your niece. Can't you paste this thing with the Indian back together?"

"Kirke!"

"It really is too bad. What of the baby boy?"

"I know the Massachuseuck." Gil had Tame Deer in mind. "He is being well-raised."

"That's not enough for him! Or for her! Hell, what's to happen to your land if you can't find him?"

"Your voice, please, sir."

Its volume was not lowered. "Has anyone confronted him? Has anyone made a demand of him now the emotion of the event is out of the way?"

"Out of the way!" Gil's own voice came like cannon. "She has almost died over it! She teeters on the precipice!"

Kirke's tone went low. "I did not notice any of that and we talked a good long time last night."

Worth's voice carried up the stairs. "One convivial evening does not undo two years of deathly turmoil. She must be carefully handled, gently handled. And understood!"

Kirke yelled back, "She's not the cripple you make her!"

Then Gil took on the mantle of his genealogy. "With all due respect to your age and to your genius, you are beyond your rights to come here and tell us our business. No one," here his already deep voice deepened with meaning, "no one, not even he, will be allowed to gallop in here and tear her down." He damned Kirke's gold and its seepage toward Elizabeth.

Kirke surprised him by resting a hand on his shoulder. "Are you sure she didn't start feeling better when she began to support herself?"

Gil shook loose of him. "How dare you insinuate that we all mean less to her than a few gold pieces in her trunk!"

"Thirty pieces to be exact."

"Blackguard!"

"Don't call me names!"

They were shouting again.

"Your man Locke inspired her to do it!"

"And do you suppose she took Locke up on the offer to sell out her dream? No! With every cross of the threads she pulled her own fibre together to be ready to have the Indian back!"

Gil stood stripped of retorts.

"That is what she wants. What she should want. However polite she is. You do not serve her by making her forget!"

Hanna hurried to the kitchen. "Matthew! Matthew! Matthew, you must do something. If I go in to stop them it will live on!"

Matthew bolted from that quarter. But instead of quelling the argument, he bounded up the small staircase to Elizabeth's room. He stood, black as black in the white hall, his burl of muscle showing through his summer baize. "Mistress Beth?"

"Matthew!" Came from inside. "Open!"

He stepped into the room, his broad back the block between her and the terrible silence that had overtaken the lower floor. He saw her flattened against the window as if pushed there by wind. Her face was hard. Tight. It helped him say, "Mistress, would you like it if I drove you to the Stirlings'? Would you like to leave right now? I could take you, if you choose, to Dowland House, and come back for your luggage."

"I had better go. But not yet. But it is a good, kind thought."

"Give me the order! We'll be gone!"

"Not ready!" She closed her eyes.

"Marley will pack. I'll bring everything to you."

"I am not to be pushed out by other people's concerns."

"I am sorry, Mistress, that I let the man go as far as he did. I should have risked my master's displeasure and shut the visitor up!"

"It is not Mr. Kirke in the wrong." She left her glass bulwark. "If you would help me, Matthew, please let them know that I am coming down to breakfast. I like my morning meal and I expect this will be a memorable one."

In each year there was an uncomfortable day in the summer dining room. This day was the one. The convulsion of the seasons left the skin tight on the face. Since the architect had been a purist there was no fireplace to forestall the emergency of August. The chairs yelped as they were pulled out. The air was dry and, for no apparent reason, it smelled of apples. Everything and everybody sparkled like iced water. Behind the clangor of their spoons were suspicions of autumn approaching.

Kirke had been placed at the end far opposite Elizabeth. She was beatified in the light of the eastern window, the sunlight illuminating her shoulders.

Kirke broke the ice. "Sorry for my way. It proved not a gentle change from last night to this morning."

Gil was disarmed. "Stay a little longer and it will seem summer again."

"Ah, yes. Indian summer." Kirke drowned his bowl of blackberries in cream.

Gil and Hanna, close by virtue of the table's dimensions, touched toes in commiseration.

Elizabeth looked down the table, her eyes beaming. "We do not use that expression in this house."

"Unpleasant reference." Kirke shook his head over the reasonableness of it.

Gil used his napkin to cover his expression.

Hanna turned fully and slowly on Kirke. "We do not say 'Indian summer' because it is a one-sided and improper view of the Indians using the last of the colored foliage to hide their fighting their way back onto their lands. It is not nice to hint treachery for such a natural desire, and, it does not speak well for the English."

"Appreciated. Yet, I say, if a questionable expression has lost its original meaning, as most nasty things do, it is usable."

Elizabeth took it up. "I disagree."

"We disagree." Kirke's mother-of-pearl eyes gave her a stern look but his mouth took a merry slant. Another droplet made a diamond on his nose. He breathed in hard to clear his passages. "That's good. Disagreement. Makes us family. It's nice to be here among you. I do not think I could stand to be among empty-headed people at a time like this."

They all laughed outright.

"A time like what?" Elizabeth asked.

"For your information, it is the end of the world."

He was hilarious. They laughed again.

"I'm dead serious! This fish is excellent, madam," he turned to Hanna, "mild but excellent. I've brought you ginger. Interesting on almost any food. I'll go get it." He stretched and took his leave and went upstairs. He did not return with the gift but went to sleep.

Later, looking for her needles, Elizabeth passed his room. The door was open. His shoes were tucked neatly under the bed. His coat hung on the post. So tired he had not even pulled the quilt from its fold to cover himself, he lay in his breeches and shirt in a strange cessation, his limbs like lumber thrown in a heap for later use. His eyes and his lips surprised her; they had not seemed equipped to close down but had. His flighty hands had the look of wings folded. Only his forehead showed a remnant of his waking animation. At intervals, his brow quivered as if a light inside were being carried temple to temple - his mind's standard against unconsciousness.

Fascinated, Elizabeth stepped in. To her he did not look like a grandfather, or a father, or an uncle, not old. He looked like a man of many years lying still.

They walked in the late afternoon.

Kirke asked. "What will you do?"

"To keep the world from ending?"

"Aye, it's what I meant."

Her eyes shone at his response. "Plant. Trees."

He jumped in the grassy field. "Well! Where?"

"At Dowland Farm."

"Trees? Orchards?"

"Not at all. I would make a forest out of some of it again."

"But the house in the middle. It will decay."

"Not as I will plant. The trees will make a deeper border. They will be a sign that my father's Will still protects the People should they return someday. Who knows? My son may find a use for them."

"That is quite a plan. I have another. Why not travel with me and your aunt and uncle? Let's go after the Indian together. We'll find what is to be found."

"No, Viti...."
"What did you say?"
"I said, no."
"No! What did you call me?"
"Viti!"
"Mistress Dowland. Be careful of me."
She turned away.
"I must confess I forget you are a woman."
She turned to him again.
"You are more my familiar."
"You, Merlin, and I your cat?"
"More a spirit comfortably around me. Do you mind?" His eyes were inebriated with the pastoral gloaming, blue and purple and green.

Leave-taking the next day was simultaneous. Elizabeth's chaise turned southeast to Sandwich. Kirke's coach, on its way to Wareham, followed. He overtook her at the crossroads.

Kirke shouted from his window, "Mistress Liz, it may take a year, but I'll be over to see you! I'll have news for you by then, you can buy stock in that! Remember, seek remedy! And you, Matthew Freeman, think of yourself as a leaf of tea!"

The Worths met at sunset in the sitting room.

Gil knelt before a Chinese chest of rosewood and worked the key. Hanna lounged on the Celadon couch.

"I think it was better in true white." Hanna.

"I was hoping you would say it." Gil pulled out five shallow drawers, each about half the breadth of a keyboard, each lined with foil made of hammered gold. "We'll tear everything out in the morning and get the brushes going." His adept fingers opened one seal after another.

"We could paint the fireplace surround a tint of gray."

"Definition. So much better than the ivory wash." Gil weighed a drawerful of ground ginger. The next drawer held as much of saffron. A third was filled with ground cinnamon. The fourth with powdered seng, the fifth with cardamom out of India. "I feel as if we have been visited by the Magi!"

Hanna licked a fingertip and touched it to the ginger and tasted. "Thomas Kirke is a philosopher!" Her smile unsettled Gil, based as it seemed to be on some experience apart from him. "Should we have gone with him to Maine, Gillie?"

"No! No for principle's sake. Look how Beth stands her ground. No, because I've two harvests to manage and all the paperwork besides, and no because you are not strong enough yet to travel."

"Of course I am. And the spices will help."

"Then let's think of going away. Sicily?

"We've something new to attend to."

Gil gave that a moment. He said huskily, "What do you think of your prospective nephew-in-law?"

Hanna looked at Gil.

Gil returned her fraught gaze. "Distinguished looking relic, isn't he?"

"I think so."

"Oh, you think so, do you?"

The wife came to his side. "I was not thinking of Thomas Kirke."

CHAPTER EIGHT

Fall 1750

The world went up in a golden smoke. The mountains piercing the sky and the land below were suddenly not green. The lake water looked on fire. The gods had set it afire the same as the trees. The leaves were flames that burned without destroying the trees and without heating the world.

The way to keep warm was to run, run up the hills to the sky-high rocks and tall trees that were always green. Qunneke said that these trees with rods for bodies and needles for leaves were "cowaw," but Pequawus said, "the pine." They smelled as spicy as burning wood but they never fooled a man with false fire after the hot weather was gone or lost their skinny leaves. That was why they stood at the top like the headmen of all other kinds of trees. Dark, and tall, and quiet.

Moses Bluehill ran and lost himself among them until he cried, and, when he gave up crying for laughing, he allowed his half-sister and his cousins to pull him down through the mehtugquash, the rows of trees whose heads were decorated with feathers of fire.

The colored leaves paled, and curled, and crumbled, and turned to dust in his palm. The trees without their leaves looked like men to him, tall and naked and smooth, muscled and cold and breathing the thin air patiently.

This was the first remembered fall of Wakwa's half-white son, Wolf-of-the-mist He-hopes, Muckquashim-ouwan Noh-annoosu. That and Moses Bluehill were his names. He had two names while his friends had one. From his names he knew all about himself and everybody knew all about him.

He had been born in a mist at nunnowa, the time when the old sun rubbed the leaves till they glowed like a kettle, when the women stored the berries and the corn and the fish and the meat and the herbs. It was also true that he was wild and alone like the wolf. Had his father not left him on his own on the mountain under the moon? Wolf-of-the-mist had meaning. Noh-annoosu, He-hopes, meant something too; something as fine as the green trees that pointed up always, that were ever-green, that lived like sachimmauog rooted among the rocks.

One of his other names, Bluehill, was the name of the place of his birth that he had never seen, no, that he could not remember having seen although he had lived there when he had had two mothers.

He was one man with two mothers. How did he know? His sister, Sequan, whispered it to him after Qunneke was asleep. Black-haired, black-eyed Sequan, the first child of his father, the first child of Qunneke, born three springs before their father was the husband of two wives, came under Wolf's blanket with fruit and nuts which she shared with him while telling him a story that had many parts. When she told it with a single difference from the way she had told it before, he, from Bluehill, made fists and pounded her plump arms and she pulled his strangely colored hair until he stopped. And then the story would come out right, from the beginning, night-by-night, until they reached the end. And reaching the end would make him shed loud tears and Qunneke would wake up and be angry with them both but would never scold. She showed them her back. And this was family life.

Sequan's story was the truth of why his hair grew in rings tighter than a squirrel's tail. Awepu told him the English called these 'curls.' Qunneke cut one of his curls off with her knife and tucked it into a tiny bag of doeskin and hid it in her basket of prized things - strange things - a vessel that looked like a swan, its beak for pouring, its tail curved for holding, and made of the skin of a star. Silver! The silver swan was a ewer, which had served his white mother for a breast so that she could keep him alive when she had lost her milk.

Two other things, twins, also formed of silver, were at the bottom of the basket; ugly, heavy things looking like vines of wild roses tied in a circle and frozen into ice. These were buckles, an adornment for English shoes. They rotted, turning black in the basket, the ewer and the buckles, and Qunneke would take them out when she thought he was asleep and rub them with a paste until they gleamed again.

But Qunneke especially cherished the cut curl, which, like all Bluehill's curls, was the color of the dead needles of the pines that built a silence under them. This curl was for him the great sign of his aloneness and his difference from his family and of something else that he did not understand and which left him thirsty no matter how much water or milk he drank. The name for the something else was Moses.

He was Moses. Moses was also the name of a man of another great tribe of thousands of falls-of-leaf ago in a far place whose mother had left him in a basket in a river. A second mother, the daughter of a pharaoh, just as Sequan was the daughter of a sachim, had come and scooped the Jewish Moses from the reedy waterway and had taken him to her home and loved him and raised him into a man.

When he was alone, covered in the brown needles under the green pines, Moses Bluehill wept that mothers gave away their sons called Moses. Bitter was his crying that the mother from whom he had emerged and his father who had put him in her would have given him that name.

Moses, at the age of three, taught lessons to the dispersion of the Massachuseuck. When the last rattle of that Taquonk season's leaves quieted and lay dead underfoot soaked in cold rain, Moses walked with Qunneke and Sequan and his young brother, Lightfoot, the second child of Qunneke, who was bound onto Qunneke's back. Moses held Qunneke's hand. Some of the other women came out of their houses to look. They bowed their heads. And Moses Bluehill let go. In dropping the hand of the woman who had folded him in her arms after his first mother had left him, he stood as himself, alone in front of them.

When the smell of snow struck the mountain, Moses heard pounding and thought it was his heart. He put his hand on his breast and felt it but its rhythm was apart from the beat that enthralled him, that came through his bones. He put his ear to the ground and was afraid of the pounding that moved faster and faster toward him as if a giant buck and his hinds were scarring the earth with the force and speed of their huge, cloven feet.

The people in the mountain otan began scurrying, calling out, the mothers collecting the children, the guards running off in all directions to fetch back the hunters. Even Qunneke almost knocked him over running for her comb. Her serving girls raced away to the half-frozen stream for fresh water.

Moses told Sequan about the sound of the terrible deer and she laughed at him, her eyes, as he had never seen them, as bright as two suns. Sequan told him that the noise was from horses, taller, thicker, slower, stronger than deer, but not freeborn, and so not able to refuse a man upon their backs. She said their father had a horse, and Awepu, and Qunneke had one too which had thundered away with the others to the West. Only the bad cousin of their father, a man called Weeping Heart, had a horse that he did not share with the People. And all these horses had been gifts from a man so white that his hair was as yellow as butterflies' wings. And this white man was the uncle-by-marriage of Moses' white mother. And Qunneke kept a snippet of *his* hair just as she kept one of Moses.

The beat, like hands beating against wet bark, faster than any hands should move, made him run from the women and the babies. Moses ran up his mountain to his pine trees to be alone with the sound and to see and he slipped and slid on the wet leaves under the gray sky and urine spilled out of him in droplets and he did not squeeze it off and it heated his round smooth leg in a golden river.

Moses knew from the time that he knew anything that he, Wolf-of-the-mist He-hopes, was important - that the People held his house as special. Meat was brought to their door by every hunter the tribe had left to it. The women would watch Qunneke's slow, definite stride the way the wise-sayer watched the stars. The old men would frown when Moses sat his grandfather's arm, his father's father, Pequawus, the Gray Fox, the man second to the old sachim, Waban. Moses' old great-uncle, Waban, the Wind, sat in the key of any circle of men and he spoke long speeches. When he laughed, other men also laughed. Moses held no picture in his mind of that circle with his grandfather laughing or with his father laughing.

The hoof-beats broke into the clearing and shrieking as from joyous birds filled the air. The camp was a lake of people pooling around the horses. They danced like Waban's second son, these deer with uncloven hooves, these fleet moose without antlers, these Manittowock, godly creatures, with long, thick snakes for necks and frog's eyes and massive headdresses of hair.

A serving girl took Moses by a back entry to be bathed and cleanly dressed and Sequan with her newly shining eyes would not stay close to him.

Moses sat in the wetu next to Qunneke and was staring at a bent knee and a thigh in the firelight and this perfect leg was his father's. He knew so by the man's voice flowing softly against every soft part of him. The voice was also the explanation to Moses why the family was held above others.

A long arm extended toward him. A big, graceful hand summoned him. Moses struck back at Qunneke as she helped him to stand. He moved around the fire toward his father in front of his grandfather who he loved and his great-uncle who frightened him with his laughter. He hardly saw them for his father. His curls shook with the look on this man. He felt all the family watching him shake. He saw them watching the face of his father.

His father's eyes were like the lake water, dark under the sun, filled with silver birds of light that perch on the wet, sink, and, tah! reappear on another ripple. His father was crying with no noise and no running tears. Moses watched his father's mouth turn and twist when he looked at him as if he were swallowing some rancid food. Moses' high opinion of himself sank into his father's eyes among the silver birds winking bright to black.

The unfamiliar hand came behind his head and it exerted force, gradual force, bringing him closer and closer to the large, perfect chest. Moses fell forward onto his father's neck and was crushed in arms so strong that he thought two pine trees had collapsed on him and had pinned him there forever. A humming set up in his father's throat so near to Moses' ear, and over the hum the child heard his father gulp the tears before they could drop, until they were gone.

Qunneke cried out and the others who were crowded into the house of exile clapped their hands together sounding like leaves battling the wind, like horses' hoofs.

Moses' stomach turned, he was so high off the ground when his father stood with him in his arms and went outside. And the whole town, waiting there in the cold, began to clap and sing a chant as if it were a wedding.

While Wakwa was away in the West, the camp had held its breath over Moses Bluehill. Now they knew not only that it was right to accept him but also that they must. Easily, so easily, they could have deposed the young sachim who had thrown away their ancient lands with his heart. Yet Wakwa was a spokesman like no other and they saw him as their headman when Waban would slip away into old age and death. Wakwa had behaved like a man and he still had the stomach to love the child of risk. He had accepted the child to his breast and that was enough for them. They cheered him. Again. Again.

The cheers were muffled for Moses nestled low against the slick, flat scars that were his perfect father's only marring. He never wanted to leave his father's embrace.

Moses, tucked away to sleep, watched Qunneke and Wakwa. Even to the boy so young, it was clear that Qunneke was happy that Wakwa had shed the grime of his journey. The heat of the pesuponk, the sweat hut, had melted some of the terror out of Wakwa's muscles. It was clear to see. Fright had poured out onto Wakwa's skin and down him into the stream to become part of the lake at the foot of the mountain. Wakwa smiled at everything Qunneke whispered to him; he listened hard to her.

Moses half-sat in the half-darkness when his father sighed and stretched. Wakwa looked like other men who wanted to sleep. Moses was amazed that his father should have such a common need and he was pleased. Qunneke became busy putting warm water into a dish of clay and untying Wakwa's jacket as if she were his mother. Moses was aghast that she intended to wash a grown man, a grown man who had already washed.

Moses crashed down on his mat to avoid sight of his father looking down at Qunneke and doing exactly what she asked. Their voices, soft under the bitching of the fire, made their way to him. He heard Sequan's name and his own and a sound of complaint from Qunneke. Wakwa's voice persuaded in the soft tongue of the Ninnuock, "It is only three days' walk and it is important for him to be with me. He must be seen as part of the great moments of this tribe from the beginning of his life. And that is nothing new for Moses!"

So! He was leaving the mountain with his mighty father. Moses looked up. His father was naked, pulling the thick, red blanket over his silken skin, and Qunneke, bare to the waist, was washing herself in front of Wakwa now. Moses crushed his face against his pillow and then, without knowing when, he looked up. He watched them.

The bowls of washing clay were abandoned on the firestones. The red blanket pointed sharply like a lean-to. It collapsed about Qunneke as she slipped under Wakwa's arm. Moses watched his father's hands smooth Qunneke's black hair back from her forehead to the beginning of her braid. One hand, and then the other, one hand, and then the other. Qunneke made the sounds of a dove.

Sequan had told Moses that many winters ago her mother's hair had been longer than anyone else's in the world. Its ends trailed on the ground. It took three people to wash it and comb it and Qunneke did so with all her helpers under the waterfall in the blue hills of the Massachuseuck. Sequan remembered the day that her mother had cut off her hair for Moses' mother's sake. Qunneke's hair had grown again. In the two years since it had been shorn it had attained the bottom of her shoulder blades.

Wakwa's hands circled the plait and worked down over it and over it until Qunneke's honey-colored arms emerged and wrapped Wakwa as if he were a suckling boy. How awful Moses thought it was that his father pretended to be an infant. And he was a shy one, his mouth touching the woman's face, and throat, and mouth, places that could not and would never give milk.

Those places gave his father something else, Moses saw. Wakwa seemed to be feeding on the honey of Qunneke's skin, and Qunneke, who was not small, seemed small. She disappeared against Wakwa's body the way Moses did against the mountainside. Wakwa ate her away and Qunneke folded down against his neck and his side and went limp as if he had sucked all the honey from her, had drunk all the pap out of her through her skin and her eyes and her mouth. Moses would have gone to show his father where to suck but Wakwa seemed pleased with the nourishment he got and looked bigger, stronger, frighteningly strong drinking from her in this way.

And then, things changed. Wakwa seemed twice his great height after all his tasting. He pushed up many times against Qunneke as if he would feed her back. Wakwa was as horrible as a fallen tree trying to rise off the earth. But Qunneke looked unafraid and she made sucking sounds although her mouth was nowhere near Wakwa, nowhere near a place where food or milk could come. They were suddenly very still, dangling there like moist foliage. In a blink they were resting side by side as they did when they were not feeding on one another in this strange, difficult way that seemed to bring them so many good tastes. Then it was Wakwa washing her for she seemed to spill his food from between her legs. Moses himself felt full now and he drifted from his watch into sleep.

His rest broke sharply. Qunneke slept, but Wakwa lay on his side stiffly away from her, his hands holding his own head, the skin of his cheeks pushed down like an old man's or a monster's. Wakwa bit his lips, his mouth wide, his teeth white and shining like a wall of wet shells. Squeals pushed past them, coming out of his belly, chest, and throat although he tried to stop them. Wakwa was weeping like children who had lost their way in the woods. Wet sprayed when he snorted. Wakwa punished the dirt floor with the side of his hand. Once.

Moses wondered if Wakwa wanted to eat and to feed Qunneke again. He tried to figure how often a man must do this in the night. Qunneke neither woke nor moved. Moses cried out wondering if his starving father had killed her.

Wakwa hurried to him and invaded his small bed. "Do not wake your mother, little Wolf, this is a sleep she must have." His hand lost itself in Moses' curls.

"Qunneke is not my mother!" Moses squeezed his eyes shut. "Sequan says!" He was sick at feeling Wakwa's hand slowly withdraw. He lay next to his very still father, the sachim, smelling a new smell on him, a sweet smell, a smell like boiled corn and rotting berries. It was as if Wakwa had just been baked.

CHAPTER NINE

Fall 1750 and Spring 1751

Kirke just moved in the direction he was going. Messages sent ahead nearly always seemed a waste of time. They must travel his route and, especially when he was rushing, would arrive with him if not after. So the surprise when the white-haired master of Pemaquid Bluff galloped up the sandy road through the pines to his barn.

V.T. Kirke walked through the enclosed passageway joining the stables to the main house, let himself in, and was half through reading the post heaped on a salver in the vestibule by the time Claude de St. Aubin descended the stairs and discovered him.

Kirke looked up with no greeting other than, "Claude, you could say I am a demented old ass for not realizing that Locke would send me this tray full of letters but why not to London? That's where I was. I crossed an ocean just to get word!"

"Thomas, you have never said one extraordinary thing in your life. That observation is no exception. How do you do, darling fellow?" From the steps Claude blessed him, then stomped across the floor to embrace him.

On being freed, Kirke rationalized, "I suppose it makes some sense since Locke is in the Ohio country, as he says here, 'engaged in rescuing some of our property from the confusion of several small wars.' Imagine, Claude, men dying heroes' deaths over the personal interests of private parties!"

"Neither is that insight startling, dear boy."

"Go to the devil, will you?"

"I've already done it, haven't I, living with Dire?" Claude laughed and exuded charm and took Kirke in to the black and green room made blacker and greener by the woods showing through its windows. "Have I told you what heaven this house is in the wintertime?"

"Heaven? Never gave it a thought until several weeks ago."

"Thomas, you are not under the weather?"

"I am, indeed. A nicer September I have never experienced."

"Touché!" Claude's steps toward the Cognac shook every object in the room not bolted down. He was pouring and thinking. Kirke was talking.

"I came to America to find an Indian called Silent Fox."

The liquor splashed Claude's thick hand. He shook it off, rocketing drops against the walls. "You flew here on your broom, you know so much already!" Claude hid behind irritability.

"What do I know? What is there to know? What's wrong with you?"

"I am working on him. You are not to go near him."

"Are you telling me you know this man?"

"But, of course." Claude seemed put out. "Anybody who is anybody knows Renard!" Claude's chin came up and stayed up as he made his way to Kirke with a snifter. He bumped his shins on the furniture.

"You know where he is?" Kirke's eyes were white-hot.

"Naturellement!"

"Why are all the answers in this house?"

"Strange question from the head of a trading company, n'est-ce pas? What do you want with Renard?"

"Never mind! Get me to him!"

"Humph!" Claude sipped his drink.

Kirke collapsed into an enormous chair. "I have lately met his Colonial wife."

Claude whirled away but said affectionately, "You are not a shrewd man, Thomas, but you are a great one."

"What? What are you talking about?" Kirke's parchment brow crumpled.

"You are ahead of us all." Claude was almost sorry at making this slight hole in Wakwa's and Dire's secret.

"'Ahead?' You're speaking very funny English for a Jesuit Father. Ahead? What does that mean?"

Claude turned back. Slowly he came to sitting. He watched Kirke's glance travel from Locke's letters to the bogus bishop's ring he wore, to the pearls joining his own shirt cuffs.

"I might expect some chicanery from Locke and you, may you both rot in hell, but from *HIM*? You both know where *he* is and all of you know where *she* is and you lot don't tell that girl dying of him?" Kirke folded up small like the idiot Claude made him out to be.

Claude took pity but shrugged, "Come, come, Thomas! I am a priest."

Kirke swallowed the remark hard. "If you won't explain then I'll get myself to the Ohio and put it to him myself."

"You Irish are a mystery! Thomas, you say you 'ave met a woman. What do you want with the husband that she had? Tell me! What is she like?"

"The French! And you the master of many souls! Shall I drool over the virtues of a precious young woman as if she were an emerald I could grab on the cheap?"

"It will not be on the cheap, my lamb. That I can say. It will be a trust exacting your blood, as that in the chalice upstairs. And, if you understand your position, why go to the West where Dire has moved from anyway because he is coming 'ere, and why disturb the hero, Renard? It is bad enough for the Fox, non?"

"Their child!"

"When he is older."

Again Kirke learned from cryptic comment as if from an illuminated text. Elizabeth was young, very young. There was plenty of time for - everything. Kirke puzzled over whom else might have taken that into account. He saw his place in a grand scheme but the schemers evaded him. "Do you think Elizabeth Dowland has it figured out?"

Claude looked steadily at Kirke. "You see my robes. I cannot claim to be an expert about women least of all about Renard's former wife since you will not tell me about her. However, just as I know she is innocent of all things leading to this moment, I also know she has made no move to find Renard or the babe."

"It seems unnatural."

"Mutton head! She plays out the rein and by that device does not strain it, or break it, or let it go. She 'as somezing figured out!"

Elizabeth never really lived in the barn again. She made it her atelier but stayed with Dr. Stirling. It was a delicate tenancy. She brought her small work to his fireside after supper to sweeten his evening with the rhythm of her stitches. He cast aside his ledgers or his music to follow the thread of her thoughts.

Stirling was angry at the world on several counts and his ire burned his health away. He was upset with Israel for obsessive study and felt insulted by Worth for entertaining such a houseguest as Thomas Kirke and not including him. He was jealous of Dire Locke's salubrious influence on Elizabeth and his heart batted irregularly from the prospect of her being dished new disappointment if brought into contact with the Indian. He fumed not only over the loss of the child, Moses, but also over his being shut off from learning anymore of herbs from Qunneke. Together they had concocted quite a pharmacy. Worst of all was his frustration that with his wife deceased, the only person who had him as her sole interest was his housekeeper of thirty years who was no use as an ally in his labor of love, the curing of Elizabeth Dowland, because the Scotswoman was constitutionally so ill-natured.

She, least of anybody, Stirling thought, had anything to make her nasty considering her light responsibilities. There was virtually no entertaining to prepare for and his house was supremely plain and comfortable, taking all its beauty from the sea outside. It was light and almost every room was square. The salt on its many windows and the roar of the wind in the chimneys made complaints he supposed, but any self-respecting Scot should take such in stride. The walls, shelves, settles, tables, were of painted pine. Big chairs, dark and solid, built of English wood in the century before were paired on small rugs scattered over the bare floorboards. A bit of wax took care of it. Ivy festooned the high corners and cascaded to the baseboards out of round, colored bowls.

Stirling and Elizabeth passed the winter in these pleasant surroundings like a father and daughter who had quarrelled long before and forgotten over what. By spring they achieved mutual restlessness.

One morning late in March, Kirke tapped at Stirling's glass-paned door. The housekeeper made no rush to answer. Kirke made a dash for Stirling's barn. Working the latch up with the skill of a felon, he looked in and yelled, short and loud, "Liz!"

The interior was as dark as country night except for one spear of sun hurtling to nowhere. A surprised scream revealed that she was there.

"Where are you?" he demanded. Blindly, the merchant held his hands out. Elizabeth's hands gripped his. Kirke screamed in turn.

"Hello!" she said. "You frightened me!"

"Good God!" Kirke was not sensibly dressed for March. The Cape Cod sunlight had fooled him into silk, a raw-woven suit of fair weight, yet no combatant for the wind and fitful sun. The muscles in his neck jumped with cold. "How do you feel?"

"I? What of you? You are shivering! I could have made a fire. I did not know you were coming!"

"Why not?"

"I got no letter."

"I told you I would come."

"In a year!"

"Shall I go back to Maine then and wait the time out?" His blue hands passed across each of her cheeks and then cupped her head. She drew away.

"Forgive me!" He hurried. "I've thought of you every day, all day, an old man's fancy that you would have been doing the same and would have known that I got aboard the first boat that could cut through the ice."

Shamed, she looked down. In disbelief she saw the dirt floor. "What wrecks we are!"

"You think I'm a wreck?"

"Not you!"

"You can't take that back just like that. You said something."

"I did not mean quite what I said."

"You did too! I know what you meant. We are so...alive... so...dead. Lost. I know. I know what you meant. 'Tis enough! Elizabeth, it does not have to be perfect."

She looked past him sadly. "Does it not?"

He brought her into an embrace so delicate it pained her.

She looked full into his face. "You have been in Maine. Did you find...what you wanted?"

He kept holding her, fencing her from the rest of the world. The look on his face was doom to her most cherished ideal. "It is this wretched barn so quiet, so private." He choked out, "You'd better tie up at the throat; this place is so big and so cold."

"What of you?" She turned his collar up and tried to make a muffler of his stock.

He slid her hood over her head.

The bell from the faraway kitchen rang irritably.

He did not smile. "You look so good."

"I do?"

"I'm going soon."

"Aren't you staying for lunch?"

"Liz! Are you a dunce? I am going away forever. I want you with me." He let her go.

"I think we'd better talk up at the house."

"I don't feel like eating just now." Kirke explored the place, acclimated to the shade, seeing the work on her loom.

"Do you never stay still a minute?"

He was back suddenly and took hold of her arm at its pit, a bit too hard. "Mistress, I am sixty-one now. I am a merchant. I thought you understood that."

"I do." She said. She pulled free and ran away out of the barn toward the house, leading him, shouting back in the March bluster, "I feel like a genius! I sensed you would come and here you are! Your place has been set for days!"

He caught up with her and loved the way she lied about her tears shooting sideways, saying they were from the wind.

Dr. Mac watched from the window and retreated just in time.

"You drive a man mad." Kirke said the following noon. He sat on a bench outside the barn. "I know a few things, Lisbeth. I know the man. Met the man when your boy was born. Oh, come. Oh, come." He would not brook her groaning. "I know the man from long ago. He is a fine man. A good man. A good and quiet red man. A true man. And true. And knowing you, I...."

"You know me hardly at all."

"And knowing you utterly well, though hardly at all, I see how you have driven him mad. Into his mind, as it were. And being there, he is the madder for having no room for you."

"You dare...!"

"Oh, I will." He reached down for her as she struggled to rise off the sweetening grass.

"I will say what's on my mind for I'm old enough not to credit what you may do in retaliation."

"What gives you the right...!"

He cut her off. "Now, listen to me, little girl, it is now 1751. March. The New Year. You have lived in this haven of animals since January '48 or '49 if you reckon by the new calendar. And you have lived alone. I thought about that while I was away. I have so few years to give you. Such a few. Ten? Twenty? You'll be forty-two. The priest up there saw me with paper in my hands always, scratching numbers in a line with my pencil and he thought I was keeping daybooks, I suppose, or adding dividends, but I was not!" Kirke sounded peculiarly Irish in his intensity. "I calculated years, ages, and possibilities and expectancies. It's a low appeal, I know, but it seemed to me up there with the waves reaching like hands of death that I must refuse to die. More so must you."

"Don't depend on me for anything."

"I will!"

"You have no right!"

"That again!" He moved away leaving her on her own. "Nobody has a right in a thing like this. That's the whole idea. It's just that one says, 'please,' and one says, 'yes.' Or, 'no.' But the doing of the thing is the yes. The act is not a right. Rights are between the lender and the debtor. The prisoner in his cell and the society getting its due. I talk of a yes. A simple yes. An occasional *yes*. 'Yes, Viti, I will break my fast with you. Yes, we will sup together on hard-wrought honey. No. Tonight I feel unwell, but there will be yes. In some tomorrow.' I'm talking of a hope of yes. Of life. Life before eternity. And heaven in your pocket. And those who live a living death over saying no will roast in hell when their lives are over."

"No!"

"There's my religion, Liz. Shall I see you at the luncheon table?"

She stood with him. She looked past the cloth of his shirt to his pounding heart; it shook the trim of his neckcloth. She put her hand against his chest as if it were the broadside of a sunken ship, a shipwreck. She did not look into his eyes and her shawl fell clinging to both of them as it slipped.

The great slowness with which the busy man turned her face up to his caused her fibre to twist. The scent and taste of his cheek came to her as he modestly caressed her face with his face keeping his lips away.

He wished that he could pick her up, could move her even with his eyes, but he resigned himself to the limitations of his spine and looked down at her, more pink than he had been before.

She stood there cut by memory - Wakwa lifting her and burying himself in her. She pressed her cheek against the hard little buttons of Kirke's shirt.

Holding her shoulders, he stepped back and did kiss her on her mouth leaving a syrup for her tongue to take in. And when she did, he whispered, "Yes? And what does that mean?"

"I am a woman married. I will always be. My 'yes' was to someone else."

"You will kill me!" He pushed her away, took her back, then let her go. He left her and leaned his forehead against the worn edge of the barn door. "God in heaven!"

"Oh, I know!"

"You do not." Disdain kept his mouth nearly closed. "Jesus!" he kept saying and sat back on his bench.

Elizabeth rushed to him. "You are a lovely man, Viti, a lovely man."

"I know. I know."

Softly, she laughed.

But she laughed, and he held her arms at this sign. His ageing face was transformed into itself, into no age. His diamond eyes split a light from inside. "I know that nothing I say will take his hook out of your heart. I leave it in! But see you let the tissue grow over it. Let it be round as before. I am not such an ass as to try to tear out his prong and then wallow in the wound. My purpose is not to make you pain."

"I am so sorry. You do not know me. I am proud, I am persistent, I am vain!"

"I know. I know."

She did not laugh but saw that she could have laughed at his opinion of her.

"Show me some of it!" His speckled hand dropped to his breeches buttons, then sank down. "How I wish Locke were here to speak for me!"

"You do not need help, Viti. But for Wakwa to explain my part."

"He would not do it."

She shunned him and stood straight, seeming tall.

Kirke stood taller. "I do not apologize. It is true." Kirke admitted modestly, "His reluctance is what permits me to stand here and so close to you." Kirke came closer still and he set his hands upon her shoulders like epaulets, badges of distinction. "The proposal is for us to have a dalliance. For what years remain to us. The way it can be done best is to marry. Let us fool the world. Be his wife but my amour and we will have a marriage that is what a marriage should be!"

She stood alone.

Kirke, regained her side, wrapped her in his arms and moved her cordially, stepping toward the barn. "Just lie down with me. Rest with me. My time is short! He cursed their shaky way up the rungs to the loft.

"You lie down. You rest." Came from her.

He threw his coat aside and rid himself of clothes to the waist. He lay down on his back and cast his arm across his eyes. "This is a hell of a vicious bed."

To this she could agree. She said only, "I was cleaning it away yesterday when you came. I do not use it anymore."

He moved his arm. His eyes were jade and full of play. "Once more."

She sat. At the edge. She sat with him but faced away several storeys above the floor of the barn. Kirke put his pale arm out, claiming her, leaving her no choice but to lie down. He heard her sigh and sigh again as she lay in her woolen clothes on the white of his chest.

"So," he asked disregarding her sorrowful sounds, "is it yes?"

"I am bound. Tenderly bound. I gave no consent to a divorce. How can I say yes to you?"

"You have to, little girl. There's no way out of it."

She pulled away from him and sat upright shivering without his body's heat.

"Presuming of course you want...what I want. Then of course you have to say yes otherwise the authorities will probably hang you!" He laughed.

"How dare you! How dare you take...everything so lightly."

"Not you, Liz."

"Marriage then. You mock it."

He came up on one arm. "I do not mock marriage but put it in its place." All kindness, he drew her near to him again, away from the drop. "Young woman, you surprise me. I thought you more grown up at heart than that."

As if weighed by stones, her neck bent downward and her face was hidden against the woolen covering her knees.

"Eliza, listen! Marriage is not something to take seriously. Say you'll believe me. Try to believe me! One takes one's hairdresser seriously."

Offended, her shoulders hunched.

"One takes one's horse seriously. Do you get me? At times, one takes one's banker seriously. All in that order."

She looked up, tears running back along her temples, into her ears. What a man she had known. Where was he?

Kirke barged ahead not knowing where her attention rested or sensing too well where it homed. "Take marriage seriously, Betty? Take your overcoat seriously! Your cloak is a matter of life or death but marriage may come and marriage may go and we live on. We eat, sleep, start anew!"

Elizabeth's hands caressed her own arms needing solace at Kirke's onslaught.

He reached for her and firmly turned her toward him and required through his clean, friendly hands that she lie against his heart. "Lizzie! Marriage is like a ship. It is a floating thing. It must be buoyant, big, displacing more trouble than it holds. Do not ever anchor marriage to the bottom with seriousness if you want to cruise about in her. By God, marriage is a vessel in which we follow stars but the ship must move!"

She cried in his arms at that.

He asked, sure of his opinion, "Can marriage be weighed down with sighs and tears and catch any wind in its sails?" He swallowed a torrent of words, then forced himself to speak, but carefully, softly, gently, "You know that it cannot." He waited for her to stop moaning, then chucked her under the chin. "Frolic on her decks, mend her when she springs a leak, drink and eat and play solitaire at her board, watch for the dinghy of your mate on the horizon with a sense of expectancy, deliriously plot her charts, but Lord, don't give marriage the time of day." Before Elizabeth could object, Kirke pounced on her reason. "What has marriage ever done for you that you should give it the slightest bit of personal attention? What is it anyway? A thing? A person? A place? Marriage barely qualifies as a respectable noun!"

She drew back to say, "But it is something!"

He moved slowly toward her face, which lingered sadly near his shoulder. Gently his kiss quieted anything she might say. "Liz, Liz!" Kirke's voice roughened in an uncustomary whisper. "Marriage is an illusion. And that's something. Enough anyway. Everything! More than beings of flesh should expect. Marriage is eternal because it can be classified about the same as you can classify a nice fog, or ghosts, or God."

She felt him begin to take solace in her. She felt his hand and then his hands perform the ritual, not hackneyed but refined, moving on his intent, which was to overlay her figure with the figures of his affection. His old hands worked at coaxing her anger to lie down. They ventured peaceably to her waist and below. He brought her close, hating the straw. He said nothing. He made no sound. He exerted force, the kindly arm in league with the bony knee insisting that she turn, that she give up her defense. A tender sun, he spread above her, the overturned turtle. "Help a little?"

Not pitiless, she acquiesced although slightly – allowed sight of her breast and her skin to him. And she regretted and regretted his finding beauty there. She watched his aged throat and wept against it.

He sought to say something comforting but only managed, "It would be nice to wash but I do wash every day. My feet in a bucket morning and night and pertinent places night and day."

"I am sure, I am sure!" She kept repeating not wanting any hand but one where his had come.

He took time from habit or wish. He leaned lazily on one arm and looked within himself although his eyes were trained on her. "Would it help if you considered me to be a road? A route? A highway? You can choose to follow me for the road and the traveller are always goin' to the same place."

"Stop!"

"I can't. I just roll along like every other road and in my case, don't you know, the surveyors have gotten to me first and laid out my course although a road is not supposed to know that kind of thing. What I do know is there'll be pleasant places to stop along the way, and heights from which to observe the scene below. Much can be learned in touring, the objective being to arrive refreshed at your destination."

Clothes began to litter the loft. Her hose and skirts bunched near the ladder like a woman contemplating suicide.

Elizabeth found herself pressed by man's shape after so long. She pulled back to verify by sight what closeness told her. She remarked him, witnessed a member encased in elegantly thin skin as white as he, blushing from foretaste of love. She was enlightened by the fact of its color, considering the husband she had had. There was nothing unremitting about the phallus so close, nothing weapon-hard. This part of this elder man was flesh filled full enough to give. She permitted it to inveigh on her as Kirke took her against him. She was impressed by its definite message free of the bristling of youth.

He brought her up from hiding to sit on him. That she refused. He set her down against the straw to judge her face.

"Thomas, I will not!"

He looked. Confirmed. "Not." Kirke lay down himself. "Liz, my dear, I will not be deterred." Kirke made his own embrace. He lost himself in his need. He watched her watching him take himself. He did not punish her by this lonely exhibition. He locked her wrist in the crook of his arm and pulled, and pulled, and pulled, and he drew up some love for himself out of his impacted store. He smiled sweetly at her as he worked.

"I am sorry!" She said near his ear.

"Hush! Hush! Hush! Hush!"

She drew herself over him like a coverlet, her hands sheltering his eyes to spare him from sight of his solitude. He was as absorbed as an idiot but suffered her kindly hand to cup the surge of his semen when it came.

The housekeeper's bell shrilled.

Kirke turned them front against slippery front bathing them both in his defeat. They lay together, primed with the liquor he had forcibly extracted. And her heart shook that its smell brought saliva into her mouth like the smell of an unnamed cologne.

His drugged, wet hand was upon her face and she tasted from it in sorrow for the taste she had once known. Kirke stroked her face, the liquid of his seed shimmering on her like a paint. His mouth, twisting and wry, he brushed her forehead, her nose, her cheekbones, her chin with his finger, etching her features, as if for battle. She was so stained with the Indian.

The bell scolded like a biddy again.

Kirke teased it, "I am here!"

This was profound. As a drowning person acknowledges the blessing of a rock, a branch by which to cling fast to life, Elizabeth acknowledged the blessing of Kirke, holding him around his neck. And with good grace, he accepted her clinging to the goodness of human touch and, he desperately hoped, to some goodness in him.

"A thousand welcomes," he smiled at her, "nine thousand welcomes. I shall tell you that Irish story someday."

They fought over who would get water from the well. Kirke insisted on the task. Elizabeth stayed adamant that it was her place.

"You're to be an Irishman's wife, woman. There will be different courtesies, no doubt, than those you were habituated to."

"You presume much in your statement."

Kirke buttoned the minimum of his clothing over his steamy body. "I won't be taken for granted. If we are going to continue this affair, it shan't be done in barns but in our own house. All legal. If the world wants a porthole on our happiness - give it to 'em. For God's sake, at least we'll be warm and have water in the stand!"

"Thomas, I said I'd go."

"That's not enough! We must never have this particular opportunity for disagreement again. How can you blandly say, 'I said I'd go.' At least blush about our activities of this forenoon."

"*You* should blush! I would be in the stocks if anyone had witnessed today."

"Thus, Bettina, I am off to your uncle to settle our marriage deep in his mind."

"Thomas...."

"Say it?"

She sighed. "Viti...."

"Ah!"

"Viti, I may admire you, treasure you, even love you, but I will never marry you."

He took her forearm gruffly. "Don't say that now you've taken my virginity."

"Scoff at my condition!?" She blazed at him.

He put his cold shoes on without his stockings. Disregarding her torment, he said sagely, softly, "Lisbeth, you've loved with your whole self before. I had not." He paused for a moment in mortal danger from his honesty. "I can see now it is not a thing one gives up easily. There is a rightness in your struggle." This said, a better humor overtook him. "That is why you'd better twist what you said before. You will marry me, Liz, but love me? We shall see." He climbed down carefully, damning the bucket. "What you've got to think about, Lizzie, is - what is perfection?"

When he finally could speak, Gilbert Worth commented, "Locke once told me you were barely conversant with English, yet I sit the victim of a vivacity of language that paralyzes reason."

"Mr. Worth," Kirke said formally, earnestly, "I speak from the heart which may explain why my talk sounds like a foreign tongue to Dire."

Gil let a shout of delight slip out.

"I've the gut and no wit to say nothing but the truth in as many ways as possible."

Gil felt drowned in the pool of gold the sun made out of his chair. "Kirke! Your ages!"

Kirke's eyes narrowed. He was not a callow boy but a man with a fortune, a staggering fortune, for whom many mothers of marriageable daughters would gladly overthrow their delicacy about social position. He regarded Gil's objection as a ploy. But he cajoled with passable skill. "She is grandmotherly but I'll cure her of that. And she lives dangerously. If she doesn't look out, I'll outlive her."

"I wish you both long lives. Yet, they do not, necessarily, have to be lived together."

"Good. We could live them apart and be miserable for a long time."

Gil went silent. He recollected this sort of scene, Elizabeth's father in his place, and an Indian in front of him, brave as the dawn, and Charles Dowland despising the enormity of the act of consent. "Kirke...."

"Don't be formal," Kirke was sardonic, "call me Thomas."

"As you wish. Thomas. You have to know something about our Beth."

"I know everything about her."

Gil stopped, then forged on. "I do not mean her history from bliss to the day of horrors with Hudson. I mean her peculiar talent for loyalty. She is fixed upon her first partner. Wouldn't you be letting both her and yourself in for a deal of the worst kind of grief with this suit?"

Kirke thought this kind on Worth's part and while he searched for a fitting reply Worth continued.

"I suspect you are looking for a full and blossomed marriage."

"I flatter myself, no."

"Forgive the suggestion then. But a marriage of convenience will place her soul and future on the rack more stringently than it is now."

"Sir, I am not looking for a marriage of convenience. I am sixty-one not one hundred."

"But you said...."

"*You* said it!" Kirke shot to his feet and paced. "Marriage full and blossomed, as I imagine you imagine it, is impossible with her and even with me, considering the lives we have lead. But it doesn't mean she's ruled out gladness in the flesh, and it doesn't mean that we cannot build a marriage. Of some good design."

Gil watched him and tried to remember if, like Kirke and Wakwa, he had paced in front of Charles when he had sued for Hanna's hand.

"I take it kindly that you are concerned for her...as a woman. We'll be friends when you care somewhat about me. I am the fellow who's going to abide her come what may and never have her to myself for the Indian will be in our bed with us till I'm dead!"

"If you are aggrieved even now...."

"Aggrieved?! These are the facts of life! I am Thomas Kirke. Kirke Company is an integral part of your lives. As for the

Indian – Kirke Company is the whole support of his tribe, of his life, of his children's lives, of his first wife's life, and of his plans for his folk! I will be welcoming them all under the sheets and that includes you and your dear, gracious spouse, and Locke and the Frenchwoman and the lawyer and his motherless kid and the Jesuit, and the ghosts, and the skeletons, the lot of you." Kirke choked aloud on the mouthful of them.

Gil nearly tipped his chair over scrambling to his feet to take Kirke on. "Kirke Company can never buy 'the lot of us,' including Elizabeth, so you can have the pleasure of my niece in your dotage!"

"What else is it but buying and at a high rate! Although, considering our ages, your fine point, leasing is the more accurate term. It does not take a great mind to see the advantage to this Silent Fox in my relation to her. Not a move the House makes will ignore his monetary needs or his aims for his People with Elizabeth as my wife!"

"You presume the pleasure, sir!"

"I already have the pleasure, sir."

Gil froze. His lips lost color. "You crude...!"

Hanna slipped into their conference through Matthew's office.

Kirke took her presence in but dove ahead. "Don't you hear me?! How could she know her mind unless she could give herself to me? I could leave it at that with no blame from her, more, with her blessing, and be sailing free from these constraints but I am not."

"Who is holding you?"

"You tell me! I give you the benefit that you did not engineer a match between Elizabeth and me since you seem to hate the idea of her loving anyone but Silent Fox. But you were made aware, you were poured into a mold just as I was by Locke and this monumental lover who's got better things to do than make it up to her! I know that's not fair, for Elizabeth and that man are too high quality to embezzle my money by pumping my heart or other parts of my anatomy but the advantage to the Indian is obvious! Raw good business! The Trade is on an uncharted course yet the King'd bring me breakfast in bed if I let him because of the corner I've got on Chinese gold. With me as the OTHER HUSBAND, the Indian's made a mute alliance with the Crown! That keeps his reputation among the French enemy, saves his face among the independent tribes, and his neck among the Iroquois who for over a hundred years have been cannily in league with the English, the Grand Oppressor! This is a complex man with a project so sweeping I cannot see to the ends of it."

Worth could not refute the truth. "I am her guardian. I have...I want to...continue to help her."

Kirke slowed and softened at Gil's plaint. "Mr. Worth, face the fact that no matter what dowry you'll tack onto Elizabeth which I will oppose 'cause you'll lose her for me for you know she'd hate it, it's Kirke and his ships floating on every sea on the face of the Earth who's dished the job of protecting some dream - whatever it is, I appraise it as good and worth every penny. I'll be footing the bill, Mr. Gilbert Worth, not to purchase a wife but to ransom my soul. It's been a long life." Kirke dug the heels of his hands into his eyes for an instant. Then, manfully, those eyes sought and held the eyes of Worth. "Forgive how I told you we'd come together. I was more than crude, I was cruel. For I know you love her much and I know the secrets of this house, and they are frightening and knightly ones and safe with me. I alone am not allowed to love her apart from her love for him. And so, I move over for him. And for both of you. And for the rest of the crew!"

Gil became aware of Hanna at his side and also that he wanted to laugh.

"For out of her will, and her grace about the matter of time, and her wildness, and her great good humor and pity, and her sense of the connection among us all, your niece will have me not without happiness if *you* recommend it."

Gil's head sank low.

Hanna said, "Thomas, that was beautifully put."

"I made a mess of it. I can't stand having to explain myself. But the image of the horde of us in the buff, rumpling the sheeting in one hot bed on our desperate voyage to God-knows-where makes me howl and will get me through the roughness of it."

Gil prepared Kirke's proposal to Elizabeth in writing, the old fashioned, sensible way. He delivered it himself and alone.

From the thinness of the ink laid on by an incredulous quill, Elizabeth could tell her uncle's hesitation. "Do you think I am mad still?"

"Never did. Just overwrought with sorrow. But what will you think of me when I tell you what Wakwa and I should have confessed nearly three years ago?" Gil made a clean breast of everything, his guilt increasing at adding to her burden.

But Elizabeth saw through the coil of crimes, some of them her own, without which Wakwa might have been hanged. She walked into the shallows and dug for clams. She fed Worth as she had fed herself alone for years. And they talked as they used to with no bar between them.

They watched the scattered pines on the beach, monstrosities of wind-tortured wood and needles clutching dunes that shifted but did not blow away.

The Psyche's captain wed Thomas Kirke to Elizabeth Dowland aboard ship a little out to sea in June. With sober visage, Gil gave the bride away. She wore a gown of the linen she had made. Sea gulls were the bridesmaids in white and gray lined up along the rail. There was no society but the Stirlings and Locke.

Kirke held his young wife there after the vows to hear the compliment of the crew who sang a chantey, their blue caps held low in roughened hands, their steady feet spread wide apart. His arm supported her through the punishment of the words.

> SHALLER BROWN, YOU'RE GOING TO LEAVE ME
> SHALLER BROWN, DON'T NE'ER DECEIVE ME
> YOU'RE GOING AWAY ACROST THE OCEAN
> YOU'LL EVER BE MY HEART'S DEVOTION
> FOR YOUR RETURN MY HEART IS BURNING, BURNING
> SHALLER BROWN YOU'RE GOING TO LEAVE ME

The end of the verse left a shocking silence, just the lapping of the waves.

The gulls screamed their surprise and fluttered westward to inland. Their shout was - KAYASKWA! KAYASKWA! But for Kirke's warm, strong, thin arm steadying her and Dire's ocean-blue eyes skewering her to the deck with a message of consensus, consent, vivid benediction, Elizabeth would have followed the sound of her Indian name over the side.

CHAPTER TEN

July, August 1751

"She must have written as they were coming into port, Gil!" Hanna sang out and broke the seal of a letter Matthew brought to them in late July as they were enjoying strawberries. "Do you want to read?"

"No. No."

"I'll read it to you, dear!"

"Thank you, Ana. I'll read it in quiet. Later."

The letter lay between them. In covering Gil's hand with hers, Hanna caught the handle of his spoon with her wrist. Cream was everywhere. Gil licked her hand for a kiss but rose to take his afternoon walk.

Gil tended toward the northwest side of his farm, past the greenhouse dome, past Matthew's cabin, toward untilled space. With his back to Sweetwood at the south, Gil could look at the land as it was before the Massachuseuck or the Wampanoag or any other tribe had accepted payment from the English for using their ground.

Worth had let Nature continue her romp here. Deer kept in mown, birds kept it cheerful and fertile, the sun kept it clean, the rain kept it fed. The forest with its heartbeat kept it sacred. This was his temple of peace with no preacher, no elder or congregation, no dogma - only creation and the room it gave him to contemplate a Creator.

He was unhappy in his Eden. His niece wheeled free of home. She had become a writer of letters. Locke was gone like a genie after a lot of patting of hands and winking and nodding at Elizabeth's wedding to Kirke. Hanna furtively missed two children, the kick of hope banished forever by Gil's confirmed sterility and her part in its confirmation. His heart was clotted with disappointment. He ambled across the meadow with the ennui of the bees at the buttercups.

The best he could do was sit on a stone and wait until his vitals craved food, or sleep, or the solace of Hanna. Without youth around, without the proximity of the Indians' communal life, without festivals to plan, wrongs to avenge, without even a spark between Hanna's maid and the local carpenter, Gil felt the morbidity of possessing the ground he had once planted with enthusiasm. He felt the weight of the chewing cattle, the agony of the ripening peaches, the pinch of the sowers and the pickers, the anxiety of his servants and the young minister and his wife. He dragged himself home, a man dying.

Hanna met him as he let himself into the sitting room to plug away at his harp. "She says Thomas is having papers drawn to make her a full partner in the Company."

"What?"

"She's hardly more than a child, but as Thomas' partner her orders will carry weight when he's away."

"What!" Gil said differently. "He pulls her out of solitary confinement in a barn to put her in the same predicament in a palace! Elizabeth is going it alone in Venice!?"

Hanna passed him by for the desk and the letter. "Thomas' bank, in which he wants to include you, hinges on his going away from time to time. Try to see, Gillie, it is far-reaching!"

He forced himself to play something lighthearted.

For the first time in their life together, Hanna stopped his hands on the strings. "How much Thomas Kirke is like you! Can't you see? Bit by bit he's making Moses his heir by this! Aside from enormous wealth, Beth's son, if he chooses to, will have command of the seas and affect the course of history!"

Bested even in magnanimity, Gil quit the room to take his bath.

Blue night came out of a gray day that ended in a tantrum rain. Until the summer squall, the citizens of Venice made their way between the houses and over the white bridges in the mist as if through endless folds of silk.

Elizabeth's window was high in the wall. It framed a white dome and, across the canal, the closely-coiffed Italian trees and the portico of a marble building.

The upset of the neutral afternoon by wind and wet had lasted a long time, long enough for night to show as the storm wasted away. It was virgin night unmolested by any force outside its own maturing. Its face was vibrant blue. It flushed bluer as if at its own beauty. Its difference from the white stone became real and became great with its blueness. The white dome was found against the deep, living blue. The marble took on a magnificent pallor like a breast in a lover's eye. The water and the sky fed each other blue with such passion that the fugitive color was made fast. The dome and the trees and the portico took it. Venice lost the stamp of man and was as simple as any slip of land lapped by water as the dark ate all that showed.

While still in exile, Moses became sophisticated in the matter of windows and of doors and of corners. With his father, Wakwa, and his kinsman, Awepu, he visited the house touched by the morning sun before any other dwelling or living thing. The house of V.T. Kirke.

Their journey without women, without Qunneke, for whom Moses wept unreproached by Wakwa, brought them to Pemaquid where the great man, Kirke, had built a house shaped like a storage trunk made of long, flat pieces of wood. The house surveyed in calmness the swaying water that grasped at it over the rocks. It possessed many glazed eyes. It was gray like an old man.

When Moses murmured these impressions to his father, Wakwa murmured back that they were true and that the house was like its master - the great one - Thomas Kirke.

Moses walked the rooms without the trembling he suffered in the makeshift sachimmaacommock up the mountain. And his father, quiet and as strange on Agiocochook, seemed far happier in V.T. Kirke's house. Not happy but at ease.

The-Friend, Dire Locke, who had stayed in their lodge in the winter, was there. While Dire and his father talked, and Awepu smoked in a chair, a priest in a black cassock slipped Moses sugar-coated chestnuts wrapped in gold paper. The foil, finer than the scrolls of bark the People drew on with charcoal, glistened like raindrops on new leaves. The chestnuts were sticky and as sweet as maple syrup. Pereclaude said they were 'glazed.' Moses loved him neither for the glazed chestnuts alone nor for the priest's big stomach or his bulging eyes but for the way he spoke. He had Ninnuock words, English words, and words called Francais. He had Latin words and showed Moses his writing of them and told him that Latin was the language of educated men.

As tenderly as a woman the priest took Moses' hand and walked him through the rooms and explained in the words of four languages the treasures in the house, most of them new to Moses, except the telescope. Wakwa had bought one for Awepu's son before Moses was born and it had been used to guard the mountainside and to bring the stars close. Claude spoke with his round eyes as well, and they shed a rain of pity. "Pauvre enfant! Pauvre Elisabet! Pauvre Renard!"

Moses imitated his father in climbing the stairs and prepared for sleep in a feather bed. Wakwa motioned him to a wide blue and white washing bowl high off the floor in front of a fire that burned inside an empty square in the wall. Moses loved the house.

"Wolf, let me lift you to the water." Wakwa used English.

Moses understood the words and also that his father used English words as the tools of his work the way the hunters used ropes and rocks and weirs and guns. When he spoke of family matters, when he said a thing like 'love,' Wakwa said 'cowammaunsh.' Moses lifted his head, alert.

"Come."

Moses felt it cruel to be addressed as a foreigner.

"What is it, my son?"

Moses hid his heart. He raised his chin.

"You are sleepy."

Moses shied.

Wakwa folded the washing cloth. He sat in a chair and waved Moses to him. "I am right to bring you on important meetings. You know how to behave. Your Nature tells you. Now sit with me."

Moses took a step closer to his father.

"Sit with me."

Moses could not shake the pain of the hard-edged English. He stood where he was.

Wakwa watched him, saw his son balk. "My son, my heart, I know you understand me. All the time I was away your grandfather taught you English as he taught me when I was your age. He saith you draw letters from the holy black book; you learn to write and to read. Two moons from now you will have finished four years of your life. Your mind is keen and keen for words. So, if you understand me and hold back, you are waiting for something. I am the Black Fox Who-Waits. We are alike."

"I am not like you!" Moses paid his sire in English and marched past him to the window. He watched the moon as he had never seen it, spread like milk in the moving hollows and on the backs of the stretching waves.

Stung, Wakwa stood up. But his voice was sad not angry as he allowed, "Mayhap not, but you are very like your mother, Elizabeth."

At this first mention of her name between them since she had been gone, since Moses could remember anything, the father and son, unmoving, exchanged glances not hard but bright and swift like the water-trapped moon.

"Nunnaumon!" Wakwa said, 'My son!'

Moses softened his stance.

Wakwa walked to him. He squatted and looked out the window with his child. Again he took up English. "Does it hurt you that I speak to you as I would to the Governor?"

"Why do you?"

"Because of the days we live in. Beside that, English is part of your spirit. Teach all you know to the women and to little Lightfoot for their safety. That is the cloak I wrap around you. At fall-of-the-leaf, I go away."

Moses reared back. "Then you are like my mother, too!"

Wakwa knelt there bowed. Eventually, his arm circled Moses' slender form. Wakwa put his cheek against his first son's cheek and he knew when the boy felt his smile starting. "If that is so, then you and I are alike after all."

This father! Moses swooned into his arms and let Wakwa carry him to the chair and stayed balled against his chest as they savored the logic.

"I go for a short time by ship, ten days walk from our old home south of here, with Dire to Philadelphia. The City of Brotherly Love."

"I like that! Take me!"

"Matta. No. A great thing is happening to you. You will at last know what it is to live as Massachuseuck. We are headed south now it is summer and we are free to go home."

"Free?"

"Moses! I am going to tell you. Others may tell you but remember that I told you first."

Moses knelt on the surface of his father's strong legs, facing him. His small hands rested on Wakwa's breast, feeling his heart beat through the fragile doeskin of his shirt. Wakwa took hold of Moses' wrists and knew the impulse of his blood.

"The world did not love that Elizabeth loves me...."

"Loves?"

"Yes. Yes! And I her!"

Moses drank the words as if he were drinking delicious liquid from a forbidden cup.

"The world would hurt her for loving me and bearing you. I could not let that be. I gave her back to keep her safe. She did not wish to go!"

Moses sat back on his heels. He could hardly bear Wakwa's face suddenly young, like a boy's pleading for pity.

"My work for the People put her in danger. The talking that I do to bring peace to these parts goes against our Submission to the English King. Now, the King's man, a great judge in the city, has swept aside all complaints against me. So, I say, we are free. And free to go home!"

Moses brightened. "Then she will be there? Waiting for me when we go south?"

"Aah! Nunnaumon!" Wakwa caught Moses close and whispered at his ear, "My son! I gave her to the care of the Great One - the man whose house this is - the man who never hurt us - who will not hurt her. They have sailed across kehtoh, the great water, called the ocean, to live on the other side! I do not know when we will see her again!"

Moses slipped out of that embrace. He ran and reached the open window and gasped to get air past the ice that blocked his throat. He gripped the sill and looked across the heaving, lighted deep. "Where did the Great-Kirke take her?!"

Wakwa was there sheltering him. "You want to go to her, little one!"

"Do not you?"

"It is all I want!"

Moses felt an arrow here.

"But I will not until I change this place! Until I make it new. It is not just that loving us she is put to shame. It is an injustice for us!"

Moses let his sight travel where he could not - east across the sea. "Hurry, father!" And then he hid his eyes against the scar on Wakwa's neck. "Father, I love you!" Odd. The words did not sound hard in the English.

August. In the slowest, most honeyed hour before sunset, in the third week of the calendar's majestic eighth month, Gilbert Worth walked the fallow field at the top of his farm. He sensed the land with the acuity of an insect. Moving in the circle of wild grasses, following their sound and scent, he took the moment in as if it were nectar.

His resort to the undeveloped ground produced thought about his bond to the ground itself. Gil came to see his thought as truth: what had made his brain tick and his heart leap and had fired his masculine urge was not lust for a man, not lust. It was the ecstasy of sharing ground with the red man.

Gil's drive was the product of the ideal emigration, the enfolding of the voyager by the native, complete generosity and absolute gratitude blending into a harmony of earth and heart and principle. That marriage gave a man liberty. It gave a man a country. And Elizabeth with Wakwa gave that country its future and its fire.

Gil's lonely husbandry in that hot, static season had unearthed the secret of his impotence - the stoppage of the communion of blood. He had gone to the land's breast to listen for a heartbeat and had come away with the secret of the New World. Gil wanted to shout it. He vowed to tell Mac, to bring him to Sweetwood, to stand him in heaven's pasture so the Scot could know the thrill of it.

The north quarter was suddenly streaked with black. Out of the pine-tree border, a bulk, darker than the dark under the trees at night, raced past him. It bunched, stretched, rippled in flight like a giant evening stole. Gil recognized Sucki, Black, the Kirke-bred stallion.

Gil called out of a hell of memories and the beast came to a standstill. They drifted together, the blond man and the black horse. Worth's voice caught and snagged on native words familiar to the great steed who was gentle from kind treatment by strong hands. The ruffs circling the ankles of the mighty charger, the fabulous mane and tail, quaked like the fringe of a hunter's doeskin clothes.

The forbidden names of people Gil had learned to love left his throat like roots torn out. Sucki - Black; Awepu - Calm; Qunneke - Tame Deer; Wakwa - the Black Fox. The master's sound. "Where is he?" Gil begged the dumb animal.

Slowly it came to Gil that Sucki was saddled. The Englishman planted his foot in the silver stirrup and in spite of a shaking knee he heaved himself aboard the black mountain. From this high place, Gil surveyed the field. He watched in the sun.

Wakwa came across the campus. The horse danced. Wakwa came carefully not to distress the wind's singing in the hay.

Leaner, graver than he had been, the Indian walked like a man brooking a tide. He neared, watching the whiteman's eyes which matched the green and yellow meadow behind him. He walked on until the horse's side stopped him like a barricade. Pressing his hands against the sleek ribs and belly, Wakwa slid down onto his knees. His hands wrapped Gil's boot and the stirrup for support.

"God!" Gil cried. "Stand!"

Wakwa complied. Blood vessels broke under his skin lighting the glow that life had snuffed out of him. Tall though he was, he looked up at Gil.

"Speak!" Gil commanded.

"By what name shall I call you?"

Aside from the rightness of leaving their future behavior to Gil's discretion, the grace in the neat turning of the challenge into a challenge for clemency assured Gil that anyone who depended on this spokesman, even now, even Elizabeth, would never be waste.

"Call me...Uncle!"

Gil threw his hat to the ground and Wakwa pulled him out of his dismount. They shared the same turf. Worth wept openly. Wakwa stood with chin high and eyes closed and an open smile spreading.

Gil's heart split over his niece. By the Devil she had been torn from grace, from intimacy with an eloquence of spirit ideally a king's, from the touch of a man who could turn such a creature as a horse into an ambassador. By a word Gil had him back and Beth did not.

"You must not go there, Gil."

"I knew you'd say that, Ana."

"I am right!"

"I know."

"Will you go?"

Husband and wife took each other's measure.

"I cannot help myself." Worth was honest.

Instead of confronting him, Charles Dowland's sister walked the bright sitting room, her hands hidden in the pockets of her sewing apron. She glowed with emergency, her brown eyes round with concentration.

"You must admit he's done everything right." Gil added. "Approached us just on his arrival as a neighbor of any significance must. *He* made the first gesture. He came alone, taking his chances, unprotected, without anyone to witness or defend him from a harsh reaction on my part."

"He is a very smart man."

"He is more than that!"

"Yes. It hurts to think how good he is. How wise. So, I do not understand his expecting us to betray Elizabeth! If he had come twelve weeks sooner...."

"Ana. It is clear he was marking his calendar with precision. He was with us on *The Psyche*. I am quite sure."

Hanna shook her head unable to justify Wakwa's reticence. "To take up with him and mingle with...without her there!"

"She is there. Always will be. And she is in Moses."

Hanna stopped. "You are right."

"This connection more than any other drove him out of the woods onto this farm. Think of the love!"

"A cynic would say something else."

"Discounting the pain."

Hanna whispered not without sadness, "How is Qunneke? Did she have a healthy lying in?"

"We must find that out."

"He did not say?"

"I did not ask."

Hanna stood in the beam of the swinging sun. "Tame Deer was so good to Beth when you think about it. Imagine, she has held and fed and cleaned and taught Beth's baby for years now. Tame Deer has kept him alive. The child of her husband and our Beth is alive. We owe her much. All this heartache has some purpose. The Dowland line continues. Our heir is alive! My brother's heir is alive!"

"I presume. Wakwa was silent on the point of his family. He broached nothing. Seemly. I thought. He talked only of matters that could affect the whole colony."

Hanna whipped in and out of the light. "I am through tolerating his - separation of his family from his life! He was not like this before! It is not - Indian in him! I am going to tell him the trouble will not stop until he... becomes... more like you!"

Gil, a man alive again, devoured this great flattery like a lion at his feast. He thought it a good thing for the moment to stick to his news. "He and Locke and a tight group of Philadelphians and New Yorkers are going after some sort of unification among colonial governments and are aiming at a place for a conference."

"Here?"

"Not here."

"And you asked him nothing?"

"I said, 'Is all well with you, Wakwa?' And he said, 'Well enough.'"

"He said that?" Then she filled Worth's arms. Her face was wet against his. "This man! What heart! What genius! He makes us long to talk to him! To comfort him! But we must not go in. Get Doctor Mac to do it!"

"What inspires you?"

"Mac is a healer. A physician. He will be accepted by all factions. I won't have them despise us for being the wounded party. Which we are as much as they! Mac will see to them. They must not be found by us in any broken condition. Not a cut finger! We will meet them on equal footing."

"Ana! You are a great woman! Stirling marches in, the advance guard, and we follow in all pomp and propriety and at a distance!"

"Oh, no!" Hanna stopped him. "They will come here. Every one. The entire tribe will pay fealty. This will be the treaty ground. This will teach the Sachim! We will play their rules to win."

They danced a bit. Strangely. Like swans. Very close and slow.

CHAPTER ELEVEN

September 1751

Hanna's demand set off a sea-turn in the Massachuseuck soul, that shifting of the waters by the southwest wind blowing clockwise, full circle in a day. In terms of the Ninnuock, they turned swiftly from hiding to exposure, accepting as a stringent obligation assembling on the lawns of their English relations to pay their respects. Because they did, nothing would ever be the same. The southwest god saw to it.

The old sachim, Waban, the Wind, had resisted returning home from the mountains. Cloistered with his tribe on the unfamiliar peaks that rode above the fractiousness, the murders, the pitched battles breaking out between the English and the French-allied Indians in the northern region, he had had plenty of time to frame a decision. Seventy, not old among the People but definitely not young, and long past his middle age, Waban, the Wind, as he always had, ultimately, decided to cling to practicality.

He had made some fine decisions in the past. Foremost, in his own mind, was his approval of the nomination of his nephew, Wakwa, to be the young sachim. Awepu and others of his talents were fine to serve as atauskowauog, dependable counsellors to leaders, but the Wind had supplied the People with a future led by Wakwa Manunnappu, a man who was fluent in all things English.

Another decision, actually only a suggestion of Waban's to which Wakwa had responded with flare, was that Wakwa take a second wife to produce him a son since one did not seem to be forthcoming from Tame Deer. Waban had not anticipated that Wakwa of all people would cooperate with such alacrity or that the second wife would be Elizabeth Dowland, a New-English woman.

But the wind dips in its courses, speeds and slows and turns around, exactly Waban's nature. Therefore, Waban decided without any handwringing to let Elizabeth make her life among the Massachuseuck. As he justified it, she was the daughter of a respectable family, peaceful, hardworking, and rich in land and in something else - understanding. Her father had proven to be a high wall keeping back the poachers and the bounty hunters, who, for a short time, had hunted with legal sanction the hair of the tribe's young men.

Waban could taste on his tongue the sweetness of his permissiveness with Wakwa; Elizabeth had brought forth Moses Bluehill. The tribe was secure. In his golden years, Waban rode high.

Naturally, before deciding about a return to their ancestral grounds outside Sweetwood, Waban cogitated upon what had driven them to the mountains in the first place. When Wakwa wanted to talk with the Abnaki and the other northern tribes, a desire in opposition to the English King's rules set down in black ink in the Treaty of Submission, Waban acceded cautiously, just as he had accepted the large grants of land from the Dowland estate and from Gilbert Worth in the name of Elizabeth's son. Born into Waban was the certitude that these things - the right to discuss mutual interests and rights to the land - were natural not special allowances and bequests as the English made them out to be.

Nevertheless, it was the English who had them by the balls and it was Waban's chosen - Wakwa - helping them to wriggle free.

Much good had come of the younger sachim's energies - a new, lucrative trade in man root, the leasing of an island by the French Indians to Kirke Company for the building of ships (a diplomatic feat showing the fulminating war to be ridiculous) and a promise of safe passage no matter how the political tide swung. The Massachuseuck had already tapped that good-will concession in their flight from home onto the mountain!

Full-circle: the reason for their needing a hiding place extended from other decisions of Waban's which he preferred not to review. But, necessarily, he looked backward, wondering why it was that his nephew rather than his own sons was blessed by Manit so liberally. No man could approach Wakwa in speech and grace and looks and fortitude and physical and spiritual prowess. Even a slender, winsome white girl produced him stout male issue and brought material benefit to a People diminishing until Wakwa married her.

Waban could not answer the worming question of how his brother-in-law, Pequawus, Wakwa's father, such as he was, had made a great son. For Waban, the root of the conundrum went back years to the night when, as a young man, Pequawus lost the election as sachim to him.

The sun was sinking and Waban was locked in public, verbal contest with Pequawus. Then Nippisse, who was Waban's sister and Pequawus' wife, and newly the mother of Wakwa, decided to go gathering and got herself killed by a rabid bear. To Waban's way of thinking, the bear, whatever else he did, handed Waban the victory.

When Nippisse slipped away from the debate alone so she might wander unencumbered as the perfume of night descended over the otan, Pequawus, ardent and concerned, excused himself from the council fire to follow his wife. The bear reached her first. Surprising her on the ridge above the river, the bear wrapped her in his arms like a husband might and feasted on her delicate face. While Waban admitted the horror of Nippisse's beautiful person motionless in the hairy grasp of the bear, high above them against the moon, he condemned Pequawus' reaction.

Pequawus raced up the hill, gathered Nippisse in his arms where the bear dropped her, and cradled her until her spirit flew and she was dead. Waban did not even need to make a decision; his instinct drove him to hunt the bear and toss his mangy carcass at the People's feet. He had secured the otan and told them so. The People cast their votes for him.

Yet, Silent Fox always maintained that without his father's, the Gray Fox's, affectionate heart, the bear never would have been startled in the midst of his crime and many more people would have died when the monster finished with Nippisse and tore through the otan. Waban had to admit that in some ways Wakwa was his father's son. The truth rankled.

Added to this, Waban knew all too well that the reason for toiling through the woods up Agiocochook with winter coming on had to do with one of his own sons; both his offspring and their deeds were repugnant to him. Waban took the responsibility for teaching both sons wrongly although he was at a loss to pinpoint the error in his rearing of them.

One, his first, Wuttah Mauo, Weeping Heart, was a drunkard, the other, Nuppohwunow, was a dancer and a father to girls. Now, there was nothing wrong with that. Waban's second son made life bearable in these days of privation on the mountain with his happy soul and his eloquent body and his sweet daughters. But where was Waban's blood in a drunkard and a dancing man?

As Waban saw history, the one who had gone sour on alcohol, so keen of wit before, had gotten himself cuckolded by a white strumpet from Sweetwood oddly named Prudence, had kicked aside a bond with a beautiful, if tarnished, woman from the otan, and had basely implicated an innocent man, the great one, Wakwa, in some tawdry business on the docks in Boston. This at the time of Wakwa's delicate negotiations to the north and just at the conveyance of the Dowland lands into Moses' hands. What a stupid, his Weeping Heart! And on top of that, Weeping Heart, like a Judas, the betrayer from the holy book which Wakwa and his father could read, had given the news about Wakwa's journey north to the white priest who lived obsessed with Elizabeth and would not forgive Wakwa or her for their love.

And so the great net of safety the gods had woven through Wakwa began to unravel fast. King George fingered Wakwa for a traitor. Hence their trek north into hiding.

Decisions. One bad decision leaning upon another had brought them away from their secure, ancient home to this windy precipice, Agiocochook, the White Mountains.

When Panther Eye, Weeping Heart's secret lover, a convicted fornicator, set her torch to Elizabeth almost killing her, it was Waban's decision to put Panther Eye to death.

And when Stirling, the man of medicine, had come with his son to care for Elizabeth, and the Scotsman had cut open Panther Eye's corpse to teach his son, Israel, the parts, Waban was shocked to learn there was a child in her womb - a grandchild of his - a boy. Waban had made the decision on the spot to seal his lips about it.

To save his knowledge for a darker day. And although that day had come months later, much damage was already done by his black silence.

Such pain it was to admit even to himself that he, a sachim of experience and of years had been insufficient in his office! That he was a murderer of innocents! That he would do better to slit his throat than to make any more decisions!

Waban had to admit to himself that executing Panther Eye without waiting, without deliberating with Wakwa when he got home from the northern woods, had been a poor decision compounded by his silence about the unborn boy. He had killed his own, heinous enough, but also had frustrated a possible successor of full Massachuseuck blood.

No matter what decision he made after that, everything got shoved over the line to Wakwa's half-white son, Moses. The decisions had a life of their own.

The bleak day came when Weeping Heart, in front of all the important men who had to do with Wakwa, white and red, was pressed to admit his role in giving to the Boston Court the names of those who had gone north, Wakwa among them, exposing even Wakwa to the hangman's rope. Waban had quickly made the decision to release the fiendish tidbit about Panther Eye's babe to distract the assembly from Weeping Heart's sin against Wakwa, against the tribe. At Weeping Heart's summit of agony over that mess, Waban had bludgeoned him, his firstborn, with a club, turning a drunkard into an imbecile so that his own competence, his own loyalty to the tribe, would never be brought into question by his association with a son who was a traitor. Waban decided in a twinkling to put out the light of his firstborn so that Wakwa and worse, Pequawus, would not know that he, Waban, was short-sighted, so that Wakwa and his wise, silent father would not see that the drunkard and the dancing man were the fitting offspring of the Wind.

Then instead of advising Wakwa to go to the court at Boston to confront the English judge with reason and the truth, to dare, to risk as he always had and won, Waban made the decision to reassume control; he broke Wakwa's heart by breaking his and Elizabeth's marriage reeds. Stupid decision that one! How could anyone break a marriage where there was love?

And to prove it, even while he sat like a lump on the mountain and Wakwa travelled among the head-eaters to the West and did great deeds, Wakwa, without consulting him, had gotten around the wreckage of his heart and secured the tribe again, linking lovely Elizabeth to Thomas Kirke - a superior lifeline. Two husbands for her and two wives for Wakwa although they could not live in the same sachimmaacommock.

Waban sighed over the young people who were not passionate the way they used to be in his day. Just look at Pequawus almost forty years before, rocking the bleeding, mutilated Nippisse until her spirit rose away from the earth into the southwest among the great ones, and her blood turned to plum-colored crystal in the cold fall night.

Therefore, Waban refused to decide about going home to the south when Wakwa, hard and thin and burning-eyed, arrived on Agiocochook with his men and his horses and Kirke's man, Locke, who informed them that they were free.

An old sachim and a young one were supposed to operate in agreement. Waban felt it keenly when Wakwa said nothing, did nothing to support his, the older sachim's, indecision. The Wind bowed his head in defeat. He knew if he looked Wakwa in the eye, Wakwa would be all over him with words and truss him with words and drag him off the mountain and home in a trap of thoughtful words.

Waban found it difficult to eat on the journey home. He had no time for food - he was in the throes of decision. But after the tribe had made camp on their ancestral grounds outside Sweetwood at the tail-end of summer, and Doctor J. Macmillan Stirling rode over the hillock and crossed the river with his red-headed son in tow and delivered the ultimatum that the tribe do obeisance to Wakwa's white uncle at Worth Farm, Waban's final decision galloped upon him.

"How long have ye no' been eating?" Stirling asked of Waban. Stirling's trust was not made easier by his Hippocratic oath. He was loathe to set foot on the Massachuseuck grounds without Beth there. Yet he could not look at Silent Fox with blame. No charlatan with a barber's knack for cutting flesh, Stirling called on the best in contemporary medical arts for a diagnosis. "How long. About?" The Scottish doctor asked again in the big, central room of Waban's great lodging.

Waban's granddaughters sparkled here and there and his wife and his second son, gravely concerned, hung on each question and Waban's answers.

Waban groaned evasively, "I take a little water in the morning. When I lie down at night I drink water. You must open me up, white taupowaw. I have a hard thing inside me. It hurts me. I am in pain."

Stirling's bushy eyebrows rumpled. "Aye? And your powaw? Wha' has he go' to say?"

The Sachim contested the Scot. "I have great respect for his healing powers. I have received comfort from his prayers. I would never dispute his great abilities. See how fine is his work that Wakwa's scars are healed so smooth."

Stirling locked glances with the canny chieftain. "Aye! It is a credit to them both that wounds so deep do not horrify the onlooker."

Waban's mouth changed and his features grew overcast as if a gale were brewing. "That is why I want your services! The taupowaw heals. I need someone to look inside! I cannot sleep."

"Can you not?" This from Stirling had such an edge that it prompted Israel's steadying hand on his shoulder. Such sleepless nights as he had seen Beth through brought poison to old Stirling's lips. He sucked it back, tucked it in his cheek for spitting at a better time. "Canno' Tame Deer help you? She is well versed in the use of plants. Indeed, I take suggestion from her!" The reluctant doctor had a method to his reserve.

Waban, once a hunter of merit, looked into Stirling's trap. "My body is old. It requires the complete attention of skilled hands. Qunneke is much distracted by her responsibilities. She has the new camp to settle, and the Sachim to see to...."

"And an extra child to watch...."

Waban decided to toss away the insult. He had no notion of being foiled in his great design by the taunts of the red-faced, white-haired coatman whom he desired to use and quickly. "You speak truth. I look to her to save us in Moses."

Israel's sweat made cautious tracks down his neck. The elder Stirling stayed silent in perverse admiration for Waban's control, his agility. He gathered truth from Waban's responses as he gathered the herbs of his pharmacopoeia. Waban was too cogent to be sick.

"Is our house too rude for your arts, Doctor? Does the presence of my dear family impede your knife?"

A hush fell on the room.

"Go away!" Waban dismissed his loved ones. "And farewell!"

Stirling marked the death wish. He fetched his black bag and marched back to the old man's bedside. He took Waban's pulse. The pulse raced but the bronze face did not change nor did the dilation of Waban's glittering eyes. "The house is perfectly adequate, Sachim. And as to yer family, I say you can never have too many relatives about. There isn't a man who's got one to spare."

Waban lay thinking about this last sarcasm.

Stirling made a thorough examination. He pressed and probed and listened. He continued coy. "My preliminary findings are that you are sound in your muscles and in your system. The stresses of your journey, your great responsibilities tha' do not abate could be causin' your wan appetite and the distress of your sleep."

Waban caught the physician around his neck and drew him down. He said gruffly in Stirling's ear, "Open me!"

Stirling motioned for something from his case. Israel came quickly with a vial and a pewter dish. Mac explained, "We call this a bleedin' bowl. What you need is a renewal of your blood."

Waban's glance locked his.

"Your body will cure itself."

Frustrated, Waban tossed on his couch, a stiff but well-appointed bed of mats and blankets raised away from the nicely covered floor. "Is it you have not the skill to cut me open and look about for the heavy thing I carry that stops my food from going down?"

Stirling debated turning his back on Waban or snapping at this evil opportunity. "Tha's it! My surgery's no' so advanced tha' I can open you and peek around and guarantee no harm."

"You cut the bad woman, Panther Eye, with a finer hand than I have seen among the best of our hunters. Not a part was damaged."

Stirling purred without pause, "But she was dead. I could cause her no more harm than had already been done."

"Yesss!" The Wind hissed.

"You understand?"

"Do you?"

Stirling fidgeted now feeling himself pushed along and whirled about as he had many times when the seaside gusts had had their way with him. "I could kill you by trying to save you!"

Waban smiled invitingly. "I am strong as you say. Open me and then sew me up with a silken thread. Kautantowwit, the southwest god, will take me when he is ready for me. I will not die before."

Stirling was in a corner although there was not a right angle in the place. "Don't you think we should call in Silent Fox?"

"What for?" Waban rose up off his bed. "Is he a doctor, too!"

Both the Stirlings were frozen by the blast of spite.

More resilient on account of youth, Israel attempted reason. "Sachim, as my father says, you are generally in good order. Why bring on yourself all the pains and doubts and dangers of a surgery exploratory before the meeting with Gilbert Worth? Won't afterward be time enough?"

Waban gave the speaker the answer he sought by engaging his blue eyes.

And so they knew. Waban's gall was the last remnant of his pride.

Stirling stropped his scalpel on his thumb, wishing in his darkest soul to sever Waban from life.

Israel said, "We've got a way of making - pills."

"Yes...? Waban's skin went taut.

Stirling gazed at his son.

The carrot-haired apprentice bore on. "It would seem you need sleep worse than anything. We have a way to make a powder of certain roots and press it into a tiny, hard ball with a little syrup that makes the medicine inside less bitter...."

"Go on!" Waban hurried him along.

"Less bitter to the tongue so that you can swallow it and let the plant work its wonder inside of you."

The Sachim smiled.

"And if your wont is rest, and rest would be the preparation for any action that you took, surgery, for instance, the pills given in the proper dose would grant you sleep...."

"Sleep?"

"As deep as you like."

In gratitude, Waban grabbed onto the freckled wrist. "Israel! You will become a great man! A great...what is your word...."

"Physician!" Israel whispered ruefully. He squared his broad shoulders, cautioning, "There is danger in the pills in that an improper dose can seize the heart. My father and I would not, will not, cannot prescribe an improper dose."

Waban scowled like a child betrayed.

Stirling took on the mantle. "What m' boy is tryin' to explain is that we'll start you slow with a gentle dose and then increase it till we know your tolerance. And you will get sleep." Here Stirling admonished, "Then you can think properly about your best course of action with regard to the surgery." Stirling threw his paraphernalia in his bag and lumbered toward the door.

"How shall I swallow this medicine?"

Stirling turned on his heel and tossed back, "The way you swallow everything else!"

Waban asked for quiet after this interview and lay alone in his amber room eager for his medication and a visit from Wakwa. He could stand the Scot's snarling with very little trouble. Stirling understood his function - that was the pith of it. There was no point in arguing with the Scot when he, Waban, was getting his way. Waban lay back lazily, his stocky body, once vital, given over to indolence. He admired the patterns on the hangings that gave the room its character. His wife had a fine eye and hand with the mats that lined the domed rooms. She painted sometimes to the exclusion of everything else, to the neglect of her household. The serving girls had to manage themselves. She indulged her love of paint with almost the same intensity Wuttah Mauo indulged his taste for rum or Nuppohwunnau devised a new dance. Perhaps his sons took their flaws from their mother.

Unlike his habit of years past, Wakwa seldom came to Waban's sachimmaacommock. He had become quite agile in his avoidance - his reasons were good and his timing was perfect. Wakwa was nearly exhausted evading the man who had destroyed his happiness. This languid summer night Wakwa entered the room with Moses.

"At last!" Waban sighed in satisfaction as Wakwa greeted him in the dutiful way, touching his lips to Waban's shoulders.

"Uncle?"

"At last you come to say good-bye."

"I am not close to leaving. First, I am preparing the town for the walk to Gilbert's farm. And I prepare Moses to meet another of his great-uncles."

"I did not say you were leaving. I said good-bye."

Wakwa showed concern. "Have not Mac and Israel been here? Can they not salve your pain?"

"They can."

Wakwa cast his glance beyond Waban to the darkest regions of the room.

Waban took advantage of his apparent distraction to seize Moses' arm. "My delight! My blood! Will you stay a while by me? Your father is preoccupied with his great plans. Sit by me till the white powaw brings me my draught."

Moses let his gold-washed eyes rest on this relative.

Waban gave a nervous laugh.

Wakwa observed his dead mother's brother. He meshed his fingers then let them part. "I will not delay them."

"Go! Go! You have things to do! You will do them well. I know. Go! But leave me Moses." It was not a request but a command.

Wakwa's eyes were steel. "He shall stay with you until I call him." Then after slight hesitation, "I hope you come well, Uncle."

Waban pursed his lips at Wakwa's coldness, his formality, and his insufferable politeness. From Wakwa's tone of voice, Waban could tell the younger sachim meant what he said.

Moses Bluehill sat near Waban's couch, erect, his head high, his posture patterned after the wolves. Waban noticed. He let it pass. When the curtain no longer moved after Wakwa's exit, Waban turned on the boy. He changed like the wind he was, turned cold and insistent.

"Muckquashim! Wolf!"

Moses deigned to direct his attention toward his great-uncle who told others when to laugh.

"Good. Do something for your father! *I* am telling you to do it. Your father obeys *me* while I live. So must you. Do you hear? Understand?"

Moses nodded. But he pulled back.

Roughly Waban jerked him near. "Come near and listen to me!"

Moses was left no choice, his slip of a body easy to take. The uncouth lips were at his ear. The words, plain, flew on a breath that stank of ice and of flesh.

"Go to your new friend, Doctor Mac, and see where he keeps the pills. Come tell me. That is all. If you help me you will help your father. Do you have the heart for it? Or are you like him?"

Moses scampered out. He raced away from Waban. Naked, not old enough for a breechclout, he blended with and passed other boys of his age enjoying the soft summer night on their bare skin. He hardly saw them or heard the quiet laughter of the families gathered at fires in the open air preparing their food, or the pretty trees bending their arms back and sighing like girls. He entirely missed the scent of night flowers and sight of the silver dots in a sky no longer light. He wanted his mountains for a place to hide but the land here rolled like the ocean under his bare feet. The purple evening went black for him. He ran straight into Stirling's breeches.

"You look like you've seen a ghost, bairn!" The old man knelt on one knee. He stroked Moses' face, recognizing his look, stroking the loathing away. "Won't you come with me to my wetu? Your Papa's there. Israel too!"

Inside, the place was bright with candlewood, chunks of pine rich with pitch, making fine working light. Moses sat his father's arm and watched the doctors bend over their work, a cauldron steaming, a makeshift table set up for the forming of the balls of medicine.

"What will you give him?" Wakwa was curious.

"Tha's the great question. Poppies to make him happy or hemlock to make him sleep."

"Mayhap if you mixed the two...." Wakwa's smile was wistful.

"We'll have to mix them but not with one another." Israel cautioned. "Hemlock is deadly. The dose must be minute." He worked over the compound under his father's eye. "I'll keep the jar of them in my pocket to avoid confusion or, as in the fairy tale, the old man will sleep a hundred years."

Moses covered his ears and trembled.

"Are you cold?" Wakwa asked. "Let us get you fed and put you in some clothes."

Moses took Wakwa's face between his hands. "Nosh, must I go back to Uncle Waban? He told me to."

"It is too late! And you are not to go to see him again without me."

The racket of the nighttime woods, the riot of creatures who preferred darkness to day, distracted the mind, prevented easy sleep, promoted waking nightmares or drove one into a beloved's arms. The hubbub of late summer midnight broke Waban's rest. Dizzily he rose, disappointed in the delicate boy who had let him down. How lonely it was! All he had for allies were the frenzied little creatures who crawled and slithered and darted. He shuffled out of his carpeted lodge. He passed his sleeping guards and blessed them for their deafness and their fatigue. He boldly lifted the mat of Stirling's wetu in the din and did not hear the rustle himself.

The last of the candlewood blazed, lighting the small lodge low to the floor. Waban saw the black bag. He moved toward it.

He may as well have been dreaming for the soundlessness of his steps amid the deafening ecstasy of creatures too small to see. He saw Stirling. The old Scot was covered like a corpse to keep the bugs off. Disgusting. Sleeping under his blanket in the clothes he had worn all day. And his boy, Israel, white as deer fat, lay with an open book on his breast. His fiery hair poked out of his nightcap and his coat dangled from a longpole.

It would not be a good thing to wake the doctors. The practical thing was to reach for what was closest. Bumps in the pockets of Israel's coat excited Waban's hand. One pottery jar sealed with a cork, like the corks in the rum bottles Wuttah Mauo had strewn on the forest floor, came to hand. Waban dropped the coat to no notice because of the infernal noise. Summer hell bleated all around him as with shaking fingers he coaxed the cork from the bottle's neck.

His perseverance and practicality were paid by the god of the Zephyr. Here was the cache of pills. Thirty days supply. Hemlock coated in licorice powder and dipped in sweet sugar. Waban downed the lot right there, without water to drink. Bitter was not the word for how the candied pills tasted as they crowded down. They were the gallstones of his sins, putrid green things, fistfuls of them, the Devil's tears. Bitter? No viper had venom like these pills.

The orgy of the insects rendered silent Waban's choking and chewing and gasping as he staggered out under the stars. Wind buffeted him as he strove for the pond, his keen eyes clouded, his legs turned to stone, and his broken heart suddenly still.

CHAPTER TWELVE

Harvest 1751

The Ninnuock sifted through the woods to Worth Farm like a wave toward the sand. They progressed over the scant distance easily, a pleasurable walk. The scents were so delicious they left the human heart happy for creatures whose gift it was to know life by scent. Vines laden with wild grape spiralled pillars of scrub oak and beech and trees heavy and rosy with apples and pears. The fruit held the fragrance of the flowers that had birthed them, recapturing the springs the Ninnuock had missed in these environs, soft of earth and air.

The sound of their natal woods, like a mother's breath near her infant's ear, surpassed any other forest they had known or that might exist. Under the sighing of the leaves, they murmured their admiration for the place they had abandoned when old Waban had torn Elizabeth Dowland up by her tender new roots and thrown her away like a weed.

Now three hundred in number, they moved lightly, grateful that the man they were going to greet loved them and had stood by their wild woods in their absence.

The men preceded their wives, the children walking in between. Alert for interlopers, man or beast, the men held back branches for their families following, tested the ground, handed those under their protection over obstacles to safe footing. The young couples, their babies still on boards, the youth, the widowed, the elders, the straight and the bent parted the branches and found their way like grain through the sieve. By this means, they would all ring Gilbert Worth's northwest meadow in the same instant and advance onto his fields and his lawns to the house. Then straight as arrows the great men and women would file out of the woods through the tribe to Worth's door, appearing last, arriving first.

They passed the landmarks of their lives. In a low voice Awepu told Moses of the history of the place and Moses responded softly, "Noowahteouun. I know."

Awepu whispered about the spot where Elizabeth used to sing and sew before coming to the otan to live. He pointed out the place of the winter feast on the last night of which Moses was conceived. Moses knew.

"Your feet are touching the very trail Elizabeth walked east to visit her farm and her father in her first winter in the woods. She was not even carrying you yet! And on this very path she walked back to us when her father could not tell her apart from the snow."

"Noowahteouun!"

"I rode through these pines on Gilbert's horse to tell your father and Elizabeth that your grandfather...my friend...Charles Dowland...had died in my arms!"

"Noowahteouun." Moses lisped, awed by the break in Awepu's voice.

"See there! The place Elizabeth lay laboring to bring you forth. I know because I was at her side."

"Noowahteouun."

"And do you know that here your father lay with the wound in his neck between death and life over ten days' time?"

"Noowahteouun!"

"Wakwa has taught you much, Moses, in the few days since we have been home."

They passed a large area of fire-blackened trunks and sprightly new undergrowth that marked a burial ground Awepu would not speak of. Moses knew it was the death-site of the men who had tried to kill his father but he would not speak of it either.

"Awepu?"

"OO?"

"Did you know, this is the path my mother rode east, tied to a horse, when Uncle Waban sent her away from me forever?"

Shocked and sorry at the reminder of that night, Awepu, choked out, "Noowahteouun!" How he knew!

Worth Farm, by design and in modesty considering Moses' claim on it, was introduced to Moses only as they emerged from the woods. Wakwa did not direct Moses' vision to the vast green property but toward the white house caught against the hill like a feather drifting.

Dotting the cultivated grass near the house were gaily-colored tents erected over tables laden with food, some of which the Massachuseuck had sent, but Wakwa took no notice of them and neither did his son.

Tutored for Waban's funeral, the boy assumed a regal pace at Wakwa's side and they walked down and over and up and across the green skirts of the house and found themselves standing on great stones bordered by roses that glittered as if from a private rain. Raising his eyes from the flowers, Moses forgot his studied detachment and reached for Wakwa's hand when he beheld Gilbert Worth just outside the door.

Here was a small man like Locke yet Gilbert Worth was not like the factor. Like Claude's eyes, Worth's eyes spoke with no voice but were nothing like the priest's. This man, Worth, this uncle-by-marriage of Wakwa's and of Elizabeth's, related by blood to no one, seemed to be bursting apart, releasing light like the sun. He was like a wildcat in this his lair. He seemed ready to run, to fight, to dance, to laugh and weep all at once. His hair was stiffened corn silk and his clothes were woven of colors that made him disappear against his ornately fruited fields and the sea beyond.

At his side was a creature with softly curling hair and skirts that ran everywhere as if all her flowers had melted about her hips.

They had done Elizabeth's child up in a crossing of styles, the soft collar of a linen shirt resting open on a stiff little English jacket tailored of buckskin. His breechclout and leggings were edged with unadorned fringe fine-cut to play with the breezes. Riding his hip was a pouch gorgeous with quillwork and containing gold pieces and a small silver-handled knife. It was supported by princely bands of blue-black suckauhock. Because his fawn-colored curls could not pleasingly set off feathers or fur, Qunneke had fixed the down of an egret to the ties of his moccasins.

Hanna saw these as her eyes swept him. Moses saw what she saw and rolled his eyes. That was how they fell in love.

Wakwa stayed still, breathed several breaths, not releasing Moses. Then the Black Fox Who-waits moved. He walked forward to Gil, freeing himself of Moses' small hand in order to hold the Englishman's upper arms and to bend to him to kiss his shoulders. "My service to thee!" Then he used the name which Pequawus had given Gil on the night they took him as their own, when they had announced Worth's soul's relation to them, the night they knew he had taken the law into his hands for Wakwa's sake. "Summagunem Wunnutcheg! He-holds-out His Hand."

Moses heard Wakwa add the words, "Nissese, forgive!" and trembled at the blond man's voice which was clear and cool and dark and deep like cave water. "Nephew, forgive me!"

Then Wakwa did a shocking thing. He pitched down on one knee before Worth's wife. Here was a stance they had never seen. The black-feathered headdress of mourning, of his state, made Wakwa a giant of over seven feet. Suddenly, he was cut down to half his size, by his will, in front of a woman, in front of his tribe. The headdress, the emblem of his denial of her niece, tumbled off at Hanna's catching him close. It was as if Wakwa's skull would bore through her body to fill the emptiness of her womb. Pressed to her belly, they shared sharp cries, forced back, never cutting the air. The cries found the throats of those looking on.

It was just four. The etiquette of Hanna's tea was to receive in the sitting room. The homage took time. The tribe's containment, their good humor, their consistent quiet, their color, the sway of their clothes seen through the great window as they arced across the lawn waiting their turn, enchanted the hosts. The treasures of the house, the shape of rooms, the silence of rugs, precious metal and cut glass struck by the sun awed the guests. Two languages collided, mingled.

Bred to endure, to stand before others, Wakwa's children kept Qunneke's side. They did not look toward the bright outdoors or seem to hear the sounds of other children's games. They studied with polite gaze the divergence between the life of this house and their own. Oddly, Qunneke appeared familiar with what she saw.

Gil said into a lull, "Wakwa, with all respect to your late uncle, it must be a relief to reign alone. At last you've got control. You are free to work."

Wakwa came back in an acrid voice, "From his grave the old man ties me! With him gone who is there to care for all these people?" He snorted. "How can I travel any distance when they need council, help of every kind. Who will bury them, marry them, judge them, punish them? Protect them? Feed them? If he thought so little of his place and of his life that he killed himself, why did he wait till now? Why not step down when Elizabeth was still mine? Why ruin us and then change his climate?!!"

Heartened that Wakwa's pain over Elizabeth was sharp, Gil ventured only, "All those pills. Most odd." Then, "Why not get an alternate as he did with you? Take on a younger man to rule with you. And then be off!"

"I have suffered with the sharing of power. Never again! I would withdraw rather than answer to someone else."

"So, you'll stay put and negate your role as spokesman. For what then did you sacrifice Beth?"

"So, you see me stuck on Waban's spear. He rules. Only he does not have the work of it! It interests me that my mother's brother did this just after Elizabeth went away with Kirke!"

Gil chanced a barb, "Look at it this way. You are granted time to know your children."

Moses eased away to Stirling who slumped exhausted in a chair. The Scot's hand descended to Moses' curls. The skull's structure was defined against Mac's hand. He turned Moses' face up. Mac judged the bones, marking their similarity to the paternal line while the mother's subtle influence blurred the prime sculpture. The effect of him was pure delight. Moses' eyes were cast in gold. His skin looked toasted by summer. Mac tested the devil in him.

"Little feller, you wouldn't have heard Israel tell your father where the pills were?"

"Yes, Mackie."

Mac cleared his throat. "Did you now? And what did Old King Windy say, eh? You spent some time with him. Would you mind tellin' me?"

The fright came back. The man who never could make Wakwa laugh was as good as in the room.

"You don't have to say. But I'd like to know. Did the old Sachim ask you to get him the information?

"Yes!"

"Did he force it out o' you?"

Moses looked into the blue eyes. "No!"

Mac gathered Moses onto his lap and brought him against his chest. Moses heard the strange rhythm of Mac's heart.

Mac spoke near his ear. "Tha' was brave. The man was the big sachim."

Moses hid his face.

"You didno' warn your sire? You didno' say old Uncle Waban was curious about the location of the pills? Well! Well...I won't tell your father either. Good riddance! The King's dead. Long live the King!"

An odd alliance - the old man and the little boy.

When darkness became established, the People lit torches and slipped behind the tree line. Matthew struck the tents and cleared away the surplus for a cold party for the neighboring farms.

It was midnight when Gil came down the stairs to the sitting room. "I thought I'd find you in this room." "You don't mind if I join you?"

Wakwa, seated in the wing chair in the dark, replied, "Please! Come in!"

Gil took the settee. His slipper dipped into a silver pool formed by the moon. "You should take the master bedroom. It's empty. Bed's untouched. The ladies are in yours and will talk all night I would suppose, though what they're saying when they can't understand each other's words, I'll never know."

"They understand. Somehow. And we know."

Gil's breath shot out. "You cannot live like this!"

"I have been three years thus."

"Well. You can't go on."

"Why? Why do you want to break me down?"

Gil struck his own arms for warmth. "Would you mind a fire?"

At first silent, Wakwa offered. "As you wish. I will walk. I will stretch my legs. The moon is up."

"You sound like her! That's all Beth ever did. Walk! Walked till she got stuck in Locke's web."

Wakwa swung out of his chair and moved beyond the reach of the moonlight.

Gil tried to make amends. "I've never seen you so unsettled."

"You have never seen me angry."

"This is since the old man took his life?"

"Since he took mine."

"You're overwrought. You need sleep!"

Wakwa crossed the rug to him and squatted by his side. Simply clad, he looked younger than in the afternoon. "I wait until I am so tired, I cannot recall my dreams."

"Bad idea. If your dream is Beth."

Wounded, Wakwa backed away. He struck against the harp. It complained and teetered and the two men rushed to right her.

Close to him, Gil seized Wakwa's wrist. "Kirke slept at the dining table his first night here. It's true there are ghosts on the second storey. Of the living and the dead. They keep people downstairs till they get used to them. Wakwa! Undo it. Annul it! Whatever arrangement they've made between them it's by your grace. You can write! Write to her! You can talk better than any Cicero. Tell me what you want to say. I will write the letter. You've matched her with an extraordinary person. If she asked, he'd let her go!"

Wakwa's eyes found Gil's in the pearl-light. "Elizabeth would never ask of him what I asked of her."

Gil dropped his gaze. "I have not changed."

"Nor has she. That is why I do not sleep. Come. Walk with me, Gilbert."

As the moon pulls the waves, the moon pulled the men. Avoiding the forbidding crest of the grassy spill that led to the manse, they took the lunar lure leading them brightly toward Dowland House.

"I have missed your high spirit!" Wakwa said. "What would you think if I place my father in my stead in my absences? Then I could continue to speak for the tribes as the peace requires."

Worth, sparked by the flattery confided, "I thought, tonight, when all your folk went home or be forced to sleep on my lawn, that I should build a longhouse. North field. White clapboard. A big central room for any sort of meeting. Would hold fifty. A hundred. Meetings, receptions. Bed chambers above. Say, ten of good size. Could have three to four beds in each. And a cellar dug deep. Wine. Stuffs. More beds. Or anything volatile wanting storage."

Wakwa stopped to take him in.

"Good kitchen." Gil planned as he went, "And water in the Roman way. We'll get heat without the warning smoke of fires and flush the waste-water out in pipes. Isn't it worth a try?"

"Miawene here? Meetings with the men of Boston, of Philadelphia? Uncle, it will cost you gold. I cannot let you do it."

"It's not your say, Nephew. More, I am investing in some ventures of Kirke's. To increase my capital."

Panting behind them, the rustle of small feet on the grass, the cry of, "Nosh!"

Wakwa laughed at last. He swung Moses up.

Gil cried, "Everything back to normal! Not a soul where he or she should be!"

They talked softly after that. They came upon tall Dowland house bright white under the moon's flare. They passed Israel and Priscilla chatting in chairs at the kitchen door. They saw Mac asleep in Dowland's window in his vigil over them.

They entered by the front door, quietly. From Elizabeth's room, Wakwa and Moses discovered the pine saplings she had planted, illumined.

GULL

CHAPTER THIRTEEN

August 1752

"Viti! You must sleep!"

Kirke bent over a map in the room with the blue window. He cursed the hot wax that pelted him from the candelabrum hung strategically over the stone table where he sometimes worked, sometimes ate, sometimes slept.

Elizabeth rose from the enormous, low mattress and wandered barefoot over the stone floor and behind him. She came to his elbow but Kirke blocked her view of his chart. Elizabeth left him without a noise.

She descended the ten slick marble steps to the ground level and crossed a vast salon to its long doors thrown open onto the canal. Moonlight passed through the fabric of her nightdress and strands of her loosened hair, even her fingertips and ear lobes, turning her unearthly.

Definitely without the luxury of the disembodied state, she felt keenly the guilt of her existence and the constant affirmation of its appetites. They were modest enough - food, materials to work with, steadfast companionship. But in Venice with Thomas

Kirke the essential requirements of human life were transformed by circumstance into pleasures with no root in the soil of struggle or of cold survival. The elegant local fare, the seemingly limitless resources of Kirke Company and of Venice herself, and the solace of the kindness in Kirke's sharp, seasoned eyes conspired to bury the pang she honed in her heart. Her temptations were the vice of ingratitude for such gifts - and implacable remembrance.

She heard him come down the stairs and across the floor to her, his unselfconscious throat-clearing, watch-case snapping, coin-clanking stride so opposed to Wakwa's quiet appearances with a step direct and soft.

Kirke put his spotted hand on her shoulder. "Rough night?"

"Beautiful moon."

He stood away, advancing beyond her onto the balcony. He stuck the toe of his shoe between the posts of the balustrade. "You noticed. Good." He turned back to her, his disordered hair making him lunatic in the silver light. "Didn't mean to be rude up there. I was finishing something."

"Finished now?"

"It's not to my advantage to answer but I will for you're my wife and my partner and you asked."

Elizabeth moved close to him as if toward the safety of a pillar.

Kirke said, holding to the stone rail, striking a pose of nonchalance, "You've got to consider just how many English subjects there are in your American colonies."

"What?"

"You take your map and trace with your finger where all those people are going to fit. The Scots and Irish are pouring into Pennsylvania from Britain at an alarming rate. They're sure not sailin' back to Europe ever! It's expensive on the coastline and so they push west. They want to get rich quick. They're all after peltry never mind the touchy situation with the Indians and the French. But I'll get to that. Where was I?"

"Moving west." She whispered.

"Right! Wrong it is in my opinion." Kirke's arms crossed his chest and his hands gripped his rib cage through his coat. "There's a line established these so-called pioneers should not be crossing. But they are. Oh! It's all connected!"

"Because Dire Locke and...HE...had something to do with making the line?"

"Elizabeth, you've got to understand! The damned Chinese are after peltry. The European sources are thinner now and expensive to 'em. So the race is on to supply 'em from America and I'm not about to let Levy, Franks & Simon or the Shippens and Lawrences of this world beat us out of it."

"You're so upset. There is bad news?"

He ticked his tongue at her and drew her against his breast. "Not at all. Not yet. Not as far as my information goes. But picture the map of Pennsylvania and the Ohio country and the line that's not supposed to be crossed by families wanting to chop down the forests to lay down farms. And the line is bulging, straining, pushed farther every day and when it finally gives and breaks open, a flood of these clods is going to inundate the Illinois, pouring over the Blue Mountains cutting down the trade, French or no French, Indians or no Indians, Kirke or no Kirke."

"Then drop this trade! If the settlements WILL happen we'll lose by the western trade no matter what we do."

"You're so bright!" Kirke grabbed her so his agitation could jump any gaps between them. "If we drop it, what of our supplying China and what of our source of supply in Canton, what of my kung-hang's payment in gold for the ginseng? Sure, there's the New York fur fields but they're all connected after all by the turf, by the Indians, by the English. If we drop the fur trade, what of our major scheme to have our merchant bank and tons of gold at the ready for the ventures of our souls? If we drop it, the French will overrun the West and there will be a war between France and England bloodier than any yet and it won't be confined to the banks of the Ohio but will rage anywhere there is loyalty to Louis! The Continent will be on fire! If we drop it or do NOT drop it, England will crook her finger for our gold to pay for a fight to defend! And, if we refuse to supply the Crown because we'd prefer to manage our own business, we'll swing for two traitors. And if we supply gold to the King, whatever our politics, we'll never get it back and go under! We are in a bind. I'm mad as hell after a lifetime of profitable business and good planning to be in this position! And the Indians are getting mad as they perceive the bind they're in. They hunt and live by the trade therefrom. And the Trade brings the greedy and the poachers and the rotgut and the guns and the end of the supply and, of course, the pioneers! The Indians are acutely aware they have a hand in their own destruction! What else can they do but try to push all of us out? Whatever stripe!"

"Then, I'll say it again, *they* must stop trading and so must *we*! We must gradually stop trading."

He held her tightly. "It doesn't matter! An Indian war is inevitable. It will be the end of them. Some leader will arise out of the Six Nations or out of a western tribe, out of somewhere and he will be abetted by his brothers from the northeast, and a pox on their allegiance to England! He will be brave. He will be valiant. He will win many battles. He will be crushed by farmers! There are so many of them! There will come a treaty. Locke and...other...

particularly good traders and agents and...chiefs...will be there to make it fair. It will be fair. And like the hedgehogs they are, the farmers will pop up regardless and the Westward march will push the natives out of the way to the corners. And then England'll choke me and Levy, Simon & Franks, and Shippens and Lawrence, et al. And then we'll see the taxes on imports and exports and duties and fees far too heavy and the stupid, inadvertent strangulation of all profitable business especially of the carrying trade!"

"Viti! What will we do?"

"We will let England dismember us with painstaking slowness and arouse no suspicions nor instigate a loss of confidence in our abilities!"

"Viti, *you* are brilliant! But all your long days! It is like toiling over a thing of beauty and then - burning it up!" Then she remembered when such a thing had happened to her.

He knew her story and moralized, "As long as it's done to a purpose, Liz. The American colonies will stand on their feet like Colossus out of their unaccustomed financial depression resulting from the eruption I describe, and there will be yet another war unlike any war ever begun, mark that, and unless the Americans can afford to succeed with it, I cannot see from here where it will end. Or if I can ever get you home!" He clung to her but tossed this way and that in the rush of insight as if it would fell him. "I must keep on. I must succeed! I must have the gold!"

She wrapped his waist and drew him up the stairs and unbuttoned his clothes and lay in the crook of his arm and waited very still.

Instead of a caress he gave her news. "Pick's Town on the Ohio was, six weeks ago, overrun by the French. It is yet undeclared, but the war with France is started. And sure as hell your Massachusetts man, the Fox, Silent Fox, your man, Wakwa, will have to take a stand. Shall I take you back? The ports will close."

Elizabeth quivered, going cold although Kirke held her.

"His chief, Waban, is dead." Kirke stroked her hair. "Will you want to go there now?"

Elizabeth shied from his hand.

Kirke pretended not to notice.

"When did Waban die?"

"About this time last year. September, actually."

With violence, she twisted to face him. "How long have you known?"

Kirke freed himself of her not liking her implication. "I found out today. When Locke's map arrived." Then he took her back and added, "The old Sachim was a suicide."

The clock ticked the passing of an hour. Their words to one another were as clipped and as inexorable as the pendulum.

"Half a dozen letters from Uncle Gil! Nothing of this!"

Kirke listened to the minutes pass, then offered, "Your Uncle Worth is a gentleman. Bred. Wasn't his news to tell."

"Not news! Responsibility!"

"To whom!" Kirke parried.

Considering the men, the interrelations, the political situation, she could reasonably announce, "Out of the question."

"Out of season."

The candles wept their last onto the map and sputtered out.

Elizabeth kissed Kirke's hand before they slept. "Viti, reconsider? Take me to China. I'll disguise myself as a man. The Chinese and the English will never know!"

Kirke laughed an Irish laugh.

"Will you think about it?"

"You think about this, Liz - how to pack our cargo of gold on the way back so the pirates don't steal it!"

In its heyday, Palazzo Asolo had absorbed the attention of many servants of permanent employ: a kitchen staff of ten, as many housemaids, half a dozen laundresses, two keepers of the gate, several gondoliers. In excess of that, there were the personal servants, the ladies' maids and valets, whose numbers were adjusted to the number of family members. There were, as well, resident and itinerant musicians, the wine steward, and a man for basic repairs loftily titled, "l'architetto - the architect." A captain, that is, the major domo, keeper of the keys, coordinated all of them. Now, with the family diminished and the great house leased out to Kirke, housekeeping at Asolo limped along on seven.

That parsimony was reason enough why soft-cheeked Cecilia, who oversaw the current, modest operation, nursed a reserved opinion of her mistress. Worse than closed rooms and understaffing was the advantage Donna Kirke took of her delightful husband. A man of parts. A man of humor. A man who had mastered the Italian tongue and used it like a feather to tickle and cause blushes. A man of wealth and business. Rarest of all - a faithful husband always at her side. And his wife? A thing of bisque who never gave him children. Who never went to church but observed satanic rites, crossing her arms over her breast facing in the direction of the Adriatic every sunset. She rarely laughed. In fact, she often wept in secret. What had she to weep for? For the balls she did not hold?

For the people she did not welcome? For the wine she did not drink or the dancing she was shy of? Where had Sior Tomaso found such a wife? She was like a stone he had stooped for on the beach.

What use was she, this Elisabetta? Sitting in the kitchen with Asunta with her hands in the flour learning to cook! Ordinarily a good trait in a person of quality, work with the hands except for dainty stitchery was out of character for an English lady. That! She was not really a lady, her husband relegated to the merchant class. She was not really English, born in a primitive place, America, a land of savages and of Protestants!

Cecilia could have gone on all day about the shortcomings of Donna Lisa as that fool of a steward, Luigi, cared to call their mistress. She was like a bitch pup clamped onto the master's heels dawn to dusk until he was so vexed by her that he would pull his hair and throw her off and then come to pet her where she stood in the corner licking her wounds. She worked on man's work all day and then while Sior Tomaso Kirke snored in a chair, she bent in the firelight over a table in the upper chamber, once a library that looked beyond the city at the sea, cutting her own clothes! It was degrading to serve a servant. Cecilia sealed her lips about that part of life at Palazzo Asolo. After all, she made a very fine salary. But the rest was fair game for gossip - the mistress sitting at her desk, writing letter after letter and then walking out of the house alone like a stray to post them! Surely she had a clandestine fire in her bosom *such as it was*. Surely she had a lover. Indecent thing! She should have him set up in residence like other wives whose husbands had passed September.

Elizabeth loved Venice. It was a dream of fantastic outcroppings of mind. The wilderness of streets leading to magic wells of buildings and bridges was to her much like the woods. The light shifting, the mist floating, made a different place out of a place one had walked before. There were the sounds of happy people. A kindly pattern of early rising and siesta and afternoon activity gave way to the air ringing with the clatter of pots and pans and singing and a bright babble of conversation. It was communal life that cheered her. The freedom of the Indian town seemed the foundation of this city. Just as foreign to Venetians as she had been to Ninnuock, she ventured among them mute from lack of vocabulary but trusting.

The morning after she learned from Kirke that another principal impediment to her restoration to Massachusetts had passed and been passed over she turned a corner not far from Saint Mark's and was lost. It was the way in a place where the light played games and instead of shadows there was mist.

She stopped in front of a bridge that arced toward the doorstep of a shop. The building stood astride an offshoot of a canal or that was how it seemed in the clearing formed out of sun and stone. A gilded lion's face stared from its hook near the door. Elizabeth went up the gangway and in. Her pleasure was keen at finding a maskmaker's shop in this illusory way.

Two square rooms plastered gesso-white fed into one another. The first one where she stood was deserted except for golden faces with empty eyes lining the walls. Alone among the effigies of animals and men, she admired the masks at leisure. She took one down from the wall to examine it closely.

These were not the ordinary carnival masks she had seen displayed even at the butcher's, made light and attached to a stick for feigning mystery or flirting in earnest the night before Lent. These were life-sized sculptures. Some were formed of the usual papier-mâché. Some were carved of wood.

The lion guarding the door and the mask she held were sculpted of some tree, light in color and light in weight yet weighty enough for durability and hard on a knife. One could not wear it. The mask was thick through. It was rough-hewn inside but finished as smooth as skin on its surface. Plain wood on the inside, pure gold out. Elizabeth regarded the face. No hook-nosed *Frachinappa*, it was serene. Its forehead was high, broad, its eyes almond and large, its nose long and sweeping smoothly from its arched brows. Its nostrils were sweetly made, curved for beauty, not flared with passion. Its lips were bowed and promised much if the gilt wood could pucker and kiss. What face was this? Its resemblance to Wakwa's about the cheek bones gripped her but there was another element also ancient, lost in time, that stunned her senses and blinded her to the live man stooping to pass under the door lintel and then standing straight before her.

"Bon giorno, Madama!" The tall man said. He wiped white sizing off his hands with a Turkish towel.

Elizabeth responded, "Bon giorno!" But she did not hear herself speak the well-practiced stock greeting, rapt as she was with his large eyes, his forehead and nose and his mouth identical to the mask in her hands. In English and fractured Italian she stammered, "Is this a Venetian face?"

The maskmaker smiled but looked behind her, out the door into the sunspots. Then, returning to their subject, he let her know by gesture and word it was a reproduction of the image of the original mask, the facsimile-prototype of the mask in Italy. It was a pagan mask, a face drawn from the farthest past. The forehead, he pointed out, was Etruscan. The mask's name – *Sirmolo*.

The maskmaker looked beyond her. Once more he smiled. He relieved her of the piece and showed her other masks regretting the lack of language between them. Elizabeth took *Sirmolo* back and nestled him in the crook of her arm. She began to choose fancifully painted masks, tiny ones; the lion came off his post. A beak-nosed comedian was added to the pile.

The maskmaker tallied the large purchase. Elizabeth watched the fantastic mound, *Sirmolo* secure against her side. She looked at the masks the way she looked at flowers before she picked them to make them into dye. She sensed they were teaching her, informing and opening her mind.

While the maskmaker left her for a moment to peer out the door, she moved to the second room. A metal vat half-full of opaque white liquid for undercoating the gold stood in the center of the gesso-spotted floor. She whirled on the proprietor with an idea. English burst from her. "Can you put the gesso on top of gold? Can you mask gold with gesso?"

"Gesso. Si!" But the craftsman wrestled with the unknown words. He scratched his balding head. He looked toward a back room and called a name. There was no reply. He was without help in speaking to her. Troubled, he passed through the outside door, down his steps and up the narrow street. He shrugged, coming back in.

Elizabeth knew then he was searching for her escort. He was upset that she had been left alone by a servant. In the manner of the Italians he could not conceive that she had ventured into the streets without a companion.

At his curious almost condemnatory look, she blurted, "Do you have a barrow? Oh, find a barrow and we will make it worth your while!"

His brow furrowed. He licked his lips wet. He could not understand a single word of what she had just said. With a deep bow and a vaguely anxious expression, he offered her the bill with his compliments and his name, which was Dario Ipato. He described her purchases clearly, naming them item-by-item, counting, "Uno, due, tre, quattro, cinque, sie...." A fifth of his stock was heaped for packing.

In her life, Elizabeth had never carried money. It was neither necessary nor was it appropriate to her station in the Dowland neighborhood. She had been reared in an atmosphere of self-sufficiency and the absence of the luxe. What was bought outright such as peddler's goods or those items imported and delivered to the house like porcelain, pewterware, or furniture, had been paid for out of her father's till ensconced in a trunk in the root cellar. Anything bought in Sweetwood or Wareham was simply sent home and placed on the merchant's account with a quarterly reckoning.

Until she had known Silent Fox, who was obliged to wear belts of money as a sign of his affluence and for practicality in trading in the towns and among the Ninnuock, Elizabeth had regarded money with misgiving. She disliked watching her father's vexation with receiving paper money in payment for his crops or using those same bills to pay his own debts. Old Tenor, Middle Tenor and following those, New and Second New Tenor bills of credit turned him into a wounded beast from a quiet deliberate man tender over the calving or delighting in the corn yield. "A good Queen Anne dollar is all that is necessary!" She remembered his irate and frequent cry, for he kept up with the changes in currency not to be ruined by depreciating values.

Elizabeth did not understand the ephemeral appeal of the provincial Tenor or why the Crown fostered its printing and use. How one paper bill could be worth anything let alone be worth any more than another paper bill when neither could be redeemed for coin but merely for paper escaped her. And when finally the Equity Bill declared a set value for the exchange of the bills for silver, the race to redeem them left her father distraught over the fraud against all parties concerned. And so, when Wakwa paid periwinkle shells for a yard of cloth she found such commerce to be profoundly rational.

Earnestly, she prevailed on Dario in broken Italian, "Please send, uh, prego manda...tutto...everything to...Palazzo Asolo!"

Dario moved forward slowly, his glance darting to the rear room for packing straw. "Asolo? Per ordire de chi?" He asked on whose authority he should deliver the objects created by his hands and who might be paying him.

"Send them in my husband's care. Sior Thomas Kirke. Mio mario...my husband!"

The maskmaker clasped his hands and caught his breath. "Su mario?" El Sior Tomaso Kirke?!! El gran mercante! Su mario?!!" All excitement that the great merchant was her husband, he broke into an intricate dance step.

"Hurry! Hurry! I must get to him and tell him my idea!"

"Hurry! Hurry!" Dario repeated without knowledge of the word.

Their hands caught and they laughed, she for joy over her inspiration, so simple it could save the Company and all its ambitions, he because of this connection to the world-famous merchant, a complete surprise, so Venetian. She urged him toward the door. He dropped her hands, hastened for his coat, then remembering the masks, bundled the mountain of golden faces deftly with tissue and straw, packed them into an enormous basket which he slung over his shoulder. With a jaunty stride, he escorted her home.

Minutes later, Cecilia caught sight of them walking and talking fast. She noticed Donna Lisa's expressive use of her hands, painting the air, and wondered at such passion from such a person and how her hands had learned to talk so suddenly. Cecilia left the window to prepare her master for the worst.

"Find her a young man but not this! Do not let her drag them home!"

Kirke dropped his pen, its body and nib one solid piece of glass. Ink spattered all over his note to Locke. "Damn! Swallow your tongue, Cecilia, or I'll stow you in a trunk on a boat to Boston and send you to the savages who'll boil you and it for supper!"

She curled her lip, shook her head over an old fool, and stalked away.

Luigi opened the gate. Kirke came smartly down to greet the excited pair. As fast as they could with their burden, Elizabeth and the maskmaker made their way across the inner bridge, and through the high front doors.

"Yes?!" Kirke accosted her. He was on guard at her breathless, happy look.

Unfettered by sadness or sorrow, Elizabeth threw her arms around his neck and swung him into a brief and happy dance. "I've got it, solved it! What do you think?" She spilled introductions and ideas out of some store of hidden sunlight.

Kirke was astounded at her mood, her quick step, the life bubbling from her.

"Meet Dario Ipato." She ran to the maskmaker and begged him to set the heavy basket down. While the men shook hands, she rifled through the cache of masks. She seized *Sirmolo* with a shout of satisfaction and held the handsome face of gold aloft. "Varda! Oro! Behold! Gold!!"

She placed the mask in Kirke's hands and then with effort channeled her excitement into her message. "Instead of gilding masks, let us mask the gold. Take the bars, the coins, and right aboard ship melt them down and cast the liquid gold as masks - cover them with gesso and paint the faces and stack them in the hold! We could cast other things - bowls, why not? Cups! Saucers! And paint them blue and white like the trade China. Throw molten gold as shoe heels and soles, and cover them with gesso and size and paint them too! Form gold into golden whalebone for corsets! I'll buy every corset in Venice and tear out the stays and as soon as the gold ones are made, they could simply be slipped in! Beat the gold into sheets and fix it onto screens then size and paint the panels as if they were made of wood. Mask the gold! I defy any pirate to board us and find it!"

"Elizabeth Dowland!" Kirke's eyes burned her up in adoration. "I've never seen you...never seen you!"

She flushed, magnified by the success of her invention, not hearing Kirke's real commendation. "Dario is an artist. A craftsman...."

"Dario! Yes!" Grasping her thought without words, Kirke turned to him, ushered him in, and in swift, sweet Italian straightened him out about what was wanted and what service would be appreciated. Kirke reassured as subtly as if throwing a noose around the Venetian's neck, "You'll eat at the captain's table. The voyage is but six hundred days! I'll pay you in pure gold. No alloy! You can choose your own assistants - as long as they've got closed mouths. The mandarins won't accept foreign women so you'll have to give that up for a while but just think of how glorious times will be when we lower anchor once more in the Lagoon!"

"Donne!" Dario held his adept hands in front of his face in real horror at the thought of female companionship.

Kirke surmised, "You can't do without one?!"

"Le donne son molto brave! Bravissime!" Dario looked at Elizabeth but kept his praise in bounds, careful, artful, balancing insult and implication. Dario made the sign of the cross as if asking the indulgence of God and of particular saints concerning his artists' integrity. "God and St. Luke pity me and St. Anthony too!" Then bravely flying his flag, he stated in carefully couched Venetian, "I cannot have women and know my task."

"What do you mean?" Kirke floundered, out of his depth.

Dario looked into the palms of his adept hands. "Sir, it is not given to the artist to know women."

Kirke regarded him with a curious confidence. "You say that?" Kirke's reputation was built on his ability to seize the advantage. "Then a ship is the place for you!" Then for Elizabeth's benefit, "A ship is the place for him, Betty!" He continued his persuasions in split monologue. "We'll set you up in large quarters and get your alchemy going on deck. As many assistants as you require! We're 200 tons, over 1000 tons burden, and sport a crew of 190. We've got room for your manufactory. Let me see the things you do!" Kirke viewed the pieces Elizabeth was spreading on the floor. Kirke finished, "Without women."

Dario balked. He rubbed one hand inside the other.

Kirke looked at the exceptional work, all minor works of art, but he saw the vats of molten gold, smelled the smoke of the pitch fires on deck, felt the sea spray. He caught wind of the problems attendant on talent and temperament and men undesirous of women imprisoned for quarters of the year with sailors undressed above their waists laboring with supple muscle in the salt air and stars and sun. Kirke gambled. "Take my offer? Come?"

Dario let off an urbane light. He bowed. He backed away.

"You want more money?" Kirke admonished, "Man, I'm setting you up for life!"

Dario pleaded for compassion. "Sir, please understand, I see your offer as more than generous. It is fair and fair is more than generous for what you require - the time away from my beautiful city - the risks to my health - the dangers of the sea - from marauders - from disease - from filth! Please understand there is a pride, a line that cannot be abridged in art. I must sustain my household, yes. But to work *just* for money, for the most precious commodity, for gold? For hire alone? I will either lose my skill or my soul and I do not know which would be worse!'"

Kirke turned to Elizabeth. "He thinks I'm trying to buy his soul. What do I do?"

"Tell him he's to help us in a cause! One greater than the gold. Something holy! It is the truth." Her eyes shone with it.

Kirke wrought the idea in Italian.

Dario pulled away, gained the door. He asked for time to think.

Kirke gave him until morning.

Elizabeth put her hand in Kirke's. "He will accept!" Her hand, unconstrained for the first time, made its hot impression on Thomas Kirke as if she were of molten stuff and poured into the shape he gave her.

He implored, "Let us have this night!"

They fled the world up the slippery stairs and that once were alone.

They took their breakfast on the bedchamber balcony at four the following afternoon. It was hot on the shimmering street of water far below. Cecilia, with darting eyes prying for the secret of them, served them melon with lemon ice in debacle in its hollow and custard wrapped in pastry powdered like babies' bottoms. Lido crystal chimed with chunks of ice floated in coffee and making islands for seas of cream.

"No word from Dario." Kirke perused the morning news.

Elizabeth looked kindly on his distraction. "I have been thinking."

"Good!" Kirke threw the paper down.

His cool eyes intently studying their object had potential to frighten but she was glad of their focus. "I think you will not hear from him."

"Damn!" Kirke took as fact whatever she said. "Whom to get then?"

"Dario."

"It's like living with Locke."

Their glances engaged.

"Not quite!" Kirke's skin turned rosy.

"Quite like my thinking in its way." She blushed in turn. "I have a friend."

Kirke jerked in his chair.

"His name is Stephen Poore." She told him the story from her girlhood and finished, "Had my parents matched me with him rather than...the way they did...with Annanias Hudson...Stephen and I might have...."

With an impatient hand, Kirke hurried her along.

"I might never have...loved...married...a red man."

"Nonsense."

"You are right." But her eyes veered left into memories. "Stephen loved me. He never fought for me. Never!" She laughed.

Kirke observed. Tried to catch at the information that she cast like seed from the pouch of her past.

"Stephen loves me! I love him. We are...."

"Amici?"

"Yes, Viti. Friends with no gender. It is wonderful!"

"No gender at all?"

"Almost none. Or is it - gender without the flesh? That is more like - it is lively sympathy."

"Why do we need him?" A haggard look came over the man who just hours before had been rejuvenated by this woman.

She reached across the cold slab of the tabletop and took his shaking hands. "Thomas, dear...."

His face was set.

She corrected herself, "Viti! "He lives in Paris now. Like Dario does here."

Kirke's bright eyes brightened with concentration. "He doesn't mince...surely not?"

"I want to include Stephen in our work. He is a scholar of language. Invaluable! Michael Beckett knows how to reach him. We could have letters in his hands in a few weeks. Stephen could accompany you to the East! He would be our brother. I worry about him - spending his life alone. And...."

"And?"

"His understanding Dario's...way...might make the artist trust us."

"Introduce them?"

"It occurred to me! Dario Ipato is...handsome, charming."

Kirke revived somewhat. "Betty, putting them together, two men - is it evil?"

She looked at him long. Softly she returned, "Love is never evil."

Cecilia found them still there in the evening, the dishes scattered to the four corners of the table, their pens scratching quickly across parchment. A ship of the master's was straining at anchor to embark for the Strait of Gibraltar and north to England. Good as gold those letters would be on it. Cecilia cleared. They disregarded her and kept writing. She prayed the next tenants would not be merchants but something more polite, more conventional.

CHAPTER FOURTEEN

September 1752

Stephen Poore, Jr. never hurried when he walked. His stride was slow but charged with purpose and so not lax. On a frame of three inches over six feet he carried much weight but even as a slender child he had moved methodically - seldom running toward his objective.

Twenty-four days after Kirke's ship left Venice with letters to him, Poore bore down the front path of his parents' house in Mayfair without haste, curious but not excited at glimpsing a pair of merchant ship's officers through the ground floor windows.

Stephen had come to London to join his mother, Gwynn, for an indefinite period, and, incidentally, his father of whom he was not fond. At twenty-seven, a scholar in the service of language, associated with no university, living mostly in Paris quietly but without privation as one might judge from his waistline, he had sailed the Channel to calm Gwynn Poore who did not like his living out of England with war threatening.

"Darling, one never knows with the French," was her persuasion to bring him home.

Poore's agreement with her on that point was, ironically, his main attraction to Paris. Nevertheless, after a month or two, he had come along and had just gotten settled with them on Cork Street when Kirke's Captain Dray and his first-mate docked themselves in the drawing room.

Stephen entered and hoped he could pass up the stairs without attracting any notice because he had a dinner engagement and wanted to take time with his toilette.

"Stephen!" Gwynn rustled into the vestibule as he began the climb. "Two men to see you!"

"Oh?!" Poore delighted in bolts out of the blue.

He observed that the uniformed pair had experienced his father's hospitality, that is to say, none. No cup or glass was in evidence. "How do you do?" Poore greeted them affably, avoiding looking at the clock on the mantel although he was anxious about the time. "May we offer you some refreshment? Sherry?"

Poore the senior clouded the farthest corner. "They are here representing Kirke Company. THEY say. And that's all they'll say."

Stephen blushed for his sire. "Quite right since they are here to see me! Shall we sit?" Thunder in his ears from the sound of the Kirke name and its connection to Elizabeth distracted him to the degree that he left it up to the guests, or really as he thought about it, Kirke's emissaries, whether to sit or stand.

Dray enjoyed divulging, "My ship waits at anchor for you. There is no time to sit!" Dray received a pouch of tooled Florentine leather from his senior officer and presented it to Stephen.

Stephen's blood had not rushed through his heart as it now did since his first visit to America and Worth Farm where he had met Elizabeth Dowland when she was only ten. "How did you find me, Commander?"

"The Company has its contacts in the shires, sir. We came into port yesterday, relayed a letter to Cambridgeshire, to Michael Beckett, Esquire."

Poore the senior barked, "Beckett?!"

"His reply received no more than an hour ago brought us here."

"What's come over him? Giving out my address? Must be in Kirke's pay!"

"Or in his debt, Father." Stephen turned back to Captain Dray. "The wind is good. We'll be pleased to weigh anchor by sunset."

"What!" The elder Poore was furious.

Stephen swept over to his mother's small desk and struggled with the bag and the parchment. "Mother, the Sherry!"

She rang.

He fumbled in extracting the stiff papers, knocking over small, delicate objects in his effort to be quick. Shuffling a large pair of folded letters to assess which to open first, he enquired, "Is Mrs. Kirke all right?"

"She is in safe harbor, Mr. Poore."

"Thank you. How are you sure?"

"I officiated at their wedding. And Venice seems to agree."

Immediately, Stephen slit the seal of Thomas Kirke's correspondence saving Elizabeth's for last.

His father fumed, "Venice! Perfect. Nothing to do there but play. And thieve. And whore! Who is Kirke to send ships to steal my son! Why doesn't he get one of his own to ferry about? That woman! Witch! Little wonder the savage threw her out!"

Stephen winced, remembering the summer of '48, the beach at Sandy Neck on Cape Cod, Qunneke by his side telling him her words for things while he scribbled in his notebook, his spectacles slipping down his nose, and Elizabeth, barefoot in the sand, with her hand so firmly held by Wakwa's, the pair seemed welded, a study in copper and alabaster.

"Dear!" Gwynn, hovering over the passing of the tray, silenced her husband. "She's of fine stock and the native is highly placed. Hanna Worth said in her letter...."

"Mrs. Poore, I've told you not to mention those people to me!"

"Hanna's letter states the whole thing was very complicated, very political."

"So's this new alliance, no doubt!"

Gwynn disregarded her husband. "Frankly, I think Beth is a marvel not to shoot herself being without her son."

"Ha! The wolf pack has kept her wolfling back from civilization! Good!" The senior Poore sniped.

Gwynn did her best against him. "Husband, our Stephen was and is quite fond of her and, if he had spoken up, she might have been in this house this instant, your daughter-in-law, and had no problem in the world!"

Stephen looked up from his study. "She would have had some problem, Mother."

"Insolence!" The insulted father stalked toward the door. "Daughter-in-law! Presbyterians! All she had was a great hunk of land around her neck. Stephen was smart enough not to sink himself under that. Imagine, my son living in that place! Near that renegade, Worth. *She* won't even do it!" He turned on Captain Dray. "What cargo do you carry that you can sweep in and out of port like this?"

"No cargo." Dray did not honor him with direct address. "Just the required number of cannon and crew to meet the Venetian statute and deter the Barbary pirates. My voyage is strictly on your son's account."

The elder Poore choked on his own air. "Crass display! I want to know what Kirke's extravagance is to cost me?"

Stephen had completed both letters. He answered for Dray. "Your only progeny."

Gwynn stood confused, her peach-tinted ruffles quivering.

"Not to be unreasonable, Mr. Poore," Dray spoke directly to the younger Stephen, "our orders are to embark immediately if you agree to come."

Stephen, moving his three hundred-fifty pounds with the swiftness of a thin man called back, "Yes, I'll come. I'll be your ballast. Give me a quarter hour!"

Captain Dray saluted.

The senior Poore offered cruelly to his wife, "Shall I get the gun?"

A skiff, cut loose at sunset from Dray's Psyche, scampered bravely through the pre-dawn fog. She was eager in her northward slicing of the silver Adriatic. Just as the sun swam out of the smoky water to starboard, licking her sides pink, the little boat slid up the center of the Canal Della Grazia racing past the white-domed church of St. George in sight of the palaces hugging the Molo. Daylight caught in her rippling ensign brightly tracing the picture of her name - a golden butterfly. The Psyche's child was here to tell Thomas Kirke that Stephen Poore was a day away.

Kirke caught the signal - a scarlet pennant. He sent patrol boats to verify. He and Elizabeth gulped breakfast on the balcony watching their good news grow closer and closer.

"Cecilia!" Kirke bellowed.

The housekeeper popped her head out of the kitchen door aptly located directly below the balcony. She walked out onto the miniature pier far enough so that Kirke could see her curtsey.

Kirke pointed to the incoming boat. The woman turned toward it, then, with grim determination to perform her office thoroughly, appeared after two minutes at Kirke's side.

He informed her that a guest, a friend of the family's, was due and would be staying on indefinitely.

What sort of guest? A woman? A man?

An English gentleman.

And his wife?

A bachelor.

"Ahh!" Cecilia nestled her hands at her bosom. She even inclined her head in Elizabeth's direction. She asked if the cicisbeo inglese would take the room over the master's bedchamber.

"Elisabetta?" Kirke appealed to her.

"Can't we get another housekeeper, Viti?" Elizabeth longed for Cooke.

"It's not to our advantage to play the Puritan, Liz. She wants an answer."

Elizabeth thought, then said, "Tell her, before she murders me in my bed, that Stephen is to stay in the room adjoining ours."

"Is he, Mrs. Kirke?! I don't know if it's to our advantage to play the Venetian either!"

The next day, the last day of summer, they met Stephen at the quay. Luigi, and the boatman, and the present "architect" were on hand with a three-wheeled cart to transport the luggage of the new household member.

Kirke had arranged for a local street band to blow a tune of welcome, which they did with gusto as Poore negotiated the gangway. The scholar's vital but deliberate stride moving his startling bulk led Kirke to remark, "Isn't he grand! He's the Chinese god of good fortune on a sturdy pair of legs!"

Elizabeth touched Kirke's arm happy with his powers yet the moment of sighting Stephen was not easy. So many memories played on the glowing, dancing water that Kirke had to coax her the few steps to the pier's edge.

Stephen estimated and re-estimated them as he stepped along. At first, the gaunt, gray Kirke seemed like a specter blighting Elizabeth. She, strangely beautiful in a gauze gown of chartreuse, like a bud refusing to open, looked damned by her nearness to age. As he drew closer he perceived them as two islands joined by a bridge of intricate tracery, its piles driven deep. When Poore was upon them, the perversity of their bond of age and youth and the taint of their souls' bigamy burst like bubbles. Was it Venice and her similar sins who forgave them? Or was it the Venetian air graced with peace and freedom?

All Stephen heard was the fanfare, all he saw was white pigeons' wings, all he felt was one of Kirke's firm hands set at the back of his neck and the other gripping a hand of his in a hard, dry shake. Wakwa's ghost slipped past and Poore warmly returned Kirke's handclasp. And then came Elizabeth's lips on his and on his eyelids and on his cheek.

They collected a crowd - the brass band accounting for some of the attention, a minor procession the adjunct to the daily gaiety in St. Mark's Square. But even on the thronged landing the trio bred curiosity, the huge young man lead by the occupants of the Asolo, the old merchant's quite young bride laughing and pulling the newcomer by his hand like an innocent and the merchant himself never releasing him all the way to the palazzo, jabbering in English without a pause.

The house had a heartbeat as soon as Stephen set foot in the door. Luigi and his men were favorably impressed by the large stranger, since only a single trunk and a satchel comprised his baggage. Behavior so concise foretold a happy tenancy. Cecilia and the rest of the staff lined up at the entrance to greet him. She gave him a full-bosomed curtsey and called him, "milord," for what else was he? Not a merchant, not a neophyte on his Grand Tour, obvious from his age and his size. He was a man of fortunate birth and fully English, not mongrel like her employers. Asunta, the cook, parted from her kitchen for the reception of the guest, almost sang when she saw Poore's generous figure anticipating his appreciation for what she would create for him.

Nevertheless, for the principals, the arrangement felt brittle and clouded like a thing of glass in the making.

"I must thank Dray for managing the business in seven weeks." Kirke offered at the welcome-luncheon served immediately. "I suppose we'd better have him to supper tonight."

"Viti, shouldn't we take time with Stephen this first day? He accepted us on a moment's notice."

Kirke beamed, "The captain to dinner, Liz. Stephen has read between the lines. A pretty good scholar, I'd say."

Stephen's attention swerved to Elizabeth unsure where her ease stemmed from. "Your enticement, Mr. Kirke...."

"Thomas."

Stephen looked to Elizabeth for her opinion.

"V.T. pleases him."

Kirke watched their communication.

"Very well...." Stephen flinched. "Those successive consonants. What would you think of just 'T', sir?"

"That'll be fine. It's shorter!"

Laughing at this hint from a busy man, Stephen went on quickly, "Your bait, Mr. Kirke, I will try to say T, that I might study Chinese firsthand hardly fooled me. That's exciting enough and there's a hidden adventure here I'd have been an ass to reject. But it was plain you would not put me under solitary escort merely to augment my notebooks. 'Mighty plans' was the phrase from you, sir. And Beth, to be told after an interval of four years' dead silence that all your dreams turned on my joining you both here...." His blue eyes brightly took in Kirke and then caught and held Elizabeth. "Well...! Since we understand each other and agree on what's important - they must be my dreams too." He reached out to her, his stout hands open on the tabletop. "To be needed! I am yours!"

"Steph!"

Kirke cleared his throat and pulled out his purse. "Stephen, you left London not at your convenience. You'll need capital, I suspect, so far from your ordinary sources."

Poore eyed the bulging pouch but demurred, "You're very kind but I'll find some situation to tide me over till I can lay hold of my funds."

"*If* you can."

"Viti!" From Elizabeth.

"His sire's cut him off. I am right?"

"How could you know, sir?"

"Were he another sort of man, Liz would have put him on my list of possible partners. No. You travelled light on our account and you'll need immediate outfitting for we want to sail by January."

"I am sure if I write to our solicitor...."

Kirke overrode him. "That's Beckett, so I say not. Not discreet. Not yet at least. Not for a long while. No. Your father could cause me trouble. He's got you stuck. I hope the repercussions are not too great for your future...."

Stephen beamed, "You mean - the WILL?" He tossed his handsome head. "I don't live for it."

Kirke glanced at Elizabeth. "So. We have a new member of the family. See here, Stephen Poore the Junior! I'm run ragged without my chief factor who's mired in the colonies for a time. Take this purse as a sign of my trust...."

"But, Sir!"

"No sirring!"

"I'm sorry. T. But...!"

Kirke's mottled hands quelled all arguments. He took back the bag of coins and extracted his personal cheques from a pocket. With his forefinger he scrawled an amount to be made visible later in ink. "My personal note on a standard of sterling not some devalued paper currency. I'm not offering to buy you, son, but to re-enfranchise you. You're over twenty-one! Take this and make your own arrangements, if you want. And if you'll stay and be secretary to the Company, Grand Secretary, as the Chinese put it, there'll be a monthly stipend. And a sharing in the profits. This is a rough sketch, particulars later. There is only one request. Your utter silence about the Company's activities. Which are the Trade. As she develops. 'Silence is golden' is a good adage. If I were you, I wouldn't give another thought to money."

Stephen Poore stood, speechless. His expansive middle gave him the statesman's air but he was mute.

Elizabeth slipped over to him and took his hand.

Stephen regarded her newly then turned back to Kirke. "Are we involved in treason?"

Kirke stood. "Thanks for the 'we.' We are charted on that course considering the Royal wind."

Stephen smiled his small smile. "The mighty plan and the dream."

"Yes!" Elizabeth said.

"Part of it." Kirke added thinking of the Indian.

Stephen saw then the struts of their marriage as incorruptible and was troubled by it.

"What do you say?" Kirke put it to him.

Stephen looked straight at him. "I wonder how it will change me?"

Elizabeth asked, "China?"

"Having a father."

Kirke's eyes sparkled so that Elizabeth knew shame at any reluctance of hers as his wife.

Kirke led them away from the table to the library to find his desk and his writing materials. He remarked, "I've often said that Elizabeth and I have taken a great assortment of people in bed with us. We'll have to shore up the mattress with you in it, Steve, but at least there's room!"

Stephen trilled a laugh in fine counter-tenor.

After a look, Kirke went on, "You should know, the servants think I brought you here to be Lisbeth's lover."

Stephen blushed a shiny red at Kirke's freedom in front of a woman - a wife - he could not think of her as exclusively Kirke's. He informed them, "That's the way my father took it. Mother's opinion of us is better."

"Is it? The Venetians think it would be decent."

Poore's small mouth twisted prettily. "Then, how shall we... satisfy...the situation? Should we whisper in the stairwells, Beth? Would that be enough?"

No answer came from her.

Kirke said, "Keep them on pins and needles. No sign of anything. That'll make the gossip lively but not mean." He bent to the inkwell and began writing.

Stephen was past the topic, strolling the room, taking in its connecting halls, measuring its grandeur.

"Been to Venice before?" Kirke tested.

"Once for half a year."

"Grand Tour."

"Nothing so grand as this. I just wonder with such walls, why there are no paintings?"

"The seminal question! Glad to have you on board! The Asolo family sold them. Not to me. To that Englishman. What's-his-name. And then George the Second, he just crooks his finger, writes a cheque for a paltry twenty thousand, and suddenly the priceless paintings are hanging in his house!"

"Palace, Viti!" Elizabeth corrected.

"What difference?" Kirke growled. "It happened with Who's-it's *library*. For ten!"

"His books?" Poore was horrified.

"Every one! Ultimately with no cheque at all, I predict, His Highness will acquire What's-his-name's and Who's-it's heads. So why not evade the Crown, if not defy it openly by owning nothing?"

"I agree...." Stephen marked his perturbation in moderate steps across the rug.

"Yet...suppose...."

Kirke paid him strict attention.

"You say this man, Dario, paints? He must know legions of unrecognized artists around the Lagoon. It might not take a great outlay to buy their stuff and frame it."

Kirke and Elizabeth looked puzzled.

"In gold."

"Framed in gold." Kirke mused.

"Not in leaf."

"The gold itself? Live with it in the open! The exact opposite of Elizabeth's notion!"

Elizabeth caught the idea, "No king would want work of unproven value."

Stephen embellished. "This Dario could dull the frames down, do what he must to make the concept work."

"We are depending a great deal on Dario." Elizabeth cautioned.

Kirke added, "We've heard nothing from him. How do we get him?"

Poore divided himself from them with a darkling grin. Almost coldly he demanded,

"What does he look like?"

Kirke could not speak.

Elizabeth simply pointed to the mask, *Sirmolo*.

CHAPTER FIFTEEN

November 1752

Aware that the service waited upon his arrival, Gilbert Worth walked smartly down the center aisle of the church and assumed his seat in the first pew. It was the Dowland pew, never relinquished on the death of Charles.

As head of the two great properties of Sippicon, Dowland Farm and his own, as an heir to Dowland's estate, as the sustainer and a member of the family heading the list of the Elect, Worth had never sat in any other place. Besides, he was an elder. Elders served for life.

Gil had been named to governance of the Presbyterian Church after his first year in America. Quickly, he had learned to despise Sweetwood's minister, Annanias Hudson, and as quickly had left the Session so as not to taint his picture of the Deity, which was pleasantly abstract and nicely suited to a life devoted to reason. Only after Reverend Hudson's bleak death had Worth reassumed his responsibilities to his neighbors and to the Synod.

Sweetwood's new minister, Mayhew Low, and his wife, Dorothy, rated Worth's loyalty not only for Low's fresh viewpoint but also for Dorothy's divine silence about the circumstances of Hudson's demise. And while the young Mrs. Low's witting dumbness did not have to be bought or otherwise expensively maintained, Worth's gesture of regular attendance supported Low in his unorthodox proclivities and preachments. Hence Gil's consternation about his tardiness.

Without the staunch blankness between Dorothy and Mayhew about what had actually transpired the night of Hudson's misalliance with Elizabeth, any par-blind investigation would link Silent Fox with the dead minister's mutilated corpse.

Cooper, the tither, the Town's Eye, as he was commonly called, on the witness of Mayhew and his wife, Dolly, as she was affectionately called, glibly put down the cause of death as '*mortal wounding by a transient*.' This deposition sedulously construed the corpse sans tongue and intestines (and its silver shoe buckles) as evidence not of murder but of manslaughter, pending evidence that could either justify such thorough battery or lay at the doorstep of God or of the Devil this undesired excitement in Cooper's placid jurisdiction.

And while The Reverend Mr. Low was protected by his discreet wife from any knowledge of who may have been Hudson's executioner, the new pastor was aware of Hudson's crimes and thus he disregarded at no cost to his conscience the peremptory justice God had dealt the cleric-run-amok.

This day, the fire burning in his vitals sent Mayhew Low up the pulpit steps without Bible or notes when the Order of Worship yielded to the sermon. Dolly Low, so large-souled with Elizabeth in the terrible dawn after Hudson's passing, caught Gil's eye from her place across the aisle not in the slightest damaging their composure.

The interior of the white-spired church declared the Calvinist ideal. Walls of Jasper-blue, mouldings and wainscot of pure white, windows of clear glass, cushionless pews and side chairs of ageing cherry and mahogany, and a floor of random-width pine shivered the soul. The Communion table, of spare use, sheathed in snowy linen, supported a cross forged locally of iron and was flanked in the cold season by baskets of evergreen boughs. Heat was found in the light, the Word, and the words of the preacher.

"You should ask my resignation if I quote from the Testament this morning." Mayhew coolly outwitted the congregation's collective gasp. "I would ask withdrawal from membership of any who would expect that I make Scripture the struts of today's homily."

Gil wished intently that he were stationed at the rear of the church to enjoy the sight of Sweetwood scandalized. The grim, red-eyed silence rewarding Low's opening filled Worth with perverse joy. Hanna at his side would have helped immensely as a sensor but she was at home with Moses whose unexplained presence in the pew could bring down Low's ministry. Dolly's droll eyes were Gil's only source of contact and Gil took from them that this was to be a significant preachment.

"It is not my plan for any Sabbath to abuse Holy Scripture as a sugar syrup with which to dose you with truth. My message, coursing your veins from the womb, is self-evident. It is a spoken prayer, an audible meditation. We do not need to throw a rope around the Redeemer to justify our thought. But if we think and think clearly - it is my idea that He will smile on our works. Hear me!"

Dolly's eyes closed and her hands clenched. Her tight, hay-colored curls trembled. Gil remained straight and still as a goad to the congregation behind and flanking him. He breathed deeply of the fresh wind Mayhew Low dared to let loose.

Low's style over the four years since Hudson had swaggered in the pulpit had been limpid and inoffensive, cooling with a gracious humor the fever of a village reeling from sudden change: its first family decimated and shadowed by mystery, its notable clergyman killed in his pasture, a girl of the parish gone mad and stung to death in her apiary, and the odd exodus and then the migration home of the local Indians.

Low had been quick to plumb the depth of Sweetwood's villagers. War with the French and the trend toward land speculation in farthest Pennsylvania were peripheral matters. Life was strictly local.

Low found his fuel there. "If I have ever been tempted, it is to be a Congregationalist!"

Low's confession, thrown among them like a snake, caused the appropriate reaction. The people pressed away from him against the hardwood, aghast. Gil crossed his legs and smiled at the shiny toe of his boot.

"It is they who have the foresight, nay, the brains to oppose openly the persistent, unflagging, undying attempt of the Crown to set upon this Continent a bishop of royal appointing and little-by-little to drag money out of all denominations for his support!"

Coughing told of relief, their disengagement intact.

"Such was attempted with the Presbyterians in Scotland and we all know what became of the offending King Charles the First. All that aside, I think not ill of the Papist!"

Gasps. What had happened to their bright young man? The man whose stipend they laid out with pretty good grace. Men had been flogged, banished, burnt alive, drawn and quartered for saying less. They leaned forward for signs of drunkenness, of strain. Was the manse haunted by the unhappy ghost of Low's predecessor?

"I think not ill of Anglicans and Episcopalians!"

Grumbling became audible.

"I think not ill of Jews."

A farmer stood to leave.

"Our Savior was a Jew!" Mayhew held him up. "And a good one. Up to a point. It is that point we have reached as Christians!"

The irate landholder was pulled down by his pew-mates.

"I think not ill of Moslems. Or of Buddhists or of the Hindu."

Real concern crossed the faces of some elders and deacons. One began to take notes.

"I think. I think and therefore my objection is to STATE RELIGIONS rather than to religious people."

Here was food for thought. They quieted only to be stirred like a Flip.

"I would like to think that not only CONGREGATIONALISTS can think! Can YOU think? Can you realize that you must fight with words, fight with whatever force will gain the notice of His Majesty, fight in any way this insatiable slug swimming the seas toward our shores."

Grumbling from the men and whispering from the women.

"'This what?' you ask." His name is, Archbishop! His See is Unlimited Submission!"

Low quickly laid the problem before them. If, as he was attempting, the Archbishop of Canterbury were to appoint and send to America prelates, men of luxurious habit and perquisites, to ordain American Episcopal clergy, the venal connection with the power of the Crown might, as was already happening, siphon members from the Calvinist churches to the Episcopal one. Revenues leaking indirectly from a softening populace or directly from taxes levied on all colonies into the coffers of the state-sponsored religion were the bone of contention. The result of current and anticipated defections toward the pomp and splendor

241

of the English system would ultimately divide and destroy the backbone of New England. With the back broken, the independent mind would die. Their colonial charters which gave room for their self-governing assemblies ran the risk of revocation bringing each chartered colony, Catholic, Episcopalian, Protestant, Puritan, Quaker, right back to where it had begun before the Pilgrims' lonely voyage to the wilderness.

"Most of you, because you were born here, cannot but imagine a citizen speaking his mind, a town levying taxes or not levying as suits its fancy, its plans, its hopes and dreams. You do not know the yoke of the English way. But I do! Just four years ago I quit England for Massachusetts. Very sharp still is the pain of parting but sharper is the delight of our freedoms here. Here, I am a man! There, I was a pawn. Even in the Church! And so, I left first for the Presbytery and then for America. My dear mother's last words were a malediction to Calvinist ears - 'May God place in your hands our dear Prayer Book and grant that you return to the Church of England!' How I still love her! Would that I never had a thirst for my soul! She would have died happy! Would that I never hungered for the exercise of my free will to do the will of the Creator. I would live happy and fat! But I THINK the will of the Creator is definitely not bound up with archbishoprics and the neatness of all paying tithes upward and taxes upward and nothing to show!"

Gil applauded in his heart this recitation of his own emigration discounting the maternal curse. In the family Gil had left behind for America, religious quarrels were dismissed as ploys for kings and the cud of the commoner.

Gil could only wonder why, with Low's undoctrinal approach and after four years of restraint, the minister had chosen this November day to roll out his cannon and shoot it.

Low's good tenor rang through the building. "Any religious incursion is an incursion on Everyman! Thereby, any religious incursion is a sin against humanity let alone against God! Without exception, from this day forward, every dictum from Whitehall must be tested between our teeth for rottenness. Every rotten design must be challenged to the death!"

Gil, neither a public nor a pious man, moved in his seat in his agitation. Sermons like this were fit for the press, fit for the Boston pulpits. They divided communities and fractured families. He knew before Sweetwood tested their king they would test their pastor, grind him in their molars before they would be duped out of an hour's peace or a penny for the sake of an ambitious man. Gil was unsure how quiet the skeletons in the Dowland closet would stay if their seal, to wit, Mayhew Low, placed himself under the scrutiny of people who called themselves saints.

Mayhew's passion evened and deepened. "I talk about a lifetime battle of free men not a fleeting pastime for malcontents. I propose a parish committee open to ALL in this neighborhood to gather and read any information about the proposed American bishops with a view toward taking action and joining the action of other churches against such an incursion. We will meet bi-monthly.

"I pray you, *think*. *I* have thought. I have no choice but to forge ahead. I am afraid in this fight unless you hold my hand. Hold my hand!"

Gil nearly whistled aloud at Low's skill of rhetoric. He wondered why he thought just then of the lobster and the pot. But the bait was excellent and the fisher pure and his hunger real.

Low descended the pulpit steps and walked out of the chancel and stood in the center aisle at the premier pews looking not like an orator or demagogue or minister, but like their son - a man a shade over thirty, slim and white and scrawny-necked, his forehead high and packed with learning, his blue eyes dark with energy. He stretched out his right hand. His fingers, callused from the pastoral pen, were short, dry, steady and open.

Gil stood. He seized Low's offered hand with his right one. What choice did he have if he wanted his choices? Dolly held fast to Mayhew's left. The people responded in stream-like fashion. Some flowed quickly to the fore, some slowly, some stagnated on the sidelines grimly silent, some eddied at the fringes full of comment, most pooled around their pastor holding to one another.

"Well they may!" Gil muttered. He extricated himself without asking the Lows to supper. The minister's frail barque newly launched might suffer from the weight of too close partnership with Worth's unconventional household.

"And," Gil whispered to his Arabian Bay as he mounted, "My first allegiance is to Wakwa."

Gil had the distinct sense of Elizabeth's presence as he passed Dowland House on his ride home. True, it was November, her month, moreover, it was the first, marking her natal day, always a time of ruddy cheeks, rising smoke, blue-gray skies, ashen but discursive leaves, and the glory of apples and quick blood.

Elizabeth had not yet been conceived when Worth bought his property from Charles Dowland who had married well and late. But, in '28, on Gil's and Hanna's return from their honeymoon in England, Beth was born and became to Worth Farm a delayed wedding gift. Reminiscence aside, his feeling this day that she was as close as his sitting room engorged his heart with blood and pain.

Grandee swept up the last hill and made an arc northeast toward the barn. A hubbub greeted horse and rider. Wakwa's impressive black stallion, Locke's blue roan, and two grays belonging to the Stirlings, father and son, were creating a stir among the usual occupants at their Sabbath hay.

Gil tossed his rein to the frantic stable boy, scraped his boots as fast as clockwork and dashed to the kitchen door. "Cooke!" Gil found the housekeeper working at double-speed over dough. "Is she here!?"

Cooke seemed to know what he meant. The slight waver of her eyelids made a negative response. She said obtusely, "Matthew's adding a board to the table in the winter dining hall. Mistress Worth is in the sitting room with the Stirlings and Mr. Locke and the Sachim."

"I'm on my way!" Worth crashed by her table and the hanging pots and pans.

"Marley's with them *at* tea."

Worth's heels dug at the slate. "'AT tea?'"

"*At* tea, sir."

"Not serving tea?"

"She's become engaged."

Gil tossed his hat into a corner of the room.

Then Cooke smiled, not quitting her work. "I baked pink cake yesterday for Master Moses which he gobbled but all these people are a surprise! I thought the occasion called for apples."

"Of course, apples!" Gil stood behind her agreeing, unsure why. "Who's the bridegroom, damn him? I thought we were shed of Carpenter Spinney!"

"It's not Sam, sir."

"Whomsoever!" Gil was hot. "And where are we going to get another Pris! I like her in the house!"

Wiping her hands, Cooke prepared him. "Master, Israel Stirling is the man."

"What!!"

"He's so shaken by the duty of speaking to you, she has no other family, he's spilled his cup twice already."

"He'd better not have." Gil groused lewdly. Then Gil's keen pain from Elizabeth's absence took him over. "I'm very disappointed."

Cooke mistook him. "Oh, Master Worth. She never abused your trust."

"Well, of course not!" Gil was surprised Cooke should bother to say this of Charles Dowland's daughter.

"She never took a minute off her duties or played coquette."

"This is a bit unnecessary."

"Only on her free day would Mr. Stirling walk with her. And he spoke of his interest to Mistress Worth immediately he felt it."

"Israel did?" Worth's conscious mind was pulled this way and that.

"He's going to be a fine doctor. A good provider. And loyal to her."

"You mean to Priscilla."

"Yes. Sir. What else? He throbs with love for her. How good for Pris to graduate from your service in such a happy way!"

"With all his shaking and spilling and throbbing, remind me, Cooke, never to have Israel Stirling perform my surgery!"

Cooke's head bowed so low to hide her laughter, Gil saw the crown of her sheer bonnet.

"With respect, Master, he is the son of your great, good friend."

"That is his saving grace."

"And he was attentive to Mistress Beth. And now she prospers."

"I know." Gil fell into a chair.

Cooke fed him slices of an apple in a blatant quest for information. "It were best for Marley that I know your objection."

Gil chewed the fruit like medicine. "It's a wonderful match. Priscilla Marley is a gentlewoman at her heart. Strong and brave." He thought of the secrets even she shared with him about Hudson. "Discretion is not the least of her virtues. She'll be perfect as a physician's wife."

"But the gentleman?"

Gil swallowed. "He's got red hair."

Cooke raised a questioning right shoulder.

"Well! You know what that means!" Gil's whisper was so harsh Cooke stepped back.

The woman kept her silence.

"What annoys me most is his fear of me!"

Cooke walked toward the door and placed her hand on the latch. "A master as thoughtful and gentle as you have always been to us, sir, cannot be feared."

Gil whirled on her.

"But marked."

November was ordinarily a respite in the life of a farm. The harvest was in. The wood was stacked. The jellies and pickled stuffs stood on their shelves. The smokehouse was hung like a grotto with meat. The cider was pressed. The seeds gathered. November was the time to burrow in. To feast. To make music. To attend to the life of the mind, to correspond with friends before the snow locked the letters in, to spin, to weave, to ply the needle. There were always the animals to care for but without their dependence a farmer could soften. Alert early in the day to their lowing and bleating, by tea dreams had been dreamt and plans drawn. November was the month when time halted. When the board groaned. November was a time to build the blood.

In the few steps down the hallway, Gil lost the sense of the season. He threw open the sitting room door onto the chaos of spring. Wakwa, farthest from the fire, peered southwest over the meadow toward Dowland Farm through a slit in the drape. Stirling sat between Priscilla and Hanna, his knees covered by the excess of their petticoats. Israel paced in front of them. Dire Locke, hands clasped behind him, oversaw Moses at the writing table where the child was absorbed in some exercise with a quill.

Everyone turned, quieted, rose.

"Somehow, I expect I'll skip the afternoon service!" Gil greeted them all at once with a laugh, fighting an undefined weight on his heart.

They surrounded him. He kissed Hanna, embraced Wakwa, shook Locke's hand and held on to it while he searched Dire's wintry eyes. He patted Priscilla's cheek and slapped Mac on the back. He congratulated Israel.

"But, sir...!" Israel's freckled face went red under his orange hair.

"Cooke did us both an incalculable kindness but stole none of your thunder. We will talk somehow and today."

Hanna left with Priscilla to aid Cooke with the meal and the tone in the room changed. Men's voices fuming with news darkened the atmosphere. Gil left Wakwa for Moses at the double writing table. Moses, greatly changed in the year he had lived in Massachusetts, edged off the chair, came briefly to hug his English uncle, his only uncle now, then climbed back and continued to work. His curls were gone. The light brown hair had straightened and turned to jet. His tender flesh held the tone of young muscle built by his life in the woods. Natural and inculcated talents were displayed in his lengthening fingers now holding a pen, more often grasping a knife, a net, a rope, a joint of meat, a stone, the bow and arrow, the hatchet, the branch and vine. His eyes were the same - a canine gold.

"Now, Wolf, I haven't seen your father or any of these fine people, save Mistress Marley, for moons and moons. Before I talk to them, tell me what you are doing?"

Moses looked at Dire who glanced away despondently. The five-year old turned his square of paper toward Gil. On the sheet were matched columns of figures, monetary equivalents, revealing the current values of varied currencies. The native sukauhock and wampum were matched to English sterling and Queen Anne and Spanish dollars, and the livres of the French. Kernels of dried corn and dried beans in discrete heaps on the polished desktop were the makings of his abacus.

"This is astounding!" The uncle grabbed the sheet. "Writing one's numbers is one thing...you did this yourself, Moses?"

Moses caught Gil with his bright glance. "Yes, Uncle."

"These equivalents are correct." Gil appealed to Wakwa.

Wakwa cast a smile their way.

"Dire? Did you teach him this?"

Locke tipped a hand toward Wakwa implicating him.

Moses explained, "Dire says figures should never be written down!"

"Ha! Like him!" Gil waved the sheet at Stirling. "Mac! Take a look! It's not by rote. This boy, my great-nephew, is calculating currency exchanges. With grain!"

Stirling obligingly admired the feat and sat the prodigy on his knee. Excited, lifted out of dreary presentiment by youth's brilliance, Gil joined Silent Fox and the factor. "And what have you got to top that!?"

Wakwa replied wanly, "It is November."

"Oh!" Gil blinked at this vacuous revelation. He confronted Locke almost harshly. "Is this what you found out in Philadelphia?"

"Have some pity, Worth."

"If you'll both pity me." Gil stood with them completing a triangle, their gazes lowered as if at the base of a shrine. "And that heartbreaking boy."

"You will see." Wakwa murmured.

Locke cut into the arc of Wakwa's delivery. "The grab is on for land to the west. Granted, that's not news. But the dirty business is intensified. The French are moving down the rivers and building forts on grounds clearly not marked out for them on any agreement with anyone. They're setting brass plaques in the ground! The English traders of whom I am one, you will not be surprised to note, are losing their shirts."

"But not their eye for acreage."

"You have the gist."

Wakwa intervened. "The Iroquois, the great friends of the English who helped me lose my ground one hundred years ago, have closed their eyes to their English friends of so many long seasons and have declared - neutrality."

"Incredible!" Worth was shocked.

"Astute." Locke corrected.

Gil surmised, "They want to be bought!"

"Not quite." Locke caught him on the point. "They're not impressed by the Crown's lack of a hard policy in this exigency, its neglect, its penny-pinching, the lack of good guns to stave off the French, its lack of protection of them, their rights, and of the suffering English traders. All of which destroys the Trade. The Iroquois are not overjoyed with premature English settlements which eat into their hunting grounds."

"They are a great people of five great Nations." Wakwa intoned obliquely. "Only a few summers before my birth the Tuscarora moved north and made them six."

Locke simplified it. "They are all over the map. With their numbers and their acumen and their very balls they can swing the Continent any way they want."

"Except towards themselves." Wakwa's face was strict. "Unless the plan we are speaking for in Philadelphia comes to the notice of King George and is put into practice."

Gil concluded cynically, "Well! As good as done. Judging from the Crown's sensitivity in the past. Let's drink to it! Beer? Scotch and water? Beckett's favorite, a Flip?"

Dire disregarded his mood. "It will take a year or two before the wheels of the Board of Trade and the Parliament synchronize themselves. By then...."

"By then we could all be killed in our beds!" Gil exclaimed.

Moses looked up. Stirling hushed the huddle of men. Israel paced.

"You speak the truth." Wakwa said, his eyes taking on the shine of pride. "We told all we understand of these matters to the men at Philadelphia. We must now persuade the top men in all the colonies of the merit of the Franklin Plan. There is strong hope that

King George will call a great council in New York. Unless we, the Ninnuock, are satisfied in our rightful desire for a voice in what happens to us, the English stand to lose all to the French."

Worth repeated, "Killed in our beds."

"And so I have joined the neutral stand of the Iroquois."

Worth looked confused. "You have always maintained neutrality. What do you have to do with them? They've been allies of England up till now. They've been your enemies from before Columbus!"

"The times change, Uncle. I must be at that conference with Dire! We of Massachusetts are too small in numbers to be delegates unless we are partners with the Iroquois. We Algonkins make alliance over this one matter."

Gil snorted his disapproval. "Do you suppose the Iroquois will sit idly by if war breaks out officially here between France and England? You'll have to fight cheek by jowl with Mohawks no matter whose side they're on!"

"Uncle, if the Iroquois fight, their neutrality is no more and our agreement with them broken. In that event, I will break with our history and declare for the English."

"The English??!"

"I have no choice."

Gil despaired for his niece and lost his patience. "Forgive an impertinence, but you do say that at every critical juncture!"

Wakwa watched him and carefully queried, "Uncle?"

"You said it to Charles Dowland when you announced you had taken Beth to wife, you said it to me when you wanted to live with two, you said it to Beckett when Waban broke off your marriage to my niece, you said it to Elizabeth implicitly by saying nothing to her at all when you came home, no doubt you've said it to Moses regarding his mother, and now you're saying it to the bloody Six Nations!"

Wakwa stepped a small distance away, moving backward, never taking his eyes from Gil's face.

Worth followed, pressing his point, although Locke ticked his tongue in disapproval. "You've got to admit it! It's a lot to swallow."

Locke stood between them stroking his thin lips with a thin forefinger.

Wakwa said low again, "Uncle, I have no choice."

"At least you are consistent!" Gil remained sharp.

Shuddering from the past dredged up by Worth, Wakwa summoned all good memories of this man. He said, "I do not have a choice...because Kirke Company is English."

Gil instantly saw his own grave error. For a moment his hand shaded his eyes. Worth raked his hair with both hands. "I am sorry! Sorry! I'm always needing to say that to you. Of course, you reminded me of November." He forced his eyes to Wakwa's. "Never will I criticize you again." Then he added, very slowly with a stabbing pause between each word, "I...am...sorry!"

Wakwa stayed aloof. Pain impassible, mutually owned, kept him back.

Dire stepped in. "During this phase of Kirke's building his bank, of his stockpiling precious metals, the Company must have all our support. If you agree, Mr. Worth, that free commerce is the fuel of free conscience, you can see that Silent Fox cannot stand idly by while Kirke plays hide and seek with the Board of Trade. He must put himself in a position to help the Company. A success at the Albany Council could quell war with the French. Usher in a new era. Bring the People into partnership with you colonials and both factions with the King. Preparing for that meeting means preventing full-scale hostilities. It wants time. Thus the neutrality. But at the borders, it will be a long and bloody while."

Gil threw himself into the wing chair.

Matthew entered and served cups of hot cider.

Israel refused any, closed in and started his suit, "Mr. Worth...."

Gil held him there by his coat cuff and looked around Israel's earnest figure and announced to Wakwa and Locke, "I was planning to take Hanna abroad. Leave both farms in Matthew's hands. Shall I abandon that plan? We could be stranded in Europe by sparring navies." Gil was grateful when Wakwa ventured close to him and took a seat. Dire moved toward them postulating, "More likely a blockade."

Israel broke in, "Sir, if might please...."

"Israel, I haven't forgotten!" Worth dismissed him with a trace of annoyance and confided to Wakwa, "I had the idea we'd take Moses with us. Perhaps when we came to Venice...?"

Wakwa's face, impassive in political conference twisted with personal torment. "As you wish. But do not delay your voyage. Nissese, I have a favor to ask of you."

"Anything!"

Wakwa said no more.

It was Dire who explained, "Claude must be gotten out. He is not safe in the Pemaquid house."

"It has been attacked?!"

Locke commented dryly, "I think even the French know better. At this point." Then turning his head fully toward Worth, smoothly, slowly in his predatory way, Dire divulged, "Claude has resigned his post."

"What?!" Gil looked from one to the other. "What of his 'lambs.' His Indians. Priests don't cut and run."

Locke elucidated. "His Indians are gone, gone with Bienville to take possession of the Ohio Valley. Their wives are off to Canada to press the linen of the aristocrats. There are no communicants, there is no Trade. More, the Jesuits are in disarray. They are already banned in places. Venice is one. Plus, the Order is under heavy attack from Rome for its mission-work in China."

"A flop?"

"Anything but."

Gil pressed the heels of his hands into his temples. "The world is such a muddle!"

"It takes surprisingly few men to straighten it out."

Gil grabbed the gauntlet. "What can I do?"

Pleased with him, Locke minced no words. "Get Pere Claude to Venice. Thomas Kirke needs him. And something else...."

"You are both obsessed." Worth interrupted. "Elizabeth's child visiting, hah!, an afterthought, yet, for business...!"

Dire punished Worth with his message. "Kirke's off to China. Claude is quite subtle in the Trade and I would trust him to run the business from Venice while I act on...things here."

"Beth is going to China?"

"No. Foreign wives are not allowed. By special edict from Peking. Thomas Kirke is going to China for a couple of years and...."

"A couple of years!" The idea drove Gil to his feet. "For this she was joined to him with considerable agony of soul seventeen long months ago?!"

Moses started from Mac's lap. Gil, Wakwa, and Dire shrank into silence. Irritated with all three, the elder Stirling ushered Moses out.

"Kirke is being accompanied by Young Poore." Locke pressed on. "Stephen's broken with his father to do so. The Company's adopted him."

"Wait! Wait! Claude is trading in his collar and his country and shattered families strew the globe for - The Company?!!"

"You are getting a sense of it." With lifted eyebrow Locke finished, "As she resides in Italy, your niece requires a man's presence in the house. A priest seemed like a good idea to me."

The four men in the sitting room elected not to lunch. The women pulled chairs up to the kitchen fire for Moses and Dr. Stirling and shared the meal with them and with Cooke and Matthew.

Ignorant of what had changed the mood, Hanna reassured Priscilla, Cooke ladled her a double portion, and Matthew volunteered to investigate. Mac seemed content with the fireplace heat and his lunch of lobster bisque and corn bread. The pies were on their oven shelf bubbling and baking and sending up a fragrance that turned the northeastern room into Paradise.

They heard the front door slam. Shortly after, it opened and closed more quietly.

Priscilla twisted her napkin then darted from her chair. "Excuse me!"

Moses ran after her, reaching the door before she did. Together they stood on the stone step catching sight of Wakwa as he slowly strode the field in Israel's wake.

"What shall I do! What have I done?" Priscilla looked into the eyes of Elizabeth's child.

Moses smiled at the purposeful gait of his father and pulled Marley back into the house by both hands.

"Leave it to him?" She sighed a shaking sigh.

Worth ignored the maid and the child retracing their steps to the kitchen. "Dire, you said there was something else."

Locke was at his elbow. "I should not have said, 'else.' It might be put better - in addition."

Gil's strong, musician's hands clamped the arms of his chair. "Fine. What 'in addition' does Kirke require of me!"

"If there were another course he could take to accomplish his purpose he would never think of enjoining you to do his business. He wants that understood."

Impatient for the revelation, Worth sustained The Company's aggression. "It is understood."

Locke sat. He crossed his legs. He looked Gil straight in the eye. "Kirke wants you to use your influence in Lords in his behalf. The Crown wants to knight him. They may even go so far as to create him an earl. The Company will not have it."

"Not?" Gil crossed his arms and pressed against the soft back of the wing chair. "No one ever threatened me with a knighthood! Or an earldom. What's Kirke's trouble with it?"

"Surely that is apparent. He will lose his independence entirely. The honor implies impressment into a brotherhood of British wealth and blue blood. Elevated, Kirke cannot think a thought different from the Crown's and not be a traitor! To follow his lights would land Kirke on the gallows in a year's time. Less."

"Is he a smuggler?"

Locke shot back, "We are all smugglers! The East India Company are smugglers. Sanctioned ones. If the King bows Kirke's head and claps that sword upon his shoulders, Thomas Kirke becomes an adjunct of the Crown less free than any fish monger in the street."

"You make your point." Worth said brusquely, considering his lineage.

"My point is yet to come! This is a life and death matter. Please, understand. They want to cut Kirke off. The East India gentlemen are envious and suspicious of his smooth sailing and his world-wide interests which are Byzantine in their complexity."

"They want a chunk of it."

"They want it all. Now..." Locke joined his fingertips, "...to gun him down in a Venetian alley is quite workable but then they don't get at the House itself."

"Unless they get you."

"Or Elizabeth."

"This coil!"

"Thus his petition that you scuttle the thing in Lords! Never deceive yourself that it would be good for your niece to achieve such pale power as Kirke's elevation would bring. The King and his ministers don't care about a half-Irish, unschooled ruffian and his nimble-fingered, idealistic, colonial wife. They've been after Thomas Kirke and all he has for years and they're getting closer as war with France in America bursts upon them. They don't like my gnawing at them about passing a law, or, at the least, handing down an American trade policy that will stick! More than they want Kirke dead, they want him in their pocket. Let him perform the labor and drop the fruit into the Royal treasury like a toady. Then put him out to pasture in some countryhouse. And *that* would kill him."

"But I hardly know anyone anymore!"

"With respect, your brother has inherited a seat in the House of Lords!"

"Ha!" Gil let go a puff of air at this effrontery. "The Commons have the pull with the Throne these days in any case."

"Therefore, sir, the lower house must not get a whiff of this sublimation otherwise Kirke's cause is lost. Lord Worth has only to influence his peers against it. He is, above all else, your brother."

"He thinks I'm an ass or worse for living here."

Dire's lips pursed. He looked at the golden harp, the books, the gorgeous rug and then at Gil. "Surely not. And better if he does. It would taste sweet to Lord Worth then to talk down this investiture. Whisper it to death. After all, Kirke is an inconvenient relative for him to have socially and possibly a dangerous one considering the times. He might consider your hint to him a great fraternal service and take you to his bosom."

Gil waved the unappealing prospect away. "Can't I just introduce you?"

Dire's eyelids lowered. "What do you think your brother's confreres would make of my pedigree, English Jew and Welsh Baptist?"

"Foolish suggestion."

Dire's cool eyes flared. "You are called 'Honorable' just for living, Mr. Worth! You were *born* to the task."

Worth's mind wandered the family lore - Romanized, then Christianized Britons shattered and scattered by the Saxon onslaught. Arthurian in their stance against the invaders, the family did not compromise their blood or end their quest until, with the Vatican's whisper in their ear, they served the Saxon House of Wessex against the Viking horde. Later they served Wessex kings. Drawing the line at Danes succeeding to the throne, Worths backed William's claim and, near their home ground, helped the Norman change his name from Bastard to Conqueror. In William's cause, the broken family, carefully preserved in far-flung places, was swept together and restored like a cup of fine clay. King William named them barons. English barons made it their business to rebel. Runnymede came to mind.

Dry-throated, Gil responded. "I will try."

"Succeed. So much floats on the accomplishment of your mission!"

Gil quit the tall chair and sought the solace of his harp. He held its forepillar and observed, "There is planning to be done. I must have much information from you or muff the job. It's going to take time."

Dire bit down hard. "Kirke's pushing for a January departure."

"Next January."

"This January."

"This coming January!? January '53?"

"Possibly late January. As soon as your boat arrives."

"How can I book passage, notify family in England, pack, and...."

"No need. If you're willing, you and your party, including Claude, will travel aboard a new ship of Kirke's built on that island Wakwa secured him."

A flash of pride gave way to objections. "But the season! Hardly what I had in mind for Hanna."

"Kirke's aware of the grave responsibility. You'll sail in the flagship of a fleet of three. You'll have the wind behind you, plenty of stores, comfortable quarters, three good captains, a crack crew, including a Florentine chef, and...."

"And?"

"I hesitate to mention...it is free."

Gil seemed to take tarnish in the firelight.

"You are family."

Gil assessed the factor with eyes murky as algae.

Dire waded through these marshes with caution. "The Merriweather will carry a thousand ton burden of seng and shingles and other items. And eighty cannon. There is no monetary justification to let staterooms. And you would be doing him a great courtesy. And...."

Gil smiled at last. "And?"

"There is the matter of Jeanette."

"Matter? Something else? 'In addition'?! She's still settled with Beckett, I presume."

"Correct."

"She is still your wife?"

Dire's face barely changed. But it changed. "She needs looking in on."

"I draw the line. I am not visiting Beckett on any account. Not even yours. Or Kirke's *or* Elizabeth's. You have no idea...."

"I do."

"You cannot possibly."

Locke turned silent, broke away like an iceberg, took to the colder part of the room. His narrow shoulder brushed the drapery, which swayed like a woman's skirt.

Worth stood still, thinking with pain of some need of Hanna's possibly prompting an indiscreet confidence about her miscarriage.

"The settee." Locke quashed false deduction.

Gil looked aghast at the tattletale couch sporting its new upholstery. "That's all?"

"No. It made a confirmation."

Gil's mind scrambled for Locke's connection to his intimate biography of three and a half years before. "Jeanette."

"Precisely." Locke poured both of them Claret. "Beckett is a lonely man and a drinker. But in time, he might be useful in some legitimate capacity. He owes me and The Company an enormous debt of gratitude for the survival of his son and of his line under Jeanette's care. Besides, his loyalty to England is unquestioned. Very useful to Kirke."

"And Jeanette's loyalty?"

"The Company is her country." Locke passed the stemmed glasses. "All Kirke desires is that you make a social call on the Esquire. Verify that all is...." here Locke chose his way carefully, "as it was arranged to be."

"Kirke wants me to spy for him?"

"I don't favor that word." Locke wrinkled his aquiline nose. "Let us simply say that Kirke is expert at keeping open communications with all parties, all factions. You speak French. Jeanette speaks French. Claude *is* French. When sensitive messages must be relayed...it is essential that there be no break in the chain."

"The chain being attached to what?"

"Mr. Worth, there are Frenchmen of wealth who will outlive their nation's claim on America. I don't believe things will go

France's way. Their enthusiasm, their gallantry, should not be wasted. It is an exciting time."

Gil gratefully sipped the wine. "Too exciting for me! Just this morning in the church, the minister advised a rebellion against the King on account of a scheme by the Archbishop of Canterbury which promises to outdo all the land speculators and merchants and Indians and Frenchmen combined."

Locke snapped alert. "I want his text."

"He's not suicidal, Locke. He didn't write it down!"

Their joining in laughter over this reference led Gil to say brightly, "We have the wedding of Priscilla Marley to settle. We could have Low up here!"

Locke took this for his acceptance and downed his drink.

Worth rubbed his hands over their minor espionage, went to the rack for his coat, and coaxed Dire into the autumn bluster.

Israel slowed his steps at the farm's northwest quarter, which had turned, now that it was chill weather, into brambles and poisonous berries of scarlet.

Wakwa was soon beside him. "Twice I made the discourse you desire with Gilbert."

"I don't envy you." Israel kicked at the clods of dirt around sun-bleached markers of the projected lodge - an undertaking put off for lack of time. The unbuilt meetingplace for statesmen of many cultures awoke the young doctor's manners. "Sir!"

Wakwa smiled secretly.

Israel enquired, moodily polite. "How did you fare, Sachim?"

"Well. You saw for yourself, I kept both wives." Wakwa was suddenly absorbed in tracking the dimensions of the future walls of the building. "For a beautiful season."

"But Mr. Worth won't let me talk to him!"

"You gave him no warning. Now you have stormed away, you are not near enough to him to speak."

"You saw him put me off!"

"My English uncle was occupied with matters involving the lives of many."

"He was rude."

Wakwa repeated. "You gave him no warning."

"He hates me!"

"Gilbert Worth hates no good man. He is quick. And quick to anger."

Israel looked across to Wakwa wondering how he should find comfort or courage there. "You saw how angry he is with me."

"And with me! You who have not injured him but helped him should feel much braver in his presence than you do."

Israel seized hold of Wakwa's last counsel. He dropped the topic of Gilbert Worth and walked with Wakwa through the phantom first floor of the meeting hall. He had viewed the architect's drawings. The building was designed with two storeys, as well as an upper promenade with a tower-like enclosure, and a complex cellar, chimneys up the center and at both ends. Rooms on the upper levels without fireplaces were to use the new exterior German furnaces for heat. Skylights would capture the sun. The dome of the greenhouse erected in the days of Wakwa's marriage to Elizabeth etched the gray sky. "Another of his follies!"

Wakwa turned his collar up against the wind. "We are asking him to cross the cold ocean in winter."

Taciturn by nature, Israel's suppressed words were robbed of emotion by the time they escaped him. "I could see to it. Oversee the construction. I rebuilt my father's barn."

Both men stopped over that, the recollection quite fresh of its latest use as Elizabeth's sanctuary.

Quietly, Wakwa instigated ideas. "And the Littlemaid? Your Priscilla?"

Israel looked to Wakwa's soft, figured shoes. Then tenderly, "We'd have to marry before the Worths went away. Nip her preparations. Pris could continue work. At least till they get back. Why not? It is unfair to Mr. Worth to make him hire someone in her place all of a sudden. And I...I could settle father here. There'd be Matthew and Cooke to bolster him. I've got to make progress. I've got to concentrate. I could study at Dowland Farm. And be of service. Sandwich could be boarded up. Sold. Rented out. Turned to flax and worked." Shyly, Israel faced the Indian.

"Eatch keen anawayean. Let it all be as you say. But first you must share with Gilbert what you have shared with me!"

Beyond Wakwa, Israel saw spidery Locke and fiery Worth half-pushed, half running toward them in the risen wind.

It turned into a gala evening. Israel proudly drove the cart down to fetch the parson. Gladly, gratefully, Mayhew and Dolly escaped the manse for the Worths' hospitality. Wakwa kept Moses close, telling him softly in two tongues to be happy for love. Mac ate and drank his fill, young with the prospect of his family's resurgence after many widowed seasons. Locke supped on the minister's perspective as a hungry man might down a chop. Cooke and Matthew served with flair and friendship seeing the withered household becoming taut with life. Hanna looked beyond the company to the sitting room imagining it crowded with wedding guests - glad to override with laughter the sorrows she had lived through there.

Gil raised the toast to Marley, once the Dowland's maid and a prime witness to Hudson's sins. "Braver than any ten soldiers, purer than any ten saints, prettier than any rare rose, I salute Priscilla, the maiden and the bride!"

By morning, the place buzzed with preparation for epic journeys - marriage, mercy, war.

CHAPTER SIXTEEN

December 1752

"Juhetteke!" Wakwa tore the call, "Fight!" from his middle and hurled it into the throats of his audience like a hatchet.

Wakwa was using the Nickommo, traditionally a time of reunions and fattening and jubilation and priestly ritual, to jolt the gathered tribes out of a pacific state of mind. Because they had honored the Treaty of Submission to the English since the days of their grandfathers, they had not disciplined their will toward the destruction of an enemy.

The spacious longhouse, annually constructed for the winter feast, held a thousand. Two hundred feet in length, lofty, it normally rang with the clamor of copper bells and laughter and applause as each celebrant earned his seat with dancing and gifts to the needy. Money was lost and won in convivial nights of gambling with rushes and plum stones. The hosting sachim welcomed and blessed his guests before the outdoor games and struck the keynote of that year's feast with talk that lived in the ear until the next winter.

Today, the speaker was Who-Waits, the elusive Black Fox, a man of peace, a conciliatory man, or so the tribe and their guests had thought. He was waiting no more. The first word out of his mouth as the sole sachim of his tribe was - Juhetteke!

Ten hundred sat in a silent test of the man not yet forty. He was blessed with an open charm and good looks and ability with foreign tongues and people. He not only saw the trouble threatening the Ninnuock but also, it was rumored, had an appetite for it. And here they were at his feast.

This great occasion had been anticipated like an elixir, tribes from all over flocking to Twisting River, dances rehearsed, money and benefactions ready, emotions high. The assembly saw Wakwa's family, his stately wife, Tame Deer, older than he was, and next to her, his daughter and son by her, and his half-white son, guarded by a score of men. The guards around the family of the great man of the Massachuseuck chilled everyone.

The day was cold. Snow whitened the skies but did not fall. Wakwa looked at his skeptical tribesmen and his relatives and at his neighbors and their headmen and pulled Elizabeth's scream from his gut, "Fight for me! Fight for our life! Fight for right!"

Dressed like a god he was, robed in tokens of power. Doeskins flowed like a falls from his broad shoulders to his knees. His legs were wrapped in the softly napped skins. His high mockussinchass were stiff with black and white money dripping in excess from his calves and clacking a harsh music when he moved. Seductive, responsive fringe fell the length of his person when he raised his arms in his passion to persuade them. His hair, not sullied by a single gray strand and grown long since his peaceable mission to the Indians in the northern woods, spread gleaming black. Eagles had died in the making of his headdress, as had a stag. But the element of his costume that grazed their hearts was a mantle of strowd, superb red English trade wool cast over his breast and backward reaching behind to his heels.

The Ninnuock listened, rapt, to his recitation of history and of current events, his connecting the past to the present and that to days not yet dawned - days of proscription or of mastery - the choice was theirs.

The choice was always the People's. The Ninnuock chose a leader and then they chose by his virtues, day-by-day, whether or not to follow him. This was their notion of government.

They listened for bitterness; they would not follow a man who had undergone such trials as Wakwa's and had emerged soured on life. They listened for avarice; the Massachuseuck Sachim, the young successor to shrewd, affable Waban, was rich. He owned and bred horses, alien animals of ancient, priceless bloodlines. The man had ties to blooded and wealthy Englishmen, to the House of Kirke itself. The very King of England had recognized a claim to thousands of acres of land in the name of Wakwa's mixed-blood son. They would run him out if they detected greed on his part for yet more land to the West as the French and English hunger for land was driving them all to the edge of war. They listened for deceit. A man who had risked all for peace and was now pushing them to risk all for war could be thought at least inconsistent. Had he been obedient to his late Sachim and a servant of the People? Had he lost his favorite wife for their sakes or was Wakwa Manunnappu so hungry for power that his foxy claws had torn his own household asunder?

But to listen to him! To his voice! It would have held beauty if it had spoken curses. It spoke nothing of the kind. Wakwa's was a call to discipline, forethought, planning, to development of their bodies and their minds. Theirs was to be a life of hard training for the taking of life and hard work to avoid the necessity of taking it. He reasoned with them sharply without fanning hate about the forces spoiling their way of life. They placed their trust in him for that.

Wakwa's grave, careful father, Pequawus, sat behind him, his eyes displaying his approval. Awepu, Wakwa's cousin, named for calm weather, sat behind him, always behind him, always calm, always on his mark with a gun. Behind Wakwa was Kirke's factor, Dire Locke, a proven friend, the sallow-cheeked, thin-lipped supplier of what was needed. Behind Wakwa was the golden man, Worth, the Englishman who, with a German fowling piece, had killed two Indians to keep the young sachim alive. The four, so different from one another, shared scars on account of Wakwa's past daring and yet they looked at him with reverence. There was no sidestepping it. Wakwa was Manittoo - he had gods in him and he would be followed.

"I ask you to wait with me but not to sleep! I ask you make your bodies into iron to protect your tender hearts! I ask you to seize between your teeth the Plan of Union and if it crumbles, I ask you to strip away the life of any enemy to our dominion. Train with me! Wait with me! Walk with me! Hope with me! Pray with me! And, if I call - FIGHT!"

The men found themselves on their feet howling the timeless battle cry, "JUHETTEKE!!!"

The noise suddenly ceased. At the height of the tumult, a great creature stepped through the doorway stealing all sound. Streamers of feathers were wound in his hair, fixed to his naked shoulders, wrapped around his narrow waist, and tied to his legs. Bells circled his ankles and wooden clacks covered his fingertips, and his right hand gripped a rattle. A herald of unity, Waban's second son, Nuppohwunow, soared from a standstill and hung in the air like a falcon before deigning to dance on his feet.

Four riders, Gil and Hanna, Dire and Moses, dashed east the next day from the Massachuseuck village. They were bound for the coach waiting to take them to Plymouth Harbor. In the unkind breath of the late December dawn, Wakwa stayed at his door with his wife and children of pure Massachuseuck blood.

"You will miss your harp!" Wakwa said to Worth as they parted, his gratitude for Worth's sacrifices drowning fuller speech.

From Grandee's back, Gil touched a gloved hand to Wakwa's face, "I will miss *you*!"

Qunneke groaned when Wakwa lifted Moses out of her arms and placed him firmly in front of Worth. A small sword in its scabbard jutted back from Moses' hip. His coat and breeches were of wool the color of a black plum and lined in damson silk. The ruffles of his white shirt were partially obscured by a waistcoat of fawn-colored damask and his white hose were lost entirely to his tall boots. His cocked hat, the hue of his coat, sported a citrine plume.

Tame Deer pressed close, captured Moses' hand and poured the pudding of her sorrowful voice against his fingers.

Gil asked of Wakwa, "Bring her to Plymouth! See us off!"

"Matta. I must stay here. We practice our moves on the open field."

Gil was displeased. "Moves? What moves are those?"

"Fetching off heads, Uncle."

Gil snapped erect at the frightful image.

"As for Moses and me...it might go hard for him if I did not board the ship and sail with him. It would be painful for him to leave me on the shore."

"I see!" Gil wondered for whom it would be more difficult, the father or the son.

"Hawunschech, Muckquashim!" Wakwa placed a hand on Moses' knee. "Take care of the fine clothes your Uncle Gilbert has provided for you. Remember - inside them you are the same man you are by Twisting River."

Moses caressed his new coat.

"Wolf, your hunt has begun earlier than it does for most boys. Someday you will return to me and teach me the wonders you are about to learn."

Moses leaned down and hid his eyes against Wakwa's hair.

But Wakwa sat him straight. "I lay on you this charge - that you ask the priest, in my name, to give you the tool which learned men use to unlock many strange and beautiful secrets. Give Pere Claude this belt as a token for teaching you the tongue called Latin."

Wakwa unravelled a broad money belt from around his forearm. It was splendidly made with dangling fobs in geometric patterns and loops of tiny, white, whole, perfect, perfectly matched shells from the South strung into tinkling tassels. He invested Moses with it, resting the heavy thing over one shoulder and across his breast like an honors sash. "Come back, sweet son, the master of what you learn over the sea."

Moses swayed but the encumbrance settled. He pierced Wakwa with gold darts from both eyes.

"Say!" Wakwa pressed Elizabeth's son.

"Nosh, will you really fetch off men's heads?!"

CHAPTER SEVENTEEN

Winter 1752-1753

They hurried out of the woods, stopping briefly at Worth Farm to take their leave of Mac and to trade their mounts for the coach that stood poised for flight at the end of the path. Priscilla clambered inside with the Worths. Israel, muffled to the eyes, mounted the box with Matthew.

Magician-quick, Dr. Mac tucked a gold coin into Moses' fist. "Fair voyage and get the most you can outa this!" The door slammed shut.

The coach rumbled south down the gravel road, past Dowland House, and picked up the Post Road at the tavern. At a crack of the whip Worth's pair of Cleveland Bays opened up turning them seaward.

The frozen, hard-packed, highway made a fast track and except for impediments such as stray swine, an abandoned carriage in their lane, a flimsy bridge crossing a marsh, and a pause for watering, they might have reached Plymouth Harbor in two hours not their dismal three hours, twenty minutes. At each successive crisis or slow-down, hog-related or not, "Sack the hog-reeve!" rang from their throats. Ultimately, they crossed the twenty odd miles to the site of the Pilgrims' landing. From the last hill they saw the bowl of the harbor floating white ice.

Speedy embraces, a few glancing tears and last minute instructions freed Hanna, Gil, and Moses to the protective factoring of Dire Locke. He set his hawk-eye on the crewmen from the *Merriweather* who stowed the luggage and the precious human cargo into launches and rowed like madmen to the ship moored three quarters of a mile out.

"It looks like Venice already!" Gil hailed the merchant ship touched with gilt and yellow and black paint and snapping with parti-colored pennants in their honor.

"A bear!" Moses shrieked, sighting a tall round figure wrapped head to toe in shaggy, brown fur and pacing the deck.

Dire almost smiled, liking this beginning. "Pere Claude waits upon you!"

Hanna tore off her travelling mask, opened her arms and laughed, "I want to bring everyone!"

Locke watched her from the recesses of his hood. He saw how she was related to Elizabeth, how Gilbert Worth could cleave to her and her neighborhood and, how disappointed Michael Beckett must be.

Contemplation sank to the bottom like lost treasure. Human tissue thrilled to the ringing of the rigging, the friction of wood married to the waves, the whispers of sails, men's voices cutting wind and water like the Sirens.

Ropes as thick as Moses' thighs lashed a case of stairs snugly to the side. Seamen stationed at intervals handed Dire, then Hanna, safely up. A burly arm lifted Moses away from Gil.

"Watch out for him! He's a real, live prince!"

The sailor proceeded confidently up the side.

On deck, surrounded by their trunks and bandboxes, Locke introduced them to *Merriweather's* captain, a Welshman by the name of Leopold Jones.

While Jones was occupied in the opening pleasantries with his passengers, Locke transferred a pouch of documents to Claude de St. Aubin. Moving in close, he murmured, "The minute you see Kirke, tell him to ship Worth's wife two pair of every select rose bush he can get out of the Chinese. Do not fail! He can take the bow. Just make sure he gets it done!"

Claude raised an eyebrow. "Thomas knows nothing about roses!"

"Then get him to set Poore on the project. It will not be without consequence."

"Tell me!"

Locke pointed to his temple. "It is not here." Grasping Claude's plump warm hand with his cold, thin one, he pushed it against his narrow belly. "It is here!" Dire disembarked after issuing orders to his sub-factors and briskly showing *Merriweather's* guests the way to their quarters.

Shortly after, the flagship weighed anchor and caught the following wind. She skated free then bucked and pitched. Her figurehead, a woman with doves in her hair and a determined chin, sprayed seawater sternward. Finding her channel, *Merriweather* steadied and glided like a tern, to east.

The cold bit them hard but the Worths and St. Aubin suffered the leave-taking with Moses from the quarterdeck. The boy watched the land shrink as the water grew. The harbor buildings scattered into foam flecks. People were no more. Gulls whirled away from the ship screaming warnings of what lay before the prow. When land disappeared entirely, Moses' skin took a green cast. Gil carried him below.

Pushing the limits of the contemporary naval architecture, rooms were strung like beads along *Merriweather's* sides as on the arc of a wishbone. The Worths' quarters were leeward and hearkened back to the longrooms of old where a whole day's activities could comfortably pass.

Gil set Moses down gingerly on a bed of polished pine built Scandinavian fashion attached to the inner wall. A panel on its open side could be drawn up and latched in place making a safe haven in heavy seas. The mattress was thick, the pillows plentiful and soft. Yellow velvet drapery hung by brass grommets and hooks, and easily fastened back, transformed the bed into a divan for use in daytime.

Gil sat at Moses' feet, Hanna at his head. Silent with the wrenching from earth to water, each observed the walls of a hardwood unknown to them. Full-length mirrors framed in gold created illusory space and light. Tapestries stanched the draught and damp. Windows fitted with thick Venetian glass imbued with gold wire could admit air or defend against the aggressions of the ocean. Drawers veneered in larch were built into one wall for a highboy. A table, banquettes, and a settee were bolted to the walls or to the floor. Persian rugs were scattered underfoot for comfort and color. A folding screen of Chinese lacquer secreted two narrow palettes and a table, all wall-hung, creating a private alcove for a nurse, a maid, a child. A cubicle, partitioned on the outside wall where the portholes ranged, served as a water closet.

Hanna absently rose, opened her handcase and arranged her combs and brushes on a maple wood coiffeuse inlaid with marquetry of pinecones. "Thomas is tender for detail. Good portent for Beth."

Keeping his own counsel, Gil roamed toward a carved door. He tried its ornate latch and was greeted not by a passageway but by another room.

"Hanna! We have a suite!"

A drawing room lay before them. Like children in an enchanted castle they explored its charms. A finely made cabinet-front was actually the underside of a bed easily adapted for a night's rest by pulling it down as one might open a secret compartment in a secretary.

Gil discovered along another wall expansive, gleaming doors, which he took to hide a repository for rugs or spirits or dishes or tankards. Tugging the gilded brass knob of one door, he revealed instead a collection of flutes. Astounded, Gil threw every door wide, four in all, each compartment lined with cedar to protect an array of instruments from the ravages of the salt air. There were stringed instruments of every family, the viols, the guitars, the mandolins and lutes. Hung by pegs in the lower section was a plainly made, single-action harp. Its size was small enough for portability, large enough to produce full sound.

Gil stood dumbstruck. Then burst out, "Kirke's knighthood is a fact whether he is elevated or not! I've a mind to recommend him for the Order of the Garter instead of quashing the business." He looked at his wife. "What need does he see? What has he made? A prison for princes? A fugitive's palace? Who's it for?"

Hanna considered. "It is for you."

Gil paled. "Listen to what you've said!"

Hanna passed over the intimation. "Beth has had something to do with this."

"Is her collusion with him so ripe already!" Gil sighed but stepped back to view the collection.

"It is a magnificent hospitality!" Hanna chided. "An act of love."

"Then why do I shudder?" Gil lurched into the adjoining room with the roll of the sea. Remembering Moses, he moved toward the bed to gather him up and show him Kirke's gift. "He's gone!"

With one stricken look toward the glittering windows, they rushed into the narrow hall outside their main door. They dismissed a case of stairs leading to decks fore and aft. A corridor, no wider than a deer path, flush with their vestibule bisected the ship. Of one mind and in silence, Hanna and Gil ran this straight artery to starboard.

They were rewarded by the sight of Claude, chin in palm, elbow supported by the crown of a chairback. Thinking he might be praying, they hesitated.

Claude motioned them into a much different apartment than their own. His was one big room, the walls pocked with rosewood cubes for his books and priestly truck. Rush rugs carpeted the floor under scattered Chinese carpets. A refectory table served also as an altar. A bed carved hauntingly of dark, heavy wood stood out into the space. The duvet was covered in purple brocade.

Claude drew them close to the bedside. "He has been resting like that almost since he came in." The Jesuit's glance wandered to the seat of the chair. It held the money belt.

Hanna felt Moses' forehead. She took up his limp hands and a small ball wrapped in gold paper tumbled to the sheets.

Claude explained, "He likes the candied chestnuts. He could not even bite one."

She glanced up at the priest at a loss.

"He is young! The sea is rough. He needs a cup of hot bouillon and rest." Claude dismissed her fear.

Hanna looked to the child. "We couldn't have waited! This is his golden chance to see his mother before...God knows what." She blushed, "Pardon me, Father." Then she appealed to the priest, "Have we hurt him?"

Claude evaded, "I 'ave stocked zis tub with chickens from Thomas' Pemaquid house. If his Italian chef cannot squeeze out a cup of broth from one, I will do it myself!" Claude saw her eyes twinkling and her lips pressing back laughter. He placed her hand on Gil's. "Take him to rest. He has many weights on his shoulders, does my little Ghilbear! Moses cannot sleep too long. I understand from him that Le Renard would have him fluent in the mother tongue in four weeks time!"

They found themselves in the corridor. Claude shut the door smartly.

Gil stroked Hanna's naked shoulder. He said softly in her ear, "Does it occur, Ana, we have not lain so carefree in a bed since the first time we crossed the Atlantic together?"

"I was eighteen!"

"You are not much older than that now."

"By two dozen years." She scoffed at his flattery.

"A matter of minutes." He insisted.

"Eons in experience."

Worth let that pass although he guessed she had not meant what it meant to him. "Imagine! A year from this coming June marks our *twenty-fifth* anniversary. We've timed this excursion just right. Oh! Timing."

She felt his meaning seep out of him. She kissed his hand. "We will enjoy this voyage!"

He engulfed her determination.

At last, lying on their left sides, Gil commented, "Like two spoons in a drawer."

Hanna let *Merriweather* rock her. "Ahh! To never leave this room! To float forever!"

Gil grunted in thought not in agreement.

Hanna corrected her vision. "Better for us to swim home and ship the world with all its troubles out to sea and let it sink!"

Gil disliked her mood and brushed wet ringlets off her brow. "I've left you...unhappy."

"I'm worried about Moses."

Worth sighed. "He'll come 'round. We're going to England! The land of milk and honey and cows and daisies and music and salons and kings and footmen and lords and the Board of Trade."

"And Michael Beckett." Her voice deepened, darkened.

"A blot on the landscape. I'll give you that. But we cannot let the grand jurist dog our lives. It's what he'd love." Worth looked for her agreement but met only silence. He continued with bravado, "We'll be in England! We'll have the gardens, the countryside, the green." Then he kissed her. "We'll taste the dew!"

Hanna said hoarsely, "You're going home! I'm leaving mine."

"Dear! Just a visit. Just a short while. It's where I first drew breath!"

"Yes! Yes!" Her hand planed his arm. For over a quarter of a century she had known of his existence and known him in the flesh almost that long and only for one long season had he stilled, his vibrant body as stationary as fat, his eyes gone to seed, his husbanding of her blighted. As she wished she had done almost four years before, Hanna put her soul into stoking his heat.

Wondering what he had said or done to produce her passion, Gil received it with a will. After, with only the energy to push stray hairs out of his eyes with little puffs of breath, he panted, "I've a plan. I'll set you like a jewel in West Sussex or in London, whichever you like, it is high season, and I'll trot up to Cambridgeshire to do Locke's errand on my own."

She circled her arms loosely about him. "No!"

He rolled her over like a boy would his sweetheart in the grass. "What's wrong?"

"Nothing! I just thought of his baby."

"Not a baby anymore. Horace is Moses' senior by nine months."

"It's what I mean! He'll have forgotten." Her voice broke.

Gil's face was pinched. "Is there anything else?"

She felt his question like a crop. But she cradled Gil's face as if it were a buttercup. "I wouldn't want...I won't have...Michael can be a stupid man sometimes...he drinks too much and loses all his...."

"Manners?"

"If you like. He can be cruel. I refuse to have him bait you. I do not think you'll disregard his insults again."

Gil rolled away and set himself up on a brace of pillows like a sultan. "A duel! Now there's an interesting idea. I'd win. That'd sink his ship!"

"And Ho's."

"True." Gil studied his hands now folded. He mused, "The boy would probably rather come to live with us. Hmmn! So you want to come up there with me? Don't trust me?"

She laughed and joined him on his high seat. "Not entirely."

Gil loved her for that. He reached for her just as the ship gave a heave. They tumbled from their pinnacle onto the floor. Tangled, tossed, they squawked in pleasure.

Pounding at the door checked them. Hanna tossed him the quilt.

Gil opened onto Claude. "Sorry to be slow, Pater. *Merriweather* jostled us out of a sound sleep."

"Tut! At your age!" Claude closed his eyes and shook his head. "Ghilbert, as soon as is convenient, have your wife visit Moses. She might like to be there." Claude turned away, then turned back. "Imp! In the morning I'll expect *you*."

"I'm not much of a nurse, but I'll try, Father."

"Nurse! I am hearing your confession!"

Claude talked to Hanna Worth from across his bed. He sat on the edge. He had watched her maternal offices, her gentle removal of Moses' clothing, her washing him in fragranced soap, her pulling a nightrail of challis over the child's head and settling it underneath him so that no wrinkle would vex his rest. Her fingers on his temples stroked away a tormented dream. Claude witnessed her kiss Moses' lips.

"The Young Wolf is fortunate in his mothers!" Claude began.

"I am not that, Father Claude. Never that!" Her voice was husky as she began to fold Moses' clean clothes and pile those to launder in a white heap.

Claude kept conversation aloft. "I find it remarkable that you brought no maid along to help you."

"The sea is so easy." She looked back to Moses. "With nothing to do but eat and sleep...."

"Provided one is not nauseous or fearful, or breaking up, or sinking, or attacked by pirates...." Claude fixed her with his Gaullic eyes. Then he laughed.

"Our maid was married to Israel Stirling days before we left. We thought of taking the bridal pair but Israel is studying and running the farms...." Again her voice slipped away. She felt Moses' forehead with her wrist.

"Better you leave Stirling home. A leeching is not what this boy needs."

Hanna looked directly at the Frenchman. "No!" She rose and stirred the copper pot simmering over Claude's brazier. She dipped soup into a cup and brought it to him. "You should take a little nourishment yourself."

He caught her wrist and said genuinely, "I find you remarkable, Puritan woman!"

"Puritan!" Hanna scoffed at herself and drifted back to the kettle. Seated again, she sank a silver spoon into the sheer liquid, observed a shiny island of fat grow denser as it cooled. Then she tasted it.

"Posterior conscience. Do I make myself understood? Posterior conscience deals with the past. I suspect your trouble comes from that, Madame?"

Hanna looked up from the comfort of the broth.

"Some virtue is active. Some inactive. You ask, 'Pere Claude, an example, si'il vous plait!'"

She had not.

"I give you one. Chastity. What is it? An act or an inward cleanness?"

Hanna placed the warm cup against her stomacher.

"*I* am not a Puritan by *any* means." Claude puffed out his puffy cheeks. "If that means a believer in absolute morality. There are Dominicans who subscribe to that. Absolute morality." Claude shrugged. "There are Dominicans who do not. The probabiliorists, a little Latin," he gave a quick smile, "justify not observing a law, natural or positive, if arguments for not observing are weightier than those for observance!"

Hanna choked as she swallowed, because of the motion of the ship she told herself.

"And they go further, these Dominicans, brushing and blowing at the ungainly shape of morality like fussy sculptors over their clay. They say, if the arguments for or against non-observance of a law are equal, then one does not 'ave to observe! You understand the equiprobabilists, Madame Worth?"

She withheld a reply.

"Then there is the master of them all, more than two 'undred years ago, Vitoria...."

"I've heard of him!"

"Non!" Claude was astounded.

"Mr. Beckett...."

"Oui?"

"Our solicitor...."

"Oui...."

Hanna paid close attention to his tone but bravely tried to finish, "He used Vitoria...to try to set a precedent in the land conveyance...to Moses...."

Claude swung his bulk off the bed and spoke as he danced on the impetus of the waves. "Vitoria is useful in that way. But we Jesuits, we who risk the displeasure of kings, of popes, of our flocks, of our brothers in the Church and, I might add, of Puritans, say that an act can be moral, or immoral, or amoral."

"Amoral?" Hanna strained to understand the term.

Claude lumbered toward her. "Oh, Ghilbert has chosen himself a wife! You shall save him!"

"I?"

"You." Claude insisted crossly.

Hanna looked away from him and did not know why she stayed on.

Claude waded with skill across the motile room and lowered himself onto the trunk at the foot of the bed. Very near her, his glance cast modestly to the side, Claude taught her soft-voiced. "If the fruit is not animated and the pregnancy is dangerous to her, a woman may procure abortion, either directly or indirectly."

Hanna stared at the priest.

"If the fruit is already animated and she would die of bearing the child, she may take such remedies as indirectly harm the child and directly aid her."

"If Gilbert...!"

"He did not!" Claude took her trembling hands. "Airault, a Jesuit, holds this opinion. Do you hear what I say? Opinion. Reason. Conscience. Circumstance. Absolute morality itself is an opinion!"

"You believe this!?"

"Vitoria says, 'If an educated man considers two opinions to be probable then no matter which one of the two he follows he does not sin.'"

"And a woman? Does she have this privilege?" Hanna spoke softly.

"Consideration of one's acts is an obligation not a privilege if you are human. And you are magnificently so!"

Hanna pressed the back of her head against the back of her chair attempting to crush the memories in her brain.

"I believe you would die without your honor. Death is not the way of honor in every circumstance." He leaned toward her and breathed, "Nor is life."

She watched him then.

"I believe your honor lies there." He looked at Moses. "You have been caught in the coil of a war that knows no country. You have been a soldier for your family. Does any of what I have said bring your conscience any comfort, Madame Worth?

"Comfort?" She asked, amazed. "The pretence that I have not sinned makes my penance every day."

Claude let a moment pass before he murmured, "If God forgives, surely we humans, his creatures, can forgive ourselves.'" He retrieved his Breviary. "Puritan woman, let us pray."

Claude admitted Gilbert Worth to his room. Night had closed around the ship. Fresh from sleep and a bath, dressed finely for Hanna's sake, Gil's natural hair and his ginger-colored silks sizzled under the lantern light.

Singalling for Worth's silence, Claude led Gil to the bed where Hanna worked over Moses. "She is superb with him."

"Still, we should have brought a maid. A doctor!"

Claude lifted his brows then indicated the large, cushioned chair. "It is more comfortable than it looks. Thomas must 'ave known I would never lie in bed."

"But you must! You must sleep. We'll take Moses to our stateroom! To his own bed!"

Claude rolled his globular eyes. "He's sea sick." Then he watched with satisfaction as Gil slowly bent to the child, wrapping his wife's shoulders then her waist. It was minutes before he freed her. Claude approved Gil's whispering Moses' Indian name. "Muckquashim!" The boy's eyes fluttered open. Claude's heart caught at the effort Moses made to reach for the strong, white hand of the Englishman. Moses' hand fell back never closing on its objective.

Claude flew to the door at another knock. A steward announced dinner with the captain in his quarters.

"Bon! Very festive! Do not count on me!" Claude turned away from him and said in a powerful whisper to the Worths, "You two, go! Go eat and drink wine and sleep it off. Moses will be absolutely fine by the time the sun is up."

Gil suggested, "Can't they send a supper in here?"

Claude ticked his tongue. "The boy will wretch with the smell of food. Go! Go on." He turned on the steward, "And please! More bouillon!"

Captain Jones appeared. Promising the full resources of the kitchen and the apothecary and more, his own valet, he left with the Worths to dine. "We have a surgeon in the fleet. We'll stop and board him whenever you want!" His accent, suet thick and coal dark gave them comfort.

Never ceasing, wind-driven, star-directed, *Merriweather* rode the waves. Claude nodded in his vigil, his heavy eyes seeing the mixed-blood child, the room, all the rooms, the crew, the officers, the Worths, the furnishings, the clean, stout beams in one blink of his eyes. Everyone, everything, rested in *Merriweather's* belly. And she rolled along, unafraid for the fate of her burden as is a woman with child. Her sails soothed them with sighs.

Claude bounced awake. He stood by benefit of the ship's lurching. His brazier had burned out which explained his convulsion. Without the moon he would have been blind. St. Aubin, not a coddled man, was shocked at the cold. He found the hulk of the bed and searched for Moses with jittering hands. Prepared to find a block of ice, he pulled his hands back as if they had been burned. He escaped into the shaft of moonlight and rummaged for his watch, an uncertain thing, but better than the quartermaster's sand glass. Trois heure! He damned his weak flesh for his losing track of time. No stopping the fleet for the surgeon now. And what would he do anyway? Leech the boy? The Jesuit thought of the Worths and of Captain Jones. But what could they do at this hour he could not? Better to let them sleep. Perhaps by dawn the fever would pass. Perhaps.

Claude's pumping heart supplied him heat to organize himself for a fight. He struck a flint, achieved workable illumination, mended his brazier fire and the burner. He chipped a hole in the pitcher's skin of ice and poured viscous water into the porcelain bowl and dipped his face in it, scrubbed his hands, brushed his teeth. He washed his feet. Trembling in the bitter night, he steadfastly removed his secular suit and threw open his trunk and drew out his cassock. He donned cleric's dress, employing a scapula lined with martin to cape his shoulders. He settled the silk cord of his crucifix around his neck.

Foregoing food for himself, he lifted the soup cauldron into place and hacked at the frozen broth with the ladle. He got it simmering in order to have the steam in the room, seeing clearly that Moses Bluehill would not be eating. He went to listen for Moses' breath. The child's chest was still. His shallow reception of the frosted air would not ruffle a chick's down.

With a curse for his bravado with the Sachim's son, Claude de St. Aubin bent back the lid of the case he carried on sick calls. Having no time for probabilities, nor of a mind to lose the boy to the Devil or to death, he ensured the Last Sacrament with the first, a lightning-quick Baptism, Dominican in orthodoxy, Franciscan in mysticism, Jesuitical in resolve. Drops of Holy Water, wads of cotton drenched with oil, salt for the tip of the tongue, and the words of welcome to the Church and of the Extreme Unction mingled. Claude was no party to superstition. But he had learned over years in the priesthood that sometimes, something in the sacrament effected, on occasion, what earthly medicines did not - a peace of spirit - which seemed to call the dying back.

As he cleared away the mess, Claude became sure that Moses had no disease to be sucked out. No compress or concoction could heal him. Moses was the dis-ease. His spirit, hammered thin as foil by his tragedy, glittered wildly through his eyes. In the darkness of the turgid night, Claude watched the thin ghost of the motherless child flaring, struggling against the wind that carried him away from what he knew. Moses burned like a solitary candle. The trouble with candles, Claude realized, was that they burned out.

Like all desperate men, Claude prayed to his God. Lifting his face from his hands, the old priest caught sight of the money belt hanging from a hook. He bowed his head before this swift answer. He had accepted the offering of Silent Fox. His mission was to teach Latin. Claude tugged at the monster chair Kirke had installed and bullied it over the wrinkles in the rug. He swore at Kirke for the work he caused. Then he sat in that chair and reached for Moses' closest hand, his left, and in a voice less musical than tender, he began to sing. He prayed in plainsong, the Latin words clear and easily discerned. So like the chants of woodland men, Claude's antiphon entered Moses' ear. Claude sang an ancient Mass. The Preface, the Introit, The Gloria, the Kyrie. Five O'clock showed on the watch's face. Moses' head turned from the black windows toward the darkness of the wall. Claude turned to the mother of Jesus with a catch in his throat.

Salve Regina misericordiae,
    vita dulcedo et spes nostra, salve.

"Hail, queen of mercy, sweetness in life and our hope, hail!"

Ad te clamamus exules filii Hevae,
    ad te suspiramus gementes
    et flentes in hac lacrimarum valle.

"Exiled children of Eve, we cry out to you, we sigh for you, groaning and weeping in this vale of tears."

Eya ergo advocata nostra,
    illos tuos misericordes
    oculos ad nos converte.

"Then come now, our advocate, turn your merciful eyes toward us."

Et Jesum benedictum
> fructum ventris tui nobis
> post hoc exilium ostende.

"And show us Jesus, the blessed fruit of your womb, after this time of our exile...."

The Jesuit chanted every trope. When it was complete, he continued pouring out the audible incense with another song, "Inviolata, integra et casta es, Maria...." The Latin words, one following another, threaded their way to the rafters and dangled there.

Claude pressed Moses' fist against his forehead. "Lupus Nebularum Sperarat!" He whispered Moses' native name in the Latin.

Day broke the black sky. Claude felt the young fingers quicken; he gloried in their pressure on his paw. He knelt on the bed and clutched the small body, lifting it.

Moses opened his eyes.

"You have recognized the mother of us all. And she has smiled on you!" Claude gathered Moses into his lap and sang on.

Hanna left her husband asleep in their warm bed, bundled into her cloak, and shivered down the hall. Claude's door hung ajar. Singing like she had never heard slipped into the corridor. Her mind and senses told her it was the music of the monastery, the convent. Dread made her push open the door.

"Charmant!" He greeted her. "I am teaching him about the ideal mother."

"Is there such a thing?"

He disregarded her. "I sat here all night wondering about her."

"The Virgin?"

"Non. Elizabeth."

"I can tell you all about her."

"Can you tell me how, if she meets her son again, she will let him go? Can you tell me what will be the voyage back if Moses Bluehill leaves her behind?"

CHAPTER EIGHTEEN

27 January 1753

Merriweather burst out of fog onto the platinum brilliance of London in late January. She and her sisters had drifted bewildered for days on entering the Channel where soundings were taken, mathematics applied, the divider exercised, and in desperation, coins tossed to decide whether to proceed blind to London or to moor themselves off the Normandy coast. Not Welsh for nothing, Jones was leery of wallowing for an indefinite period so near Guernsey and the other forsworn islands in the Channel whose major income stemmed from pirating passing ships perceived to be in opposition to the Crown. Not captain for nothing, Jones concluded tersely, "We'll stay our course." And so the bouncing entrance into the Old World, the landing born of mists like Moses.

The crossing had been enjoyable apart from its beginning. The more Claude sang his Latin, the stronger Moses grew. In fact, after he was up and around, the Worths barely saw him but could always find him in the Jesuit's tow. Moses frequently turned up in the afternoon in the Worths' drawing room interrupting Gil's harp to sing the chant he had learned that morning. Just to grasp onto him for a while, Worth put a quill in his hand and taught Moses to draw the black squares of Gregorian notation on a staff. Hanna bound the resulting manuscript with needle and thread.

The formalities of trade, customs, tariffs, above board and under the table kept the sub-factors busy. Moses, snugly wedged between his great-aunt and uncle on the foredeck, absorbed sights and sounds the more fantastic for his having been so quietly and for so long at sea.

"Claude will stay aboard." Gil murmured to Hanna. "French Catholics are not the fashion in houseguests here. I will send a note to our brother, Cecil, and hope it finds him. We cannot land upon him unannounced like a flock of pigeons."

Hanna smiled, "What will your note say?"

"The truth. Cecil will, of course, not believe it."

And Lord Worth did not. Found at his club by Captain Jones' first mate, Cecil Lord Worth listened to the man's short, strange preamble, testily reached for the sealed letterpaper, unmistakably Gilbert's, read of the abrupt arrival of his youngest brother with his American wife and his half-Indian nephew, and shouted out, "Nephew, my ass!"

Members looked up. Lean, tallish, and gray, Lord Worth scrawled the fraternal response, "Come ahead, damn you!" on the back of Gil's card and swiftly carved his way out of the room of men and chairs.

Within two and a half hours of docking, Moses was being scrutinized along with Hanna and Gilbert Worth in the center hall of Cecil's townhouse.

"Hardly a letter from you in six years, Gib." He clubbed Gil with the odd diminutive. "What have you done now?!" Lord Worth waved his butler into action and the doors to a long, brightly lit salon opened. He commented to Hanna, "You look just fine after nearly a quarter century with the runt of the litter, Sister-in-law. Must be something in the Massachusetts air."

"It is, Brother-in-law." Hanna responded nicely.

Cecil studied the stationary trio in front of him.

Gil, ruing that he had let his English contacts slide, forcing him on his brother's prickly hospitality, introduced Moses. "Lord Worth, may I present, Wolf-of-the-mist He-hopes, a.k.a. Moses Bluehill, my nephew and heir! Moses, Cecil Lord Worth."

Moses, his father's son, bowed deeply after the Ninnuock manner. His clear, young voice piped, "It is my honor, sir!"

Cecil stood graven to the spot. The boy's sun-touched good looks, his cheekbones, his fashionable clothes, his eyes, his eyes of gold, canine eyes, his hair - black - black unnatural, his air, aplomb without arrogance, condescension sublime, and no years on him to speak of, not more than five...."Master Bluehill!" Cecil acknowledged Moses' greeting, then barked, "He doesn't look a thing like you, Gibber."

"It is impossible that he should." Gil responded coolly. "He is in the Dowland line. And the son of a prince of the native people of the Dowland neighborhood."

At that, Lord Worth looked aghast at his youngest brother. "Heir?!"

"Mine and Charles Dowland's. The legacy cost Moses his mother and has changed history. I thought you should know."

His look still fixed on Gil, Cecil pointed to the wide-flung doors. "In!" His glance fell on Moses when the child did not move to follow his uncle and aunt. The peer's peremptory hand and wrist turned, palm open, fingers more graceful in their invitation.

Moses did not budge. Cecil dropped to one knee to get closer to Moses' face. He reached for and held the slender arms. Moses pulled back, unused to the touch of strangers.

Cecil released him but stayed level with him, intent on the secret of Moses' pride. "My wife should have met him!"

Gil asked from the doorway, "And why should she not, Cil?"

Cecil looked up blankly. "I've lost her. She's dead." Cecil turned a hand against his face for seconds only. "I should have written!"

Hanna gave a bird's cry. Gil moved toward his brother and then to his wife. But Moses wormed his hand into Cecil's and walked him at a solemn pace into the sitting room.

Moses only half-heard the adult talk that followed. Swinging his legs as he sat a settee, he concentrated on the house, different from his father's, from Awepu's, from The-Kirke's house, from his Uncle Gilbert's, from sober Dowland House, from the ship. Here was a tall narrow place to live with stairs winding ever upward. He felt as if he were inside a hollow tree composed of polished stone, glass, and plaster, and stocked with silver and silken things instead of nuts and nests. The London-Towners lived like fancy owls, Moses thought and he privately gave Cecil that name, Ohomous.

Gil's arm encircled Moses. "This is much in one day for you, Wolf."

"I like it here!"

"Do you, truly?" Vague disappointment crept into Gil's voice.

"If Claudius were here...." Moses' thought needed no finish.

Gil turned the child's face up. "Like your father you shoot gracefully as a sun ray to the heart of the problem." Gil announced, "It is dangerous for Claude here presently. And your Claudius has another purpose. He is doing your father and the entire family a great service. We must leave before night to sail with him."

Moses asked, "Where will we go?"

"I've told you! I've told you. To Italy."

Moses set his chin. "Where is Italy?"

"I've tried to tell you many times. Here!" Worth rose and led Moses to the fireside where a globe stood on its axis in a stand. It affected Gil that his brother might resort to it from time to time, might spin it to west to get a sense of the Atlantic and how far Massachusetts was from home. "Here we are in London, there's the River Thames, there the Channel where we passed by my family's ground at Heathersley, West Sussex, which we could not see because of the stupid fog, then out into the broad Atlantic and south to the Gibraltar Straits, past the Barbary pirates, we hope and pray. On to the Mediterranean, past the toe and the heel of Italy...."

"It is a boot!"

"The boot is Italy! And then up the Adriatic and thence to Venice." Gil snapped his fingers as if the journey were that easy.

Moses gazed at the landmasses curved over the blue-painted seas. "It is not far away - for a bird."

Gilbert kissed the top of Moses' head. "I wish I were a bird! I wish we were all birds!"

As if he were his father building onto the long house, Moses took measure of the sphere with his fingers. Marking eight progressions to Venice, he worked his way back across the Atlantic in ten to Plymouth. Abruptly, Moses veered away from the orb and the uncle he loved.

"Moses!"

"It is far. Almost as far as we came to England." Moses turned to Gil. "The way to Venice is curled around itself. It is not straight."

"No!" Gil whispered his agreement. "Not straight at all." He reached the boy and held him. "With a good wind it could be accomplished in half the time it took us to reach London. Claude must stay behind to help...Kirke." Gil chanced, "And your mother, Elizabeth!" He dug his fingers into the child's coat. "Claude must stay with her. But *we* will come back. In six weeks. Think, Moses. Would you like to go to see her? See your mother?"

The child stood suspended, his uncle's arm cutting across his chest like the windowsill in Pemaquid over which he had peered with Wakwa. He saw the rocking water, day-bright under the moon, and heard the scraping of his father's voice as he said all he wanted was to go to Elizabeth. *It is all I want. All I want*!

Gil whispered his question, "Don't you want to see her?"

Moses' eyes went molten but, turned as he was, Gil could not see their melting. Moses did not move. He did not speak.

Gil whispered into the silence, "Never? Not this time? Next time? If there is a next time? When!! If you won't come, what shall I say when I bring Claude to her as her helper? I cannot hide that you are here. What shall I tell her? What *shall* I tell her? What shall I say!"

A tear boiled over Moses' lashes onto Worth's hand.

Gil bent, bowed at this sign of a heart he had not been sure existed. "Say yes! Come to Italy!"

Moses twisted to see but the acid of his own tears blinded him to Worth's face.

"Show your Papa the way! You must want to see her!"

"I want...what Father said!"

Gil faced him. "What did your father say?"

"Everything ready!"

Gil's strong fingers hurt the boy's arms even through his thick coat.

Music seethed inside the boy, then issued like smoke. It climbed and writhed in the air.

Then the words came.

Gloriosa dei mater, cuius natus exat pater, ora pro nobis omnibus, qui tui memoriam agimus. O pulchra.

Gil stood away. "What does this mean?!" He meant the fresh denial.

Moses reached into his coat for the small, bound notebook, his hand quick, his tears smearing the black ink of the cantor's text he had scratched down in Gil's stateroom. He sang it over and over like a drowning choirboy as he opened to the proper page:

Radiant mother of God,
 whose Son is the Father,
 pray for all of us,
 who are mindful of you,
 O beautiful one.

He stood quivering in front of the fire with his back to them all. Singing.

Gil was gone.

Cecil mounted the stairs. A book under his arm and a glass of Sherry in hand, he stopped abruptly at sight of Hanna seated outside Moses' room. "Ah! Madam!"

Hanna placed a finger on her lips.

Cecil offered her the wine. She demurred. He took a sip and offered it again. She accepted and drank. They were friends.

"The boy sleeps?"

"He weeps."

"You'll kill yourself keeping up with this thing! This family... tragedy...comedy." Cecil sniffed at the whole affair. "High comedy."

"I hadn't thought of it that way." Hanna reprimanded gently.

"You should have travelled with a nurse for him and a maid for yourself. Are you and Gib in straits?"

"We have plenty, at present, thank you, Cecil."

"What words are these? Plenty? At present? There is foreboding there. It's like something one's solicitor would say!"

Hanna drank deeply of the Olorosso.

"Is it a problem with the natives? They haven't burned you out? I don't wish to offend but I have got to know."

Hanna began to tell him in brief the story from Elizabeth's flight to the present.

"So I have it straight, sister-in-law, the child in my guestroom has legal title to 3,400 acres of American ground?"

"Seventeen hundred until Gil's death."

Lord Worth waved the detail away. "Then I ought to be poking about for a baronetage for him!"

"Just the opposite! The threat of one is at his mother's door. She is now the wife of Thomas Kirke!"

"Not *the* Kirke? Kirke himself?"

"May I tell you?" She mapped it for her influential relative. "Gil and I and Elizabeth have secured our few thousand acres to Moses who has a moral right to them not counting all the lands on his ancestral range amounting to hundreds of square miles! A kingdom!"

"George Two won't like that."

"Precisely, Cecil. What harm it would do to a free people already impinged upon by the English kings, and Gil and myself, and all the colonials, to lay unfulfillable obligations on Moses' back by an honorary title! Or to shackle him through a knighthood for his mother's very rich, very independent husband, Thomas Kirke."

"Who's talking about *him*?!"

"The House of Commons."

Cecil sputtered.

"The Board of Trade."

"Those are Whigs! Those are my friends!"

Hanna simply smiled her summery smile.

The widower scented strawberries.

"We know you have nothing to do with Commons."

"I certainly do not!"

"But many lords are connected with the Board of Trade. You would know how to discourage them from honoring Mr. Kirke."

"This is very odd."

Hanna's blanket slipped down.

Lord Worth swept it up and spoke while tucking it about her, extremely vexed that she sat exposed to January's cold in his hallway. "Odd because most people will trample others to death for a title and you want me to let two fine opportunities slip away! Why, if anyone catches wind of my spurning of fortune, they'll think me a fool, worse an idiot, perhaps decrepit and unworthy of my seat! I'd have to give it over to my eldest. Impossible lad. Then where would I live?"

"You could come to live with us. In Massachusetts."

"You are serious."

"Never have I been more so."

Cecil paced. The rich runner under his feet, the portraits peopling the walls told a tale of loyalty to kings. "If I have enemies, which of course I must, and if they get wind I've scotched Kirke's elevation, his now being connected loosely to the family and all, their noses will tell them falsely that I am a traitor."

"Not falsely." Hanna admitted.

Cecil wheeled on her, drew himself up. "What possessed you to say that!"

Hanna kept silence.

"Let me see." The master of Heathersley retraced her mute train of thought. "If I acquiesce in this wriggling away from public ties to the Crown, if I assist Kirke, a perfect stranger to me, in turning his back on the duties implicit in elevation, I trumpet independence of spirit, let alone of pocket, and that could be construed as treason. If I arrange to free him of his obligation, I am placed in revolution against the monarchy. Against *monarchy*!" He confronted her. "I wish you and my brother needed money." Then his outrage flared, "This other is a bit unfair!!!"

Hanna rose off the wooden seat. Not far from Moses' door, they heard him howl. A hair-raising cry. In the civilized corridor it sounded as if a lion were housed in the neighboring room.

Cecil asked, "Spoiled?"

"Not by his natural parents." Hanna quipped.

"Leave him to me. This is Gibert's fault!" With that he left her for Moses and shut the door.

Cecil stood against the chest of drawers, his arms folded. Moses' keening stopped instantly. He skittered out of the sheets and pressed himself against the headboard. "Better cover up, young man. It's a cold time of the year."

Sweating, Moses obeyed.

"You show good sense." Cecil took a step nearer. Then, seeming distracted by the strained starlight, he pulled his shawl around him and moved close to the window. "I've felt like that, Master Bluehill. Quite a bit like that. Not when I was young like you but recently. I wish I could roar it! Does it make you feel better?"

Moses answered, "No, my Lord!"

Cecil sighed. "I thought not. Then don't do it anymore, there's a fine fellow." At that Cecil approached the bed where a candle stub burned in a lamp. "I want you to tell me anytime you are uncomfortable. Let me know what I can do. There are no people your age in the house. If you wish some I might arrange it."

Moses' eyes veered to his right then they became fixed on his host.

"Not the problem, eh? Never mind! You might still want children about."

Moses shivered.

Cecil sat on the bed. "I want you to do me a favor tomorrow morning. I want you to tell me, starting at breakfast - at which there will be eggs, and ham, and sausages, and a creamed fish, and cakes, and currant jelly, and tea and even coffee - I want you to tell me about home."

Moses moved back.

"About Massachusetts. The farms and the forest. We won't let your aunt interrupt or embellish. I want it straight from you. I've got a decision to make. I depend on your utter honesty. You know the word? Good." Cecil caught up Moses' abandoned nightcap and refitted it on his head. Black, straight-shafted hair slipped like silk across his wrist. "You've seen Englishmen before, Bluehill. I've not touched an Indian till tonight."

Cecil stood stiffly promising Moses a Sherry. When it arrived, Moses was soundly asleep.

Breakfast was arrayed along the short wall of the winter dining room. It steamed and bubbled, cooled and gelled but the talk went on.

Cecil consumed the details Moses provided in answer to his questions. Then he offered, "Not so many hundreds of years ago, Moses, Britons lived around their fires."

"They did not!"

"It's quite true. And strangers came, some better some worse. Some burned and stole, some built roads and walls and baths. And the Britons, some of them, the smartest of them, our family included, survived it all intact. Looked about and chose the best."

"As at buffet." Moses summarized.

Cecil regarded him severely for a moment then turned to Hanna. "He is enchanting to have about."

Cecil ordered his coach for the early afternoon to treat Moses and Hanna to a whirlwind tour of London. He said aside to Hanna, "How will he keep up his Latin?"

"By letter from the Jesuit."

Cecil scowled, "That could be dangerous. Certainly it will be slow. Three weeks up and three weeks down and three weeks up again with the priest's comments and another written lesson starting its route is an improbable tutelage."

"Cecil! It cannot be that Moses lose his mother and Pere Claude too. More, lose him to her! They must remain in contact!"

"Well they should. But in the interim there must be someone steeped in the Classics to help him along day-by-day. We should go to Heathersley. In the country the Catholics are somewhat freer. They keep priests like relics, as it were, of the age gone by. There must be a choir. Masses to be served...."

"Cecil, you are more like Gilbert than either of you knows."

"I beg your pardon!"

Hanna laughed at him. "There must be a tutor. Young men must know Latin for college."

"College! Has your husband so like me, you think, given that a thought? I thought not. When's he going to register the boy, when the list for his year is closed? We'll go to Oxford, you and I and the Indian's son, and set him in the record. It'll cost real money but you are late, very late."

"You're probably right but I can't say...."

"Of course you can. The boy's in the Dowland line. Cambridge is not a possibility. Worths and their relations, and, may I stress, their *heirs*, go to Oxford. Cambridge is out!"

"But what of Silent Fox? He is the father."

Stumped momentarily, Lord Worth countered, "He is the one with the brains to set the child to Latin!"

That night when the city twinkled like fairy dust, they sat at dinner in a second storey room.

"Why not finish the winter in West Sussex, Sister-in-law? When Gib is back in the spring you'll want to dart to the London shops and stroll at Vauxhall and use my tickets at the opera and all of that. Right now...."

"I don't have the heart for it either."

"Are you sure, Hanna?"

"Very sure."

"We could ask people down. People with children...." Then, off the cuff, "Preferably people conversant in Latin!" He laughed at his joke.

Hanna colored.

"What is it?"

"When Gil comes." She said. "It'll wait till Gil comes."

Cecil leaned forward, his lace grazing his meat. "Sister, never wait!"

It was then that Hanna confided, "There is a family, a father, a Michael Beckett, who is a solicitor, and Horace, his dear, orphaned son, whom we are supposed to go visit."

"Let's do! A solicitor must be up on his Cicero!"

Her history with Michael and the careful doing of Dire's sticky business backed Hanna away from something so natural. "In the spring when Gil comes home will be a better time to go to Cambridgeshire."

"Cambridgeshire!?"

"That's where Becketts live. And go to school."

"Madam, I think *you* are like my brother!"

CHAPTER NINETEEN

February 1753

The fleet sped southward on the winter wind at a clip, Captain Jones assured, of one hundred ninety-two miles a day. A twenty-four hour day. Skidding and bucking at Gibraltar and then off Sicily, they broke their slick run but they shouldered boisterous waters where two seas met, found the Adriatic, and wafted into Venice with the snow.

The shore was necklaced by white and gilded domes and spires under a falling veil of sparkling silver. The anchor dropped into the Lagoon, as viscous and as shiny as mercury. The fleet lolled in its luminous bed, loquacious in the silence of the Venetian dawn.

Gil spent his life in impatience. Hanna told him it had to do with his upbringing. His desires swiftly seen to had, in her opinion, given him an unrealistic view of the world.

His breeding reared its head now. Whipped by Kirke's fleet thirty-two hundred miles through the roaring ocean in twenty days flat, Gil went nearly mad at tarrying over breakfast with the Jesuit in Jones' quarters instead of speeding ashore.

Claude de St. Aubin attempted to calm him. "Our able Captain Zhones...."

"Jones! Captain Jones."

"Did I not say Zhones?"

Worth curled his lip.

"Very well, then. Zhones must prepare Thomas and his wife for our coming, make his report of business matters...."

"I thought that's what I was bringing *you* here for!" Gil savaged the priest's excuses.

"My dear, if I may finish...Zhones will make the necessary reports and the lady of the household will have time to assemble herself and greet us with whatever civility she can muster on so short notice."

Gil's green-eyed look poisoned the atmosphere.

"Ghilbert! Eat this delightful fish that swam but an hour ago into the net. The lady awaiting you and me will find no comfort if we arrive famished and cold and harried. We are to be a calming force, a sign of good things to come!"

Sealing his lips and swallowing hard, Gil swerved out of his chair and pressed close to the window glass. Retired or not, Claude retained the confessor's air and earned the respect of his calling. Gil complained marginally less irritably, "This pace!"

"What pace? We are chewing."

"My point!" Worth entirely lost the battle for patience. "Suppose Jones gets knocked on the head on the way to Kirke's palazzo and he never arrives! We'll linger here and chew ourselves to death!" Gil jabbed the wooden inner wall with the heel of his hand.

Claude pushed his chair back and with effort stood, spilling nothing on the table. At Worth's side he said, "It will not 'appen."

"How can you be so sure?" Gil sniffed.

"Captain Zhones is not you."

Gil pranced out of reach in resentment.

Claude remarked, "What a sight Venice is in the snow!"

The hour did pass. And another half of one. A sun no bigger than a gold ducat dotted the sky. It created slippery shadows and littered the Molo with intangible, metallic refuse. Small boats coming to life at the water's edge appeared no more distinct than a cloud of dragonflies.

Gil became fearful of what Jones might have found or not found at the Asolo. The priest hovered, afraid for Gil; he believed the Englishman's soul was drawn as tight as a soul could get without ripping a fatal hole in the body. Their distracted game of chess begun in desperation was broken by calls from the water, from the crow's nest, from the water again. Men's voices tossed tidings back and forth. Gil and Claude scrambled up the stairs and on deck.

Portside, clearing the remnants of mist, pelted by dazzling crystals gone gold in the morning sun, was Kirke's yacht. Standing in the prow was Jones and behind him, Elizabeth.

She did not simply stand. She paced the rail, nearing Jones, backing away, turning, striding toward the keel and, breaking sideways, traced the cross-ribs of the small boat.

Worth broke from Claude recognizing her figure. He trumpeted her name without stopping. "Beth! Beth! Beth!"

She heard him, then saw him. She seized the rail with one hand and threw off her hood with the other. She called, "Uncle Gil!" open-throated as a bird.

Claude noted that she had a good voice. It possessed a speaker's not a singer's power. His work for Kirke would have been an infernal penance had she sounded strident.

As the Butterfly drew close and cut her sail, Claude squinted at Elizabeth, a swirl of wool and fur. The yacht was secured. A sailor handed her into Jones' care.

Claude supposed the captain and the wife of The Company boarded but somehow he missed the motions; she was there. She was all there was. She was a bit of white arm peeking from a luxurious sleeve, she was a back, a flowing cloak, bound-up hair unwinding auburn, laughter, boot-toes, arms of steel hugging Worth breathless, lips branding his.

"And Aunt Hanna?"

Gil spun her toward the priest. "Beth! Here is Father Claude!"

She gasped, holding hard to her uncle's arm. Head up, surprised out of her embrace, she planted her feet squarely on the quivering deck. She faced the Catholic cleric who years before had pronounced Wakwa in heaven for having two wives who loved one another. She knew nothing else about the Jesuit. She stepped toward him and reached up and brushed his cheek with her lips in welcome.

Close, touched by her, her electric pulse loose against him, Claude breathed, "Je comprend! I understand!"

Elizabeth, not understanding what it was he understood, gazed on him.

Claude found it exquisitely painful that she, at twenty-four, had such depth of regard. Her eyes were bright but in their recesses were the black layers of morbid matter, leaves of memory sodden from cold tears. Claude saw she had a clear grasp of reality. Of her misfortune Claude said again, "Je comprend." He bent his bulk to kiss her hand.

She inclined her head welcoming him. "Thomas cannot wait to see you! He is pacing up and down the jetty!"

Claude carped, "So he can scamper off! The rabbit!"

Elizabeth filled with laughter.

Claude was hers. No notch in any man's belt, she was a free spirit, rather, a spirit freed, dangerous and endangered in a world of frill-brained women and cocky men. Claude was sure she would make excellent company. He wondered if she played whist.

Her hands still in Claude's, Elizabeth turned to Worth. "Let us gather up Aunt Hanna and...."

Gil closed tight on her, firmly clasping her shoulders, "You look so well! I want to hear everything. Thomas Kirke is a good man!"

Elizabeth asked flatly, "What's wrong with Hanna?"

Both men closed her between them as if the truth would dash her off the deck.

"Hanna stayed behind."

"What!!"

"In London."

"She's ill."

"She's fine."

Claude made a rumble in his throat.

Gil corrected, "She's rabid to see you but had to stay behind. We'll see. Mayhap she'll come. My brother's wife just died. Hanna's with him and...."

Claude held tighter to Elizabeth's cold fingers, cold through her gloves.

"And...." Words failed Worth.

"And?" Her voice lost its command. It slid up a scale dizzyingly high with hope.

Gil crushed her to him again, his face against hers, his lips at her ear. "And Moses."

Elizabeth did not see Worth or the priest. She strained to remember her child's face, a child thirteen months, with tiny teeth and light eyes.

"He could not come. I'm sorry to tell you...in this way...." Gil trailed off.

Elizabeth listed against the priest.

"He is five now. I had hoped it would be easy. That he would come along. But he does not take to sea travel...."

Wordlessly, Elizabeth scorned the excuse.

"He had a difficult crossing! Claude saved the day."

"Then I will go to him!" She caught onto Worth's arms, intent, maternal.

Claude studied the decking.

Gil attempted grace. "Moses is a smart little thing. He knows he couldn't leave you if he...met you...."

The dank blackness behind her eyes stirred. "He's refused?"

"Something holds him back. The same thing!"

Elizabeth whispered, "I had flowers brought from Africa for Aunt Hanna's dressing table. And cologne of jasmine from Taormina. On this boat are English yarns for crewel work I thought we'd start together...as we once were wont in winter."

Gil and Claude looked at each other over Elizabeth's bent back. She curled against the rail.

"That is not to say you'll never see him. It needs more time!" Gil pleaded Moses' case.

Captain Jones rid the deck of sailors, sending them to the hold to work. He himself withdrew to a discreet distance.

Elizabeth let loose a song of sorrow, a mother's croon. The men kept her between them but drew apart somewhat, horrified, when she finished off with laughter.

The snow seemed whiter, colder. They sheltered below decks for the short sail to the dock.

His size, the brazier's heat, prompted Claude to open his cloak. His crucifix showed. He saw to it that she saw it although she sat frozen in aspect. "Daughter!" Claude stroked her glove. "You and I will 'ave plenty of time to talk of Moses. What each of us knows. All of it. Every single thing. Plenty of time. But we will now put into your hands somezing he send you. Somezing he make."

With perceptible reluctance, Worth produced the book of cantos Moses had penned. Claude directed him to open it to the red ribbon marker.

Elizabeth received the curling pages into her lap. She removed her gloves in clumsy courtesy to touch the red satin. Elizabeth ran her fingertips along the lines of black undecipherable to her. "The ink has run." She wondered aloud.

"With tears. His for you. For this...situation."

Not even looking at Worth, she demanded strictly, "What are you trying to do to me?!"

Gil shrank in his seat. After their mutual suffering, after waging terse, bitter battles for the truth, after their reunion, next their parting by the sea, their yearning for letters and replies from one another, for contact, for touch, his faith in humanity was battered that she found it possible to freeze him out. He recalled she had done it from the first. For weeks after her disappearance he had searched for her, not knowing Wakwa or that he had taken her under his protection. When Worth actually entered her hiding place, standing inches from her, she had willfully stayed hidden. She allowed him to trudge away in failure and broken-hearted.

Gil turned on her, a vein standing out in his neck, "I'm doing my best! It's a hell for everybody! I *begged* Moses to come. To reconsider and come down with Hanna later! He is as stubborn as you! As his father! Read the words, Beth. Moses *sang* the words. For *you. To* you. In his little voice. With the tears streaming down his round little cheeks. The words are in his stead! He handed me the book expressly to bring to you. I will say it! Wakwa...," Gil's hand shook against his mouth as he broke the ban against using the name, then his hand, still shaking, dropped to the comfort of his kersey coat. Again, he looked at her and again he said it. "Wakwa - wants him taught Latin. Moses is learning. From Claude. But on his own he knows *how* to sing and *what* to sing and *when* to sing it!"

 Elizabeth braved the outraged eyes of the uncle who without a blood bond had shown more devotion to her than a parent. She covered the brazen vein in his neck with her cold hand until it calmed then she turned her attention to the text, printed amazingly by a child's hand, her child's hand, in the Latin and in the English. "...'O beautiful one.'!" She looked to Gilbert Worth but spoke to Claude, "Father, am I evil?"

 "Dear girl!"

 "It makes me happy that he cried!" She touched the traces of Moses' tears. "Happy he cried for me!"

 Kirke stuck his head out of the window of his coach. Then he swung the door open and hopped down suspicious of the smallness of the party. Kirke's un-Venetian clothes of dusky wool, black leather boots, a plain stock, a small white peruke sheltering under a black three corner, gave way in the matter of his cloak, a brocaded claret silk over Russian sable. Kirke fumed in place.

Elizabeth slowed and stopped, standing across the jetty from him. Worth moved on, adrift between them, hailing his host with his hat. Claude labored behind him and obliterated Gil's greeting shouting, "'Ello, Thomas! I 'ave a message for you from Locke!"

Kirke bypassed the priest growling, "Later, Claude." He extended his hand to Worth, to Kirke's practical mind a sort of father-in-law. "A good crossing I hope? How was the food? I don't think the Florentines know good bread."

Poore was at his elbow.

Elizabeth swept past them all and up into the coach. She commanded, "Viti!"

"Trouble." V.T. Kirke mounted the two steps and the footman snapped the door shut behind him.

A second carriage boarded Gil, Claude, and Poore and rocked along to Palazzo Asolo.

CHAPTER TWENTY

February 1753

Moses rocketed from window to window in Lord Worth's coach, witnessing London dissolve into hedgerows and pasture and stands of ancient trees.

The fifty mile journey to the home where Gilbert Worth's soul had found its form took the better part of two days, not long considering a fall of snow, their heavy baggage, a stop for tea, and then an overnight stay at a half-timbered cottage Cecil kept up for convenience enroute to Heathersley. The interruption to their momentum did not quell at all Moses' pulsing expectation for his first sight of the place where his Uncle Gilbert had been born.

Bearing south and slightly west, virtually to the Channel, the team strained toward the vestiges of day. The coachman whooped and hallooed and laid on the nudging lash and they caught sight of the mansion just as its edges lost their sharpness to an inky sky and its marble walls were fired red-violet from the sinking sun.

Built, crumbled, and rebuilt in tireless continuance since the fourth century when Worths were British decurions from Chichester in the Roman system, there was something holy about the vast villa wrapped around a garden. Set on a tray of land held aloft by an arm of white rock gently sleeved with grass adorned by heather, the palace promised dwellers with hearts not brutal but brave. Meadows billowed to fat tenant farms.

Moses begged them to open the window. He pulled cold, damp, briny, rushing air into his lungs scenting what his eyes were losing to the bloodstone sky.

Wolf-of-the-mist entered the gateway like a young king. The Heathersley servants greeting their master and his guests in the portentious twilight, were conquered by the child of exotic coloring and regal manner.

It was a cold season to be introduced to a home of sixty rooms on a bluff above the English Channel. Moses found no trouble in it. His natal palace was the forest. At the age of five he could easily walk all day under the snow-laden trees, light a fire, unearth food Qunneke had buried in the Fall. He could fish through ice and, however imperfectly, work a knife under the steaming hide of his father's kill. He was versed in managing in cold climbs. The trees made chimneys for fire and exuded pitch to patch a torn canoe. Thus, in a day, he had reduced the plan of the villa to his experience; four three-storeyed longhouses joined at right angles and grouped protectively about a camp of yew hedges and pointed trees and a pool and a fountain and benches for sitting and stands of lavender and roses. Nevertheless, his curiosity was fed for weeks by the marble walls setting off countless long, glittering windows, the sunswept floors of a million tiny tiles of cobalt and saffron and alabaster and gold patterned into faces and fish and flowers, the painted panels, the many-chambered bath with its hypocaust for heating. By mid-month, he absented himself at will from the temperate east wing and the sun, to explore alone or apparently so Heathersley's summer quarters, the west and north apartments.

These segments of the house beckoned Moses. In the whistling loneliness of the venerable interior, Moses stalked what he could not quite remember from his infant past.

Cecil followed, fluttering mutely between the two remote segments of the house, roosting here and there in a chair, pondering the rambles of the Sachim's son who damaged nothing but brushed close to everything.

One afternoon, Cecil lost sight of the boy in a room of books and pillars and jutting alcoves and high-backed chairs. Lord Worth made for the corridor nervously and looked right and left. He reentered the maze, darted to the corners. He cleared his throat to break the news of his presence with the least possible shock for the child who must be there and who must not lose himself fatally to the enveloping cold and the enticements of the collected curiosities. Cecil called, "Master Bluehill!"

"Ohomous!" Moses shrieked from behind.

Cecil yelled, turned, caught the scampering boy and dropped into a chair with him. They clung, sweating slightly in the chill.

"That was not very polite to come up behind me." Cecil reprimanded.

"I beg your pardon, m'lord." Contrition settled unsuccessfully over Moses' features. "But you have been behind me for days!"

Cecil was at no loss. "I was worried. A youngster trotting alone through this labyrinth of ancient bric-a-brac." Thinking his words inept if not insulting, he admitted, "I didn't want to lose you!"

Happiness rose in Moses' eyes yet he resisted when Cecil tried to draw him near.

Spurned, Cecil responded coldly. "It's time for tea."

Moses did not move a muscle but stayed ensconced on Cecil's knee like a bit of porcelain on a pedestal.

Slowly, Cecil sorted through what had occurred. "I did follow you first. I might have frightened you. Please excuse my behavior, Moses."

At that Moses melted against him. He took a deep whiff of Cecil's skin, its own and added perfumes. "Ohomous! You smell very like my Uncle Gil!"

"I assume his smell is pleasant. And what is this you call me? I'm Lord Worth to you, young man."

"You are also Owl." Moses' hands turned, palms to ceiling, "You have proved it. You live high above the ground. Your shawl makes the sound of wings when you move close to the walls. You keep your eyes on me. Like an owl with his eyes upon the mouse. You search me out in the dark. In the frost." Moses settled back onto Cecil's shoulder.

Cecil remarked after a brief pause, "From the little I know of your folk it is something of an honor to be given a name. I thank you. Owl! I like that. It is said *how*, Mouse?"

Moses laughed then instructed, "It is said, Ohomous!"

Cecil allowed the briefest of smiles then sniffed, "I suppose my brother, Gil, has a name as well."

"Sumagunum Wunutcheg. Who-holds-out-his-hand."

Cecil pounced on that, considering Gil's entail. "That the does!"

Arriving late for the evening meal, Cecil and Moses caught Hanna staring at a folded piece of letterpaper on a salver at her place.

Cecil swept in. "What does Gib have to say?!" He settled himself in his seat.

Hanna answered as if she were one of his statues forced to speak. "A letter. Not from Gil."

Cecil offered, "I'll open it if you'd rather."

Hanna reached for the letter. "It's from Cambridgeshire. I'd better look at it first." Sickened by the imprint in the wax, she slit Beckett's seal.

The widower watched his brother's wife. He watched her narrowly.

After a moment's reading, a sound escaped from her like a pop from a pistol.

> *The Honorable Hanna Worth*
> *Heathersley*
> *West Sussex*
>
>   17 February
>
> *Dear Madam,*
>
>   *It has come to my attention that you and Mr. Worth are in residence with your nephew, Moses, at Heathersley. A renewed acquaintance would be most beneficial to my son who fares poorly. If it is not disagreeable we will follow this post by a week.*
>
>   *Your respectful and dutiful, etc.,*
>
> *Michael Beckett, Esq.*
> *P.S. We are a party of three.*
> *M.B.*

The twenty-fourth day of February, standing in an upper window, Moses caught sight of some glistening thing not made of ice. Like a stroke of wet ink it raced down the tree-lined alley scoring Heathersley's park. Pale daylight glanced off the bit of onyx which blossomed into a coach and four, the vehicle black, of course, and its horses, two wondrous blacks and two star whites.

Moses raced through rooms of ancient glass, the vases ringing. He rounded the stairwell crazily in his leather-soled pumps and hurtled down the second staircase to the Great Hall and through it, calling his call, forgetting civilized form, losing words to meaning, telling his aunt in canine yelps that the Becketts had arrived.

The sound of hooves and carriage wheels carried into the house.

"Ani! Come to the door!"

Hanna caught up with him and admonished, "Moses! Remember where you are!" Garbed in ochre wool and silk, she left the impression of sweet butter burned. Her unpowdered hair was drawn softly back into a knob. Several strands of gray flew free of the gleaming auburn. Some cheer was shed by a circle of Italian ribbon at the summit of her throat just under her chin. Her shoes were of biscuit-colored kid. Only her stockings hinted at life. Brilliant life. When she gathered her quilted petticoat to meet Moses in his rush, lapis and ivory stripes painted her feet, her ankles and calves. Moses stopped. It had never occurred to him that under her skirts his New English aunt had legs that led upward. She led Moses out of the hall into a receiving room.

Cecil poked at his neckcloth in the mirror. "They'll be shown in, Wolf. When in Rome...."

"In my father's house we go to the door." Moses grumbled, confined to the tall windows. "I see a man, a boy, and a small woman!"

Hanna swayed and sat.

Cecil caught her shock in a mirror. It told him a tale. He turned away, vowing to watch Beckett like a hawk - like an owl.

It took some time for Michael Beckett to appear.

"Why don't they come?!" Hanna fretted.

From his post behind Moses, Cecil observed a tall, graceful man instructing Heathersley's groom. A woman was visible in the coach, dainty, with a capped head of dark curls, sheltering someone in her cape.

"Punctilious about the horses. Dashed insulting." From Cecil.

Hanna snapped, "Little Horace hates the cold!"

Cecil's eyebrows rose. He refrained from speech.

Moses skittered away from the window and danced along the walls of the large room. "Little Horace hates the cold! Hates the cold! Hates the cold!"

Cecil admonished, "Wolf! Our guests are nearing the house."

Beckett's stride on the marble floor was heard. Frigid air from the main hall trailing words of French slipped in. Hanna gripped the arms of her chair. Her brother-in-law stood behind her, a hand on her shoulder. As he pranced by, Moses ran his hand along the strings of the harp. Its confused and wounded cry magnified against the walls of stone. Beckett's steps halted. His sharp, cool voice ordered, "Horace!" and light footfalls pattered.

Hubbard, Worth's butler, delivered Beckett's card and, at the master's word, threw open the double doors and stood just within them. "Michael Beckett, Esquire! Master Horace Beckett! Mrs.

Dire Locke!" The last name electrified Moses and dashed the tension from Hanna's face. Her relief made Cecil scowl.

Beckett's manner was perfect. "Lord Worth." His head tilted with a tantalizing arrogance.

Cecil made a crisp salutation and remarked Beckett's prompt setting aside of his normal schedule for the quietude of Heathersley. Watching for barbs in the baronial welcome, Beckett responded with turgid care that no activity could take precedence over Lord Worth's gracious response to his request to visit.

Hanna was surprised at Beckett's bow, his clasping her fingers, his bringing her hand briefly to his lips. He broke four years' silence with her saying, "Mrs. Worth!" They shared a glassy look that shattered.

She said thinking of Horace, "It is good that you have come."

Beckett, aghast at how four years had gentled her, loosed his glance to the room. His excuse for his lapse of attention was made to Cecil not to Hanna. "I heard the harp, Lord Worth."

Almost amused, Cecil informed him, "Master Bluehill tickled it in his uncle's absence."

"Absence? You did not say he would not be here, Mrs. Worth!"

"Oh, do say Hanna, Michael!" She scolded.

Cecil trusted her after that.

Beckett turned on Moses, resenting being fooled by a child particularly that one. "Gilbert Worth is your tutor, Master Bluehill?"

Moses smiled at the widower, "No, Mr. Beckett. Ani says you know Latin so I suppose *you* are my tutor!"

The contrast between the boys was stunning. One was impish, the other constrained. One was vivid, the other pale to transparency. One was brave to brashness, the other made stubborn by corked courage. One gleamed with health, the other was faded by frailty. Their separate blood and nature and experience told in their persons but their eyes, painted differently and differently shining, held the same motherless craving. It made them twins.

Hanna bent to Horace. Her muted clothes blended with Nature's bleaching of him. Their affection appeared fated. Beckett did not miss, nor did Cecil overlook the phenomenon. Shy Horace intended toward Hanna, a stray stalk inclining toward the sheaf. Horace's brown eyes even sparkled momentarily.

Hanna left him for his governess. She moved freely toward the small, dark-haired, dark-eyed, sharp-featured woman whose defiant shoulders sported the burdens of her love for Dire. "Let us go upstairs and settle you in the nursery. There are wonderful things there for your bath!" She slipped an arm around the younger woman to guide her.

"Orase!" Jeanette called her charge in a voice like a bell.

Beckett seconded. "Run along, Ho."

Horace stroked the carpet with the toe of his boot, deliberately lagging.

"Dear! Beckett ordered. "Now!"

With consummate politeness, Lord Worth intervened. "Wolf, shall we all throw back a Sherry, then you and I show our guests about the place?"

Michael Beckett fought to control a tick in his neck.

Under Cecil's guidance they drifted southwest then due west and north. They remained on the first floor in easy view of the garden wrapped in a pall of frost.

"You have accomplished great work for my brother's family." Cecil pressed gently against Beckett's belligerence.

"We simply upheld the law, Lord Worth. The Dowland estate went to the worthier title, i.e., the male one, i.e., to Moses Bluehill."

"You don't appear to be modest, but you are."

Beckett's mouth slipped into a smile, which he quickly ended. "The privilege of your keenness is rare for me, Lord Worth."

"My brother chose his solicitor well." Cecil put Beckett in his place.

Beckett struck back, "Actually, his wife sought me."

Lord Worth blinked the sally away.

Moses, asked, one foot already on the stairs, "My Lord, may I show Horace *my* wing?"

"Well, Wolf," Cecil consulted his pocket watch, "if this reads right you have precious little time before tea."

"We'll run!"

Beckett fussed as he had over his Thoroughbreds. "Horace tires easily. It might be cold there for him if the rooms are closed for winter. He wants a wash before coming to table."

"The hypocaust! We'll bathe together!" Moses appealed to Cecil and then to Beckett. "But first, we'll see my wing!"

As the boys dashed upstairs, Beckett jabbed, "My Lord, you really ought to have the Sachim here sometime."

Heathersley possessed the triple virtues of grandeur, intimacy, and privacy.

Not over-furnished, its massive pieces were on a scale to contain everything and afford comfort to everyone without clutter. There was space in which to move no matter how preposterous the hoop of a skirt or how crowded the guest list. With only half a dozen souls in the villa besides the servants that winter, night walking was free of bruises, stubbed toes, crashing statuary. There was room at Heathersley to wander, and best, the floors were heated in the Roman way.

Midnight strolls in the Winter-wing with its amenities of radiant heat and lamplight became, without Gil, Hanna's field of meditation. Alone, gowned for bed, wrapped and capped and slippered, she seemed to walk without her body and to anywhere she willed.

She thought nothing of rising from her chair in the exquisite hour and venturing down the hall. She had not gone far when she heard bitter weeping. Hanna moved quickly toward it.

A shaft of yellow light cut the main corridor and Beckett stepped into it, slamming Jeanette's door behind him. Loosely dressed in his day-clothes, he took the stairs to the ground floor.

Tempted to recede to her room, slink into bed and coax her eyeshade over her braid, Hanna joined Jeanette instead. Hard on herself, Hanna judged the bed's disarray and could not disregard the perfumes that hung in the air. She folded into a chair. "Dire loves you, Jeanette. He sent you to us. Do you understand? Good!"

Jeanette slipped to her knees in front of Hanna. "Ee is nearby?!"

"No! He is in America preparing for war."

Jeanette's eyes looked within.

"Claude is in Venice."

Jeanette gripped Hanna's hem.

Gingerly Hanna let her hand rest on Jeanette's head. "Dire wants you to stay at your post."

Jeanette stifled a sob.

"Are you mistreated?"

"Non." Then more trustingly, "Not often!"

Hanna cupped the younger woman's face in her hands. "It is not good for Horace. Do you understand what you have to do?"

Jeanette glanced away.

"And what you do not have to do?"

Jeanette, too proud to weep, staggered away from the bed.

"You and Mr. Locke have done great service for Mr. Beckett. Mr. Beckett may be of great service to Kirke Company one day. I thought you should be aware." Hanna left her.

Beckett swirled the liquor in his glass and spoke with his back to Hanna as she entered the Great Hall minutes later. "I never knew you to sleepwalk, Madam."

"You never knew me well."

Beckett slowly wheeled on her. "Quite well enough." He toasted her silently then said, "Jeanette begged me to let her speak with you about Kirke's Most Glorious Factor. I refused. Hence her keening which woke you."

"It brought me, not woke me."

Cecil roosted on the gallery, in the shadows, unseen. Sound carried to him along the stone promontory as at the theatre.

Beckett switched the subject. "May I ask where Gilbert is? Along the byways picking up...folk tunes?"

"Michael, I love my husband and he loves me." Her voice struggled out of a swamp of memories.

"Seeing this place and remembering Sweetwood, I would concur." He batted his lashes at her and invited her to sit.

She continued to stand. "I do not follow."

Beckett made a sound at her obtuseness, bent his elbow and gulped his whiskey. "To have all this at his disposal and to live across the sea in a glorified cottage! Surely you can follow that?"

"Above all, Gilbert Worth is English. His passion is the land. I am indivisible from it."

"Lucky you!" Beckett set down his drink with a thump and came her way.

Hanna backed against a pillar. "Do not prey on Jeanette out of your groundless frustration, Michael. The child senses it. All is not well with Ho."

"I submit, Mrs. Quick-in-the-Saddle, you have no right to preach to me about what harms children!"

Hanna gave a shout and turned away. Beckett caught up with her and pawed at her arms. "I'm stinking drunk. Don't mind what I say! We'll have another! Another time!"

Speechless, motionless, Hanna endured his collapse about her shoulders and down her bosom and the front of her gown. Through her nightclothes she felt his forehead against her crux.

"Why did you allow me to come?" He begged in a whisper.

"For Moses. For Ho. It was selfish on my part. Feel free to go home."

Beckett reeled into the lobby. "Oh! Hanna! Do you see how lonely you have made me?"

"I do!"

Her blunt declaration, not without sympathy, rallied him. He burbled, "I can reform. I've done it many times before."

She rejected the cruelty of laughing. "Promise then to leave Mrs. Locke, your son's governess and another man's wife, to herself...."

"But...!" Beckett issued a wet-mouthed cry.

"Keep your quarters even at home...."

"If you knew what a dungeon that place is...!"

"Devote yourself to some worthy cause. Whether it is the law or your horses but do not dissipate your precious life anymore."

Beckett, quick to restoration, accused, "Virtue! It tells on one. I saw it squatting all over you this afternoon. I hadn't been so sick to my stomach since the late Mrs. Beckett gave birth. All the guts gone! Where's my filly with the wild eye?" His hand lingered in the air then dropped towards her.

Hanna placed a toe of her slipper on the stair. "Michael, it is far more attractive in a man to revere a woman as the soil to be tilled than to approach her..." mounting a few steps, she finished smartly, "like a horse's ass!"

Cecil was at the top step. He offered her his arm.

CHAPTER TWENTY-ONE

25 February 1753

Inspired by an overnight thaw and a high-caste sense of humor, Lord Worth crowned Beckett's surfeit with a summons to follow the huntsman next-day in exercising the hounds. They rode at 7 A.M. under a slight drizzle.

Beckett was wan and, for him, contrite about his brutal performance of the night before. But he was neither so stricken nor so vain of his equestrian skills that he misjudged which of his horses to ride on the slippery turf. His predictable, brown-coated Cleveland Bay that had followed his coach to Heathersley did him fine. The lord of Heathersley was content with an Irish-bred Cob whose nimble, white legs teased the yelping, slavering dogs.

Beckett nicely held his gelding half-a-nose behind his host's horse. Cecil maintained his pace, honoring Beckett's deference.

Turning slightly in his saddle, Lord Worth remarked, "No better hunters around than these steady fellows!"

Seeing dangerous fences and chasms to jump in each baronial word, Beckett ventured, "They suit the neighborhood exactly."

Riding, as he was, slightly ahead, Cecil easily concealed his smile over Beckett's Midlands snobbery about terrain.

After they had covered a bit of country, Beckett tried to recoup their conversation. He began as carefully as in court, "May I invite you to try my black or white in finer weather, Lord Worth?" Then flickering with pride, "Their grandfather is the Godolphin Arabian."

"How does someone like you...!"

Mistaking his reaction for mocking, Beckett cut in, "*My* fifteen guineas is as good as anyone's! By next year Matchem won't cover a mare for less than twenty-five, and his stud price will only go up! And...," Beckett paused for effect, "...as Lord Godolphin's estate is hard by my house, sending my mares to stud as soon as they're in heat again will be a wisdom from both a monetary and a breeding point of view."

Cecil ignored the steaming pile of facts. "I meant, why squander precious time over hot-blooded stallions when you are a solicitor of uncommon skill. What's more, you've already perfected the Yorkshire breed!" Cecil gestured in respect, touching his crop to the dripping brim of his hat.

Beckett acknowledged the compliment bitterly, "At least we know my indulging my passion does not interfere with a wife." His remark unfortunately, if not intentionally, dredged up everything despicable in his diary.

Using his crop against the Cob's flank, Cecil showed Beckett his back.

Michael's pounding head throbbed in annoyance at his mistakes with Gilbert's august brother. Again, he attempted through his hung-over haze to say or do something handsome. "Please understand I indulge in the law as a pastime."

Cecil shot him a sour look.

Beckett cut his own pomposity by adding, "My Lord, I am not rich. I breed horses for much of my living. I supply the hunt in the Shires. My father before me was more the scholar - he left me with a mouldering house and piles of good books and good rugs. The rest is up to me."

"Pity!"

Beckett mistook Lord Worth again and responded with pique, "You saw my Thoroughbreds...."

"Hitched to your carriage!" Cecil spat in outrage.

"I am testing their tempers!" Beckett fairly shouted. "This first cross has produced four animals out of four native mares with the speed and style of royal racers and the bone and heart of cold-blooded, Dark Age steeds of war. In two years, my Thoroughbreds will rival anything out of Godolphin's Gogmaggog estate! The Thoroughbred will be a breed one day, my Lord. My word on it! Capital T!"

Cecil halted on a chalky shelf above the Channel. The tall, noisy dogs scrambled down the dunes absurdly baying some empty victory. Cecil observed, "My brother, Gilbert, never liked the hunt. Found it cruel."

"Oh?" Beckett reacted archly. "In Massachusetts he has been known to bag some pretty big game with his fowling piece."

Cecil studied the deep and writhing waters. "Fair game, I have no doubt."

"Right you are!" Bested, Beckett twisted the knife, "Considering your native kindness, my Lord, I cannot imagine your kennels and stables stocked for the chase."

Cecil swung his snowy-coated Cob due west where rode the obscured sea. Beckett trotted close beside him.

With forethought Cecil said, "Titles force certain habits, Mr. Beckett. It is my brother who does important things with his time."

Beckett balked at his rhetorical setbacks. "Seeing all that the Honorable Mr. Worth left for a life in the wild, his accomplishments could be deemed madness."

"Mr. Beckett! Madness comes when we trifle with our talent."

Embarrassed, Beckett studied with infinite attention the formation of his hunter's hooves. He looked up when Cecil's hand descended on his arm.

"How long have you been a widower, Mr. Beckett?"

After a pause, Michael admitted, "Since Horace was born!"

"It is a lonely thing." Lord Worth agreed. "A man needs to occupy his mind. Would you take the bit and do service for your King, if you had the chance?"

Beckett did not mistake the trumpet-call of patronage. "At any time!" His answer was right but he ran it long. "I cannot say how sorry I am over my excess last night."

"Do not mention it." Cecil's voice froze at Beckett's crude timing. He urged his horse into a walk away from the water.

Beckett caught up, concerned, out of breath. "Your forgiveness?"

"You did not offend *me*!"

"I've written Hanna a...I plan to write a note to her to beg pardon for my offenses."

Lord Worth brought his horse around, "If by a note you can recover your character with a lady of such goodness, I'd advise you despatch it today!" He spurred his horse and the Cob carried him away in an exquisite closed gallop that put any Thoroughbred's canter to shame.

Moses and Horace went together as naturally as blackberries and cream - as blood and tears. Their remeeting ended for each a strained half-life.

Moses could have been jealous of Hanna's sympathy with Ho. But, the half-Massachuseuck boy had been reared otherwise. Wetu and sachimmaacommock were places of welcome and shared love and responsibility. More, since Horace seemed like a newly hatched bird, Moses took a protective stance toward him and was not bothered by Hanna's special attentions to Michael Beckett's son. Like Sequan had done for him, Moses accepted Horace as a wounded brother needing special care until he could claim a place among the able.

Horace did possess one strongpoint. He was an excellent horseman. In the saddle since the cradle, Horace taught Moses to ride with grace, to whisper in the equine ear, to balance off the saddle toward his pony's neck like the Italian riders and, soft on the bit, race down the hills of sand.

One thing only came between them. A single topic brought on dismay, revulsion for Horace's puny gut. A single prod unleashed Moses' bleak sulk, the injured air, the precious stare. Yet Horace bravely asked his question from time to time. "Moses, if your mother lives, why won't you see her?"

VaughanThomas Kirke complained to Gil, "You made good time but you're later than expected and Captain Dray is pacing *Psyche's* deck. We've got go as soon as the wind is up. And now this! This poor lad. My poor wife!"

Gil shuddered.

"Who's idea was it to bring the kid?" Kirke mentally accused Silent Fox.

"The idea was mine."

"God, Gilbert!"

"Thomas, I had no idea Moses would refuse to come to Venice."

"And what if he'd accepted? On the eve of my leaving for two years?"

"Thomas, you know better than I when the King will throw his blockade. I had to take the chance."

"Aye. I see it!" Kirke stayed fierce, put out, in perfect agreement with takers of risk.

"See this. I am bound to deliver a message to you. From Wakwa's other..." Worth stammered and flushed at his error, "...from his wife." Worth pulled a reticule of skin from an inner pocket of his coat. "Tame Deer charged me to explain to you and you alone that there are other things in storage with her, Elizabeth's things, which she once treasured and used. Tame Deer said to tell you expressly that she is holding them for Beth."

"The Sachim's wife sent a message to me?" Long seconds passed then a light came from nowhere and settled across Kirke's face. He looked directly at Gil. "That is the best news I've had in years!"

"I can't keep up." Worth complained.

A smile burst briefly out of Kirke's dry inside. "If I don't make this voyage, that is, if I don't return, if the Cohong doesn't like my squeeze, what we call the personal presents he's expectin', and he takes me for a swim with a stone 'round my neck, the Indians'll take Liz in!"

"It's not a question of her having no place to go!" Worth drew himself up.

"I know. And so does Tame Deer." Thomas Kirke's hand reached slowly, took the skin purse into his grasp, and reached in with long fingers for the relics. One was a bound lock of straight black hair that dashed his smile, kicked him in his most tender region.

Late the next morning, with only ten days left to February, Elizabeth ran at Kirke's side to the dock. The coveted wind dusted up the mist to be incinerated in shafts of sun. Kirke was the last to board *Psyche*. With a repeated, downward motion of his hand Kirke tried to quell Elizabeth's mothering him.

"Viti, I've had four extra cases of soap brought aboard. Wash yourself, wash your hands, boil the water, wash anything that touches your lips! Every cup, every fork!"

"The Chinese don't use forks."

"Say you'll use the soap, Viti!"

"Liz! On our table there's a list of places you are to be seen with your uncle and Claude. Be sure to go!"

"I'm dreadful at those evenings."

"Liz! We've got a quota to meet in our sales of shares. The bank must be up and running by the time I'm back. Your uncle has the particulars. Cooperate!"

"Suppose...!"

They stopped.

Vaguely put out, Kirke supplied, "I've always gotten back from China before! I'm aiming for eighteen months but you never know the pace of the Imperial Deputy or how big his pockets have grown since the last time they were lined. I could be surer of my return with Locke at my side...but he's not! I'll stay stuck outside Canton with the factors just so long. The trick is gettin' the gold payment past the Chinese pirates offshore once the tradin's done. If I'm not on this spot in twenty-four months, count me dead. No matter what, before George, our idiot-king, closes the American ports, get yourself home!"

She fought him. "Massachusetts? I am not wanted!"

"You are." He resumed his march to the gangway.

"I am not!"

"Yes, you are."

"They are all, *all*, quite relieved by my absence. Has there been one word to the contrary? One, single...."

He stopped, took her shoulders and swallowed her outrage at its source. His lips left hers for her ear. He whispered, "There's a bag in my highboy. Open it. It's from Tame Deer."

Before Elizabeth could speak, before any tears, Thomas Kirke mounted the gang, storeys high. Not waiting for the sails to fill, he disappeared.

CHAPTER TWENTY-TWO

February and March 1753

They stood an hour at the pier. Large, looming, *Psyche* bore away from land and behind her the smaller ships, the mothership with her children tagging on her skirts of foam. Treading the crowded port with care and with grace she whistled her farewell and grew small. She was a spot. She slipped over the curve of Earth, even her disturbance of the Adriatic lost like a dream.

Elizabeth stood alone for the ripping away of the ships. Two years and eight months of frenzied life with Kirke tumbled under. She faced a span of time without him of almost equal length. Compromised by the secret he had released into her ear, she watched her husband's leave-taking in shame.

Elizabeth took her guests under her wing. She led de St. Aubin and Worth calmly up the stairs from the ground floor, the Asolo's temple of commerce and housekeeping, to the living quarters. She ordered the luncheon served, carried a steaming broth to them herself, then, with nicely made excuses, she retired up another flight to the room she shared with Kirke.

Elizabeth did not rush toward the thing in the drawer. She bolted the door. She washed her hands. She dashed her face with clear water. She changed into plainer clothes. She sat on the edge of the bed remembering Thomas Kirke, remembering further back in her history. Then she fled across the floor with the same abandon she had shown dashing off the path between the Worths' and her father's house in the mesmerizing Massachusetts heat never emerging from the forest until Waban and, if truth be told, Wakwa cast her out.

She pulled the handles of the drawer Kirke had designated. The softly folded purse leaped at her. Her hands were on it, it pressed her mouth, its smell of balsam and smoke clotted her breath, sent her down on her knees onto stone. The bag splayed open to her groping. She saw locks of human hair - baby hair in gradations of color from black to fawn to black again bound in ribbons denoting the mood of the times in which the hair was cut. She apprehended a diary of years in seconds. She saw the bound locks as what they were - signs of a life dripping with honey - a life remarked in gentle detail, a life of joy which superseded hardship - a life she had embraced when little more than a child - and now she sprawled with it against her chest and rolled with it away from the door, away from kindly hands, until she struck against the wall under the windows.

Asunta grew uneasy. She spoke to Cecilia about the mistress' mid-day meal going cold. Cecilia, wakened from siesta, shrugged the cook off as late as three. At last, Luigi was called. After all, he held the master keys. His shrewd suggestion was to ask the two gentlemen guests if Donna Lisa had perchance left instructions, anything the staff should know. His next move would depend on their answer.

All three servants acted to preserve the dignity of Palazzo Asolo. Asunta arranged small pastries on a plate, Cecilia armed herself with the afternoon's post, Luigi raided the wine cellar for a bitter liqueur to serve as a digestive. With these subtle covers for their anxiety, they presented themselves in the second storey dining room where Gil and Claude lingered hours after the table had been cleared.

It was the high point of the late winter sun. The silvered-rose of Venice, post-meridian, filtered through the windows of the dining hall. In bad combination came the blunt hoots of the gondoliers propelling their barques to the kitchens along the Grand Canal. An uncouth joke and raucous laughter from the common-bred crews floating by marred the servants' diplomatic expedition.

Luigi had mastered enough English to observe Elizabeth's simple orders. He vaulted into fluency in the household emergency. Gilbert Worth was delighted to revive the Italian of his student days although time had buried idiom. Claude's Italian was hampered by an accent but not one so ornate that he could not make himself understood.

Luigi poured two cordials. "Signores, with sorrow to break your conversation, may I ask...Senora Kirke is not downstairs since returning from the Molo...." Luigi looked about the room as if his mistress should be hung like a mirror over the credenza. "Is... command from her?"

"None." Gil responded, curious about the bottle.

"Non!" Claude took the goblet stem between two thick fingers. "The cordial, my good man?"

Luigi lowered his eyes against their hardness.

Cecilia curtseyed and laid the bundle of mail before Claude.

"Thomas ordered up the post for our dessert!" Claude scooped up the folded notes and papers and pouches.

Worth took a taste of the liqueur, held his glass to the light. The draught showed ebony. "Bitter. Very nice!"

"One day, you will be serious, Ghilbert. In any case, I cannot linger, it being trois heures, **None**. I shall go up and pray."

A rough shout from outside and guttural laughter interrupted.

Asunta made the sign of the cross. She darted forward and passed a footed dish of sweets. In her soft, almost hoarse voice she bemoaned Donna Lisa's fast.

Unrewarded by any reaction from Worth or St. Aubin, Luigi cleared his throat and ordered Asunta to carry a tray upstairs. No need for the gentlemen to bother. After all, Luigi held the keys.

Gil looked up. The Jesuit scowled.

Worth remarked, "They are fussing."

"They are fussing over bonbons. If they feed her like this everyday she will get as big as I am!"

Gil said to Claude, "I'm more worried about the cold, Claude. If she's asleep she'll catch her death without a fire in this mausoleum!"

"Even if she is not asleep."

"Forgive me to break your conversation." Luigi grew more insistent. "Her husband, her...young...man...they go away. A woman so sad...with many cares...?" Luigi nudged their imaginations to see the problem. He wanted no bloodied daggers striking the floor, no fatal romantic gestures from Donna Lisa on his watch.

Worth eyed the timepiece in his pocket. "After three. Luigi's right."

"Fuss!" Claude ticked his tongue and pushed himself up from the table. "The little lady is asleep. Who would not need rest after three years with Thomas Kirke! Up half the night over a pile of papers and then God knows what else!"

"Honestly, Claude!"

"And with that reticule...." The priest took a moment then he started briskly for the stairs.

"God!" Gil slipped past him and bounded up first.

The priest shouted, "I am coming, Blasphemer! It was my idea!"

Luigi and the women brought up the rear.

The door was an uncommon barrier. Twelve feet high, slab-thick, deeply carved, gilded, locked, moreover, locked from inside, it made a crypt of the room beyond.

Frustrated by the fruitlessness of polite knocking, Gil paced until Claude made the stairs. The servants infiltrated the landing. Luigi pulled a small lever, which he explained rang a silver bell inside. They all waited in silence, heads cocked, ears primed.

"Absurd!" Claude carped.

"Send a boy up the trellis on the outside wall and we'll get in through the window!" Gil prodded.

Luigi moved toward the lock making a good deal of noise with his heavy ring of keys.

Cecilia, under full sail, cut a swath between the houseguests even elbowing Luigi aside. She was a woman, give her the keys, what if the lady were in some distress or dishabille, please remove to the top stair, and Asunta, come close behind.

"I had a housekeeper like her once." Gil dourly recalled Mrs. Winke.

"Out of my way!" Claude turned on the staff, seized the keys and snarled, "Madame is trying to rest. I am 'ere on the express wish of her 'usband to assist her in running this establishment. Stand back!"

For fear of him and their posts they did.

Gil put in, "It is nice they show concern, Claude."

"Pah! Venetians!" Claude pounded on the door with the butt of one key. The pounding made no impression on the wood or on the occupant. He thrust the key into the lock. Not knowing the turn for the deadbolt, his frantic motions made the marble corridor clatter like a prison. Finally, the interior lock moved and the high, heavy door sighed on its hinges. "Elisabet?" Claude purred.

The servants crowded around the door. "Is she dead? Is she on the floor?" From Cecilia and Luigi. Asunta whispered prayers into her hands. Claude edged through the portal, Gil on his heels. The excluded trio vied for position to see inside.

In a square, carved chair set before the bright casement like a throne, there sat a gray figure. The arm straight out, the bone-white hand straight up warding off intruders, the sunken eyes ringed with puce. A tan bundle showed against the breast. Out of the swollen mouth the words - "Mine! Mine!" It was Elizabeth.

Claude stood petrified.

Gil said, "Shit!"

Claude ordered, "Leave! Leave her to me!"

"I know this! I've seen this! Except this is my fault. Was before!"

"I must help her!"

"*I* am her uncle."

"*I* am a priest."

"She is not a Catholic!"

"Get out!"

"The servants!"

Claude rolled his eyes toward the door. Remaining inside, Gil shut it with a thud.

The Frenchman announced to Elizabeth, "*We* are keeping you company."

Elizabeth started to speak but her voice failed.

Gil turned to light the fire. The orange flame caught and danced. He crouched at the hearth's enormous mouth. How all life depended on fire! It was the constant benefice across countries and cultures. Aside from this general source of heat and light he searched for a single constant in his niece's life. It would not be found in Silent Fox or Kirke. They were about the world's great business. It was not in her child. He was learning to be a man. Gil, himself, was their willing messenger, their accomplice - Hanna too. There was no mother, no father, no immutable affection, no stable force. No infinite, unchanging God in Kirke's temple of gold save the gold and that made precious little comfort. There was only fire, Elizabeth's often unlit. He looked at her face gaunt with sorrow, riding above the doeskin bundle. He saw what was constant - fire, sorrow, and Qunneke.

Gil faced the room and found Claude sputtering his Office. Elizabeth was sitting still, her feet tucked under her, her bosom shielded by the skin bag. Her eyes turned to take Gil in.

He viewed the slight movement as a fragile invitation and knelt beside her and stroked her cheek. "I thought I was, but she is your greatest friend!"

Elizabeth could not stir to acknowledge what he had said. The truth threatened to cut her, to bring up blood.

There was no moment so sacred in Elizabeth's day as the opening of the shutters in the morning. When sleep ceased, her ritual was to lift back her corner of the coverlet, seek her slippers with her toes, feel her way down the expanse of the enormous bed then push off into the blackness. Seeing with her hands, she would pass the table without bruising her legs, discover the carved chair, perceive the lesser darkness, reach, find, and lift the latch, and part the shutters, backing out of their way.

Spread across the placid water there appeared daily a landscape of human and Divine creation; an alabaster structure, sculpted trees, terra-cotta soil. White, green, red, birthed by Nature or Art, were made pale by the Venetian dawn. Wedded to the sight, to the custom, she could appreciate Thomas' jilted cry from his pillow, "Carry a candle, Liz!" After all, it was like nothing else on the face of the earth more than the beach of the Nausets on Cape Cod.

The morning after Kirke sailed, Elizabeth took her moment at the southeast window, bathed, dressed and was at work in the ground floor library with Claude by the time Worth stepped in.

Thrilled to see her functioning, Gil remarked as he entered, "No one breakfasts till noon at my brother's house! I'd forgot how early the Italians get started. I should go back to bed!"

"Uncle Gil!" Elizabeth, showing no melancholy or madness, came to his side, kissed his cheeks, and slipped a book of names into his hands nabbing him for the Company's work even while he breakfasted.

Worth studied the list of salons where Kirk's letters of introduction would make him welcome, chose those most advantageous to attend. Good will between families was founded or dismantled at these musical evenings along the Grand Canal. Gil's gifts - his physical appeal, his proficiency in music, best, his pedigree - were the perfect lures to attract wealthy Venetians and British and Continental ex-patriates to Kirke Company. Gil called it "extended farming," that is, tilling the social soil to produce the fruit that fed The Company's maw: news of kings, whispers of trade, tracings of the transcontinental gigue of precious metals, and tangibly, ducats for financing far-ranging investments and loans, and not least, private transactions for Kirke's guarantee, yielding commissions to be poured into his secret stockpile of gold.

After a brief meal of a shell-shaped pastry the crust of which unwound like the braid on a perfume bottle, a small cup of black coffee and a fan of Sicilian blood-orange slices, Gil stepped back into the library where Claude and Elizabeth were sorting correspondence, devising replies, recording information, writing directives to factors and their subalterns and keeping Kirke's files. He shuddered at their instant partnership, utterly disciplined, and he retreated to the music room across the great hall. He was not fooled by the waiting harp as an accouterment of civilization in Kirke's rented house. It stood polished and ready like a long gun in a besieged stockade.

Gil was surprised by the indolence of his life heretofore, issuing orders to Matthew, watching the cherries ripen, and turning the profit from his crops back into the soil. This palazzo of Kirke's was a workhouse, an engine of the future the parts of which would rust if not oiled every day and night, all day and all night, with ideas and labor. A man who had no inclination toward business, Gilbert Worth that morning felt snagged in the teeth of Kirke's power machine. Better to be in its mangle than spat out on the dusty roadside when the times turned.

The ground and second floors fell dead as a museum. Claude could be heard snoring away his siesta on the third-storey hallway. The hours of respite, one through three, were respected even by The Company.

Accustomed to a Puritanical regimen, Worth labored over his first letter to Hanna. The writing was slow. It was Gil's second day in Venice, barely twenty-four hours after Thomas Kirke had sailed for the Orient. Except for the brief scene on the Butterfly and the bad hours over Qunneke's packet in her bedchamber, Elizabeth had said nothing of Moses, nothing of the past, made no inquiry about the farms or Massachusetts. Gil wasted paper crossing out observations that made his communication with his wife into no more than a travelogue.

When the bell at his door jingled unexpectedly, he gladly stuck his quill upright in its stand and went to answer. Elizabeth was waiting in the corridor.

"I'm so glad you're awake!" She whispered. "I knew you would be. Would you like to follow me?"

The stairs were narrower, the flight shorter than any other staircase in the Asolo. She unlocked the door at the top with a key she drew from her sleeve. The door yielded to the pressure of her shoulder. The meagre landing forced Elizabeth to stand down a step to admit her uncle. She locked them in.

Gil turned to a wall of windows. Far below them and stretching southeast was the Adriatic; on the opposite shore shrouded in mist was land extending due east for thousands of miles to Peking. "So, this is your ivory tower!"

She slipped her hands through the armholes of a pale gray smock with a bib as wide as wings and looped its narrow belt through a slit at its waist. Pulling, she created crossed panels at her back and a closed full skirt replete with pockets, every edge framed in broad appliqué of white and yellow linen.

Gil turned toward her, admiring her inventiveness with clothes, a thing reminiscent of her days in the woods.

A spinning wheel, spindles of some glossy thread, a loom with work unfinished on it, a library table littered with strange implements like jewelers' tools and pens and sheaves of paper, leather boxes sealed shut, captured Gil's attention.

"You have noticed we keep no dogs?"

He caught his breath at this non-sequitor.

She took his arm and stood with him in the enveloping sunlight. "Listen!"

Gil cupped his hands behind his ears and was rewarded by a whirring and chortling as if old women were gossiping on the window ledge. "Pigeons?"

"Viti calls them Rock Doves."

Always jarred by the tenderness in her voice when she referred to Kirke, Gil paused then postulated, "You love him don't you?"

She turned as if to avoid a shadow behind her. Very softly she said, "We forego the company of dogs, although we'd love a pair of Italian Greyhounds, for nothing must interfere with the birds." She tapped softly with her fingernails on the glass, in polite warning, opened a casement and coaxed Gil half outside.

In a cage of decent length and breadth, that Gil would have testified was formed of gold wire, two pigeons nestled and sighed and warbled. One hopped through the open door onto the ledge and crooked its head. Elizabeth cooed and coaxed and the iridescent creature bobbed near for a caress.

"Tomorrow or the next day or the next, I don't know quite when, there will be three." She searched Gil's eyes for his appreciation of what that meant. Casting some millet on the ledge, she dropped another clue. "As the months go by there will be four. And when the cage is full again, Thomas' ship will appear there!" Her slender arm pointed to the horizon.

"Are you telling me....!?"

"They home! Thomas is not the first to try this but I'm so glad he did! His pigeons find their way from his ships to his house, wherever he's living. The captains tie tiny messages to their legs and the birds deliver them." Her eyes held the wonder of it.

"So!" Worth surmised. "That is how he gets the first news from everywhere and anywhere. And I thought Locke was clairvoyant!"

"Dire is." She laughed. "But that's beside the point. The Company has used pigeons between Pemaquid and Boston, London and Scotland. And since we came here we've been training these. Oh, they are so wonderful to have near!" She crooned and petted the birds' blue-gray breasts.

Agitated by the effect of the merchant on her, Gil strutted away. "Wonders! Next Kirke, himself, will sprout wings."

Elizabeth said strictly, "I wish he would. He is going a voyage of thirty thousand miles when you count both ways and with no diversions from the route!"

"I know. I'm sorry."

"With wings," she started to smile and calculate on her fingers, "he could travel overland and China would be only five thousand miles from this very room; ten thousand in all."

Gil thought of Moses saying a similar thing about his sojourn to Venice but could find no gentle way to introduce the topic.

"One-third the total and one-third the peril."

Gil trained his eyes on her glistening threads. "I suppose you would not be his wife if you did not love him. So, I do not know why I find it so hard to accept. Since loving two is no rarity in this family."

She turned her back on the birds and the window.

Gil fingered the distaff. "I speak of myself."

They both saw the woods, the lodge on the day of Moses' birth, Tame Deer in the doorway.

He said, "And of Qunneke."

A wayward smile fluttered from Elizabeth.

Ashamed at how he had nudged his wife toward it, Gil divulged, "Hanna as well."

"Oh, Uncle!" She passed Beckett's spectre and took her seat at her wheel. "I knew."

"Did you!" Gil made a bitter noise. "Then there is Wakwa." He cuffed her with that.

"You are sure?!" She was acrid in turn.

As glad of her torment as of Moses' sorrow, both signs of sanity, Worth insisted, "I am very sure!"

She resisted his lead as if denying an addiction. She hid her face in self-disgust, came close to the elixir of Wakwa's memory, then quickly locked it out of sight in some cabinet of the mind.

"And now there is you."

Instead of carping, she touched his hand and noted its gold hairs fighting silver.

"Thomas is the lone exception."

He swallowed her admonition. "Proves my rule."

They sat together, he in a side chair, she at her wheel. She pulled kid gloves from her pocket and drew them on.

"Dry skin from the work?" He speculated.

She only smiled.

Relaxed, he would have smoked, but he thought Wakwa's pipe and the scent of his tobacco a cruelty to her. Gil sang to her instead, as he used to do.

She combined two strands of stuff, one sheer as spider's silk, the other like a scratch of ink from a gold-dipped pen. A single thread like a corn tassel wrapped the spindle.

"Beautiful!" He did not flatter. "What will you weave of it?"

"Weaving is a useless skill."

Gil teased to preserve her happy mood. "Without it we'd be Adam and Eve dressed in foliage."

She let him make her laugh then said, "Or in skins."

"Beth...." He cautioned.

She insisted, "Hand-weaving is obsolete!"

"It was not too long ago you taught the women of the otan to spin and weave."

"I meant it kindly."

"Beth!" Gil soothed. "I know!"

"You know it did no good. Caused so much trouble."

Between his teeth he hissed, "Wasn't the weaving did that."

She covered her wounds with a confidence. "Thomas has bought part interest in an invention. An automated loom."

"A what!?"

"Uncle," she leaned away from her work toward him never stopping the rhythm of her fingers, her arms, or her practiced foot. "Uncle dear...there is a man in Scotland working all night, every night on an engine that runs on steam. He attaches this to a set of wheels and...."

"A steam loom?"

She laughed again. "No! He's making a coach without horses. The engine alone makes the wheels turn."

"I know something about this...."

"It is not perfected, but soon. One year, ten years, fifty years! Soon."

"Child, if you think fifty years is soon...."

"But not soon enough for me. You know I've never been a rider really. I'd love to pilot myself from place to place on vapor only!"

Worth looked at her building the diaphanous thread and said, "Don't ever go to Salem."

They laughed once more. In fact, they laughed as they spoke and they laughed as they listened.

She. "Horses are obsolete."

He. "Don't tell old Beckett."

They had joy at his expense.

"The plough horses and fancy coach hacks are to be turned out to pasture. We'll be steaming from place to place on wheels and the horses, bless them for their patience with us, will be the gentlemen of creation with nothing for labor but...."

"Fox hunts!" Gil supplied.

She waited out his unfortunate phrase.

Worth cleared his throat.

Elizabeth began more quietly. "Hand weaving is outmoded. There are too many people to weave for with too little money to repay the weaver's skill. It simply takes too long to make a yard of cloth for the return. Thomas says...."

"But your hands!" Gil protested. "Thomas *must* see what you produce! It was your weaving brought him to you." Gil rose, bent over her chair, stayed the wheel. "It looks spun of gold. Fairies' work."

"It is!"

"But I see you spinning it myself."

Again, she laughed. "I'm saying it *is* gold! Thus the gloves. I'd be cut to ribbons. The thread is formed of gold and undyed silk."

Gil looked about the room testing whether her art were a recurrence of her grief-madness.

She did not miss his panic.

"Elizabeth! We need you. Your son needs.... Very soon things may change...Wakwa is straining to...and you could...if you wished...if you and Thomas wish...you might come home! But you sit in a tower room weaving gold?"

Without pity she announced, "I am charged by Kirke Company to change the form of a certain store of gold which Thomas comes by in trade or by securing others' trade. I help The Company administer his work, I play the clerk, but I have this room up here where I come to dream...."

Worth implored, "Do you dream of us?"

"I work with my hands...."

"Do you think of the farms? Remember cows?"

"I take gold melted and shriven into finest wire and weave it into many disguises. I mask gold."

"Such work will send you mad. You know it will. Alone. Up here. Doesn't Thomas see that this artificial life...."

"I disguise gold behind its highest properties. I protect it from itself."

He whispered, "I can see!"

"Look!" She swung off her chair and hunched over the long, heavy table. She sorted through the mixture of stuffs and found scrolls of drawing paper that she spread open to him. "I've not got my dead brother's skill with a pen but my designs are clear enough. See! Pots with a middle layer of gold. Golden teeth for the empty gum. Teapots lined in gold and painted over. Inside! Sheer stockings of the stuff!"

"Holy God."

"Walking sticks. The works of music boxes. Gold candles with the wax within! Shoe heels. Clockworks. Here! My latest! Maps with all the country lines and the rivers and the mountains drawn by gold thread pressed in."

"Cages for birds?"

"Those as well. And all the obvious things, forks, knives, plate, goblets...masked. I invent the prototype and artisans in Dario's shop produce in quantity."

"Kirke has harnessed the finesse of your imagination to produce contraband?!"

"The gold is legally gotten."

"I didn't say it wasn't! But it is not legally gotten past customs."

"Uncle Gil! The gold must not fall to the King. The gold must be gotten to America for rendering into bars."

"But this!" Gil could not dismiss his terror of the madcap project glowing on the spool.

She pulled a length of gossamer off the spindle looped it around her hand like yarn, tied one side with a ribbon and cut the other with a razor. She held the shining bundle high and shook it. "Hair!" It blew and trembled like a Dutch infant's bob.

"You and Qunneke."

She gulped that insight. "I've refined this over six months' time. We'll fix it to dolls' heads. The dolls themselves of gold. Pack hundreds to the crate. We must ship all the gold we get before an embargo!"

He held her tight. "Hurry! Weave it into draperies instead of this time-consuming stuff and factor it over yourself!"

"Oh! For an automated loom!"

CHAPTER TWENTY-THREE

April 1753

Wakwa's agony of expectation was as like birth as anything could be for a man. His responsibilities should have blinded him to spring. He had business in Philadelphia with Locke, yet he waited in the otan for the season to unfold.

Occurrences of green, ice broken by sun-shafts, mild afternoons that grew fangs by sunset charged him with hope and despair. He was committed to staying in his territory until the appearance of a certain blue flower. Its blossoming in profusion along the riverbank would signal the ninth cycle since his daughter's birth. Wakwa was stubbornly set on picking those flowers with her, feasting the otan in her honor, and presenting her with a small canoe he had built and decorated for her over the winter.

The daughter Tame Deer had conceived with him was only two when Elizabeth Dowland had been received into their life and a tender and sentient three when the white woman was arbitrarily barred from it. Springs had passed and now within the fulfillment of a few more, Sequan's body, at least, would be a woman's. In a time of bourgeoning war, Wakwa refused to miss the last moments of Sequan's girlhood. The flowers lingered in bud, binding him exquisitely to home.

On an afternoon when Wakwa was running his lines and teaching other men's sons to hunt, he heard a horse on the deer path from the direction of Worth Farm. He dropped his work, chose by the speed of the hooves a place to head off the rider, and raced to the spot through the trees. He was waiting with his guard by the time Israel Stirling rode into view.

Blunt and shy, with hardly more than a "Heigh!" not even dismounting, Israel pushed a mail pouch into Wakwa's hands.

The Sachim gave the pouch into the keeping of Mosq and politely asked after Dr. Mac and the progress of the new building in Worth's north quarter.

Israel nipped the civilities. "Sir, that packet's off a Kirke ship docked last evening at Plymouth. I'd look into it."

Wakwa was pleased with the young doctor's directness. "Plymouth? Why not Wareham?" Wakwa looked away from Israel to the pouch. Almost languidly he stretched his arm for the mailbag.

"Matthew wanted to run it in to you but he's making some subfactor comfortable at the Worths'."

Wakwa's eyes kindled on this information. With a motion of his hand Wakwa sent his men to a discreet distance. His eyes lowered briefly, hungrily, to the bag then rose to Israel's. "Was there any spoken message?"

"None. Just the trader, breathless."

Wakwa turned into the trees with a set face, made his way straight to a clearing as if it were his office. With a tilt of his head he invited Israel into the glade. "And the trader's eyes?"

Israel said, "His eyes? Oh. A little bloodshot from his early ride and I suspect from the sea. And rum. Nothing to his eyes."

Wakwa's relief was cautious. "I may need your eyes, Israel. Stay by me." He emptied the pouch of three letters, studied and sorted them. One was from Hanna. Another, closed with a massive seal, was in a hand he did not recognize. Wakwa ran his fingertips over the last letter, a thick sheaf decorated in fanciful printing.

He read his own name on the front of the folded parchment. "He wrote! Moses wrote his father's name!"

Israel studied Wakwa's face, every feature washed with pride, hope, happiness.

"Look at it, Israel!" Wakwa shared the sight of the phonetic tour-de-force. "With no letters for writing his own tongue he has let the sound of my name go through his English ear to his mind into his fingers through his quill to the paper to *my* eyes and out my mouth! 'Wakwa Manunnappu.' See you!"

Israel dropped his glance to the folded sheaf. Two lines of printing marched their mostly measured way in a slant to the upper right. Out of a profusion of W's and N's and P's he deciphered the Massachuseuck name. On the line below he saw in English, "The Black Fox Who-Waits."

"Ah! Qunneke is right." Wakwa seemed free of all burdens. "She saith to be patient under the seasons and they will reward a man. If I had run off to Philadelphia with Locke, would I have received this letter? All these letters? By the time I came back they would have been yellow with age and meant nothing."

"They're at least six weeks old as it is."

Wakwa sent a look Israel's way, slit the wax that bore no seal and became engrossed.

> *My Father Wakwa Who Loves Me and Who I Love,*
> *One hundred times have I risen in the mornings*
> *not seeing your beautiful face, Mother Tame-Deer,*
> *my brother, Lightfoot, my sister, Spring. The*

cloud, see it, is full of a shower of kisses for her day. Slit it with Big-Knife, shake it over her. She will feel many pecks of love float down upon her shoulders and her sweet face. Twist Lightfoot's nose.

Wakwa emitted a satisfied sound as if he had just eaten sweets, cream from Gilbert's table, cakes, sugar-laden tea, fruit with no seeds or stones or blemish or blight.

I live in the biggest house in the world. Beautiful to see. My Uncle's brother whose house it is I call Lord Owl. Lord Strix in Latin. Owl loves me.

"Gilbert's brother? The one he so dislikes? Is this good to call an English lord by such a name?" Wakwa returned to the text.

I ride by myself. See the horse? See me? Ho B. is my teacher.

"Ho? Ho B.?"

"Ho." Israel grunted. "I only know one individual goes by the name."

"Not Horace Beckett! Michaelbeckett's son? They cannot be together!"

I love Horace. May I bring him home?

Wakwa handed the letter off to Israel. He dug the heels of his hands into his eyes.

Israel cleared his throat and read aloud.

Michaelbeckett teaches me Latin. Ani told him to.

Each man searched the other's face. Israel returned to the business at hand.

Bear-Claude has gone away with Uncle Gil.
To the boot. To Italy....

Israel's steady voice trailed off.
Wakwa looked to Israel, breath quickened, color up. "Read!"

...to Italy where my real mother lives. Around
its toe and heel and up behind it to the cuff.
I went not. I said no! See my face? So ugly?

Israel returned the stiff page to Wakwa. "He's made a drawing."
Wakwa glimpsed it but was unable dwell on his son's agony marked in knotted, twisted, blotted pen strokes. Wakwa struggled to the end.

This letter took eight days to write. Mo.

P.S. - that stands for post script, Latin for
I thought of something else to say after I
signed my name - P.S. Does Manit smile on
your fixing up the world???

Wakwa put distance between himself and his son's query. "What sort of name is Mo?"

But Israel brushed his breeches off in silence and left the space. He saw to his mare. He checked her shoes. He pulled twigs from her mane.

After an interval, Wakwa joined him, his face closed, his head high, his voice dropped to diplomatic temperature. "The message is repeated twice more. Once in Latin. It must be for I cannot read it. Once in Indianne onontoowonk. The best he could. Without native letters. It is much work for one so young."

"That it is." Stirling, not given to conversation, made a sparce reply.

Mist spread, hushing the woods. Wakwa was grateful for this soft outcome of the argument between winter and spring. It absolved him of seeing his neighbors clearly or of speaking to them as he crossed the camp with Israel. The band of them, the Sachim and his guards and the son of Gilbert's great friend, moved across the otan like figures in a dream.

Wakwa brought Israel into his big house, a composition of four domes. They entered a circular place meant for public use, the reception of friends, official visitors, the kenoonuenuog or counsellors. He deposited the younger Stirling in the rotunda beyond that one with Qunneke, the quarter that faced the river, the family's sanctum. Then through a short connecting corridor Wakwa slipped into to a room reserved for private talk. He passed through a second, longer passageway and lifted a curtain at the end admitting himself into a huge, empty, inverted cup with only rush floormats against the cold and a ring of stones marking the place for the fire. He got up a flame with punk and the wood always laid there, always ready.

This was not a room with a ghost; it was the ghost of a room. It was built to the exact proportion and in the exact place of Elizabeth's room when she was Saunks, exactly opposite Qunneke's. A tended garden had begun to green between them.

The Ninnuock quieted their voices when near the sachimmaacommock. And they gave wide berth to the derelict dome, as they saw it, half their Sachim's heart, to which they were never admitted. Wakwa, himself, visited the vacant room only spasmodically, a shrine of weird whispers pushed into its smoke hole by the wind. The vault was to him what mirrors are to felons.

Again, he delved into the bag of letters. He saved Hanna's for last, dreading the complications of whatever news it held. He devoted himself to the large, square communiqué with the baronial seal.

An arm, young, long, slender wound Wakwa's neck. He gasped. Turned. Then his right arm slipped around his daughter's waist.

Tall for her age, Sequan knelt against him where he sat, his lap obscured by papers. She guessed, "You thought I was Zabeth!"

He stopped settling stray hairs from her single braid. "Your mother sent you?"

The nine year old closed her eyes as Qunneke always did in response to his skillful evasions. "Is there a message from Zabeth?"

"Sequan!" He warned.

"About Zabeth?!"

The hope in her voice pushed him to candor. "Yes!"

Sequan fell forward, vine-like, toward the letters and reached for the letter uppermost.

He placed his cheek against her cheek. "How is it you came here?"

Her silence told him.

"You have been in this room before!"

In his fashion, Sequan dodged his question. "Should I not come here?"

Wakwa steered away from answers. "This one is from Hanna."

"Ani!" Sequan kissed the parchment as if it were Hanna's face. "I want to read it!"

He ran his thumb over Sequan's cheek. "When do you come here? Why?"

"Every day. And when you are gone, I sleep here."

"What! Your mother allows this?!" Wakwa rumbled with anger.

"Nosh! My mother does not forget!"

The father closed down that line of thought. "So. You would learn to read?"

Sequan loosed herself to retrieve Hanna's letter. "I do read! Some few words. Ani taught me. But I want to read like grandfather and you. Perfectly."

"Perfectly! A girl!"

"Zabeth reads! Perfectly. She's a girl!"

"Sequan." Wakwa begged her. "Stop." He tried to draw her into his embrace to silence her.

Sequan squirmed away. "Why cannot I say her name to you? I am not...." her free hand made a disparaging gesture toward the town of roundhouses outside. "I am your daughter!"

"Yes! You are!" He agreed roundly. "Only never make little the folk of this town. They are more important together than I or you or...any one person."

Sequan scooted away on her hands.

"Do you understand?"

She stayed quiet with the puzzle.

"Now, I will hear you read - I will help you."

Flushed at the vastness of his love for her, she extracted Cecil's letter from Wakwa's right hand. "What is this? She ran her fingers over the wax as Wakwa had done over Moses' printing. "What a beautiful sign! What does it mean? Who is this from, Father?"

Wakwa drew his daughter to himself delighting in her warmth in the cold cell of memories. "The sign is called a Coat of Arms."

Sequan observed, "It is a small coat!"

Wakwa chuckled. "It is a picture of a warrior's story...."

"Oh! Like Mother's paintings on your cloak."

"But handed down from father to son...."

"Oh! Like the coat you have stored in your basket for Moses - the one Zabeth made you with her needles!"

Wakwa forgave his daughter's indiscretion. "A Coat of Arms is given an Englishman by his king. And forever it is the sign of a family. This were the Worth Coat of Arms."

Her fingers traced a thorny cane bent by two laughing lions into a heart wound with roses. "The paper then is from Gilbert?"

"The paper is called a letter...."

"But it is made of many, many letters, Father!"

"Sequan, all the letters together are called..." Wakwa waited although it did not help, "...a letter."

Sequan made a face.

"This letter-of-many-letters is sent to me from Gilbert's eldest brother. An English lord."

"Oh!" Sequan's small, bright eyes brightened more. "He must be a warrior then. Like a Mohawk!"

Wakwa laughed outright, creating an unfamiliar echo in the desolate room. "Gilbert is more like a Mohawk than any ten of his brothers could be!"

But Sequan's eyes dimmed with worry. "Is Gilbert sick? Why did he not write the letter-of-letters?"

Wakwa spoke with dry voice. "Because...he is with...."

Sequan looked down and said without sound, "Zabeth." Then, catching fire with an idea she seized her father's hands, "Moses too?!"

Wakwa petted the hands in his. "No! Moses refused."

Very slowly, very firmly, Sequan pulled her hands away.

After due pause, Wakwa tried to turn the topic. "Lord Worth invites me to London to speak to a council of English lords."

"Take me?"

Wakwa looked at her newly. "I would like to!"

"But you will not."

"I will not go."

"You must!" Sequan did not berate but encouraged him. She crouched in front of him like an instructor of runners in the Taquonk races. "Father! You must!"

"How shall I go to London to the House-of-the-Lords to speak for the Ninnuock?" He snorted at the idea. "I cannot speak for all."

Sequan looked into his eyes. "You speak the best!"

He smiled. "Every Nation on this great island, the English call a Continent," he stopped, he thought of Moses' second page and wondered if the word were Latin, "each Nation has a spokesman. We must all be invited to London before I can speak."

Sequan leaned away from him in disbelief.

He reached for her hands but she withheld them.

"Understand. Daughter. If I go to London to argue that the English should leave us alone, or give back our lands, or grant us a say with the New English people in governing these blue hills and get them to agree in all the terms I lay out for them, all the other sachimmauog out to and beyond the Ohio River would have to agree. I do not hold the reeds of all the spokesmen for all the tribes. I cannot act alone! I am a man among many. No king or god."

Sequan wilted. "If you do not reach out your hand, Father, how will all these other headmen know to put their voting reeds into it?"

His eyebrows rose at her attainment. "I leave you after your flowers bloom to make just such a thing happen."

"Go now! Don't wait! Not for that!"

He crooned and touched his daughter's face. "You will never be saunks..." he finished when she reared back, "but a warrior-woman. Before that season comes I want you to know how you, you and your mother and my sons, are more important to me than all these others." His own hand drifted toward the outside.

"But you said before they were more important than we! Which I do not understand, since we are all of one. That is what we believe! So what you do or say against any one is against all!"

Wakwa was stymied.

"And if that be *not* so, is it not wrong to say it *is* so just to get your way at times?"

"Be quiet now. There are things you do not understand!"

Sequan stood. "I understand enough even without perfect reading! What must Zabeth think? You tricked her! You told her that you love her and then threw her out for those...folk out there! Will you do that to me someday whether you stay for the blue flowers or not?" She threw Cecil's letter to the mat.

"Pick it up, Sequan." Wakwa was severe.

A tear started and then a matching one. She scraped them away, brave in front of her formidable sire, who was powerful, tall, even seated, and with a look on his face she had never seen before. "I do not understand!"

"Pick the letter up." His back stayed stiff, his head high.

She obeyed. She salvaged the folded sheet and brought it to him. Penitent but proud, she kissed each of his shoulders.

Wakwa said out of horror, "I am your father before I am your sachim. I would prefer your kiss upon my cheek." He set his gaze on her.

Sequan melted against him, wrapped her arms around his neck and kissed his lips.

He clung to her, supporting them both in the ghastly gray light. "I am born a speaker. Winning wars with words takes time." With a sigh he spoke the forbidden name. "Elizabeth...could have hidden. Been ours secretly. But she would not. She stood stiff-necked for what is right!"

"Zabeth is a warrior!"

Wakwa kissed the child's forehead. "Sequan! Now you understand."

Night was richly wrapped around the otan before Wakwa appeared among his family.

He was thirty-nine, fresh enough to repudiate the decisions of old men like Waban, ripe enough to be criticized by the young ones seething at his feet. It had not occurred to him before his talk with Sequan that his motives, so selfless, could attract anything but sympathetic responses, especially from his own blood. He had read the correspondence from Hanna, Lord Worth, and Moses over and over in the far room. He would need the rest of the night to write his replies and had decided to send them with Israel at daybreak to catch the sub-factor before he left for Plymouth.

Israel was just shedding his muffler and tam after the obligatory rounds of each wetu where his services were needed, pulling teeth mostly or performing slight surgeries leaving the more serious medical problems for his father.

They shared supper simply and at Qunneke's fire since it was late and the serving girls had been sent home. Sequan's grace in bringing the washing bowls and their water cups and their stew made Wakwa proud although he was aware that Sequan had as much to offer as any of his counsellors.

Wakwa commented to Israel, "I wish your own daughter will be like Sequan, able about her work, loving, and keen of mind!"

Israel went beet red and looked to his bowl. "How did you know? I haven't told anyone but father!"

Wakwa hooted. "True? You will be a father?!"

"I shouldn't say." Israel's glance could find no resting place. "It's only two months along, but Priscilla...!"

Qunneke clapped her hands. She needed no translation. Just the young man's color, the mention of his bride, the sound of her own child's name.

"Pris has only Cooke to guide her..." Israel looked balefully at Wakwa and Qunneke, "Cooke is so...English! I've hoped you would come to see her, Ma'am." Israel had considerable trouble leaping the conventions of his culture.

Tame Deer was so full of delight she emitted English. "Ma'am, yes!"

Wakwa was amazed.

Settled near Qunneke on their mat, watching the red embers darken to ash, Wakwa whispered not to waken the children. "It pains me worse than I can say that Moses will not see his mother's face. To see...her face. He does this because I hang back. Not to see her face! Not to have her face in his memory!"

Tame Deer's arm fell across his heart.

"Hanna writes she will travel with Gilbert's brother, Cecil, to an old and great place of schooling in England to place Moses' name in their roll, the matricula, it is called. Again, Latin. It will require 30 L. immediately and 200 to 300 each year he studies there and that doth not pay them yet for his taking an honors degree!"

Tame Deer sat straight up.

Wakwa's hand patted her knee. "Lie thee down. It will be many years before Moses leaves us. When he is a man. Sixteen, seventeen. It was Lord Worth who thought of it. How shall I reply?"

Qunneke nestled against him for strength and warmth. "How shall you repay?!"

Wakwa and Israel rode to Worth Farm in the morning. They paused at the construction site of Gil's longhouse. Mounds of earth ten feet high marred the meadow.

Israel's intense silence begged Wakwa's opinion.

Wakwa managed to say only, "It is a big hole!"

A rare smile scudded across Israel's face and disappeared. "Try to get anyone to dig it! I don't know what Mr. Worth would say if he were here and saw only the cellar dug and not even the storage chambers and groundbreaking four weeks gone."

"He would dig it himself!" Wakwa laughed.

"What do you think Matthew and I do every night till we cannot lift another shovel? And Pris! She pitches bits of dirt into little buckets and hands them up to Cooke and my father just has fits over the women and dances like a dervish at the edge of the pit."

"Israel! Why have you not come to me for help?"

"Well..." Israel hedged. "I did not think...it's not the sort of work...your folk...!"

"This house is to benefit the Ninnuock! I have a hundred young men under me training for battle. Their backs might improve with this digging!"

"Mr. Worth wouldn't like that. I know that. He did hire hands...."

"The sun is up! Where are they?"

"Back to Boston, I shouldn't doubt. The Irish are a superstitious lot. The job's been poisoned."

"Poisoned?"

Israel rubbed his considerable jaw. "That fellow, Spinney is back."

"Spinney. Sam Spinney. The carpenter."

With pique, Israel corrected, "Not much of a carpenter. Got thousands out of Gilbert Worth for his furniture manufactory but had the nerve to fail at the business and come back here bleating that it's Pris's fault for not marrying him!" Israel added with a glint in his eye, "Can't get along without her."

Smiling a sardonic smile, Wakwa said, "I have sorry experience of that sort of Englishman."

"Well, he walked right up Mr. Worth's front path, got access by Cooke, and demanded a loan even in Mr. Worth's absence!"

"I do not like the sound of that." Wakwa frowned.

"Father nearly had a stroke! Matthew Freeman who keeps the cash box, as it were, in Mr. Worth's absence, told Spinney *no*, point blank! So Spinney left in a huff, found *my wife* at Dowlands' and pressed her for old time's sake to wheedle *me* for a job as head carpenter on this project!" Israel's veins poked out on his temples.

Wakwa could not stand still in his impatience. "You gave him this work?"

Israel's outrage tied his tongue.

"Israel, it were good you denied Spinney."

"Maybe. Maybe not!"

Wakwa took him around his shoulders and said solemnly, "It were good. That man was working at the manse the night the Reverend Hudson died." And after a pause, "So cruelly."

Israel garnered information unspoken. He chanced, "Then you should know that Matthew Freeman heard from Cooper, the tither, when he stopped at the public house to fetch the regular post, that Spinney's been spinning some tall tales over his beer. After which our laborers quit in a body. Haven't been seen."

Wakwa gripped his own arms. "What did Spinney say?"

"He said anything to do with the Dowland neighborhood were cursed. That Hudson's ghost walks at night. Other gibberish." Compelled by Wakwa's silence, Israel went on, "That the new minister's wife, Dolly, is made barren by living in the manse. That strange lights can be seen on the hill over the church on foggy nights."

Wakwa's face was stone.

"And that..." at last Israel hesitated.

"Yes?!" Wakwa lifted his chin as if for the final blow.

"That Indians live too close to Worth Farm for safety and that is why Worth himself has left his house with his wife!"

Wakwa was overcome with shadow.

"Spinney's not stupid. He knows we cannot touch him without a lot of stink about the past. But it could come to that."

Wakwa looked toward the drop that led to the manse that Hudson once occupied. "We must find a way around Spinney quickly. Strong as she is, your little wife is in danger."

"You think so?"

Wakwa panted on their way to the house, "Why have you kept all this from me!"

Israel sputtered, "We've been so...busy...the baby coming...the digging, Father's illness...."

Wakwa reined in Sucki. "Illness?"

Israel held up. His lips trembled when he said, "He's getting old."

"Not so old! My father is ten winters older at least!"

"Father lives a different life! He's a different person. He is more tender of health than the Sagamore!"

"You are a doctor. Can you not fix him?"

"All I've got against it are sugar of roses and saffron cordials!"

Wakwa's eyes, turned on Israel, would have frightened a lesser man. "What is *it*?"

"His heart." Israel stopped again. "He had heart-stroke a week ago Sunday."

Wakwa bent slightly at this blow the bore down on the rambling house. For the first time he admitted himself without knocking. He did wait in the hall, his chest heaving.

J. Macmillan Stirling, bundled in the wing chair in the sitting room, saw Wakwa flash by. He fumbled with his rug calling out,

"Take 'er easy, Laddie!" He staggered up and into the center hall with the plaid still clinging to him, rocking on swollen feet right into Wakwa's embrace. "Wha' is it? Wha's the matter?"

Wakwa held the old doctor tight against him, heartbeat against heartbeat. "And if Israel had not come with letters for me...how would I know...?" Wakwa drew back and looked into the bleached blue eyes.

"No' that! Come in! Cool off!" Mac thundered, "Cooke! Bring tea!"

Wakwa helped the elder Stirling to sit again and swaddled him tightly in his coverings.

"Look a' you! Look a' your face! You'd think I died! Angina pectoris is wha' it is. An inconvenience. Not nearly as bad as what you're sufferin' vicariously. Can't an old man ge' a pain in his chest without you moonin' over him?" Mac burst out again covering Wakwa's gloom, "Think of it as interestin'! Good training for Israel. I canno' live forever and I may as well serve some purpose whilst I'm here!" Mac leaned down as far as he could out of the tightly wound rug. Softly, he murmured, "I know wha' you're thinkin'. Tha' you won't accomplish all you've got to in time for me to see Beth's bonnie face again." The old blue eyes swam painfully. "I'm watchin' for it. I'm cheerin' you from the front row. But ge' your play on the stage, Lad, an' soon, before m'chair is empty!"

Wakwa's hold of Mac's feet slipped. He took to the window-wall and surveyed the grounds outside.

"I won't bow out tomorrow." Stirling kept to his metaphor. "Heart-stroke gives a man time to think." His hand wandered to his chest. "Think over the acts he can't take back. Tell me the news! Shouldn't you be in The City of Brotherly Love by now?"

Wakwa changed the subject. "Your attack...."

"Heart-stroke. Much different."

"Your heart-stroke, Doctor Mac, came before or after Samuel Spinney made his request?"

Mac's jaw jutted.

Wakwa concluded, "After. So! I ruin *you*, too!"

"Now, you're makin' no sense." Mac grumped.

"Doctor Mac, you are afraid for me. Afraid Hudson's unholy hand points at me from the grave."

"You've always had a way with words."

Wakwa swept over to him. "Not only with words. Samuel Spinney must not be allowed to stain Priscilla, or frighten her or Dolly Low, or frighten Sweetwood Village."

"Good thing Gil's not here. He'd hand Spinney his head!"

Wakwa turned sharply to him.

"That is not a prescription, mind you!" Mac's blue eyes bulged.

"I could not drink that cup if it were! How many times can I act for justice alone by myself? How many secret graves must be dug?"

Mac balked at debating Wakwa's swift justice of years before. He reflected, "This month, nay, this day, the twenty-third of April, marks the birthday of a singular fellow."

"A friend of yours?"

"A poet. Wrote plays. Mostly. Said the truth."

"Then he must be singular."

"Ever heard o' Will Shakespeare?"

Wakwa said not without pride, "I have his book from Gilbert."

"Have you! If you can make sense of the meter, read it. He says, "Murder will out!""

After some minutes studying white wisps in the sky collecting into clouds, Wakwa said as if to himself, "It were not murder."

"Ask Hudson wha' he thinks abou' that!"

Wakwa turned a strict eye on the Scot.

Stirling soothed, "I agree with you. On all counts! You did a great an' necessary service. Bu' it's back to haunt you."

"Would you have me confess to the Boston court?"

"Hell, no!"

"Then what? I cannot 'hand Spinney his head' as you put it. My skin will not allow another such act - by me. And Spinney's offense is not the same as Hudson's! Spinney is a small man. A talker. Hudson was an evil-doer of the highest order."

"Go on."

"What think you of granting Spinney the payment he seeks?"

"Hell no, again! Blackmail is wa' i' is! He'll drink it away or piss it away and be back for more! Remember Shakespeare!" Mac shook his gnarled finger Wakwa's way. "Gilbert Worth can't buy your way out of this."

"I agree. But the carpenter cannot live here with his bitterness."

"An' it's no' so much about you but my newlywed son. I warned Israel about marrying a girl with no family, no protection! No matter how nice a girl she is. An' she is. Bu' she's prey to this sor' o' thing."

Wakwa faced the Scot fully. "I married one with all the family and protection a woman could have and look what good it did her or me!"

His reason defeated, Mac's hand roamed the table at his side for a Bible. But this was Worth's house and the thing was out of reach, out of sight, and locked away.

"I could arrange Spinney's removal to another place."

"Oh, fine. Abduct him. Your minions will end killing him anyway. Spinney's strong as an ox and has a mean streak. And if you'll excuse me, you don't do so well with dirty hands."

"How do you know, Doctor Mac?" Wakwa moved to the other side of the window to see if Pequawus were coming along with Sequan and Qunneke.

"Pah!" The Scot spat his frustration. "If you could lick Spinney up on your silver tongue and swallow him alive, I'd say do it! With my blessing. I've go' a grandchild on the way, remember!"

Wakwa watched the sloping land dipping and rising to the greening woods. This privileged tract, his first son's birthright on both sides, seemed suddenly narrow. "I have an invitation to London, Doctor Mac."

"Aye!?" Mac's tired eyes brightened. Hope leaped in them.

Wakwa turned away from the sight of the familiar fields. "Not from her...." Wakwa's eyes closed as he painfully corrected himself. "Not from them. But from Gilbert's brother, to speak before the House of Lords."

"Holy Cow!"

Wakwa laughed outright at the oath. "But I must first go to Philadelphia."

"Why first?"

Wakwa turned back to the land. "I must be delegated by the other tribes as their spokesman, and...."

"And?"

"Suppose that from there, I lick this Spinney up and spit him out somewhere else."

"My heart is pumpin'. Tell me quick."

"Spinney is strong and hungry and has a skill in building, so far as it goes. Such a man might burn to make his fortune along the Ohio."

"Wha' are you talking about?"

"Spinney has lost his woman. Is he not burning to fight someone? Anyone? To make his name great since he will have no sons to do that for him."

"At least no' any sons ou' o' Priscilla." Mac settled that.

Wakwa stopped in his tracks to clearly form his strategy. "The French make incursion every day in the West, building forts and seducing the tribes thereabouts to their service. For trade. The English do not want to spend the money to build forts to hold the French back. As well, the colonial assemblies refuse to vote the money because they cannot agree together on anything. Not yet." Wakwa turned toward Stirling. "But they will soon vote to collect the money or the French will overrun their English towns putting torches in Indian hands to burn them out!"

"Aye?" Stirling led him.

"I have it in my power to find Carpenter Spinney work. Away from here." A little smile flitted over Wakwa's lips.

Mac followed, "Wha' work? Where?

"Building. Among the head-eaters on the Ohio."

Mac held his heart.

"War has started on one side. The other side must soon defend. Spinney will find honor in the work." Wakwa finished fiercely. "And might even kill himself an Indian!"

"Christ. You have a cold center in you no' apparent to the casual eye."

Wakwa cast a look in the direction of the manse.

"You're going to buy tha' n'er-do-well a commission?"

Wakwa responded quickly, keenly. "Spinney hath not the learning nor the family for that honor. But as you say, he possesses a strong arm and a black will. He can work for day wages for the illegal settlers while he waits the governors' call for foot soldiers. Locke can guarantee him work. I will get him on the Governor's list of fearless volunteers. He need not know who any of his benefactors are. And when the call goes up and the wages are in the treasury, and the war is declared and the trees need knocking down for cart roads for the militias, Spinney can ply his trade in the service of his King."

"You *are* goin' ta kill him!"

Wakwa resisted, "I give him a chance to make a man of himself amid real dangers not among women and ghosts of preachers! If he lives, Carpenter Spinney could become a warrior. A great man among his ilk. Even a rich one. Dear friend, I do not kill him but give him lease not to kill himself!"

Mac gasped. "How long does it take women to boil water?!"

Wakwa came to Stirling's side. He sank to one knee and gently put his hand over Stirling's heart. "Old friend?"

"I've go' some pills in my bag like the ones Waban feasted on. Maybe I should put some in a cup o' tea for Spinney?"

Wakwa whispered in Mac's ear, "You have a cold center in you not apparent to the casual eye!"

It was the nature of Worth's house never to be at rest. It held by ten O'clock, eleven people, bee-like. Qunneke brewed herbs into incense for Stirling. Cooke bent over pot and skillet. Matthew Freeman labored with pencil and ledger. The old men, Pequawus and Stirling, chewed over the problem of Spinney's threats. Israel calmed Priscilla who could speak only of the Lows, "Dorothy's lost another babe!" Lightfoot, like his name, quick with nuance, laced himself nimbly through pairs of buckled shoes, slippered feet, and moccasins as if binding them. Wakwa spoke softly to Awepu organizing a quicker exit from the otan than he had anticipated.

Sequan thinned their number, skipping away to the river to watch alone for its banks to quiver blue.

CHAPTER TWENTY-FOUR

Spring 1753

They dressed. The drawing on of each stocking and the tightening of each stay made them thrum. The vibration was less in the ears or about the heart than in their vitals, as if they were each free of the past and all attachments. Elizabeth and Gilbert were, in their putting on of clothing exquisite, not niece and uncle - they were actors about to take a foreign stage where improvisation was the dramatic form and fraught with failure.

Before Elizabeth Dowland's winsome side had been crushed by the marriage contract with the cleric, Hudson, Gilbert Worth flirted with the idea of introducing her into civilized company for pleasure alone. He had no idea at all of shepherding her into marriage for marriage's sake - he was early wise to her self-respect.

That - her self-respect, had overridden his dreams of musical evenings under chandeliers among gentle friends with her on one arm and Hanna on the other. Beth's prime virtue had driven her out of his kitchen door, across the meadow, away from Hudson, into the woods, never to reappear until Waban had expertly torn her from her happiness with Wakwa and tossed her like poison ivy over the back fence.

There had been one exception - the evening in Boston at the merchant's, Mr. Crosswhite's, which she had attended with

Wakwa. Begun with joy and promise, the music fete was diluted by tangential calamities into a mere distraction. Best forgotten. Nor had Worth attended another since. No wonder Worth blessed Kirke's golden leash tugging at them to be seen in society.

Venetian society was arranged about the Falier salon like a tableau. Cultivated faces were sweetly shaped, finely featured, female and male. Women dripped embroidered ribbons weighty as a bishop's vestments. Elegant linen and lace at the throat, breast, wrist, were subordinated to cuff, collar or shawl, a fabulous waste (sinful because it was conscious). Silvered glass framed by silvered glass to which florets of silvered glass were fixed, reflected by millions the clusters of patricians in their costumes of indigo, pink, blue-black, tangerine, their hair white, whitened, golden, umber, and rust. The female silhouettes, hooped as round as the bubbles in sparkling wine, revealed slender waists and ankles and feet caressed by stockings and slippers of bright silk. Men's nicely turned calves were crowned at the knees by circlets of ermine or gold-edged galloon. Language replicating the hidden lace, the spread silks, and as subtly and as shockingly colored, hinted of the satyr and the faun.

Here was music! Not since his Oxford days, had Worth swum in such sound. Not even then. Instruments, all varieties, bulbous, sleek, long-necked, arched, all beautiful, sang. And what they sang! Gil gloried in being alive and in attendance at this great house in the heart of the century in the heart of the musical world where the passionate thrust of musical expression left the appetites sated without taste of meat or wine or carnal intimacy. The Venetian stamp, a many-colored mark, lay upon the notes vibrating through the air into bodies. The courtesies, introductions and small talk, were swift and cheerful, mere wavelettes flirting with a beach. Lady Music absorbed them like a sand of jewels.

The host had compellingly placed a harp for Worth on the circumference of the great ballroom. Gil politely set down his guitar and pulled the harp between his thighs. He drew a crowd, typically Venetian, admiring, analytical, stunned by his mastery, ultimately unconcerned.

Gil kept Elizabeth clearly in sight. She stood with Claude. She was clothed in clay-hued velvet with an over-gown of stiff, sheer, seaweed-colored silk, throat to train.

The large priest wore his non-clerical gray brocade. Appreciating the women who were appreciating the cut and colors of Elizabeth's gown, Claude remarked, "I must give Thomas some credit for settling in Italy." Elizabeth stayed rooted at Claude's side.

A young man stepped forward - the youngest son of the host. His deep bow to Elizabeth showed a trim waist, the legs of a rider, the feet of a dancer, the shoulders of a wrestler. When he stood erect, his face presented the mask of civilization.

"Madama Kirke," he said in careful, stilted English, "what a gracious soul is your husband to honor us citizens of Serenissima with your presence while he...follows her other calling." His pause was calculated and his phrase formed a brilliant summary of the intertwined interests of the House of Kirke with the old families of the Republic. It was followed by another bow. Longer. Deeper.

Elizabeth exchanged glances with Claude and, after an instant's hesitation, she curtseyed to this man whose position in the line forbade his marrying. The legal device, unique to Venice, preserved the family fortune to the eldest son during life and beyond, and, thus, power to the family. Young Falier, like all younger sons, squandered time and, to support a pointless existence, the family's loosely tied purse.

Elizabeth dropped and rose slowly, her bosom etched by black-green shadows under the rigid, transparent silk. "How gracious your family are to receive us!"

"Bellissima!" He put her hand to his lips. Shapely lips and mobile.

Dismayed, she stepped back against Claude's vast belly.

The young Falier took a step back himself as if fencing. His hand did not release hers.

Worth made no mistakes. His fingers kept pace with the music but his eyes were filled with the picture of innocence in its death throes.

Claude let his pudgy hand fall on Elizabeth's waist.

Falier saw as a Venetian and assumed he understood the gesture.

St. Aubin informed him without charm, "Thomas Kirke, my friend of many years, left 'is wife in my keeping!"

Without the least clutter of emotion or words, the young man said, "Then, monsieur, I ask *you* if I may dance with the lady."

Elizabeth broke in, fearful. "Don Falier, I do not dance. I have never danced in my life!"

At last Sebastiano Falier faltered. He paused. Swallowed his disbelief. He recovered, "Because you are so young, Madonna." He bowed to St. Aubin. "With your permission!"

Claude wished for Locke's quick tongue right then but he whipped Falier back with, "This is a Puritan woman. It is she must give permission!"

Falier, ever artful, ignored Claude's social error. He seamlessly turned his attention on Elizabeth. "Madama Kirke, I should have realized. For pure you look!" His glance delved hers. "Honor me! For I am at your mercy." Sebastiano Falier sank to one knee revealing a crescent of revelers behind him tittering at his difficulty in achieving a dance with Kirke's mysterious wife.

Gilbert Worth silenced the harp, seized his guitar, and nearing, played with extreme delicacy.

Elizabeth's heart softened toward Sebastiano when she saw him mocked. "Claude, tell Don Falier...he may...teach me the step, if I may talk to him about America."

Claude's brows arced. It was as if Devil Locke had brushed her soul. Kirke's ensign
surely waved behind her words. And then the prime negotiator, Elizabeth's grand passion, the Indian, came to Claude's mind. Whatever its source, the Jesuit was glad to strike her bargain. Accepted, it got Falier off his knees and in an investor's posture.

Sebastiano Falier led her lightly to the center of the marble floor. For long minutes coaching and coaxing, he was rewarded by the feeling of her skin heating and her body following the lure of the guitar joined irresistibly by other instruments. Falier praised, "The Puritan lady does dance!" His comment elicited a smile from her the like of which she had never given another man.

Dancing, that is, the adherence to prescribed maneuvres with the feet, the raising of the arms in public in rhythm with another body, caused surges of rare fluids through her organs. The pushing refrain of the music tore a creed too cold, planted in her the germ of play. A kindness for diversion took root.

Worth played without regret that with the dance a little of the world had invaded her to keep her quick, alive, and wanting.

CHAPTER TWENTY-FIVE

April 1753

Gilbert Worth wobbled in his first steps on the pier. For golden moments he watched his wife dashing across the lawn toward him, her shawl floating away on the wind off the Channel. Then regardless of the awkward gift he bore, he ran toward her. Two boys hooted hello as they tried in vain to outrun Hanna.

In the window from where they observed Gil's arrival, Beckett said disgustedly to Cecil, "Nothing drives a wedge between them – no event is awful enough to break their bond!"

"Then why not stop trying?"

Beckett turned toward and away from his host. He decided against any retort.

"I intend to keep you so busy you won't have time to chafe, Mr. Beckett."

Beckett turned back to Cecil. "How do you mean, Lord Worth?"

"The chafing or the workload?"

Beckett permitted a brief grin to slide across his well-made lips. "Both." He watched his son a few steps behind Moses nearing the entwined pair and Gil's burden, a square encumbrance covered in heavy cloth and swinging from a ring.

Cecil took the scene in with thoroughness. "How would you say Moses is doing in his Latin lessons?"

Bleakly, Beckett allowed, "Wonderfully well. As he does everything. My son taught him the fine points of riding and in that too the Indian kid excels. He's outstripped his trainer." Then archly, "Like his father, Wolf-of-the-Mist is a quick study."

Instead of taking up the argumentative line, Cecil ruminated, "I should like to meet the Sachim one day. In fact, it may soon be more than a wish."

Beckett's attention to the scene below snapped.

"Horace and Moses have been petitioning for a journey together to Massachusetts."

Beckett groaned. "I know."

"I wish I could accompany them."

"Moses, perhaps, not Horace. There is no chance that my son will go jaunting off to America."

"No?"

"With all due respect, Lord Worth, "I can't afford the fares. It is unthinkable that I would let Gilbert toss money at me! Even if I had no concerns about cutting into my reserves, I can't afford the time. Heavens! At foaling?!"

"I do not think you follow, Mr. Beckett. Your son will travel without you."

Beckett seemed to foam at the mouth. "Preposterous!"

Cecil watched Gilbert remove the drapery from his burden revealing a cage that caught the sun like gold. Cecil was convinced even at their distance that it was gold. "I am glad to hear you feel close to your son, but weren't it better for him to have a healthful sea voyage with his governess rather than be shut up on your Cambridgeshire donjon?"

Beckett let the bit about the governess slide. "You see his weakness. I could lose him!"

Cecil replied, "I see him stronger since coming to Heathersley."

Beckett countered, "There is war coming on! The seas will close!"

"That is precisely why I need you in London. You have knowledge of the law and first-hand experience of America. There's policy to decide, war or peace. Agree to come. If not, I'll find someone else. Think about it and think about them. You and I are lonely men. Shall we make two others?"

Gilbert placed the cage on the stone and half knelt to embrace the boys. He crushed Moses to him. "She gives you time. She gives. You'll get there!"

They all crouched to see the pair of pigeons, survivors of the journey from Venice. Small fingers found the feathers through the wires. Gil nabbed one bird and took a ring of gold foil from its skinny leg.

"Can you read this? Elizabeth had to write very small!"

Cherish them. They'll fly home.

The English spring with its mud, its moist blue skies traversed by ships of gray cloud, its citrine grass and soft air coaxing flowers into bud, its black rains, its blooms thick with color and perfume, borders resisting wind to burst with spikes and circlets and trembling with blue and white, and bees and honey everywhere, was subordinate in Moses' mind to the pigeons in their cage of gold. Never far from them, often netting them from their roost on Cecil's bookcases and confining them to their flimsy house, he took them riding, included them in picnics, toted them up the rocks over the Channel.

He never named them. They were so alike he would have called them the same name if he had had the heart to laugh. He knew from his mother's message that they knew how to fly and they knew their way home. Those talents made him hate them some days. He with all his study could only yearn, look up at the stars not understanding how to make certain things be. But the gold message of tiny letters pressed in with a needle bade him cherish them. His Uncle Gil had explained the word. If feeding them, cleaning them, letting them fly Cecil's galleries, talking to them, keeping them close, meant cherishing them, he had not dishonored Elizabeth Dowland's desire. He stroked their breasts, warm from their hurried hearts, as she might have stroked them, the oil from her skin mingling with the oil from his on the pigeons' luminous feathers.

The moon above him, white as milk, made delicious reflections in the hollows of the Channel. It was a kindly night. Not cold. Not rough. *Cherish them. They'll fly home.* Moses understood each thought, not how it fit with its fellow. But sorrow for the captive birds who knew more than he prompted him to swing open the cage door and kiss each pearly head as it peeked out. He held the heavy beings on each of his outstretched palms. He said to each, "I love thee!" They cocked their heads, needing to be sure of his message. Then Moses threw them to the wind and watched their wonderful wings.

CHAPTER TWENTY-SIX

1753 to 1754

Simply and sensibly, Wakwa revealed himself at last to the greatest whitemen of the day.

So rationally, so deftly did he present Ninnuock requirements in the face of world war and his People's extinction, the colonial leaders recognized him against the brilliance of their own political dawn. As in the legend of the black fox, his namesake, Wakwa was visible briefly then he vanished from their sight unharmed.

Wakwa, himself, was amazed at what a sheen his words took on in front of the meeting in the City of Brotherly Love, the words being so simple and the idea behind them growing in him since childhood. From the days when he had first become aware that there were colonial assemblies and that they functioned not unlike the tribal councils of the Ninnuock, Wakwa thought that delegates from the Crown, from the colonies, and from the tribes, should meet once each season to resolve their current differences. What could be simpler?

The traditional treaties around far-flung fires did not approach the symmetry of the congress he envisioned. To his mind, pacification of ills with treaty-presents and promises in place of a workable policy accomplished nothing but humiliation and bad will.

With Dire's help, Wakwa laid a plan before the prime men of Massachusetts Bay, Pennsylvania, Connecticut, New York, and Maryland. And those powerful men, some with reluctance, some with enthusiasm, some with respect, grudging or otherwise, incorporated his idea with others' ideas into the body of a plan for unified action against the French.

They would all think about the plan, named for the great man, Benjamin Franklin, and convene after the winter in larger numbers at Albany for discussion and a vote. If the *Franklin Plan* survived Albany, it would be transformed into the *Albany Plan*, and introduced quickly to every colony. Like any new child, it would live or die on the acceptance or rejection of its nurturers - in this instance, the colonial assemblies.

The signature Wakwa left on the *Franklin Plan* was his style of transforming differences into agreement and agreement into action. Wakwa argued that any resolutions proposed by a tri-part Congress would be put to a vote: one vote by the Crown, one by all the colonies, one by all the native Nations. Three votes. The outcome would legally bind all factions to comply. And each faction, royal, colonial, native, unified within faction in order to have the right to vote, would be more likely to set about complying.

Some of the delegates at Philadelphia said his plan was too simple. Some said it was simply elegant. Some said it was revolutionary. But its simple turn in the relations between red and white, counting them equal, made Wakwa's plan an elegant revolution.

Silent Fox went home and basked in the sun of his success all July. In the last days of August, Dire Locke rode into the otan.

"*The Merriweather* is not two weeks behind me." Locke's announcement was flat and dour although the day dripped gold and blackberries in a fresh breeze off the sea.

Wakwa lit with delight. "Gilbert has a way! A fine sense of the season. What a harvest we shall have! My Moses will step on shore just at his birth-time. Oh, we shall feast!"

Locke avoided jubilation. "I would not have expected them till winter. The Company set Worth some difficult business to accomplish. He's either a genius or he's neglected his charge. Nor am I convinced he is aware of the delicacy of your position. I've got a copy of the passenger list. It includes a woman unnamed."

Wakwa heard. "Unnamed?" Without his knowing it, a free, broad smile cast his features as his younger self. "Claude has reunited mother and son after all?"

Locke snapped that line of thought. "It is not Elizabeth."

Hints of age crept back. "I see!" His hands involuntarily smoothed his lower face planing it of telltale lines, puckers of hope or turmoil. "I see."

"I am sorry."

Wakwa clung to reason. "If she is unnamed, how can you be sure the woman is not Elizabeth?"

"You know Gilbert Worth better than I. You don't think he would put...Mrs. Kirke...aboard...and not tell you?"

Wakwa swallowed. "I think not."

"Horace Beckett is on the list!"

"Husseh! The woman unnamed is your wife!"

"I cannot think who else it would be besides Jeanette." Dire said without joy.

Locke produced the rolled list from his famous inner pocket, snapped it against Wakwa's outstretched palm, and paced the floor mat. "I don't know if I like it. Something's gone all too well. And not a syllable from Worth about the mission I set him!"

Wakwa looked from the list to Locke.

"Not that he should write about that, but some indication. My fault! We should have set up a code. Some musical notation would have sufficed!"

"Dire. You are so vexed! We will take your wife in. Sweetwood is no place for her."

Locke remembered his manners. "I thank you for your offer but I'll manage Jeanette. I've finally found a property."

"West?"

"I will not drop a half-penny in the West until the Albany Plan is passed. Wetomp, my little spot is not fifty-two miles from where we stand!"

Wakwa was baffled.

"I bought a tract on Rhode Island. Can you imagine? A place to hang my hat. I've got a house underway already."

"But there is Pemaquid!"

"Is there? If Albany fails, God forbid, the Maine will be a battleground and the seas around her. No. No. We need a position here smack in the middle of English ground to snag what ships and news float into Wareham Harbor. And I need a place to stop." Dire pulled his peruke off. "And where I'm not the only Jew for a thousand miles!"

Wakwa made a sound of sympathy. "Nux, Dire. Your tribe is in Rhode Island." He prevailed on the factor to sit.

Dire held his forefinger and thumb a tiny bit apart. "There is just a chance that happiness could be ours!"

Wakwa resisted, "When have you ever before said the word happiness in my presence?"

"It was an overstatement."

Wakwa shook his head to the contrary. "Annoosuonk. You hope."

"Hope is not a word in my vocabulary."

"There is another English word...you are...."

"Optimistic?" Locke shrugged. "I would not go that far. I am...prepared."

"Prepared...?" Here Wakwa's color deepened. "Prepared for what?"

"Business as usual."

"Truly as usual?"

"Very nearly." Dire exploded, "Except for Worth and his impetuosity! Now the house won't be ready and Jeanette delivered out of season."

Wakwa swallowed Locke's sureness that the mysterious passenger was not Elizabeth. "Dire. She is your woman that you love."

"Fox, I've things to do! I did not expect to deal with a woman so soon!"

Wakwa looked at his friend. "Dire, it were better they force her upon you for if you wait as I do, you may never see your woman again."

Locke took his point in silence.

Wakwa asked politely, "My dear friend, where on Rhode Island is this half-built house?"

"Hah! Half-Built House it shall be called! In fact, I'm building two. My personal house and one standing near, a place for business, for guests." Locke's words bounced out of him like bubbles. "It's at Newport. A boat ride of a few miles and then about forty more on horseback. Or, in a good wind off Sakonnet, one bilious day on Rhode Island Sound and down Buzzards Bay to Wareham!"

Wakwa watched the factor's expression closely. "So that I understand, wetomp, you are building what? A trading post? Not in these times. Kirke bade you purchase ground on the sea and build on it a house? Two houses?" A rising blood-darkness tinted Wakwa's jaw.

"Kirke has nothing to do with it. He knows nothing about it. It's my money. My land. My house. My idea, and my business!" Then, as Wakwa's probe hit home, Dire scurried close and spoke low, "But if he should want or need to come there...he'd, she'd, be most welcome!"

Wakwa looked worriedly into Dire's face, "Dire, I have things to accomplish first!"

In light of the fleet's imminent arrival, and with a secret hope that sickened him like fear, Wakwa called a council of the elders, men and women, to organize a welcome for the travellers.

He set the scene for them. "Out of the water, out of the mist, the masts grow like the pines they are, as if coming back to life over the great bodies of three black merchant ships throwing painted gold back to the sun!"

The miawene applauded his poetry.

Wakwa got down to business. "With my father, Pequawus, Awepu, and Dire Locke, I will greet them from the shore. Our brave young men shall keep our largest canoes poised on the crests of the waves so that our presence will be clear to them. When Gilbert and Hanna and the two children walk down the gangway, the men will sing to make the voyagers' hearts light. Ah!" His arm struck his breast in anticipation.

The council chamber stayed quiet. The women smoothed their hands and looked at their covered knees. The men shifted their crossed ankles.

Wakwa said more persuasively, "This is a plan of which I am fond."

The women counselors wrinkled their noses and made dove's noises at his irresistible and rare smile. Yet, they countered, "Shall only men see the masts rising out of the water? And what of the stuffs to be brought onto land? Who will carry? Men?" This last raised some laughter. "If you have a glad song you will need bells! And if you have bells you must have women!"

Someone called out, "Nuppohwunau should dance!"

"No, no!" There was disagreement among the women's council. "The song should be deep and mighty, even sad. No bells. No dance."

Wakwa gasped his frustration. "Must I weep season after season? Cannot there be a moment of summer for me? For us? For the children of this town who have had too many summers of downcast eyes and whispering?"

Men and women looked down. No one whispered.

Wakwa fumed.

Qunneke's mother brushed stray locks away from the curve of her neck. "Sachim, my son of old, my son-in-law, do we know who is on those ships? Whether they suffer disease? Sorrow? Who is on the ships? Who was left behind?"

Wakwa flinched.

"Listen to those who caution you to greet the boats with reserve." Her regard was strict and strictly on him.

Wakwa addressed them all but he looked only at the mother of his wife. "Your sachim is a man. His heart can be lighter than air. At times. Yet he thanks you for weighing down his heart. He yearns for a light heart but his advisors load ice into it. Rake hot stones into it. Both make it heavy. It is most proper."

When no one came to his rescue, Wakwa spread his gaze around the circle of faces, "Had I been asked this very dawn if I lived my life caring for the lightness of others' hearts ahead of mine, I could have answered, 'Yes!' I do admit today I have a care for the lightness of my own."

Wakwa spoke no more and the only sound was Qunneke's mother clearing her throat a bit sharply for a day at the start of Nunnowa, a gentle season.

Awepu filled the stark silence. "Sachim, would it please you if Matthew Freeman and Israel Stirling went with your father and me to meet the ship? That way they could give care if there are any ill, there would be someone to lift their trunks of clothes, and your chief counselors would be there to show the travellers love and respect. Canoes could be hidden there to carry everyone upriver to you."

Wakwa answered sharply, "Israel cannot leave Worth Farm. He has a wife near to birthing his child. Doctor Mac is not so strong. Matthew is needed at home with them for it is harvest. And then, I *want* to be there. *I* want to see the ship float into port!"

Awepu shook his head sadly, knowing who Wakwa desired to be aboard.

A concerned elder spoke up. "Sachim, why? Why put yourself at risk among the drunkards of the town?"

Wakwa snapped, "I did not see my son leave from Plymouth Harbor. I stayed here preparing us for war. Now there is a chance for peace! Or, at the least, for help in our defense! I will turn my eyes from fighting for an afternoon. I will watch the ship arrive!"

Another loyal man continued the theme. "Look toward Albany! Let us your counselors take the risks and bring your family home for you."

Wakwa could not believe his ears. "I spend half my life at Wareham. A little town of sheds and mice!"

A new, young council member warned, "Sachim! Listen to them. There may be risk. A man can fight a war better than he can dodge broken bottles from behind."

This Wakwa could not brook. "With you at my back, Raven, what have I to worry about?"

Nothing cowed, Raven defended his point, "A man who has success also has enemies. You have told us yourself there is talk against us in Sweetwood."

"I have taken care of that. As you are aware."

Pushed to it, Raven added provocatively, "What proof have you that Carpenter Spinney has parted for the Ohio? It was not so long ago that other enemies of yours made calamity in your house and set us on the road to the mountains. They may not like we are come home!"

Wakwa pegged this bleak speech as subversive. "It is the nature of the raven to feed upon dead matter." That settled that.

A woman ventured subtly, "If you go, Sachim, will you bring your wife and her children?"

While Wakwa gathered himself to reply, another woman interjected, "And if the Sachim cannot know the moment the ships arrive, will the Saunks make camp on the sand in front of sailors and shopkeepers? There is no decent way for them to live!"

Wakwa closed his eyes. "Thus I had thought the women's council and the Saunks should wait here ready to receive our English family, their guests and my son, Moses. Is it not more natural the women prepare here for the travellers?"

Qunneke's mother flared, "I do anything you ask of me, son-in-law, but I am not content my daughter who has spent herself raising another woman's son should be burdened over cooking pots the very day the child again enters her care!"

Wakwa slapped his knees at her bitching.

And so it went until the beautiful summer afternoon silvered as it waned. Chilled, they drew on shirts and shawls and lit a fire. A meal was served, blueberries lost in cornbread, a stew of fish, a ruddy heap of heartberries, and a steaming pudding of the first pumpkins inundated with maple syrup.

When the pipes glowed, Wakwa looked at the two-score people, the struts of their tribe. He pulled on his pipe and let smoke rings ascend to the bowed ceiling, toward the smokehole where stars could be seen as if pinned to the sky with quills. One diaphanous circle framed a star and Wakwa took it as his signal to speak.

"It is wondrous, is it not, how the mist lifts away by this time at night?"

The forty-odd counselors, alert for a signal, sat erect.

Pequawus, pleased with his supper, with his pipe, knew keener pleasure at Wakwa's remark. He did not let his face change, did not search out anyone's eye or throw an elbow into anyone's ribs as old Waban might have done. He only sucked the neck of his pipe like a connoisseur.

"I decided...."

The factions of them took breath, squared their shoulders.

"I determined in the spring just past to write my first son's name on the matricula at Oxford."

No one spoke; no interruption was attempted. But the keen advisors around the fire crossed glances with one another. They had been speaking of the welcome of *The Merriweather*!

As if he did not see their confusion, Wakwa sent up another smoke ring. "There on the British island, Moses Bluehill will meet another wisdom. As our sons separate from their families to listen to the forest for their life's direction, the English send their sons away to study at the feet of learned men. You know this as the truth. You also know my first son, who is sailing toward us seeing these same stars from a different place, has two souls. Red and white. Both must be fed. And by his devouring all knowledge, ours and that of his...," Wakwa veered away from reference to the maternal side, absolutely refused to cast Elizabeth's name before them like a tattered blanket, "and that of his European forbears, Wolf-of-the-mist He-hopes will become a strongman, a saviour to you, your children, to any future of this withered People. That is he whom we greet in fourteen dawns or so. Our hope! I would have told you this earlier but I felt that you were aware of all these things without my telling you because you love me."

If etiquette had permitted smiles, they would have smiled. He had trapped them in his graceful net.

"And since you love me so that our souls are one, you know how it will be the day the ships appear! My father, Pequawus, my cousin, Awepu, and I, your servant and chiefmost man, with suitable guards, not many, and in silence, will watch the landing. And the great canoes will ride the waves so that from the distance our family coming home can see our love of them. The small canoes will be waiting to speed them home. But as my cousin, Awepu, saw, a solemn, sweet, singing by the young men paddling will set up as we push off. And at the places where the river bends, other canoes will slip into the water, men and women...singing, the singing growing. At each turn of the river more canoes will join and the sound become larger, the song dark and rich like gut-meat to feed the travellers' souls starved for home, and by the time our roundhouses come in view, the trees behind them red and gold, every Massachuseuck, young and old, with bells jingling, shall be present on the water or on the riverbank singing! We shall bring the journeyers home and feed them and rest them and hear their stories until they slip into our arms to dream."

No one dared object. Instead they laughed inside with pride at the grace of Wakwa's mastery over them - the leader they had voted in. All their wishes incorporated, all his desires met. They knew all too well how his plan of union had been swallowed at Philadelphia.

Sighting his mother-in-law, the woman who had nursed him at her breast when he had been, like Moses, an infant without a mother, Wakwa added, "As for Qunneke, the Saunks, *she* shall choose where she will be." He raised his arms blessing them. "We are then content with this?"

Qunneke's mother presumed to comment, "We will pray, Sachim, it does not rain."

It did not rain. Qunneke chose to watch the landing and chose to have her children and Awepu's second son, Tamoccon, with her. They sheltered in the barrens at the river and only made their quiet entrance onto the sands near the dock after Kirke's colors could be seen on the horizon. With the aid of Tamoccon and his telescope they saw in miraculous detail the fleet of three surge into Wareham Harbor.

"Husseh!" Qunneke breathed, the long glass tight on a boy with hair as white as down.

Horace Beckett breathed in, breathed, breathed to pull the Massachusetts brine, the pine, the silver dust of the New World sand into his lungs. He strained to see the people on the shore but in the delicate light of sunrise could glean only the splendidly straight silhouettes of faceless men. Horace stepped down the gangway arm-in-arm with Moses. The tall, straight people, black before the sun, moved forward and turned the healthy color of flowerpots; their clothes of skin trembled like summer dressing gowns. The tallest man went down on one knee and held out his arms.

Ho felt Moses pull away. Leaping, skipping, scampering, Moses quickly touched his lips to the shoulders of the man he called, "Nosh." Ho thought the gesture strange as it broke Bluehill's progress into Nosh's embrace. Then for minutes, minutes, there was no face, only the man's black hair blowing and blending with Bluehill's.

Ho felt Hanna's firm hand on his shoulder, "Wakwa, see how Horace Beckett has grown! Ho, this is the Sachim, Moses' father, Wakwa."

Uncoached, Ho bowed. He straightened to discover very close to his own face, man's skin, sun-brightened, smooth, no stubble, no beard, teeth lightning white, no eye-tooth-fangs as in English mouths, sparse black silk for brows, cheeks and nose strong with bone, bottomless, black, India tea for eyes. Ho looked for what was not there in the hollows of Wakwa's face - Michael Beckett's bitterness.

Wakwa turned to Gilbert Worth.

Worth's voice was hoarse, as if he had been shouting for hours. He said, "Wakwa! Everything is as you ordained!"

Ho escaped the men's embrace and was confronted by skin of beige silk wrinkling in a smile. A woman's cool-water voice, called him, "Wushowunan!"

Wakwa let Gil go and laughed in two languages, "Hawk is a warrior's name, Tame Deer. Not for Michaelbeckett's son who looks a mild man."

Qunneke spoke again.

Wakwa translated, "Qunneke saith his hair is the color of the she-hawk's child and that a sachim should know it is the tame hawks scare away the birds who steal the corn!"

That broke the spell. Beckett's son laughed, his platinum self suddenly as alive as the sun on the sea.

"Let us take you home, Hawk!" Wakwa placed one hand on Ho's head. "Let us take you home."

Ho dug his boot heels into the sand. "Jeanette!"

A coach and four, shining black against the backdrop of the pale gray port stood above them on the quay.

Wakwa pointed to the carriage. "Dire has come."

A woman's skirts filled the doorway of the coach and were engulfed by its darkness. The door snapped shut.

With the river in view, Wakwa worked an iron spade. A number of his tribesmen returned to Twisting River with fish and shellfish from the arm of land thrust into the ocean that the English called Cape Cod.

O, there was cod! That was only the beginning. Bass, haddock, bream, eel, and the sturgeon with roe fit for kings crowded the take, and best of all, the oyster, clam, and lobster filled the baskets.

Wakwa stood opposite to and twenty paces away from the newest member of the men's council, who happened to be Raven. Each senior member of the council faced his next newest counterpart twenty paces away. The exactness of their circle seemed uncanny. It was not. It was geometrical.

Wakwa sank the spade into the soil near the riverbank. He pushed on it with his foot and scooped out a heap of reddish earth. Delighted applause met his ceremonial act. Wakwa passed the shovel to his father, his father passed it to Awpeu, and so on through the men's council until an accurately cut ring of earth existed twenty paces across.

Moses and Horace and the children of the counsellors were treated to a turn with child-sized tools, all giggling and gasping, each expected to turn the heavy soil and contribute to the mound of earth outside the ring. The less illustrious completed the work, digging a shallow pit inside the ring for the baking of the feast.

The sun had just climbed out of morning when Qunneke ordered the women to bring the seaweed. The men lined the open oven with stones; they piled on hardwood and fruitwood. Wakwa touched a raging torch to the wood. The scent that rose infiltrated memory.

The Worths declined to leave the otan. Awepu went to Worth Farm to collect the Stirlings and the Lows. Matthew could hardly control the horses he loaded down with bushels of apples. Dr. Mac stashed surgical tools in jars of gin. Priscilla turned a deaf ear to Israel and shouldered a pouch of pills and medications and led the party down the deer path. And for the first time, Cooke followed them into the woods. She went armed with paring knife, flour, butter and board, and bags of Kirke's ginger and cinnamon. No Indian feast was so satisfying, she maintained, that it could not be improved by her pastry.

The stones turned red-hot. The hundreds of pounds of fish and shellfish, icy cold from their storage in the river in baskets, were at hand. Just-picked corn in the husk filled baskets at the edge of the pit.

At last the smoke burned white. Wakwa gave the signal. Fresh water flew, dousing the flames. The stones sizzled. Men drew a layer of seaweed over them as a bed for the vertebrate fish, and the bass heads bundled in scarves of seagrass. A layer of seaweed covered that. Jade and opal and jet – the lobsters, clams, oysters, and muscles were tossed onto the pyre. Another blanket of the briny grass was spread, more shellfish loaded on, until there were no more. Onto and under coverlets of seaweed went the corn. Abockquosinash, birch mats weighted with stones, closed in the steam. The kiln of seafood was abandoned to its agony.

The slow baking of the fish left the women time to stir the meal for the cornbread. Squash and cubes of deer meat and cress were dotted with bear fat, encased in cedar bark and grilled over open fires. Puddings of pumpkin and pound upon pound of maple sugar were perfected in big copper pots set over tripods on the plane.

This slowly cooking food produced an aromatic mist that veiled history, misunderstandings, murders, war, blood, venom, stone fences, fear and hate. One could not partake of such goodness and not acknowledge the source unless stark mad.

Moses and Horace ran in a heaven of fragrance of the bake and of the cool, bright air of the woods. They took off with the Massachuseuck boys for the forest and played at hunting. Lightfoot, Wakwa's second son, was too young for the game but his name, Wautuckques, meant quick in the rabbit's way, warm, observant, fleet, so he was permitted to join. Privately, his grandmother called him not Wautuckques, but Noowan-anumukquog, her impression of his place in Wakwa's and Qunneke's eyes. To her he was, *They-Forget-Me*.

Used to the fringes, fiercely attached to following a secret path, Lightfoot naturally played the prey on the occasion of his half-brother's return from the Old World. He thought it was fine to be caught by Moses and his friends when he was playing the part of any animal other than the one linked to his soul. They could truss him and turn him on a spit if they could overpower him. In fact, he let them, giggling, for his friend-cousin- brother-hunters brought him grapes and blackberries and maple sugar to console him after they were done feasting on his carcass.

But one boy-hunter sighted *rabbit*. Lightfoot was off. He moved so fast he never heard Moses bring down the mischief-maker, never heard the boy's pleas for help against Wolf-of-the Mist, the half-white predator with eyes of gold. Lightfoot felt his bones cold, his lips blue as he evaded the insult.

The boys called him. They told him the game was over. They called to him of corn parched till it popped open into puffballs, of luscious fruit, and bowls of nuts they would crack open for him. They tracked him. Silence reigned in the green glades. Their tapping on the trees, voicelessly begged him to reveal himself. From high in a tree he watched them cutting back and forth, going in pairs, lifting sodden logs, disturbing summer insects in their death throes.

Lightfoot was practiced in avoidance. He hid expertly and changed his hiding place. His flight led him toward the farms, away from the feast, and onto turf where a frost of ghosts not many seasons old always clung. Instinct carried him to the pinewoods behind Dowland Farm. None of the hunters' sons would follow him to the tall, empty house which, if one stood quite still, could be heard to groan at twilight in fall-of-leaf.

To be captured as what he was, was death. His rabbit-soul abhorred disgrace. Abhorred disgracing his name. Very little sun slanted through the pine boughs. Quaking from his cooling sweat, from his fright of capture, from his other fright of angering his brother, his mother and father, Lightfoot turned toward Dowland House. Too many pitfalls lay in the way of his gaining the kitchen door undetected. He turned back to the woods. He blinked.

In a white lance of sunshine against the shade was the English boy, Horace. His hair and skin white, his white shirt open at the neck, his blue knee britches and black boots lost against the boughs, disembodied him. "Hill!" the apparition called softly as it beheld the Puritan house for the first time.

Moses broke free of the woods as if he had forgotten why he had come there. Lightfoot made a discrete circle south through the woods, then east over the short grass in front of the house. Sprinting close to the ground, he gained the northeast corner. Then he popped up on the kitchen steps. Panting. Ready to run, his heart pumping, redeemed by his prowess, he crossed his arms over his chest meeting face on two who loved him.

Moses saw Lightfoot and came along, trotting. Never rushing but transfixing Lightfoot with his bright eyes, Moses reached for his half-brother and held him. Ho Beckett jogged near and stood panting.

"Want to come inside?" Moses asked them.

As the three of them walked through the rooms, Ho asked, "There's another name for rabbit. Do you think he'll mind if I call him Coney?"

"Okasu!" Wakwa came across his mother-in-law surrounded by girls, Sequan included. These were children a few seasons too young for flirting with the boys.

Qunneke's mother held them fascinated with a story but she broke off when the Sachim, greeted her.

"You look happy, Mother!"

Neechippog, named with some humor for the morning dew, her cold, clear wisdom like a daily medicine, smiled, "I am grateful Tame Deer is strong enough to bear the new weight."

Wakwa gave no more time to her; he moved at a sober pace toward his wife. He was conscious Neechipog was watching him. Tame Deer looked up, met his eyes. One of her hands lightly fingered a necklace of unalloyed gold, gold hammered into a deep collar of scales which moved like chain or mail - a mermaid's tail.

Wakwa stood speechless.

The ingot, reformed into a bold decoration for a beautiful neck and bosom, was much more. The "blessing given by Elizabeth," according to Qunneke, was, to Wakwa, Elizabeth herself, recast in the stuff of power. His voice was nothing like his own when he enquired in their tongue, "Was there any writing with it?"

"Matta." Qunneke said, no.

Wakwa's hand ached to touch the queenly piece that Elizabeth had surely created and as surely had touched when it was smithed. He withheld his hand.

Instead he ordered his men to dismantle the cover of the pit. Lobster gone scarlet, clams and oysters and muscles sprung open, slabs of whitemeat fish and spears of tender corn filled everyone with their aromas before a bite was taken. He walked to a height to taste of the twilight scene. Then he slipped away home.

Gil found him in the rotunda. "I've brought you a portion. Eat! It is sublime. There is nothing, nothing in Europe's complex kitchens can approach it."

Wakwa looked at the blond man. "She does not forget this. She smells the air full of our smoke. She will return."

Worth bit his lip.

Horace Beckett could not sleep. Bluehill breathed steadily only inches from him although the fire cracked like cannon. From his grass mat, Ho tried to make out the voices of the men who spoke sometimes in English sometimes in the native language. Wakwa's voice was clear. Gilbert Worth's was deep. Another voice, nasal, whipping Indian syllables into submission with an adroit tongue must be Dire Locke's. There was a quieter voice, a mystery until Ho thought of Awepu. Ho wriggled out of his hard, flat bed on his belly. He lifted the corner of the reed curtain and saw men talking and laughing and smoking.

The room where they sat was red and umber, breast-round. The Sachim faced east - exactly the direction of Qunneke's room, exactly the direction of Ho's curious face. Gilbert sat at Wakwa's left, his heart's side, Pequawus at Wakwa's right, the side of power. Awepu sat opposite the Sachim, his back to the quivering curtain.

Doctor Mac, sleeping, wrapped in fur, muttered into the fire. Locke faced north.

"Come. Come in. Come to me, Hawk!" Wakwa motioned to Ho.

Ho could only shake with shame. Discovered eavesdropping! He had pried only to match sight with sound, save the picture in his eyes forever.

"Ho! Don't be afraid." It was Gilbert Worth. "Come ahead. We're inconsiderately noisy."

Ho stood die-straight in his white nightgown.

Wakwa unbent his legs and walked to him, a tower moving. He lifted Ho's chin.

Ho Beckett flinched.

"We wakened you!" Wakwa apologized.

"Father would be so upset!"

Wakwa squatted down and held Ho's shoulders. "I praise you for hunting out the voices which disturbed your rest. Come sit with the men!"

"Me?"

"You."

Awepu twisted around. "You and Moses. Wake up your friend, Hawk. A good name!"

Gil, softhearted when it came to Qunneke's son, said, "Don't forget Lightfoot."

Qunneke's necklace was discussed.

"What does it mean besides its value?" Wakwa wanted to know.

Locke said, "It's at least as significant as the belt of wampum you sent Claude. Not to mention its monetary value."

Wakwa ruminated. "I asked Claude to favor me with a great service."

Worth submitted, "Tame Deer favors my niece with a great service every day. Look at Moses!"

Locke said tartly, "Look at all *you* do for him. Did Elizabeth give *you* a bar of gold?"

Worth was stumped. "You make too much of it."

Pequawus spoke, "I do not think he does. There is heat in this gift. Touch it! It is pure, soft, giving, entrancing to see. It is like a good mother, a source of life and comfort. The giver..." Pequawus bowed his head in memory, "Moses' mother..." he paused then went on, "a woman...has placed our future in Qunneke's hands."

Wakwa's eyes changed with this complication.

Even Locke objected, "With all respect, Sagamore, I cannot think the gift was sent to undermine Silent Fox."

Awepu raised a hand. "We know this of the English, no matter which way their minds turn they always turn about a core of gold."

"There is the mark I must hit at Albany!" Wakwa cried out. "Convince them on terms they can understand. Convince the King the favor of our neutrality is a luxury he must pay for not in money or trinkets or stuffs or supplies but in fair treatment!"

Locke summed up. "The necklace inspires you. Then King George's future is in the hands of *two* women."

Ho felt as if he had had too much sherry. Around a humble fire, men sitting on the ground talked of convincing kings of things those kings must do. It amazed him that men could think to convince kings of things the king must do, more, that men could think they had a right to put their notion of right on the same level as Divine Right.

Gil caught Ho's scandalized look. "It's a strategy, Horace, not a plot. Do you know the word treason?"

"Yes, sir!"

"A Beckett through and through!"

"Father says trying to take away the King's power is treason."

"Then you'll hang with us, if caught." Worth winked. He turned back to the men.

"Treason!" Ho whispered in Moses' ear.

Moses yawned, "They do this every night, Ho. It's no great thing!"

But it was.

CHAPTER TWENTY-SEVEN

November 1753

"For a childless house, we've got a marvelous number of children all over it!" Gilbert Worth paced his sitting room replete with males, juvenile and adult.

Lightfoot was, as usual, weaving his way through the chair legs desperate for the notice of Moses and Ho who were sprawled on the rug absorbed in the hilarity of speaking untutored French. Tamoccon, twelve, poked through the window drapery with his telescope.

"And soon there will be one more!" Locke grimaced.

Priscilla Marley lay in labor in a hastily organized birthing room up the short staircase.

Gil threw three new logs onto the fire. "Our collection of young folk cries out for a girl!"

Wakwa looked up from the desk where he was writing in his labored style. "I supplied us one in Sequan."

"Gloriously! But where is she?" Gil groused, "I'd like her here!"

A groan bumped down the stairs like a metal object.

The boys' antics ceased. Wakwa stood straight out of his chair. Gil was quick to snap the double doors shut. Locke seemed to develop a tick in his neck.

A guttural cry struck the closed doors.

"I have three children. I have never heard such sounds." Wakwa came to center floor.

Locke stated, "I don't believe men are supposed to witness these events."

Wakwa rhapsodized, "I heard her call like a bird in the sky! A beautiful call. Then Tame Deer and I came to the clearing and saw Awepu holding him! In his hands! My son yet attached to...by her... by the cord!"

Moses looked curiously at his father.

Now a scream, long and jagged.

Gil paled. "One would never guess how dainty she is!"

Locke insisted, "That is why she is in distress, yes? Men simply do not listen to these things!"

"Mac and Israel are so doing." Gil made a point.

Wakwa seconded, "Awepu did. And gave us Moses safe and sound."

Dire finished smartly, "Not to mention a convincing witness in your land conveyance." A shout seemed to crack the walls of the birthing room. "How about a walk in the freezing cold?"

Men and boys milled in the hall pulling on cloak and coat, jacket and strowd, hat and muffler.

The four boys raced ahead and disappeared inside the cellars of the new Meetinghouse, barely finished. September had seen the outer walls go up, the roof shingles hammered into place, glass installed. October's foliage had been a gorgeous sight from the building's capitol, a pair of tall half-moon rooms forming one complete circle sparkling from floor to ceiling with leaded panes. Autumn's voice was the clamor of sanding, hammering, yelling, as floorboards were nailed, sanded, stained, lath and plaster and wainscot stuck in place, and the German furnace fixed into a flue on the exterior northeast wall. November's great work was the completion of the deep cellar, a floor of brick set in cement on a sub-floor supported by massive hardwood beams, creating a ceiling for the secret vault beneath. Gil and Hanna planned to receive a ship in December carrying the carpets, the brasswares, the armchairs, the tables, while the building settled into the cold earth.

Gil remarked, pulling his muffler tighter around his chin. "Too bad about Spinney. Had he been better at his trade he might at least have made the banisters."

Tersely, Wakwa said, "Were Spinney a better man he might have been a better carpenter."

They entered the empty structure, their footsteps echoing, their lungs taking in the fragrance of new construction. The innovative furnace, a thing never yet seen outside northern Europe, was commuting its task nicely. The interior was quite pleasantly, evenly temperate.

Locke praised, "This is the greatest innovation I've ever seen in building! Why haven't I got a German furnace in my Newport compound? I've got to get furnaces installed."

Wakwa commented, "Warmth without smoke."

Gil cautioned wryly, "Don't let the village gossips get wind of it. They'll haul me out to the stocks for witchcraft."

Locke said, "Priscilla Marley ought to be giving birth here for comfort's sake."

"I should have thought of that." Gil started the climb to the cupola to view the land. "Let's see if there's a signal from Matthew. She may have done it by now!"

"It takes Englishwomen more time." Wakwa said tight-lipped.

"I'm still not clear on how we'll manage if the Stirlings remove to Sandwich." Gil fretted. "We've depended on little Pris for such a long time. I'm loathe to hire from outside - our family being...more interesting than most."

Wakwa said, faintly smiling, "After Albany it may not be so hard to own friendship with an Indian."

"I did not mean exactly...."

"I mean it!"

"Dowland House is the place for them." Gil was impatient with the notion of the Stirlings in Sandwich.

Wakwa asked, "How shall Israel manage the Sterling Farm and Dowland Farm *and* learn his medicine?"

"He's always been a problem!" Gil chafed.

Horace sucked in air and said on its release, "Why don't they live here?"

"What's that, young Beckett?" Locke turned full on him.

Horace stuttered but clung to his thought. "The...the...Stirlings. After the chairs come. There are so many rooms...the unwell could stay here too. And Dr. Israel would not even have to step out of doors!"

Worth asked absently, "What are you saying, Ho?"

But Wakwa understood. "Manittoo! House them here! Section a part for Israel and his little wife and babe and Grandfather Mac, if he would want it! Oh, mighty Hawk!" Wakwa lifted Beckett's son into the tower's bright sky, "You see all from on high! We will make this a place to bring the sick of the village. Farmers, hunters, all."

"Wait a minute!" Gil stuck out his jaw.

"Oh, yes!" Wakwa cut in. "Like me! The black fox! Hiding in the glare of the sun! Gilbert. This could be a working infirmary.

Israel could learn. Help many. Dr. Mac could have new reason to live beyond the baby! He could preside over the surgery."

Worth was deflated. "What about the Meetinghouse? This was to be a place to plan. To create. In a bit of style!"

"In great style." Wakwa persuaded. "What better way to keep our secret? Physicians' supplies coming in and in."

Worth finally saw it and continued in a trance of delight, "Under their noses, these talkative Sweetwooders! Private conferences up a case of stairs. Lights burning late in the cellars. No witchcraft or sedition. Just the *infirmary*. Symbolic! The birthing and the healing place of body and of thought!"

Wakwa set Ho down.

Worth shook the boy's hand. "What are you, young Beckett? A poet? A philosopher?"

Unsure of his terms, Ho said humbly, "I don't feel able, sir."

"Well you've got ability in my book, Beck!"

Wakwa praised the boy, "Your sire must be proud of such a son."

Horace Beckett giggled at that assessmenet. "Father thinks I'm a girl."

Tamoccon made repeated sweeps of the treeline and the farm. "Natoncks!" He called his cousin, Wakwa, to put his eye to the lens. Matthew Freeman was loping toward the Meetinghouse. They could not scramble down the stairs and out fast enough to hear the news of the birth.

Moses pulled Horace toward Sweetwood Village.

"Come back!" Gil motioned.

"Stay here!" Wakwa commanded.

Moses ran away shouting, "Moce-nanippeeam! I will come bye and bye! Sequan!"

Wakwa sent Tamoccon down the hill after Moses. "Noh pasoo! Bring him!"

Worth tried to pacify the worried father. "They're not going far. Sequan is at the manse. Dolly Low is needed now!"

All Wakwa would say as they ran was, "Think you the boys know that?"

Lightfoot skipped over the field biding his time. When his father neared Worth's house, Lightfoot scampered over the crest of the hill and down the slope.

As the trio stamped into the house, Matthew relieved them of their coats and announced, "Mother and daughter safe!"

Gil was transported, "A girl! A girl!"

Locke blotted his eyes. "Jeanette can stay on as nursemaid."

Gil started for the stairs calling gleefully, "Locke, you humbug! You're crying over the newborn!"

Locke sniffed, "Au contraire, Worth, "There's a great lot of smoke from your fire!"

Gil called back, "Wakwa! Fix the fire!"

Worth invaded the linen draped room. He moved aside for Hanna, carrying away a pail of the shiny, amorphous matter that had been the newborn's lifeline only minutes before.

Israel detained her, "Don't burn it, Mrs. Worth! Have Matthew put it in the ice house!"

"Oh, yes!"

Gil was momentarily distracted by an early darkening of the sky.

Qunneke stirred a pot of something viscous over the fire and tested a spot of it on her inner wrist. Jeanette sorted sheets drenched with the fluids of birth. Priscilla lay in the guest bed, her bright hair dark from sweat, her young face the repository of all knowledge. On her breast, a tiny bundle breathed, topped by a furze of orange red.

Mac held her hand and turned to the visitors. "My daughter-in-law's the heroine of a breach delivery!"

Gilbert Worth approached the bed. "So, the family has a new daughter!"

Her smile at his inclusion of her was of a higher realm. "I'll call her Anniebeth," she blushed, "Ann Elizabeth, if I may, sir!"

"Oh, you may!" Worth looked around for Wakwa and Dire Locke.

They were at the window, peering toward the village.

Wakwa rushed downstairs without a word. Locke followed on his heels. Matthew shouted, "Master!" Doors slammed. Worth reluctantly left the hive of new life.

Outside, dun colored air polluted the lungs. Instead of snow, black particles fell from the sky. The stillness of frost was broken by roaring and screaming, as if the ocean had rolled overland to Worth's door. Gil looked right, west, toward the Meetinghouse but Matthew nearly ran him down with the cart shouting, "The manse!" Gil leaped in. His farm laborers, gripping wooden buckets by the fistful, clattered downhill.

In the premature darkness, they passed Locke, mounted and sidestepping down the dale. Wakwa's shoulders and hair could be seen on the rill and then the bottomland swallowed him. Worth caught the reins out of Matthew's hands and lay on the whip.

"Sir! Sir!" Matthew begged as the cart swerved and teetered off the road onto uneven ground.

The whip cracked again and they careened down the bank pulling abreast of Silent Fox who ran like a soul possessed.

Gil screamed, "Go back! Don't go unguarded!"

"My children!" Wakwa streaked ahead.

Gil dove out of the wagon. His cold-weather boots stood his ankles well against the unyielding soil. He took off after the Sachim.

The artificial night was set aglow by the burning manse. Villagers surrounded it, hopelessly tossing water at the blaze. Books strewed the road. Mayhew Low reeled around a corner, his arms filled with some smoking salvage of his library. Dolly and Sequan scooped up volumes where he tossed them and ran up the rise to Dowland House depositing them in a growing mound. They ran back for more. Matthew brought the cart to a halt near the heap of books. He ran toward the flames.

The manse glared and groaned and twisted until it snapped, the ground floor melting into its foundation, the upper storey defying collapse, floating boards through the sky, curtains flying free on wings of flame.

Hanna, arriving out of nowhere, screamed to Sequan, "Moses!"

Sequan pointed to the barn, the building closest to the minister's house.

"No!!!" Hanna matched the fire's scream. She battled her way through Sweetwood's women to reach the boys.

Raw-skinned, square-jawed, hollow-cheeked, their modest caps askew, the goodwives of Sweetwood poured over the incendiary parcel of land still referred to as Hudson's Farm.

In the dark shot with flame instead of stars, Sequan collided with a village wife. "Excuse me, Mrs.!"

Sequan's oval face, her soft skin clothes, her black, shimmering hair, her poised speech, struck the housewife ill. "Brazen thing!" she bellowed, the veins in her neck distended, "Filthy Indian!"

Dolly Low pulled Sequan into the cart and took the reins. She drove uphill as a burning window frame showing chards of purple glass in its mullions was hurled above them on the energy of fire.

Hanna crossed paths with Locke's stymied roan. He reached down to aid her onto his saddle.

"An' who's he?" The women demanded of Hanna. "There's always somethin' goin' on!"

Locke looked down on the village females as if on a yardful of geese. "And who are you? Move off!" Locke pointed the way.

They babbled their outrage. Men, parched and soot-smeared, gasped for air near the clutch of women. They yelled at Locke, "Get on with ye! The manse's explodin'. If you ain't helpin', you scarecrow, get goin'!"

Like the fire feeding and fattening on its own fury, each belligerence boiled into the next. "I see *you* trespassing!" Locke pounded them.

"What accent is that?"

"Bumpkins!" Locke set his cosmopolitan heel on their insular necks. "Get off this ground!" Locke raised his crop.

Hanna, struggling for the stirrup, warned, "Dire! Dire!"

"Beelzebub!" They pointed at Locke and a farmer grabbed for the roan's bridle.

Locke whirled his horse and cleared himself space. "Get gone! All of you! You have no business here!"

"No more have you! This is church land!"

"That it's not!"

"How dare!" The farmers turned on Hanna. "You Worths'll answer!"

"Careful! Locke shouted into the din. "You rail against an Elder and his wife!" Again, he reached for Hanna, again the townspeople got in the way. "Goddamn it!"

"You blaspheme on holy ground!"

"As real property is sacred, I blaspheme! Move off!"

Hanna gazed at Locke confused.

People yelled, "Property? This is our church!"

Locke spat at them. "Who owns the church?"

Shocked, they gasped, "No one, you Lucifer! Consistory paid and the parish built her! The Synod gave permission."

"Who owns the manse?"

"If you belonged here, you'd know!"

"Who owns the manse?!"

"The same as the church!"

"And the barn?"

"That's different!"

"And don't I know it!"

One man, sharper than the rest, specified, "The barn is Hudson's."

"Not!" Locke spared him one word.

"It's his land! Bought it from Dowland. Built the barn!"

"And where is this Hudson!" Locke shouted above the fire.

"Over there! In the churchyard!"

"Six feet under and deader than a mackerel!" Locke gloried in the fact.

"Murdered! Foully murdered!"

Locke shouted back, "Immaterial to the disposition of his ground! The church property was already vested in Mr. Low when Hudson resigned months before his death! The rest of the place got from Dowland, a good thousand acres, several hundred square feet of which you are all presently taking up, is now a freehold estate in abeyance and you are trespassing upon it!"

"What're you talkin' about!!!" "What's he sayin'?"

Lock pressed them. "Has this estate gone to probate?"

"What!?"

"Whose is it?!!" Locke persisted.

"Move him off!" They slapped the roan's flanks.

Locke beat them with his crop. "Do we have a Will?!"

"Troublemaker!"

"An Executor?"

"Shut him up!" The women screeched.

"An heir?"

"Hudson left no children behind. No daughters! No sons!"

Evilly, Locke spewed the truth. "No living sons!"

If thunder had rolled over them and rain had poured out of the sky putting out the fire, they could not have been more stunned.

"Who are you?!" A woman stepped forward.

"Who am I?" Locke spun his horse again as if to show them every inch of his being. "I'm the man who's going to be granted letters of administration to save this fat parcel from reverting to the Crown since I see no kindred leaping for the job!"

"What's yer name?" They yelled, they screamed like the pitch geysering from the flames. "Who are ye?" "Get his name." "Do you have a name?" "What's yer name?"

Locke tore them to shreds. "Your chief creditor, that's who I am, you chattel!" Locke gave a hyena's laugh. "You're all in hock to me! Which makes me first in line to do the honors over this estate, and, failing heirs, take the spoils!"

"Who is he? What's his name?"

"Dire Locke's the name! I'm chief factor for Kirke Company! And my eye's on you!" Locke's pockmarked cheek stretched with merriment at their milling confusion. "Hudson's widow is Thomas Kirke's wife now, and you all owe him money!"

"Dire! Dire!" Hanna pulled at his coat.

The shouting started up. "What's he mean, 'widow'?" "Dowland's girl? She drowned! Never! Went mad!"

"Elizabeth Dowland with Thomas Kirke is the head of the House! You were ever in her father's debt and now you are in hers!"

"Don't believe ye! An' Thomas Kirke's got nothin' to do with us!"

"You turds! Without The Company there's not a cup of tea on your table or a cup for that matter or sugar to sweeten your pot! Not a bolt of calico on your horizon or a gun in your belt! Mr. Kirke's got an Irish temper. I'd not encroach on his or his wife's business were I you!"

Hanna, rendered speechless, listed against the roan's breast.

Locke began to ease his horse out of the circle. "Who takes the profits from the harvest, eh? Who's been getting the profits since Hudson croaked?"

"Congregation! Proper procedure."

"Not for this length of time! I will tell the governor that instead of trying to contact possible legal heirs of the farm, members of this parish are, season after abundant season, enjoying the profits illegally."

The Presbyterians came right back, "Someone set the manse on fire and you sit high and mighty talkin' money!"

Locke kept them down. "Then you've got attempted murder on your hands. *And* trespass!"

Locke handed Hanna up to ride sidesaddle. He called back over his shoulder, "Innocent people were in the manse when it was set ablaze. The clues to this arson are incinerating while you dicker with me!"

The woman so angry when she saw Sequan, screamed after them, "Savages running all over! They started this!"

Dire Locke turned to memorize the features of her face. "You've already insulted the daughter of the Sachim. A public apology is in order! I'll be at Sunday meeting to hear it whether the church burns or not!" He trotted toward the fire rejoicing that, as he showed the crowd his horse's rump, chaos stimulated the beast to void.

Hanna complained, "Dire, we've taken such pains to keep things quiet!"

Locke seethed. "Discretion is done. This is exactly the moment to clarify the status of this legacy. I blame myself for letting it slide this long. Elizabeth could get her pound of flesh and Moses his due!"

"She'll get nothing but grief from this. There was no civil ceremony, Dire. None but a church registry."

"Who was responsible for that oversight?!"

Hanna's silence made her confession. "I thought that way it would be easier to annul."

Locke strained to be kind. "You did your best. Henceforward, the word is Hudson's death came too soon for the law to be satisfied in every particular. The brute, Hudson, sealed the fate of his land consummating his marriage to Elizabeth *after his fashion*." Then Wakwa's wisdom bared its fangs. "I'll call in a favor Beckett owes me for saving his son with Jeanette. He will steer us around it."

Wakwa functioned among the Sweetwooders, building a firewall. He captained construction of an incendiary arc of baled hay and boards, corncribs, the corn still in them, anything that would burn. He and Gil threw likely fuel from the hayloft in the barn to the scavenging men and boys on the ground outside. They lugged it to the brittle works at the southwest end of the property. Men, women, children, dug with spades, with pitchforks, with, stones, their bare hands, to open a trench between the burning house and the threatened church. Strapping young men heaved stones into the shallow gorge. The girls they were courting commandeered the milk pails and raced to Hudson's brook then back to fill the stone-lined gutter.

Locke trotted to and fro searching for Moses, as frantic as Hanna that no evil befall Elizabeth's son, not to mention Beckett's. There was the matter of Tamoccon, but unspoken and with a guilty twist of gut they each felt the full Massachuseuck boy possessed inborn skills of survival.

A chandler filled a boy's arms with staves and watched him build up the works fronting the bridle path that divided Hudson's land from Dowland's huge parcel. With a coarse laugh, he pointed the effort out to Dire Locke and Hanna Worth. "You'd think it was his, the way he goes at it!"

Dire's glance fell on Moses.

Hanna cried out to him. Moses turned for an instant and saw her. Without a sign Moses went back to work. Hanna burrowed against Dire. "Absolutely his mother's son!"

With surprising gentleness Locke asked, "Shan't I take you home?"

"The barn!"

As they turned from the churchyard, a small figure on horseback appeared. He was the lone rider among some farmhands who were prodding cattle up the hill toward Worth Farm. The little horseman urged his mount expertly into a sheepdog's role, herding goats and rams and ewes, Hereford cows and bull, the plough horses. The Lows' pair flanked him, hitched to his saddlehorn.

Locke and Hanna made a victory cry at the sight of Horace on the hillside.

Dire observed injudiciously, "Like his father, a rider."

Hanna concentrated on the feat Horace was performing, "He'll not be seven till April."

Farmers fanned away from the completed firebreak to climb into the bell portico of the church. With water buckets, hand to hand, they soaked the cedar roof. Dire and Hanna wove through the mob. Wakwa, burning torch in hand, ready to set the tinder wall on fire, passed them booming, "Get the children! All the children! Count the children!"

Hanna slipped down, sought them and fought for them and pulled them away from their desperate tasks and delivered them to Locke who nudged them like lambs uphill to an open place a safe distance from the flames.

Wakwa touched a torch to the parched wall. Fire caught its fuel and chewed it like a lion does meat. An orange line burst into existence. The villagers intoned their awe. The roaring wall of fire braved the inferno advancing toward it over the corpse of the frame house.

Hanna wildly sorted through the neighborhood children; the small ones caught up in the older ones' arms. She left Locke with the youth of Sweetwood and gained the barn. Hanna heard whispering. "Moses!"

He hunched over a pile of straw.

Her hands saw for her a bundle covered in a saddle blanket. "What is it?"

Moses panted. "This is Lightfoot." The darkness, the smoke, the small mass of him made it impossible to recognize Wakwa's second son. "I did not know he followed me!"

Hanna reached for the nephew she loved boundlessly.

Moses drew away. "I'm to blame!"

Hanna turned to Lightfoot. Her eyes, dilated in the fitful darkness, identified a body on its side, still and staring. She put her arms around him and gathered him up. She uttered a cry of disgust and nearly dropped him. Lightfoot's once perfect head was lopsided, in places twice, three times its normal size. His head was like an enormous sea sponge, his scalp not holding its shape against his skull. A lump above his right ear, large as a goose's egg, turned him monstrous. "Life continues hard. Find your father now and bring him!"

Moses shuffled for his footing in the dung and the hay.

"Wait! Kiss me!"

Moses' lips brushed hers, then he stumbled out of the barn.

Israel had torn himself away from his wife and newborn daughter to be of use to the village. His footsteps on the barn floor brought Hanna's face around.

She whispered, frightened, "What is wrong with him?"

Israel's heavy hands saw for him. "I do not know!"

"You must!" Hanna knelt in the straw. "Why doesn't he speak? Cry?"

Well-trained by his father, Israel's fingers explored the child's neck, tested the vertebrae, passed down his spine, his legs, spread his limp arms. They tested Lightfoot's face, his jaw, his nose, his brow. They slipped sideways and stopped. Trembled momentarily. Went damp. Lingered over the right temple. The large lump seemed precariously balanced over a cleft in Lightfoot's skull. Lightfoot's entire head had turned boggy, the warm wetness of flowing blood flooding from the wound under his scalp. His once shapely head was a grotesque tangle of black hair spiking out of bulbous softness. Israel diagnosed tersely, "Blood's spreading from a fracture to his skull."

"Fracture! Oh, God!" Hanna breathed out. "Broken through?"

"Tis."

She stifled a cry. "How does one fix a...fractured skull?"

"We have no way."

Hanna cried out.

"I am afraid to move him." Yet Israel pushed his arms under the light body, his big bones a palette for the spine, his elbow a niche to cradle Lightfoot's wounded head. "It's the nerves that worry me."

Hanna steadied the young doctor as he rose to his feet. She shrouded Lightfoot's head and body in her shawl. Guiding Israel in her embrace without looking back, as if they were fleeing Sodom, they picked a path toward the wide doorway.

A long, dark figure filled its center and passed in. Wakwa canted the name Lightfoot, "Wautuckques!"

They had not heard him cry this way before. They had witnessed his graceful weeping in joy at Moses' birth, his scalding, self-punishing, wet-eyed hysteria at his failure to keep Elizabeth, but not this disembodied sorrow, this spiralling downward. Only his voice, plumetting, had strength. Without having seen his injured son, Wakwa seemed to replicate him, slack, powerless, desperately reduced. And broken.

Hanna left Israel for Wakwa. "Wakwa! Dear. Listen to me!"

But Wakwa kept calling, "Wautuckques!" and he struggled against the impediment of Hanna's arms.

She guided Wakwa to Israel's side and gathered the soft wool away revealing Lightfoot's head briefly visible in the carmine afterglow of the flames.

Wakwa's keening coalesced into voiceless tears that glanced off the child's immobile face. Lightfoot blinked. Wakwa leaned over him, capped the swollen mass of his child's skull with his hand, calling in his truest voice, "Wautuckques, nip-Wautuckques! Lightfoot, my Lightfoot!"

At that, Lightfoot's arms shot out hideously, his fingers rigid: he poked Wakwa away. Lightfoot remained in that living rigormortis and Wakwa fell back into the shadows.

"The child's gone mad!" Hanna called, aghast.

Israel worked with the evidence. "The brain responded!"

Moses gasped, "Shall I get Mr. Locke?"

"He cannot go on horseback! We cannot take him in the cart." Israel was firm.

"Like this?" Hanna suggested.

"Carrying him could be worse."

As they teetered out with their awkward bundle, they heard Wakwa hitting his own head against the silvered wood of the barn wall.

Matthew and Mosq, searching for Worth and Wakwa filled the void. A palette was quickly made, Mosq's wide buckskin shirt tied at its four corners to the poles of two hoes. Together they bore the Sachim's son shoulder high, their gait swinging like the water in a womb. No harp was heard that night. For a long time, Gilbert Worth did not appear, nor Wakwa, nor Moses, nor Dire, nor Awepu's son, Tamoccon.

Lightfoot lay in the sitting room chiselled in the posture of rejection. Qunneke kept the corner, observing their work over him, waiting for the universe to speak.

CHAPTER TWENTY-EIGHT

November 1753

Wakwa settled onto the floor of the barn, his back against the wall. It was a position he had never expected to occupy. He bloodied his heart on the tips of Lightfoot's splayed fingers. For the first time in his life, Wakwa felt accused of sin and banished for it. The mere sound of his voice had summoned Lightfoot out of coma to fend him off. Wakwa drank from Elizabeth's fate and joined her in the darkness where he had cast her years before. Not having her to hold, to hold him up, their broken link drew him under.

"I do not like the look of it." Locke murmured to Worth.

Gil half knelt at Wakwa's side. "Nephew, I beg you! Listen to me! There is much to do!"

Torchlight pained Wakwa's eyes. His hand burned. He drew it quickly back and saw Moses kneeling at his feet holding out a steaming mug.

"Nosh! The townspeople sent this in to you. Drink!"

Wakwa smelled the spiced cider and he placed his hands around this thing called a mug, an oddly named vessel, he had always thought. Moses' fingers touched his as they released the mug's handle. Wakwa held them fast. "You wish me to drink this?"

Moses shook his head, not able to speak to the vacant-eyed man who sounded and looked like his father but who was no longer his father.

Wakwa raised the cup to his lips. His empty stomach sickened on the not unfamiliar rotted taste of himself. He gulped and shouted in pain.

"Slowly! It is hot!" Moses taught him.

"Quickly!" Gil urged. They want to talk to you!"

Drawn gradually into the real, Wakwa scented the fragrant cup. Watching Moses, he sipped, guttered the amber fluid with his breath, then drained the liquid to its sediment. He gasped at its power to raise the image of Elizabeth, her perfume.

Wakwa stood outside the barn where the ground and the grass and the overarching tree limbs were black from fire. The fire had sated itself on the firewall and was slowly suffocating under thousands of shovelsful of cold-hardened soil. The smell of destruction contained, and of the land largely unharmed, agitated the villagers almost to cheerfulness.

Gilbert Worth shook Wakwa's shoulder. "Because he knows you, the tither's been chosen to speak for Sweetwood tonight over any of the selectmen."

Cooper, tither and shire-reeve, possessed of political acumen exactly suited to his rural surroundings, stepped up to his sensitive duty with an air of confidence. "If I may say, Sachim, there's no one in Sweetwood that is not grateful to you for the work you did to save the church."

Wakwa inclined his head. His hair, dulled with ash and stuck with foreign matter, slipped stiffly forward onto his breast.

"They appreciate your ability with fire and its moods saved their farms."

Wakwa came more alert, wary, grateful to feel Moses against his leg. He let his hand rest on Elizabeth's child.

Gil encouraged, "Your point, Coop?"

Undaunted, Cooper proceeded steadfastly, "And knowing that certain children were visiting the manse when the fire broke out, they are grateful to Providence as well, for it is supposed their presence brought you to Hudson's Farm."

Wakwa's eyes narrowed.

Locke struck his boot with his crop. "It is not Hudson's Farm!"

Cooper blinked away the interruption. "Further, there's a goodwife here, one Martha Bawtry, who has somewhat to say." Cooper signalled her with his elbow, a tilt of his head.

Mrs. Bawtry stood forward, her lips working hard to disguise her nervousness, her dress torn at the waist and scorched to tatters. "I've never had to do with...anyone like...you...or...yourn. Just...town Indians." Her throat gave in to dryness and she gulped like a frog. "In my surprise to see an Indian girl with the minister's wife, I said things unworthy a Christian. And seeing what you're made of, I'm that sorry."

His spirit forced back into him by their presumption of his soundness, Wakwa listened intently.

The Reverend Mayhew Low made an impatient entry into the speaker's circle. "You do mean, Martha, what you said against Sequan was unworthy of the child."

A furrow ran the length of Wakwa's brow.

She shook her head in the affirmative, hiding her trembling mouth in the crux of one fist.

Wakwa did not let the moment escape them. "Be easy, woman." A step brought him close to her. The men drew in, grumbling.

She looked up at him in terror. He touched her cheek with his grazed and bloodied knuckles.

"Stand back!" Men shouted but they did not move against him.

Wakwa's benediction was very tender, very telling. His words mirrored his touch. "You and I are black and weary from the same cause. Only, woman, forget it not tomorrow."

Her wind left her lungs. She gasped, "You had a boy injured!" Her chin stuck out from toughness.

Wakwa twisted back toward the barn.

Cooper took advantage. "That brings us handily to the subject of how the fire started, Sachim. Have you any idea? It strikes the assembly here it could have been accidental."

Worth pointed an accusatory finger. "Cooper! You said a tribute! An apology! Hasn't he done enough for you?"

"Have you any idea?" Cooper chiselled away.

Wakwa used full voice, "It were not an accident."

The crowd dropped a heavy sound.

Cooper piped, "How do you mean?"

Wakwa turned away again toward the barn and again turned back. And his turning, and the agony of his turning seized the hearts of the townspeople.

Locke polished the wooden butt of his pistol with his palm.

"Now," Cooper reasoned loudly, "if she were set, would she not have been set when there were a wind? So she'd spread faster and damage more? You do see my point?"

"Tither, your point would find its mark only if the setter wished the fire to spread. And rapidly."

Locke breathed deeply, relieved to hear Wakwa beginning his minuet with the motley village mind.

Cooper set his feet in the sandy loam. "I think Mr. Worth was right. We're all fagged. We need a night's sleep and until that house is charcoal we're not due for any o' that. Shall we talk further in a few days' time? By your leave, Sagamore."

"Shire-reeve, my youngest son, who lies without speech or sight or movement, has no such leisure. Is it meet that we take ours?" Wakwa tethered them.

Worth and Locke went to him to advise him to wait. Wakwa said with no fanfare that waiting was done.

"Should we get us some chairs?" Cooper smiled through the weird light.

Wakwa's face, long in design, and backed by the black November night, appeared like a banner of sorrow. He said, "Neighbor! Let us share a comfortable hour together when all this is settled. Right now, we can reason on our feet, can we not?"

Some of the farmers dug their torches into the ground and crossed their arms, eager to see firsthand something akin to the councils etched into their plantation's history and not so long ago daily printed up in the newssheets.

Cooper changed his tack, backed up a step. "Please! Speak!"

Wakwa's hands folded momentarily as if in prayer then he revealed, "I have a grievance against Sweetwood. More than one. Each time there has been an offense against the Ninnuock, the offense sprang from this place where we stand. I mean to say the Massachuseuck have run afoul of your church on more than one occasion."

His audience complained in cries and calls like crows.

Wakwa raised the hand closest to his heart and silenced them. "The first was when your minister," he coughed up his next word as if it were chimney dust, "Hudson, incited your number against our celebration of winter, the Nickommo, soon to come again...."

"It's too late for that subject," Cooper smoothly deflected the complaint.

Wakwa seemed not to hear him. "Nickommo is the time when we pray and eat and dance and play games of skill to keep our spirit high through the cold, and thankful for the abundance the gods have granted us...."

"That's all well and good, but the man's dead, lying just over there, and can't defend himself or his opinion. And by the way, there are those that say his murder was...."

Dire Locke clipped him short. "If the cleric's bones are no good to you, ship them back to Boston where he came from! He's taking up valuable real estate!"

The assembly made their internal shock felt across the barnyard in a sound emitted as one.

"Letters have come." Cooper admitted. "Letters of inquiry."

"What letters?" Worth demanded. "You never mentioned any correspondence to me!"

"You've been abroad." Cooper ably deflected the patrician wrath. "Away. And when here - so busy. I've been holdin' them."

"You've been reading them, Cooper!"

Cooper's stringy neck stuck out, his sooty face went red. "They wasn't addressed to you. Exactly."

Locke took him on. "To whom were they addressed?"

"To the Town of Sweetwood, which, I may say, however humbly, is *me*."

Worth sniggered, "We shall see next election."

Locke stuck to business. "You did not answer them?"

Cooper stood tall. "I did."

"Imbecile!" Worth squawked and beat his arms against his sides.

"I only said the Town would look into the matter, that is of the ownership. You should be grateful you've got a shire-reeve who can read and write!"

"Eternally." Worth stabbed in baritone.

"With your permission, sir," Cooper gave a polite nod, "We've got a matter comes before that." He gave way to Wakwa.

"The matters are not separate!" Wakwa caught him. "Hudson and his folk would continue to bleed Sweetwood and us of our peace and our land. Your minister, now gone, committed offense against our holy custom eight winters ago and the wound he made has lived on like a sore every season since. Again, this very day," Wakwa's voice rose and thinned, "all three, my children and a son of my cousin, Awepu, who you know from his friendship with Charles Dowland, and another child, an English boy, a visitor, the son of a powerful English lawyer, were exposed to death by fire at your minister's house."

Cooper bypassed the accusation, saying, "I had met him before. This man at law. A Mr. Beckett, was it not? Hadn't I the pleasure, Sagamore? In your town?"

"Cooperrrr!" Gil warned.

Wakwa's voice descended into the pit of himself. "It were a grave thing. There is no reparation you can make if my youngest is not restored to me and his mother, nor even if he is."

"Now, see here!" Cooper raised his hands and lowered them as if to press a lid down against a boiling pot. "There are those who think the lads themselves through some mischance or accident may have spread a spark and put all of us at risk."

Moses spoke without invitation. "Smoke was already rolling up the hill when we came to find my sister!"

Wakwa looked down curiously at his son.

Cooper studied Moses; the cut of his face, the metal glint of his eyes. "Your little brother might have caused the smoke even as you went to the house."

Wakwa opened his mouth too late.

Moses spoke for himself. "The fire was making the smoke! Don't you know that about fire? Fire was already climbing the back of the house!"

"Sachim," Cooper read the village mind, "the lad speaks well, if a bit forward, but it is a lad. We have but the word of..." here he trod with care, "of...a little boy."

"If the truth would rest on the greatness of one's size, tither," Wakwa, halfway between six and seven feet himself, finished, "how should I believe a single thing you say!"

And so Sweetwood laughed.

"Now, now!" Cooper drew himself up.

"Would you believe your present priest?" Wakwa asked the official. "Would you believe him and his little wife, even though they are not tall, but were surprised by the same danger that has reduced, mayhap forever, my littlest child?"

Locke gloried in the language molten on Wakwa's tongue.

Gil murmured, "He'd better not go too far."

"What is your idea, then?" Cooper would not be beaten. "For sorry though we are that your boy is hurt, it were not fire hurt him."

Wakwa changed. A cry fought to burst from his lungs but his office and his breeding went against it and he stood with eyes closed.

"How do we know the plucky lad, that Beckett boy who cleared the barn of cattle, did not run over your boy in the dark?"

Not seeing the assembled people, Wakwa saw inside the structure. Saw himself sitting, looking at the spot where Lightfoot had lain, from where he had been lifted by Israel Stirling. Wakwa moved into the thick of the crowd, speaking to them, addressing the tithing man. "As I was in that barn, Mr. Cooper, and saw no son of mine, and, myself, directed young Beckett to remove the horses and other cattle, my idea is that the fire at the minister's house was lighted in malice and that five children were put at mortal risk, and two people grown, your holyman and his wife. No one knew the children were there - no one knew - therefore, my idea is that none could have wished them ill." Wakwa appealed to the crowd. "But they did know your preacher was at home. Sunnamatta? Is that not so?"

The villagers were absolutely quiet.

Low spoke. "I write each day in the afternoon in that same chair in that same room. It is well known."

Wakwa turned slowly on the spiritual leader. "Is it not also true, good priest, that your people, from time to time, are wont to slay those who are different in their thoughts from themselves? This has happened."

Now Low was deadly quiet.

"It has happened with the Quaker. The Catholic. The Presbyterian. Among all Christians and against the French. The Jew. And against their own in the place called Salem."

Mayhew Low took in the faces six deep around him.

Wakwa's face took light. Again he addressed the entire assembly. "Is there no truth in my idea that the setter of the fire chose a day without wind to toss his burning branch against your minister's lodging so that no one would be hurt, so no farms or money be lost, just your minister shaken, warned, discouraged, even silenced, or fled in fear of speaking his mind in his church?"

Worth's mind flew with his fellow members to the past November when Mayhew had railed against the Church of England. They all wondered.

"I see one of your number missing. Put a name on him. I cannot. I see one of your number doing his angry, cowardly work. Then! He is surprised by a houseful of children. Indian children! Mainly Indian children. Dangerous to endanger - especially in these times."

Someone muttered, "He threatened us."

Cooper croaked out, "It don't have to be one of us."

"Who then?" Wakwa settled his gaze on the official. "Find the man. Whoever he is! Is it not true, were that fire-setter you, you would take to horse? The horse skittish at the smoke and the fire's sparks against his haunch? The horse lifts his frighted, heavy body up and paws the air and you bring him down so you can get away, when your horse," Wakwa's voice deepened further as his sight of the event neared the darkest part, "your faithful mount, afraid of fire, bucks, rebels against the punishment of the bit, of the spur, kicks with his iron-shod hoof. The noise! Like a jar of precious substance - cracking." Wakwa's breath heaved out and out making him lightheaded, but he saw on. "You look. There lies a tiny boy. One who had seen your face and had turned to run for home." In a whisper wet with tears, Wakwa added. "To tell his father." Wakwa gasped, "But he runs no more."

"No! No!" Martha Bawtry moaned. "Not one of us!"

Wakwa came back to them. He used Martha as his focus. "Is it not the truth you wanted no one hurt? Even you, who set afire another man's house, would not stand the child's being swallowed by the flames."

She shook her head and her hand rubbed back and forth across the air near her face to wipe the images out.

Wakwa turned his eyes on one and then another farmer or farmwife. "You dismount. You gather up the young one. You cannot regain your saddle without further hurting the boy. You place the little body over your horse's back like a blanket and urge the wild-eyed beast along through the tall stumps of the corn and away. You watch in the cold for a chance to rid yourself of the little body where he will be found."

Cooper tried to stop him but Wakwa did not or would not hear.

Even Low said, "It does not have to be any member of this parish, Silent Fox. My remarks are more discussed in the tavern than in undercrofts or houses. My words could well have lit the torch of someone from afar! Someone from as far away as... Boston!"

Wakwa did not answer the minister. He stood unsupported, his eyes seeing beyond the gathering. "The day turns into night. Men run out of the barn. The horses and cattle are driven to safety up the hills. You see your chance and you carry the child through the shadows and lay him, not ungently, on the cold, unclean floor, cover him with a little hay. You are gone." Slowly the vision came to rest and he faced the crowd, exposing his stricken features to full view.

Moses hung his head, but Wakwa's hand was there to receive the quivering face, to catch his first son's shame in his palm.

Gil reached them and said, "Come home."

Wakwa disregarded him and appealed to Cooper. "Will you put a name on him?"

Cooper yelled, "How can I do that?! We have only your imaginings!"

Wakwa stalked away. Then he twisted back viciously. "Get you the word of young Horace Beckett, if you will not accept my charitable vision! Perhaps the word of two boys one atop the other will be as true as the word of one red man!"

The others broke their lines, some to see to their own children, some promising among themselves to take up a search in the morning. Some of the farmers eyed Wakwa's passion narrowly, some remarked on such warmth from a leader with a reputation for a cool and iron will. But Cooper knew his business and trudged off with some of them and the Reverend Mr. Low to Worth Farm.

Wakwa slipped back into the barn. He thought he was alone. He wrapped himself in a saddle blanket in the frosty night. Again, he used the wall for support. Free to remember his swift little son, he saw only the bulk of idle harnesses and saddles, felt the disturbance he, himself, had made in the order of the great building tearing out its fixtures to feed the advancing flames. Wakwa remained in the darkness. Listening.

Sound first came to him from the loft. Wakwa became aware of a faint disturbance of the breath of the barn. Faint friction. The tips of wings against the siding. An owl flying from its roost to sup on a mouse. That Silent Fox had heard no mouse caused the roots of his hair to prick. He lowered his head and closed his eyes. He saw himself from above in the posture of listening. His blood came alive and he knew he was not alone. His teeth ground, he so desired his hidden companion in the barn to be the man who had changed his family's life forever.

Wakwa moved his hand to the hilt of his knife. Steps rewarded his slight movement. Light steps. Indian in lightness. Feet, softly shod, rushed across the boards and stiff hay.

Wakwa opened his eyes. Shades of black, different densities of the void, were the only information his eyes recorded. He remained as still as the wood all about him. He soundlessly breathed the scorched air.

The steps were suspended, then a body alighted, weight supported by almost silent feet touched the packed earth of the barn floor. "Sachim!"

Wakwa heard his title. Without remembering rising, he was standing, facing the advancing shoulders, chest, nose and jaw of a Massachuseuck. Livid firelight leaked through a chink in the siding just long enough to inform him.

"Raven!" Wakwa sheathed his knife in disgust. "I am not dead yet!"

Raven said, "I have been watching."

"What else!" Wakwa was sardonic.

"Many of us came to help. Your father and Awepu and many of the women are at your English uncle's new long house."

Wakwa seized Raven's forearms worried.

"Awepu sent me. People of Sweetwood are burned and hurt. They are streaming to the farm to find the Scottish doctors. The farmwives and our women are setting out mats and blankets. Everyone is flocking there."

"Not you."

"I acted on Awepu's word."

"To what end? You are not bred for a guard."

"To watch. While you spoke to the farmers, I watched from the roof. I saw in a circle. And out of this place, from under me, strutted a man, dressed in dark clothes and with a gut on him. I watched him into the corn."

"Yes!?" Wakwa shrugged off visions of the dead Annanias Hudson.

"He vanished. Like smoke."

"A spirit!?"

Raven gave a laugh. "He was real enough."

"You watched? Did nothing? Did not stop him? Was he a farmer?"

"I sent men. There is no trail of him, no horse, no sound of a bridle, not a rustle or whinney or bent leaf or a broken husk. There is no trace of the man."

"A living man leaves some sign, Raven. He swallows, coughs, breathes hard! You did not hear a tear of remorse? Not a running step or a fall? Not even the hiss of his water passing?"

"It is as if the ground swallowed him."

"Oh! Do not tell me that!"

Raven crossed his arms over his chest to restrain himself from holding the man who headed the tribe. "Do not go mad over your pains. It is no spirit. The man is flesh and walking. We need you!"

Wakwa took hold of his advisor's shoulder. He looked into Raven's face. "You saw a man? A living man?"

Raven's black eyes glinted with confidence. "I saw a white face and curly hair and a flat black hat, that gut, and pale stockings."

Wakwa saw only the dead Annanias Hudson.

Raven insisted, "He is real. He is somewhere. Shall we go together? We could keep the roof till dawn."

Wakwa let him go. "I want this man."

Raven hunched under an idea. "Give him over to the women, would you?"

"I do not want his drawn fingernails in a tray before me or the tip of his tongue or of anything else! I want this man. Whole. I will give him to the church. Give him to Low and the tither. Let them hear him explain. Let them throw him on their fire! If twenty winters must pass so he may be found, let them pass. I will have him!"

"Shall I go with you?"

Wakwa waited. He placed his hand over his heart turned to pulp by Lightfoot. "I have much to see to. This...is yours!"

Consumed with the pleasure of a trust so personal, Raven cried out. He made the old fashioned obeisance, shedding a kiss on each of Wakwa's shoulders.

Wakwa raised him up. He looked into Raven's eyes. "That sound you made gave me the first happy moment of my service!"

Lightfoot lay in subdued light on the pale green settee. Mac was haggard, his hands slowed by his gross fatigue. He was trimming and shaving off Lightfoot's hair. Qunneke, oddly unresponsive, hugged the wall outside Matthew Freeman's empty office. Her mother held Lightfoot's hand. Awepu and Pequawus kept to the inner reaches of the room, cornered by the books. Tamoccon's continued absence was the subject of their discussion. Moses knelt at Lightfoot's feet, his forehead pressed against the wooden arm of the settee. Locke stood half in the room and half in the front hall scratching in his notebook with a pencil.

Worth asked crisply, "Your observations, Dire?"

Locke arched his eyebrows. "A note to myself. You'll be needing more Celadon silk for the settee. That is the color you'd like to continue with? Or would you rather, tapestry?"

A bitter smile distorted Worth's face. "Do you suppose if we got rid of the couch, there would be fewer emergencies in this room?"

Locke rejoined with finesse, "It is you they come to, Mr. Worth. Not your chair. And we wouldn't want to get rid of *you*!"

Gil's eyes were splashed with emeralds. "We've got Sheriff Cooper swatting about the lawns with a six-year-old trying to keep Hudson's sheep out of the roses." He opened the door onto muted pandemonium, goats leaping under the black sky and smudged stars, the cows plodding through the frozen flower borders, displeased not to be cosseted in their barn. "This is exactly how my brother must picture my living!" Gil steamed. "We have strangers traipsing all over the place but the most precious members of my family are lost to me!"

Dire stepped into the doorway with Gil. "Never lost! Only not present is all."

They saw Wakwa mount the summit of the hill at that moment.

Locke jotted. "Would a peacock blue be a nice variance?"

Gil lowered his face to his hands and wept.

Wakwa confused their tenderness of mood with disaster.

Worth said hoarsely, "No change."

Locke asserted, "Silent Fox, I do not find children easy to like. Yet, I like your Lightfoot immensely. He is a personage. He will come round."

Wakwa broke for Qunneke who stood alone. He held her in one arm and surveyed her face. "Will he come back to us? Can you forgive me?"

She turned away but leaned against him and Wakwa received her weight like a reprieve. Over her crown of braids, Wakwa saw his mother-in-law. He left his wife for the older woman's side. She was stroking Lightfoot's hand but her cold, clear eye was cast on Moses.

"Do not blame him." Wakwa spoke in his softest voice. "This has to do with me."

"I do not blame him," she said in their language. "Or you. If you want strict obedience get you a son named Dog!" She looked him in the eye. "You never shall. Not with *your* will which is the feature of you that made me vote for you for headman no matter how my heart broke for my daughter when I did it!"

Wakwa's chin rose as if defending against a blow.

"Your Wolf," she sniffed again, "who is Moses, another lone wanderer and bewitcher, is as he is from both sides of him. His mother followed her own will to the center of your heart...." She raised a hand against his protest. "And if her son, your Moses, had not blood in his veins thick with willfulness, he would not have gone for his sister! Sequan and the priest, Low, and his wife, and the lands and the buildings which are Moses' by blood on both sides might have been ashes." Here her glance returned tenderly to her grandson of full blood. Her crystalline eyes shone with tears that vanished quickly like the dew for which she was named.

"Then I am to blame. Me and my wife-that-was."

"Why must we blame someone?" She argued. "Moses disobeyed you, Lightfoot ran after him! Speak sense. Moses heard his sister's need in his veins. He went to her. Lightfoot followed, unknown to his brother, then ran to find you. Fleet as he is, something outran him! That is what I see."

"Mother, a man was observed coming from the barn while I talked to the townspeople. He went away on no horse. Raven says the earth seemed to swallow him."

She cocked an eyebrow at this. "Him?"

Wakwa blinked. A dawn.

Wakwa left the house to find Will Cooper, the shire-reeve. The task was not difficult. Wakwa saw Cooper's lantern swinging from his staff and the tither darting in its halo, prodding errant goats and cows toward the white fence of Worth's pasture.

Horace Beckett, still mounted, walked his horse among the beasts, shepherding them patiently, one by one toward the gate. Worth and Locke aided on foot. Awepu and Pequawus looked on troubled.

Cooper huffed up to them, sweating. "Come on, gents, help us get these here penned, and then we'll talk in the kitchen! I've yet to say three words to the Beckett lad, let alone hear his story what happened down there."

Ho slapped his mare's withers and kicked her sides, shouting back as he continued work, "What happened is all right with me!"

"Hold on!" Cooper could not believe his ears. "Get down now and explain yerself!"

"Watch out, Cooper!" Gil warned. "You're ordering a gentleman's son about!"

"I'm that sorry, I surely am, Mr. Worth, sir. But it's necessary considering the words just come out his mouth!"

Ho reeled over on his swayback. Mischief filled him. He scattered small animals setting them bleating.

"Like father like son." Gil murmured to Dire with odd delight.

Dire saw no humor in it.

Wakwa held the rein and lifted Ho down in one motion. He set him on his feet. "Speak, Hawk."

Michael Beckett's son looked into the assortment of faces. "The house should have burned. And had it not, it would have been my suggestion that the village set it afire on its own!"

"Ho?" Gil questioned.

Cooper slapped his thigh. "Hear that?"

Dire held a warning finger to his lips.

Ho crossed his arms over his chest. He spread his feet. Peculiarly like his father about to sum up an argument, Ho threw out, "It was an awful house. Deserved to burn down. My house in England is of stone and warmer than that!" Ho turned momentarily to the peppery glow lingering below the hill. "Moses banged on the door. They let us in. We hauled everybody out. I ran in and out with their stuff. I was hardly in the house at all and felt numb. Suffocated...."

"The smoke, boy."

Ho ignored Cooper for the others. "It was a bad house. Had a rotten breath."

Cooper intoned. "Some say it were haunted."

For the first time, Ho shivered. "Then I'm even gladder it's in cinders!"

Wakwa seized Ho's hands. "And before Moses pounded on the door? What did you see? What did you do?"

"We were chanting on the hillside...."

"Chanting?" Cooper waxed suspicious.

"Shut up, Cooper! There's a good fellow." From Gil.

Ho watched the men and sagely said, "Some hymn. And all of a sudden there was a whoosh! And fire flared out of the long, thin shed. Like a fire in a frying pan."

"What would a gentleman's son know about frying pans?"

"I'm warning you, Cooper..." Gil kicked a passing ram.

Wakwa dredged them out of trouble, "Hawk. Did you see a man run from the fire?"

Ho shook his head, no. "We saw the flames and smoke. We stood still as posts then we took off for the manse."

Wakwa laid Ho a trap. "Did you look after Lightfoot? Did your eyes follow him up the hill?"

Ho looked quizzically at the Sachim. "Lightfoot wasn't there at all. We ran for the door. Tamoccon ran to the village for help."

Awepu knew no relief.

"And at the barn? When you and the others went for the animals?"

Ho laughed outright. "It stank of manure! As if no one had forked it clean all day."

Now Gil knelt near him. "Did you see Coney there? Or anyone you did not recognize?"

Ho's eyes caught the light from the oil lamp. "I saw you, sir. And the Sachim. Don't you remember? The Sachim told me to get the animals out."

"And there was no one else there? Not Coney? No villager?"

I don't know anybody from this village. They're all strangers to me."

Locke took note of Beckett's child.

Cooper leaned toward Ho. "Was there anyone in the barn?"

For the first time in his life Ho wished his father were at his side. "The animals all atremble from the fire! I looked everywhere so I wouldn't leave a mouse behind. I had a lamp! I left that barn empty!"

There was something about the word of a Beckett that shut Cooper down.

The medical theory was to let Lightfoot heal through rest. J. Macmillan Stirling declared it firmly when Wakwa and the others entered the room.

Then the taupowaw arrived. He did not touch the swollen head or peer at the dent marking the impact of the iron shoe against Lightfoot's skull. With eyes closed, he meditated over the boy at first silently, then with a rising crescendo of expressed grief. He suddenly ceased.

Hanna was heard weeping in the adjoining room.

The taupowaw's dictum was for Lightfoot to be brought to pesuponk to breathe the incense of alder and then be doused in the cold river.

Mac shrugged, "As good as anything else. When he can be moved."

"When will that be?" The taupowaw enquired archly through Pequawus.

"Not yet!" The embarrassed Scot stared his rival down. "Or, take him off my hands! You put the boy's life on <u>your</u> head now, why don't you!"

The Massachuseuck doctor-priest made mute answer by unfolding an envelope of deerskin revealing a fabric of a blue-green color. Gently, with his knife, he lifted segments of the damp, mossy offal of aged acorn meal, then laid the mold with infinite care over Lightfoot's balded, distended, spongy scalp. He matched the segments like patches of a quilt, planing the seams with his blade.

"Wet it with a little water." The Indian priest said to Stirling through Wakwa's father. "I await you at the sweat cave." He bowed, turned away, then called back ironically, "When he can be moved!"

Lightfoot lay supine, capped like a rotted orange.

Dire Locke and Gilbert Worth went into the cold morning unfed and on foot. From the peak of the hill, they caught a view of the scorched patch that was all that remained of the manse. They made out figures moving within its smoking perimeter and hurried down, their rich, dishevelled clothes serving well against the wind. They watched women wade through the field of char, heard the clink of salvage as it fell into the vast pocket each woman had made of her petticoat.

Dire snarled, "This scavenging must stop!"

Gil was lost in the pastoral image of women young and old, bending to their task, their backs covered in hooded capes, their heads protected by winter hats, their skirts tied up under their aprons creating bulges of drapery at front. "Look at them, Dire. They could be harvesting sunflowers on some great Mediterranean canvas of the Renaissance."

Dire squinted. "Look like a crowd of beefeaters to me. Terrible legs. More like portly men in bonnets than females!"

Gil gripped Dire's arm.

Locke's blue eyes sparked coldly; a pair of north stars.

"Raven's man." Worth drew the picture. "The man was a woman, pulled a string and the skirt spread down. She faded into the crowd! Answers the riddle of carrying the child unnoticed and then vaporizing."

"Worth, what kind of woman...."

"I might know one, Dire."

"I am shocked!"

"I once had a housekeeper. Put her out for narrowness of mind and looseness of lip. Sent her packing to empty Dowland Farm just after Moses was born." Worth concentrated on the sequence of events. "The next summer, I cancelled her contract, with pay of course, and recommended her for Hudson's service since she got on with him so well."

Locke displayed his disapproval.

"I know. I know." Worth plunged on. "Hanna had the sense to turn the housekeeper out when Beth went down to marry the fiend, Hudson. Never saw Widow Winke again."

Locke made a sound of dismay and looked away. "And you do not know exactly where she went?"

"What difference can that make? It has been years since."

"You should have made sure!" Locke started for the charred squares and rectangles that marked the former shape of the immolated house. He turned back to observe, "I find country people difficult to decipher." Locke approached the avaricious townswomen. He stepped gingerly through the ruins in his handsome black boots. "Ladies! A fine day, if a bit cold! This wind is cleaning up the environs wonderfully well. Not to mention you. The Lows and the church cannot thank you enough! What a great public service you render! You are the model for the colony.

Fighting the flames all night and then preserving what you can from the wreckage."

"Is this your business too?" One square-jawed matron confronted Locke.

"Your pastor has made it so!" Locke lied a bluestreak. "He is given up to charities for the injured and sent me to thank you for yours. What Christian hearts! Master Worth and I have been observing your labors for the good of all. Oh, no, your activities here this bitter morn have not gone unnoticed!"

The dozen or so women had straightened by now, their aprons pregnant with booty.

Locke waltzed around their belligerence like a champion skater on familiar ice. "As the farm is barren of equipment now, such as a cart or wagon, I suggest, to prevent physical strain, that you goodwives deposit what you've found right in the church! That way every last item will get to its rightful owner with no fuss. Here! I'll take down a list and keep a bill of lading, as it were," he winked at them, "and good Mr. Low will read it out on Sunday next, so even Heaven will know the tally of your good will!"

Gilbert Worth stood haggard in the wind, watching Kirke's man take control.

"Come on, dig in everyone! A Spanish dollar to she who finds the most!"

Their losses blunted although their fun was ruined, Sweetwood's women were goaded to cutthroat competition. But the wives of the more substantial farmers assumed a disdain for any payment. They marched as regally as possible under their clumsy loads toward the shut-up church.

Worth stayed solitary, more and more amazed at the scene unfolding. The strong, plump figures bent again with a will, the women's hands turning raw and black with their ferreting in the freezing char. He heard his name ring out, Locke calling on him as an elder to open the church. Gil obliged Dire, affecting an attitude crisp and disinterested. He was released from soul-searching, and Locke's cataloguing, by the sound of approaching horses. In moments, he was mounted and riding in company with Matthew and Awepu to track down Tamoccon.

CHAPTER TWENTY-NINE

Fall, Winter 1753

Dr. Mac threw open the sitting room doors onto Hanna and Tame Deer huddled on the stairs. "I'm ready to dunk him in the river as the taupowaw said!" Stirling turned back into the room, the strip of sodden linen he held dripping onto the rug. He tried to force this wick between Lightfoot's teeth. "If I canno' get some water in him, he'll burn up!"

"More ice?" Hanna volunteered.

The Scot grumbled.

Her servants occupied at the Meetinghouse, Hanna stuck a pick and a mallet in her own apron band and made for the icehouse with the Saunks of the Massachuseuck. In a quick quarter hour they returned with a small block.

Moses slickly relieved his aunt of the pick and exposed it to Horace.

"What've you got there, lads? Don't go makin' holes in yourselves! I've enough to do! Dr. Mac hovered over Lightfoot, melting ice against his lips, packing him in ice like a fish at market. "Fox! Can you see Moses and Horace don't puncture an artery?"

Wakwa, facing into a corner, slowly turned and rose.

Moses probed one of the doctor's elderberry branches with the pick. "I'm only making a flute."

Wakwa heard. He watched the inexpert jabbings of the pick against the pith. His eyes began to make sense of the picture they showed him. He drew the ice pick away. "Moses, Hawk, go for a thinner stick!"

The boys hurried, the consequence of disobedience fresh before them.

Wakwa repeatedly used the fire to make the new sprit hot. With each firing, he worked it against the poisonous pith of the thicker branch, then cleared the hardwood of its internal matter as if scraping the marrow out of a bone. After a long while, Wakwa offered the straight, cleaned tube to Dr. Mac.

Moses said, puzzled, "I do not see any holes."

Mac frowned, turned the pipe end-over-end, looked through it. "You've cauterized it. But without holes what use is it? It won't play a tune!"

Wakwa held the reed to his lips and forced air through it. The silver hairs rose over the back of Stirling's hand.

The physician studied Wakwa's face with piercing candor. "Of course! A straw!"

Respectfully, Wakwa submitted, "With this sort of tube we empty the sap of the maple for our sugar."

Mac took the reed back. "Empty? You tap the syrup. Suck it out not wi' your mouth but by a physical force. So...instead of Lightfoot's sucking water out of a cup wi' this, which he canno' do, you'd have me blow the water into him!" The old doctor yelled, "Moses! Get the women!"

Mac submerged one end of the hollowed stick in the basin. He sucked water into it and then closed off the base of the straw with a stubby forefinger. "Tame Deer! Support his back! Hanna! Work your finger 'tween his teeth!" Stirling struggled to insert the pipe.

"If the bairn don't swallow, he'll flood with the water. Drown on a drop, as it were. Hanna! Beat his back when I tell you. Fox! When I say, take his ankles and hold 'im upside-down! Ho and Moses, stay oota the way!"

As Mac managed to force the hollow reed against the roof of Lightfoot's mouth, his thumb on the upper end made a vacuum that held the liquid fast. Then, as he would if playing the flute, he lifted his thumb a trifle. Water slipped into Lightfoot's mouth. Stirling pressed his thumb down to stop the flow. "More now." Quiet-voiced, Mac set the pace. His thumb shot up, stayed up. The vacuum broke. Mac put his lips to the hole and blew like Pan.

Lightfoot gasped, twisted, gurgled, choked. His eyes rolled back. He thrashed like a hooked fish. "Hanna!" Mac cried, refilling the tube in the basin.

Hanna gave blows.

"Fox!"

Wakwa took hold of Lightfoot's ankles to suspend him like a carcass.

Before he could, Lightfoot gulped in agony. His jaw unlocked. Eyes open, not seeing, his body went limp.

Into the family's horror, Mac whispered, "Get me a cup! We've go'a chance!"

The metallic sky was scarred with violet, a tease of spring color, as night fell. An impatient knock struck the door interrupting the rhythm inside Worth's house. Hours before, Hanna had stoked the embers under the gridiron in the kitchen and pushed a long-handled copper frying pan on. She and Qunneke braised a deer rump in the splashing fat. It took them both to lift and slide the heavy roast out of the pan into the Worths' forty-pound iron cauldron, suspended from a hook above the flames. They added quarts of well water. Shining with sweat, they paused, panted.

"I've got juniper berries." Hanna said without hope of Qunneke's comprehending.

"Root! Root!" Qunneke looked longingly toward the woods.

Hanna seized Tame Deer's hand and led her to the cellar. Here were onions, beets, potatoes, turnips, parsnips, carrots, the summer's harvest of tubers, and fruit dried, and, to Qunneke's satisfaction, the horseradish root she was looking for. They lavished some on the pot with salt and sprays of the juniper for style.

"I am, forthwith, raising Cooke's salary!" Hanna laughed as she mixed a cornmeal batter for bread.

Qunneke turned the batter blue with huckleberries. Hanna spooned it into a pan, set a convex cover on, loading that with hot coals.

The mistress of the house laid the long kitchen table with fourteen pewter places. The Sachim's wife set red apples on a gleaming fire-dog of shining cutout steel. Perfumed juice began to bubble. Inspired by the fragrance, Hanna peeled the cobalt-colored paper from what remained of that year's sugar cone. She stood over a salver with her shears, cutting twenty-eight even pieces, two for each place. When she was done, hardly a granule wasted, she lifted each piece with silver tongs into a China bowl to serve with tea.

Cooke and Millie, Sequan, and Dolly Low, finally closed the emptied surgery and wove across the north field to the kitchen door with Israel. Hanna and Tame Deer boiled water for the baths.

Cooke said abashed, "Mistress Worth, you have done my work!" Then, "Did you remember to sift the flour for the gravy?"

Hanna soothed without success, "The Sachim's wife has put in cornmeal for thickening instead."

When the five were bundled off to rest, Hanna and Qunneke took refuge on the staircase. Sharing the same step as in the morning, wrapped in the same shawl against the chill, both looked at the sitting room doors and listened to the voice of a flute.

Put in mind of her husband, Hanna sighed, "Where is Gilbert?"

Qunneke sighed for him as well.

A rap on the front door brought Hanna to her feet. Dire stood on the threshold. He announced through frozen lips, "You've guests coming. Uninvited." He pushed a sooty iron frying pan into Hanna's clean hands. "Funny. I found it in back of the tool shed. Hide it away. Evidence." Dire threw open the white panelled doors.

Mac sputtered.

Locke saw Wakwa at the fireside, the completed flute to his lips."Wakwa!" Locke scolded, "There are Mohawk runners in the otan waitng for your attention."

Wakwa looked up reluctantly. After thought he replied, "They should wait. We have waited more than a hundred winters for them."

Displeased at this reaction, Dire Locke stepped backward into the hall. He turned on the women. "They'll cut us all! Can't you do something about him!?"

They called Jeanette to prepare Dire's lavation.

Singly and in pairs and groups the company assembled. Mayhew Low knocked at the kitchen door. Worth and Matthew Freeman galloped to the block. The master stamped into his polished vestibule after a perfunctory scraping, the houseman tended their mounts.

"Where is Wakwa?!" Gil was winded and, like his Bay, close to foaming at the mouth.

Hanna summoned the crowd into the kitchen. Master, mistress, family, guests, the newborn, and the servants shared the table. Grace was said. The venison, the bread and butter went around. Hanna made plates for the men and boys who were keeping watch in the sickroom. She flattered, "You found Tamoccon very quickly, husband."

Worth scolded, "Moses and Ho should be at table."

Matthew said from his corner place, "Awepu's boy found *us*. Spied us from a room in a storehouse in the port. Dropped into the street right in front of us. Like a leaf."

Worth cut the tender meat with a vengeance. "Was a woman did this thing. Awepu's son saw half the story. We'll fill in the rest." Music interrupted him. A dragging fiddle, a weeping flute. "What is Mac doing in there?! Hanna let me bring those things!" Gil pulled the tray out of her hands while Matthew scrambled too late to perform the office.

Hanna softly opened the room. Bleary, his collar tossed aside, Mac continued to improvise. Moses' attempt with the flute died in a slow whistle. Horace Beckett, sprawled in front of the fire, came alert. Wakwa got to his feet.

Breathing hard, Worth demanded, "How is he?"

Stirling pulled his fiddle off his shoulder and slammed it across his knees. "Quiet!"

Wakwa moved his hand toward Lightfoot. "He can take water now."

"It was Winke." Worth bit out.

Wakwa worked at coalescing the sparse declaration into information. "Did this?" He looked again at Lightfoot. "Your maid?"

Worth amended archly, "Hudson's at last count! Look here, Tamoccon saw a stout woman riding past him down the road. He saw her hitch her horse at the first fence in the village then double back on foot. Didn't like the look of it. Then he lost sight of her for he had a crier's job to do. But he remembered her, sought her out by and by. Used his glass. Fought no fire. Just trained that lens on faces. Discovered her flat face under a man's three-corner hat, stout stockinged legs exposed, and a front heavy as if - *with child*. He saw her hobble into the barn under the weight."

"No!" Hanna pushed the picture from herself. "No."

"Not having to move a step because of his telescope you so wisely bought him years ago, Fox, Tamoccon followed the androgynous creature out again with his glass and into the corn. Lost her. Just as Raven did. But Tamoccon spied that pug visage again against the flames with her gown down at her ankles where it belonged!"

Mac interrupted, "How do you know, Gil? What's to prove it was that starchy maid and not someone else? Or a man dressed up in *woman's* garb?!"

Gil's eyes turned murky with shame. "It was the person I hired to care for this house and then got rid of - but not well enough."

Mac questioned again, "You are so sure, Gil!"

"Risking his neck to the noose, Tamoccon filched a horse from the tavern, borrowing on short-term, and rode behind the wretch all the way to Wareham in the near dark! He stalked her to the public house where the bitch calmly spent the night. Snoring as she did here, no doubt!"

Mac batted the anecdote away. "An' so what!"

Gil's voice soared high. "Tamoccon kept his vigil. Saw her pay her fare and board a boat. She sailed out of harbor like a queen. Cooper is right now drawing a warrant for her arrest!"

Hanna touched his arm. "Gillie, is that the cautious thing?"

Worth exploded, "I've done with caution! What is wrong with all of you!"

Hanna braved his ire. "Why say it was Winke?"

"Hanna! What do you think of me? After hearing Tamoccon's tale, I approached the dock, discovered the name of the tub she was on, bribed the owner for a look at the passenger list and saw written in her brazen hand, her name - Hulda Winke."

Wakwa had followed Gil's statements closely. "And by this is proven...?"

Gil went silent and sullen. "Nothing, I grant you. Dammit! But Awepu's observant son, used to probing the planets with his telescope, took a look at her horse with his bare eyes when she first hitched it in Sweetwood. Found this on the shoe of its left, *front* hoof." Studiously but with a shaking hand, Gil drew a black circlet from his coat pocket. "It is hair."

Mac rose. "Front hoof?"

"Ah!" Air escaped Wakwa and his body rocked as if he had been kicked.

Mac assessed the evidence. "Front. Then it was a deliberate act!"

"Not necessarily." Hanna checked him.

"Tamoccon cleaned the shoe of it and made this neat bracelet. Until we have her in chains we can only surmise that the harridan saw Lightfoot sprinting away from the burning house and ran him down."

Hanna insisted on fairness, "Or the horse was running and ran over Lightfoot and Winke tried to rectify the situation by leaving him in the barn!"

"To die!" Gil turned quite cold. "Really, Hanna. Your objectivity is quite out of place."

"Consider, Gil..." Mac thought aloud, "the fracture is in front over his right temple."

"It gives me pain to suggest that a person my wife and I once trusted bore down on the boy when he turned to judge how fast her mount was gaining on him."

At last Hanna breathed in horror. "Huldah Winke!"

"Yes." Gil bowed his head. "This well-named weasel of a woman!" Worth slipped the circle of hair onto Wakwa's wrist.

"Let me see it!" The doctor demanded. "I'll compare it!" The doctor hurried to the writing table. "Who cleaned this room without my permission! Where is the newssheet with Coney's hair!?"

Hanna found her voice. "I'll find it in the refuse."

"Oh, Hanna!" Gil slapped his thigh in frustration.

"Matthew hasn't burnt it yet. Having been gone all day with you, he's not had the time." Her tired face did not spare him.

Gil complained, "I do not understand you!"

After a moment's eloquent silence, she commented, "I do not understand why Winke would set the manse on fire."

"Just a small amount of imagination!" Gil chided. "There is something in that house. Of value. Was."

Hanna's youth seemed to drift away. Yet she responded, "Or was never."

Mac lumbered over. "You've go' a sharp tongue tonight, Gil."

"I'm sorry. But...."

"Don't say it to me!"

"Oh, it's all right!" Hanna spoke wearily making for the door.

"Hanna." Gil's deep voice stopped her. "Darling."

Her face grew more pained at his endearment.

"Why did you say, 'was never'?"

She turned on him. "Leaning more heavily on reason than imagination, Gilbert, I would say any treasure, benefice, or inheritance Winke might seek from The Reverend Mr. Hudson would exist documented and in copy or *not at all*. Perhaps she knew she had been overlooked. Try at his aunt's or at his attorneys' in Boston. And do not fail to open my late brother's strongbox in his root cellar." She parted from him sadly. "Come. I have cut you sugar."

Wakwa mounted the stairs to the public hall of the Meetinghouse well after his counsellors, his chosen guests, and the emissaries from the Mohawk had been seated on their blankets on the floor.

Voices struck the plaster, the wood, the glass, the way ice might, the way eggs might. Wakwa put no spring in his step but made his bone and muscle count, appearing at the open door, weighted with a leader's wealth of care, crossing in front of the assembly to Worth's wing chair hastily carried over and placed with its back to one of the two glowing fireplaces. The German furnace did the work of warming.

The Iroquois in attendance experienced no awe at the architectural arrangements. Their frame structures for living and assembly might not display the elegance of Worth's, but gave up to it nothing in size, tightness, or strength. The Iroquois' fortifications staving off the French for a century were a matter of wonderment in Europe. Yet, there was no comparison between Mohawk castles and the Meetinghouse high above the ground, glass windows viewing forest, field, farm. Without a word, or the whir of an arrow, the new hall taught by eye the lesson Wakwa held in mind for the full-faced Mohawk warriors in front of him whose vassals the Algonkins had never become.

The Iroquois audacity folded under the etiquette of the council; one man nicely presented Wakwa with a handsome belt of white. Not as precious as Wakwa's black money which he was wearing around his forehead and forward over his breast, the Five Nations' gift would, in their minds, more than do for a man who was, after all, merely a sachim of the tiny remnant of the obscure Massachuseuck.

Wakwa's glance would wander during their delivery of their message. Nothing the Mohawk proffered could appear to be a surprise. He worked to control his lips, his chin, his brow, the muscles in his cheeks and yet not look like stone.

Then they made a request of him that made him angry. Their language, dissimilar to his but not unintelligible, caused him to turn to Locke for precise interpolation. The Black Fox Who-Waits stunned them with his reply. "I welcome you to this neuter place. Yet, all that your eyes rest on beyond the walls of this greathouse, every building, every animal, every tree, every furrow, every tongue of grass, every brook and pond and woods up to and across the Twisting River to the west, is not neutral but is the keep of my first son."

To a man, the Mohawk were puzzled.

Gilbert Worth drummed his fingers against his lips discouraging this confidence. The tick in Dire Locke's neck returned.

Wakwa went on, "When he is a man, Moses Bluehill will hold sway over all this place by his mother's Will."

The Iroquois sat straighter as their confusion increased. For although authority and land came through the maternal line in Iroquois culture, they could see Manunnappu was definitely not an Iroquois. The Mohawk spokesman derived, "Then the mother of your son is one of us. Who is she?" He chanced a sneer, "A Seneca?"

Wakwa dropped it like a cannonball. "Moses' mother is English."

The fact blew them back.

Wakwa glutted their open mouths with concepts. "Your greatest alliance, like an unbroken shaft of sun, has been with the English. Mine with Moses' mother," Wakwa chose his tense with care, "has been such an one." After respectful pause, he finished forcefully, "For this reason and this reason only, the Onondaga fire and mine burn together."

Wakwa waved Moses to him and dubbed him, resting a hand on Moses' shiny hair. "Wadchau!" He called out, explaining, "Today, on top of his other names, I name him - Saviour."

The Iroquois stirred at their places. Their speaker got to his feet and threw out in English, "Brother! You ask for our protection but offer us no ground in return!"

Wakwa parried, "*I* protect this place, not anyone else. Nor is the ground mine to give. For discourse on that, the Iroquois must wait for Moses Bluehill to be a man. I ask you for nothing. It is *you* who today have asked *me* for help."

Wakwa's father bit the inside of his lip to hide his gladness over his son's force of mind, which protected them better than arrows and guns. Better than the Five Nations.

Wakwa granted his first smile. A small one. "Mohawk! As you aptly say, we are brothers. Although lately." Wakwa dug at the unhealed wound of Iroquois complicity with the English that had inspired Philip's War and permanently dispossessed the Massachusetts tribes of their ground.

Everyone grew cold despite the two hearths and the furnace duct.

To be clear, to be cautious, to be responsible, Wakwa restated the matter the Mohawk had brought to him. "As you are Iroquois and children of the English King who often brings your great men across the water to dine them and honor them and let them bend his ear, your coming to me is a great moment." Wakwa judged through miniscule sound, through men's very breaths, the crowd's understanding his real meaning. He decided to draw the matter in plainer style.

"You say we are brothers against the French? So I have agreed in council with the united nations of the Iroquois and with the Algonkin tribes." He saw the Mohawk men fuming, aware their feet were about to feel his flame. Wakwa turned severe. "Today, you come to me for Pennsylvania's governor. I know he is a good man. You ask my help to push the Frenchmen back to the Ohio. Because the good governor of Pennsylvania needs help. You say that out of his own pocket will come guns. Powder. Will you also tell me why I want these? Why would I want guns and powder *now*?"

Wakwa let them gape. He allowed the room full of Iroquois and his own folk to ring with objections, reflections. "Brothers from the Long-House! Tell me! Where shall we keep the governor's ammunition when we stand on his soil? Where keep the guns? Is it possible you have not thought through to the end of this question? Are the Pennsylvanians or the English building stronghouses for the Iroquois fighters and their allies? No? Where will the sons of the English be whilst you and I, exposed, fight the well-supplied French protected in their forts? Where shall we find the sons of the Pennsylvania landholders? At our side? Again, it is no! Is there pay for our doing this bloody work alone? No, again! Know you why the English and the colonials will not give these things, especially not their blood?"

The Mohawk envoys grew surly. Their contingent stood up, sat down, not willing to stay, not ready to leave. The spokesman set his hand on his ax.

Wakwa stood to show them his full height. "Here is your answer! The English King, your white father, wishes all his gains at no expense to himself. Perhaps he has not much gold! That makes him a weight on our backs not a father."

The Mohawk spokesman tore his hatchet from his belt and waved it. "Massachuseuck!" he derided. "Families assist one another. How is it you do not know?"

Close to reaching for his knife at the insult, Wakwa retorted, "What example did you give us when you abandoned our cause one hundred winters ago!"

The Mohawk bristled. "You pick a fight about that now?"

"It is your hatchet waves in my face. Brother, as you put your weapon in your belt, recall the compact formed between us and you. Not *against* the English King but in his aid."

The Mohawk, not without talent, smiled. "Then aid him. Fight for the good governor."

"Your headmen, and we of Massachusetts, and the governors of the colonies have forged a plan better than this ill-timed request you bring me. Soon, the colonial assemblies and the English King will consider our plan to take us out of our misery not increase it!

It is a plan not for war but for union. And you, you Five Nations, must respect the advantages of that!

"A union born of this Franklin Plan would make a settlement with France *not* a war. The new governor-general with his grand council into whose ears you and I shall be whispering, according to the Franklin Plan, will set a policy for the Trade for the first time and we all shall stop crashing one against the other like blind men in the dark!"

"That is a good Plan, brother." The Iroquois relaxed, scenting his own victory. "But if the French attack? Will the Plan stop their bullets?" He put his head on one side. His logic was irrefutable.

"Yes!" Wakwa barked back. "The Union born of the Plan, the colonies together as one, would lay on the taxes to pay for guns, for stronghouses, for powder. If the French see our strength *equal* to theirs, *unmoved* by theirs, *surpassing* theirs, *united* against theirs, they would see the benefit in honoring the treaties they have signed. I lay you a bet the French would remove with their own hands their brass plates from the floor of the forest claiming ground not their own!"

The Iroquois' brows furrowed. The man of Massachusetts was not so simple as they had assumed.

Wakwa kicked them with hard words. "Let me help you understand me. Why should I come with my bravest men *now* to do work that may need to be undone? Why should you! Do not come back here and ask for me until the Iroquois and the English throw the Plan of Union onto the fire and cheat for all time their brotherhood and their future!"

The Mohawk asked, incredulous, "That is your answer?"

"That is our *alliance*! First the Plan. Failing it - *war*."

Wakwa walked in his suit of skin and soft shoes and glittering money belts to the window looking northeast. Small specks, the innocuous beginning of a blizzard made a show. "Husseh!" The Sachim pointed, and at last smiled broadly. "It snows! Brothers, I am concerned for your welfare. Go west and north and home before you are buried!"

Gilbert Worth strode at Wakwa's side toward the house. Locke had bolted the farmland for Wareham, riding into the face of the storm with Raven to set him and two of Kirke's agents on Winke's trail and then to Boston to get Kirke Company named administrator of Hudson's estate.

Gil said, "I'm glad there is no clock in the Meetinghouse yet. That assembly was the shortest it could be and still qualify as one. What a beginning of the hall's diplomatic history! So, you can be quick!"

Wakwa walked faster without a word.

Gil turned his collar up. "What a gall they had trying to feed you to the cannon!"

"The Iroquois think very little of us men of Massachusetts." Wakwa listened to the snow's hiss. He called out over it, "I am sorry for Governor Dinwiddie of Pennsylvania that he is alone in his fight. It were better he fought first for the Plan of Union!"

"You used the Plan better than a sword against those Mohawks!"

Wakwa stopped their march and faced Gilbert Worth. "The Plan had no part in it." Wakwa brushed Gil's coat free of collecting whiteness.

"But you said up there...!"

Wakwa held the Englishman in the brace of his arms and said softly, close to his ear, "Uncle, it is Elizabeth Dowland turned them away. The truth is, I will not leave this place until Lightfoot looks at me with love."

Worth jerked back. "What are you talking about? Coney adores you! You have responsibilities!"

Wakwa moved in silence through the collecting snow, leaving pale footprints. At the door he turned to Gil again. "Once, I gave myself over to love of another. All good in my life has spread from that. It were better I were chopped into stew by a Frenchman's Indian than turn aside the child I would make secure with plans of union."

Worth felt the gladness of summer overcome him. What had broken under the iron horseshoe was something more terrible than bone - it was a hardness of spirit called duty which men of all descriptions crawled into like a shell.

The blizzard closed them in, silenced all turmoil under an arrangement of crystal on crystal in measure so great it was holy. The sound of the house was reformed from cries and clatter to melody. Gil's harp made the air sing. Music sifted into Wakwa's injured son like life's fluid.

One midnight, alone with Lightfoot, the others retired to their beds, Wakwa parted the woolen drape to look across the moonlit snow. A shadowed path northeast to the ocean was visible where Worth's ox team had broken out the spread of white vellum. He heard his name spoken with such yearning he felt Elizabeth near him. But the voice said, "Nosh!" not Wakwa.

Lightfoot reached for him, one arm extended, his hand cupped and round.

CHAPTER THIRTY

Summer through Fall 1754

"Massachuseuck, we thought you were all dead!", called an Iroquois sachim in full regalia, his arms cockily folded across his chest.

Wakwa took in the Mohawk's splendor, and let his smile fly across the lobby of New York's assembly hall. "Another of your errors about us Algonkins! I speak of your deafness when we called on you for help one hundred springs ago!"

The Mohawk clucked. "Who-Waits, see you make yourself heard today. For even *you* will be put to war should a union fail."

Wakwa's smile broadened. "I am glad we are on the same side this time. Else I would be forced to drink your blood when you fell to me!"

The man from Onondaga guffawed at this reference to ancient custom, a primitive compliment, swallowing the red, flowing blood of one's valiant, defeated enemy to ingest his courage. He clapped his hand onto Wakwa's shoulder and the pair of temporary allies entered the assembly, laughing together.

1754 was the noon of the Iroquois. The traders, the colonial governors, all appointed by the Crown, even the British secretary of state, Lord Holderness, founded all preparations for defense against France on the good opinion of the Iroquois, more accurately, the Five Nations. The Mohawk, the Cayuga, the Oneida, the Onondaga, the Seneca, had made a name for themselves in the world as fighters regardless of their perennial inability to conquer by arms or words the Algonkin tribes, including those of Massachusetts.

The Iroquois' famous acquisition of ground and power was in direct relation to their confederation two hundred fifty years before, a brilliant stroke. This signal difference between them and their individualistic neighbor-tribes had given the Five Nations the edge in Continental matters. Practiced at union and facile at parcelling out resources and credit to bind their sphere of influence, they had more than a good aim and a vested interest in victory to offer their ally, the English King.

England was keen on the congress at Albany. She saw it as the best way to secure the existing alliance between herself and the Five Nations in the face of a certain embarrassment of theirs in western Pennsylvania that past winter and spring - a loss of land to the French. Pennsylvania's governor, Dinwiddie, had made an attempt to erect a fort, undermanned and underfunded, and then a bloody skirmish on his behalf led by the callow George Washington had been markedly unsuccessful. A simple nod by the Iroquois Confederacy toward the British at this low point would, the Crown calculated, unite the colonies against the aggressor who was France.

Confederacy was also the lesson seized by certain colonials who were long thinkers. On the inspiration of the Iroquois and of William Penn's project for federation of almost sixty years before, a committee, carved from the eight colonies with sense enough to send delegates to Albany, set out the Plan of Union. Benjamin Franklin proposed the draft that he had hammered like silver out of the good ideas of all sorts of men. Wakwa and Locke, Awepu and

Pequawus, part of the delegation of Massachusetts-tribes, sweated in the onset of Albany's summer with the rest, listening, debating, refining the proposal before it was put to a vote.

With the French breathing down their necks, and the English nipping at their heels, the Congress at Albany seized responsibility. By a swift and mighty stretch of mind, it pulled the English-speaking world out of feudalism. The Albany Congress turned the world on its head. For the first time the power to thrive and to protect flooded from the people to their king. On the fourth day of July, of the year 1754, they passed the *Albany Plan of Union* - unanimously.

As other men shouted, "Hear! Hear!" Wakwa cried, "It is born!"

Pequawus wore a long face. "The babe will now be set out naked under the sun. We shall see if it survive."

Awepu, looked far away. "In any wise, there will come a war with the French. The Iroquois will not suffer being squeezed from west *and* east."

Locke's right hand pressed his chest against the pounding of his heart. "Don't you see, you *free* men, what history has been made today?"

Not the exit from the statehouse, not their parting from the men of the Five Nations, not the business of crossing southward in the great canoe the muscular Mohicannituck, (the waterway Wakwa would never refer to by its English name, the Hudson River), not the climb across the Tacquonig Mountains or the trek through two-hundred miles of summertime woods distracted Wakwa from a potential benefice of Albany's victory. He hardly spoke.

Locke broke the spell one night in mid-July. "Will you write to her?"

Wakwa left the fire for the perimeter of a nearby pond.

Locke buzzed at Wakwa's elbow, "The news is good. May never be better. It might go hard with her if the news comes from me."

Wakwa let his fingers toy with the fringe of Dire's doeskin coat.

Locke's tongue lapped the traces of a smile. "I have pen and paper along. Enough ink to write a book!"

Wakwa stated coyly, "I have in my pouch the feather of a spotted egret."

"That will do just fine!"

"I could clog the Mohicans' river with the paper I could peel just from the birches within my reach!"

Black gnats tickled the skin of the pond.

Wakwa turned to Locke, the setting sun striking his face with youth. "This is my time! My fortieth summer!"

Locke swallowed, not seeing any advantage to Wakwa's advancing age. He rescued the mood saying, "What a birthday present their honors gave to you at Albany!"

Wakwa took Locke by his thin shoulders. "Think you that?"

Locke's throat hardened. "Do you want me to go get my writing case or not?"

Wakwa spat words one and two at a time. "What shall...I see her...I could say...the land itself calls...her forgiveness...without the right to...."

"Damn that!" Locke tied off Wakwa's gaspings. "I'll get pen and ink. Once in hand you will know how to phrase it."

Wakwa was left standing alone in the afterglow.

As they got underway in the morning, Pequawus said to Wakwa in English, "I saw you writing at the water as the sun sank. Did you send a word of love to her from me?"

"I wrote no word at all."

Pequawus leaned on his son. "Now is the time. She will never get back if they close the ports."

Wakwa walked with one arm around the only parent he had known. "I made many starts. 'Dear Elizabeth....' What right have I to call her by her name? So I put down, 'Wife of my Friend-in-Trade....' I please myself to think that distant name might hurt her heart. It hurt mine. Should I say, 'Mother of my son' when her son was held away from her and kept away so he does not even know her face? I start again, 'Mrs. Kirke'. That is true and not ungentle; I do not cross it out but drop to the next line. What do I say? 'Good news! Here is the *Plan* making me very nearly equal to the rest of men. The world is safe for you and me *if* the assemblies pass it. Come home and admire how great a man I am, having done all this on the back of your sorrow! Leave the man who married you for love for the one who let you go - for love. And on and on. Much paper lies under the water. What woman would read a letter from such a man as I, or respond, or come to him? I would never have taken such a woman to wife! Father, this is not a thing to be done by letters!"

"Then while the assemblies are deciding, before England declares a war, go to her!"

Wakwa let his arm slip from around his father's shoulders and walked on ahead, alone, a more sensible formation in the forest. He stopped on their path and turned to say, "Instead, I have written to Gilbert's brother, Cecil, thanking him for his great kindness to

Elizabeth's son, eighteen moons ago. With the letter, I will send, by Dire's kindness, the canoe which carried us to the Congress."

Pequawus' eyes shone with the diplomatic possibilities. But he said wistfully, "Mayhap, Lord Worth will put her in it and send her back to us!"

Elizabeth seized a biscuit and abandoned Claude. She lifted her skirts to run from the balmy summer dining room to her tower. Her happy cries clashed against the stone stairs as she took them, laughing at the promise of the wings, the warbling, the jumble of newly arrived pigeons in the roosts on the ledges of the palace walls.

Claude clapped his cup onto its saucer making a small geyser of black coffee that scalded his hand. He cursed, anointing the tablecloth with a flick of his wrist. Standing with effort, he climbed after the girl Kirke had dared to marry. "What do you find, Elisabet?" He huffed in his haste.

A pair of pigeon-messengers poked across the sill. They giggled and bent forward to drink water and eat crumbs from her palm. Claude lingered in the doorway.

Elizabeth's hand thrilled to be near the metal anklet that held news, yet she went gently, coddled the birds who had flown unascertainable distances to home. At last she gathered them, one at a time and placed each one tenderly in its cage like a bonnet in its box.

"These coquelets belong over canapés or in a jelly! To depend on them for word!" Claude stomped across the floor. "I even prefer Dire!"

Laughing in delight over the Jesuit's tantrum, Elizabeth snipped one metal band from one tensed, red leg of the larger bird.

"You will mutilate it!"

She reported huskily, "This makes no sense." Elizabeth spread the diminutive scroll and impaled it to a board with pins. Claude crowded her. The morning light poured in and put in dark relief the tiny letters incised on the gold foil.

> *Ship total inventory fabric division; port of origin.*
> *V.T.*

The priest said, astounded, "C'est-ci?! That is all?"

Mystified, Elizabeth examined the second pigeon.

Claude chafed, "No word of love? No endearment? What would it have cost him? Thomas is such a pig's knuckle!"

Elizabeth concentrated on the cryptic message.

The old Jesuit looked over her shoulder. He said in more politic style, "The pigeons bring good news. Thomas is close to home." He drew her up and took her against himself. "We must not throw our time to the devil. We must do as Thomas bids us and quickly!"

She held onto his ursine body. "Father! We do not have a fabric division."

They closed themselves in; threw the bolt. Elizabeth sat upright in the window. Claude retreated against the wall farthest from the water-light as if into a cave or a confessional.

"He is alive." Elizabeth began.

"Bon."

"His business is done early in China...."

"Or..." Claude debated, "...he has cut it short."

"Illness?" Elizabeth showed Claude a frightened face.

"His hand was steady as it cut those letters. Non. Thomas is well." Claude paused, then asked, "We have no such division so what does he mean? Oh, Thomas is not ill. He is Irish!"

Elizabeth lost no time to Claude's wit. "The cloth we carry goes under the soft-goods division."

"An abbreviation? He wants you to create a fabric division? The fabrics are from every port, so why 'port of origin?' Whose port of origin? The fabric's? Yours?"

She stood. "*My* port of origin!"

They came together at the center of the room.

"Elisabet, *you* are the fabric division! Thomas wants *you* to take ship. To go home. The ports are subject to closure any day!"

"Total inventory!"

"Do not so much as look at me! I cannot leave just like that!" Claude snapped his pudgy fingers. "And what do I go to? My lambs are scattered. All my life up to now is in a heap of rubbish!"

The similarity of their lot brought a smile to her lips. It drifted away. "He means neither of us."

"Eh?"

"Think with me. He says the *fabric* division."

"What fabric division?" Claude gave her the cold eye. "We have no fabric division!"

"We have no fabric division. The Company knows we have no fabric division." She began to move. A step here. A step there. "Everyone part of The Company knows we have no fabric division."

"So, why does Thomas say, 'fabric division', eh?"

"Because...no one who is *not* part of The Company will know we do not have a fabric division."

"Eh?"

479

Elizabeth's bottom teeth scored her upper lip. "If our winged messenger landed on the wrong ledge - on the railing of the wrong ship to rest, to sleep...."

"Oui?" St. Aubin began to follow her thought.

"If the message said outright what Viti wants to tell us...."

"We would be...pâte fois gras!"

Her idea spun fast. "The one division no one knows The Company has is the *gold division*. The gold-fabricating, the gold stocks, the makings of our bank. Viti is saying 'fabric division' because it clearly does not exist - neither does the gold division to the public mind. Father! Don't you see?"

"It is Byzantine." He relented enough to say, "There is a light around your face! A grace from God?"

"It is time to get the gold through. Thomas is churning toward us with more. Much more. And no place to store it unless we ship what is in the warehouse. The fighting has begun!"

"With no word from Dire?"

The crack of laughter each emitted stopped abruptly.

Elizabeth amended her theory. "The war waits for the gold. War in America is - at hand."

Then Claude pulled his hair, his face red, his round eyes made rounder with rings the color of eggplant. "Where is God in this? I am sick for my lambs."

Elizabeth fell to her knees at the priest's feet. "Oh, Father, will God forgive that I am happy?"

Claude de St. Aubin, S.J. could not speculate on God's mind he was so stricken at her own.

Wakwa and his party entered the otan at twilight on the nineteenth day of July. Qunneke was upset by his unannounced arrival. Secretive movements did not speak success. Nor was there time to organize a fitting greeting from a grateful populace. In the morning he was not there; as the evening's mist overawed daylight - he was.

Wakwa dropped the reins of his stallion into the hands of a guard and greeted his neighbors. His father, Awepu, and Locke, took slow strides behind him.

Qunneke heard the slight commotion and came to watch him from her door. His smile was shy, his step cautious, but his greetings to the people who had stayed in the otan and kept it purring were gracious not brief or brusque. Tame Deer was relieved from worry enough to stand aside for Lightfoot who was clamoring to lead his father home.

Amazed at the boy's improvement in only a month's time, Wakwa stopped walking to let his youngest child run to him. He witnessed Lightfoot's quicksilver gait broken by an ungainly dangling of his left arm. It hung lifeless as a pelt. The Sachim dropped to his knees. Lightfoot was lost eternally to the forest. He looked like the future running toward the Ninnuock.

"Nunnaumon!" Wakwa swept him up, watchful of contact with the withering limb.

"It does not hurt!" Lightfoot whispered.

Wakwa took the statement into his heart like an arrow.

Massachusetts listened for a response to the Albany Congress. Farmers of the great tracts watched the newssheets for more than predictions of the weather. The quiet success of Albany rested on the breast like the humidity. Men dragged through the days in what remained of the July sun. Hope ripened, softening by the close of August. It clung heavily through harvest, rotting on the vine. By the end of a hot September, it went to seed and burst over hard clay. In October, expectation of colonial approval of the Albany Plan became an empty pod, which, by November, had dried and blown away.

"The imbeciles!" Gilbert Worth paced his sitting room.

"It's the taxes, Gil." J. Macmillan Stirling summarized the failure of Franklin's plan.

Israel sustained his father's opinion. "Mr. Worth, if the colonial assemblies turned over the taxing power which is now exclusively *theirs* to one *Grand Council*, we might all be serfs again. That governor general could turn himself into a minor king quite easily."

Worth threw himself into his wing chair. "I could see your point if the governor general, not the Grand Council, were levying the tax or if the taxing power of the Grand Council were unlimited. He is not and it is not! These ignorant assemblymen!"

Mac muttered while mixing some borage into the tea, "George II would no' like it."

"And why not?" Pugnacious, Gil wanted to know. "A tax on each colony *by* colonials *for* the colonial defense, all proceeds tossed into one central Treasury with branches in each colony for distribution of the funds, would enable us to present a united front against the French without costing the King a cent! But of course, as you say, he's not too smart."

"Tha's not wha' I said!"

Worth leaned out of his chair. "Haven't you heard that Governor Shirley in his desperation for some flow of monies is pushing the *Parliament* to levy a tax on us? For the first time in our history every colony would owe directly to the Throne! And then we'd be on our knees to get it back for our defense."

The elder Scot turned lobster red. "Ye do no' mean it!"

Gil closed his eyes and informed them in a voice of dread, "There's some requirement to pay for official stamps on Colonial business documents to create a continental treasury, since the colonies have just abdicated that responsibility and right."

"But what's the trouble with tha' sort o' tax if good is done by it?"

Gil held his head as if preventing a cerebral explosion. "The trouble is we of the colonies have no representative in the Parliament! If our money goes to England without any guarantee of return, any guarantee of at least debate, we are reduced to the serfdom Israel pictures! And by our own shirking!" Gil groaned, "Say you understand that if more good is gotten by the colonies uniting than is given up, then nothing is given up!"

Hastily, Israel added, "I agree there is some willful blindness in the unanimous ignoring of the *Plan's* possibilities. If they were sincere, the colonial assemblies might have suggested refinements to make it more agreeable to themselves."

"Cherries in the cough syrup?" From Dr. Mac.

Worth crossed his legs to hold himself still. "Joke, when your son is going for a soldier?" He sighed, "Thomas Kirke foresaw this years ago. We are every man for himself. The French are on the offense! My God! We could lose everything to them!"

Mac was up, drawing aside the green drape as if to widen his perspective.

The window revealed Wakwa running toward the house.

"Uncle!" Wakwa stood breathing hard in the entry hall, his fur cap in one hand, his jacket unevenly bulging.

"Wakwa? News? The *Plan* is passed afterall?"

"A ship...is in!"

Gil held his breath. The Stirlings held their tongues.

"A Venice ship!" Wakwa's eyes were full of the past.

"Direct?!"

"Unheard of!" Mac pondered.

Israel blurted. "Who's aboard?"

Wakwa closed his eyes. His breathing steadied. "A smith in gold. From that place." His lips formed a tight seam.

Gil led him into the sitting room. Mac invited, "Tea?"

Ignoring their hospitality, Wakwa dipped into his jacket and pulled out the figure of a girl in miniature, a plaything. He laid it across Mac's hands and it fell through the Scot's fingers to the floor with a thud.

Mac apologized. "By the devil, it's heavy!"

The quartet squatted around the beautifully wrought doll with silky hair.

"Heavy yet unbreakable." Gil analyzed.

"Like her heart!" Wakwa composed himself before looking at the semi-circle of blue and green eyes. "This you see before you is solid gold. The whole cargo is gold. In fantastic shapes. Like this poppet. All inventions of Elizabeth's hand!" Wakwa's fingers caressed the glimmering, supple hair.

Gil looked only at Wakwa. "I watched her spin it."

Israel quashed romance. "Is this to be melted down? Into bars."

"Thus the Eye-talian!" Mac pursed his lips. "How long does *he* stay?"

Worth looked up from the golden doll and asked with an edge, "Have you something against Italians, Mac?"

"I couldn't say, as I never met one, Gil. But the town of Sweetwood'll whip him down the road an' you with 'im, don't you know, without a how d'ye do! If they had trouble over me, as they did at the beginning, what are they gonna make of a Venetian?"

Wakwa appealed to them. "With this ship of Kirke's nothing will be the same as it was. Kirke is telling us! Gilbert, this gold is but the beginning. There are guns as well and powder. Good stout cloth!" Wakwa rose and made for the denuded sitting room window. "Other ships will come."

Worth went to Wakwa quickly, "They will get through! If Kirke can see from China what should be done and when - any fleet of his will get through!"

At the impersonal word 'fleet,' Wakwa became all business. "Dire directs the goods to us over the next days. Soon afterward he is gone to England with the man-root and Beckett's son and the Frenchwoman."

"And the Eye-talian?" Mac encouraged.

CHAPTER THIRTY-ONE

Winter, 1754

Gilbert Worth took aim at the purple bird. He had not shot a gun in some time. Half a dozen years before when he had employed his German fowling piece against quarry that the gun was neither made nor purchased to kill, he had shouldered it with flair. Now it was not the same.

Sweetwood had mustered. Like other towns and villages the local effort had to suffice in the face of the colonies' failure to mount a cohesive defense against the French. Gil's pedigree, his European training, his monetary substance, his holdings in land, his pew in the church, his spotless reputation, his connections and his whiplash nature, all made him the obvious choice to arrange for arming and training Sweetwood.

Once the decision had been made by the selectmen, and the honor accepted, Gil drew up orders. Allowing himself just a week to plan the garrisoning of the village and all approaches to the adjoining farms, he worked with pen and ink in the afternoons.

It had snowed. Through the long glass doors of his sitting room Worth saw the elm in the north quarter, its wet limbs black, illuminated with white. What arrested Worth's vision was the arrival of a pair of crows sharply visible against the tree's snowy windings. Larger than lap dogs, they perched in the highest branches, reviewing Worth's wintering orchards. Another bird, even bigger, flapped over, crowding them. His feathers sent off the color of a black plum.

Worth set down his quill and eyed his gun cabinet. The thought of lifting the Jaeger off its rack appalled him; the fast-actioned, straight-shooting, modern machine had been his accomplice in a secret act of justice. With that rifle, Worth had killed the two trespassers on his land who had twice nearly succeeded in killing Wakwa and had been stalking the Sachim in a third attempt on his life. Not guilty about playing the godly role given the circumstances, Gil abhorred the mess of bullet-driven death.

He willingly bore the stark consequence of killing men in exchange for Wakwa's safety. What offended Gilbert Worth was the power granted him by the pull of a trigger to blow tissue apart, break through bone, search out the soft, pulsating, blood-streaked internal organs and rip through them so that they would burst, bleed, still, and very soon rot.

Skeletons secure in his closet, his village had called him, a village in a colony loyal to its king who sat an ancient throne. Worth stuck his hands into the polished cabinet, retrieved the weapon with a grim grace and trudged out to shoot targets.

"Die, Beckett!" Gil held the colossal third crow in the accurate sight and squeezed the Jaeger's hair-trigger. The ball, shot on a sure-fire ignition of flint, was aimed true by the spiral rifling of the gun-barrel.

Worth calculated that the explosion would send any winged creature squawking off its perch so he aimed high. But the crow hunched his shoulders, gripped the tree's bark, and let out a belly laugh as the bullet soared beyond him. The bird floated down to a lower branch.

"Cocky bastard!"

"Do you hate him so much?" Wakwa had come from nowhere.

Gil squawked much like the crow then found it funny that he, with his new civic responsibility had been caught off guard. "The crow or Michael?"

"The man, Uncle."

"I'm sorry for him, really, and for that crow, because I'm going to get him. Right now." Which he did. Vindicated, Worth resettled his new coat of kersey. "Always name your target. Trues the shot."

Wakwa lifted his silky brows. Then he announced quietly, "I am gone with forty men when the snow melts."

Worth's jaunty stance changed.

"No war is yet declared. We fight it in any wise."

Gil looked into Wakwa's eyes. "Everytime you shoot, say, 'Hudson!' Kill a thousand men but get home to us!"

Wakwa took the German-made gun out of Worth's hands. He worked its lethally accurate parts and got off a shot.

"Take it with you." Worth invited. "It's not as long a gun as some but it is high calibre and it does its job." His flagrant grin and wicked green eye spoiled the innocence of his comment.

Oblivious, Wakwa touched its silver inlay of fleur-de-lis. "You should retire this piece. Its beauties will hang us."

Worth snorted, "What times! I'd overlooked the French reference. You are right. I'll bury it in the cellar till this infamy blows over."

They walked at a fast, nearly military clip toward the Meetinghouse, which rode majestically above the secret cellars.

"Dire sails at sunrise."

"Tomorrow!"

Wakwa bowed to the efficiency of English expression. "I must separate Wolf from Hawk."

In the vestibule, they caught a glimpse of two patients waiting for a consultation with Israel Stirling. They found Priscilla in the kitchen starching bibs and aprons. Dolly Low was at the table crushing a root in a mortar. Lightfoot swung his legs in the chair at her side. A tuft of black hair like a decoration shot sideways from the point of his fracture. He held a bouquet of bayberry in his good hand.

Worth looked back at Wakwa as they descended the two flights to the smithery. "Lightfoot has the makings of a taupowaw."

Wakwa smiled not at the idea but that ideas never stopped coming from Worth.

Misinterpreting, Gil amended, "Or a pharmaceutist. Look how he keeps Qunneke's side when she is collecting in the woods and how he watches the making of medicine."

At the bottom, Wakwa confided, "He will live more with you than with me in the otan. With one arm...." Wakwa looked toward the whitewashed stone labyrinth.

Worth pushed open the door of the big workroom where the gold was being rendered. The Venetian had his back to his cauldron and was bent over a workbench burnishing something. Moses and Ho were seated on little stools watching his hands intently. Four Indian apprentices, two men too old to go to war, and two boys too young for combat, cooperated over the fire.

Worth walked in, greeted them, then stopped at the bench asking in Italian, "How goes it, Eugenio?"

Eugenio Patti, the goldsmith, straightened and turned and displayed against the backdrop of his palms and fingers a slender golden thing, as if he were a midwife showing an infant just out of the womb.

"Look at this!" Gil said to Wakwa.

The smith turned the half-polished flute slowly, revealing a replica of the elderberry pipe Moses had been playing for a year. The gold one was of uniform diameter inside but its exterior bore all the subtle sculpture of peeled wood. Easy on a hand used to holding flutes from Nature, even the finger holes were hollowed knots.

Worth said in excitement, "You play! You must! You have lived with us over a month and never said!" His sigh floated the dingy jobs that had overtaken all their lives as they prepared for killing. "And tomorrow will be too late...." Gil trailed off.

Moses knew instantly. He backed toward the wall. Horace tripped toward him and hung wordlessly at his side.

Wakwa stayed mute, his office undone by the Englishman.

Worth made no apology. "Tonight. Everybody. Everybody! Eight O'clock. Sitting room! Anyone who can play anything - bring your instrument!" He turned and left, his graceful hands pushing his way through unseen interference. He skewered Wakwa with a look as he passed him, "Nephew! Mark me! And bring Tame Deer!"

Nearly thirty people from the farm and the otan filled the salon at the Worths' one last time before their lives changed forever.

CHAPTER THIRTY-TWO

September 1754 - February 1755

Like surf kicked aside, common pigeons scattered as the Jesuit walked Elizabeth briskly toward St. Mark's Basilica. "I do not suppose Thomas ever brought you in 'ere?"

"Never, Father."

"Shh! Do not say it!" Claude looked right and left, his Order banned in Venice.

She mistook him. "With *my* history how should he bring me to worship?"

"Especially with your history!!"

Confused by his Catholicism she confided, "We passed by and stopped to listen to a sung Mass. We stood outside for a long time just to hear the voices cling in the air."

"Z' Basilica is for ze eyes not for ze ears!" An early Mass for sailors had just concluded spawning a crowd of clergy and private citizens. Claude led Elizabeth through the throng pooling at the great doors.

Brought up on the spare beauty of Sweetwood's church with its white spire, Elizabeth stood stark still. The interior vastness was a wild conceit formed of the essential element of fortune. The gargantuan space was a work in actual gold in miniscule segments pieced together by obsessive skill into an unbroken skin as flawless as a serpent's. Although enormous, it seemed not alien to Elizabeth's own designs, fraught with complex symbol and handiwork. Chills broke over her. The Mosaic did as intended, lowered human eyes before a sight as overawing as Divinity.

"This is nothing!" Claude pulled her on, out of the nave and past the side altars to a case of stairs behind a wall. His girth and age were of no consequence in these environs. He climbed at a quick, even pace. Elizabeth toiled in her skirts to keep up with him.

Flight after flight spiralled them to the top. One at a time, they squeezed through a narrow wooden door. Strange it seemed that the Basilica was not dwarfed by the sky.

Elizabeth felt her way along a narrow walkway flung in the open air around a dome far above the city.

Claude pressed his side against hers assuring her balance as they moved along the parapet. Suddenly his hands were searching against the face of the cathedral for her hands. The sleeves of her gown appeared empty.

Elizabeth forgot the precarious ledge and the exquisite miniature of Venice spread below her. Her eyes recorded the stone instead, a mottled pastel of yellows, pinks, blues, greens. She opened and closed her fingers to differentiate them from the walls of the great structure. Her skin matched the native stone. Her fingers, her palms, the backs of her hands shared its mineral composition. She met her Corsican grandmother in this way. Beaming, she turned her face up to Claude's, so close. She had seen the origin of herself for the first time. And for the first time since her break from him, she flooded with sympathy for Wakwa's indivisibility from his red Massachusetts soil.

His silver hair flying, his red cape whipping the winter dawn like a sail, a pug-nosed monkey clinging to his forearm for its life, Thomas Kirke surprised Elizabeth before Venice stirred.

Asunta was working dough in the candle-lit kitchen and Luigi, yet unshaven, was sleepily favoring her, grinding the morning coffee. Cecilia shivered at the washstand in her room on the dank ground level.

The bell rang maniacally through the palace. Luigi came alert, picked a pistol from a drawer and stepped hesitantly toward the front entrance. Fearing robbers, Asunta printed the sign of the cross on herself with flour-dust. But Cecilia knew in the pit of her empty stomach that the master of the house was home. Such things happened in February, validating her lifelong opposition to the second month of the year. Caught in her skin, her hair unbraided, her corset laid out on her bed, no chance of presenting herself properly after twenty-four months of fastidious service, she tossed on a woolen negligee and ran barefoot over the cold stone screaming invective like a banshee center-floor in the Great Hall.

Elizabeth hurried past her, *New Psyche's* colors cut against the gray sky out her window. Kirke shouted to her while Luigi unfortressed the Asolo. Kirke yelled his way across the bridge although Elizabeth was merely ten feet away from him behind a gate of iron filigree.

Struggling together, Elizabeth and Luigi finally opened the black gate and she fled the house to reach Kirke. He continued loud as if against an ocean wind or from miles away. The neighborhood cats yowled complaints down the alleys.

Kirke and Elizabeth stood face to face in utter quiet. Kirke's sharp eyes, bleached by ocean light, judged Elizabeth's eagerness. She was aware of his testing and was ashamed that her naked heart dominated their marriage. All the old pain was present to them both making it fresh. They recognized one another.

He grazed her cheek with a gnarled finger. She held his wrist through his lace.

"Hope you'll want him."

They laughed as the creature clutching Kirke's sleeve raised its tail and skittered up the human limb as if it were part of a tree.

"Seta! Seta! We'll name him for silk!" Elizabeth reached for the glossy, golden monkey who hid under Kirke's neckstock.

Stephen Poore, in mandarin garb, pulled Elizabeth into an embrace. "Or name him Sera. The Roman name for China."

Worried by a dramatic decrease in his girth, she whispered, "It has not been an easy voyage for you, Steph."

"Oh, Beth! Nor has it been difficult!"

Kirke tossed the monkey toward a potted tree. "Grab on, Seraseta!"

Cecilia screamed. Kirke looked displeased to see her.

Claude cried from the staircase, "Petites imbeciles! There is a roaring fire in the piano nobile. Come there!" He raised his right hand and blessed the new arrivals while barking at the hysterical housekeeper, "Cafe! Cafe!"

Elizabeth studied Kirke for frailty. He seemed sound, strong. Like Poore, he was thinner than when he had departed for the Orient. She hovered. "I've worried. You did not come 'though the pigeons got home!"

Kirke threw her a warning look and himself into a chair near the mouth of the fireplace. He covered her remark pushing the monkey into her arms. "I could not think what to bring you that wasn't just more junk so Stephen suggested...."

Poore objected, "I merely suggested he pick something compatible with your moon nature."

She laughed, tickled by the animal's kisses. "What is a moon-nature, Steph?"

"The occult sciences are not your natural bent. Suffice it to say, you were born under the Chinese astrological sign of the Monkey. The living thing was all your husband's idea!"

The little ape leaped down and gamboled over to the Jesuit. Claude hopped away knocking something precious from a table. Pieces flew.

Cecilia ground her teeth.

Kirke laughed her way, mixing Italian and English, "Cecilia, your sensitivity makes it clear I must entrust the care of the beast to no one but you!"

"No!" She drew herself up.

"Si!"

She crossed herself and cried. "No! No! No!"

"I count on your soft, maternal heart to make him at home and clean his cage and brush his yellow hair and cocker him...."

Cecilia shook with fury.

Kirke cajoled Seraseta onto his shoulder. "Like that." Kirke stepped close to the housekeeper. The monkey snarled, showed sharp teeth. "It is smiling at you!"

Cecilia set her jaw, quit Kirke's employ in a very few words on the spot. She ran downstairs for her clothes.

Kirke stroked the animal, "I thought you would have sent her packing long before I got home, Claude, but it's taken care of now."

The strained silence that followed Kirke's slap was broken by the sweet chime of cups and spoons being carried up the stairs. Claude and Stephen departed for the dining table. Kirke ate and drank nothing. He watched Elizabeth watching the fire.

His voice trembled as he said, "Soon I will tell you why we must rid ourselves of any weak links. Do you think the remaining staff'd draw me a bath?"

Elizabeth sat against the headboard. Kirke slept nestled against her ribs. Elizabeth bore his weight, her insides misshapen by it.

Rain woke Kirke to the dusk. "Am I that old? The day is gone!"

She said gently, "I am glad you slept, Viti."

He made no reply to that. Nor did he look at her when he said, "You'd better know now that I was not permitted to come straight home."

"What do you mean? 'Not permitted.'"

"We went sailing by the Barbary coast in September. I released the birds to you from not so far away." His face twisted up toward hers. He snapped to sitting posture, free of her. "The Crown is calling upon me, an independent merchant of reputation and means, to transport through naval battlelines gold bars and guns to the Prussians who are beating up the French in some silly war." Color flooded his withered cheeks. "The Crown is smuggling all kinds of stuff as sure as we live. The fashionable term is patriotism."

"You did this?"

"*Will* do it. A tea clipper crossed our path with the summons and I went straight on to London to hear out the war ministry. Had to!"

"*Had* to? How bitter for you. I know well the having-to!"

Kirke swallowed her tone. "I did not cow-tow in China and was sure not doing it in my home city! I asked them when Pitt would succeed the Duke of Newcastle as Prime Minister."

"He is resigning?"

"I believe he will now."

"Viti! If all you have to do is say what you want, I have quite a list for their lordships!"

"I know how it reads, Elizabeth Dowland." Kirke quipped. "By heart."

"I am a brute."

He ignored her apology. "The government's not to be dismantled by an innuendo from me. Locke has been prying Newcastle loose for months on the grounds of no Trade policy and no war policy and no policy in general. Perhaps they want to hand the risky business to me as punishment for Locke's nagging!"

Kirke clucked at this new perspective.

"You will not perform this charge personally?"

"I will!"

"But don't they need an officer in the Navy?"

"Liz!" His tone was not kind. "That is exactly what they do *not* want. You must see why!"

"You could be killed!"

"I will be in any case! If the French don't shoot me, George will manage it."

She laughed at his wit.

"I'm not trying to be funny, Liz."

"But this is factor's work. You are the owner."

"No one wants to kill Dire. Therefore, he's not invited to take part."

"You are not making sense."

"Oh, but I am! The Crown is about eating us independent merchants the way the Chinese eat some feisty fish alive while they yet gasp for breath on the plate."

"Horrible!"

"I'm a thorn in their side. I turn a profit no matter what snare they lay for me. They want the seas for the East India Company, so they'll get their booty, don't you understand?"

"I don't think I do. You are an honest man!"

"Much of the time."

"You pay your tariffs. You pay your duties, your taxes!"

"But I don't pay more than is required. The Throne's got the East India Company purchasing the rights to the oceans and receiving protection in return. That's big business. No independent merchant can compete."

Elizabeth turned to him. "Is there no need for independent business?"

"Sure! They need all my experience, my business ability, my navigational experts to do this dirty business." He spoke congenially, "It's a bit like the Chinese trying to gain wisdom by standing a clever monkey under a table with a whole cut in the top and then poking through his skull to pick his living brain."

Revolted, she twisted away and off the bed.

Kirke stretched his body across the expanse, captured her hand. "It will be a good thing if the Prussians are slow with their pummelling of the French. I should be able to run the guns till the end of that war and no doubt another will start up. I will try to be useful to 'em. And if Pitt takes over, perhaps the cloud will pass. But when he does take over, and he must, or Massachusetts will go to the dogs, I will be allied with the old guard and they will kill me before Pitt gets anything out of me or uses me himself. So, if I don't do it, or I do do it, or I do it no matter who's prime minister, I am probably not to live out the normal span of my life, which has been long. I suppose." He kissed her hand. "I am leaving Locke to finesse American affairs. He had a fierce crossing. Much ice. He needs a rest. He was factoring precious cargo - the lawyer's son."

"Oh, yes?"

Not liking the sound of it, Kirke rushed, "And Jeanette, the nursemaid, Dire's wife - a very fine ear does she have for useful information, may I add. Locke also was sweating over a hold stuffed with ginseng picked by the Massachuseuck, their percentage of that harvest's profit having been advanced by us in gold and forwarded by pre-arrangement from my ship to the university at Oxford. Your son's first two years' tuition is prepaid in princely style not to mention great optimism."

Elizabeth burrowed into the bed linen.

"The King wants *my neck,* Liz. The *People* may be saved by Royal command, if I remain alert to opportunities! No more of this mad work in gold for you! You are on permanent holiday."

Of stock inured to work, she felt the pressure of 'permanent holiday' like illness or imminent death.

"Because I've obliged him in Europe, the Secretary hints, if war is declared in America, I'll be running guns and whatever else across the pond, through French lines, under the protection of the British Navy! *I'll* be the one to pocket the Royal commission and pack whatever I want into my hold and float it to the other Hemisphere. Including you! Isn't it sweet?!" Kirke turned his head against her hip and fell like a stone into sleep.

When the dawn got past the open shutters, Kirke arced above her. He woke her but disappointed himself, his flesh lax from neglect.

She harbored him for a long time. She worked out of her will not her wish to make him come to life. She was his wife.

CHAPTER THIRTY-THREE

November 1755

Huldah Winke had minded exceedingly that Annanias Hudson had asked her to witness his Last Will and Testament. She knew by the honor that she would inherit not a penny from him, her most beloved employer. At her most reasonable moments, she acknowledged to herself that the difference in their ages mitigated against her surviving him; but she had not got pneumonia, she had not gotten herself beaten by thugs, or made dangerous coach journeys in mid-winter as had he. She, Widow Winke, had, in fact, outlived the windbag. Almost more than not inheriting a portion of the minister's money, she minded that he had left her not one sentimental memento out of his personal property let alone anything of real value. Considering the shocking occurrences she had put up with in his service, which she had rewarded with her unflagging loyalty and discretion, she was furious at being so thoroughly passed over.

Winke was the childless widow of an Acushnet barber-surgeon, reduced to service by the cruel bent of English estate law. A nephew had inherited by its precepts the home she had kept during her husband's short, dull life. On her darkest nights, Winke saw, as one vaguely sees a star through a mist, that the law which had lost her her home and rightful place in society was the same law by which Annanias Hudson had profited, that is to say, without it, Elizabeth Dowland would never have been betrothed to him or perhaps to anybody.

Twice dispossessed by men, three times, if Winke counted Hudson's ingratitude, she had, after her exit from Sweetwood, preferred herself to The Reverend Hudson's widowed aunt-by-marriage in Boston and was in her service when the dowager went to her grave. Winke herself had influenced her urban mistress in her last days against pursuing any inheritance of Hudson's personal property, a few sticks of furniture and a pile of books. Obtaining these gratuitous benefices would make it necessary to dredge up Hudson's past, which was not pretty, and Winke was bound up in it.

Although Winke could not be blamed for the minister's premature demise, she was uneasy about her complicity in certain actions of his that may have invited the sorry ending to his intense existence. Her silence at his consorting with criminals outside his religious jurisdiction, her invention of the method for his pasting up the Information which had gone anonymously to the Boston Court causing incalculable havoc up and down the Coast, made her balk at investigation of her life in the manse.

Ancillary problems such as her encouragement of Nathan Hanson's daughter, Prudence, in her hopeless contest against Elizabeth Dowland for Annanias' affections, her partnership with Prue in a honey-making business which gave the imprudent Prudence the wherewithal to escape Sweetwood with the minister's out-of-wedlock bump in front, her unquestioning welcome home of the girl to the apiary, mind and baby absent, and Winke's brilliant disingenuousness when the strumpet got herself stung to death in Dowland's meadow in a roundly-deserved nightmare-death, was another tin of worms Winke wanted kept firmly shut.

The final straw, Hudson's aunt's unremarkable slide into Hades without so much as the legacy of a handkerchief for Winke to weep into, set her, a simple, able housekeeper, on a spree of vengeance.

With coins purloined from the household till, Widow Winke left Boston by boat, docked at Wareham, rode to the cornfield behind Hudson's house, that is, the manse, to wipe it off the face of the Earth. She deemed herself to be doing a public service, purging sleepy Sweetwood village of immoral influence. Among the manse's perfidious features was that purple glass set in the staircase window for Mistress Beth who had lost her soul to red-skinned spellbinders, next, those books of Hudson's, stoking the mind of his replacement, the English-born, high-flying preacher wonderfully named Low, who had been reported in the newssheets as having charity for all sects including Jews but excluding Anglicans, third, the four-poster hung with exquisite white on white linen out of Mistress Beth's bewitched needles in which the Reverend Mr. Low presently tussled with his barren English wife. There was the manse's housekeeper, Millie, whom Winke had succeeded once upon a time, now smugly re-ensconced in those coveted surroundings. One could not forget the carved furniture and the lead-lined bathtub with drainage into the meadow. The list of infamies went on in that vein. Winke had put a stop to it.

How easily she had confounded the great of the village. A slab of pork fat in a frying pan set ablaze and left behind the tool shed was all it had taken to scorch out memories, frustrations, evidence of past crimes. Knowing the cancerous tendency of the neighborhood to tolerate the Indians long cockered by her once-and-most-exquisite-master, the Honorable Gilbert Worth, she had been rendered more vindictive by the little rabbit of a savage who had scurried past her horse. He wanted getting rid of like the rest of the anachronisms about the manse. Manfully, Winke had done it.

But his moan clung with her as she galloped back toward the center of the village and uncertainty interfered with her plan. She simply could not recall whether the Indian boy's moan had come as her horse's hoof struck his skull or after the horse had run past. So the fastidious Winke turned back, hitched her horse in the cornfield, and carried the limp, red beggar out of the way. Found too early, the heathen boy might be saved, live to tattle, and she be hanged on the gallows.

The next hours had gone almost too smoothly. After a sound sleep, she boarded a boat bound for Philadelphia where she landed and disembarked like a lady. The cruise down the East Coast of the Continent was a revelation to a woman who had known few holidays. Hulda Winke was met by a doctor, a widower, who had hired her from an advertisement she had placed when her Boston mistress had gone sick.

Two things only she regretted; first, that she had not been able to watch the manse burn to the ground and, second, that she had contracted to accompany her new employer, a Quaker and most pacific, to the out towns of the City of Brotherly Love to make rounds among the crude pioneers.

While it was true her experience as a cutter's wife had procured her her new situation, it turned her stomach to extend charities to awful people who insisted on living like pigs in one room - as she thought about it - rather like the Indians.

It was then with a real lightness of heart in August of '55 that she heard the doctor exclaim in shock over continued bad news from the West. She had been tantamount to delighted by the English loss of Fresh Meadows to the French during May of '54, whetting her wish that men would be brought low by their lust for land. All she could gather as she hung the Quaker's sheets in the yard was that the by-the-book General Braddock had died at Fort Duquesne on the Monongahela with appalling numbers of colonial soldiers and that his cohort, Colonel Dunbar, had primly withdrawn from the next battle, leaving Fort Cumberland to the French. Good! It was all land Englishwomen could not have at any rate so why should she bother about it.

Proud of having arranged her life in relative security in spite of her gender, Winke kept the plain-coated man's house, went to market, even to church, without looking over her shoulder. Her pride burrowed in her future like a beetle in the heart of a rose. Massachusetts seemed quite far away.

The two Kirke sub-factors had very little trouble following in Winke's wake. There was no difficulty in finding her permanent address considering their intimate involvement in the Trade and the frequency of Winke's signature as she placed orders and ran the doctor's household errands at merchants' throughout the city. They installed Raven in a room in a neighboring house they leased under Kirke Company's name and furthered Company business while the Indian watched Winke the way any bird of prey watches potential carrion.

Raven was neither English-speaking nor literate, but he understood enough of the arrest warrant to know that he could have thrown a sack over the matron and forcibly stuck her on a ship bound for Wareham Harbor and ended his commission in short order and to high praise. But it was not in his nature to do so. To his credit, Raven was not ready to trust a colonial court with Wakwa's second son. Raven wanted to drag Winke home by the ear when she had damned herself irrevocably by injuring her own kind.

Raven watched. When he saw Winke's silhouette blowing out the candles in the Quaker's windows at night he succumbed to short sleep. By dawn his duties began again. He took exercise, following as Winke walked or drove the Quaker's phaeton to the shops. Her occasional ride to the frontier with the doctor required far more skill in tracking, for the Pennsylvanian settlers had no use for red faces. Raven travelled under the guise of messenger, cook, anything that served the sub-factors' cover conveniently. So, they wore down their horse's shoes through the city spring and into the blistering inland summer. Mosquitoes were the plague of the Pennsylvanian woods and Raven was impressed by the staunchness of Kirke's men under the daily trials brought on by his tactic of waiting for Winke to stumble mightily.

Raven knew that Wakwa Manunnappu, a waiting man himself, must have honored his pledge to the Iroquois by now and be holed up in the western woods of New York picking off Frenchmen one by one. Raven prayed that Wakwa would be preserved at least long enough to see the fulfillment of his charge.

The Quaker doctor hitched his gray horses more and more to his canvas-topped wagon. In the Quaker's moving longhouse, settlers could find a bed, gain safety away from their charred cabins, be stitched and salved and straightened into splints, or when the western tribes were at their worst, have their mutilated corpses brought to burial.

Raven had news through Kirke's men that the French had tasted many victories and their Indian aides from the Mississippi had the bloodlust. They were not ones to wait or watch. Isolated from the coast, they were deluded that the French could be managed and the British were small in number and could be wiped out with tomahawks and fire. Raven knew better. Like trees with good roots, the English would blossom heartier and thicker for their cutting.

Two years after Winke had burned the manse and run Lightfoot down with no mercy, errant French Indians rode on the out towns of Virginia and Pennsylvania with firebrand and ax. The Quaker doctor hardly slept with the numbers of desperate and wounded and dying who limped into the city from the frontier.

Raven watched. He watched not only Winke but also the bedraggled and ruined farmers with the horrors in their eyes streaming through the streets. He watched through the nights. He took turns with Kirke's men. He kept the Quaker's wagon and horses firmly in sight. He readied himself for a sudden rush down to follow Mrs. Winke into great danger.

One night, when her master asked her to pack the bandages and sheeting and tins of food for a two-week foray to the frontier, Hulda Winke drew the line. For the entire autumn she had listened to the doctor read of the terrors as she sat darning his stockings at the fireside. In the cold, with snow threatening, with no place to hide, as if one could hide, Winke thought it stupid to go inland to patch together people who had no business in the wilderness. She told her employer so, and minced no words. The Quakerish man pulled her contract from his secretary drawer and reminded her of its provisions. Well aware of her agreement, Mrs. Winke stuck out her jaw and folded her arms across her ample front. The Quaker, a man devoted to peace, informed her blandly that his only recourse in the emergency was to cart her off to the magistrate to put the matter to the Philadelphia court. Winke had come full circle.

Cornered, she squealed like a sow, she fussed, but in the end did the only thing she could - submitted to her servitude and went upstairs to pack her necessaries. She left with the Quaker in a miserable November dawn. Her neck switched with cold. Their uncomfortable ride was eerily solitary. They found no welcome at wayside cabins, most burnt to their foundations, the rest emptied out of fear. These forlorn houses made their hotels as they progressed west. The fifth night brought them to a tiny house on a hillside, rich, it seemed, because of its fresh coat of green paint. There the doctor delivered a baby whose slow advent had pinned its parents to their hill. By morning, the Irish farmers and their sleepy babe rode east.

Raven continued to trail the doctor and Winke west over the high hills. The doctor, convinced the attacks were over on account of the imminence of snow, drove his horses as far as one hundred-sixty miles from the city, then made a final stop. A few traders were the only population. Raven observed Winke heat the Quaker's sausage and gruel at the hearth of an abandoned house. She settled down for the night in some stranger's creeping bed.

Winke lay sleepless in search of a way to end her service. Fate found it for her.

In the tolerable sun of Pennsylvania's late autumn, with a northwest wind telling of snow, Winke went outside to throw their blankets over a line and beat the bugs out of them. Was it the wind or a scream racing around a corner? Winke worked on, anxious to fold things correctly and start for home. Perhaps it was the wind. But the keening grew; it spread, like fire down a firewall.

The country was open here, the mountains due west and the rolling land, rich and arable, was spread much like Sweetwood's to seed. She had a magnificent vantage of miles. Winke did not bother to look, busy as she was. The sounds of wind, of fire, of hell's pain in such a fine prospect at last persuaded her from her clothesline. She hooded her eyes from the glare and turned east to south to west to north. Some waving thin things of gold clarified, the sound sweeping fast ahead of these objects, which grew constantly bigger and brighter.

Winke did not decipher what they were until she heard hoofbeats, horses running away, east. Meaning not sight reached her brain first. The men had left. The men had abandoned her. The doctor and his wagon, and his boozing, unshaven patients on their horses, were running before a zealous, fevered horde that advanced with firebrands brandished against the miniscule town of logs, not even a church to burn.

Winke stood away from the woolen covers in the laundering yard watching God's judgment fly toward her. Bare-armed, bare-chested men of considerable physical beauty, faces obscured by delightful colors of paint, bayed hot like hungry animals, hatchets raised against her as if she were the British regulars. She - a woman, a housekeeper, alone.

Raven watched the thick, hard woman wield her wooden beater against a raider who reached down to slash her. He watched the wild man unseated, watched him pummeled by the smooth, round head of the household tool, watched him leap to his feet to seize it, saw the dizzying, tightening circle of horsemen tossing their torches onto the tar and log roofs, and, yelping, close tight on the tidy housekeeper with the square jaw.

As white as Winke's sheets, Kirke's sub-factors threw their horses down and lay behind the wall of breathing horseflesh, their long guns primed and cocked. Raven almost could not look at the woman under attack. True to his name, he forced his eyes and his mind not to waver.

He saw Winke's lips draw into an angle of rewarded expectation as the Indians took her hair. That haughty smile remained as they flayed her. The smile was fixed for eternity. The band of men withdrew leaving the scorched ground and Winke's mangled body to the mercies of winter. When Raven moved at last under starlight, pulled a blanket off the line and shrouded Winke's bled corpse, the smile glowed red.

All the way to Philadelphia with her, every wind-tossed second on the ship home, Raven contemplated Winke's validated idea of his race.

CHAPTER THIRTY-FOUR

Fall through Winter 1755

The stench of the marsh, the tattling insects, a thousand men's shoulders, chests, backs, hands slippery with ooze, muscles long, thick, hot, straining for contact, turn to stone. A thousand guts scream, AMBUSH! The French enemy spring three to one. Scouting, planning, for shit!

Pushing, ripping, piercing, burning, slicing, chopping, bodies, bayonets, arrows, bullets, swords, hatchets, blood flying delicious bands of red blinding them to who is who, staining all the same, uniting males. Such screams! Dreams clotted underfoot. Almost soundlessly the scalping knives separate skin and hair from the gray bone of skulls. The vanquished sing the violation with their final breaths.

Wakwa creeps in the haze-light through death's offal, a mud of excretions, fighting flies for a path toward Awepu; Awepu's eyes discourage Wakwa from salvaging him, mutely urge him to lie still while the victorious French tramp by.

Wakwa's knee crosses the breast of Hendrik, the Mohawk, who had argued before the British general only hours before that the scouts' count of the French was mistaken and too low, the same Hendrik who at Albany had called the English soft and open as women. Wakwa gazes at the great chief, the tactician famous far beyond his woods, Hendrik without his hair, his blood wasted.

The French press north over a thousand corpses, English and their Iroquois, virtually the whole contingent.

The handful of survivors breathe lightly, shrink away from the French into the green woods or lay as if broken and gone. They deny any voice to their grief over comrades slipping hopelessly from life's bonds.

"C'est-ci incredible!" Baron Dieskau, the French commander, scratches under his hat. The job was so easy. The English and their native allies were just what *his* Indians had predicted. Too few to win, too many to sustain loss without disgrace, surprised like sitting ducks. What sort of soldiering was this? With any more such blunders by the English, the war would be over before it officially began. Punctilious, the French commander, his force of three thousand and more, nearly intact, pushes to find Lake George, the enemy's encampment, to pull the slender root of this forest of dead English-Americans and Iroquois.

Wakwa on his belly, whole men on their bellies, slither to a shallow pond to slough off the filth, the blood, to salve their bruises, their gashed flesh, to preserve life. They tote their sure-shooting French muskets of Kirke's supply nicely above the surface. They crawl onto dry land like a frightening new form of life. Absorbed by the woods, they maneuvre behind their Lake George camp, a crude works of felled trees and mounded earth.

The French are delighted to find more English and Iroquois tucked up in their motley fort like nutmeats in their shell. Cocky from their easy win on the approach, they move in for the kill clear that with a win at Lake George, Lake Champlain to northward will be saved from the English.

Awepu was a reputed marksman. Best when he did not have to hurry a shot, he was nothing daunted by pressured aim. He bid for accuracy and thus long life by choosing a target, blowing a hole between its eyes or over its ear or through its breast or stomach, then moving his position. His climax was a lightning reload. His opponents never knew exactly where that steady, small-calibre cannon aimed from. They counted on its misses. Awepu did not miss.

Awepu pecked away with Johnson's seventeen hundred men. They were not soldiers. Not yet. These were yeomen - farmers, shopkeepers, ox drivers, cobblers, wainwrights, smiths, chandlers. They did not know enough of war to tire, to put their flesh and bones before the idea. They were young and embarrassed about the slaughter of their brothers. Hate kept them strong. Every man was five men. Their dirt castle girdled with criss-crossed tree trunks was emblematic of them.

Balls flew. The French picked boys off the summit. But, as in a nightmare, the buff-coated colonials and their Iroquois partners did not fade. Sure shots from the entrenched French made no impression. The untrained ragamuffins did not die, did not give in or up. They did not give! They were so English!

The French and their Indians grew fagged, grew fewer. Their judicious shots told a sad tale of winnowed numbers, diminished ammunition, the battle's absurd and bitter turn. At their low moment, the horrible thing happened. The American amateurs and their Indians roared over the rampart, fangs dripping and fresh as the devil.

Mon Dieu! For some saliva to spit in their faces. The English! Men without hearts! Why else had so few scurried down the path into Dieskau's jaws? Doomed by their own generals as lures? What manner of men - the English in America and their Indians - to feed one thousand souls to thirty-five hundred? And then with a measly thousand, plus some hundreds behind a mound of dirt and sticks, tear up the gallant French? Dogs! They fought hand to hand, tendons snapping, soft tissue rending, muscles ripping, life's blood spurting dark.

The Americans never tired. The French who could, scattered from the field under orders. Dieskau, himself, was claimed by the Mohawk for the stake. Johnson, generalling the Americans, told his Iroquois they would have to burn him too. The hungry flames were dashed.

His skin stinking of burnt powder, his spine pressed against the straight trunk of a sycamore, Wakwa listened to the disappointed hoots of the Mohawk. "They want to burn the French commander."

Shadows from their cooking fire danced in pairs across Awepu's face.

Poisoned on gunpowder and blood, Wakwa coughed out, "I understand them!"

Slow from surprise, Awepu blinked through the flickering flames.

"They know how to end a war. Butcher and roast your enemy and toss that meal at the feet of their king!"

"Must we talk of that now?" Awepu muttered and turned the spit that held a skinned muskrat.

"The English did this themselves. Do it yet! Pereclaude says the English burned a Frenchwoman called Joan who was given up to them. A woman! A she-general and a holywoman! From time to time they take their enemy's head and stick it on a fence post. Narragansett heads, Massachuseuck heads have surveyed the world from that high position. Sunnamatta?"

"So they say." Awepu thought it best to mix a little cornmeal in his palm with water and eat that instead of the rhodent flesh. He wiped his hands on a chamois of moss

"The Mohawk, living so far from the sea and the big cities, are pure." Wakwa theorized, training his eyes on the darkness. "They promised to defeat the French and were about doing that when William Johnson told them, nay. He did not let them burn his French brother!"

Awepu knew his cousin's rhetoric. Obediently he supplied, "Why not go and urge the Irisher to change his mind? Put the French commander to the flames."

"I? What am I? A Mohawk?" Wakwa's voice changed, tore a bit. "I am not so pure! I am not so stupid as to be pure! Or as cruel!"

"I hope the Iroquois do not hear you."

"I hope they do!" Wakwa forced himself away from his prop and stood free. He walked out of the grove toward the camp shouting, "War is not pure! War is trade! A trade has just happened before our eyes. The war is not yet declared and the French and English strike bargains as if at a treaty of peace! Awepu, you and I and all the Iroquois in the world have been traded away this night! Like the fur that is no more!"

"Wakwa." Awepu arrested him with a word. "Shall we quit this alliance? Go home and leave the war?"

"How can you say that, Awepu, you a Massachuseuck and a counselor!" Wakwa stepped back among the columns of the trees, his voice low but clear, "I will ask Johnson whether he will follow up this victory with another. If he says no and would sit hereabouts preening, then we are done with him and will offer ourselves elsewhere. I would eat the heart of the French by fighting them at Canada. Burning generals is child's play!" He stalked off.

Awepu, his appetite gone, his shoulder blue, set about oiling his gun.

By the time snow covered the forest, Wakwa was home. Johnson, just named a baronet, had made a lackluster pass at Crown Point and lost. In the words of the veterans of Lake George, their stunning victory was a "puddle of piss". The French were busy building a fort to service Lake Champlain, now, indisputably theirs. They called it *Ticonderoga*.

The Massachuseuck sachim arrived in the Dowland neighborhood eleven fighters fewer. He prepared to mourn with the families whose men had unquestioningly thrown their lives into the bottomless pit of territorial conflict. He was not prepared for Winke's corpse. Dead by days only and transported in the raw cold, Winke's well-preserved face showed plainly the curled lip of the superior being.

"This is your service to me!" Low-voiced and bitter, Wakwa took Raven to task. "I wanted her public confession!"

Raven knew better than to reply.

"If the people of Sweetwood see what was done to her - we shall have another war on our hands!"

"Sachim. The English of Sweetwood know we of Massachusetts do not do this manner of...."

"You tell them Raven!" Wakwa thundered. His rage drove him across the room. He stormed back to look at the open crate. "We did not, nor will we ever know if this woman hurt my son! *We* have done this to her! As if we held the hatchet in our hands!"

Raven stepped back.

"Guard her!" Wakwa quit the room in grief.

"So!" Wakwa rasped to Worth and the Stirlings. "What shall I do?"

Gil sighed. "For the first time I envy my brother's lot. This American coil tightens and tightens. The Quaker must eventually notify someone that Winke is missing. Her death will out! He can pass it off easily enough in Philadelphia. Say she was dragged out by Indians despite all his heroic efforts to prevent them. He'll get Governor Dinwiddie to give him a medal, you wait and see!"

Mac snapped, "Send it back! Send the damned box back with her in it. Pu'it back in his hands. Let this balless physician explain that rotten mass to the postman!"

Wakwa considered this alternative with some interest.

Israel stipulated, "I'd have Tame Deer come and spread the corpse with the oxide to preserve the body. It will effect nothing if it goes to jelly."

"Israel, please!" Gil admonished, disgusted.

But Wakwa was in favor of the suggestion. "Whether we send the body back to Philadelphia or no, it were the proper thing to do."

They did not notice Qunneke's son, the quick one, slip past them into the frigid chamber. Raven, obedient in demotion, did not dare move toward Lightfoot.

Now a boy of six, Lightfoot, or Coney as he liked being called, was like the sun, searingly bright; his light reached into everything. He moved toward Raven, a man who used to sit with Wakwa in the sachimmaacommock. Now Raven was standing at the end of the room. Coney went toward him and passed by the long, open, wooden crate commandeered as a coffin. Then the boy turned his eyes to it and never moved on.

He saw a face, made strange with the strokes of knives and hatchets and a backward peeling of skin and meat like a fruit cut for eating then thrown aside to parch. He came so close to the coffin he could see cheekbones peeking through.

Coney lifted his right hand to the horrific mask, the forefinger of this unspoiled limb drawn like a divining rod. Raven closed in on him. His move alerted the adults in the hallway. Wakwa cursed aloud and burst through the door he had left ajar.

Unflinchingly, Lightfoot studied Winke.

Wakwa softly called his son away.

Helping his withered arm with his able one, Coney grazed the corpse's wrappings at its breast as if blessing it with a broken wing.

"Wautuckques!" Wakwa whispered from his vantage point. "Come to me!"

This second son failed to take more than one leaden backward step toward his father, the sachim. He looked only at the monster laid out before him. "Koowahush!" he said in his native tongue. In English, "I know thee!"

"Wautuckques!" Wakwa insisted.

Gilbert Worth cut through the knot of men, lightly achieving Lightfoot's side. He half-knelt, his arms loosely circling the child.

Coney leaned against him, turned to whisper in his ear. "Noowahik."

Gil gripped the boy. "She knows *you*, you say?" His fine features slid and trembled as he forced himself to look at Winke's savaged face. His bass voice shook with revulsion. "Tell me again! Tell me in English!"

"I know her. She knows me." Over murmurs of the others he persisted, "I see...that...face...at night!" Lightfoot leaned forward.

Gilbert held him back. The boy's good arm broke the vice Worth made.

"I know her face!" Lightfoot said again, moving somewhat to the side as if to see the face without all its changes, as if to meld its worried parts into one smooth and normal shape.

Gil was looking at the boy now.

"Each night...I close my eyes to sleep...I see her face."

"That face?"

Coney shook his head. "Her mouth like that and her eyes!" At last the boy turned against Gil's neck to block the sight of Huldah Winke.

"Say it loud!"

"Come to me, Wautuckques!" Wakwa crooned.

Lightfoot turned to the dead woman. He accused, "I know you! You come in my dreams."

Wakwa cried out, "Only a dream, my son!"

"Matta! No!" Lightfoot contradicted his father. He backed against Gil for moral support.

Worth grasped Lightfoot's deadened hand and the live one. "Remember! Remember anything!"

Convulsing from the effort, Lightfoot blurted, "Her! A horse's eyes! Round. Round face! Her mouth like that!" He screamed, his eyes open, unblinking, as if, were his lids to drop, Winke would ride at him again. "I hurt!"

Gil uttered a sob and backed away with the boy.

Tamoccon was brought to view the corpse and match the mangled housekeeper with his memory of the face at the burning manse.

Wakwa declared, "I am satisfied!" To Raven he said bitterly without apology, "I give you the name - Justice!"

Raven looked for a long moment at Wakwa then abandoned his watch to pay homage to his sachim.

Careful in his phrasing, Wakwa commanded, "Come to council to receive your reward."

Ever politic, Raven replied, "My reward is to sit at your fire."

Wakwa watched his subordinate.

Oddly, no one made mention of the disposal of the body. A tell-tale acquisitiveness in the Stirlings' blue eyes let them all understand that Winke's best service would be to science.

CHAPTER THIRTY-FIVE

May 1756, through September 1759

Considering a world on fire, Europe at war with herself, and her colonies east and west in all latitudes swept into the bloodbath, it might seem a small thing that Michael Beckett, Esq., secured Annanias Hudson's ground to Kirke Company.

Dire Locke sagely retained him in the matter for small it was not; Locke saw in the accomplishment of the business a first crack in the wall between Elizabeth and Wakwa which had been built by Hudson's hand. Beckett was glad of the income.

Elizabeth Dowland and Thomas Kirke were delivered this Chancery gift Coram Domine Rege, that is, under *Ordinary Jurisdiction*, that is, according to the right line of the laws and statutes of the realm, by the writ De Dote.

Michael Beckett explained it to Elizabeth by letter stating that Hudson's land was like a sardonyx in a jewel box - a black gem streaked with blood-red, valuable but unsuitable to display in public, better passed on judiciously and under wraps. He advised that she immediately look to the matter of deeding the ground to some person uncontroversial in the legal sense. Such a settlement would avoid an expensive and unappealing second experiment for her with the rule of Equity in the Court of *Extraordinary Jurisdiction*, the particulars of the present case being far different from the alienation she had accomplished years before when her feet were still under Wakwa's table, so to speak, and Hudson had not yet been exterminated in his pasture.

On receipt of Elizabeth's answer by return post from Venice designating Gilbert Worth as the legatee of Hudson's farm, Locke issued Beckett a partial advance of his fee to see to the details. While Elizabeth's choice was the correct one, it could not help rubbing Beckett a bit in the wrong way. Notwithstanding, he pocketed the money.

Cecil Lord Worth affirmed his confidence in the solicitor as well. For enlightenment and persuasion in the eking of funds from the Crown to defend its American colonies against a presumptive France, Cecil needed an expert on American properties; in lieu of Silent Fox, he introduced Beckett in Lords. Naturally, no income accrued on such a lofty plane of service. Lord Worth, sensitive to Beckett's predicament, reserved out of Beckett's stables two yet unborn foals for his Heathersley estate and, not without design but with exquisite subtlety, whetted his peers' interest in Beckett's Thoroughbreds.

By one means or the other, Beckett's name began to rival that of his late father's. The lawyer was as pleased as a debutante at her coming out – pride and anxiety mating in him.

In the matter of women, he remained strapped. His personal position was too fragile to allow philandering among the playful wives of lords. Their unmarried daughters were off-limits for reasons of their superiority to him in social status and financial depth and, most important in his mind, their inferiority in beauty and character to Hanna Worth. He certainly preferred a truculent Jeanette to a plaything of rank. Consequently, Michael Beckett retreated into his work, which pleased Cecil immensely, even, and especially when, it progressed at balls and parties through a haze of alcohol. To return Lord Worth's considerable favors, Beckett exercised his genius for disparagement every chance he got to puncture Kirke's chances for an elevation.

England declared war on France officially in May.

To a solicitor, especially to Michael Beckett, all military actions were the same. He seized on the captive presence of his nine-year-old son to declaim and perfect his postulate: to wit: men of varying virtue all offered their blood and their youth on the altar of territorial right for the short-lived glory and financial gain of kings. Regardless of the location or duration or object of the battle, no matter the contenders, the stuff of combat was exertion, endurance, prowess, and a painful expansion of soul often leading to extinction. Ergo sameness.

He said to Horace one night in an embellishment of the premise, "War is sport. Deadly sport."

Ho pondered the assertion without comment.

"Give me an example, you say. Here it is! The Great Chief, Wakwa Manunnappu, applies himself to winning these competitions not only by fighting with fierceness and brains but also by choosing his competitions according to the merits of the generals in command. For the pawn to pick his knight is alien to a good British game of chess but it is the cardinal rule of his self-made war-game, for the prerogative to pick his battles feels as natural to this Indian as his balls."

Yet, by the summer of 1757, after years of grinding warfare, Michael Beckett further refined his martial theory declaring it indisputable that chance was, in the face of everything, the ruler of success.

Ten-year-old Horace made the equation: "All battles are the same for they are games of risk ruled by chance."

Beckett scowled at his son's mathematical simplification. "Examine chance! Is it merely random happenstance or more - a holy spark struck from the friction of things past?"

Ho stood by algebra. "Then, Papa, if chance is the latter, there is no such thing as chance, and all battles cannot be the same."

Sudden as a shooting star, the Marquis de Montcalm became the commander-general in America for the French. Luck was with him. He could not lose an engagement.

The news reached Silent Fox in the field. He confided with excitement, "Awepu, they say he is magnificent! A small man, but in his eye lives the strength of the pine and the fire of the eagle."

Put in mind of Gilbert Worth, Awepu looked up as if to speak, then refrained.

"More, this lion is a man learned in Latin. In Greek! He has fathered six living children of the same wife who he loves as when she was his bride."

Glad now he had refrained from comparisons, Awepu responded, "They say Montcalm will not burn English generals, yet his Indians slaughter common Englishmen against his strictest commands, prisoners-of-war, unarmed, sick. He is a bad warrior to loose control of his men."

"He has won control of much ground." From Wakwa.

Awepu's skin crawled.

From the darkness of his obscurity, of his subordination, Wakwa could see into the light - just as Montcalm in his shrewdness left the great men of the English unmolested, and the small to the mercies of a barbarous horde - Montcalm, a great one, must not be sacrificed. His ignominious death would kindle the French aristocrat's delirious army to meaningless atrocities among the ordinary. His loss would leave France hopeless, desperate, foolhardy. No one could tell what would unwind from that.

Wakwa's worst fear was total French victory. His second-worst fear was total victory for the English. Total victory for either meant total defeat for the red-skinned. Like fire struck with a firestick and a flint, the way was illumined for Silent Fox. Out of a smoky haze came the pure flame. The war must end in a draw. As if there had been no war. As if it were all the same to have fought or to have declined the fight. As if each battle the worldwide had ended in a victory for all parties. As in a game at the winter feast, each opponent should be judged equal to the other. No stalemate, but each contender striving and rewarded the same.

Montcalm must be stopped but not killed. Montcalm should live out his years with honor in Candiac in the bosom of his family; the English and the French could balance their power across a large polished table anywhere. And Indians would gain time, could sue for a fair settlement of their grievances for all time.

He told his insight to Awepu.

Awepu's head listed to the side. "This is a dangerous dream. Who will trust you if you kill and withhold from killing like the English and French generals?"

"My cousin, my counsellor! It is in a much different manner. William Johnson's mercy to Dieskau dealt Indians out of their own fate! In securing Montcalm, we Indians deal to the English and French the only possibility of lasting peace."

"A fine line. You know what they say about red men who walk lines."

Wakwa opened himself to the criticism. "All victorious men are line-walkers." He brushed the skin of his arm to illustrate, "This should make no difference!"

Having determined these things, Wakwa chose to face the French and Montcalm at the untenable English position - Fort William Henry.

The French capture a prize dispatch while the battle rages - an English general's letter: *no reinforcements due to relieve England's Colonel Monro.*

Monro is on his own. The pox enters his ranks. Fever is rampant. Monro's twenty-two hundred English regulars and Americans, so-called, and their Indians, hole up.

Eight thousand French and French Indians outside the ramparts struggle to breach Monro's defenses. It takes bloody day after bloody day. The breach is made. Montcalm takes a chance on British common sense - sends the hard-luck message in. *No reinforcements due. Capitulate with all honors.*

Heart and blood drown sense. Monro holds out! Eight more days of battle. Eight days. Nights and days. Over the succession of brave, horrible days, three hundred of his men die hard. No reinforcements due. No reinforcements. None. Never. God!

Reduced to executioner of his own troops, Monro capitulates. All honors accorded. All taken prisoner. All walk or carry their comrades on palettes to the next French fort.

Montcalm trusses his Indian headmen in agreements to ensure that the columns of English troops pass without harm. The headmen, aware of an array of honor codes, promise safe passage. But alien red youth out of the French West snarl at old men and the rules of war.

They raid the line. Grab one captive. He screams and screams. Another is taken. Another. The prisoners on the march unable to rescue their stolen comrades stumble on under threat, damning their own hearts for beating. The woods are alive with unseen monsters. The French troops, dry-mouthed, bug-eyed, sweating to death, and not from summer, make poor protectors. More than half a thousand veterans of Fort William Henry are missing from the ranks. Some of these actual, breathing men, sick from terror or sick from the pox, are chopped into stew. Tough chewing.

Wakwa fades from the fort with his band in light of the French ultimatum. The Massachusseuck stay on the loose in the August woods, strange woods, smelling of blood and echoing with male sorrow. While the young cannibals sleep off their feasts, Wakwa, the Black Fox, and his small force, cut bonds, throw doomed men over their shoulders like trade blankets and dart with them out of the shadow of the cauldron into the safety of moonlight.

Saving English soldiers, they serve Montcalm, abet his mighty effort to salvage his prisoners and his reputation. The French and the English and their Indian allies in desperate alliance drag back from the cooking pot, the stake, the knife, fully five hundred of seven hundred men; men of courage. The French, the English, and the Indians play the game on the same side. Each wins. For a time.

The last day of April 1758, saw a Kirke Company shipment of goods arrive. Wakwa was at Worth Farm making his farewells, the Massachuseuck only hours from returning to the war under Abercrombie in the New York woods. A sub-factor's appearance out of a mist taking the color of chartreuse from the forming leaves, struck Wakwa as manittoo - godlike - thus fortunate.

Preoccupied with Matthew in supervising the carting of fresh crates of guns and ammunition and gold straight to the infirmary cellar, Gil handed a flat leather pouch off to Hanna. "Read to me, dear?"

But Hanna stood dazed by a gift from Kirke – two-dozen Chinese rose bushes potted in priceless porcelain, thorny green canes already tufted. She passed the pouch to Wakwa.

By this chance, he was the first to see the message it contained. Wakwa's heart tumbled in his chest to see the flowing line of ink drawn by Elizabeth, her spirit and the movement of her body evident on the heavy paper. Wakwa's fingertips touched traces of her for the first time in nearly a decade. A man hardened by war should not have trembled or flushed from the mere sight of the script of a woman so long ago his. He should not have moaned aloud. Perhaps.

The sounds brought the Worths to his side. They read together:

> *The rarest thrive near the sea. Sir Jeffrey Amherst is the new general-in-chief for America.*
> *I love you all.*
> Beth

Wakwa gazed at the large white sheet. The letters glided and swam.

Hanna offered, "She means the roses."

Gil shrugged that off. "Then she would have said, 'This variety of rose thrives near the sea which is why Thomas sent them.' And what does Sir Jeffrey have to do with roses. No, it is something more...sensitive. This is code."

Wakwa could only repeat, "'all!'" He folded the cryptic message into his pouch.

Before nightfall, Captain Jones relayed a message from Kirke Company. "Amherst will sail from Halifax to Cape Breton Island by June to win back Louisbourg from the French. The battle for Canada is on."

Gil deduced, "Louisbourg! Near the sea! Beth guides you, Fox!"

Wakwa savored the truth. After nine long years apart, Elizabeth was alive to him - to what the war could bring them. His blood laughed to him that victory might come of this war after all.

Wakwa's choice for Amherst averted his probable slaughter under Abercrombie at Fort Ticonderoga. It was not easily done but by late July the English forces pulled down the French flag at Louisbourg forever. With that banner gone, a man could as good as see down the throat of the St. Lawrence to the heart of French power - Quebec.

The Becketts, Michael and Horace, unrolled a very large, fresh sheet of kid-finished paper, the sort an artist might use. Beckett blinked back the reference. He was a solicitor, no glory-seeking pigment-dauber, and his son was merely a motherless chap of twelve.

They noted on the wide sheets of paper the daily reports of battles won and lost the world over, one sheet per month. Twelve per year. By early summer of '59 Beckett calculated the private parlour game had begun to cost an appreciable sum, for the months rolled by, and there were battles everywhere, and the sheets came at a premium. Frankly, Beckett did not see how the wild-eyed painters did it - bought their stuffs on which to work. Probably had family money like everyone but himself.

"This war had better end soon or we'll be doodling on our backsides." Beckett neatly jotted the date, preparatory to their filling in the day's details.

Ho stopped his father's hand.

"What are you doing?!"

Always gray-faced in his father's presence, a color not in sympathy with the blandness of his hair, Ho spoke firmly. "Let's do this differently, sir. Let us see if we can end the war."

"Horace! It's going to get late, this hideous room is going to get colder still because of the rain, June or no June, and we're going to miss recording our data! By tomorrow there'll be more and we'll be...confounded."

Ho flushed coral. The tint flattered his good bone structure and sound skin. "If we only take note of what others do, we can never influence the outcome!"

Beckett eyed his son of the awkward age, let his glance travel to the sideboard of decanters, decided they were at acceptable levels and returned, "If it will curtail the expense in materials, I say, proceed, General H. Beckett!"

And Ho began to draw. Too well for his father's taste. There appeared in short order, the city of Quebec roosting on a height of rock above the meeting of two rivers, the St. Charles and the rapid

River St. Lawrence. Eight miles east, Ho's quill spilled the St. Lawrence into the sea.

"Father, you write down the problem."

"Tell it me!" Beckett was not totally oblivious to amusement.

"Prime Minister, Sir William Pitt, sets James Wolfe the impossible task...."

"Which is...?" Beckett sent a look of dark indulgence Ho's way.

"Conquer a city in the clouds from the water below. A citadel generalled by the Marquis de Montcalm."

"Evocative. You'll not make a lawyer at this rate. Nor a sachim, neither. You have yet to state the specific challenge."

"Quebec is built two hundred feet above the water."

"Better."

"The precipice is sheer."

"Good."

"Quebec cannot be captured from behind."

"Why not?" Beckett snapped, concerned that Pitt *was* looking for the impossible.

"French Canada spreads back from the old city for thousands of miles."

Beckett gazed at the son he had always thought inadequate. "That's obvious."

"The French food supply is endless. It is a factor against England's success."

"It is indeed." Beckett said more respectfully. He lowered his head and wrote.

July brought them no more specifics of offense or defense than their own reason might have.

Beckett cast *The Times* aside. "What's Wolfe doing? I hear he's got a killer of bellyache. The man's actually dying. A tragic case, but Pitt ought to get someone else on the task."

Horace stuck his shoulders back. "You have noted what Wolfe is doing."

Beckett ticked his tongue. "Chipping away at the problem."

"What would you do, Father?"

"I'd call in Kirke. Maybe Locke could fly some horses to the top of the rocks on his broom!"

"Write it down."

Beckett did. "Your turn."

Ho's lips twisted, withstood pressure from his upper teeth, finally relaxed and opened. "I approve Wolfe's action. He's seized footholds, strongholds along the river. He bombards Quebec from below. He confounds Montcalm."

"He confounds me, that is sure."

"Father, protecting shiploads of his own men under his own cannons' fire is good. He sails his troops upriver to west twenty miles, downriver to east twenty miles, up and down the river again." Ho pounded his fists on the table and warbled delight as his father recorded the English strategy.

"You are making me blot! And what's so funny about sailing to and fro all summer?!"

Ho could hardly make himself understood through his chortles. "Surely, Father, the formidable Marquis de Montcalm must wonder at Wolfe's antics. The French troops must be worn out, marching the rim of the precipice west, then east, then west, then east, to guard the entire position!"

Michael shot his son a quizzical look. "You see it all don't you? Clearly as if you were there."

Ho swallowed and looked down. "We are not there."

"Well, chin up, old son". Beckett thundered, "Jeanette!"

When she appeared, she enquired, "Time for bed? So early, mon petit?"

"Forget your *petit*." Beckett stood over the round table with quill poised. "What do you think your French general, Montcalm thinks of the English scooting up and down the river all summer?"

Jeanette held Michael Beckett firmly in her dark-eyed regard. "Eee must think of home. Eee's marriage. Eee's babes! Eee's bed! Eee must think ees trials will never end!"

Beckett curled his lip. "Enough."

"We are being led by an invalid. We will lose!" With a bad grace, Beckett filled in the August chart as to date and current status. "What Wolfe has done hardly requires a whole great new sheet!"

Ho sat with hands folded on the table's edge. "Montcalm is stymied by a ridiculous rule that intelligence can reach him only after being run through some petty official of the city. His military response is hostage to a Quebec nobody, possibly drunk, possibly corrupt!" The August breeze filtered in the open windows and riffled the pyramid of rolled charts. Resolutely, Ho unfurled them, tacked them down on the floor with books at their corners, and stood on them. His arms tight across his breast he demanded, "Put down, *Go over the top*!"

"What!"

"If I were lying on my fevered couch, and dying as James Wolfe is with the impossible to do, I should go over the top!"

"Do tell!" Beckett may as well have been Pitt.

"I should send my scouts to find a way up that palisade."

"That is hardly original."

"It has been overlooked! But Wolfe has no time left. The northern autumn may bring snow. Ice will kill any chance of climbing."

"Climbing? We have here the summit is two hundred feet above the water, and the rock, sheer."

"It is three hundred feet a few miles west of the city. And there, west, is Montcalm's weakness!"

"You outstrip me, General Ho." Beckett derided when he did not understand.

Ho held his head at his father's denseness. "Montcalm hardly guards that spot because of its height. It is his Achilles heel!"

The skin on Beckett's face tightened. "Only if there is a vein in the rock. Some foothold or other. Some way for an army to climb. And when would they do?"

Ho cast himself into a chair in disgust. "In the middle of the night, of course."

"Why didn't I think of that?" Beckett dismissed it.

"Write it down!"

Beckett did so and then stuck his pen in the well. "Right about now, with my enemy very small and very far below me, with six miles of sentries peering over the St. Lawrence, with my opposing general dying to the unconcern of the British chief-of-state, I would be planning Christmas in Provence." Beckett wiped his hands of the problem.

"I am sorry for you, Father."

"God made Montcalm his bastion five million feet in the air! God seems to be on King Louis' side. And Gilbert Worth better be packing his things, because the whole conveyance, and his farm, and Dowland Farm, and all his little ways, and his little sitting room, and his native chums are going to stink of garlic soon."

Ho stood. "There is the element of chance."

"Is chance greater than God?"

"God could create the luck the English need. That is what the great James Wolfe is counting on on his deathbed. He is casting about for a miracle."

Beckett fought the point. "Montcalm is proven great, corrupt local officials notwithstanding, and he has God on his side. He is the Catholic, and the believer in miracles. And, he is a man determined to be home for Christmas!"

Nearly with his father's disdain, Ho claimed, "Precisely why Montcalm can be foxed!"

Floating downstream like the leaves spinning across the September sky, Silent Fox joins the search for access to the plateau. The sun throws itself down, tears the mighty current, bleeds red into the river. Lost in light and color, Wakwa and Raven fight the flow of the water to steady the canoe. A path, non too cruel, is in view. Still Awepu studies the cliff's hard bronze skin through his long glass.

Shadows stripe the soaring rock. The shadows darken with the arrival of evening. The slim depressions take on depth. Awepu's arm cuts the air. "There!" His hand follows a crazed line upward. Brave bushes cling to the sheer stone. A possibility. Others paddle to the place to look.

Wolfe struggles off his bed. Inspects every find. Chooses the wide incline but is nagged by the image of the declivity, that wrinkle in stone. Wild shrubs obscure its vanishing point. Wolfe, dying of his own insides, knows this worried line in the cliff's face could be his single chance to reach Montcalm. Wolfe seizes it.

The English troops, stationed below Quebec, throw shot up the cliff into the old city herself. Wolfe's army executes diverting landings and actions along the falls and the rivers that score the eight-mile line.

Montcalm pities his desperate foe who begins two, then three losing battles. Poor English! They have no way to fight him, no chance for victory. Montcalm salutes their brazen adieu. And thanks his God.

September. Twelfth day. Sunset. Downriver from Quebec. The English stage a false landing east of the city - Montmorenci.

Montcalm, alert, suspicious, sends large numbers of his men against the incomprehensible English. Montcalm, strangely nervous, takes horse; rides the banks of the St. Charles River all night.

Thirteen September. Two hours after mid-night. A light out of nowhere flickers. Disappears. Seventeen hundred Englishmen take to the water in small boats. Float blindly downstream on the ebb tide in the blackness. A Scot twice lies to the sentinel on the shore, "Francais! De la Reine!" The current places them not at the path but at the foot of the sheer climb.

Wolfe's boat comes in line with the defile. Wolfe opens the little locket framing his betrothed's miniature, which the night obscures. He murmurs poetry to his mates, "*The paths of glory lead but to the grave!*" Seventeen hundred troops rock soundlessly on the water like babes before birth and as awake to death.

Two-dozen men volunteer to slip ashore under William Howe's command. A Highlander, a climber, goes first.

Slippery stone; perpendicular. Wakwa, one of the twenty-four climbing hand-over- hand toward small unhelpful stars, sees Kirke's roses, canes reaching, thorns latching on. His fingers find roots growing out of stone. His life balances on his toes, lodged briefly in the pockmarks of the precipice. Three hundred feet upward. Three hundred clampings of fingers of iron that leak blood. Wakwa before Awepu. Awepu followed by Raven.

The twenty-four creep in silence onto the rocky ridge where a few sentinels doze instead of the usual one hundred – two horses lame, one stolen, men off duty for the harvest. Chance! God-given luck.

Wakwa's obsidian knife circles a Frenchman's throat as if it were a buck's; he cuts deep, up, severing head from spine. Wakwa holds up the prize. "For Moses!"

The twenty-four despatch the meager French picket guard making way for Wolfe himself to tred the gentler path to the Plains of Abraham. The Boy-General Wolfe climbs away from disease to fight this fight.

Like plague, word of thirty-three hundred, good British regulars' presence on the heights spreads east and pools at Montcalm's feet. He intones at another man's miracle, "This is a very serious business."

Wolfe's invasion of the western plain cuts off French communications. Montcalm's forces spread east and west, tacked at their extremities like butterflies on a board. Montcalm accepts nobly Wolfe's stern challenge to open-field battle, an unfamiliar brand of warfare for his native and homegrown troops.

The rest of the world sleeps, uninformed.

Day breaks. British troops spill into a thin red line. March two-deep across the grassy veldt of the Quebec plateau toward the city's walls.

Rudely awakened French regiments pull their trousers on, tear through Quebec's narrow streets. Others' marching orders change. Leave one battle for another. On they plunge to The Plains of Abraham, two thousand regulars, aided by two thousand Canada militia, veterans of the woods, baffled by war in the field.

Ten O'clock. The French march out of Quebec's gates beyond Quebec's western wall, fifteen minutes, twenty minutes. Regimental colors flying, they march, they march, a thick wall of confused men. "Vive le Roi!"

The English, toy soldiers, stay stationary. The French march as close as forty yards. Minutes tick by, two, three. The French take the bait. Shoot first.

The order from the English, *"Fire!"* Two-deep, two balls ready.

Burning light! Bodies piled.

"Fire!"

Men die on dead men. Ghosts rise. Mayhem. *Charge!* White and red hands force bayonets through French hearts. Indian hearts. Kilted Highlanders scream from their bellies, sink claymores into heads, joints, ribs, viscera. The Scots' double-edged broadswords mutilate living, resisting men.

Proven French soldiers, brave men, run for Quebec's skirts. Safety stains their honor.

Montcalm saves it, roaring, *"Retreat!"*

The moment glitters.

Montcalm's horse rears, holds him high, the guidepost for the French survivors.

Wakwa forces his way toward the horse, his men fanning behind him. Push Montcalm behind the wall! Save him for another day.

WOLFE SHOT! SHOT AGAIN! DOWN. DOWN.

They have broken! WHO HAVE BROKEN? The French!

Wolfe turns on his side. "NOW I CAN DIE IN PEACE."

Wakwa nearly breaks. Slaps the French toward the gate with the butt of his gun.

Awepu prods their flight with bullets. Montcalm rides into his sight.

Wakwa begs, "He must not die!"

The small target, brilliant as a god with a lion's face, turns toward Awepu.

Wakwa screams. Screams. Screams.

Awepu spends a second. Sends a ball over Montcalm's head to move him on.

Wakwa screeches, "No!" as a hell of British gunfire sprays.

Vermilion streams down Montcalm's waistcoat. His arm slips down his gelding's neck. The horse strides, kicks, crushes his way toward the wall. The gate is open.

A magnificent man! A father of six. Scholar of Latin and Greek. Wife, babes, mother, praying their God to see him home for Christmas.

Montcalm sways close to the gate. It receives him, as do the waiting arms of his officers. Wakwa watches, "GODS! SAVE HIM!"

Raven watches his Sachim, amazed.

Wakwa's back broader than a barn.

Raven veers.

Awepu sees.

Raven pulls an arrow from his quiver. Expertly, he poises the stone point against the bow, sick of the reign of his line-walking Sachim.

Awepu has Raven in the crosshairs.

Raven's muscled arm stretches back the bowstring as far as it can go: his aim, delicate art in the hysteria. The Raven shrieks.

Awepu's longbore claps.

Raven's hand releases. Propels the missile. Raven scattered into pieces. His arrow flies amiss.

Silent Fox turns at Justice's cry.

The next day, Montcalm died.

WOLF

CHAPTER THIRTY-SIX

January 1763

Dire Locke appeared at Michael Beckett's great stone, and iron gate for the first time and without forewarning in the frigid January of the signing of the war treaty.

The climax was Quebec, after which England swept handily everything the Seven Years' War had to offer. Her golden victory, wrenched from the jaws of defeat by Prime Minister Pitt's brilliance, was burnished further by the crowning of the new George when the old George died. In a trenchant reaffirmation of the monarchy, Pitt was dismissed for being too good at his job. The post-war fiscal depression interrupted by not one peal the euphoric bells tolling England's mastery worldwide. Massachusetts was as giddy about the defeat of the French as the rest of the Americans.

The English called them that now and freely. Locke thought the appellation had much to do with the English treasury's being low and the Crown's predictable desire to fill it back up by means of taxes on their cousins across the sea. To forge the post-bellum population of Massachusetts and the other colonies as one with England might make squeezing money out of them unseemly. On the other hand, their lack of a presence in the London government could prompt a row. No, they had to be styled as connected to the Crown by the frailest of bonds, and in England's debt. Hold them at arms' length where they lived so fatly – America. Yet, to hold them too foreign, that is, independent, patently counter-productive.

Locke's business was partly to explore such dangerous political ground with the Board of Trade and partly to contribute his knowledge of Indian matters to the delegates to the Paris peace. Before the negotiations were actually concluded, Locke slipped away to tend to the Company's more personal concerns.

Moses Bluehill was sixteen and of college age. Considering his parentage and property, Moses' education and his safety while acquiring it were matters of public import. He required a companion at Oxford. Horace Beckett was the universal choice except by Michael Beckett. The September term in sight, quick resolution became a necessity. The family naturally turned to Dire Locke.

By the time his coach's wheels ground to a halt scarring the gravel fronting the dismal Beckett place, more dismal for the weather, Locke had erected a fixed pole in-mind around which to wind the solicitor - his screaming need - that of funds. Beckett unwittingly provided him another.

Locke stood in Beckett's dim, low-ceilinged study with only the trunks of the trees outside cutting long bars down the windows of diapered glass and he could not tell what season of the year it was. He opened his mouth to speak.

Beckett announced first, "I have been thinking of you, Locke."

"On what matter of business?"

"Is that all you think about?" Beckett shone with charm. "Sit down! Be comfortable!"

Locke raised his eyebrows at the morose collection of large wooden chairs.

"When Jeanette and I do not see you for a while...."

Michael Beckett's expansive, 'Jeanette and I,' rankled Locke exceedingly, yet the verbal slip blasted open a course of action wide enough for a fleet to sail through.

Still standing, Locke echoed, "Jeanette and I..." he dangled the lawyer for a long moment then let him drop a thousand feet, "will be separate no more."

"What?!"

Locke danced away with his new theme. "I've come to take her back. The war is done. My house at Newport is ready."

"How...?" A man of words, Beckett could not phrase a sentence.

"I am quite well fixed. The Trade has taken a most profitable course considering the war and its successful conclusion. And, she is my wife."

"Sit down!" Beckett boomed and came off his own chair to pace.

Locke cooperated because Beckett, mean and on his feet, was a sight to see and no tactical advantage could be gained by competing with it.

Beckett's stature was abetted by moves powerful and swift, giving Locke the impression that the man could leap to the top of his bookcases and roar and spit from there like a tiger.

Beckett pushed the old carved chairs out of his way in his terrible ramble of the room. He crossed through the window's light.

Locke traced sorrowful gutters down his face to his throat as if Beckett's stunning white skin were alabaster harrowed by acid over the years. His body and his face, so contradictory in their messages, gave him the aspect of great courage.

Locke found him disarming when serious. Beckett's smile unveiled his soul's fangs.

Beckett smiled. "So, you do think about something other than money!" He glided over to the liquor cabinet singing *Heart of Oak*, England's victory tune, in a surprisingly smooth tenor: "'*Come, cheer up my lads, 'tis to glory we steer, to add something more to this wonderful year!*' By the bye, Locke, my congratulations to Kirke Company for its part in crushing the French."

Beckett's insensitivity, considering the facts of the contest, not to mention Jeanette's heritage, made Locke pluck the Company out of the limelight. "Without the bravery of Major General Wolfe, sir, and other courageous men, Silent Fox among them, all the gold in the world were as naught."

Beckett collapsed onto his couch, howling laughter. "You humbug! Without Kirke-the-smuggler, the entire pack of noble hearts would be 'as naught'! What will you drink?"

"Anything decent." Locke committed the foul with glee.

"Well!" Beckett was up studying his rack.

Locke got an idea. "Make it Champagne. In light of events...."

"That's downstairs."

Locke looked up at his host, each blue eye marked with questions. "Oh, all right. I'll switch to it not to waste the bottle." Beckett rang, gave instructions, then sat opposite his small, thin, uninvited guest. "The truth is I do not live as luxurious a life as you are used to."

Locke closed his eyes briefly and considered reminding Beckett of his connections in Lords. The factor forbore.

"Does what I say surprise you? I am a solicitor with a non-paying clientele for the most part, as you are well aware, and the horses help me to barely break even. This big place I have from my father has leached me. His curse on me, I suppose. Takes a horde to keep it running and that horde do eat."

"A prime moment to take my Jeanette off your payroll."

"She doesn't eat so much!"

Not crowing, although the delighted cry battled up his throat, Dire remarked dryly, "You seem to want to keep her."

"She seems to like it here."

Dire quickly pulled that sword out of his vitals and stuck it into Beckett's. "But what will she have to do? Her charge is sixteen, seventeen now. Horace is ready for college."

Beckett snorted, "I don't think I'll send him. He's no genius."

"Surely you are being modest. His French must be excellent by now."

Beckett flashed his lethal smile. "Jeanette is an excellent teacher."

"Whom you cannot afford!" Locke warned Beckett off this baiting. "She is sorely needed elsewhere and a governess is a luxury for a man to keep as his son is about to incur an adult's expenses. Unless you intend that she continue in some form of tutelage with him as he assumes his manhood."

"Haw! What a thought out of a husband."

"Obviously not feasible."

"I should say not."

"For reasons of economy."

Beckett chuckled as he received two chilly bottles into his hands. "I love hearing you talk!"

"It is not just talk. You already live at Cambridge and to put two people up suitably in lodgings in the same town where you've got quite a big house would be extravagant."

"Drop it Locke."

"And it might get him expelled. You are more familiar than I with the legalities."

"I know you so little but your archness puts flesh on the legend." Beckett brought their saucers by their stems.

Toasting the third George, Locke ventured, "The time has come to part with a comfortable situation. A woman pines when underemployed."

Beckett kissed the wine with his lips and tongue. "Jeanette would not be idle much."

Locke hated him now. "Are there more children?"

Beckett stared over the glass from which he had almost sipped. "You ask that!"

Locke switched meanings the way a street swindler does shells. "You have taken your household to me at London when you have been on legal business or when you have put your only son in my charge."

"If any of your brats were running about, don't you think I'd stuff 'em in an envelope and post 'em to you?"

Locke looked into his saucer. "I should do the same with any of your manufacture."

Beckett looked darker than the dark room.

"Here! It is absurd to expect you to finance my wife anymore than my children. I'll just take her off your hands."

"Not so fast. We have a contract. There are two years left on it."

"She is nice to have around." Locke allowed.

Beckett was drinking freely now. "I am used to having her in the house."

Locke dandled his glass not partaking. "You have numerous staff. You said so yourself."

"Jeanette is different." Beckett rectified this. "She has been like a mother to Ho."

"It would be a pity to tear them apart."

"You can see that?"

Locke did not commit to it. "What does your son say?"

Beckett growled in disgust. "Oxford. He thinks and talks of nothing else. It is just like him to be contrary."

"Boys raised without their real mothers...." Locke clacked his tongue, "Headstrong."

Beckett drained his glass in agreement. "An understatement."

Locke found the lawyer to be off his guard. "Moses Bluehill is another."

"No fault of mine. He could have had his mama if the Indian had done right by her." Beckett's eyes shone with panic. "Not that husband and wife must live together at all times and under all circumstances! It is probably better for all concerned that he put her aside. It remains a knotty case."

"Let me see if I understand. You think it would be good for my Jeanette to stay so that she could tend Horace at holidays and so forth to give him a sense of continuity. And you too."

"Oh, exactly!" Beckett preened at how easily this famed negotiator was falling into his hands.

"Continuity is a subject much on my mind now that the matter of America is settled in England's favor. I must stop roaming for Kirke."

"You are retiring?!"

Locke hedged. "Adapting to the new demands of the business." He wrinkled his aquiline nose. "Notwithstanding the fur trade is flat as a pancake, Kirke Company has made me a fortune. Actually, Elizabeth Dowland has been very helpful."

"Has she?"

"Mr. Beckett, if you had some fallow money, there are commodities in which I would advise investment that could triple your stake in three months."

"High risk." Beckett doubted him.

"Not as risky as fur, more lucrative than the law. Being privy to The Company's mind helps one to know when to get out. Kirke is not only alert. He is never wrong."

"The way to be about money." Beckett licked his chops.

"I am amazed you haven't availed yourself of my services before. I'd be glad to broker any purchase."

"Very cordial of you." Beckett did not want Locke's train of thought to break. "But...."

"The money!" Dire took a deep first drink. Wincing at the wine's quality almost imperceptibly but not imperceptibly, he philosophized, "Money! You've got to be willing to take chances."

"You've got to have the money first!" Beckett cooled, then after a pause, confided, "I have thought of having Ho live here and having him ride to his college to save the cost of rooms but he would be a laughing stock and has not wit enough to go as a servitor and earn his way."

"You are being hard on him, I suspect."

"Very. He has a persevering intelligence marred by imagination. He wants me to foot the bill for an endless holiday down at Oxford - that sink! Its buildings are falling apart! There are corrupted children roaming the quadrangles. The examinations aren't worth a piss!"

"Then why does he want to go?" Locke sipped.

Beckett hesitated to say. "He says that Blackstone's there."

"The great man of law. He is." Locke raised his glass in tribute.

"But I am here...."

"Blackstone's got a name."

"So has my son. It's Beckett. Becketts go to Cambridge."

"When they can afford it." Dire dipped into the bubbles.

"Well!" Beckett raised an eyebrow.

Locke caused his other one to rise. "How are you going to come by the cash to send him?"

Untidily, Beckett declared, "That is why I have been thinking of you! I am considering selling off some things."

Locke cleared his throat. "Some of your father's things."

"They are mine now. Have been for years."

"Pity." Locke dared Beckett's eyes. "The whole thing is a damned pity."

"Some fathers do extraordinary things for their children. Of course you have no way of knowing."

"Do you say that because I am childless, or do you insult my father?"

"Please forget that I said it." Beckett swabbed his perspiring face with his handkerchief.

"I certainly will." Locke created Beckett's first real debt to him. "What shall you sell?"

Beckett sighed, "Rugs. I suppose. Big old things. Ought to keep Horace for a few years. But he doesn't want to go to school so why bother."

"He wants to go to Oxford."

"That!"

"What's to prevent you from selling your rugs for the Oxford fees?"

"Never!"

"The boy will fail if he is forced to Cambridge against his will, and then, what's in a name?"

Beckett sulked, then gathered himself to pour. "Ready?"

"Not quite." Locke doubled his meaning. He pushed on, "Moses Bluehill's of an age...."

"That! That's it." Beckett whimpered then snapped, "That ruddy sorcerer is tempting Ho to Oxford. I've been deluged with letters from him and all his fawning relations. He wants Ho at Wadham College of all places!"

"They were fast friends. 'Tis most natural."

Beckett snapped, "Bluehill's a seducer! Like his father. He'll pull out on Ho when the going gets rough. I've told my son all about the noble savage and Elizabeth Dowland."

Locke did not wonder that Beckett condemned his son for imagination, an attribute glaringly lacking in the father. Locke even toyed with the idea of informing him that it was Wakwa who had matched Elizabeth with her second husband and had sustained her new union at enormous cost to himself. But Locke simply reminded the debt-ridden man, "Elizabeth Dowland Kirke."

"Yes." Beckett watched the Welshman's eyes.

"It is a good connection."

"Kirke?"

"All of them. Moses' aunt by blood," Locke turned the knife, "you remember Hanna Worth? She is the wife of an English gentleman. A blood. A rich one. A millionaire. And generous. He would do anything to see his family happy. But why remind you?" Locke pointed his toe, turning himself into an arrow. "You have dealt with him firsthand." He paused ever so slightly. "You have experience of them both."

Beckett's clear brown eyes turned to mud.

"Of course, there is Worth's brother. No more need be said of that. And then there is Moses' mother's strain in him. Her wisdom and feeling have made her the wife of a powerful and unbelievably rich man. Moses could tap forty fortunes by sending an idle note in almost any direction. His own estate is quite princely."

"I won him that estate!"

"Then why throw away the benefit of your legal prowess? Were I in your place, I would let the Indian boy win a round and have his bosom pal with him at the college of his choosing. If I were the father of a son in your son's strategic position, I'd advise him to go to college or to any place that Moses Bluehill were going."

Michael Beckett strangled his glass by its stem.

Locke moved in. "When you please, Mr. Beckett, you fight the legal battles of people of import. Worth was born among them, and Thomas Kirke makes them all loans for one thing and another. Your son, Horace, is no dunce! He's got the world by its balls with such a bon ami as Wolf-of-the-mist He-hopes."

Beckett's brow furrowed and one of his hands covered his lips.

Locke spilled Beckett's fears. "You know what universities are. There would be no stain on your son from consorting with...an Indian...."

"After this war?" Beckett cut him off. "No matter the heroism of Mr. S-for-superfluous Fox, the Sachim has become a non-entity. Who needs him? Not the Americans. Certainly not we English! He stands in the way of progress. At best he belongs in a case of memorabilia! Or dissected in the laboratory to see what makes him so unfailingly popular with the ladies! With all his honeyed diplomatic ways, he has turned into a political and social albatross the like of which the world has never seen. Burn sugar and see what you get, a sticky, useless residue!"

Locke survived this speech, which was not a wholly inaccurate representation of the Indians' current, unfortunate position. Reserving venom, he skirted the complex topic to persuade mildly, "The colleges dote on the exotic. I have recounted you Bluehill's virtues. Mr. Beckett, there may be more than the current politics, school examinations, and architectural integrity to consider. Cambridge. Oxford. What difference? Look at the bright side. The Worths will escort the Sachim's son to England and live at Heathersley with Lord Worth and in London. Think of the society Horace will be engaged with. You will be part of the festivities. Get a rich wife out of it. Ho can have one too!" Locke drank deeply and laughed at the same time and choked endearingly. "I'd do it myself but I've got a wife!"

Beckett pomaded his hair with the dregs of his drink. He had misplaced the idea of Jeanette in his excitement. "That would be something. The half-breed lifting Horace Beckett into the aristocracy! It's such a fantastic notion, I might buy it."

"You can't pay for it!"

"I've got the rugs! Come to see them!"

Dire said delicately, "I could send someone to see them."

Beckett swallowed. "I am sorry."

"Don't worry about it. I confused you when I said I dealt in commodities."

"These rugs are no commodities. They are unique!"

"I verily believe you. All the more reason they should stay in the family. Remember, you have an awfully rich daughter-in-law to impress."

"You're a very funny man."

"Not very." Locke shot back. "Just enough." Locke held out his arid glass. "If you had an inclination to send Horace to

Oxford which appeals to me as the best investment considering the probable return, I should be able to arrange you some sort of loan on very, very easy terms. You shall invest part of the principal and accrue profit. I think you have got a plum of a situation here, Esquire. Opportunity is, as they say, 'knocking.'"

"At interest."

"All investments carry a cost!" Locke punished this parsimony. "What's to be gained after all by always paying out and getting the minimum in return?"

Beckett's eyes would have frightened a less self-confident man than the factor was. But gradually, when Locke did not modify his assessment, Beckett averted his glance. "Locke, you know, this Champagne is damned good!"

"Not bad, Beckett." Locke swallowed. "I'll take a look at those rugs."

"Will you?" Beckett brought Locke out of the study saying gratefully, "Very good of you!"

The central hall was darker than the study, passable even in daytime only by means of candles and oil lamps.

"Quite a place." Locke ventured. "Must be cool in the summer."

"As you must feel with so little meat on you, it is cool in the winter too." On the wings of this complaint, Beckett brought Locke up some stairs. "There's one."

Locke stared at a priceless tapestry six centuries old.

"The other one's outside Ho's room. Shall we?"

Locke hardly looked at the second hanging. "Both could be collateral although they would not bring a lot on the open market. They're just too big to very useful." Locke twitted him.

"I see what you mean."

Locke marvelled at how little Beckett knew of the true value of his possessions. "And they're no good at all if you cut them into smaller pieces."

The ridiculous notion set them both laughing.

"Despite the odd moth-eaten corner or the greenness of some of the backing, Kirke Company could show them as curiosities should the House claim them in a default of your payments. I would suggest you take L12,000."

"That much!"

Locke's nostrils trembled like a hound's at the scent of soft prey; three times that much would have been a steal for the House of Kirke. Then he tore Beckett to pieces. "Borrow all you can at one try. Get a good war chest. Travel. Fix up around here. Invest! Don't settle just to send Horace to school. And if you don't use the whole thing just give it back to us as payments."

Beckett reeled slightly. "It is so sudden."

"We could strike an agreement today. We must for I have to get back to Paris."

"Paris?" Beckett was dumbstruck.

Dire gave up a smile. "You know, the French capital? The treaty?" If Locke had said nothing before that moment, his dropping a hint of his taking part in the peace negotiation was enough to sweep the field.

"You have been at Paris?! I had hoped...may I ask if Lord Worth...too curious of me. Ho! Come out, darling!"

Horace Beckett, just short of his father's height, pale, and with a thatch of parchment-colored hair, opened his door politely.

"Ho! Of course you know Mr. Dire Locke! He has been at *Paris*. The peace negotiations! He is on his way back there now. What do you think of that!"

Ho was lost in a thrill of recognition. His quiet blue eyes fumed with unasked questions. "How good to see you, sir!" Aching to ask if there were a letter from Moses, he did not quite conform his answer to his father's question. "I think Montcalm and Wolfe absolutely Grecian heroes!"

Locke looked into the boy. "You have grown taller. But are unchanged. You still admire the brave."

Beckett panted, "To be at the peace treaty!"

Now Locke trussed him and roasted him. "There is a matter calling me away from Paris for an interval. I see some merit in my sending a solicitor to stand in while I take care of a bit of business in Venice." Locke hesitated, "Although I doubt it possible that you could take direct part at this late stage as the wording is set, you could record and analyze occurrences for The Company."

"Are you serious?"

"Never more so. Although you would have to put up with a few Oxford dons already shedding light."

Horace folded his arms and leaned against the stout doorframe. "No Cambridge men?"

"To be sure." Locke answered. "But one's the same as the other to me. I did not go to college at all. Neither did Thomas Kirke."

Beckett moved to seal the bargain. Extending his hand, he said, "If you need me, I am ready to serve the Crown."

Locke held off. "Your consultation, like mine, is an honor and carries no fee. Kirke Company will pay your travel, put you up, and buy your meals, however."

Beckett blinked back this information but nodded his agreement.

Locke swiveled toward Ho. "Quickly write to the Sachim's son. I have already reserved a room at Wadham for you both."

Beckett's eyes glittered resentment but only momentarily.

Ho went slack.

Beckett urged sharply, "Go on! You heard the man! You are off to Oxfordshire."

Only then did Locke extend his hand to Beckett.

When it was night and the country dead, Michael Beckett went quietly past the rugs, past his son's apartment. He made for the back stair. He did not knock at Jeanette's door but pushed it open familiarly with his knuckles. He surprised two people in the narrow bed.

Locke came up on his elbow. "You are leaving quite early, Mr. Beckett. I trust you are sufficiently packed. Good night."

"Good night!" From Beckett.

Michael Beckett went down. He passed Horace's room, the enormous rugs, entered his den, chose a bottle and a couch. He did not pour a drink. His throat was so sore with unspoken words that he could not swallow. He was not sure why in a few hours the order of his existence had been exactly reversed.

He had made clear-headed decisions: to send Ho where he wanted to study and where his social prospects could, with guidance, improve, to keep the tapestries in the family on generous terms, to accept an invitation to the Peace of Paris, a fine opportunity to grace his biography. These were good things. Why the hollow feeling - the sense that the cup of youth had tumbled from his hands?

That small body in Jeanette's bed. Her look when he, the master, had walked in on her and someone else. He had been cast off like a beggar. He had been ordered about in his own home and had acquiesced like one of his hounds thrown a bone.

Beckett lay sore of muscle, pained of heart, wondering at the slippage of his own power over his life. He nursed wine from the neck of the bottle, taking far-fetched pleasure in fantasies of Hanna in England, of her chasing him up those stairs into Jeanette's empty bed, of the divorce settlement, of adding half of Gilbert Worth's money to his newfound fortune. Entirely possible. He conjured how she had weathered the years.

The lonely man did all he could in solitude to fulfill his urge. The alcohol did not permit him a culmination. He could only hurt as when Ho's mother had given up on him and had died the sloppy death of the pox.

CHAPTER THIRTY-SEVEN

March 1763

Jeanette watched Elizabeth. The Frenchwoman was drawn by Elizabeth's untutored laugh and her grace, but finally ignored them and Elizabeth's liquid wrists, her softness and angles, in a search for the works inside.

Jeanette's curiosity unpeeled the exquisite clothing of the woman from Massachusetts, peered past flesh and bone, as if to see Elizabeth's blood pump. With surgical precision Madame Locke's eyes cut away the skull beneath Elizabeth's tiara of braids to probe the rivulets of her brain.

Jeanette could see nothing amiss. Elizabeth's healthy expense of energy built anything to which she set her mind. She had obviously set her mind to being the wife of Kirke for the marriage had taken the shape of a fortress.

Jeanette shrugged off the unevenness of age between Elizabeth and Thomas Kirke, he now seventy-two and she but thirty-five. Such marriages were not uncommon and were usually successful for the obvious and mutual benefits of money, position, fertility, beauty, not to mention the allurements of mature love.

However, two features of Kirke's wife arrested Jeanette's imagination. They were Elizabeth's face and a region lower. It seemed to Jeanette, who had lived a life both adventurous and quiet, that the woman in the Dowland line had the look of a Madonna, holy from sorrow she had not made. The lower place, the most hidden, the canal which, to Jeanette's knowledge, this woman had always been privileged to control like a toll-taker, teemed with mystery. It was one thing for Jeanette to imagine Kirke's aged flesh traversing it - it was another to realize that one of those killers, those muscled, burnished, enduring, iron-willed male creatures of the savage woods, had run that course right up to Elizabeth's eyes.

Not only did Madame Locke contemplate that terrible congress, but also the primitive seed that had found Elizabeth's womb and blown up into a child. Jeanette recalled Elizabeth's son by the Indian as a mythological creature, a spiritual gargoyle, neither fish nor fowl, his soul twisting and writhing in an agony of desire to know what and who he was.

Locke's wife admired Elizabeth's ability to run Kirke's cabinet and the vast stone house, and was grateful for Elizabeth's kindness and dignity in not plying her for details about her days with the Sachim's son. Jeanette envied Elizabeth's skill with people, particularly with the wide assortment of difficult men gathered in front of the Asolo fire - Kirke, Locke, Claude de St. Aubin and the other one, amply filling out his impeccable satins and silks, *l'homme gros*, called Poore.

Notwithstanding all Elizabeth's sterling traits, Jeanette pitied her for the soul manifest in her trammeled flesh - stood in awe of it and not a little horror.

Dire Locke left that hour with Jeanette and Pere Claude. His purpose was to rescue Claude from the danger of apprehension by Vatican agents in the suppression of the Jesuits. Kirke had elected to escort them through dangerous waters in a sister-ship. Stephen Poore remained behind.

Elizabeth passed her own apartment to look in at Stephen's door. He was engrossed in a manuscript, some rarity not having to do with the Company.

Poore threw his spectacles aside. "Join me?"

"I'd interfere with your reading. Do you need anything?""

Poore thought, smiled, then judiciously replaced his eyeglasses. "You look miserable."

She entered only slightly. "What is it I do wrong? My father barred me from his life. Silent Fox...." The sacred name rose from her like an incense.

"Beth, you don't have to say it."

But she did. "Silent Fox did the same."

Stephen crossed his arms like a Buddha.

"My own son avoids me as if I were a felon or a madwoman...!"

Stephen rolled his eyes. His glance was snared by the beauties of the ceiling.

"Viti is so little here, and now is bent on dying for a whim!"

Stephen offered politely, "For you. Same thing."

Her chin rose in resentment.

"Why not take a swim and dine with me when I've had enough of Dario?"

"Only Annanias...." she spoke his name with a fascinated loathing.

"Oh, please! Is it Champagne supper or no?"

A convoluted gust from the Adriatic sucked the room's great door closed.

"The worst man I have ever known of, or known...wanted me above all else, and ultimately wanted me without condition. What does all this say about me? I do not think I have a grasp, anymore, who I am."

"Did you ever?" His eyes were as far-seeing as a cat's. "Shocked? You have a place in life. We both do. As tools, I think. You and I are occasionally, even often, useful to the daily patterns of some admirable individuals. Male ones. Women have no use for us at all."

Elizabeth raised her chin. "Not true!" Qunneke crossed her mind. Instead, she spoke of Stephen. "Your mother worships you, and I...."

"Et tu, Beth?"

"You never spoke for me. It was not to be!"

"Not? So sure? I reasoned Fate must have stayed my tongue. My father was as least as great a deterrent as Destiny. I was as confused then as you are now. I certainly found out who I was in the dregs of my despair over your marriage contract with The Reverend Scare-the-Pants-off-'Em Hudson. To be passed over for the likes of him!"

"Steph!"

"I blame you not! I state the fact. It took a year in Paris for me to decipher my true animal nature. Only your impetuous breach of contract and your cleaving to a red Indian made my soul to breathe once more."

"At least one of us is glad!"

"You complain of men, of boys. Yet, you do nothing to move toward those you love."

She might have been stone.

Stephen made his magisterial rise and took her cold hands. "I have thought of suicide. Have you?"

She swayed and came to lean against him. "I decided long ago I did not deserve to stop the pain."

Stephen laughed his falsetto laugh. "Calvinist roots die hard!"

She laughed in pleasure at what bound them.

"I'm sorry if I hurt you. But the strain in your face! I had to speak."

"Speaking done?"

"You are a rare woman." Stephen stated.

"A singular man!" She returned.

"You will flood Old Tom's heart with your tears till he drowns to death on them. You will ignore your son's existence till his blood freezes. The land-tie is stronger in you than any other!" Without mercy, Poore whispered in her ear, "You invaded the Indian's territory, you ate him whole, you swallowed his wife, his family, his future in your insatiable Anglo Saxon need for territory. Your passion for the Indian will never die because you recognize the land is himself! Want to know what you are? You are English!"

Poore moved through the twisted alleys, his great size and dark clothes increasing his invisibility, the flame in his lamp notwithstanding. Raucous parties had only begun to infest the night with Carnivale fever. There was no welcome light in the studio window and none in Dario's apartment above. For a moment Poore felt resentment that Dario might have slipped out to celebrate without him.

Stephen stole toward the house like a gargantuan cat. A small gold mask, new to him, was tacked to the doorframe. He became conscious of a ticking sound. His pace quickened over the small bridge leading to the maskmaker's shop. The ticking was a dripping.

Stephen drew close to the small mask, a replica of the living gift Kirke had brought to Elizabeth from China. Pug nose, glittering fur, eyes very wise. He touched it and recoiled. No work of ash wood or papier mâche and gesso, the little yellow mask was the severed head of Elizabeth's monkey. Dario must have gone mad over his work, with chemicals, with the pressure The Company put on him.

What Stephen saw of Dario after he stepped through the doorway sent him back to Elizabeth fundamentally changed. He stumbled back to the Asolo, confronted now by revelers who took his wavering walk as the sign of an early start on the wine. They saluted him.

Elizabeth's large bathing chamber, centuries old, built with ancient Roman skill, featured a tile floor warm to the soles of the feet, a sunken pool, far superior to any tub, a hypocaust to heat the bathwater, ocher walls, flaming sconces, white marble benches. The water was mineral water from Sicily. Windows cut into the ceiling admitted the moon but also the sun to foster flowers and their fragrance. In such luxury she shed her shrunken soul and breathed free of her biography. Kirke called her Cleopatra. Elizabeth ignored the reference. Her spa brought her gently back to the Massachuseuck sweat hut. It was in her Venetian chamber she always repaired to think of nothing, to push from her auditory canal harsh words, from her mind wild notions, from her heart crushing events, from her eyes the faces in the theatre of her experience.

Blissfully alone without the attentions of any lady's maid, floating in amniotic grace, Elizabeth lost herself in meditation. She considered the sea roiling in its cavernous bosom, sighing into its own spray, echoing the scrape of trains of mist, giant garments of light.

The great wooden door opened letting in cold. Stephen Poore invaded. "Can you find it in your boundless heart to forgive me?"

"Stephen!" Her arms closed over her nudity.

"Beth! Nothing but harsh quarter-truths in what I said. Come. Come out of the water!" He held her robe high to baffle sight of her nakedness.

She abandoned modesty, climbed the six stairs, and was instantly wrapped in Turkish. She became aware of the color red.

He pushed her arms into the sleeves of her robe. "You denied yourself all vanity; you embraced Tame Deer; you paid for every grace of your native life with a sacrifice of your English ways. You bravely bore a child. A son! You endured his loss. You endured hell! You ENDURE! That is British in you too! I am the glutton." Stephen hurried on. "I have been insatiable since the day my silence lost you. I need your help tonight. I don't know what to do! Some...compassion. Some further compassion. Get dressed! Dario is murdered! All his beauty is cut and scattered. The gold is gone! The walls are written over in blood, *KIRKE BEWARE*!"

With reverence and repugnance and in terror of the assassin's return they collected Dario's mutilated parts into a crate that once held clay for the gesso. They laid the little monkey in with the maskmaker. They wheeled the remains to the Molo for instant loading on *Butterfly* and private burial at sea.

They scrubbed the curse from the walls. Elizabeth whitewashed the stains ingrained there and underfoot. Through the night marred by the wild sounds before Lent, they reordered Dario's beautiful tools and rehung the masks and other objects he had carved. They leaned Dario's sign against the polished front window - the sign he used whether he had stepped out for a glass of wine or had left for China: *I am not gone for long.*

There would be no complaint from the House of Kirke, no recognition of the atrocity. No arrests, no bribes, no punishments or flight. In Venice after all, the air was made of mirrors and men were formed of smoke. Only music and love were real.

CHAPTER THIRTY-EIGHT

Spring and Summer 1763

It should have been a sweet spring. Massachusetts farmers, like the city-dwellers, existed in a delirium brought on by the eclipse of the French. The war's end and the treaty sealing its outcome freed the people to dreams pent for nearly a decade. In the Dowland neighborhood, that meant building. The earth was penetrated by spades and posts, and it brought forth spanking new structures.

The Massachuseuck under Wakwa Manunnappu caught the building fever. In Wakwa's view, transforming native life into something readily recognizable by the English, static homesteads showing possession, would be better for the survival of his tribe than guns or treaties or roundhouses that could be dismantled of an afternoon so the tribe could follow the game. The revolution in their living habits was tempered by the shape of the dwellings - they were like Iroquois long-houses but small ones. Dr. Stirling enjoyed calling them *short-houses*.

Gilbert Worth's expectations soared. "By God! What a season! The Paris Peace, the planting, groundbreakings galore, Dolly Low soundly pregnant at the mere thought of having a house where Hudson never slept, and Moses and young Beckett bound for university!"

It was a sweet season if one accepted that human life was thick with complications, mischance, and endings. J. Macmillan Sterling was weakening, Qunneke was secretly and constantly bleeding and lived not in the newly constructed town but at the Meetinghouse Hospital, and Carpenter Spinney had turned up in Sweetwood.

Worth's house was full. That was the way he loved it. He hoped the hum of voices would float upstairs and give strength to Mac. At nightfall, Qunneke descended sadly from the sickroom. Soon after, Lightfoot carried a message down. Mac was calling them for farewells.

The old Scot sat feebly against the headboard. "I'm cold," he announced.

Wakwa lifted the burden of the bedclothes and viewed Mac's purpled feet. He gripped each one in each of his warm hands. "Does that help?"

"Maybe if you held my feet...."

Wakwa despaired.

"Now look!" Mac trembled. "My shins are cold. Is Gil short firewood! What's become of us?"

One-by-one, the assembled family and friends took their leave of the old Scot. By the time it was dark, Indians grouped on the lawns surrounding the house. Pequawus, over eighty, paid his respects. Even the taupowaw made his way up the stairs. Hanna abandoned herself against the sickroom chair like a shawl of pink stuff and stayed the night.

At dawn, shattering glass woke the household. A refuse of cotton and cruets was scattered on the floor. The Scot's stone-blue hand dangled off the mattress.

Hanna turned to the men crowding the doorway. "Father Claude performed a rite just at the end. Mac was peeved about it."

Stricken though Sweetwood Village was over the loss of such a useful and colorful man as the Scottish doctor had been, community life went on. Buildings were erected, crops matured, wedding bells rang, sermons were declaimed, the newssheet printed, and the post was delivered and collected. This civil service was rendered at Sweetwood's tavern.

Coney passed the town's new burial ground on his way to retrieve the mail for Worth Farm. The cemetery on the scorched soil where Hudson's manse had once stood provided the resting place for the area's numerous war-dead and its leading citizens. Sterling's grave was the freshest. The entire landscape benefitted from his interment by virtue of the addition of vital topsoil over the depleted whole and cuttings of Chinese roses set to grow at strategic intervals. Coney bowed his head as he passed the gravesite where his mentor, his savior, Dr. Sterling, was buried. Coney would rather have spent a moonless night in the graveyard among the shades than perform his simple errand at the tavern.

It happened that this hour of the afternoon was Sam Spinney's customary time to take his ease and to check if anyone had signed his work petition. The crude advertisement was blank of prospective employers' names as usual. He tore it off the wooden wall. In the post-war days of buildings going up the way dandelions grew, he had not contracted a single job in Sweetwood. He existed on his meager veterans allotment. The paper ripped, the tack popped out of its hole and, jingling along the floorboards, landed point up and ready to embed itself in the sole of someone's shoe. Spinney crushed the notice into a ball and threw it into a corner. He picked a table at room-center. Other men moved their seats, unwilling to share his company.

The Town's Eye, Cooper, had that eye on Spinney. He noted Sam's frustration but did nothing to stay the barkeep from bringing the war veteran his whiskey. Will Cooper remarked, "You're litt'r'n, Sam. Against the ord'nance."

"Litt'r'n! What of the conspiracy that I should have no work!" Sam lashed out at the tither. He pushed back in his chair, jolting the table. His whiskey heaved out of its glass like a wave at sea. The out-of-pocket carpenter cursed and did not scruple to lick the alcohol off the heel of his hand. "I opened the road through Virginia! I shot savages right and left!"

"Kill any?" A farmer jibed as he sorted through the post Cooper had spread on the sideboard near the door.

"I got no family! I come here where I give service - good service to rich people."

"'Twas a long time ago, Sam. Got to admit that." The barkeep dried a leather tankard with a square of cloth.

"No Christian hand reaches out to me!"

Cooper checked his watch. It was five in the afternoon. He snapped the case shut.

"Witchcraft it is that I can't recover from breathin' the same air as Hudson the night he was done away with."

Cooper cleared his throat. "No more talk like that, Carpenter Spinney."

"You! Who'r you to tell me what to do?" Spinney pointed an accusatory finger at the tither. "Gold watches! Velvet suits! In the pay of Bluebloods!"

The Town's Eye levelled a look on the failed craftsman. "The watch is brass, the coat's twenty year old. For my office, the villagers cast their votes one equal t'other and their pennies too for my pay. And you are drunk, m'boy, and off to jail!"

Spinney cursed the law.

The farmers, the weaver, the chandler, the smith, all suddenly developed a keen interest in their fingernails. Spinney was too pitiful a sight to watch, almost too pitiful to jail. It was little wonder Sweetwood passed him over for work. Spinney had the stink of bad luck about him. Like the ground Hudson's house had stood on, nothing prospered with Sam. After failing in his furniture manufactory and loading himself with debt to his investor, Gilbert Worth, of course, and being thrown over by Priscilla Marley, Sam had sidetracked himself among wild Virginians doing the dirty work of war. Could such a man build a firm road through virgin territory for the King's ten thousand soldiers to march safely down? Could a man like Sam kill an Indian? Better, kill the *right* Indian?

Cooper came to his feet. A small length of rusty chain dangled from his red plush pocket. He approached Spinney from his right side. Spinney shifted chairs, putting his back to the purposeful tither. Will Cooper stepped quietly around to face him.

The barkeep slammed a tumbler of cold water down in front of Sam. He saw Spinney tremble slightly as if galled by the approaching twilight, which hinted of dry leaves and snapping air and ruddy apples and himself - alone. The barkeep wiped away the spill he had made on Spinney's table.

At this juncture, the clatter of a fast horse was heard and after a brief pause, the tavern door swung open. The townsmen sent up a prayer, considering Sam's mood, that the person entering would not be hot-tempered Gilbert Worth. As if in answer, Lightfoot came in.

Taller at fourteen than any man in the room, his back and legs and chest developed like a Hercules, Lightfoot was tolerated, even liked, in Sweetwood. For years, that back and chest, those legs and his mighty right arm, had supported, cradled, lifted, and carried broken men, women large with babies, and tiny babes themselves, away from danger and sickbeds to Meetinghouse Hospital for care. But never before this afternoon had he crossed the threshold of the public house alone. It was always Mr. Gilbert Worth with him or the freedman, Matthew, on village rounds. Breathing easier, the villagers went back to their talk and their beer and disregarded the local Sachim's son.

Cooper hailed Lightfoot with his nickname. "Coney!"

Lightfoot gave a shy salute and approached the tither who remained at the center of the room, opposite the sandy-haired man doubled over his tabletop. In his whisper of a voice, he explained, "Mr. Cooper! I am come for Worth Farm's post."

"That's condescending of you! Most condescending." Cooper, ever the politician, made reference to the regal habit of the boy's father in keeping himself and his tribe well enough to avoid menial work. Albeit, some Massachuseuck men had been tapped as builders lately, and one of their higher-born fellows, Tamoccon, Awepu's son, had started a concern in Wareham, fishing, deep-sea fishing, but these were skilled endeavors, things that a soul like poor Sam could never manage. Moreover, the mongering was left to the Mashpee. The fisher and builders were backed by the coin of the realm, not wampum, and registered in the tax rolls. As long as they did not violate the Sweetwood schoolhouse with their ruddy youngsters, it was quite tolerable to Sweetwood to have a sachim on the outskirts with old-fashioned airs and fashionable abilities. "I'll sort it for ye."

A rabbity smile tickled Coney's lips. He had his mother's face, placid, oval, even, creamy smooth, his eyes clearer and blacker than licorice. "I would not trouble you, sir." He moved toward the mail table. He spoke like his father. "I can sort."

"Can you now?" Spinney spat whiskey.

Cooper barked, "Sam Spinney, mind ye business!"

Coney knew the name. From his youngest days he remembered the name the way he remembered being kicked by Winke's horse. He had never seen Spinney. He turned abruptly toward him.

Spinney, fuelled by whiskey, rattled on. "I've seen these savages peel the skin off an Englishman's skull! I've seen 'em settle down to a stewpot full of meat carved off whitemen's bones. And this one 'sorts!'" Spinney mimed a spectacled Coney daintily culling Worth's post from the rest.

"Sam." Cooper stopped him. "I read too! The Ordinance of this village. You are incitin' to riot!"

"If you say pointin' out others' airs is incitin' to riot then I'm guilty! Take me away!" Spinney held his wrists together as if bound with chains and sneered in the tither's face. He turned to the other patrons of the tavern. "I made with my own hands half a dozen trenchers for Priscilla Marley's table service. That oughta hold the food of twelve! The way a man and wife oughta eat, both out of one trencher. But! While I was away sweating over my furniture manufactory in Boston, Priscilla ups and turns into *Miss* Marley. Told me on my visit home she wanted our children, should we have any, to eat sitting at table! And each with a plate of his own! Sitting! Not standing behind, as children properly ought!" Spinney's sallow face darkened with a rising of his bile. "Under the influence of the rich, under the spell of old Dowland's daughter. Talk of airs! Mistress Elizabeth thought she was an Indian princess did she! Did anything she wanted and wherever she went was a corner cabinet chock full of porcelain dishes all matching and each person at table eating out of his and her own plates, using those Eyetalian inventions, those claw-like unnecessaries, and not of good pewter but of silver, those forks!"

It did not seem that Coney's eyes found Spinney, sitting alone, with his faded yellow hair and stubble. The barkeep would have sworn in a court of law that the Indian kid had looked for Spinney too high, too far back in the room. Of course, Coney's dead arm made a distraction for his observers. It flapped back and forth with the boy's sharp movement.

"I know for a fact, no matter how rich she gets, Elizabeth Dowland lived among the savages. I bet she e't off of trade China in the smoke huts too!"

Cooper was visibly uncomfortable with the route Spinney's tirade was taking. "Quiet about your betters, Sam! None of that's your business!"

Spinney stood. Not a deliberate, drunken rise, he shot to his feet fast and steadied himself with his fists on the tabletop. "It's my business all right!" Sam spat on the floor. "An' it's yours! Who ruined me but Mistress Elizabeth Dowland? If she hadn't of run away, poor Dowland would be alive now and a grandpa! And I'd be workin' for him, not done out of work by redskins! Who are these diviners that they can 'sort'? What right have they?"

"Shut up, Sam!" Cooper slipped a length of chain from his pocket. "I'm goin' to give you plenty of time to learn to read yourself!" He tossed the chain around Spinney's wrists as if they were the necks of dogs.

Sam Spinney stood erect, his chin high, his boyish face gone old. "Winke was the only one spoke truth in this town! Old

Dowland clammed up 'bout the savages, Worth's like a pig in mud with 'em, an' I saw it with m'own eyes, Mr. Hudson himself consortin' over lemonade with that gimp-legged one who worked at the smithy and that nasty, varmint of a sachim's son...King Something...."

Cooper took a step back and jerked his thumb. "One more word out o' you and...."

Samuel Spinney sank into his seat, unequal to the task of standing, his memory unimpaired by idleness or alcohol. "And when old Dowland's girl got tired of them red divils and came into the manse to wed, why she weren't the same as before they did their evil to her!"

"Spinney!" Cooper grabbed for the iron chain.

The gist of Spinney's crude observation was lost under the sounds of swatting. The public house reverberated as it did in summer when the June bugs blindly butted the windowpanes.

It seemed to the townsmen resting from the demands of their day's labors, that Coney kept looking for Spinney without success. It was odd because Spinney was hamstrung so-to-speak, his wrists linked together by the tithing man's chain, and the tither hard by him reading him the letter of the law about disturbing the peace and spitting on the floor.

All they knew and could report at home later around their separate supper tables was poor Coney, turning from Cooper and turning back to him, his withered left arm, stiff of bone, swinging at right angles to his body like a club. It might have been that his accident at Hudson's years before had dimmed his eyes, because Coney kept looking for Spinney. Looking without luck. Coney kept turning away from Cooper and back. In the turning and turning back, Coney's lifeless hand, heavy as a boiled brisket, struck

Spinney's unshaven cheek, struck Spinney's nose, caught his jaw, clipped his yapping mouth. With Cooper holding the carpenter fast, shouting him down for his flagrant offenses against the picayune code of the village, Coney's uncontrollable hand split Spinney's lip and turned his jaw blue.

CHAPTER THIRTY-NINE

September 1763

Qunneke had never asserted herself against her husband's will - or so it seemed when one looked over the full terrain of her long marriage. Wooed by the tribe's most eligible man, a man younger than she and raised as her brother, she made no objection, did not demur in favor of more avid women. She accepted the outcome of Wakwa's steady suit and everything that followed.

Not every Massachuseuck woman would have sustained her husband's passion for the daughter of the Dowlands, or lived under one roof with another wife, or defended the English girl against a woman of Indian blood, or suckled the half-breed son when the second wife was gone forever. Qunneke did. Not every woman would have cried over her husband's loss of his second wife. Qunneke cried.

The possible exception to Tame Deer's perfect compliance as wife and saunks was her shyness of the fleshly side of things. But, even here, she gathered courage from Gilbert Worth and came around, lay with her husband, and, late in the scheme of things, had borne to Wakwa a full-blooded Massachuseuck son. Her story was without blemish: at least, without blame. Yet, just when Manunnappu needed her cooperation most, Qunneke rejected his cause. She would not live in his new house.

Wakwa's forward-thinking plan for the longevity of the People was to tether his tribe to its hunting and planting ground by Taquonk of 1763, the feast of fall-of-the-leaf. Wakwa painted pictures with words of household fires roaring up stone chimneys, of solid roofs, of no water coming in. He engendered true excitement for his Twisting River Town and the new work the men would engage in to keep it looking fine.

Days after Moses, bound for Oxford, floated away with Locke and the Worths, Wakwa set a torch to his emptied sachimmaacommock, the last old-style house to go. He seemed particularly sensitive to the smoke from that fire which stung his eyes so badly the tears ran out of them. His folk, watching, were sure of it for he turned his back on the blazing domes before the fire had eaten very much.

Wakwa and Qunneke saw each family to its new door and promised a big feast the next day, out on the plain with gambling and dancing - no speeches - only joy.

The Sachim was the last to enter his sachimmaacommock-with-corners. Larger than the other houses, even larger than Awepu's house which had to hold so many children, it stood on the planted eastern ridge where Elizabeth had run to escape her own and been stunned by her first sight of Twisting River. Wakwa's critics quipped that the narrow bluff was the perfect place for the house of a line-walking sachim.

Qunneke had planted its garden, and orange and yellow and red flared in the last warm sun. In the center of the pumpkins and the squash and tomatoes were tufts of silver-gray and ruby berries and as many of the plants for compounding medicine as would grow under cultivation. The corn was still hoed in common fields. And the tobacco. The cranberry bogs were the doing of the gods.

No one actually saw it happen. Qunneke crossed the bridge with the Sachim, followed him to his door. But she did not go in. She strayed among the herbs, then she sifted like mist among the trees. The people of the new otan shrugged - perhaps she was praying or looking for her medicinal plants. Some knew she had, despite her age, begun to bleed again.

As London rose above the sails, Moses removed the mouthpiece of his flute to blow it clean of his saliva. Cool white arms surrounded him. A white breast burned his cheek as if he had fallen into snow. He had forgotten the city's fog.

The anchor parted the water. Moses was thrown out of the window seat as *Merriweather* bucked her tether. He cursed and crawled after the gold pipe. A knock at the door sent him flying to his mirror to neaten his hair.

The knock, again.

"Here I am!" Moses threw a towel over one shoulder to give the impression he was further along with his toilette than was the actuality.

Expecting Gilbert Worth, Moses answered the summons in only his stocking feet. He gasped, "God!"

"'Tis I." Dire Locke remarked. He was dressed for disembarkation in his typical style spreading a self-made dusk. Yet, he created a fine impression. His impeccable silk-worsted suit, perfect for the end of the English summer, was of puce color. His waistcoat of a sheenless cloth of chilly blue duplicated the hue of his intelligent eyes.

"Good morning!" Moses whispered.

Locke tested. "Good morning, Mr. Bluehill. Champagne's in your uncle's stateroom in twenty minutes." Then, answering Moses' questioning look, "True, I don't usually carry messages 'twixt the suites but I wanted a moment with you."

Moses waited for more.

Locke cleared his throat, seemed to hover, then dove. "Do you require anything?"

"No!" Moses blurted. Then blurted again, embarrassed, "Sir!"

"Are you sure?"

Moses skittered across the icy pond of Locke's possible meanings then, even more mortified than before, asked very late, "Won't you step in?"

"Into your room or your affairs? I usually do each on invitation. This morning I must decline the first part for the second." Attempting kindness, Locke enquired, "You have been passably comfortable, I hope?"

Moses darkened with shame. "I should have asked you in before. I should have thanked you. It was wondrous."

"So I heard, standing at the door." Locke jibed.

"My language! I had dropped something." He pulled the rescued flute from his waistband and turned to the luxe salon behind him, to the long mirror with its carved frame, the Persian rug, the wardrobe, the brazier, the book closet, the rosewood desk screwed to the floor, the chunky box of quills and inks, the Florentine letter-paper and choice of seals. "My quarters have been more than comfortable, Mr. Locke. I am sorry to have to leave them." Moses stammered, "My only wish is that I could have shared them with my brother and sister. Its pleasures are difficult to describe in mere letters."

"Ah! Like your father you are a diplomat. But you flatter me too much. The trifles and gawd of a drawing room sliding this way and that in a boat reeling through the north Atlantic cannot have made you *really* comfortable. And I did offer your cousin, Tamoccon, a place in the chartroom for a start, since he has always wanted a career at sea but..." Locke shook his head, "the time was not convenient as he is engaged in courting your beautiful sister."

Moses worked to appear impassive. "Some tea...a supper...I should have...but time...."

"Got the best of you." Locke waved the omission away. "Time will do that. It is good you found out in privacy. Consider it a reminder you are here to do your family proud. I am here to help you accomplish that." Locke paused. "The Worths are your *social* lifeline. *I* constitute your line of credit. And with your welcoming committee, Lord Worth and the Becketts, lined up at the dock, you will be, in very short order, too busy for instruction of a business nature."

"Please, Mr. Locke, come in!"

Locke observed the face of his ticking watch. "Another time. Another crossing." He smiled briefly. "I'll merely remind you that the House of Kirke is at your disposal while you are at school. Your credit is guaranteed by Kirke Company."

Moses' thirty-carat eyes dulled with the implication that Kirke or Elizabeth would use money to infuse themselves into his doings.

Locke, apparently blind to the change, cautioned, "Watch for overextension while wanting nothing essential to your well being."

Moses looked to his stockinged toes. "I shall be perfectly happy with a cell like a monk's and my friend, Horace."

"Frankly, I cannot imagine a young man of your parts delightedly cooped up away from the delirium of sport, the fragrance of your silent woods, the exquisite implements of your father's house, not to mention the nearby pleasures at the Worths. Let alone the company of women."

Moses protested.

Locke interrupted. "There too, I warn caution. You doubtless feel the weight of your invisible crown. Never, never, put it down!"

Perturbed by this notion, Moses squared his shoulders. "Is this dictum from the Kirkes or my Aunt and Uncle Worth?"

"It is from your father's wife. The Saunks. Qunneke." Locke passed him a skin sack containing a bottle. "From her. Against the French disease. Better would be to avoid the occasion of contracting it."

The metal of Moses' eyes went hot.

Locke did not try to calm him. "I had hoped we could discuss the matter in some fullness but now there is no time." Locke referred to his watch. Yet, he paused to achieve his next phrase. "You must never lack for your physical security while here in Europe."

Moses' face tightened at this final undermining of his excitement over a lifelong dream turning real.

Locke bowed. "With all deference, may you benefit from the parental affection on *both* sides betokened by your formal education." Locke turned and left.

Moses was rendered speechless at Locke's innuendo about a mother he did not remember, that girl in the Dowland line who had given him life and, to his mind, had blown away like the fuzz from a fairy clock. "Dire!"

Locke wheeled on him.

But Moses could only force out, "Thank you, again!"

"You know, I speak your paternal tongue. You should use it when you are with me - to keep in form. You are going to be away from its melody for a long season."

Moses stood stricken at Locke's rank shredding of his confidence into homesickness.

Locke jolted him another way. "Are you wearing a wig as you get off?"

"I...of course! Do you think it best?"

Locke returned to him to say confidentially, "While the ironies of fashion dictate flowing Indianesque locks for today's propertied young men, I think *your* abundant natural hair, however well-cut and groomed, will do you least harm if, at first, you cover it over, or wear it tied behind."

Moses finished his packing. Carelessness, untidiness, imprecision in his woodland life were antithetical to survival. For this reason, his stateroom was in perfect order. His task was easier for it.

He emptied the wardrobe. With reverence he placed his father's books, gifts to him, in his trunk. He tightened his inkwells to preserve the expensive and precious letter paper from spills in the carrying box. He smartly folded his breeches of the day before and laid them in place as with a mathematician's square. He turned to his four pair of shoes and his four pair of boots. He deemed the shoes useless footgear for disembarkation. He stuffed each into its grosgrain bag and tucked each bag into a corner. His boots came under scrutiny.

The first pair was of Massachuseuck make - soft, resilient doeskin. Finished to a dove color, they were high-cut, climbing past the knee where they melted into tassels as fine as corn silk. This was the fringe that gave a man nerves outside his body, feelers for the changing breeze, for the approach of beast or man or, as could happen, of a woman. The feet of the chamois-soft boots were figured with pastel slivers, porcupine quills sewn into delicate leaf forms. A little money out of black shells had been added to the heels to jingle like the spurs of white horsemen. Ornamental, indestructible, Moses eliminated the skin boots, not for their incongruity with his European garb which he thought suited him, but for their pliant soles. He folded them away.

Moses instantly rejected his riding boots as an absurd choice when he would be driven the few miles to Mayfair in a coach. He postponed the decision between the cavaliers his Aunt Hanna had given him for his birthday, which had occurred aboard ship, and another pair, plain black ones.

He slipped on a shirt of white linen; his breeches were tan. He buttoned on a waistcoat of brocaded cloth dyed to the hue of the sun at fall-of-leaf. He watched himself put on the tan coat completing his suit. He stood wiggling his black-stockinged toes.

The boots were reflected behind him. He ignored them and hurried his hair into a net. Out of disrespect for the custom, he stuck a gray wig on imperfectly. He liked wigs a little askew and he liked how the gray aged him to about twenty-four, the perfect period, old enough for the perquisites of manhood, too young for a quarter century. He tied a gold ribbon around the short, curled queue.

The wall hooks were empty. His sword leaned crazily against a corner. He shoved a pistol in his belt, one of a pair, a birthday gift from Gilbert Worth, whom he worshipped.

He felt a tug toward Hanna's cavaliers, high-heeled, loose at the ankle, slouching under the knee into deep cuffs. They were fawn-colored and sported clusters of garnets suggestive of roses.

Yet, the fourth pair, black, close-fitting at the calves like his riding boots, were uncuffed, squat-heeled, unembellished except for straps loosely intertwined wreathing the ankles. They did not dance by themselves like the cavaliers but they made kind walking companions on cobblestones. Moses felt the snaking straps lined in butterscotch leather circling the heel and the top of the foot. He thought of his father's prized shirt made by Elizabeth's hands, lined for comfort inside the neckband where no one could see. He drew on the least showy of his footwear with no more hesitation. Moses never saw the final effect of his costume of honey, ingot, jet, and snow. Slamming his trunks closed and securing the clasps, he grabbed a white felt hat and stepped smartly out of his stateroom. He presented himself to the Worths five minutes early.

CHAPTER FORTY

Autumn 1763

Moses Bluehill looked like he was Michael Beckett's son. Clarity of feature, loftiness of height, the tall man's curse of grace offset by an awkward slowness in crowds, and most important, a sad cynicism born of long-buried loss made them relatives under the skin and father and son to the quick passerby.

Horace Beckett, pastel of coloration, animated by an irreverent sense of humor, tendons apparently smelted of an advanced metal alloy providing his entire body with spring, was Gilbert Worth's taller reincarnation if not his real child.

But Moses was no kin of Beckett's and no blood relation of Worth's. He knew well whose son he was. He knew his sire as a man of sadness with no self-pity. A man with an endurance not touched by emotions. He was rock, a heart of granite on which a man, a house, a city could stand which would not give way. And, torn open, this rock would be riddled with veins of gold and blood, not running but rich and staid like marrow. Moses could see his father as a fellow of the college, a sage with a following. He was a man damned by race whose smile was important because of his lack of optimism. He neither cried nor caused others' tears cheaply. He was immersed in his work. The father Moses knew had a dove's eyes from love.

In the stony grandeur of the university, Moses Bluehill paled at the step and the sound of men who had no idea where he was from or from what manner of seed he had sprung. Moses saw the world he had chosen as artificial and its population as brittle and as hollow as China cups. The presupposing English made him hunger for another sort of personality. In short, Moses was immediately sick for home for home was Wakwa. All other people were ghosts of his past or of his dreams.

Moses nearly wretched when Beckett and Worth departed the college and strode across the quadrangle to their waiting coach. He did not know what to say to the young Englishman, Mr. Horace Beckett, with whom he pretended absolute familiarity. Moses wanted the company only of his magnificent father.

He tried to strike a conversational spark. "Our apartment reminds me of my father's house."

"I heartily disagree." Ho's terse reply.

Their dormitory chamber possessed a central room of square shape, thirty feet by thirty feet and twenty high. A wall of windows opened west. Two far less significant rooms, closets for sleeping were attached to the main salon, one south and one north. Locke thought this floorplan contributory to civility and study. Michael Beckett hoped it would put some distance between his son and the Indian.

Ho enlarged on his opinion. "Your father's house is as warm and red inside as the proverbial womb. Never this dripping, moldering place or my father's feudal pile."

Moses drew a rug around his shoulders. He considered Ho's opinion. "How is your money supply, Beck?"

"Why should I answer you that, *Hill*?"

"Tell me!"

"I've got L15 until April."

"That is *not* enough! You'd barely squeak by with sixty! Ever done your own washing? There's the kitchen, the buttery, the weekly food bill, the boating club, for what that's worth, the union, you've got to have that, and..." Moses threw his hands up in despair, "you'll never afford the wine club. How to pay the tailor, or the bookseller, what of the cobbler, the chemist...I'm not even talking about ever getting off the campus!"

Distinctly insulted, Ho shot back, "I suppose your purse is bottomless with such an uncle as Gilbert Worth!"

Moses grinned briefly at Ho's passion. He announced, "I have refused any money from him."

Ho's jaw dropped.

"My father has paid for my tuition, and for entering me on the college list. My uncle has provided me my clothes. Your father was generous with a horse for each of us...."

"How much have you got?" Ho demanded.

Moses threw a tiny sack of coins to Ho and watched him count.

"This is less than mine! Do you want money from me? I'll share whatever I have, but it's all pathetic!"

Moses threw the blanket aside and left the dubious comfort of the settee to measure the room by striding in his boots. "I have only to ask for funds at a certain London address. Each request shall be written on a ledger. The money in any amount shall be mine. The debt will be made good at the tribe's convenience."

Ho Beckett said in awe, "You have unlimited credit?"

"I do."

Ho was immobilized.

"I do if I want to sink my father into a nightmare of debt. Which I do not."

Ho jumped off his chair, a thing of tortuous carving. "What are we going to do? We're prisoners here! We can't even feed our horses much less go to town! What if we run out of claret?!"

Moses, laughing, cast his wig aside and poked his head into the cold mouth of the fireplace. "Do you think Wadham would clean this flue, Ho?"

"No. I do not, *Mo*." Ho was right behind him, his arms, crossed, his feet planted wide. "There are too many servitors to full-paying students. The college hasn't the money. You are thinking what?"

Moses extricated himself from the chimney. He brushed away soot and spider webs. "Do you think there are any scholars worse off than we? Any whom we could pay to clean and mend this room? All our rooms?"

"There must be one." Ho laughed at their empty pockets. "How shall we pay him? Have *him* extend us credit?"

Moses leapt straight up and let out a whoop. "Inspired!" He took his childhood friend around his shoulders and made much of him. "Beckett!"

Ho asked a second time, "You are thinking what?"

"I am thinking…aloud. What of making this cavern into something beautiful? I am thinking..." Moses' ideas seemed to knit with his restless pacing, "thinking...of charging these empty-headed aristocrats for the privilege of admiring our living quarters. I have a thought...suppose we set up gambling tables and take a percentage of the house? We could hire a man to manage, so we could wear our eyes out in the library while the fools pay our way, buy our wigs for us, and our drink and our snuff and our...good times!"

"That's a bit grandiose."

Moses defended, "Some underfunded man studying architecture could make this his laboratory! He could figure how to divert the leaks, warm the place up. Take his degree on the merits of his work instead of putting his don to sleep with term papers!"

"And the frescoes?"

Moses stood stock-still. "You are some kind of genius. I do not know yet what kind but you cannot open your mouth without some wonderful notion flying out!"

Unaccustomed to flattery, Ho turned red. "This renovation will take a detailed plan and an immediate outlay even if the actual labor is performed on speculation." Ho tossed his clothes out of his trunk to reach his supply of paper beneath.

Moses rubbed his hands together. "We could give our architect part of our share of the take, or...a high percentage of a tax on each table...."

"Tax?" Ho was spreading his chart, sharpening his pencil.

"An admittance tax. Dues." Moses shone with his fully blown idea. "To run a business at school would be against the laws of the university. The warden would have us expelled. But if we run the gaming as a club...." His tongue ran the clean edges of his white teeth.

"Elitist." Ho accused.

"Private! Justifying the admission fee." Moses would not be swerved. "Run by the same principles as Parliament. Buy one's way in or earn a place through merit or birth. No snobbery here. Poor men can get a turn at a table by a bit of sweat! Carry a tray, sweep up after everyone's gone home, keep the fire stoked...piss pots scoured clean." Moses rattled on.

Ho snapped his pencil against his palm. "Tap your bank in the City, Bluehill. We'll pay back the loan ourselves from our commission on the winnings. After that we're rolling in clover!"

Moses stagnated. "It is not a bank. It is Kirke Company."

Beckett subsided as well. He knew the implications of Kirke Company in Moses' life.

They returned to their respective seats thinking not about fathers or about money but about a brush with Moses' faceless mother.

This auspicious first night of his university career found Moses Bluehill huddled in the dark and damp in his bed while Beckett made the rounds in the dining hall. Moses' escape into sleep was so profound that he did not hear voices inside his room. More accurately, he heard the hum of people close by but did not wake. He had grown up nestling under his blanket on a mat in rooms where adults discoursed late into the night. Voices, even strange ones, soothed his rest.

Ho had returned from the dining hall with two companions and a plate for Moses. He was eager to introduce him to Gordon Brite, the Earl of Marthem, son of the Marquess of Leed, and to Ifan William, untitled, of a poor, politically important Welsh family and, most pertinently, a student of painting and architecture.

Ho's candle burned unwaveringly. He cast its light right and left in Moses' chamber, illuminating his sleeping quarters in small circles: pallid walls, the dilapidated window-seat, an ominous side chair, a warped highboy on which Moses had already set his wooden box of keepsakes.

"He must have gone walking. Exploring, you know. He'd think it unsafe not to know his surroundings." Concise in his speech, Ho, no matter how politely, set himself up as arbiter of Moses' culture and habits.

The Marquess's son had no trouble asking a question or two. Ho had no difficulty supplying the answers. Ifan nodded his head as if he had seen the places and the people of Moses' life before.

Moses turned in his sleep. The three visitors jumped back.

"Gods!" Ifan's blasphemy summed their embarrassment.

Moses twisted out of the bedding and onto the floor in the same instant. Crouching in defensive posture, his bare body showed faintly in the scant light. His loose, long, line-straight hair crosshatched his face and slipped down like glass filaments to his shoulders.

Gordon swallowed.

Ifan whispered, "Gods."

Ho stammered, "Lord Marthem, and Mr. Ifan William, may I present my American friend, the prince of the Massachuseuck people, Mr. Moses Bluehill."

Moses, now fully awake, came to his feet.

Ho added, "In all his glory."

CHAPTER FORTY-ONE

Autumn 1763, Winter 1764

Returning to Kirke Company, Ltd., London, after a few days' business to the north, Locke was not amazed to find Moses' account in arrears for one marble mantelpiece, one crystal chandelier, and a secretary of straw marquetry along with enough lumber and paint to scaffold and decorate the Sistine Chapel. He blacked out the specifics, correcting the entry to read: *improvements to the monastery*. Locke was little impressed that Moses had visited headquarters unannounced.

Moses had made his raid on his account deliberately without fanfare. He convinced himself that the pressure of time predicated against arrangements by post and the pressure of the purse made a messenger extravagant. Only in the hottest chambers of his heart did he admit to evasion of any sudden or accidental contact with his mother.

Bluehill waited at the House of Kirke in one of a series of rooms painted with a gray distemper touched here and there with twenty-four karat gold and furnished with long tables of glistening ebony over Persian rugs of blue silk. Awed by the solemn embrace of mercantile mastery, he nevertheless left elated. The leather satchel they gave him, heavy with notes and specie, shouted to him that his father, a man of elemental habit, commanded the respect of

Kirke Company to the degree that they responded without halt or confusion to their standing instructions even in the absence of the firm's central agent.

Michaelmas Term passed. The senior Beckett's nervous neck muscle switched as he thought of the months flying by and the money he owed to Locke, not to mention Moses Bluehill's ravenous appetite for his books over social opportunities. Hanna was proud of Moses' scholarly bent but was dismayed that Moses could find no time to visit her in Mayfair aside from a week's visit at Christmas. Gil was not fooled that his great-nephew-by-marriage was a bookworm. As February loomed, he took the initiative, unstuck Hanna and Cecil from their city pastimes and commanded Moses' presence in Heathersley during the post-examination break.

Moses resented missing Ifan's application of the pigmented wet plaster for the ceiling. Yet, he packed and left for the south country without audible fuss because he loved the Worths and Heathersley and Horace Beckett was an inspired superintendent of the labor.

Travelling alone, on horseback, through the soft, wet air of England's mock spring he arrived before his elders who used more cumbersome transportation. As in his first visit, he arrived at sunset although this time there was no sun.

He enjoyed the tub and his mattress wrapped in fresh linen. He took a plate of meat in the company of the great clock then retired to his bed in the empty mansion.

Moses woke at dawn, his usual time to study. He responded to the deadness by sinking back to sleep. He woke at ten to the groans of the clock. He lay awake, hungry, weighed by the weight of feathers. He remembered that he would still not be welcome in the dining hall. His hand smoothed the green satin of the comforter until eleven. He washed, dressed, appeared for breakfast punctually at noon and then walked outside to find his old haunts.

The temporary thaw transformed the estate into fool's glass. The English sun painted the shimmer a faint yellow. Moses tramped out of the park down the farm roads, past the squires' comfortable houses to the neighborhood of the tenants, a pleasing warren of stucco and thatch and pretty garden walls. Moses' black cape was taunted by the edgeless breezes that tickled the countryside.

He trespassed property rented by Cecil's tenants at fat rates now that the price of wheat was up. The only hazard of the land was the dung of roving cattle.

Moses heard singing from behind a low stone wall. The sweet bawling created a quaint music across the glowing, fallow landscape. Moses put his foot on that wall to listen as his Uncle Gil might have done. He surveyed the hut-like houses.

"Heigh!" A woman in cap and apron, her hands on her hips, appeared in the door of one of them.

Moses glanced at the tenant wife, tipped his hat, turned back to the view, but kept the wall.

"Heigh!", the woman shrewed again. "What are you?"

After a moment, Moses looked at her.

She asked not what he was doing or what he was doing with his foot up on her wall but what *was* he.

Moses threw her a smile. "You would not believe me if I told you."

The woman let out a pleased shriek. Her hair was coarse, red. It was bunched girlishly at the sides of her head by means of ribbons. "An' what are ye doin' on me wall?" She mewed.

Moses answered nothing to this more direct question. He did remove his nicely shod foot from the stone shelf.

The tenant wife angered and toiled over the muck to him. "Look at what ye done to me shoes!" Her tongue floated in her tight little mouth. The skin of her bare arms was exceedingly white and fine and stretched over such round flesh that Moses could not see it ever showing age. She was as yeasty as a baked loaf.

She looked at his cape. "Ye'r from the big house, ain't ye? I can't talk to ye 'cause I'm in the middle." She pranced back to the doorway and stripped off her shoes.

Moses pondered what she was in the middle of and why being in the middle of it would prevent her talking when, indeed, she had already spoken.

"Cum for some cider, sir, if you're too shy to ask."

The mildness of the day could not prevent the dampness from invading his bones and so Moses found himself seated tensely at the edge of a short-legged wooden chair, his hands wrapped around a steaming cider mug.

The rust-haired housewife worked over a long board under the window, her back to him and one eye on the tiny yard enclosed by a hedge from where children's screaming rose.

Red bags, unidentifiable to Moses, were arranged in neat rows amid a litter of strange crumbling matter. Moses looked away.

"It's to be brought to the big house for your supper and a damned sight of work it is to prepare."

"We shall appreciate it, I'm sure."

"I've got out o' you ye'r from the great house! Oh, lar, then you know, you're not supposed to be in here! Are you down after a mid-month rent, cutie pie?"

The tumultuous children burst in. Their noise suffused any retort. The woman, about thirty, shooed them out of her kitchen and forbade them to play in the house. They scrambled down the lane.

Moses, not understanding her question, studiously watched her tiny, thick hands manage the red, many-pointed sacks.

Palming the sacks one at a time, the tenant-wife scooped the crumbles into them. She pushed the pungent stuffing into the points of the membranous bags.

Moses smelled onions and raw beef and fat and some sort of green. The woman set a small, ruddy, now turgid bag on its open end on a baking tray where it poked brightly up like a crown.

"What are those things?"

She turned to him crossing her arms over her round belly. The spoon spilled its residue down the front of her gown. She grinned, "Cocks combs!"

Moses lurched away from the table. Striving to control his stomach, he stared out the window gouged from the thickness of the wall. He sensed her close behind him.

"Never 'ad any?"

He turned slowly toward her.

She licked the stuffing spoon.

Moses answered and was sorry. "Never."

"Go on! You've 'ad plenty. Just look at you! A dark prince you are. From the big house, eh? An' that lovely color. So who's your marm?"

Moses backed away.

"Had many an unusual banquet's my guess!"

Moses caught a whiff of her rotten meaning and staved her off with actuality. "I have drunk blood."

She discounted it. "So's everybody."

"Out of a lion's skull."

Her round, blue eyes narrowed. "You bloods! You dare come in 'ere an' scare a decent woman."

Moses sought the upper hand. "I have eaten the nose of a moose."

Her stubby hands covered her lips and the spoon fell to the floor. "An' you complain of a cocks comb!?"

Moses reached for his hat. "I am sorry if I insulted your culinary treat!"

Her fingers grazed his lace. "You can make it up. Cum fill some with me. The faster to bake them so you can taste."

"That's kind of you." Moses held his hat brim in two hands and backed toward the low door. "But you mustn't spare any to me. You've got the children and I breakfasted only an hour ago."

"Oh, yes." She looked drained. She turned fast, her little mouth in a pucker of disgust at life. She pounded her fist onto the board and one of the combs bounced on the wood and split. She walked into another room.

Moses went quickly to the board to repair what had broken. He took up the rooster's red, wrinkled, flaccid headpiece. His breakfast backed up his trachea. He plastered the pocket with the greasy puree, mending the tear with the paste of meat. He planted it upright on the tray next to the others. He searched for a rag, for water, for any decent thing on which to wipe his fingers. He licked them. The flavor of the meat was not noxious.

Moses worked his way down the few dark feet of the hallway. He saw the bottom portion of the woman through the open door of the room at the end. He called out as he approached, "I thank you for the cider, missus. I fixed your...thing. I wanted to clean my hands...."

"Don't bother."

Moses stood in the doorway. He saw the small woman roll toward him over the straw. She was a white dollop in the shadowy room. The shutters were open yet the light stayed outside. The little children's voices could be heard faraway.

The tenant wife motioned him in.

"Are you unwell?"

She rolled onto her back with a cry as if stuck. "Comin' in an' insultin' a poor man's wife. A hardworkin' mother."

Moses stood at her side wishing he had brought someone on his walk, Cecil's butler, the groom, the stable boy. "What did I say?"

She rolled back toward him, one of her breasts escaping her bodice the way a breakfast roll does its basket. "Did you ever see red hair like mine?"

Moses, perspiring, began, "A friend...."

"Don't answer!"

"I'm going now." He took a step back.

"How old are you?"

"Seventeen." He turned away from her and his cape flared behind him.

The woman caught onto it. Pulled steadily on it. He turned toward her to warn her off. He saw her pull the string of her stomacher with her left hand.

A balmy breeze, unnatural for the time of year slipped in and dried his sweating lip. The woman was perfumed with chicken fat and powerful human smells.

"There's a fine in the public court for enterin' the home of a tenant before rent time. I thought I'd do you a favor lettin' you know an' my man not at home. I shouldn't wonder you could be flogged." She pulled sharply on his cloak and he was forced to bend his knees for balance. He touched the mattress for support. She took hold of his free wrist and rested his hand on the full jelly of her breast. She cried out. The sound was light and pleasured. The red circle at center and its pointed nipple were like the cock's comb stuffed.

    Wildly, he basted her top with the paste still stuck to his hands and then devoured it with his tongue. She clucked at him and clucked and ditched the magical drapery of her skirt.

CHAPTER FORTY-TWO

February 1764

Moses came swaggering into his renovated rooms expecting to find Horace Beckett. Instead, the Earl of Marthem sat ensconced in a freshly reupholstered chair.

"Gord!" Moses tucked his riding gloves under his arm and made his way over to him, slightly distracted by the changes Ifan William and his workers had brought into being.

"Glad you're back." Marthem stood, shook Moses' hand. "The ancestors placated?"

Moses felt Marthem's query a bit close to the bone considering the manly secret he harbored. "Thank you. They are. Where's Beck?"

"Oh." Gordon looked down, his great trumpet nose twitching at the nostrils. "Walking off an argument with me."

Moses gazed at the walls, the ceiling. On the northeast wall, around the door and its massive stone pediment, were beautiful horses, Beckett's donjon far in the background. Opposite, at the room's northwest extremity was painted, not ineptly, a pine forest spelled by white birch. A ship floated on a southwesterly route around the windows. On the south wall was a rendition of Heathersley, its palatial villa, its park, its countryside, its tenant farms.

"How did Ifan....?"

Moses and Gordon walked the circuit of the chamber.

"I got him a drawing of the place from the library. It's an impressive house. One can hear chariots on the gravel I suspect. The flutter of togas on the terraces. Ours at Summerset lacks the dust of the ancients." Most subtly, Gordon added, "Ho whetted my appetite to go down and have a look."

Moses evaded him. "I can tell you, Lord Worth has better heating than we do here! Ho should have lit a fire."

"Not yet. The murals and the ceiling have to dry naturally. No ash or expanding or contracting plaster, you know."

Moses was proud of the place, so clean, so colored with Nature's and man's works, its stone floor insulated with rush carpets, its magnificent windows liberated from dirt, joining the light and the weather to the artificial scenes indoors, making a largeness and a fresh reality. Stiffly, as if he were his father in the many-domed sachimmaacommock, Moses invited the Earl to sit. "What's between you and Beckett?"

"Pontiac."

Moses felt as if a bone had broken in his neck.

Marthem enquired, "What do you make of him?"

Not deliberate like Wakwa, Moses instinctually lunged for the right answer. "Were he of my father's mind he would have known better than to start his war."

Gordon's brows rose.

"Pontiac is a purist."

Gordon enquired, "And your father is not?"

"Definitely not."

"You say this of your sire!?"

"He married my mother."

Gordon Leed nodded. He understood.

"My father is not a purist. He is pure. My father talks to all tribes of a careful peace - a peace that does not emasculate the legitimate claims of anybody."

"So. Why haven't we got such a peace?"

"Such a peace carries costs - material and spiritual. Neither England nor her American colonies will pay for it."

The young earl clapped. "Wonderfully said!"

Moses switched topics. "What do you think of the...room?"

But Marthem leaned forward out of the carved chair, his large hands wrapped around the lion's claws curving out of the arms. "I want my sister to meet you!"

Moses laughed at the painted blue sky above him.

Gordon sniffed, "Is she not highly enough placed for you? Not rich enough?"

"Forgive me, Lord Marthem. You cannot understand!"

"I understand my sister, at any rate. Lady Augusta Brite is incredibly beautiful and unaffected. She is unimpressed by the life Britain holds out to her. She requires the exotic."

"Does she!" Moses' eyes hardened into brass.

Gordon disregarded the warning. "If I am right about you both we could be brothers beyond the span of our lives!"

Moses' lips trembled at the feeling in Marthem's speech. "I have not met your sister. But I know you would make me a good brother."

Gordon smiled widely. "Then may I put you forward to her? There are picnics galore in spring and a thing we host at Summerset in May on Mother's Day."

"Gordon, if you love and respect your sister as I am sure you do, you will not want her to meet *me*."

"What an odd thing to say about yourself."

"I say nothing about myself."

"You must be mad. There isn't a man on this hall, or in this university, or in the whole damned country who wouldn't jump at the chance I am offering you! Do you know how old is our name? How sumptuous her dowry?"

"You do me too much honor." Moses observed the forms to push Marthem away.

Marthem's mouth twisted. "Spare me the humility, Bluehill. It doesn't suit you. Englishwomen of noble blood marry Greeks and Turks and Prussians and Moors! Ladies marry the most common brigands raised to the peerage by *business* or some bloody service or trickery. Quite aristocratic girls wind up waiting on prattlers in parsonages. You've got family on both sides, a fortune, brains and looks enough for ten men, and an air! What's the trouble with it?"

Moses shocked the earl by answering. "The trouble is, my father's People have a different attitude toward property than the rest of the world. We are different from you English and all the others on this point."

"Oh, come!" Gordon's hand and arm made an arc indicating the expensive and glorious setting.

"Gordon! We are not civilized."

Marthem, a lanky young man, made an unnaturally quick bounce out of his chair. "I don't believe that! Listen to yourself, Socrates!"

"We are not civilized!" Moses insisted. "We are a civilizing force."

Marthem stood still and silent, considering the depth of what had been said.

"Come with me." Moses beckoned and walked toward his room.

Gordon stayed close behind him tantalized but wary like a child in the dark.

Moses lifted something from the top drawer of the highboy, which, by Ifan's magic, now slid smoothly. In two hands, Moses cradled his father's obsidian knife.

Gordon's gaze fell on the thick black strip of vitreous lava manufactured by angry gods.

"The rest of the world is very new to us." Moses spoke as if in a sanctuary. "And its lack of simple freedoms and simple rightness is yet a matter of amusement around the fires."

Gordon put out his gray, bony hand and ran it down the cold, smooth, shapely blade of Wakwa's knife, more lethal than steel, more obdurate than granite. His voice dropped to a whisper, "It is the blackest thing, the most dangerous thing, the simplest sculpture I have ever seen!" Gordon moved back several steps. He had hardly touched the blade yet blood sprang.

Moses grinned away the possibility of noble girls.

"Bluehill! Thank you for not being a prick about it."

Minding Marthem's quick retreat, Moses patronized him, "As I said, we are a civilizing force."

Gordon accepted a handkerchief for his invisible but deep wound. "There's still no reason you can't join the party in May."

"Got to throw you out. Got to wash. Got to dress. Got an engagement with a certain Miss Tawney whom I met while dining at an inn on the way here."

Gordon shook from insult.

"She lifted her tray well. Should have a good strong back. I am less a romantic than my father."

The Earl stalked through the rooms, threw open the door and chipped the fresh plaster and paint with the latch.

"Keep a check on your temper, Lord Marthem. You've already fought with Horace Beckett today!"

Marthem whirled on him. "*He* told me how Pontiac could have generalled the war to win!"

"Then Ho's the one you should introduce to your sister!"

Leed looked back from the hallway. "But his father is a nobody."

"His father is a solicitor well-respected. A Cambridge man! He was an observer at the Treaty of Paris and is known in the right circles as *the* expert on American PROPERTY! Perhaps your father could get him dubbed Lord Something-or-other."

"You're the one I wanted, but...."

"But Beckett might do?" Hurt, Moses spoke unkindly.

Horace Beckett observed Moses leaning against the stone doorframe. They were poised for the opening of their club.

"Hill, you don't think Ifan will mind my asking him to serve tonight? It's his arm and eye have reformed our squalor."

"Ifan needs money and can't afford to gamble. He is a partner after all. He'll take a cut of everything we make."

Ho, adjusting his brown silk suit and platinum waistcoat spoke again shyly, "I thought, if you agree, that we should sit the bloods at one table to make opportunity for higher stakes."

Moses' happiness with him increased. "Where do you get your talent for this?"

Ho returned compliment for compliment. "May I say, your finery adds to the atmosphere?"

Moses wore a black velvet suit set off by lace the color of coffee overdosed with cream.

Ifan William made his appearance. A quartet of hallmates trooped in with viol, bull fiddle, violin, and flute. "They'll give us music in exchange for one free hand at cards."

Gordon came in quickly after them. Dressed in a splendid cloth of sooty gray, he advanced on Moses. He condescended to say, "You'd better know some evil tongues have told Warden Wilkes. He said he'd stop in."

Sudden heat colored Moses' face.

Ho, ignorant of their feud submitted, "Awkward."

Marthem glowered, "To say the least."

Moses said, embarrassed, "My performance of yesterday was abominable. I apologize. To you and...all concerned."

"Oh!" Marthem said acidly. "You want to reconsider."

"I want to apologize."

Horace heard trouble and distracted from it. "As you say, Gord, the Warden's coming. It's clumsy for you, your father on the Board of Governors and all. If you can't stay, we'll understand."

Gordon stood his ground. "If I go, you'll both be expelled. I'll sort it out. Why do you think I dressed like a Calvinist!" Then he allowed, "But that was thoughtful, Beckett." Gordon shot a look Moses' way.

The hallmates had heard the mallets at midnight, Ifan's trowel scraping as day broke. They had smelled the unmistakable perfumes of pigment and linseed oil. But they had no idea that students could create out of a dormitory room a salon that could have rivaled the ones they had left behind at home. The pastorale and seascape, the foreign woods, and merchant clipper encapsulated their national history without the irritation of their having to read of it. They did not mind so much now lightening their purses to enter this rarified emporium.

"Most enterprising." They were determined not to reveal excitement. "Clever fellows."

The partners mixed with their paying guests. As Moses passed from clique to clique, queries followed in his wake. Who is he? The only time I ever see him is in the library. How are he and Horace Beckett connected? What is he from? What is he called, again?

Ho leaned toward Marthem and said something in a soft voice. The earl took his suggestion and formed a table. The music struck up and whist got underway. While the lesser guests found their own places, Ifan William busied himself about the food. Beckett clicked matters off his checklist. Moses pulled his watch from his pocket. He slipped it back in. He reminded Ifan it was time for the Claret.

Round after round increased the laughter. Time between hands made the occasion for snuff. The sneezing made another opportunity for laughter.

One student, much disheveled, green from too much drink, squinted at Moses. "I didn't know we had a German on the hall." His slurred speech was so loud that for a moment it stopped all other conversation.

Talk started up again.

"Fritz!" The boy guffawed, slapping his knees.

No one paid him attention.

Moses stood at the hearth sampling tobacco freshly arrived from Massachusetts. Gordon sauntered over.

The underclassman taunted, "Turk! He's a Turk. No...Sicilian? Heigh! Sicilian!" He strutted closer to Moses. "Russian?" He was at Moses' elbow. "That's it. Oh, great Czar!" The drunken boy supported himself by holding Moses' arm with both his hands. "C'mon! What's-your-name! Tell us!" He craned back at Moses' height. Saw Moses' cheekbones, his loose, black natural hair precisely cut and curling under at his shoulders. "A Mongol? I'm right? Heigh! Everybody, meet Genghis Kahn!" He began to clap and dance in a way he could not have managed had he been sober.

Moses' silent turning toward the fool quashed all chatter.

Marthem supplied, "Mongol is much more like it, you idiot. Please leave!"

The lad grew surly. "You're not a Chinaman. You're a Sicilian."

"There is a bit of Corsican in him." Ho steered the sweating troublemaker toward the door. "There's a good fellow!" Ho ushered him out.

A few throats cleared. Moses sat. He picked up his hand. "Let's play, friends." The tables refilled. Whist resumed.

The door burst wide open. "You can't put me out! I paid for my place! I want it! I'll have it! I paid!"

Again, and with assistance from the earl, Ho ejected him from the room. The hallmates laughed, moved on to other subjects. Stories of their female conquests engendered far more excitement in them than a one-man row.

A quarter hour passed peacefully. Then something struck the bolted door hard. The blow repeated. Came again. The oak panels remained as fixed as rock. The players pushed away from their tables.

Moses listened with his ear to the panel. He waved Ho and Marthem and the others away.

Marthem confided to Ho, "I do not see how you'll have a steady crowd with so much...drama!"

The thud again. Moses jerked the latch up. He swung the door back hard, against himself. The little alcoholic was propelled forward by his own momentum brandishing a battle-ax filched from a display.

Some laughed. Some shouted. Some classmates shrank against the walls. From behind, Moses threw a kick between the troublemaker's legs.

As if at a gladiatorial contest guttural cheers overpowered a wail of pain. Moses took the weapon and pinned the offender to the floor.

Marthem came forward.

"Gordon, stand back!" Moses held him away. "We don't want your line to end over nothing."

The drunken freshman wheezed and fought for the lance. "Corsican robber! I paid. I'll have my rights!"

Moses removed his coat.

Growls of approval peppered the air.

"Garlic press! Turk!" The student struggled to his feet with madman's strength. "Can't you speak English? Say something!"

Moses spoke. "Shall I tear out your tongue?"

"You heard him! He threatened me!" The sotted boy, shorter than Moses, less well developed, unsteady on his feet and seeing double, was yet not blind to danger.

Guffaws.

Moses' stance was stable but light. His arms were balanced about waist high. His eyes burnt into his detractor who defended himself with taunts.

"Foreignor! Ignoramus! Thief! Dumb ox!"

The assembly of males not yet men hooted him down. "Shutup! Get out! Sot! Wretch!"

One step brought Moses inconveniently close to the bloodshot eyes, the stinking breath, the distended, drooling lips. A spectre of the past, some drunken cousin of his father's who had wreaked havoc for the tribe, for his father and his mother, seemed to be staring at him, not a British boy off his mind from a bottle of Clary.

Moses stepped back.

"Coward!"

Moses folded his arms across his chest. He debated within how to shut the fellow down. He stood straight, showily straight. "English is but one of my languages - friend. I am fluent as well in Italian! French! German! Greek! Latin! Among other tongues you have never heard of."

Light chuckling burbled at Moses' fantastic statement.

"Thaz not possible." The boy put out a pug jaw but his voice quavered. "You're a nobody and nothing."

A collective moan told how dangerous the company regarded this baiting to be.

Moses turned his back on his guests. He pictured snapping the fool's neck like he would a doe's he had hunted down for supper. An idea unknotted his muscles and he turned back perfectly relaxed as he would have been in his father's camp before some contest of speed or skill. He smiled. "I have no reason to explain myself to anybody, least of all you. Friend." His nose wrinkled in fun. "But if it will hasten play, let me inform you, in English, that I am a bloody Red Indian by the name of Wolf-of-the-mist He-hopes, my father is king of a nation in Massachusetts with more than fifty miles of ground and many hundreds of people under his sway. He has two wives, or had before he divorced my

English mother, an heiress of his region. She, herself, is possessed of uncountable wealth - in *gold*. My father's best friend is her English uncle-by-marriage, a peer's son and the executor of a vast American estate to which I will accede at my majority. If you have further questions, I refer you to the family solicitor whose son is your other host tonight."

Titters had begun among the company very early in this speech. They enlarged to approving laughter. A cheer went up at Moses' strong finish. Moses was laughing himself in the way he laughed, silently, with his head raised and back, his very white teeth remarkable.

The rosebud face of the heckler went purple. The crowd of silken coats and powdered wigs and stockinged calves hemmed him in.

One fellow asked with an edge, "Mr. Bluehill, with a literary bent like that don't you belong at Cambridge? That's the place for novelists and poets."

"I'm here for law. And Wadham was my uncle's college."

The student's glance wandered to the marble mantel.

Warden Wilkes filled the door. "Gentlemen, it is after ten. Would you mind explaining? There is damage to a case of Mediaeval weapons and damage to this door. It appears you are gaming. A serious offence."

Ho's throat went dry. Ifan seemed to grow even shorter.

The warden hissed, "What have you done to this room? Are there women here?"

Moses answered while pulling on his coat. "We have gone out on a limb with the paint brushes, Warden." Moses smiled at his pun and relied on the animal charm of his eyes.

The warden's glance roved the salon springing with painted trees.

Moses finished with a brief bow. "A little whist is all, among private club members."

Applause for his bravery was silently made in the hearts of his witnesses.

"All?" The warden glowered at the tables and their towers of coins.

"Well.... There is money at stake, sir. It was my idea wholly to start this...club. One enters by money or wit or work and Mr. Beckett and I take some of the winnings."

The warden's face went beet red.

Moses lied blatantly. "For charity, sir."

"What charity!"

"Why, sir!" Moses ran his hand through his dark, dark hair as if terribly puzzled. "I thought you would know of it as you are in command of all things in this college."

"Do not push me, Mr. Bluehill!"

"It is my fault. I should have set it down in a letter."

"What charity, Mr. Bluehill?!"

Moses heaved a breath not knowing where to go with his tumerous fib. "The widows and orphans, sir."

"Which widows and orphans?"

Moses' overwrought imagination froze.

Ho piped up, "From Pontiac's War."

The warden sputtered, "You are gambling on my hall to give money to bloodthirsty savages?!"

Ho strode forward, bellicose.

Moses lounged against the monstrous, carved chair Gordon favored. "Oh, sir, I don't think there are enough casualties on the

Indian side to merit an offering. Besides, the *savages* always care for their own. I know since I am half one myself. No, the money we collect here is for the families of the poor, torn English troops, the Crown's treasury being so low. We thought as loyal subjects of King George it was the least we could do."

Snorts of suppressed hilarity filled the salon.

The warden soured at Moses' adroitness.

Gordon placed his lordly hand on Moses' shoulder.

The warden was shocked. "Lord Marthem! You are here?"

Gordon had taken color. "We would be honored, sir, if you would bless these proceedings. Won't you take a look at the improvements? I must say that Bluehill and Beckett have been awfully creative in providing decent work for the servitors. Better than Oxford men blacking boots!"

The warden stepped in, cast a jaundiced eye around. He caught sight of the mar behind the door. "What's this! Is this assembly violent?!"

Again, Marthem obliged the situation. "I did it, sir. Pure clumsiness. I insist that Bluehill and Beckett allow me to pay Mr. William to repair it."

Warden Wilkes, monitor of rich men's sons, was by definition a diplomat. He stood in the middle of his students. "Whist is a gentleman's game. But I think you should add tables for chess. You can't play that so well on too much Claret. Messers. Bluehill and Beckett, kindly see me in the morning or as soon as your headaches will allow." Wilkes swept out.

A minute passed before anyone could speak. And then a cheer went up. The nucleus of their college years had formed. The gamblers took their leave, one by one, shaking the hands of their hosts. Their liberators. Their leaders. One graduate offered, "You shall have no trouble with your orals, Mr. Bluehill, when they come due."

When the room had emptied, Moses said to Marthem, "My heart is full with gratitude to you! I played fast and loose with my father's dream. You saved it. I owe you my honor."

"Well!" Gordon seemed satisfied with this acknowledgement.

Moses went on in the style of the Ninnuock, "Try me."

Marthem studied the golden eyes. "Try you? Try you? You mean as in feudal times? Test you?"

"My neck is bent to your axe."

Gordon's chin rose. "Then disappoint your waitresses and your other common female prey. That must be done! I would introduce Horace *and* you to Augusta."

CHAPTER FORTY-THREE

Winter 1764

The winter feast of the Ninnuock always coming in the bitterest weather made it count for much. The first deep snow hissing like sizzling meat was never an occasion for dread but proved to be the answer to their hunger for laughter, for ease, for sport. Faces beamed at the scent of the white crystals.

The smell of snow pervaded the Dowland neighborhood. It slipped past window mullions, through chinks in barn walls, swooped down chimneys like a bird of prey lost.

Qunneke scented it from her bed in the Meetinghouse Hospital. Her reaction to the frost and the coming whiteness was not what it had been when she was younger, when her belly was flat and firm, even four months gone with child. Now, with no baby taking form in her womb, her abdomen was large and felt peopled by stones.

Her folk dreamt of fires devouring the meat drippings, of red apples sputtering around the perimeter of the flames, of pumpkin flesh simmering for pudding in its own round, orange body. The People entertained visions of the young men dashing on the iced field averting their heels from the racquet, sending balls of doeskin to the mark, of couplings in the frozen forest and of the laughter of people in love finding home. Qunneke saw the snow out her window as her shroud.

Lightfoot made his way into her room carrying her tea tray. Qunneke looked at him thinking it odd that neither of Wakwa's sons was preparing for Nickommo.

"Nokace!" He said, 'my mother.'

She enjoyed his use of their native tongue. "Wautuckques."

Lightfoot plumped her pillows adeptly with his working arm, tied a bib over Qunneke's nightgown, set over her legs the bed table Gil and Wakwa had made for her, and arranged the cup and saucer, the tiny teapot, and the steaming supper Priscilla Stirling and her daughter, Anniebeth, nearly eleven, had prepared. "Have you decided? Will you let Israel cut out the tumor?"

Tame Deer caught Lightfoot's live hand. She spoke in the language she had known from her birth, "What use, Son? You should not even bring me to eat."

Lightfoot pulled his hand away, added wood to her fire.

"Shall I eat alone? Your father - is he not coming?"

Lightfoot tested the window for draught. The glass was cold and blue from the gathering frost and night. He saw the white ghost of Worth Farm to the northeast.

He covered his eyes with the hand that did the work of two. "I asked him not to come."

"I cannot believe...I...I...lie here like this! Alone!"

Lightfoot sent her a stricken look. "You leave him alone all the time. Yet you want him with you tonight when I am here!" He hit his dead arm with his live one and the useless limb bobbed high before falling still at his side.

Qunneke's left hand came to the ruffles of white wool at her throat.

Lightfoot saw her swift, natural, unthinking movement. "That simple act I cannot do - I do not even dream of doing what other men do. I do this!" He pulled the silver teapot away and slammed it on the lowboy.

Qunneke tried to rise and nearly upset her plate.

Lightfoot cursed in English. He resettled her and held her hand in the only way he could - with his right one. "Rest."

"There is always to do. Your father has no help from me! The feast is near!"

Lightfoot slipped to his knees, his giant body spread across the mattress; his head pressed Qunneke's swollen abdomen. "You have helped him." Quiet with the truth for a long minute, he began to speak softly as if his words might cut him if spoken in normal tones. "Before I was conceived, you took a stand in front of the full council when my father was gone to the Passamoquoddy. You saved his honor as the husband of two...."

"How do you...."

"The woman who accused him of neglecting you was she who burnt and blinded his Elizabeth! You fed Moses and his mother from your breast and kept them both alive. Was that not a help to him?"

"It was little enough...if you knew the pains I always put him through!"

Lightfoot lifted his head to see her face. He no longer wondered why the slight formality between his parents. "You helped him in other ways. Did you not burn your beautiful house to the ground at his order when they sent his other wife away?"

"Do not speak of...." Qunneke pressed her temples with fingers not so slender as they once had been.

"You did that while I was inside you!" His voice rose.

"Yes!"

"You sacrificed to the fire everything of your own yet you carried father's and this former wife's treasures on your back all the way to the mountains while lesser women ran about wailing."

"Who told you all this?"

"You made Moses your own son when my father gave up Elizabeth!"

Qunneke cried out. "What favor was that to anybody?! I should have gone to her with Moses instead. It might have brought her back among us! But I was large with you...."

Outraged at her coupling his existence with the torn condition of their family, Lightfoot snapped, "You gave me birth on a bank of snow, that was all the comfort I was granted fifteen winters ago! That was to save father from the noose! For him and Moses, you bore me in the mountains without the comforts you were used to. Without the love of other people your heart was crying for... without Uncle Gilbert!"

Her face turned rigid.

Lightfoot backed decently away from this theme. "My first winter you kept the tribe together when my father would not open his mouth to speak to you!"

"I love him."

"You love Uncle Gilbert too! I know you conceived me of the Sachim, my father, but it was because of Uncle Gilbert! Because you loved him. You love him still!"

Qunneke choked on the words massing in her mouth.

"You went to his farm for the silver vessel to feed Moses when father took Elizabeth to the forest to heal her wounds. You learned Aunt Hanna was far away, yet you stayed with Uncle Gilbert alone in his beautiful house. I would never have been started or born unless the whore, Panther Eye, had hurt Elizabeth and left her dry of milk. So, who is my mother? You? Panther Eye? Maybe Elizabeth! You love Uncle Gilbert and this farm so much you came back here and cared for strangers from the village when they were hurt in the manse fire! People who would despise to see you even in their kitchens!"

Qunneke's face sealed, closed to further trespass.

"Even with me lying at my Uncle Gilbert's nigh to death, you helped strangers for the good of my father!"

Tame Deer's forearms caressed her swollen middle. "My friend held you in his hands. My friend, Mac, brought you back to us!"

"For what?! Unlike you, I can help no one!"

Qunneke's mouth softened. "Lightfoot! You do!"

"After all these years with the plants, with the pills, with the shit and the blood and the pans and the trays, can I help you? Say it! No!"

Qunneke watched her quietest child erupt.

"Even my passing this dark hour with you is nothing to you! I am with you and you cry you are alone!"

Tame Deer pushed the standing tray down the bed and struggled to free herself from the sheets.

Lightfoot retreated to a chair much too small for his bulk. He stayed doubled over, his right hand inadvertently shielding the gnarl of bone over his right ear marking the site of his fracture.

Qunneke had never seen him favor his wounded place.

He looked up. "True - with me you *are* alone!"

Qunneke loosed herself from the bedclothes, once foreign things to her. She wobbled when she stood but steadied. She approached Lightfoot over the rag rug of red and yellow and black.

But he rose, moved away from her and turned toward the mirror. His face, hers, was yet intrinsically male. His father's stamp on him. But the slight bulge on the right playing havoc with the growth and comb of his hair and the flaccid left arm gave his image a monster's symmetry.

Qunneke's hands claimed his shoulders. "How do you know these things about me? These things from before you were born?"

Only his eyes, so like hers, turned toward her. "I may not be able to fight like other men or shoot like them or build a house like a man should, or cut the sick open with a knife and heal them, or...." he choked back some flood of inner passion.

"My son...." Qunneke's arms slid down his back.

"Or hold a woman in my arms...ever!" His voice was hard but he freed himself gently from his mother's embrace. "I may not be able to do things that other men do but I listen better than anyone with my rabbit's ears!" He smirked at his own name. "How could I not know? People talk in front of me as if my brain fell out the night that horse kicked a hole in my head!"

Qunneke would not be shocked or turned aside. "Which people!"

Lightfoot's right hand lighted with unselfconscious kindness on her shoulder even though his words seemed to lacerate the inside of his throat. "I heard the talk in our own house, I heard it at Uncle Gilbert's, I heard it from the common folk of our Twisting River town who whispered and yet whisper after us. I cannot go to the public house in Sweetwood without having rumors stuffed into my ears!"

"When did you go there!? Why did you go there?"

Lightfoot snorted at her. "You think I drink their poison?"

"You are not yourself!"

"Your husband, my father, the Sachim who fathered a girl who is as good as any man, came to Sweetwood to argue my way out of the jail in the cellar of the church for slapping this Spinney whom they then tarred and feathered and drove out of the town!"

"When! When was this?"

Lightfoot escaped her and stepped too swiftly to the stairs. Turning to look up at her caused his dead hand to swing and hit the railing hard with no inconvenience to him. "At harvest! When we were all mourning Moses' leaving at his birth-time, I went to collect the post and found myself defending *his* mother's honor - and my own - this woman I have never seen! This...*woman*! And my father who once debated terms of peace with the great men of nations red and white, is reduced to pleading for small favors from the tithing man!"

Qunneke bent forward one hand clutched between her breasts as if to pull a knife from her heart.

Lightfoot rushed away from her down the steps, his descent slightly awkward because of his compromised left side.

"Son!" Qunneke's tone brought him to a halt. She reached the landing. "Why did you tell your father to stay away? So you could tell me this about him?"

Lightfoot made a noise, small, like a squeal strangled. He hung his head. Then he spoke with his head high. "I wanted to tell you alone - I have made up my mind - I am going to ask Uncle Gilbert for a piece of ground to live on behind Dowland House."

Qunneke smoothed her hair as if her neatness would straighten their convoluted family life. "You have been afraid there all your life. You do not like that place." She chanced moving down a step toward him.

Lightfoot mounted a step toward her. "Not afraid. Sad. It makes me sad to see it alone. And Dowland's ghost alone."

Tame Deer reached for his hands, the one that could feel, and the other that could not.

"I thought of telling our priest I would follow him. Go into the woods, learn his cures, his words. Become the Massachuseuck priest."

"Yes?!"

"But I cannot even raise both arms in prayer. And then," he chanced a smile, "it seems our gods are deaf."

Qunneke let his blasphemy pass. With some pride she said, "Your voice might heal their hearing."

Lightfoot's face clouded. "I like Low's church. But I cannot follow him or his god no matter how good he is or how powerful his god is."

"Did Mayhew say this?"

"Mother! How could I stand in Low's pulpit on his holy day to talk as a Christian, when the Ninnuock can sit only in the gallery! Because of that I would never preach his god to the Massachusetts nations."

Qunneke spoke in wonder, "I never knew you thought of these things. Of priestly things."

Lightfoot retreated a step pulling his hands from hers. He let a whispery laugh escape him. "Did you think at all of what I might have thought? Or did you presume I would spend my time scrubbing Israel's surgery? Follow Israel about but never be able to doctor the sick, lacking as I do the tools for the job." He held his dead hand aloft then let it drop.

"You could grow the herbs! Make the pills!" Qunneke slid to sitting on a step.

"I could do that. But that is not a life! Making pills!"

"You could *find* cures!"

"I could do that. I might do that. But herbs are small tillage and cures long in coming." Lightfoot seated himself one step beneath her. His eyes looked beyond the confines of the stairwell and the foyer and the door and the darkened path. "I see those pines Elizabeth planted behind the house. Her little forest. Just big enough for me. I have talked to Matthew. He will teach me the way to husband Dowland Farm, to plant the way they plant, to work the numbers, to husband the cattle. All of you spend your lives trying to help her, her and Moses. I can think of no other way that I can *help*. Help all of us. Or save my Uncle Gilbert, my father-of-the-spirit, many pains." He turned his eyes on her. "And I could be the friend of the place."

She held her face in her hands.

He took them down. "I want a little house of my own. As long as I must be alone. In the long nights I can make the plants into pills for Israel. I do not forget what his father did for me. So. Now you know how I will live when you refuse to see the spring, and leave me!" With considerable grace considering his size and limitations, Lightfoot slipped away from her, down the stairs and out into the flurries.

Qunneke called to him repeatedly without a voice, "A woman will come and hold you in *her* two arms!"

Anniebeth found Qunneke soon after and helped her back to bed.

CHAPTER FORTY-FOUR

March 1763 and March 1764

With steely discipline, Elizabeth had outmaneuvered the spies, English and Venetian, by making her usual round of shops and post office instead of rushing to the dock to meet Kirke. She sent Sebastiano Falier in her stead.

Kirke had been troubled by Falier's doing the honors but had not missed his cue. He talked on with Sebastiano about the state of banking, and trade, and sparked things up with hints about speculating in the London stock market. His impulse was to thank the man for his courtesy by asking him to supper. Instead, Kirke put the appointment off and retired to wait for Elizabeth.

Not an hour later she hesitated in the tall doorway of the master bedchamber.

Regardless of the thickness of the walls or their distance from the public rooms, Kirke used a quiet tone of voice. "Once I went away for two years and when I came back I felt the earth underfoot as solid as it can be in Venice. Why, after only a dozen days out, do I feel my craw full of canal water? Where were you? Where is Poore? You send me Falier!? Am I the Venetian husband the servants have always prayed for me to be? Is it Falier then? The message delivered with 'the fine Italian hand?'"

Shaken from the sights and smells and touch of murder, she slammed the doors shut, a feat of noteworthy strength or fury. "I deserve better from you! So does Sebastiano! You sail about the clean seas, while we who stay behind are mired in your messes!" She marched off for the window.

Kirke tossed his peruke onto the seat of a chair and unbuttoned his waistcoat. "Well! Then, what, precisely, has happened?"

Elizabeth looked at her husband in his seventy-third year. "Nothing and everything."

Kirke wheeled on her in some impatience.

"I cannot be more accurate."

"I hope you shall try!" Kirke's tone was meant to graze and did.

She lashed out, "Dario has been slaughtered!"

"What?"

"All the work of his hands is stolen..."

"What are you talking about!"

"Dario! His hands! We found them...finally found them!" A scream shot out of her like the steam from a kettle. "We found his hands in his waste bin!"

"Make some sense!" Kirke demanded.

"Sense? Sense! Words written in his blood were smeared all over the walls!"

Kirke sat down hard. The tail of his peruke poked out under his panted thigh. Elizabeth stood in horrified fascination of her husband as a beast dressed as a man.

He turned only his head toward her. "This is true?"

"Is it...! Would I make up such a horror?"

Kirke shook his head back and forth taking her point. After a time, the motion became a token of confusion. Kirke concentrated on the figures in the rug and rubbed his scalp red with his fingertips. "What were the words?"

"The words?"

"The words on the wall!"

She murmured, "'KIRKE BEWARE!'"

Kirke's shoulders bowed, his spine bent under tremendous, invisible weight. His clothes appeared to have more life than he. Kirke drew in one long breath and rose gracelessly, tottering, lunging as if he were aboard ship in a storm. He faced Elizabeth. "I had never killed a man till this!"

"Thomas..."

He disregarded her use of his despised saint's-name. "As good as if I chopped him up myself!"

"Please!"

"Please?!" He began to savage the buttons and clasps and ties binding his clothes onto him. With a yet strong arm he flung his coat and neckstock, his waistcoat without care for their flight or what they struck before settling like shot birds onto the vast floor. "Who will they come for next? Stephen? Dire?"

Elizabeth stooped to retrieve the parts of his costume as they struck the stone. "It is you we are concerned for, dear."

Kirke disliked her phrase. "Are 'we'?" He strode to their bed and cast himself down on his back, his half-stripped, vulnerable parts exposed. He came up on one elbow to look at her. "I want the details."

Elizabeth stopped in mid-reach for his shirt.

"Now!"

"Details." She repeated, befuddled.

"What happened to Dario, for God's sake!"

Despising Kirke's ferocity, she walked in memory a second time into the goldsmith's shop. In groans, in shouts, with shaking, the story disgorged from her; the blood-soaked boards, the agonized eyes, the disembodied hands, the neat rows of tools hung above Dario's workbench turned butcher's block, her reach across the pooling red for a pincers big enough to lift pieces of a man hacked apart with a cleaver like a chicken disjointed for soup. Again she crated Dario's parts and the tiny, divided body of her golden monkey, two ghastly piles of flesh and fur, human and close to human. Under her nails she saw the filth of violence; she saw her bloodstained skin stiff with the milk paint. She did not see Kirke nearing her. She screamed at his slight touch.

He said in a quavering voice, "You are a strange woman and wonderful."

She opened her mouth like a fish again and again, speechless.

He petted her arm, his humble touch not nearly what she required. "You did for me...what I would not even do for myself. Haven't you always! But if Kirke Company is to be diced in little pieces and pickled in the Adriatic, I think there's nothing you or anybody else can do about it. Nothing can be done to prevent my death by the Throne falling on me. I can't even care about it! Nor can Stephen. Don't be concerned for yourself either. The Crown won't go after you. I've thought about it from time to time. They want the business. Thank your stars you're not important to them." His relief prompted his smile and a frost of tears.

She straightened and pulled away. "Not important? What of my signing power? The King would have what I have. You may have forgotten. I have land and a son. The land shall be my son's in a very few years. The King might harm Moses to seize his patrimony. Had you thought of that?"

Kirke went hot from shame. He stammered over his error, "What I thought...was...I thought...I could prevent...failure. Mine. The House's. Yours in getting what you really want...."

She doubled over. "You do kill!"

"Well, thank you, wife! You want me to say it! Fine! I've never been able to succeed with you! I married you with that look in your eye and it's stuck there worse than ever!"

Elizabeth knelt among his discarded clothes. "What right had you to try!"

"That's the bargain I made - you'd marry me and I'd make the shadows subside. Who do I think I am? How can I change the course of kings if I cannot even lighten a woman's heart after a dozen years!"

"If you think my heart a lighter challenge than some millstone of a Royal, we truly have trouble!"

Visible panic seized Kirke.

Elizabeth moved toward him. She held up.

Defeated, he turned his back on her.

She called over their gulf, "If anyone killed Dario, I did. I found him. I interested him in our work. I tied him fast with Stephen Poore who mourns him in a different way than we do tonight. I did it! I did it for The Company! What you see in my eyes is - myself."

He sighed and disrobed more deliberately, dropping his hose and shoes and underdrawers in a tidy pile. In his skin, without any material sign tying him to his century or to circumstance he was a man with the white hair and shining eyes of a prophet. "And as far as this infamy at the shop, we both know there should have been no necessity for us to hide gold like guilty children and transport it like a pair of criminals when 'twas fairly gotten. Dario died in a cause." Again, Kirke's alabaster eyes liquefied. "The problem for you and me is *he* was sacrificed in *our* cause!" Kirke wept, his tallness and timbre melting into his helplessness.

She was able to approach him, draw near, her open wounds against his open wounds. She urged him to lie under the down. "If we were in Massachusetts, Viti, we would go to pesuponk. I would build you a fire of sweet alder branches and you would shed your cares in the perfumed steam."

He took her face between his knobby hands. "Then let us talk to Young Poore about arranging it."

What at first eluded Poore was a secure exit from the stage of danger on which The Company stood. Then, as if mocking the close of their year of mourning, the Revenue Act passed Parliament in April of '64. With his scholarly sight Stephen perceived narrow paths of escape.

Stephen Poore looked up from his pencilled worksheet, figures in the right column, on the left, a chart of the movement of goods, their ports of origin to their ports of call. "The government make it look as if they are giving merchants a break on the molasses duties."

Kirke derided, "Three pence!"

"Down from the outrageous six d. per gallon. Yet..." Stephen paused strategically, "the duties will be enforced." Stephen looked up swiftly then looked back to his work.

"Oh?" Kirke smiled a bit at Poore's naïveté after ten years with the Trade. "That would be a novelty. The question is not *will the officials continue to be bribed* but how high must we go to remain in business!" Kirke laughed at the life the Trade led them.

"T., the enforcement will be under the supervision of the British Navy."

"Preposterous!"

"It is a reform of the customs service."

"Who needs one! It's creaking along passably well."

"Well, they wish to end what they term their 'salutary neglect' of the trade laws."

"Fancy words. Meaning what?"

Poore winced, "They want to improve the return by twenty times what they get now."

"Twenty times! This is worse than the Chinese! You're not serious."

"Entirely."

"That's it. Ruin! What can we do in court? That Mr. Beckett is going to get rich on this."

"Oh, T., they have set up a system bypassing the colonial courts."

Elizabeth slipped her stitch. "Bypass the courts? One has to be able to sue for what is just!"

Poore verged on impatience. "A merchant will not be able to sue for illegal seizure of his goods. That's all there is to it."

"What?" Kirke kept saying and pulling his hair.

Elizabeth debated, "If the trade laws were neglected in the past, how can the King now say he will enforce the law by trampling on law itself?"

Poore felt her precision to be out of season. He responded irritably, "The law is what the King says it is. The burden of proof and the cost of the trial will now, by law, rest on the shoulders of the merchant accused...."

Elizabeth covered her needlework with both hands. "Double ruin!"

Kirke's hands hurried them past the legal fine points.

Stephen obliged him, employing a softer tone, "They say charmingly that the whole thing is not to regulate trade but to raise revenue because of Pontiac and the expense his rebellion made the Royal Treasury. And they are watchful of trouble to come."

At this, Elizabeth gripped her hands forgetting her needle. A single drop of blood spotted the cloth. "They blame the Indians for their shortages?"

Kirke snapped, "You above all people ought to know they blame the Indians for everything!" Then to Stephen, "It's those penny-pinching colonials at fault!"

Stephen shied at Kirke's lack of diplomacy. "If the Franklin Plan had gone beyond Albany...if it had passed the Assemblies...."

"No war, no deficit of funds, no victory for the East India Company over the likes o' me."

"Hence the *doubled duties* on reshipped goods between England and the colonies."

"Doubled?" Kirke's face worked as if his pores were performing the arithmetic. "What made the list?"

Stephen began gingerly, "Along with the ordinary stuff we now have iron...."

"No." Kirke would not accept it.

"Whale fins."

"No. No. No!"

"Hides."

"This cannot be!" Kirke stood.

"There is more!"

"I do not want to hear it!"

"Then enough of the list. Let us pass on to the ban on colonial import of rum and Continental wines."

"This is a joke. You are testing me." A smile flitted briefly across Kirke's face.

"The Parliament is perfectly serious about restuffing the Treasury. Hence the higher duties on foreign sugar and English and European silk and linen and, again, wine."

Kirke rubbed his face with his palms. "What've they left me?" Then with a chard of hope, "Which wines?"

"You ask which wines?" Stephen cast about for a way to soften the blow. Without recourse, he muttered, "Madeira."

Kirke's lips went white. "Madeira?"

"Placed at L7 per double hogshead."

Kirke's attention swerved to the bookkeeper within performing a mad mathematics toward their survival.

Stephen tried to bring the old man back with humor. "That tariff should pretty well revolutionize the drinking habits of the scholars at Yale and Harvard not to mention those of their well-heeled parents!"

Kirke growled, "But lowly Port wine imported *through* England...let me guess...."

"A measly ten shillings." Stephen supplied.

"This Revenue Act is a plot against the Trade no matter what George's politicians say!"

"It is short-sighted." Poore allowed.

"Short-sighted! It's looking backward. The same old thing! We merchants have always carried the expense of the Crown's military blunders! But this Revenue Act is robbery! Assault! Assassination!

Tragedy! They are so stupid! Ruin the Trade and what has the Treasury got? Nothing! Good! Let our imbecile King go under with us like the anchor he is. Who needs the Crown's heavy weight breakin' everyone's neck!"

Elizabeth encouraged, "Viti, the new duties might hurt the small merchants but our cargoes are diverse and great in volume."

Kirke turned on her in some disgust. "How long have you had signatory power in the House? You should know we can't make up for it with heavy cargoes for the more we carry the more we pay to the Customs officials under the eye of the British Navy on their knees in front of the ramrod government of Crazy King George the Third!"

Stephen Poore cleared his throat at Kirke's unwarranted crassness.

Elizabeth studied her hands.

Stephen took one of them into his.

Kirke was hardly conscious of his offences. "Oh, they'll be boarding us and ferreting through the crew's mouldy Gorgonzola! We're not merchants anymore - we're no better than hacks in the street lugging peoples' baggage."

Poore explained gently through Kirke's diatribe, "Beth, there are now stricter registration and bonding procedures for ships no matter if they carry nonenumerated cargoes or enumerated ones. There's no getting around it. All the independent merchants are drowning together."

Kirke's hard, bright eyes probed Elizabeth but he addressed Stephen. "How strict is strict enforcement?"

Stephen looked steadily at the head of the House. "They are not to be bribed."

"We are undone!"

Stephen cut in, "All this is nothing to the new Currency Act."

"Haven't you said enough for one evening!" Kirke took it personally.

Poore twinkled and a sly grin turned his rosebud mouth up at the corner. "No paper money that is legal-tender may be issued anywhere in the American colonies."

Kirke thought Stephen's changed mood showed him unequal to the strain. "So! We are there! High priced goods and no money to buy them with. The Americans are ruined along with the Treasury and the Trade!" Then acidly, "Things are looking good for those with gold."

"Never better." From Stephen.

Elizabeth said low, "It will not look good to Massachusetts."

"Nothin' I can do about that!" Kirke said sourly.

Stephen worked to bring them together. "Beth is right. Backs are up against the rich. There have already been protests in the streets. Locke's dispatch tells of rumblings against this forcible penury and especially against backhand taxation without formal representation in London."

"Dire is going to fix this."

Poore worked hard soil. "America and Americans will need loans. The House of Kirke could survive in a new form. We must finally seek a charter and unveil our merchant bank!"

Instead of catching fire with this idea, Kirke puzzled, "How did Locke let this happen?"

Poore crossed glances with Elizabeth in quiet despair over Kirke's abstraction. "Dire says we should all three attend a meeting of the Board of Trade."

"Any particular one?" Kirke scoffed.

"The one he has been clamoring for since returning to London last September. It will mature by June - at latest sometime in July."

"Dire is slipping. The Parliament is out of session in July!"

Stephen watched the chairman narrowly. "The enforcement of the tariff closes you down. What use anymore in dodging George III? My thought is, the closer you are to the King these days, the more inconvenient it is for him to harm you. And if his Treasury is wanting, London should definitely be our next port of call."

Kirke's sharpness shone suddenly like a neglected sword. "By the Devil, that's how we'll get the charter!" He invented as he went along. "We solve the national debt by taking it over, turning it into Company shares and take an interest payment from our bloody murderer of a government in the bargain, if you please! And of course, their lordships'll need cash to float the Crown so we'll lend it to 'em."

"That's a great captial outlay, Viti!" Elizabeth commented.

"Nothing gets past you, Mrs. Kirke," Kirke said unkindly, then tore on, "We'll sell shares in the stock to the public, mark them up fifteen per cent, fifteen all right, Steve? That'll be the secret of our success. The shares must sell above their nominal value. It will be in the King's interest for us to prosper! By God, we'll swab the deck with those Acts!"

Stephen's concentration was unassailable. "I would have you entertain, at last, the elevation."

"What?!"

"A barony, an earldom, something will still be offered, for your interests are too wide, your personal service to two Georges smuggling bars of gold in the Prussian wars very recent, and your suffering silently," Poore's voice broke, "their grizzly...warning a twelvemonth ago, require they offer you quite a bit, a seat in Lords at the least in exchange for your - retirement."

"My what!!?"

"On paper, with the new trade laws, we are bankrupt."

Kirke studied the wood grain of the table but said hoarsely to Elizabeth, "What d'ye think, Countess?"

Elizabeth, stricken silent, finally spoke, "I would have to be the countess of someplace."

"Stephen, you can never speak nonsense in front of Liz for a Puritan has no sense of humor."

Elizabeth slowly rose, pushed her handwork out of the way, and submitted, "Stephen, my land will be Moses' in five years. Would it be a good idea to seek the surrounding land as Viti's?"

Kirke fell quiet.

Stephen spoke in slight confusion. "The only 'surrounding land' I know of belongs to the Massachuseuck."

Elizabeth's face was illumined. "Aye!" She appealed to her friend and her husband, "If we were to persuade...them...." she breathed and breathed, "him, the Sachim...Moses' father...to grant it to The Company, that is, to Viti, and the King made Viti, Earl Bluehill, would we not protect the tribe and my son and ourselves?"

Stephen sat dumbstruck. "Listen to yourself!"

"It is an idea!"

"Listen to yourself!" Stephen rose and backed away from her as if to go somewhere to be sick.

Kirke was alert to an electricity between them.

Short of breath, Stephen leaned against the wall. "I had you dead to rights a year ago! Cannibal!"

She crossed to him persuading and he flailed the air to warn her away.

"What is this?" Kirke strove to understand.

"While you wallowed in that pool of water and I stood by apologizing with Dario's blood piping my jabot, I wondered, wondered how I could have been so wrong about you, so mean-spirited, and now I know I was not wrong!"

"Steph! I do not want Massachuseuck land! I want Viti safe!"

"And that justifies gobbling Wakwa's ground! Well, it gives you a reason to get into the otan!"

Elizabeth petrified at this insult, not having felt so alone, so cold, so betrayed since Wakwa had turned her out. Her voice came as if from an empty vault. "I would not go in. This were not a personal matter."

"*Were* it not?" Poore challenged.

She shouted, "It would be a diplomatic expedient of a high order requiring a treaty between the tribe and the Crown. And you know it!"

"Stop right there!" Kirke asserted his authority, which they ignored totally.

"Stephen Poore," Elizabeth put him at a distance, "if the Massachuseuck grounds pass to Thomas Kirke and his heirs, the land would protect Viti while he lives and the tribe at his passing. Don't you see how perfect it is? It would go back to Indian hands."

"Just like that! Now the French are chased from virtually every corner of North America what judge in his right mind would allow a conveyance to an Indian? Another Nation!"

"Not a conveyance!" She came back. "Viti would make the Massachuseuck his heirs!"

"What earthly advantage would there be to the King giving T. the title then? The Earl of No Place! What tribute could be forthcoming from the Indians after the reading of the Will? The spoils of the French War have not gone the Indians' way - the natives have been rendered utterly expendable. Their day is past. Their sovereignty and their poverty work against them as even such a partisan as yourself must understand!"

Elizabeth could not speak.

Kirke enquired, "What pool of water, Steve?"

"What pool of water, Mrs. Kirke?" Stephen's lip curled.

Elizabeth turned for the stairs. She cut Poore out. "The spinning machine is perfected, Viti." She spoke to him as if he had not offended her minutes before. "Let us go to London to dismantle the factory and move it to Massachusetts. There is no such machine in America. If we manufacture goods there we will never be bothered by tariffs again! Let the East India Company worry about tariffs!"

Kirke looked at her in wonderment. "Remarkable. Every time I think I've struck bottom you pull me up with an idea. A practical, remarkable inspiration. Don't you think she's remarkable, Stephen?"

Stephen Poore looked at Elizabeth sadly. "More than you know!"

Kirke ignored mysteries as he spoke in a voice stubborn but soft. "I'll talk about everything else but the elevation. If they want to knight me they can write it out on a piece of paper which I will throw into the sea on our way to North America with a hold full of weaving machines never to return."

"Predicated on the merchant bank." Poore spoke only to Kirke as Elizabeth paused to hear. "Get them interested in you as a sort of continuing asset."

"I like that. I can stand that."

Elizabeth gained the door. "I shall dine alone tonight."

Stephen tried to mollify her, using her idea as the foundation for a new one of his own. "The engine of this...evasive action...a Massachusetts manufactory, will be Falier."

"Later, Steve."

"Now, T.!""

If Kirke used a stick he would have rapped it against the floor just then. "What is going on?"

"I expect my position here has suddenly become tenuous so I will speak quickly."

"Oh, don't mind Liz! And don't speak foolishness!"

Stephen wove as he went. "You will both leave soon. And I. Falier must make it seem as if you continue in residence here. Have him here daily. Make it social in premise. Make him a fixture in the Asolo. Have him pay your rent through your Venetian bankers long after you sail from London for Massachusetts. Break no lease arrangement. Maintain the few servants you have left. Especially, involve Falier in land speculation."

"What does that have to do with anything? And Sebastiano is a good man. How should I trick him into Western lands when I will not buy them myself!?"

"I suggest a *northeastern* property." Poore seemed to cull a plan from the ceiling above him. He unwisely teased Elizabeth, "In some colony that looks kindly upon dancing. Falier is a great admirer of your wife's."

From her distance, Elizabeth turned slowly, silently away from Stephen. Then she left them without a word.

Late that night, Thomas Kirke made a penitential climb up the steep flight to Elizabeth's tower room. He knocked.

She came to the door and opened it slightly leaving him stranded on the tiny landing.

"I should have defended you down there."

"Leave it alone." Elizabeth remarked coldly.

Kirke swallowed hard. "Would it help if I say I'm sorry for my tongue which proved foul *and* reluctant?" His nervous hand wrapped the edge of the door to keep her from closing it.

Elizabeth stayed quiet, watching Kirke's unstillable fingers, his liver-spotted skin. She saw other hands responding like a friend to each object they touched. She watched the phantom hands loop rope, nestle it in a basket, nudge the basket into its place against a concave wall. She said more gently, "Are you sorry for entertaining small thoughts of me?"

His answer came after delay. "I have a small way of speaking from time to time. I think no small thoughts of you."

Deciding to exact nothing more from him, she opened the door wider.

He shuffled past her in his woolen gown and robe and slippers and shawl, scolding affectionately, "What are you doin' up here?" He squinted in the minor light of her candle. "There's a fire in our bedroom!"

Elizabeth smiled.

"I do not know what is between you and Steve but I know he's sorry too."

"Let him make his own amends, husband. I am not a commodity whose feelings are so efficiently shelved. Nearly twenty years ago I ceased being the medium of exchange for property. I did so by ceasing to live an English life. I am going to write to my son. He lives in easy reach of London. I want to see him if he will grant me some time."

Kirke appeared to have contracted fever. "I told you to do just that the day I met you! But you had some complicated idea how things were supposed to work."

"Things work. No matter how many mistakes we make."

Kirke supported himself, holding to the back of a chair. "I disagree. Everything is the opposite of what it is supposed to be!"

"Not at all, Viti. I told you long ago I would love you but not marry you."

"But we are married! Does that mean you don't love me?"

It interested Kirke that she laughed and took his hand and led him to the warmth.

CHAPTER FORTY-FIVE

April 1764

Moses' scholastic reputation knew an increase. To his credit, he read prodigiously and kept his don alert. But these researches were vacant compared with his delving of his darkest self.

His occasional breach of his pledge to Gordon to abandon loose women vaguely distressed him, although that shaving of his honor could be construed as a flaw, less grimly, as an eradicable smudge on an otherwise pristine record, dissimulation of so low an order was not to be deemed fatal to the life of the soul. Nor did his spasmodic grappling for pleasure upend his self-opinion. Pleasure-seeking was, by his assessment, in the normal range of human aspiration, even pleasure briefly sustained and shallow. Its lack of moral sanction acted like a bellows to a flame. The very commonness of brainless, soulless gratification of wanton urges intrigued him and encouraged his deft dance toward and away from its pursuit.

His steeping in upper caste vice tinctured him so inconsequentially in his mind that he experienced grave shock as he passed a mirror in the loft of a storehouse where he had exchanged the sublime heat, energy, tastes, perfumes, and the dreamless aftersleep of sexual encounter with a girl of whose name he was blissfully unaware. That satyr wearing his clothes in the dark glass took his breath and caused him to touch the wooden wall for support and then flee on foot through the midnight streets of Oxford.

Moses refused the notion that he did not recognize himself because his coition was with a common, working class girl. She was not to be blamed for her birth. The face in the mirror was the trouble. Moses witnessed a vagabond's features shadowed by fear.

He ran, rather, stumbled down the road as if his feet were caught in vines tangled at the roots of weed trees, a forest of junk growth. Moses Bluehill had never known such a woods, the faces of nameless girls etched into the skinny trunks like notches on a lothario's belt. That he had come all this way at such expense to wander like a stray in a labyrinth of inferior stock astounded him. It was not the females he regarded as low, although they were low according to objective standards; it was the trackless wilderness their infinite supply propagated that dismayed him.

To think that at his age his father had slipped alone into the forest to seek himself, his name, and had emerged from the sweet woods as Wakwa, the Black Fox, a sort of fox protected from capture by the brilliant light of day, and that he, Wolf-of-the-Mist, crashed about aimlessly in a swamp he had seeded, a stinking jungle he had brought into existence. What he wanted was the woods of his infancy, the forest on the mountain; the fresh, resin-perfumed heights peopled by clean straight, conifers. He yearned for them, to be one with them, one of them, a lone pine, growing out of the welter of weeds his own debauches had planted. It took a terrible night on streets of stone, his footsteps ringing like a buoy warning ships where they should not go, for him to straighten, to stand at his full height, to resume a graceful stride, to hear the pines' message in the music the wind made in the alleys of Oxford.

Those trees of his childhood whispered he was one of them despite the miles. Dawn was not far off when, at last, he emerged out of the waste wood, a man with no mother but with a backbone. He felt, knew, had faith, was resolved, that his future would be ruled by the soul he shared with the pine. In this cleanly way he snatched his character from the maw of triviality. He would not have to say his soul's name aloud: it was of great import that he knew in his heart he was Cowaw, the Pine.

It was very little trouble to a young man of Moses' birth to gain quiet entrée to his Quad. His rooms were another matter. He turned his key in the noisy latch, closed but did not relock the door avoiding further racket. Having averted any unpleasantness related to his truancy, his sense of elation blossomed. Roused to a happiness he had never known before, he was not content to slide into the darkness of sleep from the darkness outside. He added wood to the embers in the fireplace and produced a blaze that made the room flare like mid-day. He sustained the effect by lighting the whale oil lamps and the chandelier. Uplifted by his toil away from the fearful image in the mirror, he basked in the brightness and beauty of his salon.

He took time to see the murals, to give them their due – the sea, the ship, the pastures, the trees. The graphic biography, delicately rendered, imparted a sense of security so vast that it enabled him to see as a sanctuary the grotesque valley he had just vacated. He came to regard his valley of vice as his proving ground, as sacred a labyrinth as any that received other boys of his tribe and emitted them as men. Gradually, in the fire's glow he pulled away from his wilderness. Ifan's brushwork surrounded him in beauty. The mere sight of what had been created by imagination, ability, and energy was his refreshment. He needed no liquor to clarify his mind about what honest labor and, if it need be said, money, could achieve. Without the latter, his foster mother, Tame Deer, painted wondrous hangings for the sachimmacommock but Wadham's fetid walls had required the engine of civilization, cold cash, and had benefitted by it. What might have been a dilemma crystallized; Moses determined to live not to lust. On that impulse, he made for his room. He drew open a drawer of his nightstand and retrieved the doeskin pouch from Qunneke that Locke had delivered to him. He mixed a portion of the powdered herbs with water from his pitcher and drained his goblet. Feeling fortified against disease, filled with positive and pleasant thoughts about himself, he walked back to the fire. He added wood and worked the poker to seat it. Some chunks, glowing red from inside, collapsed into a cascade of sparks. Fascinated as a wild thing in front of the flames, a commotion down the hall became confused with the spitting, tumbling wood and the screech of the iron crib as he pushed it farther back to take best advantage of the draw.

Moses rose out of his crouch. The door burst open. A fury of dark fur filled the space. Chain dragged the reed rug, caught a table, porcelain crashed, wild laughter sprang, a whistle sounded, shouting volleyed, two arms great with stinking hair embraced him.

Horace Beckett appeared in his nightrail. "For God's sake, Hill!" Then, "My God!" Ho ducked back into his room.

The doorway was quickly clogged with dumfounded adolescents and the Warden who was pointlessly brandishing a paddle.

Moses wedged his left arm between his throat and a bristling head and fangs. He strained away shaking, caught off-guard. The shaggy black monster steadied him, centrifugal force binding them as they slowly spun. Moses struggled to keep his feet, to stay tall, to avoid the horror of slipping into the posture of victim to a bear. In the crush of those powerful, dark limbs Moses' brain flashed the horror story of his father's young mother cut from life by a bear making a meal of her delicate face. Moses' right arm was pinned to his side and the limitation threw before him another bit of family history, the transformation of his father's guard into his would-be assassin when White Cat was crippled by a bear in a hunt. Seconds only passed in terrifying memories. The rabid bear bent forward, bending Moses backward as if his spine were the stem of a tulip. Moses did not hear himself scream. Screams from the young men at the door and the Warden blended with his screaming and his straining against the might of the bear.

Ho reappeared in his doorway with a gun and took aim.

"Beckett! Don't! Christ! Don't!"

Beckett's pistol was French; one his father had brought back from Paris. It was accurate of aim, but not Germanically accurate. Long hours alone in Cambridgeshire learning the gun's degrees of variance with his target had made the difficult shot possible – not sure - but possible.

The bear's head was butted against Moses' head. Shooting him from behind into the cranium was out of consideration. Into the spine, as bad. The bear's stiff muzzle prodding Moses' chin upward to find the jugular vein, much nervous movement in a small space, left Ho Beckett only a problematic shot to the temple – a moving bull's eye protected by fur. He could not take the shot from too close or risk Moses' sight, his face, his upper spine. Ho could not trust the gun from too far. A near miss could cause horrifying consequences. Horace Beckett took aim barraged by a chorus of "No! He's got to! Oh, Moses! Oh, Christ!"

A glint of platinum and a spit of flame were all Moses saw before the bear buckled on top of him. His chest seemed to tear apart. His crushed lungs wheezed air thick with animal stench and blood stench. The crowd at the open door rushed in to work the massive animal off Moses' supine body. They tugged at silk covered sticks.

Moses' mind closed on it like a hungry carp's on a hook. Legs. The sticks were his legs.

They pulled him from under the mangy body, his legs at right angles to his hips, like a girl sitting sidesaddle.

Moses reached for Ho's face. Moses clung.

"Thank God!" Marthem.

Moses breathed. He could not piece together what had happened. Behind Beckett lay a bear. The Warden was there, rasping, "You seem to attract calamity!" Club members were clapping their hands and saluting Beckett with jiggers of gin. Supported by Marthem and Beckett, Moses reached the glass doors behind which spread the dawn. Moses wolfed fresh air, surrounded it with his teeth, pushed it down his trachea with his tongue. Moses looked only at Ho. He croaked out, "Wetomp! Wosketomp! Wosketomp!"

"Is that his language?" Marthem's nightrail was soiled, the silk smeared with the bear's blood and excrement.

Ho looked only at Moses. "He's saying I am his dearest friend. He's saying I am valiant." Ho said to Moses. "I just shot it, Hill."

Moses finally stood free of help and limped toward the carcass. He exhaled raggedly, all his ribs bent to breaking, his throat sore. "Just shot it!" Then for a long time he shuddered.

The raw voices of young men, the agitated voice of the Warden and a gathering pool of dons, some muted laughter, the silence of the corpse, all impressed themselves on Moses' brain. If a small bird or a bat lost its way and flew about the higher reaches of a room what mayhem usually followed! A bear? A tall, heavy, mangy, hungry, abused and angry bear crushing one's bones? Was he mad? Had this happened? It began to occur to him that the bear was real. That the animal was not from nowhere but from somewhere and had been goaded by someone to attack him made Moses very cold. Was this a joke gone wrong? Should he be howling with laughter? Was the infringement on his peace of mind Divine retribution for his facile escape from the wild wood? No matter. Without Horace Beckett, murder or manslaughter not reckless endangerment might be the matter for the coroner and the constable.

Horace came to see his kill.

Moses fell to his knees and touched the beast. Big as a dune at Eastham, petrified with death, his small, open eyes retained their frantic regard.

Gordon hissed darkly, "What villain...?"

Moses looked at the dead bear oozing blood and fecal matter, fouling the salon floor, ruining the reed rugs. "Gord. Bring me my knife."

Gordon knew well where he could find the obsidian.

A constable joined the Warden. There was much pointing down the hall and back. *It might be a gypsy's bear. If Beckett had not had the courage to kill it we could have lost to this prank our most promising scholar. Savage hazing. Tantamount to murder. Find the criminal who did this thing! This wicked, wicked thing!*

Sweating, Moses began to skin the bear. His agility with the obsidian knife silenced all the assembled witnesses. He kept the head attached to the body pelt with refined application of the blade. Now it was his hallmates who trembled.

CHAPTER FORTY-SIX

April 1764

Dire Locke fumed. "You mock us all."

Moses barked, "*I* was mocked!"

Two brawny boys apprenticed to The Company lifted the raw, creeping bearskin out of the boardroom on a canvas stretcher. The carpet gave testimony to the filth of the bundle Moses had dropped on the floor.

"If you think your diary is not naked and open in my ledger - think again."

Moses' eyes ignited.

Locke was not to be intimidated by the outrage of an adolescent no matter his pedigree.

The factor sat close, leaned in, and rammed his message home. "Your scholastic success in the last quarter term is no blind for your wantonness, your wastefulness, your wiliness."

Moses spun out of his chair. "No one knows my scholastic record...."

"Your record is being closely followed. By me."

"I told no one!"

Locke shrugged away such a middleman's step as superfluous.

"And catting about is finished. I've given that up. You should know that before you waste your time on lecturing me."

"I see. At the age of sixteen years and seven months you have cleared your slate?"

"I have and because of a conviction firmly taken shall have a decent social life."

"You have one purpose in being here! To learn the law."

Moses' chin, cut like Elizabeth's, rose like hers in defiance. "My high scores should testify to my success at that."

"They do anything but, because they are coupled with hair-brained schemes to make money by spending money so you can debauch yourself and reduce your considerable mental powers to jelly!"

Moses backed up. His hands fenced his heart from Locke. "I am unwilling to be a burden to my father." Moses paused meaningfully. "Or to anybody."

"But you shall be. It does not matter your intent. Your actions predispose you to utter failure."

Moses was overcome by this curse. Only pride kept him standing against the tidal wave of Locke's animus.

Dire echoed the opening salvo of many a treaty between white and red. "I will say this once, the custom of your father's People. If you continue to use your intellect to best your superiors, to attract attention to your eccentric abilities, which one might ascribe to errant imagination and precocity in business, you will draw more than rabid bears to your gambling room. There will come petty duels over money, over women, over nonsense! You will be forced to break little rules, engage in deceit, until your reputation is so tarnished that no amount of praise from learned men will buff up your chances to do even infinitesimal good for your folk!"

"Mr. Locke. Are you ill?" Moses asked with some concern and sat.

Dire Locke smiled. "You have talent!" His flash of good humor cooled fast and froze. "You bear a frightening resemblance to an Indian called Weeping Heart, the alcoholic son of Waban."

"There is not the least resemblance!"

"Who by his inflated idea of his own importance and the power of money to sway events, tore your father and mother apart!"

Moses started. "If my father knew you compare me to that degenerate traitor, he would never deal with you again!"

Locke stood up and turned away to light a tobacco pipe. "Smoke?"

Moses seethed, "Perhaps another time!"

"Perhaps you are right." Locke eyed his young opponent. "The analogy fails because Weeping Heart, Wuttah Mauo, in the language you have no doubt conveniently folded away, was a scoundrel of a colossal proportion. You, on the other hand, are developing into a small-time cheat settling for a fashionable dissimulation, studying the law remarkably well to please others so that you can follow unmolested a predictable undergraduate carnality!"

Moses had no cover from the searing light Locke cast over his doings. "That side of things is done as I said."

Locke drew on his pipe and stood near Moses' left side, his heart's side. "Hear me, Wolf-of-the-mist He-hopes! To study the law is to draw upon yourself a sacred mantle. The more you know of it the less you may dodge it and all its fine points. A man of law must radiate uprightness or he will fail his trust and not inspire the same. You are being groomed as a statesman not a pettifogger or a syndicator of a gambling empire."

Raked like old coals, Moses rasped, "I am only trying to raise money. We give half away. Ask the Warden!"

"I know."

"How can you know?!"

"Oh, come! It is my business to know. You are my charge."

At this Moses stood and faced Locke squarely. "I am in the care of the Worths."

"They are my charges too."

Moses angered. "You spy on everybody!"

"True. But there is no honor or benefit in it unless good comes from my observations." Locke sat quite sociably and offered Moses his pipe.

Moses knew the ritual. Homesick at the gesture, pained at receiving it from a man who harbored such harsh thoughts of him, he balked. "I will smoke with you if you will take back that insult likening me to my father's despicable cousin."

Locke tapped the pipe's mouthpiece. "You are at a crossroads, young man. It is up to you to change my mind about the path you are traversing."

"Has my father written to you?"

Locke raised his brows, accusing subtly, "*We* correspond."

Moses hung his head. "With study there is so little time...."

"Tut. There is time for everything else. I could understand if you did not love him...."

"Has he complained?"

Locke hooted at an idea incredible.

"Dire, if you would only come to see what we have done to the rooms. How we have made a home of it. How much camaraderie comes of the gaming. I allow no faro! It would ruin the richest of them. We play whist for God's sake! We have added chess!"

"Moses...."

Moses hunched and looked up at Dire, his eyes dulled by impending submission. "You want me to close it down."

"I want you to take this pipe and consider keeping your parlour open."

"What!!!"

Locke smiled. He moved in for the kill. "I favor your turning your gross to charity. One hundred per cent."

Moses fumbled the pipe. "I shall never get out of debt. Never pay...the House."

"There is a solution to that. I will visit your splendid quarters and I will visit Warden Wilkes. I will explain to him that the House of Kirke has underwritten your repairs and will make an endowment to fix the rest of the college before it falls down."

Moses stopped the pipe on the way to his lips. "Money swaying events?"

Locke sparkled at being quoted. "Money can purchase anything but honor. And King George and all of his horses and all of his men have got it in for the House of Kirke for the King never has got any money, and honor is his from his first breath out of the womb no matter how blandly he craps upon it. It strikes me as just the time to spread The Company money around - so His Majesty will have less to steal – nothing, if I manage things aright."

Moses stopped over Locke's insinuation of a conspiracy against the Throne. Ever so cautiously he queried, "What do you want from me?"

"Nothing. As your father once said when I asked him the same question. And as he did, I now propose a trade - I shall balance my books by wiping out your monetary debt - you shall balance yours by growing up. That means approaching your life with thought and thought for others."

"I do...!" Moses began to argue.

"Thought for others *first*."

Grim and puzzled, Moses' gaze settled on the bowl of the pipe and the sweet smoke emanating from its well. In that hole, dark with the dry tobacco leaves, he felt at home. He drew deeply on the stem.

Locke sighed his gladness because he was aware how binding the wreaths of smoke were to Moses' folk. He produced two folded letters, their seals already breached. "One letter is from your father. The other is from your mother."

"Qunneke?!"

"Elizabeth."

Moses froze. "Has it to do with the Trade?"

Locke purred appreciation for Moses' sabre tooth. "No, my dear boy, Elizabeth's letter to me courteously describes the one she has written and enclosed for you. She would like to see you. What do you say?" Locke produced it.

Elizabeth's letter, written on large paper of Florentine manufacture, lay seal up on the table. The wax lozenge of pine green on the aqua paper pressed of tender fibres, tested Moses' willpower. For some minutes, he resisted the letter's beauty successfully.

Locke watched Moses' struggle.

Then like a slave to drink or any other opiate, Moses ran his fingertips lightly around the seal. Its surface ornamented with bosses was fused to the silken paper like a nipple to a breast. Recognition of it caused Moses to pull his hand back.

Locke shifted in his chair. "She and...her...she and V.T. Kirke will come to London sooner rather than later if you cannot get away to Venice for a remeeting."

Moses paid attention to Locke's voice. His tone was flat, careful, non-persuasive. It was business-like. Moses heard Locke accomplishing just another piece of business in a long business day.

Locke nudged, "I have no idea how Elizabeth expressed herself to you. As I said, her letter to me was a polite rendition of her general notion." Locke looked at Moses looking at him. Uncomfortable with being so pinioned he snapped, "Won't you open her note?"

Moses quelled a small smile. "You should study the law, Mr. Locke. You are a natural advocate. As a matter of fact, you are everybody's advocate!"

Locke gave him the Welsh jaw. "What d'you mean by that!"

"I say it with respect! You put forward the interests of many. You did so for me with Mr. Michael Beckett."

Locke stood. His sallow face flirted with color.

"But I flatter myself, sir, I am not so open as Michael Beckett to your...persuasions." Here, Moses stood, the table the bar. "I will also respect the bargain I made with you sealed with smoke. Nevertheless, that you backed me against a wall to cram this other thing down my throat distresses me!"

"You have it wrong!"

"I have had sixteen years of this shadow-mother!" Moses pointed mercilessly to the pretty letter-paper. "Do you think I am so shallow that in five minutes and for the price of some paint and sticks of furniture I swallow this momentous thing as if it were nothing! As if it were candy!" Moses stalked out and slammed the door.

Locke stood wringing his hands over the accusation so misguided but with logic so clear. Not looking where he was going in his upset, he moved toward the door.

Moses swung out of the settee in the hall where he had thrown himself to sulk and brashly turned back toward Locke's consulting room.

They crashed into one another in the doorway.

Locke seized Moses' wrists. "It was not like that. You perceive it wrong. One has nothing to do with the other!"

"I know!" Moses' voice choked.

As if he were deaf, Locke persisted, "You surprised me here today. I had no subtle plan to hoodwink you."

"I see that."

"I intended to seek the Worths' opinion to introduce the topic to you gently."

"I believe you!"

"It is true I want you to go to her. To meet her! Anywhere. Can you sympathize with her sacrifices? With her pangs? Now you are a man can you not perceive the shadows which stalk her night and day?"

"You surprise me, sir."

"How so?"

Moses grasped Locke's wrists. "That you have...."

"A heart?" Locke's face twisted. His hard blue eyes softened into rotten ice.

Moses did break. He abandoned his hold on Locke and turned away, stiff and straight as if crucified on a cross of shame. "I have been wrong about so much for so long."

Locke blotted his glowing face with his handkerchief. "Open the letter then?"

Moses bent, his fists against his forehead. He rasped, "Place the letter in your vault. You must have a vault for valuable things. Put it there!"

Locke pressed against the table's edge.

Moses said hoarsely, "I admit. I am so curious to see her! I want to touch...! Where was her letter in September? I've been here for half a year!"

"Where was yours to her? Let it go! She says she wants to see you!"

"Why now? My school record recommends me to her? She wants to get rid of money to save her husband's neck? Her own? It makes me so happy to be of some use at this late date!"

Locke snatched the letter off the table and tucked it safely in his pocket. His face was a horrified mask.

"I have thought long and hard about what I would do about seeing her."

"And this is the result of those ruminations?" Viper-dry, Locke struck.

"I wish I had never been born! This famous mother dripping with her sacrifices and her shadows and her yearnings threw the same yoke over me as her father did to her! She buried me under her father's ground as deep as if I were dead! Do you know how it hurt, how it hurts to be what I am? The cause of so much suffering? So many people's pain? She lowered me down with a load of riches and destroyed in the same motion her life as a woman! Her marriage to my father - and I do not doubt the one to poor Kirke as well!"

Locke glanced at his pocket watch there purposely being no clock on display in the room. "On this you stand?"

Moses snarled, "From my first breath like the King!"

"What a shame all the toil over you has resulted in this - self-pitying...."

"I am not! I tell you the truth! No one else will! I have a father and apparently a mother." Moses pointed to Locke's dress coat where the letter was harbored. "They should come together if they are so enamored of one another and not wait for the world or for me to do their dirty work for them. Maybe then I'll write to my father! Maybe then I'll pay court to this woman of unearthly self-control - this Puritan!"

Locke took lessons from this last outburst. "I think you are right. The time is not yet. I will do as you suggest. Keep Elizabeth's letter for you. Should I not be here and you want it, my assistant will be only too glad to put it in your hands. Now, shall we ride to Oxford together?" Locke rang a bell for his subaltern.

Moses turned from the sight of Dire Locke experiencing a rare defeat. Yet he looked over his shoulder to get a glimpse of the letter as Locke handed it away.

CHAPTER FORTY-SEVEN

May 1764

The myth of May was fulfilled. Air, flowers, sunlight, moon, were felt in the arc traced from Cambridgeshire through Oxfordshire and Berkshire to Sussex.

Michael Beckett's Thoroughbreds had raced well, winning or placing, enabling him, their owner, their author, to dispatch a healthy payment to Locke against the principal in his large Kirke Company loan and to pack his trunks for a holiday in the Turn district of Adderbourne, to wit, Summerset, the ancestral seat of William, the seventh Marquis of Leed.

Hopes sang in his ears like newborn birds. Two little flies, colorful, benign insects only, buzzed past, causing him minimal annoyance: one, his coach would sweep through the lower tip of Oxfordshire since he wanted to avoid London, and two, Hanna and Gilbert Worth had sailed for Italy and would not attend the auspicious Mothering Sunday sortie. Yet, Beckett rolled along west to southwest with smiles pulling at the corners of his mouth. He did not know or care why.

Horace and Moses had been largely silent with one another since Moses had set aside Elizabeth's invitation. They reclaimed some ease under May's influence. Like Michael, they collected shirts and knee breeches and neckcloths with the attentiveness of gardeners choosing palace bouquets. Like he had, they brushed aside the imperfections of their circumstances to catch a glimpse of the promises afloat in the atmosphere.

Lord Worth left the sea and Heathersley for a more protected shire, Berkshire, slightly to inland and north, where, in his view, good people were clustering like roses.

Locke was happy not to be part of the festivities. Although socially beneath this set, he was often a guest in the great houses where entertainment was had, information exchanged, mercantile activity stimulated, and loans produced. Locke, in solitude, took May as it came to sooty London content that Moses would suffer a forcible expansion of soul by attending such an extravaganza as Mothering Sunday. Uninterrupted by social obligation, Dire tabulated Beckett's payment in the ledger and even penned a sunny note to the solicitor advising him in future to retain his capital against events. Even May did not fool the factor into losing Beckett as an asset of The Company. Finally, astounded by the talent of his fellow-Welshman, Ifan William, after visiting Wadham College, Locke took Ifan on during holidays as an apprentice in the map-room. This corporate adoption freed William from a servitor's low status and long hours, paid some of his college bills, and began his slow insinuation into the Trade. Their contract also provided Locke another pair of eyes and ears close to Moses.

Moses looked to Horace Beckett across the coach seat. "A day as beautiful as this makes it difficult to decide. I think of going home, Ho. Not studying anymore, never taking a degree."

Ho punched Moses' arm. "Leaving would be a cruelty all 'round. A day like this makes the decision for you."

Moses gazed briefly at the pastel scene skimming past his window. "If it weren't for you, I'd tell Locke today to find me a corner on one of his ships going home."

Ho kept silence despite the flattery of Moses' statement. He thought many things behind the veil he had hung between them since meeting Augusta, daughter of the Marquess William Brite of Leed.

"I know you can't understand my constantly saying no to Mrs. Kirke's overtures."

"That's your business. She's *your* mother."

Shying from the idea of her existence, Moses justified, "I simply can't just go have *tea* in Venice with a woman I don't know and whom my father won't talk to. I wish you could see that. I hate it when you're angry with me."

"I'm not angry."

"You've been quiet."

Ho pulled himself from his reverie. "I've been thinking."

Moses changed position in his seat, interested. He studied Ho's candid face.

Ho edged his shoulders out the window to check their horses trotting tethered to the coach. Unwillingly, he slipped back down, his blond hair tangled above the silk bag covering the tip of his queue. "We should get out of here and ride. It's taking us an age to get there. Our trunks can follow."

Moses made a gesture with his hands sorting through this nonessential wish.

Ho's chin stiffened. He stated, "Hill. I'm unsuited to your kind of study. Doesn't mean the least to me - the poetry, the rhetoric, the Classics, reading law. Any of it. Even Blackstone. I've had enough of the law with Father. I don't need any more of it!"

Moses' sat erect. "What are you telling me?"

"I like to ride and shoot. I like to read of the heroes of history."

Moses evaluated Ho's prominent features; the diamond blue eyes, square jaw. "You've done that." Then he looked into his friend. "It's time to do other things."

"I want to do "*big* things."

"What is bigger than to maintain and refine a great code of law?"

"I'm thinking of going into the military service."

"Ho...!" Moses gasped.

"I'm of an age!"

"You're out of your mind. Military service is not simply strutting around in a red coat and white breeches! You've got to do someone's bidding all the time. You cannot influence the outcome of history that you like so much except by killing piles of other men!"

Ho paused then bore on, "You of all people ought to agree with me that there are cases when one must defend one's honor, the honor of one's nation!"

Moses' voice climbed very high, "They'll send you to India! I'll never see you again!"

Ho smiled briefly at this wild cry of affection. "I will do it only if I can be commissioned to America."

Moses paled, horrified. "To do what?"

Ho refused to let his glance fall before Moses' outrage. "The permanent garrison is quartered mainly in the City of New York. They don't kill Indians there."

Moses shook his head. "They do what they are told."

Horace Beckett sighed, "I've had a belly full of that!"

"Then it's a good thing you'll be a general right off!"

Ho's voice, deep and clear with honesty, covered Moses' objections. "I would fulfill a year's commission. Brilliantly! Then - having served the Crown, my father, and my reputation - I would be free...." His voice trailed off.

"Desert?!" Moses whispered.

"Idiot! Resign. I've been planning this since...."

"Would it make a difference to you if I wrote to my...to... Elizabeth Kirke? Would that make you like me better? Make it easier to stay?"

Ho rapped on the roof to stop the coach. "I've got to get out of here. Into the air!"

"Dammit, Ho! I've done nothing but study the last two months, I've taken up music again. I've stayed away from girls like a monk - all for this day! We're supposed to meet Gordon's sister together!"

With near sadness, Ho gave his secret up. "I met her. That once when you went to the City to Locke. Just the sight of her has changed my life. I've got to distinguish myself. Quickly. Will you help me talk to Father?"

Moses sat stunned as the coach slowed and teetered to a stop. "Well! You can't really be free from lawyers can you?"

They felt better out of the rattling box and on horseback. They raced one another through the Turn district to the Brites' great manor, Summerset. Sighting the immense manor house they pulled up, their hearts beating fast from more than exercise.

Moses asked out of breath, "Tell me. If your parents had been separated against their wills, and your father whom you didn't even remember wrote you after nearly twenty years out of the blue sky and asked to see you, would you do it? Drop everything to meet him?"

"Probably not."

They walked their mounts side-by-side up the tree-lined allé, little leaves spinning out of bud in a haze of green.

Ho broke their unanimity when he added, "Then again, we both know what Father is."

Gordon surprised them in the middle of the admittance ritual. He looked out of character half-dressed in linen breeches, riding boots and a plain shirt open at the neck and no cravat, waistcoat, or coat. He cut off the butler's formulaic dronings. "The Marquess is expecting you!" Gordon led the way through a small salon, then down a corridor that broke open into a dark, polished library glowering at a lawn undulating to the horizon line.

Moses bayed softly and said, "It looks like America!"

Near the drapery of the immense window, a dark figure crowned by an old-fashioned brown wig moved, turned, stood against the light. "I take that as a compliment from a sachim's son."

"Oh, Father!" Gordon squirmed.

Moses could not see anything in the Marquess' comment but deference.

Disregarding his son, Leed continued, "The lawn's that way because I use it for golf." With the exception of his jocular eyes, he looked like Gordon with forty more years on him. He came forward, although his station could have saved him the steps. Those witty eyes performed instantaneous surgery on Moses, peeling and slicing, unmasking.

The introduction was made.

Moses took a breath before responding to Leed's greeting but his speech was cut off by the Marquess.

"I have a daughter. Lady Augusta Brite. She is a problem. Won't touch the game. Always in the tower with a book or up to her elbows in peat moss and roses by the ha-ha."

Gordon interpreted for Moses, "That's a ditch."

The Marquess sighed mightily.

Moses remained silent, divining what this eccentric bend in the normal course of thought could mean.

Gordon and Ho watched the spectacle.

"I like it," Lord Leed snapped, "that you are not a talker. Your eyes reveal you as extremely well read."

Moses found no reason to interrupt.

"I am fascinated by what my son tells me about you. And that young man," Leed's dark-coated arm rose and indicated Ho, "has a reverence for your father bordering on worship."

Moses looked slightly right to Ho with a pleased expression.

"Might I ask, Wolf, I like that, may I call you Wolf instead of the other name? Can you tell me - is your father an educated man?"

Moses had been granted a good amount of time to collect himself. Not altering his straight pose, he responded, "With respect, Lord Leed...my father is one who educates."

"Wonderfully said! He is then educated!" Leed insisted.

"If by that you mean, is he well-read, I can say, yes."

"Astounding. You've a good voice, by the 'bye. I can't get the picture of a savage warrior-prince who wins medals for valor in another king's wars pulling up to the fire with his pipe and his setter for a good read!"

Gordon sank into a chair mortified. Ho stayed sharply alert.

Moses took courage from forced memory of Wakwa. Mildly wickedly, he explained, "My father has read but three books, sir."

"I knew it! Which?"

"The Eliot Bible, the tragedies of Shakespeare, and the Republic of Plato."

Leed's eyes, varnished with laughter, showed him handsome about laughing at himself. "I have read many more books than that, Mr. Wolf Bluehill, but none that did me any more good!"

The topic finished, Moses' joints went to jelly.

Gordon attempted blatantly to leave. "Papa, perhaps we should introduce Mr. Bluehill to Mother?"

Lord Leed shrugged and turned away. He turned back. "Do you play golf, Mr. Bluehill?"

I play the flute!" Moses' answer came too quickly, too sharply. He added, "Unfortunately."

"Then do you play the flute badly?"

"No, Your Lordship! Adequately."

"Alak! That is how I play golf. You may come to use my library at any time you wish, Wolf. *If* you wish!"

The acres of bookshelves mounting to the ceiling, crammed with exquisite oddities alongside essential collections, raised saliva in Moses' mouth.

The young men took their leave.

The Marquess called after them. "Grand of you to join us for Mothering Sunday when I'm told your own mother's only in Italy. We would have had her here, dear boy, if we'd known in time!"

Gordon appeared faint. Ho set his hand on the hilt of his sword. Moses hesitated at the door, toying with the idea of pretending he had not heard.

Moses turned back. "Mother's Day is not known in America, Lord Leed."

Marthem paused to speak. Instead he sat at a table and lost himself in a book.

~M~

"Mothering Sunday," The Marchioness of Leed accepted Moses' arm as they walked, "goes straight back to Rome. The Matronalia, you know. Those golden days of golden jewelry, tinted glass, and clothes that did not bind but fluttered in the breeze...."

Moses slowed and smiled at the grass daring to interrupt. "Such clothes as you describe, Lady Leed, remind me of my People's clothes...."

The Marchioness corrected gently, "Your father's People, I suppose you mean."

"Yes, I do, Lady Leed."

Her steps slowed even more. "The Roman mother in her flowing toga would, once a year in May, before it got too hot you see, would abase herself, I suppose you could say, and would bake a large, flat, round, rich cake for her household, a *simila cake* with twelve sweet balls set upon it, we call it a Shrewsbury simnel using the same twelve marzipan balls, well not precisely the same, you understand..."

"*Simila balls*, Mother?" Gordon sassed her.

The Marchioness fluttered her lashes at her son and forged on, "She would place, artistically round the border of the cake, twelve perfect balls in respect to the Olympian gods, I would guess, for after all the day was dedicated to Juno, the protectress of the home." Wistfully, Catherine added, "The Roman lady would receive presents from her husband..." again she sighed, "a new toga perhaps, and baubles of gold and precious stones...."

"You hint of this every May, Mother, but when I offer you a toga...."

With severe eye Catherine bore on, "She would cook many other fine things as well, I imagine, for you cannot give people a feast of cake alone, and most important, she would give her slaves a day of rest!"

Moses looked swiftly her way and then back to the green, green lawn. "Good of her, Your Ladyship."

Gordon opined, "Imagine the prodigious work the slaves had beforehand, swabbing the marble, shining the pots, and generally busting their...necks...to earn an afternoon off."

"Oh, Gord!" His mother scolded. "You've ruined it! They would have done that anyway. The important thing is, this great lady in her villa with the clean marble floors and shining copper pots nurtured her whole household! Her slaves, their children, her family and their children! They all mixed as equals on that one day!"

Gordon rolled his eyes. "Classical Whiggery!"

Horace and Moses listened intently.

"That one gracious day that let the mistress and the servant feel fully human. Complaisant together. They must have looked forward to that day all year long!"

Gordon teased, "On Sunday, then, dearest Mum, shall we mix as equals with the servants?"

"Dearheart! We don't hold slaves!"

They laughed hard. The incongruity flooded them until like wine it dwindled and left them quieted and thinking.

Moses dressed early for dinner. He slipped away from Ho's pacing and practicing for his reintroduction to Gordon's sister.

Viewed from the house, Moses, in lavender gray, was hardly visible as he strolled across the fairway in the twilight. He felt so much like his old, hungry, burning, sad self in this perfected place of pruned foliage that he searched for something wild. An alabaster statue pointed toward a hedge. He followed the stone finger's directive and walked gingerly along the hedge's base, as wide where it met the velvet grass as if it were the gown of a giantess.

Another sort of world greeted him on the hedge's inner side - long grass, dense trees, roses in heavy bud on tall, old bushes, green archways leading to spaces etched silver by water slipping past in its channel.

A human form mounted into one of the grottoes, took its middle, a dark blue gown flying back on the night breeze.

Moses was startled by the figure's vivacity and delicacy of stride. No ghost, the very alive female took the long grass like a faun.

One slight sound - an intake of breath at sight of him - told of her self-command.

The fabric and color of their clothes blended with the coming night. They saw only each other's face and each other's eyes.

Moses bowed his head. Only his head. He kept it low. He always avoided European gallantry like a plague. He gave respect.

Her voice, water clear, rippled a little but only a little, and brought his eyes back to hers. "I am Lady Augusta Brite."

"I am Wolf-of-the-mist He-hopes."

"Ahh!" She smiled. Her smile spread to her skin, her nerves, her bones. Her deep blue dress blew back and its gleam differentiated it from the soft night.

Moses came forward then and offered her his arm. "The footing on the lawn is not easy in your shoes."

Polite form distressed the intensity of the meeting. Each wanted only to sit or lie on the shadowed grass wrapped about the other.

Moses escorted her as far as the terrace outside Leed's library. The doors were open. She left him there for comb and brush. Moses lagged behind, watching the emerald fairway inked black by night. A warm gust caused a snow of petals to rise all around him, to mount into the firmament as if they would be stars. While they floated back to earth, he contemplated the story of his father's discovering Elizabeth in a wood, their silence marked by a few polite phrases.

He trembled as if from cold and went up to his room to collect Ho.

CHAPTER FORTY-EIGHT

May 1764

Israel Stirling sat in his big kitchen at the Meetinghouse Hospital. His wife, Priscilla, could be found there much of the day at all seasons of the year.

The kitchen made an excellent observatory, with windows spanning the west and north walls showing any traffic on the meadow from or to Worth Farm. The room was also a conservatory. Growing out of clay pots and tinware, out of bowls of colored glass (a sumptuosity in the minds of the low-bred of the village) was an herbal pharmacopoeia producing masses of silvery leaves of all shapes. Often throughout the year lavender flowers or white or pink or yellow sprang into blossom out of these diverse containers decorating the plain, clean room as if with calico.

One day in early May, with sweet air moving through the front hall into the kitchen and out to the meadow, Israel sat at the stout wooden table which Matthew had painted cream. The freedman's brush had continued over the walls and the cupboards and the floor making it look like the milk bucket had toppled over spilling its rich contents evenly over everything. The chairs were a pale green.

The kitchen, a retreat as sustaining as one of Priscilla's custards, may as well have been a fetid alley in a faraway city that day. Israel struck his fist against the enameled tabletop, jolting Priscilla from her polishing of the copper sink.

"I should have continued in Divinity school. Not turned to doctoring. Should have turned to music and gone back to Europe. Aye, that is what I ought t' have done."

"Israel?" She came to him, still fair-haired, unwithered, drying a blue dish with a blue cloth.

The Younger-Doctor, as the Sweetwood villagers still called Israel regardless of the elder Stirling's death, stared at the herb pots and muttered, "Plantain and rose-water, honey and crushed roses, they smell nice, then we have poultices of red onions...they don't smell nice. Try four grains of arsenic in a pint of water against so-called canker...and that's for the breast and no good to the ovaries as far as anyone can tell!"

Priscilla sat with him. She took his hands and would not let him pull them away to hide his face. "Is it Tame Deer?"

"I am stumped! I know not what to do for her."

"The cures help some."

"The field madder gives her strength. But grasses and cold water make no impression on the tumors at this stage, the weight of them, the pain. I could just as well blow my trumpet and expect her cancer to go away." Israel freed himself and went to sulk in the doorway.

Priscilla braved his mood. "She did not tell you till so late."

"Pris!" Israel cried out. "I am not concerned about myself in this - that *I* cure her! I am wracked there is no cure at all!"

Priscilla turned in her seat and looked across the room to his eyes under his brow, growing craggy like his father's. "Your master in surgery was great."

Israel, approaching merely forty, shuffled outside like an old man. He sat on the cold stone stoop.

Priscilla followed. "Your father taught you brilliantly. Can those lessons not help her?"

Israel stayed next to his wife until her warmth through her thin woolen dress and cotton apron communicated a measure of life into his flesh through his clothes and his skin. He threw his big-boned arm around her shoulders. "Father never performed such a surgery as this. It's one thing to remove organs neatly from cadavers and quite another to cut out the cancered parts while the patient lives!"

Priscilla turned her face up to his.

"The point of it is this, Priscilla. Will even a *successful* surgery help? If she does not die of shock, or bleeding, or infection, will she, after much agony, still have the cancer?"

"Could she?"

"I've thought long about this. It would not be so bad if the disease encroached upon one part, which I could then remove. But what if it has taken root elsewhere in her?"

"Could it?"

"It might. It might reach like the crab and claw on. It might not be a matter of that but of a spontaneous growth."

"I don't understand."

"Another growth - one with no connection to the cancer already there or concomitantly arising. Like mushrooms appearing at the far ends of the same log."

"If that has happened to her...."

"Absolutely correct! I cannot gut her like a mackerel! I must wonder if the surrounding tissue is imbued with tumor...so small I cannot see. For tumors must be born like everything else - from some seed albeit invisible." Israel hid his reddened face in the crook of his arm. "If I do nothing she will die miserably - if I cut her open I will kill her with my scalpel!"

Priscilla steered him quickly away from this shoal. "What does the Sachim say? Has he an opinion?"

"He says she wants to visit the sea."

"Oh, that's good!"

"She wants to watch the water."

"That is a good cure."

"Not for what she has."

"Mayhap not. Yet...."

"Aye?"

"A cure to her may not mean what a cure means to you."

Israel shook off her cryptic notion.

Priscilla said nothing more, afraid to sway his medical decision. Priscilla Marley, married into the Stirling name, rose, shook out her skirts, and ran her fingers through her husband's graying carrot-colored hair. "No matter what you decide to do, Israel, take her first to the sea. And dear, carry along your trumpet."

They pretended it was summer. They left the otan in Awepu's charge. Under his calm, clear-eyed supervision would come the sowing of the beans and the squash and the tobacco, the foaling of the horses they had begun to sell for a livelihood, the arbitration of differences, attention to the demands of Sweetwood village and of the colonial assembly. The Sachim, the Black Fox Who-waits, took his dying wife to the sea.

In former times they might simply have struck east on foot for the ocean, carrying their mishoonash, the big, dugout, oaken sea-going boats. Wakwa was too young to have known those times of open access to the coast. Even Wakwa's father had only heard the stories of their land unbroken by fences, lanes, streets, and the static cultivation of crops and the pasturing of those peculiarly passive animals, domestic cattle.

Instead of an easterly overland approach, Qunneke, gaunt and burning-eyed, was borne away from the hospital into the woods to Twisting River to west. She travelled gently, enthroned in a basket strung from the shoulders of two of Wakwa's guards. Bark canoes lined the river's edge to fly them the few miles southeast and downstream to Wareham. They reached the waters of Buzzards Bay before afternoon fog could smoke up the land and close them in. A portage was necessary over the swamps they followed east to the broad beaches and the open sea.

Once across the marsh and on the Cape, they stopped at Stirling's Farm at Sandwich. Since the spring of '53 when the Stirlings moved permanently to Sweetwood, their Cape Cod acreage had been turned to flax. May made it a rippling sea of blue flowers mimicking the rolling blue ocean spreading to the lip of the blue sky.

Israel launched into a clinical account of Elizabeth's mad period there after her exile by the Massachuseuck. Wakwa endured the details as staunchly and grimly as he would a whipping. Galled past patience, he left to his second son the translating for Qunneke.

Qunneke admired aloud the whiteness and stoutness of the old Scot's farmhouse, its eyes fastened on what had come to be known in the neighborhood as Stirling's Bay. She turned her back on the house and walked toward the barn. Wakwa hung back, dreading to sample the air of the strange sanctuary to which he had driven Elizabeth as with a stick.

No cattle had been admitted to the barn since Elizabeth Dowland had made up her mind to live there an outcast. The great building was solid, the air it enclosed riven only by shafts of white light fanning downward through the loose loft-shutter, which banged against the siding. The shelter meant for animals was inhabited instead by the shadows and the sighs of invisible currents of energy from tragedy, and from the daily tides straining toward its beach. Wakwa felt keenly the burden of Qunneke's dissipated flesh and muscle as the burden of a lifetime. In that barn, the touch of her flooded him with disgust. He sobbed from shame.

Qunneke would not hear him. She hobbled, nearly bent in two, toward a spindly chair showing a mended leg. Thinking she wanted to sit there, Wakwa wrapped her waist with his arms, lowering her. She bent out of his embrace until her knees touched the dirt floor. Qunneke rested her head on the chair's wooden seat and wrapped its wounded leg with her fingers. She took many breaths in that position. More than a hundred fillings and emptyings of her lungs yielded to a look of enjoyment. Her once beautiful hands stroked the floor as if someone precious lay there asleep.

"Taubotneanawayean, Wakwa." She thanked him for bringing her there. Over his noisy battle with any release of his own grief, a plosive panting, Qunneke thanked him. "Taubotne aunanamean!" She thanked him for his love in taking her to a spot where Elizabeth, the Englishwoman with whom she had shared him, had left so strong a ghost.

From Sandwich they embarked east at dawn for the beach of the Nausets. While others scrambled above the dunes to build shelters in the old way, Wakwa held Qunneke in his lap in the belly of the big canoe. Tamoccon, named for storms, took the forepaddle. Lightfoot sat behind his brother-in-law-to-be watching for hazards. Sequan, soon to be a bride, took the rear.

Wisps of words hovered then glided away on the wind. Flashes of meaning made for instants of blindness to the passing scene. The canoe bravely cut toward the open ocean. Three-thousand miles to England? What are miles? One-thousand of the small journeys from the otan to Wareham. Oh, for a swampland! We could walk to the English shore. Not so far. One-thousand small journeys to the small island of the English. Gilbert Worth shimmered at the horizon.

Qunneke arched her back. Wakwa remembered her fulsome figure perfumed in the firelight, he behind her, her arms reaching. Her arms reached for him. His fingers held her under her waist and he bent into the bowels of the canoe to hear her. She said no words. She looked into his eyes, his eyes above hers upside-down. He felt Qunneke's spine elongate and he sank his teeth lightly into the diminished flesh of her upturned arm. She turned her head aside and watched the bosom of the salt-sea.

He gulped, "I shall call Gilbert back from England. You should have him with you."

And she lightly kissed her husband's lips in gratitude.

Tamoccon suddenly cut south. Sequan, the rudder, swung them parallel with the beach to return to Israel and Priscilla who were fighting the constant wind rippling the pages of a notebook.

Israel watched the flotilla, the great boats and the little, speeding like seagulls and then tracing half a circle to skim the shore beyond the surf.

"It is how I imagine Egypt."

Priscilla blinked, wishing she knew what he meant.

"Her funeral procession."

This Priscilla understood. "There will be no treatment then?"

"Oh, yes. I shall operate."

Again confused, Priscilla asked, "How do you feel?"

"Hollow. Like those boats. Nothing in me but what I've been fashioned to do."

"Then you are not afraid anymore."

"Not for my skill. I am afraid for my soul."

"No!"

The Younger-Doctor carefully retrieved his pencil from a pocket half-full of sand. "We have come to a strange pass when I must seek out solace from Gilbert Worth in time of personal trouble." Israel began to sketch the beginnings of a letter.

Priscilla stayed his hand. "It is he who will need solace of you."

CHAPTER FORTY-NINE

May 1764

Mothering Sunday got underway officially with a service at St. Anne's, the Episcopal Church tucked into a far corner of Summerset Park and near the road that cut through the countryside. Immediately after, the married ladies of the party sequestered themselves from the spring sun and wind. Their husbands were concerned with clubs and balls on Summerset's greens, whiling away the hours between church and Catherine's picnic with its famed Matronalia cake.

Gordon, Ifan, and Ho were absent, concocting some mysterious amusement. Moses sat playing his flute on the grass above the lake. Surrounded by little girls dressed in white, he seemed like a bronze of Pan set in a flower border.

That day, Bluehill did not bother with music written by man but reproduced sylvan sounds; owls and wolves, terns and the winds they rode, streams bubbling and throstles nesting. He made a guessing game for the giggling girls about what noise came through his flute.

The bishop's wife commented to Catherine and her guests that, according to Aristotle, no moral good could come of listening to the flute. Nevertheless, the young mothers glanced with gratitude and interest through the drawing room windows at the exotic freshman, who was rendering them and the governesses a peerless service. The adolescent females who had arranged themselves on rugs dotted over the hillside more than glanced at Moses.

The man-made lake below, lay as flat as a coin. The sun cast a bright aureole around its perimeter. Into this natural stage-light, from behind a curtain of over-arching willows, glided a miniature barge. Manned by half a dozen Wadham men, the flat boat supported Gordon with a viol between his knees, Ifan seated at a harpsichord, Ho singing, holding to the sailless mast sporting an ensign of peonies.

The little girls deserted Moses and darted down the slope toward the floating stage.

Lady Leed laughed and led the women out to have a look. "Think of coming with us, Gus." Catherine urged.

Gordon's sister stayed in the window instead, seeing down the lawn to the hilarious trio, then concentrating on Moses who lounged on the knoll just beyond the terrace. She passed through the doorway and stood at his side.

"Mr. Bluehill, they are calling you."

Her voice brought Moses to his feet instantly. "Lady Augusta!"

"My brother's nearly going over backward waving you down. It appears they want you to make them a quartet."

Moses smiled away what she had said.

She smiled at his smile.

The lake magnified the screaming of the friends on the barge.

"Don't you want to play?" Augusta reached for Moses' strange, gold instrument.

Moses witnessed her appraisal of the flute. He lifted his brows when she questioned him without words about its modelling on a natural branch, its weighty gold.

The bellowing from the barge was echoed by the little girls, and then by the grown ones. The collation of guests looked toward Moses and Augusta.

"They make it impossible." Augusta said.

"Perhaps."

Augusta colored. Her eyes strayed beyond Moses to the horde of middle-aged men who had abandoned the links, anxious for the buffet. From the corner of his eye, Moses saw Michael Beckett walking in Cecil's and the Marquess's company. He burned to have his Uncle Gil in the middle of them. He took Augusta's arm and started down the grass with her without haste but quickly enough to avoid the absurdities of conventional conversation with parental figures.

She felt pleasure in his calculation. "Will you sit with me for lunch, Mr. Bluehill?"

"Will you call me Wolf?"

She caught her breath. "I should like to hear you say Augusta."

"Augusta." He did what she asked.

Each smiled.

"I'm afraid we have a secret. Wolf-of-the-mist!"

He turned to her then. "I am not afraid." With that he brought her to her mother. He backed away as if she were of royal blood.

"Come on, Hill!" Ho Beckett complained as the ensemble wobbled along without its fourth.

From the keyboard, Ifan directed one of the oarsmen to pick Moses up in the dinghy they had in tow. "*Teacup* to the rescue!"

Moses watched his hall-mate leap to the task. He heard the calls of the girls and the women, the mumblings of the men. His bright eyes lost perspective in the refracted light. On the ridges of the water, he saw his first remembered home, Agiocochook. In the absence of Wakwa and Elizabeth, its spring-fed lake had quenched, bathed, soothed, floated him, like amniotic fluid. He had first beheld himself in that lake. How had its marvels been supplanted by this puddle dug by gardeners?

The screams of encouragement, the laughter, the slap of oars on the freshwater, the melody bouncing off the barge brought him sharply alert to the compromise he sensed in civilized pleasure. Moses started to walk. He crunched over the gravel strand, stepped into the water without breaking stride, his instrument flaunted like an arrow. Mosses walked. The screams changed. The little girls and the adolescents bleated like frightened lambs. Moses walked. The musicians played. Without regard for his mulberry pumps, or his white silk hose, or his platinum silk-serge suit, or his lace, or the tail of his wig, he bore down on the barge, his neckstock floating, then lost, his grin closing, then submerged. Moses did not cease his march against the lakewater; his eyes and his brows could no longer be seen. Only his hand rode high with the flute, unsullied, gold.

He could see the bottom of the barge through the water. He worked the fingers of his left hand around the barge's shallow hull, then folded his legs against his chest in fetal position and sprang open, thrusting himself up, his elbows catching the edge of the boat, others' hands hauling him aboard like a net full of fish. And he stood on the flower-strewn deck streaming water like the central figure in a fountain in a piazza. Someone on shore swooned.

Moses saw Horace Beckett glowering with resentment, and turned from him. He shook his head and his natural hair broke loose from its net and spread over his shoulders scattering water everywhere. Moses Bluehill began to play.

The Marchioness, close to her husband and Cecil and Beckett, murmured, "I like extravagance in a man."

Augusta listened to her mother.

The Marquess mulled over what he had witnessed. "I shouldn't wonder if he's spoiled his suit."

Beckett thought this an idiocy. Then perceiving something far-reaching for Horace by it, he excused himself remarking, "Brilliant, Lord Leed."

Leed turned to Cecil, "Worth, is that man a sycophant or an ironist?"

Cecil sputtered, "Beckett? Absolutely honest!"

"Now I don't know what he meant at all!"

Augusta lunched with Horace Beckett. Lord Worth detained Moses.

"I have never disapproved of you before, Wolf."

Moses, wrapped in a Turkish robe, stood in front of Cecil. "I went too far with my joke."

"Dear boy! It was wonderfully carried off. It would have been fine if the ten-year-old daughter of Lord Whomsoever had not fainted."

Moses shivered in silence.

"Does it not occur that you should apologize to her mother?"

Moses chewed the inside of his cheek. He levelled his glance on his uncle's elder brother. "I was thinking first to make amends to *Augusta's* mother."

"What's this?"

Moses bowed his head and said while memorizing the pattern in the carpet, "Lady Augusta Brite's mother, Lord Worth."

"All these silly titles."

"Do you think so?"

"From time to time. In my Whiggish way, I like when you call me simply - Owl." Lord Worth studied Moses in turn. "It is intimate."

"Have you gone over to them then? You are officially on the side of natural rights?"

"Sit."

Moses obeyed, miserable.

"If you have done nothing to offend the Marchioness through her daughter, I would definitely not apologize. However, you are not descended from churls. You might make amends to your hostess for your startling her guests. A nicety. Was that your thought?"

"I thought, think, you should do something for the Becketts."

"Eh?"

Moses explained. "There is no fortune behind Ho. At least there must be honor. In the English mode. Ho's commission is but half of what's needed. Michael Beckett must be titled if there's to be a match for his son with...Augusta."

"I see it. You make an extraordinary friend."

Moses could not smile.

"The only reason I would act, besides Mr. Michael Beckett's intrinsic value to Britain, is to even the competition between you and young Horace. As I see it, if you half-try, he won't have a chance at the prize. And surely she is a plum of a prize."

"Brother of my uncle?"

"Wolf, you have put yourself in a most wonderful and wonderfully dangerous position. Therein lies my displeasure with you. You cannot interest a family of such influence and substance as the Brites of Leed without carrying through. Do you see it?"

Moses licked his dry lips. "I think so."

"Do not insult Lady Augusta. You will hurt everyone you know."

Moses brightened inexplicably.

"So! Into the lists with the Becketts."

"I hope this elevation will happen and without too much inconvenience for you, Owl."

"Everyone's saying that to me these days."

Moses leaned toward his mentor.

"I've been approached by my brother by letter from Venice asking me to resuscitate the elevation of Thomas Kirke. Gil who once thought a title would kill the merchant, thinks now it will save his neck! I do believe he means it." Cecil Worth, of Heathersley, forgot his lunch waiting on a tray and left for London before the cake was served.

Orals interfered with spring weekends but by June the party switched to Heathersley. Moses and Ho rode with Augusta and Gordon over the ancient grounds. The potent setting inspired awe in sister and brother. The weathered, Roman pile, faithfully held together and rebuilt over the centuries under the blast of the west wind, the Channel boiling by into the Strait of Dover, the oceanic palette of olive, silver, and aquamarine splashed with the blood of the waterside sunsets, was utterly unrelated to the emerald green and pale tints of Summerset.

Rain socked them in. The servants were shaken out of their usual rhythm to cater to the demands of the large, housebound party. The adults congregated in the drawing rooms and dining hall to enjoy the radiant heating system. They became unduly interested in reading, taking turns to visit the rambling library. There, against the west-facing wall of windows, Cecil had put Wakwa's canoe on display.

How a thing so primitive can be so beautiful...! I'm sure the Sachim has had no formal art training. The whispers went around. *Damn savages. Cost us money! Not to mention our darling boys. The new tariffs and the currency law will squeeze something out of all those pinchpenny colonials on the other side of the herring-pond. And the Whigs beating their breasts over them! I shouldn't wonder if Cecil hasn't got 'twixt the sheets with 'em. Can you fathom Catherine throwing her only daughter in that half-breed's way? With <u>their</u> property? Of course, there's never enough when you've got to maintain a place like Summerset. I've heard the pretty redskin boy has a mysterious mother sooo rich.... Some think she's a royal. Then how rich can she be? Catholic they say. Related to James Two? A Scot? He won't be getting much out of her, you can be sure. No. no! She's a Presbyterian. My point holds. Dear Cecil is playing with fire. No wonder he's got this crate up here off the beaten path!*

The young ones slipped away to the dripping woods. Fires under the yew trees, Moses' flute and Ho's naïf voice by the rain-pocked brook, horseraces on the sand, whispers and laughter at table, secret wagers for dancing partners, culminated in emotional confusion more satisfying than beefsteak or Madeira or the obligatory whiff of snuff.

The fortnight drew to a close to the sound of coach wheels spinning in the mud as the guests, single, couples, families, departed. Cecil and the Marquess had obligated themselves for the last weeks of that session of Parliament. Leed rolled away with Cecil silently troubled.

Lord Leed said, "Worth, I think it wise of Lords to quell any public discussion of the trade taxes and their connection to the expense of the Pontiac War."

Cecil replied, "I very much agree, Leed. What use in sensation when the taxes could be eased if only the trade problem itself were solved."

"Then are you willing to stay all summer?" Leed fingered his brown wig.

"We've had *all winter* to consider a quite feasible plan sent up by the merchants. Why not slip something through after Parliament quits? Shouldn't take more than the middle of July. We can settle on a policy, the clerks can scratch it out on a sheepskin, and like all unfair laws, the trade laws will gather dust. The Board of Trade will certainly agree to getting-up a ball to celebrate our coming to terms. That will bring the women to town."

William Brite, Marquess of Leed, turned a glittering eye on Cecil. "While we're on the subject of balls, I'll use the time in London to have some new ones made. The feathers are sticking out of mine. I will attend your Board-of-Trade Ball. Nothing will deter me from the greens after that! Will it?"

CHAPTER FIFTY

Middle June 1764

The day was cold, the sky over the Channel a blue dark enough to immerse the cliffs in untimely twilight. The guest count at Heathersly had winnowed.

Horace Beckett carried the tenor part for Moses' flute, Gordon's viol, Augusta's spinette. Catherine watched her pretty shoes.

Hubbard made his subtle entrance and presented the Kirke Company card to Moses. The Company's insignia, a black and gold ship under full sail, swept over Moses like a fever yet Dire Locke's name, engraved underneath the symbol, steadied him from his signal fear - intrusion by his natural mother. Ifan's name scrawled across the face of the card led him to cry out, "Trouble!"

The amateurs' session stopped raggedly. Moses quit. Catherine rose. Augusta seized the case of the keyboard. Gordon despatched his bow and viol and stood in a protective stance near the ladies. Horace Beckett murmured, "Excuse me!" and pursued Moses. Augusta tore after him.

Two seasoned sub-factors flanked Ifan William in the Great Hall. Ifan pulled a sealed letter from his coat. Moses recognized his father's peculiar hand. He broke away, avoiding Horace and Augusta.

Moses gained the cliff. He read into the wind. Tabled by the rock and the water and the sight of Augusta's mantle as she climbed the slabs of white stone alone, Moses sank to his knees to breathe, to breathe as best he could, not wanting to draw his father's message into his lungs. Qunneke dying? Stay up at school? The knife looming on July the first, yet he was told to linger over cakes and music in the salons? Held at arm's length by his father for the first time in memory. For the first time, Moses stood alone. Nearly alone. He shared his dark corner with Elizabeth.

Augusta appeared in parts, her mantle, her hair, her shoulders, her gowned hips, her arms and the tips of her shoes. He pulled her over the last shelf of stone. A star or two braved the uncertain sky. Moses watched them burn. His lips twisted then relaxed. She waited. Moses handed the letter to her.

Augusta touched the strangely made characters, read and reread them. "So! This is your father's hand."

"Unmistakably!"

"I am sorry at his news. I thought perhaps to meet your family somehow."

I've imagined it."

Her fingertips came suddenly to his lips.

Moses seized her ungloved hand. "Oh! Lady Augsuta!"

"It will happen if we want it to."

Moses felt tears and fought them, grateful for the darkness.

"I'm so sorry you have trouble now."

Moses gave a single sob. He pulled her down to the hard rock. "What you should know is I always have trouble."

"I knew that when I first saw you!"

Moses swung away.

"Moses! You need me. You'll need me more and more."

Moses came level with her and they sat hip to hip. "Beware of me!"

She laughed at him. "Beware of the big, bad wolf!"

Moses pressed the knuckles of his two fists together. "I mean beware for yourself. I could love you...."

"Could!"

"I could win your blood-red heart, promise you the moon, worse, promise you a life with me and seal it all by tipping you over like a wine glass here and now! And I do very much doubt you would get over it."

"How very proud!"

"Not proud." He hung his head.

She ran her fingers through the straying locks of her black hair.

Moses looked into the southeast wind as if to Venice.

"Oh, Moses! My father leaves me to my own devices with much pique, for they are not the devices he would wish were mine. He'd have me run with the ton, a bit you know like mother. He must suffer awfully when I appear at dinner, every exposed inch of skin scratched by thorns and not a care for society or fun." She turned Moses' face to hers, her fingers lingering on its contours. "But when I leave a rose for him I have grafted - a rose the like of which has never been seen on Earth - you should see his eyes!"

Moses could not grasp her meaning.

"Defy the Sachim and appear next to him if that is what you want to do. Support him! He is your father. He's too proud to ask, and very willing to understand if you cannot."

Moses stood and pulled her up against him. "May I kiss you?"

Her lips gave each corner of his mouth slow and tender pressure.

Moses responded as tenderly, then caught her near, branded her lips and the hollow of her throat with fierce heat. He forced himself away, keeping them apart with his arms locked straight out, his hands a pair of vices at her shoulders. "This must never happen again!"

As his strength continued to keep them separate, she became like the white stone on which they stood.

CHAPTER FIFTY-ONE

Middle June 1764

After weeks spent at Summerset and Heathersley, it seemed ludicrous to Moses that London could designate as a city park a scrap of green no bigger than a lap rug. He made his way to the single bench squarely under a street light, the glare of which was spread by a stinking metropolitan mist. The most propitious feature of the so-called park was that it and the bench were situated directly across the street from Kirke Company's offices.

Closed for the night, the black shutters slick with rain, no movement apparent, no sound audible, Moses anticipated not rescue, only shame from the ruination of his horse by too hard riding, exposure, and no feed. Derelict, without father or mother or lover or home, Moses felt, as he felt the creeping cold of the bench, his kinship with his father's hapless cousin, Weeping Heart, that miscreant, bludgeoned brainless for treason against his tribe and cast onto the mercies of the Boston docks to rot.

A drunken man attired in rags slogged across the square of unkempt lawn and sat on Moses' boots. Through Moses' ensuing revulsion and withdrawal of his well-shod feet from under the wretch's posterior, he became conscious of a continued and repeated refrain leaking from the drunk's mouth - "*Jesus' blood never failed me yet!*"

From the counting room at Kirke's, Dire Locke heard the all too familiar disturbance. He shut the wall-safe and cracked the black shutters. He saw two weakly lit figures instead of the usual solo apparition. There was the familiar lump of cloth crying eloquently about the Son of God, the other appeared to be an individual extremely similar to Moses Bluehill in style and cut. The trembling horse was of fine flesh.

Locke poured two cups of steaming tea. "You'll need the tailor when the sun comes up. As I understand it, Moses, you have ruined not one but two suits recently."

Moses looked at the factor sharply but said, "Mr. Locke, if you had not been here...."

"You would have trotted down the cobblestones to Mayfair and a nice hot bath and a whiskey at Cecil Worth's townhouse." Locke downplayed any charity on his part.

Stripped of his soaked clothes and garbed in a robe of Locke's, too small and too short, Moses concentrated on what Locke had said. "I never thought of it. Never would have."

Locke was intrigued by Moses' admission.

"My horse!" Moses came to his bare feet. "My boots!"

"Moses, you are quite overwrought. Sit back! Everything is under control."

"No. No!" Moses tried without success to frame a sentence of concern for the man in the rain.

"The Jesus-fellow got his pennies and his flask refilled and his bed in the basement. The nightly ritual. All is well."

"No!" Moses searched Locke's bathrobe pockets in vain for Wakwa's sodden, rumpled letter. "Do you have it? Do you know what it says?"

Locke bypassed Moses' emotions for the demands of his tobacco pipe. Between the vice of his teeth he commented, "I take this event as a positive development."

"You must be mad!"

"I am not any such thing."

Moses threw himself to the floor. "Tell me what to do! I am not wanted by my father!"

Locke threw his head back and exhaled. "I have no practice in telling people what to do."

"Yet they do as you ordain!"

A smile threatened but was defeated. "Get up." He waited. "There, now. Next, see your mother, Elizabeth. Sail to Qunneke's deathbed no matter what your father says. Return to Oxford so you can be some earthly use to somebody eventually, and that includes yourself. And that includes giving the Becketts some resistance in this affair of Lady Augusta!"

Moses swung toward the settee and rested his cheek against the silk. "I would like nothing better. And the way Lady Augusta feels about me," he painfully corrected himself, "felt about me, there would be no contest. There *is* no contest. Tonight, I handed her on a silver platter to Horace." Moses held the sides of his head as if to keep it from bursting.

Locke paid him serious attention. And he led him. "You have good reason, of course."

"If Tame Deer were well, I could have invited Gordon and his sister to stay with the Worths in Sweetwood. I would have taken Augusta to meet my folk...to see the ground that is the People's and that which is mine, and then...Dowland House...and then somewhere in the woods, or, better, in my Uncle's sitting room, propose that when I was finished with my studies and situated, we marry."

Locke moved with consummate care. "It sounds an amiable plan. It is not impossible that it happen even though our much revered Qunneke is succumbing to her quite long illness."

Moses straightened. He gulped back a yelp of distress. "I would come to England and ask her father for her hand and present him money belts to charm him and lay before him the conveyance to be mine at my majority. And though it were a pittance to what Augusta has got, he would be satisfied for he wants nothing more for her than her utter happiness."

Locke made a sound akin to the sigh of having eaten a meal of excellent meat. "A very good man! A very good man to know, indeed!"

"He says...," Moses paused, overcome.

"What does Lord Leed say, Mr. Bluehill?"

In a voice not unlike the ruined man's in the rain, Moses finished, "He says...he says it over and over every noontide with his breakfast...'One should never hurry over cream.'"

"Hmmn!" Locke glowed like an oil lamp. "You have encountered profundity. This were a fine prospect for a father-in-law."

"He might...he very likely *would* enlarge his daughter's prospects by offering me position through his peers...make me an earl like his son, he could do no less for his only daughter! And I could practice the law on a very high plane, I could in time vie for a post in which I could exert myself in behalf of my tribe, of my home country."

"Your own father may have this in mind, Moses. Thus he urges you to stay on. Dear boy, Qunneke knows you love her whether you ply the waves to her sickbed or stay here cudgeling your brains at school."

"You are telling me to do this thing?"

"Your motives are good. The love is real."

Moses stood, strode toward the room's center, then took to the walls. "Are they! Is it? Lady Augusta Brite is no quiet daughter of a Sippicon farmer. I cannot do with her what my father did with Elizabeth." Moses swallowed as if he swallowed a jagged blade.

"I am glad to hear you use her name."

"How glad would everyone be if I took an English aristocrat to wife, dividing me forever from them?"

"I would not put it so strongly, although it might take some adjustment...."

"Adjustment!" Moses took to the walls, burned away the shadows. "Tell me! In a union with Augusta...I may be thinking amiss...but...would I not be creating an alliance...a greatly inappropriate alliance between my father's People and the Crown?"

Locke's icy eyes were fixed on Moses' tortured face. "The war is over. Times have been better for the Ninnuock. Perhaps you would be doing them a favor."

The sachim's son thrashed through the large room roving, turning, turning back with each thought as it formed and was born in words. "Would I not be creating an alliance the People might have to break! Would I not be linking myself indivisibly with English wealth and power just when the laws of England have turned ugly against the House of Kirke, against Gilbert and Hanna Worth, against every Indian and colonial who yet walks upright!" Moses closed his eyes to see. "Bathed in the limelight, the slightest dissent in Massachusetts could be regarded by the English as sedition, treason, cause the exile of my People again - or their deaths!" Moses looked openly at Locke and cried out, "For my personal pleasure!"

"Well!" Locke's sallow cheeks shone with respect.

"Has all this pain, all this learning, all this money been expended on me so that I can turn myself and the Ninnuock into courtiers?"

"Be careful in your reasoning." Locke felt youth carrying Moses Bluehill too far.

"What should I say to Tame Deer as her soul passes away from us?" Moses gave an agonized shout. "Shall I tell her she kept me alive and tended me all my youth so that I could do my father one better?"

Locke stood. His hands hung at his sides. As if officiating at a rite of passage he said solemnly, "You are become a man. What a pity Mr. Michael Beckett cannot hear you! What a pity everything will fall to the Becketts, father and son and per stirpes."

"No, Dire! That is the *joke*. The *pity* is I will never know Augusta!"

Locke's coach carried them to Mayfair. "What happened since I last saw you to...change you so?"

"Am I changed?" Moses was scrupulous in his grief. "Until that filthy man came along prating of Jesus, I was...of many minds. But he broke my heart. How simple it all became when I let it break!"

After moments passed in silence, Locke murmured, "I am loading a special and secret cargo of textile-making machines for shipment in July to Massachusetts. By it Kirke Company may be able to survive and prosper in America. Ifan William will learn the job of super-cargo on this voyage. I would be honored if you would travel with me."

"Thank you, Mr. Locke. I must leave before that. My mother lies dying."

"Never forget, sir, you have two."

Moses studied the neutral shapes and colors of the pre-dawn landscape.

"May I suggest you reconsider your agenda?"

"Reconsider?" Moses studied the small, sage man buffeted by the coach's progress over the cobblestones.

"How can I say this without seeming hard? Young Dr. Stirling has put the surgery off till July to give you all time to assemble because there is so little hope that opening her sooner will prolong her life. As I read his lines she is slipping away smoothly without the provocation of the knife. The surgery will be the last desperate measure. The proof is that Gilbert Worth has set out from Venice for Wareham already. Word arrived this evening on the wing."

Moses studied a map he visualized on his palms. "I might get there just in time if I left today."

Locke dug in. "You would be late."

"What's the use in my staying here in any case?"

Dire Locke spread a broad net. "There has come at long last a trade agreement, no new law, mind you, but a policy. It has been a lifetime in the making. I have it from the Board of Trade there will be a celebratory ball. It would be helpful to the entire family effort if you would attend. You have chosen your path. You have found your star. I will be by you as you move toward its light. Your career is to be a public and an unselfish one. Leed will be there with his coterie of Whigs, Lord Worth, his new recruit, with him. Right now someone must represent the American side of things. We can't leave *that* to Cecil. And I, of course, am not of Jesus' blood."

Moses threw back at him, "Oh, Mr. Locke, but you are!"

CHAPTER FIFTY-TWO

July 1764

Seeefour Aitchten OH. C4 H10 O! Ohhhhhhhhh, ohhhh.... Eeethur, eeeeethur, suuulfer, sulfurickeeeeethur.

Qunneke's hands strained to lift the gauze mask for a whiff of unadulterated air. Bound cruelly tightly, she thrashed her head gasping for life.

A woman's hands, cool white hands, Dolly Low's once kind hands, locked the mask in place.

Wakwa heard the rattle from Qunneke's throat. His crash through the surgery door brought a long look from Israel gently lifting the mask from Tame Deer, suspended in unnatural sleep. Anniebeth took Wakwa's hand and led him down to the kitchen to calm him with a cup of tea.

Floating in the blue were swipes of yellow, yellow strong, too strong, stinking of rotting bones burning. The world was the sky and the air of the sky was soaked in the stink of yellow rottenness and strokes of too-yellow yellow floating by. Tame Deer, still, Still Deer, distilled into the sky of yellow, heard the thunder of human voices rolling like cannon through the sickening yellow. As the heat of sharpness invaded her, the ether-soaked gauze squatted on her face, a vicious animal, voiding odors unspeakable, which leaked into the yolk-smeared sky and the boiling, fuming, rottenness of putrefied bones. Qunneke dreamed of a doe falling to her knees and then with consuming care stepping away and bounding into the woods thrilling on the sweetness of real air.

It was night. The sky was deepest blue. The sharp points of small summer stars hurt the eye. Qunneke lay in a room different from her hospital room and the surgery, an empty room except for the bed, two painted chairs and a tiny table. The darkness rolled in on heavy summer breezes. Qunneke could see the sky through the several windows behind her because her head was lower than her feet. She could see her feet and her legs and her thighs wound in white cloths like the dead and just above her crux an uneven patch of black spreading, which, if it were dawn, would show absolute red.

CHAPTER FIFTY-THREE

July 1764

Horace Beckett lingered. Dazzled by the glittering tide of guests flowing a full storey beneath him, trussed by rainbows thrown by scores of crystal chandeliers, Horace remained in place on the gallery after he was announced. A tall figure gowned in white stopped his roving gaze; it was Augusta alone as an iceberg and she was watching him.

Ho descended and cut like a sword through the perfumed mob. "Lady Augusta, allow me to fill your card with my name!" He added, marginally less aggressively, "If you choose to dance tonight."

Augusta let the blank booklet fall open. "Mr. Beckett, don't you see your name written across the page?"

His heart skipped at her avidity. He bent to kiss her hand. Doused in a rain of light, his powdered hair, (the King was invited), his ivory skin, his chiselled jaw, his silver coat matched him to her.

Lady Leed cautioned, "Gustie! Not a line left for your brother or...his band?"

Augusta's gaze dwelled on Ho's broad back still bent in homage. "Mother, anyone else will just have to...cut in."

The blood rose in Beckett's face.

The Marchioness tested, "Mr. Beckett, what do you think of Lady Augusta's improvements to this barn?"

Green and white Chinese urns set serpentine on a table as magnificently long as a road, housed the trunks of young ash trees wound with streamers of ivy, trembling, reaching, catching hold of the vines of the trees to either side like partners in a Minuet. The trees meandering through delectables laid out on a cloth of tissue-linen, were crowned with motley blossoms like trees in a dream, roses as great as cabbages, black-red, to chrome-yellow, to star-white.

No tree could produce from its head, like a Zeus, roses of different colors, roses of disparate origins, renowned or new to the world, roses, offspring of exotic grafting. For the Board of Trade Ball the impossible had been surpassed. The point of the Ball, the celebration of the Trade treaty among the red, yellow, and white races was boldly made. Augusta's achievement exhibited a horticultural, an intellectual, and an executive mastery to be remarked. The table set in duplicate so that the diners could choose the same fare from either side of the sinuous division engraved ever so subtly upon the crowd's mind the Treaty's equitability.

Horace looked squarely at the Marchioness. "Her creation can never be imitated, Lady Leed."

After a moment, Catherine commented, "An extremely interesting answer, Mr. Beckett. Extremely satisfying. I think you should dance with my daughter as much as she will allow."

Beckett bowed, kissing *her* hand now and profiting from another influx of high color. "If I do not tear myself from you ladies to find Gordon's band, there will be no intermezzo!"

Mother spoke to daughter when he had left them. "Gus, how *will* you decide between the cogent Mr. Beckett and the dangerous Mr. Bluehill?"

Augusta replied after thought, "Mater, I do not know that a decision is necessary."

At first puzzled, Catherine ultimately breathed scandalized, "Daughter!"

Augusta smiled for the first time that evening.

Her father confided to Cecil Worth, "Beckett and Bluehill! It is refreshing to see young men who move like men not like these cream puffs in waistcoats society is churning out."

Cecil did not repress laughter but offered innocuously, "Refreshing is the word."

Like a pikeman, Leed stuck Cecil on his blandness. "You careful Worths. You can't deliver us two plums like Michael Beckett and Thomas Kirke and expect to escape to West Sussex to your Cobs and your hounds and your books and your canoe with no change to *your* title. You can't remain at the same level ad infinatum. You know."

"I know."

"Say you're a Whig and be done with it, for you most certainly are one and to a fault."

"Call me whatever you like as long as I don't lose Heathersley by it. And if you raise me up, hadn't you better raise yourself?"

"Flotsam?"

"As for declaring for you Whigs, Leed, I think it safer for my brother, Gilbert, in his present situation, if I grant your party my vote publicly without officially...."

"Putting on a Whig?"

Cecil clucked and said pleasantly, "We wouldn't want our crazed King George to sense his Crown tipping too precariously to the left."

In the reluctant darkness of July night, Moses viewed the coaches rolling in single file to the base of the palace's marble staircase. He noted Locke's black chaise, his pair of blacks at rest, the solid gold Kirke Company bridle rings and bits setting them apart from those of even the handsomest of stables. Moses snapped open his watchcase. The carriage was here, where was Ifan William? Ifan's lateness distressed him. Ifan William was dependable. He was on clavier and was late for rehearsal. Leed's little band was scheduled to perform interludes between the professional musicians playing for the dancing. If The Company's business was keeping Ifan away from the Board of Trade Ball, Moses despaired for more than the quartet.

Horace Beckett found not Moses but Michael in one of three anterooms that studded the western circumference of the ballroom. Michael Beckett, in powder and a raisin-colored suit, looked more like a peer than the peers who surrounded him. Horace signalled to his father but was rebuffed by severe movement of the paternal eyebrows.

Ho waited his turn, edging near enough to hear Michael insist, "That conveyance to the half-breed is my masterpiece! How should I deny its integrity for a...for an honor so great as a peerage... and call myself a peer, gentlemen? The honor would have lost its basis!"

Ho held his breath.

The peers quibbled over the point.

Beckett returned, "It is not professional vanity that speaks here! To nullify and repudiate the just, and, may I add, the important ruling of His Majesty's Court at Boston in order to let that parcel revert to the Crown as a daub of salve on Treasury's transient woes, will not save the Crown embarrassment but cause it!"

Ho heard grumbles and throat-clearings and was conscious of some members of the group stepping back from his tall, handsome father, doubtless rubbing them the wrong way.

Michael Beckett lowered his voice. "Despite the savage provenance of the proven heir of Charles Dowland's body, His Majesty and His Majesty's ministers, and begging, your pardons, the House of Lords, would find themselves, by such a travesty of justice, in nettlesome abrogation of long-honored treaties of," Beckett counted, "neutrality, Submission, wartime alliance with that same influential chieftain who sired Mr. Bluehill and to whom we English owe much of the victory at Quebec! More, the Crown would strike a treasonable posture, however unwitting, in the face of both natural and English common law, not to mention the Constitutional law!"

Horace observed the lords of the realm huddling like public school boys before a match. He left them to his father's mercy.

Snuffling and sneezing almost assured him Gordon was in the second salon. Ho was rewarded by the sight of Gordon's gamba propped carelessly against a spindly chair; he heard the little voice of the Earl's enamelled, musical snuffbox.

"Pinch?" Gordon offered from the settee where he was ensconced like a pasha and employing a stained handkerchief.

"A word."

Gordon turned his back. He embraced a decanter. "If it's about Ifan and the music," he began with loosened tongue, "I don't know what to tell you. He's quite undependable lately."

Ho might have sidestepped responsibility but offered, "Do you really think the combination of Cognac and snuff is a good idea tonight? Moses delayed going home to a dying mother just to play for this frolic."

Gordon huffed, "Apologize! You penniless, tea-sucking, gold-digging nobody!"

Ho did not budge in his shock. "Apologize to *me*! Lord Marthem!"

Gordon belched. "I should never do this shit and drink at the same time. Sick as a...dog." He swung himself off the small couch and hung onto Ho.

Ho quivered in anger but stood still as a block of granite.

"What do you want!" Gordon demanded irritably. "Get me outside. Oh, God!" Gordon's skin went green.

Ho cut a swath with Gordon through the crush of the drunk and the drugged.

Gordon gulped. "Should never have...stupid...so sick...I...I'm sorry...do forgive...feel like an ass!"

On their desperate way to the garden, they were forced to pass through the last room stuffed with matrons in pastel stuck like candy to a contingent of Mohawk chiefs in full regalia. Ho lingered an instant, remembering. Gordon gagged. Ho half-dragged, half-carried him outside and shoved him over the rim of the pool that caught the overflow of the fountain. When he was sure Marthem would not drown retching into the once sparkling water, he re-entered the ballroom.

"I need help!" He marshalled Augusta and her mother. "Lady Leed, Lady Augusta, if you would pass through the gardens to look for Mr. William, I would appreciate it vastly on Moses' account. And my Lords," he said to William Brite and Cecil Worth, "we've a disaster brewing if I don't find Moses! How do I get out of this room without drawing attention to myself?" Ho stared at the soaring staircase between him and the main doors.

The Lords led the commoner by another way.

Moses turned from the black sky and polished steps into the gilded glow of the palace. He fell in with Ho and his guides just inside the doors. In the clamor, Moses could not speak of his morbid assumption that Locke's ship had glided out of port and away from London with Ifan William playing super-cargo before he, himself, could board. The four walked at a good clip the way they had come.

Moses extracted his flute from a pocket. He commented innocently, "Gordon's viol should be enough to carry the baseline."

Ho dared, "Don't count on Gordon."

"You would do well to put your mind somewhat to music!" Moses said irritably as he hurried down the corridor. "A blockflute and a gamba will do just fine."

Ho endured his successive bruisings. "If you want a gamba for your baseline, go get a gamba player from below floors! Your precious Gordon's stinking drunk and high besides!"

Moses scarred the glistening floor with the heel of one pump. "What shall we do?"

"What shall we…?!" Moses made his way to the polished platform. He did not acknowledge Augusta and her mother re-entering after their turn about the garden. He allowed sadly, "My flute and your voice...too much the same tone." Then sadly, "I shall solo."

Michael Beckett stalked out of the room of his inquisition in time to see Augusta, her powdered hair sweet-looking as spun sugar, send a starved look Moses' way as he lifted the old-style flute to his lips. Michael spoke low to William Leed and Cecil Worth. "Your Lordships, I should be proud to bear the title Lords attempts to bestow on me, but with all due respect, and I am sure without your knowledge or consent, the terms laid before me are untenable. Some other device must be found in my elevation than to negate the conveyance of the Dowland estate to Bluehill! Had I agreed, I would be eviscerating Britain's sacred code of law and the one good thing I managed to do despite myself!"

Leed contradicted, "You've reared a fine son."

Beckett mused over the mind of the man of greater status.

Ho's pleasure was keen.

Augusta held Ho's arm. Her eyes drank in only Moses who was garbed in the color of blood spilled long ago, his black hair covered in a wig of gray that aged him along with his dejection plain to see as he played. A lachrymose tune snaked out, not at all what was requisite at a ball where an elite were celebrating a historic moment of their own making.

Moses blew a hymn to disillusionment, to love lost irretrievably. His choice of composer and song were a slap in the face to the assembly. Not a person in attendance was ignorant of the tragical lyrics or the composer's storied defiance of the Crown.

FLOW MY TEARS, FALL FROM YOUR SPRINGS, EXILED FOREVER, LET ME MOURNE WHERE NIGHT'S BLACK BIRD HER INFAMY SINGS, THERE LET ME LIVE FORLORNE....

Gordon emerged from the far room guiltily clutching his viol. Too late not to disrupt, too sick to be of use, he slid down against the wall behind a row of dowagers.

A rest in the music freed Moses to notice his surroundings. He took in air perfumed, air lighted. His tutored lungs slowly emptied through his instrument. His audience knew the lyric without its being sung.

DOWN VAIN LIGHTS SHINE YOU NO MORE, NO NIGHTS ARE DARK ENOUGH FOR THOSE THAT IN DESPAIR THEIR

LOST FORTUNES DEPLORE. LIGHT DOTH BUT SHAME DISCLOSE.

The song was an old one. Any person in the room who had ever sung anything could have sung John Dowland's words. And for those who knew Moses' ancestry, his choice of Dowland made a bitter reference; his choice of the irredeemably sad made an affront against the drafters of the long-desired Indian policy.

Catherine's hands hid the pulse in her throat. The Marquess scratched under his wig and looked around for an explanation from Cecil whose head was high but whose mouth was taut with disapproval as it used to be in Gilbert's presence.

NEVER MAY MY WOES BE RELIEVED, SINCE PITY IS FLED, AND TEARS, AND SIGHS, AND GROANS MY WEARY DAYS OF ALL JOYS HAVE DEPRIVED.

Augusta released Ho's arm and moved a step toward Moses.

Moses sipped air. He was conscious of the Leeds at a small distance; in front of them, the Becketts and Cecil Worth. He was aware of people mingling, circling his platform, listening, moving away, sharing soft conversation, whispering and fluctuating like eddies in a tidepool. There was a glow apparent to him on his left side. A hummingbird's green-gold. Moses turned so that as he played he could find its source.

FROM THE HIGHEST SPIRE OF CONTENTMENT, MY FORTUNE IS THROWN....

A voice, uninvited, ascended from the assembly supplying the lyrics, a female-seeming voice, an unearthly, genderless, angelic voice, a thrilling, driving counter-tenor. The words it sang pricked blood from the wound.

Moses played and sought the singer. His gaze was arrested by a mist of gold, a mist of fine golden lines, a weaving of dull gold threads just stiff enough to cage the wearer. A woman gowned in gray beneath a mesh bubble of Venetian gold, actual gold, stood rapt in front of him.

...AND FEAR, AND GRIEF, AND PAIN FOR MY DESERTS, ARE MY HOPE SINCE HOPE IS GONE.

The voice rising secretly from the crowd clouded at the last phrase, not breaking, but breaking the heart that heard it.

Moses observed a heaving of the woman's breast. He felt barbaric having hurt her with his favorite song. He stopped for breath, to wipe his mouth with the back of his hand. He sent her a smile from his eyes.

She reached out with a movement as small as a flutter of feathers. Oddly naked of jewelry, glitter such as the sun scatters was caught in the weave of her metallic overgown; the glitter was from diamonds. Her hair without powder in modesty was braided at the nape of her neck and captured in a snood, also gold, also a trap for precious stones.

HARK YOU SHADOWS THAT IN DARKNESS DWELL. LEARN TO CONTEMN LIGHT....

Moses could not move his eyes from her face, line and contour lost in one another. Her throat arced upward as she listened for the last of the melody. That swan's or lion's movement twisted his insides. Moses realized that he had stopped playing. The woman encouraged him with a smile and a nod. The crowd was drawn to the little drama. A grossly stout man in lavender-blue stood close to her. Horrified, Moses put his lips to the mouthpiece. The lavender-man sang. He was the counter-tenor!

HAPPY, HAPPY THEY THAT IN HELL FEEL NOT THE WORLD'S DESPITE!

As the song melted away, applause for the impromptu duet peppered the room over an announcement by the page: *Sahtomuskrkbart!*

Moses saw the woman snared in gold hesitate, turn away, turn back, place her hand on the arm of the enormous counter-tenor, then cross the floor with him toward the stairs where a crisp, white-haired old man stepped down as smartly as a crow.

Moses saw her transfer her ungloved hand to the old gentleman's arm. *Sahtomuskrk*! The abrupt beat of the name drummed in Moses' ears. Thomas Kirke! And the woman - ELIZABETH.

CHAPTER FIFTY-FOUR

July 1764

Cecil Worth shook with aggrievement on Moses' account. "Who would do such a thing?"

Catherine turned from Cecil to her husband, "Do what, William?"

"Catherine, please!" Leed looked at Cecil and followed his pained gaze to Moses who had bolted off the platform into the crowd. "Something's gravely amiss."

On Leed's understatement, Michael Beckett shouldered past the entire party to prove by eye what his ears had heard. "By God! Elizabeth Dowland!"

"But isn't Moses' mother a Dowland?" Catherine mused aloud to nobody.

Gordon, dog-sick with excess, cranked along toward Moses.

Catherine caught Augusta by the elbow. "Whatever's happening, daughter, be like wood!"

Like wood, Augusta heard nothing. She watched Moses instead, astounded by the distortion of his beautiful face.

Everyone else's attention was nailed on the legendary merchant and the rather young woman at his side. "Venetian style!" Sniffed a ballgoer of the disparity of ages and the magnificence of her gown.

Moses lunged for the exit.

Ho followed on his heels. "No one knew!"

Moses shed a look of contempt on his dearest friend.

Ho skipped and shied to avoid colliding with clusters of guests, "It's...it's got to be...it's a...glorious accident! But now she's here haven't you *got* to stay and meet her?!"

Moses tore through the hall.

Ho kept up. "Go back! She wouldn't have stood there while you played if she knew it was you! Do you think she would have come at all if she knew she might see you?" Ho went paler than was his norm. "I didn't mean...I mean...goddamn! You must know what I mean! Stop! God help me, she's beautiful!"

Moses tore off his wig and threw it hard at Ho. They fell together and struggled.

"She's your mother!" Ho grappled for Moses' arms. "You jackass!"

Gordon lumbered into them gasping. Moses tore out of Beckett's hold.

Horace bellowed after him, "Do you know what I would give!" He crushed the wig against his chest.

They saw Moses' white stockings through the spokes of the coach wheels. The stockings disappeared. Marthem and Beckett took the steps madly down, two, three at a time. A whip cracked and the black coach lurched forward pelting loitering coachmen with gravel.

Gordon moaned, "Moses!"

Ho held up tight-lipped.

"Hawk, talk to me, for God's sake! I think Augusta may favor you. If it's true, we're brothers. How shall we manage if you won't let me make amends?"

Hawk Beckett did not miss his chance. "Get your father to do right by mine."

Kirke allowed Michael Beckett to propel him and Elizabeth toward the Brites and Cecil Worth, while casting a glance at two young men crossing the dance floor toward them. One in blue with a greenish face hung back, the other, silver as steel, interrupted their progress.

"Madam!" Ho addressed Elizabeth. "I am Michael Beckett's son, Horace." He baldly watched her face, her eyes.

Elizabeth sank into bewilderment. Like a leaf falling with exquisite slowness, her mind lighted on his meaning. "Baby Horace?"

Michael's eyebrows did their dance. Horace bowed. Propelled toward the knot of waiting kin, Kirke searched the ballroom with his sharp old eyes. Not finding who he was looking for he reverted impatiently to Beckett's social flourishes.

"*Sir* Thomas, Lady Elizabeth - it is my honor to present you to the Marquess and Marchioness of Leed! I tell you with joy, Lord and Lady Leed, that the remarkable Mr. Bluehill, so warmly received by you and your family, is the son of Lady Elizabeth, nee Elizabeth Dowland, and the Sachim of the Massachuseuck." Michael Beckett delivered this coup de grace with fiendish delight. Then he had the remarkable pleasure of damning Moses' chances further by a simple issuance of fact. "And Sir Thomas, the renowned *merchant*, is Moses' stepfather."

With a knowing eye on Cecil, Leed kept his counsel.

Kirke erupted with the minimal greeting, "Lorrrd and Lady Leed!"

Beckett cleared his throat as a cue to Elizabeth, which she missed while wondering, wondering.

William ventured into the void, "Sir Thomas, when we recommended for your title we never expected the pleasure of your company as soon as tonight." He smoothly added, "Of course your presence could not be more appropriate considering the Board of Trade is sponsoring this celebration."

Kirke astounded everyone by grasping the peer with one hand at his collar the other on his forearm, "My wife and I are honored more than you can know, more than we deserve by my elevation as a baronet," and softly he added, "realizing you kept it modest to keep the boy free of implications. The Board of Trade are always amiable toward The Company, but were intercepted enroute to Ireland only this noon and are here at the *Throne's order* of not two hours ago!"

Behind the shocked glances crossing between Leed and Worth, Catherine whispered to Augusta, "And did she just pull such a gown as that off a hook! Do you see her minaudiere!"

"Hush, Mother!"

The small purse, lustrous as lighted wax, was shaped like a pair of nesting pigeons with eyes of topaz and onyx. It roosted in Elizabeth's cupped hands.

The Marchioness went on sotto voce, "As sure as I am Catherine DeLay Brite we are looking at blue chalcedony the like of which this Court has never seen!"

Augusta fell victim to beauty. She whispered, "Set off by the crystals, those lavender stones give the illusion of real feathers, Mother!"

"You must peek out of your greenhouse from time to time!" Catherine scoffed. "Those *crystals* are diamonds out of India or I do not know anything!"

Beckett gave up on Elizabeth, as he usually did, and presented her and Kirke to Cecil.

Cecil's memory was very sharp of his brother fresh from Venice with a live pair of birds such as the inanimate ones Elizabeth now cradled. He looked at the woman adorned in a web of the most valuable element. He saw an original mind operating dangerously outside and above the society he was used to. And material wealth resting in the palms of her hands.

Elizabeth stepped over the small distance between herself and Cecil. She curtseyed deeply and long. She looked into his eyes as he reached for her hands. "The brother of my Uncle Gil!" She wrapped him in her arms.

Shocked by her, Cecil embraced her, rescuing her, saying, "Kinswoman!" He was amazed by the tender hand of the fabric he touched, the dull gold threads wedded with something soft, the high neck showing her throat beneath, the golden net exposing and covering her, the silk of her undergown, slipping down her figure - a daring design revealing and masking.

She whispered in Cecil's ear, "Is he here?"

Cecil stepped back from her but retained her hands. "You saw him. He made music just for you."

She turned shakily to the place where Moses had stood.

Stephen Poore moved to support her, "Beth!" He addressed the tightly gathered group. "It's best we all go to that room over there. For some peace."

Kirke crooked his finger, motioning Elizabeth to him. "Lady Liz!"

Catherine Leed remarked to her husband as Augusta broke for the Kirkes, "What outlandish manners that man has!"

Leed said, "We've got ourselves a Whig, I'm sure of it!"

Onlookers ate the scene.

Moses did not waste time looking for Locke in the City. He ordered the coachman directly to the docks.

Familiar with his passenger, knowing his dependency on Locke, the driver spent himself in gaining the pier fast. Their ride to the water was reckless. "*New Psyche's* up-river, Mr. Bluehill. Weighed anchor 'bout sunset!" With considerable agility for his years, the coachman vacated the box.

Moses was ahead of him, roving the wharf already, growling, "Wild horses couldn't drag Ifan from his obligations. But Dire Locke...!"

The coachman whistled to The Company's watchman. Money changed hands. In turn, Moses stuffed money into the coachman's pocket.

"Can't take this! Wouldn't take...." Kirke's driver mounted the box as Moses boarded a cutter expertly manned twenty-four hours a day, every day. The carriage turned on the planking; the racket it made challenged the clang and creak of the fittings and the cutter's sails swiftly marshalled to their purpose.

Kirke moved past the anteroom's center. Spying an inner door, guessing that it opened onto a passage leading outside, he whirled and backed toward it, facing the oncoming Marquess and his wife, the young Earl and Cecil Worth and the Becketts. Poore circled behind, his hand reaching for the gilded door-latch.

Elizabeth stood in the heart of the room. Her abstraction complete, she did not know it was Augusta's hand stealing into hers.

Kirke clattered on. "I want you all to be the firrrst to know we are in the process of dissolving Kirke Company."

Gasps.

"My wife and I hope you will all be our dinner guests as soon as convenient. But at the moment, there is a family matter to attend to. It is clear to me," Kirke amended, "clear to my lady and me, that her son has taken summary leave of the Ball an' I do not blame him. Pooorrrr lad! With no preparation for the first sight of his mother since his infancy. An' I am sure the Throne would be sorry to know of this abrupt manner of reintroducing mother and son, a matter of such political and personal import and delicacy it has not been accomplished in these fifteen years even by me! I'll hate to leave your gentle company so soon after introduction but I go to find the son of my wife."

Cecil Worth was upon him. "Sir Thomas, I'll go. The boy knows me!"

"Lord Worth, do me a mercy?" Kirke had reached the inner door, "Take Elizabeth Dowland in your conveyance right now to West Sussex. Not Mayfair. Ride at night."

"Sir Thomas?"

Kirke, as tall, taller than Cecil, said in his ear, "The knives are out for me! The baubles she wears are for her expenses. In perpetuity."

"So glum, your prospect?!"

"That is a matter of opinion, Lord Worth." To the general hearing he added, "I'll ride with my solicitor, if you please, Mr. Michael Beckett!"

Beckett planted his fists against his hips, fighting the urge to applaud the old man's command and his soaring apprehension. Anything Kirke did, witnessed by his attorney, would be privileged information - no witness at all. And he had retained one, the best, in record time.

Kirke pattered along. "And you fine friends, you Brites of Summerset, whatever I can do to answer the courtesies you have offered Moses or will offer us Kirkes, consider arrrrranged."

Catherine stepped forward grandly. "Sir Thomas! We are not accustomed to bartering courtesy for courtesy and *certainly* not in the instance of dear Moses."

Kirke was tied there by her resistance. "Lady! Mr. Moses Bluehill is ten minutes ahead of me."

"Sir Thomas, he's taken your coach!" Gordon blurted in concern for Kirke's mission.

Kirke stopped. Took Gordon's measure. Kirke's sparkling eyes reviewed the implications parading by. "Noted." Kirke glossed over Moses' theft. "Quite natural of him. The Company's at his disposal. He knows that. Always has."

Catherine was delighted. She sent a look toward William.

Gordon said again, "Moses took your coach, Sir Thomas. You need our help! Quickly! I'll bring you out to ours. Bring Moses back to us. Please!""

The Marquess seconded, "Please!"

Kirke cracked the smallest of smiles in Gordon's direction. "I am grateful."

Stephen opened the door.

Kirke shot a glance down the tunnel-hall.

The circle cleared for Elizabeth.

Leed interrupted their silence. "Sir Thomas! What can I do more?"

Kirke turned only his eyes toward the Marquess. "It is imperative for your safety you return without fanfare to Summerset at first light. Too bad I've no time to stop to see for myself. What does the place lack?"

Kirke's directness, his proprietary arrogance, shocked Catherine and amused and informed the Marquess.

Leed laughed, "Good golf balls, Sir Tom! Godspeed!"

Kirke set Elizabeth on the matter with a glance.

Elizabeth took a step toward him. He raised a hand to stop her then kept raising it as if the motion were only his casual farewell.

"Viti?" The endearment spilled from her instead of tears. She tottered toward him.

Kirke swung halfway into the corridor, Beckett leading him. Kirke winked.

Elizabeth froze. She watched Kirke go, watched the cut of his back as he progressed away from her.

CHAPTER FIFTY-FIVE

August 1764

"Have we lost her?" Gilbert Worth seized Matthew Freeman at the top of the gangway. He saw nothing of Wareham bustling beneath the tall ship.

"She is hanging on, Master."

"Thank God!" Gil called to no deity in particular. "Let's go!"

"Word came through Newport that your *Merriweather* was sailing up the Bay. He was torn, but the Sachim stayed behind with her...."

"Well, of course!"

"Doctor Stirling asks me to explain, Master, that he cannot leave her."

"Well, of course not!"

As the master and the freedman vied for the hand luggage, Hanna became vaguely conscious of the unsuitability of her clothes. What had been an appropriate travelling costume one short year before, felt busy, overdone. The few women she saw were dressed with severe simplicity, all the old graces of trimmings and ribbons and richness of color and fabric dissolved into the drab. There was not a wig or a peruke in evidence. Natural, unpowdered hair poked out of plain bonnets or tri-corner hats and workmen's caps.

"Sippicon has converted to Quakerism!" Hanna declared as she attempted to subtly cover her millefiore earrings, prizes from Venice.

Gil, almost giddy that their captain's slick dodging of the winds had gotten them home while Qunneke still lived, ignored the irrelevancy and hurried Hanna along the sandy wharf.

"Gillie, why don't you ride on ahead? I'll see to the baggage with Matthew."

Gil saw for the first time a colt tied to the coach, tossing his rein.

"Don't get thrown!" Hanna called after him.

Gilbert Worth rode free - freed. He kicked his spurless heels into the sides of a Bay called, Littleson, a virtual stranger to him. This grandson of his great Arabian, Grandee, carried him wildly. Worth used his hand for a whip and his voice for a checkrein. Both horse and man threw themselves against the grueling climb, so gradual it surprised the heart.

Worth had even more difficulty with his surroundings than with his mount. Untrammeled fields but twelve months before were now cluttered with houses. Angry at their existence, he crossed the countryside where he willed, curses following in his dust. "Last year, they would have been jailed for such oaths!" Gil hooted to his horse. He did not know the invective was made against the fineness of his suit, the telltale lace streaming behind him, and his apparent disregard for private property. His high and mighty bon ton attitude was intolerable to men who had trounced the French for good.

Gil galloped past Sweetwood's church and shunned the road to Dowland House although he could see its cedar roof over the rill. He jumped the stone fence of his own pasture, chopping up the turf, and whirled in a victory whoop at his front door.

Just as he dismounted, a slender girl with hair like copper wire appeared on the stone steps and, as in a race, waved him on to Meetinghouse Hospital, a dust cloth for her flag.

Littleson pranced away naughtily, aiming to lose his bit, so Gil sprinted for the hospital on foot. He crashed into the hall without a knock, pouring sweat and holding his splitting heart. The big place echoed. Gil's elation dimmed, Europe definitely behind him and home feeling not like home.

Wakwa knew this wife. She had been his sister in their childhood, and, as a woman, the witness for him. She had given him back his character at cost to her own. She had preserved him and his authority although slaying his adversary with a word as surely as Waban had done with his knife. She had torn herself asunder in his behalf and admitted into the open part the heat of human passion against her lifelong virginal habit. It was not Gilbert Worth who alone had inspired her to conceive the second of her two full-blooded Massachuseuck children but she who had inspired Gilbert to inspire her. The longer Wakwa stayed in the sunlit room, the more he recalled her as a nubile girl, then a fulsome woman, then pregnant as an apple blossom with his seed and giving suck. Now hollowed, shrunken, bled, she sucked in his muscle and the air in his lungs as if they were milk, meat. He waned. He dissolved cell by cell into her. Their unity brought her disease into him. They lost life together.

That realization brought him to his feet. He put a room's length between himself and Qunneke's sickbed. He slipped into the corridor. He closed the door. The Black Fox Who-Waits waited at the top of the stairs overcome by a new and ineradicable guilt over the pain he had caused and continued to cause the two women he loved.

During the small hours of the night of Gil's and Hanna's return, Wakwa and Hanna sat shoulder to shoulder in the hallway outside Qunneke's room. Wakwa moved on the settle and the slight response of the wood roused Hanna from thought.

"I know now how my Kayaskwa felt when she was caught in the passageway one night, and from care for us could not move forward or back...she was forced to watch, to listen to me and Qunneke together!"

Hanna raised her eyes to his. It was the first time in nearly two decades she had heard him use Elizabeth's Indian name, her affectionate name. It was the first time anything had been admitted of Elizabeth's agony as the second wife of two. More, it was the first time he had made open reference to the amity between Worth and Tame Deer. And never before had Wakwa admitted to the pang it gave him.

Hanna whispered, "I'll bring him out. He's probably fallen asleep in the chair."

Wakwa shed a disbelieving look on Worth's wife. "Leave them. They have been good to us all these years. As good as they could be." He took one of Hanna's hands in both of his and held it against his chest.

Hanna felt his beauty through his shirt. His slow heart made its impression on her. She leaned against him and felt herself gathered like a doll, a puppy, an infant, an orphan. She spent the remainder of the dark hours curled in Wakwa's embrace.

They said nothing else. Each felt Gil's vigil over Tame Deer like a pick. Each hurt for disparate transgressions of the flesh or of the spirit without which their bones would not have carried them all these years.

Qunneke did not waver in her attention to Gil's face. He looked beyond hers into the impenetrable night sky. From time to time he watched their hands softly entwined.

Hers were of wax - yet warm. His were of ice, showing blue veins and red lines running under the skin.

Sometimes she smiled and the variation in the muscles of her face brought his eyes around to her. He was punished by the absence of the flesh that had given her face sweetness. He smiled at her because her bones refused defeat by her predatory disease. He came to know her facial structure as her Maker knew it. Her skull defined the poetry of the oval: the bone of her forehead magnanimously wide, her cheekbones, nearly so. They dominated her now, the rule of her genealogy. Her nose, notable for its simplicity of nostril, had seemed to grow in importance. Her jawbone, equal to her cheekbones, made the impression of a lonely coastline narrowing to a small round chin. Her little teeth were now fearsomely set in her delicate mouth, missing the constant minute dance of cheerful muscle.

She laughed at herself and him from time to time, their control the only reward of their unrequited yearning to know one another in infinitesimal detail.

It killed him that her female hub, her ovaries, had festered and been expertly cut away - this part that no man held inside his pelvis, wells of female power, magnets to man, the kernels of the race. What had those black eyes seen, foreseen, that had discouraged her flesh to death? Was it the creation of fewer and fewer sons, fewer daughters especially, teeming with Ninnuock blood and the mysterious juices of all women? Perhaps she had succumbed to the earth of Massachusetts overrun, devoid of her past, her shape, her submissive welcome, her soul, her woman-gods.

"You are a goddess!" Gil spoke and bent to her soured breath and breathed it in as deeply as he could receive it. His palms on hers felt her last flicker of excitement.

Whale oil gave them a steady light - saw them through until the sun poured in the eastern window frying the liquid across their corneas, making it hurt to see.

Qunneke lived another day and, with the Englishman's hands in hers, she gave up life on the next.

September found Gil slumped against the column of his harp, pierced by that month's peculiarly golden light.

"Can you deny yourself the joy of music forever?" Hanna persuaded.

"It has been but a month." Worth defended forlornly.

"It is your soul." She amended, "A big part of it. You mustn't let it wither!"

He gathered himself to play. His fingers, little willing, made a clumsy run across the strings. "I do not think I can do this anymore!" He cried out.

"Try!"

Gil made no effort.

Matthew saved them. "The Reverend Mr. Mayhew Low!"

Hanna hurried to say, "We saw little Mayhew and Dolly yesterday. We are enjoying her beach plum jelly."

Mayhew made a distracted bow.

Gil sorted through his memory for any form of politeness." Your stopping to comfort us in harvest time is a great compliment. Can you take tea?"

"Gilbert, I cannot take credit where none is due. I came not to comfort you."

"Mayhew." Hanna rose and said incongruously, "Please sit!"

He did so to cooperate but maintained only the outermost edge of the settee. "I have come with a need."

Fired as always by such a statement, Gil looked slightly less haggard. "Speak!"

"A group of ministers is to meet...."

"Meet?"

"We are not from the same denominations."

"Meet on a battlefield?" Gil actually laughed.

"Gil...." Hanna sent him a frown.

"I thought of the hospital. It's not overcrowded right now."

"Overcrowded?" Gil snorted. "There isn't a person in it! If Israel had not his flax to get in at Sandwich, I doubt he'd be making a farthing this fall."

Mayhew cleared his throat. "That topic is something we would like to address with you. Mayhap when the harvest is in. Mayhap when we can think it through over a warm cup of cider." Mayhew took the time for a short smile.

Gil snapped, "I've thought it through. Took half a second. I had not even gotten up the stairs where Qunneke lay dying to figure it out. Either the populace have lost confidence in Stirling because his patient was failing after surgery or they're too good to convalesce in the same house with an Indian squaw!"

"Saunks!" Hanna shouted.

"I know that!" Worth hissed. "But do they? It's not enough Wakwa broke the tribe's treaty of neutrality to fight their stupid French War. It's not enough that Tame Deer nursed their whining wives and their pukey kids - they have to shit upon her memory! Oh, I have thought about it Reverend Mr. Low and I am sick over it!"

"I have...written...a series of sermons for Advent...."

"Oh, good. That'll do it."

Low winced at the slight.

Hanna stood out of her chair. "I'll get the tea."

Low looked at her surprised.

"It is not new purchase, Mayhew. It is tinned from before the Revenue Act. But I will have Cooke put in sassafras bark, if you prefer."

"The latter. I thank you." Mayhew returned to the matter at hand. "Gilbert. I believe the confusion of the parish over the Indians is part and parcel of the confusion in the Parliament, in the shipping trade, in religion."

Gil felt he had to say something. "You are a beam of light cutting through the waste."

Low trained his clear gaze on this wayward sheep. "The other ministers and I hope to do so. With your permission we could start using the hospital for its original intent. There is a crisis of the bishops I spoke of years ago. The Throne clamps down on us in every possible way. We are like a collection of butterflies pinned only we are still alive."

"You do not require my permission for your ecumenist exercise, Mayhew. It's a simple matter of scheduling. We'll look in the agenda. I can assure you it is perfectly blank."

"No longer, sir!" Low eagerly followed Worth to view the book. "We are instituting a writing campaign. Signed letters going to important people."

"Oh, that sort of person!" Worth continued ill-humored.

"Essays to the newssheets. Pamphlets to be distributed in the schools, in the taverns, in the churches, in society in general."

"My, my!"

"We need your pen."

Gil handed him a quill.

Low bypassed humor. "We need your brains and we need your sharpness of tongue."

Worth smiled. "You are awfully good at what you do. Why we called you. You will engage my passions in the political tempest to move me over the hump of my grief."

"Not so."

"Not?"

"In any weather I would be here asking your aid. What we are launching is greater than persons. All persons."

"Oh, Mayhew!" Gil dipped his quill to enter the date of the meeting. "Your movement will die if you do not see that there is nothing greater than persons. Any person."

CHAPTER FIFTY-SIX

July 1764

Signal lights told Dire the story. In a series of flashes from the cutter, a code of man-made moons, Locke was made aware of a terrible twist in his plans. He had Moses Bluehill plucked from the pilot boat and dangled above the roiling water of the Channel, then had him dropped onto deck like a basket of poison fruit.

Moses extricated himself from the rope chair and faced Locke with the acrimony of seventeen years distorting his face. "You!" He brandished the flute still clutched in his hand.

Captain Dray pulled his beard and ordered his men to their watches.

"Take care, Mr. Bluehill." Locke instructed. "You are somewhat ahead of schedule. We had an agreement. Have you scratched it?"

"Schemer!"

Locke turned his back on Moses then waved him on like a schoolmaster with an unruly pupil. "Follow me below."

"Look at me!"

"Drunk are we?" Locke tried to save face in front of the crew. He closed in on him. Not touching Moses, he came uncomfortably close, forcing a lowering of their voices. "I'm always glad to arrange matters to your liking. How have my so-called schemes failed you, Mr. Bluehill?"

Moses looked to the heavens for witness. "You persuade me not to sail to my dying mother but to carry the family cross to a blasted Trade Ball. I cooperate against the innermost commands of my soul and you set me face to face with Kirke and...*her*...without warning!"

"What!" Locke gasped disbelieving.

"Without any warning!" Moses, mistaking him, screamed.

The captain threatened the lash for any seaman caught gawking instead of setting to work.

Ifan William materialized next to Dire.

Moses saw him and coldly ignored him.

Dire wheezed, "Are you telling me the Kirkes appeared at the...?"

"Don't pretend you didn't know!" Moses curled his lip at Dire's uncharacteristic lack of composure. "You threw me at them like a piece of raw meat!" Tears melted Moses' eyes.

"Good God." Dire turned to Dray. "Get that cutter back to home port NOW! The Company is doubtless stranded there! And if he's not, I want information!"

Moses hissed, "You don't know what's going on?"

Dire opened and closed his mouth like a fish. "I certainly do not know. I am struggling to make an intelligent guess!"

"Liar! You always know!" Moses raved.

"That's all I'll take from you, I don't care whose son you are!" Locke leveled Moses with a glance. "You'll find me in my quarters." He turned on his heel and went below.

The newest of the *New Psyche* vessels was not so luxurious as the *Merriweather* line. Thinly disguised as a trade ship, *New Psyche II* was agile, armed to the teeth, a frigate of war.

"See here!" Locke offered no hospitality. "I will overlook your monstrous behavior to me on deck only because you seem to be the victim of a monumental cross-up. But not of my making!" Locke took quick small steps in the close quarters. "You were to sail with me at daylight as planned. We crept up-river as a precaution...."

Moses let a sullen look fall on the factor. "You also abducted Ifan. He was supposed to play!"

Locke kept up his crisp walk, seeking the facts through reason. "Kirke and your mother sailed from Venice on the *Merriweather* due in Dublin for restocking and then on to Newport. Kirke is out of the Royal favor. What turned them to London? I had the weaving machines dismantled. They lie crated on this vessel. I needed Ifan to supervise that activity. This to keep the Kirkes *out* of London." Locke stopped in realization. "Thomas was forced to that Ball. He is in gravest danger of his life. He must separate himself from Elizabeth. Does he sense it?"

Moses struck his head hard on the crossbeam. "Goddamn! You've kept me away from my own for weeks but encumber me with two people utterly unconnected the situation!"

"Only days ago I gave you credit for maturity. I admit an error *there*." Locke drew himself up. "The Kirkes are inextricable from the life of your native family! I could justify their loss at the hands of the King's men but if anything should happen to you...! And now you've had this forced meeting...! I am out of alternatives, ideas! *Schemes*." Locke sputtered.

Moses looked at his own feet with loathing. "There was no meeting."

"Eh?"

"I saw them...I saw her. I heard Kirke announced. I ran out."

"God above!" Locke sat and let his hands fall between his knees. "Did that poor girl see you?"

Moses looked curiously at Locke.

Locke snapped, "Did she see you?"

Moses did not know how long he thought and remembered. But as the ship rocked on the Thames, he answered Locke's query. "I was playing solo. I saw her...she watched me! There was no way for one to recognize the other – till I heard Kirke announced." Moses wandered the cabin as if lost in a strange city. "They announced Kirke. But she bided her time leaving me."

"Oh! She abides!" Locke bit out.

"I heard his name...."

"Tell me exactly!"

"Sir Thomas Kirke."

"Exactly?"

"Sir Thomas Kirke, Bart."

"They've got him then!" Locke strangled the finial of a chair. "With a cheap little baronetcy!" Then came his slanted smile. "But he's got them too. For a while. Even a short while would do. And Cecil Worth's nobody's fool. They kept the honor small to keep you clear of Kirke's troubles."

Moses swayed. "I have never seen anyone like her."

Locke said fairly gently, "There is no one like her."

They stood at attention by the rail. The captain, the factor, the apprentice super-cargo, and the Sachim's son. Kirke's face was all they could see of him in the lamplight against the gathering fog. The sailors disengaged him from the ropes; Kirke waved away assistance as the ship bucked her anchor. He had no trouble picking Moses out of the welcoming party.

"Your mother thought I left to bring you back to her. Of course, by now she's figured me out. On another matter, I need you. I want you to talk to your father for me. Details at supper."

Locke attempted an introduction.

"Hush, man! I know who he is. And he knows me! And everyone back there has his and her assignment to keep things quiet and his mother safe. And if there be any untied ends, young Bluehill, you tell me of them while we eat and we'll see what can be done. Locke always has the answer." Busy, Kirke hurried past Moses, then corrected himself and shook his hand.

CHAPTER FIFTY-SEVEN

September 1764

Each man lifted his face to an incomparable, lingering gold. Captain Dray had assembled Kirke, Locke, Moses, and Ifan on the quarterdeck for the bath of light. Sailors off watch turned out of their hammocks and stood by the rail mid-ship to leeward.

As if it were honey spilled from the bowl of the sky, a rich yellow light coated everything with graceful unevenness. It welled, displacing portions of shadow, it dripped from the rocks along the shore and clung to things that the wind moved, reeds, wild vines, pine boughs. Gold stuck to their fingertips.

In the wonderful shine, Dray took pleasure tutoring the helmsman in bringing the newest *New Psyche* close into the cleft that marked Sippicon in Massachusetts.

With reverence very odd for him, Kirke whispered to Moses, "As many times as I sail into this place at this season of the year, the light forces me into contemplation of God!"

Moses abstractedly adjusted Kirke's shawl. He could not take his eyes from the sight of Massachusetts.

It amazed Locke how close the two had drawn over the weeks. A stranger might have taken them for grandfather and grandson, for foster-father and ward, and, to super-cargo-Locke's way of thinking, for super-father and son, the old man responsible for the young man's entire past, present, and future.

"Moses," Kirke confided, "I broke these same waves fourteen years ago just about this time of year. It's when I met your mother." Kirke smiled to himself and then jabbed silent Moses in the ribs. "Here, out of the air, is where I got the idea for the merchant bank. For the gold!"

Intense effort had been expended to sail west fast against the contentious wind. Captain, crew, from sailmaker to cook, had maintained a preoccupation with the ship's race against the elements and time. Locke, himself, had administered the preparation of the cargo for easy inspection.

Kirke called out, "Dire! Get Mr. Bluehill to shore in a boat of his own! What's more, release our brilliant Welshman from his drudgery. Ifan William! Sketch me this scene, would you? Can you make it in colored chalk?"

"Sir Thomas, watercolor would be faster. William dashed for paper and paints.

Kirke relished observing the factoring of the crates containing pieces of strange, new German steel. The spinning machines of this improved alloy had been taken down and the order of the parts blasted in their crates, rendering the muddle of metal impossible to link to any commercial purpose.

Above the seagulls' shrieks, Dray could be heard bringing them in, finding the deepest channel.

"Ships astern!" Came the watch's call. "Revenue cutters!"

Wakwa may have been reduced in his sphere of influence by the Paris Treaty but he was not without his common sense. He had stationed runners at Plymouth and Wareham ready to carry news inland at first sight of any Kirke ships as they hove in to port.

During that golden afternoon in Nunnowa, a contingent arrived bringing news of a single great ship on the horizon. That information rousted Wakwa out of his lonely house and prompted his order to his guards to find Gilbert Worth. As he and Awepu mounted, they were surrounded by the second wave of messengers with a tale from the harbor that sent them and a small band of fighting men at breakneck speed the few miles east to Wareham.

Locke, as factor, ordered Captain Dray to trim *Psyche's* sails and anchor her off Wareham.

"Moses, you'll have to wait the King's pleasure." Locke took a look through the glass at the crews on the cutters' aft-decks.

Moses chafed at the delay. His clothes borrowed from Kirke fit surprisingly well, a shirt, a buff coat and breeches, boots - just right for the dinghy.

Locke admonished, "Haste carries consequences."

Moses came back with cheek, "If it please the King."

Kirke strained to see through the glare of gold on blue. "They're shouting something. What are they shouting? *Why* are they shouting?"

A nerve in Locke's neck tightened and brought his head about toward Kirke and away from the cutters, which were blocking any exit from the harbor. "I don't like that they're shouting." As a precaution, Locke ordered two launches into the water.

Kirke looked through the telescope. "Shouldn't they be approaching from port? Should be sending an officer aboard and do their dance and set the duty and off we go. Is it in the law that they set their cannon on us? Stephen Poore would know."

The captain relieved Kirke of the scope. "Sir Thomas...."

"That!"

"Sir! Permission to prime and load the guns."

"Is that all right?" Oddly, Kirke stammered. "We...never have done that before! Locke? What do you make of it?"

"It is peculiar. I'm not familiar with anything in the new regulations requiring their cannon. Dray, do I hear them correctly?"

"They say they've word we're carrying contraband." The captain puzzled.

Kirke said irritably, "Well, tell them they're incorrect!"

Locke turned to Moses who was reading a fluttering parchment - ship's copy of the Acts. "Moses, I think you should go."

Moses looked to land, longing to complete his journey. He looked at Kirke. "Sir, illegal seizure might occasion the use of cannon. On their parts. No mention of cannon in regular inspection. Of course, you'd have to prove illegal seizure in the court at Halifax. I'm going nowhere till you're all right."

"You're goin'!"

"Respectfully decline, sir!"

"Declination denied. Dray, order him off!"

"Father Kirke, come with me!"

Kirke left Locke and Dray conferring. "That was nice to hear, Moses, but your mother's a hard woman. I'd advise you to go while the goin's good. If they throw me in the brig, so what? If they lock you up she'd never forgive me. An' you have to set things right with your father for me."

Moses looked once again toward Wareham.

"Go on! You've got a fifteen-year mess to sweep up! Speak to the Sachim. Prepare us a place!"

Locke strained toward Moses. "Get help!"

That plea pierced reluctance. "Hawunshech, farewell!" Moses embraced the old man and took himself over the side.

Kirke yelled encouragement.

Dray interrupted, "They say surrender the ship or they'll fire."

Kirke seized the telescope. "They'll what? Why should I? It's mine!" He did some shouting of his own. "Hooligans! Send your dogs over to sniff around! We'll pay the King's duty! Always have!"

The response, loud and clear, "Surrender or we'll fire!"

"Present credentials!" Captain Dray bellowed. "We are carrying a peer of the realm! Sir Thomas Kirke! Ship's owner!"

Locke commented dryly, "I think that was a mistake, Captain."

The revenue cutters brazenly rode the waves made garish by the sinking sun. Their big guns swiveled into position.

"We might have outrun them to port but it's too late." Dray castigated himself. Again he demanded credentials.

Kirke's white eyebrows went mad. "Pirates! That's what you are! Show papers or we'll show *you* cannon!"

A flame flared against the darkling blue.

"Tom!" Locke made rare use of Kirke's given name. "Save yourself!"

"It's not come to that!"

The whine of a warning shot tore their eardrums. A geyser of saltwater drenched the deck as the ball breached the water and sank.

Kirke stubbornly wiped his face of spray.

Dray was a commercial captain not of military training. But he could manage the winds and had a voice like a bugle. He raised anchor. He shouted to his gunners, "Take aim at those cutters! Prepare to fire!" All hands took their orders and the fast ship began to move.

Dray anticipated a change in the weather, silver washing over the gold. Fog overtook them in the time it might take a cloud to pass over the sun. The merchantman's captain was absolutely prepared for the demands of slipping between ships on the slightest gust, sails blending with sails, identities merging, making his ship a ghost of a target. While he had size and firepower, he declined to crack the Crown's cutters in half with cannon as he sailed between them - an offensive action would bring Kirke to the gallows. He sought the skirts of the shore.

"Hoist every inch of sail!"

Dray's first-mate countered, "You'll run us aground!"

"Exactly!"

On they flew.

A second warning ball from the nearer government boat whistled overhead, plummetting recklessly among the ships at anchor, making a neat hole in the bow of one and starting her on fire.

By that orange light, which tore the fog aside like the curtain in a theatre, the arrogant revenue boats, and New Psyche II, and the little harbor town, could see sailors rowing the launches madly toward shore. Gunshots peppered the water and one cutter beat in closer.

Dray said, "They'll cut us off! They'll sink those launches!"

"Christ. What have I done?" Locke muttered.

Dray bellowed to the midshipmen and quickly the configuration of the sails changed, throwing *New Psyche's* body between the aggressors and the tenders.

A cannon ball sang then fell. Moses dropped into the water like a stone. Oars, limbs, boards, cascaded from the silvered sky. For an interminable minute, Moses churned like an empty shell deep under the violated bay, then, with all the strength of his hips and legs and will, he catapulted to the surface for air. The flotsam of the shattered launch stymied his first strokes above water. A disembodied arm jarred his neck. He screamed and lunged forward on the tide. His gut drove him away from sounds such as he had never heard. Instinct to survive impelled him to breathe, to stroke, to kick, to breathe, to stroke, to kick. He burst out of the water and scrambled along the sand like a crab.

Wakwa heard the second round of shots, smelled the stink of the powder charge. He gave a war whoop and he and his men descended on Wareham.

He saw a launch blown sky high. Wakwa's heart paused. His horse spun sand in his face at his dismount. Jostled by the town's officials, by the blowsy drinkers emptying the taverns, by the local farmers cluttering the lanes, he heard another sound, the sickening scream of *New Psyche II* scraping bottom, her hull pried open.

A growl of outrage from the townspeople boiled into bloodthirsty yells, raised fists, threats, as Kirke's ship listed in the muck, the jaws of the sea encircling her great body.

"What's this about?" An observer looked to Wakwa for news, too shocked to care he was an Indian.

Wakwa dropped silently off the pier onto the beach. He half-dragged Moses out of the salt water.

Locke pleaded with Kirke to get into a lifeboat.

"I think not!" Kirke stuck his chest out and strutted to starboard. One cutter was so near as to make the use of the mouth horn superfluous. "I hope you're happy you martinet!" Kirke shook his fist at her young captain. "Your boss with the crown on his head owes me a damned sight more than I'd fairly pay in duties, you horse's ass! The Crown'll rebuild or I'm not V.T. Kirke!"

"Tom! Come!" Locke fairly foamed at the mouth.

Ifan William wrapped Kirke's middle with one arm and tried to guide him leeward.

The cutter's captain insisted loudly that *Psyche* rode low with ordnance.

"You could have come aboard to see for yourself but I'll be damned if I let you on what's left of my ship!" Kirke hugged Ifan to him. "William! Get in the boat!"

Cannon shot burned the air above Kirke's head. Dray responded, disabling the closer cutter with a broadside. Gunfire played. The bullets did not stop. Kirke buckled as his left shoulder split. Ifan William threw himself across Kirke's breast. Kirke sheltered him with his one good arm but Ifan never moved again.

Worth rode with Low and Stirling at the head of a stream of Sweetwooders. He saw the flames, heard *New Psyche* groaning aground, the revenue cutters crowding her and spewing bullets. "This is madness!"

Low said coldly, "This is war."

Minutes later Matthew and the women and children clattered up in the cart. Kirke was plainly visible, a foreshortened figure gesticulating on the slanted deck. They saw him cut down.

A fishing boat skimmed the choppy waters through a rain of streaming shot, no more visible than a spirit in the billowing smoke. Tamoccon struggled against the undertow while Wakwa and Moses climbed *Psyche's* side. The fishing boat moved on, floating Awepu and his fellow marksmen to their positions. Cannon on the shore blew off one cutter's mast, made splinters of her figurehead. The farther cutter took on water. Buzzards Bay threatened to gulp her down. Bullets, seemingly from nowhere, nudged British personnel over the side. Sailors, screaming English, dotted the black water like terns.

The doorway of Kirke's stateroom filled with a figure like a statue in a burial ground, dark and strong and sad. Wakwa advanced from the entry to where Kirke lay. "Come with me. A doctor waits to heal you, Greatkirke."

"I like the name!" Kirke lolled back on his pillow soaked scarlet and as soft as a heart with his blood. "Better any day than, 'Sir Thomas!'" A punctured artery pumped blood in wild disregard of Locke's labors with a tourniquet.

Locke murmured, "Just carry him off! She's going down!"

"I hear you!" Kirke complained. He gave his hands into Wakwa's. "Old Fox! I figured it out."

Wakwa smiled.

Kirke's theory glowingly confirmed, he turned his head to Locke and caroled the pain the motion gave him. "Dire! You trickster! Go to London. Declare for the Stamp Tax."

"What?!" Dire appealed to Wakwa, "Delirium. Carry him off!"

Kirke came back, "Fight for it in my name!"

Locke fought the dying man. "The hell I'll fight for the Stamp Tax! It's everything we hate. It'll destroy whatever's left of the Trade! There'll be blood in the streets! Massachusetts will rebel!"

Kirke turned his eyes to Wakwa's. "You understand?"

"I believe so."

Kirke sighed, "Thank you. Liz'll survive the foment." His gaze lingered over Wakwa's form and face. "She'll be happy at last."

Wakwa's glance wavered first.

Kirke cackled to himself.

Dray came to the door. "Last call!"

"Nosh!" Moses begged Wakwa. "Bring him!"

Wakwa cradled Kirke and whispered in his ear, "A fine doctor awaits. Your desire?"

"Tie me to the bed!"

Wakwa grabbed him closer.

Captain Dray snapped, "Now!"

"Tom!" Locke cried out.

Kirke's lilting voice was reduced to a squeak. "Do it! I'll ride her down. Alone. Decently."

Dray protested on captain's prerogative.

"Don't be stupid, Dray!" Kirke berated. "Your witness will be better believed than mine!"

Wakwa turned on Dray and on Locke and on his son. "Get gone!"

Wakwa made Kirke fast, like a baby on a board. He laid Kirke out straight, covered his bleeding body with thick red strowd, and, criss-crossing the rope, lashed his limbs tight, his feet against the footboard for support.

"Forgive me for this office, Greatkirke!" Wakwa pleaded in parting. "I like not binding you to this bed!" And his voice failed him and he ran his hands over Kirke's body.

Tears cut facets into Kirke's diamond eyes. "It's nothing you haven't done before!"

CHAPTER FIFTY-EIGHT

Summer and Autumn 1764

Cecil Worth had not gotten used to Elizabeth's presence in over two weeks. An inward excitement in her charged her outline. To him, she was like a boat in the moonlight, anchored but thrumming with every ripple of the tide.

He accompanied Elizabeth to the Turn district through the penultimate day of July. She regarded the invitation to Summerset as an ultimatum and said so to Cecil. He called Catherine's note instead a portentous opportunity for someone or other.

Elizabeth turned to Cecil, blotted her brow, and smiled. "They would not have dared drag you from your sea breezes except they have some need of The Company, although it is melting away." At that, she laughed.

"That you can laugh...considering...the...uncertainties...." Cecil let the thought drift.

Summerset's library, mercifully open to whatever moving air was to be had inland, was transformed into a warehouse. The Marquess, apparently unperturbed, worked over decanters of liqueurs giving glasses of fresh limeade some character. "Magnanimous is the word for it, Lady Elizabeth."

"Please. Just *Elizabeth*!"

Displeasure darkened his countenance. "My man tells me - *Elizabeth* - these five crates house sixty boxes, a dozen balls to a box. That is seven hundred-twenty featheries. I am overjoyed at your gift unless you suspect me of losing balls." The Marquess sniggered.

Disturbed by Leed's raw diction, hardly a trait of his, Cecil felt obliged to strike back. "Are you then saying you have lost your balls?"

Leed started. "Really, Cecil! Be mindful of company! In fact, I do not lose my balls. I have lacked *good* balls is all. That is, if they were to be had, I would have had good balls! That is, I slice into the things when they're soggy. Anybody would! Madam, you do understand me?"

Elizabeth, not to become victim to the inanities of sport or of wordplay, tempered, "Kirke Company is aware it *will* rain in Britain, my Lord."

"Spoken like a lady." The Marquess drank to her in response.

But as she once had with Dire Locke, Elizabeth moved in hard. "The balls are of Italian manufacture."

Leed worked to be generous. "A fine imitation of a St. Andrews ball, no doubt!"

"With deference, Lord Leed, the St. Andrews kind was designed after the Italian. I have been taught much about the game of golf by the warehouse master over the past week."

"A whole week?" Leed's challenge abandoned any good humor.

She took the bait. "In the preparation of the leather, the balls sent you by Kirke Company represent an innovation over the original design *and* the St. Andrews balls. You will find they 'play longer.'"

"Is that so?" Marthem fought her poise.

"Something about the thickness of the leather, its sewing and soaking. Kirke Company's golf balls are certified to dry slowly and thus not to crack so easily as others will or, if you'll pardon me, not to slit when struck when wet. The Company, quite simply, has the best balls." Elizabeth unleashed her smile.

"Touché!" Cecil hailed her agility and good humor.

The Marquess of Leed himself brought them their glasses, then faced Elizabeth. "Madam, you say repeatedly - 'Kirke Company.' I must ask if your grand gift is personal or...something else?"

"What else?"

Leed thought the heat might be wearing him down so he asked her to sit as he sat. "An ordinary ball costs half a Crown. Seven hundred twenty featheries carry a value of sixty pounds at minimum! These! Of extraordinary manufacture! Heaven only knows their value! White as babies' teeth! That! They've got teeth all right and spring...."

"Did a small box arrive?" Elizabeth broke his train of thought.

Leed rose, moved to his desk and retrieved a square box. He walked it to her and let the lid fall open on its leather hinges. "I wanted to ask you about this." A small hammer lay in a packing of velvet. The hammer of solid gold was engraved with the Leed crest.

"Lord Leed, it is my invention." Elizabeth looked down briefly in modesty. "I understand one taps the leather casing to keep the ball as round as can be. That the hammer be high karat to gentle its timbre seemed a worthy experiment to me. One would be tapping forever with an *unkind* tool."

"'Gentle its timbre.'" Leed scowled.

"May I?" Cecil took up the hammer and turned it over in his hand. He shed a soft look on Elizabeth. "*This* is the gift."

"I see." Leed scowled even more darkly.

Elizabeth returned the hammer to the Marquess. "The *gift* is the love you and your family have shown my lost son."

Leed looked at her and did not break his contemplation of her pain as he turned the precious tool over and over against his palm. "My daughter's struck hard by his absence. We brought you here with some suddenness at her insistence."

Elizabeth looked stricken.

Contrite for his roughness, William added in haste, "She yearns to know you!"

Cecil allowed, "Moses and Lady Augusta seem kindred spirits."

Worry diminished Elizabeth's poise.

"They have exchanged no promises." Leed cut off any possible comment. "Moses has behaved entirely honorably, a credit to Cecil, to the Worths in America...to his education...."

"To his father! With all respect."

"It interests me you are never at a loss."

"If that be true, it is because I know what I have lost." Elizabeth went pale, transparent.

"The truth is that Moses would not pull my daughter into a... complicated situation. Thus, Augusta's distress. She is besotted with him."

Elizabeth moved as if something lived inside her.

"With such an estimable sire, do you predict Moses will know a change of heart?"

Elizabeth tried to speak. She looked dumbly into the aristocrat's eyes, her lips parting as she tried to keep from slipping and dying under glorious memories and the guilt of forced decisions.

Leed, a reader, read the code of her stricken silence. He brought himself to say, "Let us find the ladies shall we?" He ushered Elizabeth from his sanctum into a labyrinth of sun-spattered corridors.

Augusta and Catherine waited for them in a small room near a flight of stairs and open to the flower gardens.

Elizabeth found herself in their care, taking the first step up to the salon where her clothes had been laid out and a bath was waiting. She turned from their pleasantries to witness the men's dialogue.

The Marquess was saying to Cecil as they walked away, "How much do you suppose can be done for Michael Beckett?"

⁕

By mid-August, Elizabeth confided in Cecil Worth, "Tame Deer came to me in a dream last night. I have failed her. I vowed to see her again."

"And so you have, my dear." He held her hand and brought her into the now familiar west wing where Wakwa's canoe remained dominant among the paintings, the statues, and the curios. Firmly, he led her to it. The canoe floated by means of blocks. Cecil urged her to mount a short ladder then joined her in the birch bark boat.

Elizabeth caressed the ribs, the frame. She quivered to think that Wakwa's place had been where they now sat, at middle, protected front and rear by his men.

Cecil revealed, "It never occurred to me when he sent it that it should carry you back. Even symbolically. Not 'till now. Dense of me! But when you talked of Moses' step-mother, the boat came to mind."

"I will go home."

"Oh." Worth's expression lost its radiance. "Odd. Gilbert's wife is as jolly to have around as a dish of blackberries but I shall miss you more - you are - starlight!"

She slowly turned to him, taken by his poetry. "I want you to come with me."

"To Massachusetts?"

"To Massachusetts."

"To stay?"

Elizabeth persuaded, "Civilization has much to recommend it - I have torn myself from Venice! But there is a world across the water needs watching. And you watch so well."

Worth spoke out of a brief silence, "I will do better to keep guard over the old men in London and that way protect my wayward brother, Gib, from himself. We Whigs, declared or undeclared, are in the crucial last moments of the fight against the Stamp Tax."

Elizabeth could not look at him.

Sails could be defined in the fog. Cecil saw the ghost of a ship and the Kirke Company ensign. Hopeful of news, he went down to witness a single passenger transferred to a tender.

Michael Beckett vacated the launch and marched up the wharf. "Lord Worth! I am flattered at such a reception! I don't suppose there's anything from Kirke yet?"

Cecil lowered his glance. "Nothing."

"Intriguing way to operate. I've enjoyed it. Feel absolutely Lockeian! Say what you will about Venice and Venetians, I say Sebastiano Falier is in his soul an Englishman. He is so... organized!"

Cecil declined to dispute the point. "Lord Beckett, any comments regarding her business should be made to Lady Elizabeth."

Beckett refused to enter Worth's coach. "What did you call me?"

"Actually, skipping a few steps because of neglect, his Gracious Etc. has bumped me up to First Marquess of Heathersley. Leed is now a duke, the spot vacated on his father's recent passing. *You* are a baron."

"Elevation is an apparent contagion in this group! I respectfully declined Lords' offer of a simple knighthood in favor of the Dowland conveyance. I will be hanged if I will turn my back on my best work! Our Constitution...."

"Get in." Cecil's order was given in a civil tone. "The conveyance stands. Moses Bluehill is in no way disinherited by your good fortune."

"And what *is* my good fortune?"

"Your elevation bears with it the elegant burden of a judgeship. Your jurisdiction and your barony shall be in His Majesty's colony of - New Jersey!"

"Exile!" Beckett was dangerously red in the face.

"Property has been granted you there handsome enough that you may breed your horses in a style befitting your rank."

Dubious, Beckett responded with starch. "This great benefice does have one advantage. I would be within a stone's throw of New York where Falier will be engaged with Kirke's bank. I presume I would serve as judge by *good behavior*, as they say?"

"No. Your tenure will be, as they say, *at the king's pleasure*."

Beckett fidgeted. "But then, I must refuse! You must see, Lord Worth, how this puts me at a complete disadvantage in a colony which has jealously insisted on its right to save itself from unsuitable royal commissions, to wit, *to judge the judges*. As well they should! I can imagine how I would feel if some wooden-headed appointee had the power of life and death over me, *at the king's pleasure*! Would that not shake one's confidence in the Crown itself?"

"It's the only thing that will assure your salary. The colonial Assemblies can be moody *and* are parsimonious."

"A chief justice DIED in New York from his caseload when no other judge would agree to serve with him *at the king's pleasure. Good-behavior tenure* is a hard won right of Englishmen about which I stand inflexible!"

"You are then, Lord Beckett, beginning your tenure in America at a most opportune juncture in its history. You can influence the outcome of this critical matter while serving justice. Note bene! Justice is never served by inflexibility."

Beckett lowered his handsome head. His clear voice clouded. "May I ask which jurisdiction it is?"

"On the New York - Pennsylvania road. At Princeton. We know you like living near an institution of higher learning so...."

Beckett scoffed, "The College of New Jersey!" He bore into Worth with his lawyerly look. "Elizabeth Dowland did this!"

"Not intentionally." Cecil's oblique reference to Elizabeth's reticence in front of Leed was lost on Beckett. "Look, here! Horace and Augusta have come for your blessing - they want to be married before he takes ship for Amherst's New York garrison. It seemed right to the Duke you reside nearby."

Bewilderment settled on the man of law. "A duke's daughter? Highly unsuitable!"

Cecil Worth gave up and laughed, "You are a most unusual man, Beckett. You will make an unusual judge for you are naturally incorruptible!"

Beckett stayed quiet all the way to the villa. His lips darkened to liver color when he spoke. "My son has bowed my head. And not for the first time. Put in this posture by his ambition or his insouciance, I humbly and proudly accept my elevation and will serve as Justice at Princeton *at the king's pleasure*. But I do not know if I like this daughter-in-law!"

"Why would you not?" Cecil demanded.

"She seems too much the pragmatist, throwing the race with Elizabeth's son and making book on mine merely for Horace's lighter handicap."

That afternoon, Beckett interviewed the hopeful pair in the marble drawing room with the tessellated floor where many years before Hanna had bested him. Beckett sat. Augusta sat facing him. Horace hung back, standing at the hearth, supporting himself with one hand on the mantle. He shielded his eyes with that hand.

Beckett cleared his throat to speak.

Augusta spoke instead. "We hope for your blessing, Lord Beckett."

Beckett rolled his eyes. "If I give it you will be marrying down, for Horace is, by virtue of *my* title, merely a callow baronet. How nice for him and me, Lady Augusta."

"Marrying Horace Beckett were never marrying down. As you must know, noble titles and nobility are vastly different."

Michael Beckett replied nothing to this thrust.

Augusta filled the frightening silence. "Horace will distinguish himself in the colonies and his military rank be high and he shall earn a better title equal with mine."

Beckett smirked, "We Becketts must run to keep up with you of Leed or run amuck."

Ho buried his face in both his hands.

"Lady Augusta, I accepted the elevation simply to be able to hold this discussion with you. I hope that I will be swept along on my son's coattails or my grandchildren be embarrassed to sit on my knee!"

Ho stepped closer. "Father! Take care!"

"I wish *you* had, Bart." Beckett disregarded Horace for another piercing look at his incipient daughter-in-law. He judged her beauty too rich for his son. He gave her the hard eye. "Why this rush?" Beckett insinuated then eased, "My son is young...."

Ho interrupted, "I'm old enough to fight Amherst's wars for him!"

"And old enough to leave school. Perhaps if you had attended Cambridge, university might have held your interest."

"My dream was to study with Moses."

"Ah! I trust this new dream shall be longer-lived!"

"Please don't!" Ho struck a fist against his mouth. He moved a step toward Augusta who was studying Michael with incredulity born of kinder parental treatment. Ho pressed, "My living with Bluehill helped me know at last what I wanted to do in life. Your leniency about my going to Oxford has had a good effect."

Beckett shook his head in admiration, "There is the germ of a jurist in you yet. What a shame to risk it to the rigors of the military service. And do not deceive yourself about my leniency! Your going to Oxford was a matter of finances. The House of

Kirke had its way with me, for the civilized world seems to be in the thrall of that half-breed!"

Augusta cut Michael off. "I am as well!"

"Well!"

August persisted, "Moses moved me, however painfully, to understand that I require what is real. Horace is reality! And I love him for it!"

Beckett nearly whistled at her skill. "Lady Augusta! Horace turned eighteen in June."

Augusta was unflappable. "I turned nineteen in August."

"August. Naturally, August!" Michael savored the Brites' genius for the literal. "You and my son are then virtually of an age."

Ho straightened with hope. Augusta stayed immobile.

Beckett accomplished some quick arithmetic on the tips of his fingers. "He is in arrears to you some four hundred days. How shall we even things up to your purpose?"

"Father!" Ho blanched at this slap.

But Augusta was not so fragile. "We know that we cannot. What Horace lacks in years he makes up in forthrightness." Her blow did not seem deliberate. "My *purpose*, as you call it, is to have Horace Beckett for my husband for my life. We would marry before he undertakes his patriotic duty far from home."

Beckett's fingers now met as a Gothic arch. "This haste is what befuddles me." His clear gaze concentrated on Augusta's stomacher.

Ho swept over to his father. "Father, I pray you consider your words to the lady with care!"

Beckett said nothing.

Augusta spoke calmly into the void. "I am a virgin."

Beckett rocked forward in his chair.

"And so I shall remain until I am the legal wife of Horace Beckett whether it take ten days or ten years."

Beckett blinked. He blinked repeatedly. "You...are...very... incisive."

Augusta leaned toward him across the table made of polished stone. She took hold of Beckett's hands. "My idea is that you give consent to Ho's marrying me now while there is cheer to our desire and that you and I will travel as father and daughter to America where I will help you establish your new home! I'll serve as your hostess in the New Jersey colony. There will pleasant society for you too, I am sure! Afterall, they say Princeton is not so far from the Island of Manhattan!" Augusta smiled.

Beckett changed his mind about her similarity to other-worldly Elizabeth. Augusta's sensibilities were ingrained with charm - she possessed the art of joy. To his mind she was more like Hanna. Michael Beckett quaked with resentment that his son should engage himself to Hanna's facsimile.

Ho held to the back of Augusta's chair. "Agree, Father! I have never asked for much!"

"No?!" Beckett threw back his head. "You simply get your way in the few things important to you."

"This is the most important!"

Beckett rose and dismissed them with, "I shall decide soon. I will tell my decision first to the Duke."

Beckett looked up as the pair reentered the room after hours of agonized suspense. "There is one proviso." He saw their eyes resplendent with victory. "You and I, Lady Augusta, will travel first to Massachusetts." Beckett sublimated a smile. "I have professional and personal courtesies to pay. And there is only one man to design the edifice you will grace during Ho's service. The Honorable Mr. Gilbert Worth. Besides, I think it important that you visit Dowland House - the place which gave Ho his love of the region."

"But Father!" Ho objected. "Moses is there!"

Augusta grew pink of cheek.

Michael Beckett said strictly, yet with poisonous eye, "We can hope, old son. We can hope Moses is well and not at the bottom of sea!"

Augusta never lost control. "Horace, it is a small thing Justice Lord Beckett asks." Amending her expression she said, "Father Beckett, your proviso is accepted!"

The wedding took place quietly in Adderbourne's church the first day of October. A dinner for eighteen was the signal festivity.

William Leed looked down his table pleased that his daughter was wedded to a gentleman who could provide her nothing but adventure. It would have pleased him more if the adventure promised more primitive but then men like Moses were difficult to net.

Michael Beckett was pleased by the sensible celebration more than he was pleased by the repeated ineffectuality of his own truculence. It seemed to him as a result of his failures at dictating terms that his son habitually fed himself to implacable individuals with more money than he. On the matter of feeding however, the Leeds' pheasant salad did slip down easily in the company of an extraordinary Champagne.

CHAPTER FIFTY-NINE

All Hallows and November 1764

Stephen Poore sickened at news relayed by an East India clipper that an Admiralty Court had been set up at Wareham the past September over a violent incident relating to a Kirke Company ship and His Majesty's revenue cutter, *Eocha*. And where were the pigeons with the details? Poore abandoned Locke's now nearly vacant London office, threw his cape over his shoulders and ordered The Company's coach directly to Heathersley.

That same morning, Lord Worth's butler brought him a verbal tidbit with his Guernsey frog legs. A retired captain in the Channel Islands had over a pint given some gossip to the fisher who supplied the frogs to the fishmonger on the mainland at Sussex to the effect that a merchant ship sporting Kirke's yellow ensign had been sighted recently wrestling a giant storm which had bullied her more than thirty miles off course toward the Gulf of St. Malo.

Immediately, Cecil searched out Elizabeth. She was working late in her apartment on the correspondence to the Kirke boatworks in Maine in an effort to arrange employment for a number of The Company's staff.

Elizabeth worried her quill between her thumb and forefinger. "It could be Viti! Or, Uncle Gil with difficult news of Tame Deer.

Could it be Viti sending for me? I doubt that. It would be awkward for everyone if I returned...."

Cecil dashed cold water over her theories. "It could be Moses bound for Oxford."

Robbed of breath and speech at this, Elizabeth thought and finally said aloud, "If it is...he...will...come here! I should not stay."

In agreement, Cecil said with some shame, "I shouldn't like you to rush off. Sir Thomas and Moses sailed west together as we know. It could be simply word of them. Some word."

She whispered, "It could be!"

Out of respect for the custom of Heathersley, Elizabeth did not appear dressed at 7 A.M., as her habit had been in Italy. Instead, she began her work in private, clothed in a morning gown. In this way she accomplished a day's duties before the master's noon breakfast.

Poore knocked, walked in, took his seat. Their disagreement over the safe disposition of Massacuseuck ground long settled with respect to her alleged Anglo Saxon avariciousness nevertheless left Stephen extremely careful in his approach to her. Quite simply he still hurt from his being in the wrong. "You're nice to look at today!" Poore encouraged. "I like that...thing you are wearing."

Her negligee was made of a weightless fabric woven with loft so that she seemed clothed in the furze of a newborn chick. "That ship might dock today."

"Might it?" Poore kept his misgivings about *Eocha* to himself and cast about for a way to distract her from the storm-tossed ship with the yellow ensign. "I thought you'd done up for me." He looked at her under heavy lids.

She stayed quiet and then let slip, "It is my birthday."

"I had hoped you wouldn't mention it! Poore swung out of his wide chair. "I had my eye on a gift for you but am empty-handed because I stopped for nothing when the East India Company put the fear of God in me!"

"An unfounded fear." Elizabeth proclaimed. "You do agree?"

Stephen warned, "Optimism is premature."

"Pessimism would have killed me long ago."

"Then like a sensible girl – suspend judgment."

Elizabeth suspended conversation until a smile broke over her. "Steph? What was the gift!?"

Poore noted her smile - it was her smile as it had been when she was ten - light deliciously shadowed, the light winning. He marched over to her, fragile objects in the room chiming to his step. He took her in his arms and placed a kiss on her forehead. Locking her in his embrace, he said near her ear, "It was a hat."

She burst out laughing.

He held her by her shoulders so that he could see her expression. "A hat of extraordinary originality! Black, stiff tulle piled up like a meringue with skinny black plumes bobbing all over it. There was green and purple in the feathers which I thought would be magic with your eyes...."

Shrieking from outside for Cecil's man, Hubbard, sheared her away from Poore. Stephen cranked open a casement and together they squeezed through its frame. Over some hedges and beyond an enclosure, an overturned basket of linens was the pivot for a nimbus of serving girls who were moving in an erratic circle confused and excited, not knowing whether to run after Hubbard or pick up the spillage.

Elizabeth gasped, "The ship is in!"

Poore craned hard to the left. "I see some sail."

Elizabeth dashed into the corridor. She stayed panting on the gallery. Voices echoed.

Hubbard tapped briskly up the stone steps. Seeing Elizabeth he nodded, "My Lady! There is a ship. Byrne has been sent for news."

Elizabeth clung to the marble rail and then forged her way along the corridor to her rooms. She told Stephen, "It's here! No details."

"God! I must dress!" Poore fell over his own feet; angry at his gracelessness, he hurried out, but carefully.

Elizabeth stayed in the center of her room soothing her hands, their joints suddenly painful. With a jerking movement she crossed the carpet and lifted a bottle from the console. The crash of glass against stone brought Elizabeth to her knees in a pool of pale green liquid. "No!"

"Elizabeth." Cecil stood in the open door.

Elizabeth recognized him. His eyes were ringed in red.

He stepped in.

She mourned, "I've broken it! Thomas gave me perfume. He thought of it himself! Thomas gave it to me!" She knelt among the pieces of the shattered flacon. She saw herself in the breakage. And yet, the air was drenched in the scent of lilies.

"My dear! There is a yellow pennant. That is all I know."

She grabbed at her delicate collar, missing the location of its little buttons. Her adept fingers inexplicably useless, she stumbled toward the dressing room.

Cecil moved next to her, then, passed her for her closet. He paged through half a dozen cold-weather petticoats and removed from its hook a simple dress made in one piece from cloth of a chestnut-dye. "At times, I would choose for my wife. I'll send your maid." He left her kneeling, her woolen collar askew. He saw her dip her fingers gingerly into the tiny pond of precious scent and touch them to her throat.

    Cecil cautioned against their going to meet the ship. Instead, the trio gathered in the Gray Drawing Room. An hour of terse expectancy set in. Some tea and biscuits and creamed fish were brought.

    Elizabeth took the tea out of courtesy. Poore gravitated listlessly toward the biscuits.

    After a few negligible bites of the herring, Cecil had the impromptu breakfast carried away. Words died of their own lightness, never gaining the weight of conversation.

    "This could be the good news we've been wanting." Cecil checked his watch.

    Poore posited a theory, "It is only the sky so gray and the rain threatening throws our mood." He exchanged glances with Cecil when nothing either of them said broke Elizabeth's abstraction.

    Like a music box wound, she produced sound. "With fashionable women's hair what it is, and the die-hard wig, how could my birthday hat be worn? Hair must change!"

    Humoring her, the men leaned back as if to see a new image of women on the ceiling.

    "Everything must change." Elizabeth amended.

    "Less volume." Cecil missed her larger social statement.

    "Smaller hair." Poore chuckled.

    "My hat is a harbinger."

As if her pronouncement had been heard by the spheres, hooves pounded up the allé of leafless trees. Cecil turned toward the long windows as diffidently as he might do in the dining hall of his club to catch a discreet glimpse of newcomers. "I don't recognize the chap but he's pushing hard and not holding his saddle very well."

Elizabeth flitted across the acute angle of the room. "It's the captain's mate or the captain then. Not a good sign. Especially if it's Captain Dray."

"I met a Jones once. A Captain Jones came to my club with a note to the effect that Gib and Hanna were in town with a child named Wolf." Catching her torn look, he added, "These men age. Even Hubbard! I hardly recognize him sometimes!"

Elizabeth circled near him and brushed his hand with hers.

Doors opened smartly, their snap louder as Hubbard neared with the salver. "My Lord, compliments of Captain Webster of the *Lionet*."

"*The Lionet*!" Elizabeth said aloud. "No wonder she went astray in rough weather! Captain Webster has not nearly the experience of Captain Dray. Thomas is in trouble!

Cecil snapped up the folded paper. The young captain's card lay underneath. Cecil completed reading his short note. "Hubbard, have Captain Webster wait for me in the receiving room. Send Byrne back with the coach for Mr. Bluehill." Cecil's words came crisp but he had trouble rising and moving toward Elizabeth as if his body were rebelling under a load too heavy to carry. "Elizabeth, some terrible fortune has overtaken Sir Thomas. I am not clear as to its exact nature. Wolf asks, if you are still at Heathersley, that he may deliver to you personally a letter written you from his father. *Are* you still at Heathersley?"

Elizabeth was conscious of a slight blue streak cutting across the November sky and of her voice as loud as the ocean. "Why, yes!"

Elizabeth sat alone in the Gray Room under possibilities as if they were stone slabs. As a result, she knew that if it were not for her cap, the ruffles of which fell to her chin, she would appear as a lizard, flat at the crown, eyes bright and bulging.

As with most of Cecil's house, there was very little of the current age surrounding her. The hewn stone of the walls and floors created a cathedral hush. One could read, write, invent here. One could listen well in this room and, by extension, speak well. Chair frames gilded silver, black veins running white marble tabletops, might have seemed cold, but myriad lamps of ancient date casting a blushing light through satin-glass made asceticism sing. The Gray Room, admitting the mural of the seasons through its extravagant windows, imposed reverence on flesh-and-blood beings.

Elizabeth heard a verbal struggle. Men's voices gruffly contended as the gigantic doors were cracked then pushed open wider by degrees. She could see Stephen Poore attempting to arbitrate a disagreement between Cecil and a beautiful young man.

Cecil implored, "I simply want to make it easy."

The young man staunchly held his conviction. "It cannot be easy!"

Stephen. "Could I not buffer...?"

"I was there! I must speak first!"

"Logical, surely, but so sudden!"

Moses turned into the room. "Hardly!"

Cecil insisted, "Wolf! At least let Hubbard announce you!"

Moses pulled the doors open before Hubbard could and closed them smartly behind himself. His back to the panels shutting all others out, his chest rising and falling to compensate his lungs for his rush, Moses floundered, "This is the worst possible...nothing could be more painful to me...I mean to say I am thoroughly sorry that we are to reunite under such circumstances! Lady Elizabeth...I am...Moses Bluehill...my tidings are ill!" At the visceral sound she made he stepped into the room, a chamber oddly grown many times its original size in his absence.

Elizabeth was balanced sideways on a bench. She rose. The heavy silk she wore made no sound and she progressed toward him like an apparition. She choked out, "From what you say, you should not call me, 'Lady Elizabeth'." Her hand wandered to her white linen cap and pulled it down and off. This subtle revelation, as if somehow he should recognize her better by the absence of a scrap of cloth, affected him, broke his heart over her.

Tears blocked the sight of her son from her. The hand which had pulled the cap away, now dug into each of her eyes. "*I* am sorry! I cannot explain how sorry I am for this...pass we are come to."

Moses cursed his fate and reached into his long coat. He offered her a sealed letter. Only the length of the stiff, folded letterpaper remained between them and yet they did not touch.

"Madam!" Moses extended the hand holding the message.

Her name in the labored script of Silent Fox was clearly visible. Sketched by him in sepia, the letters were angular, joining like twigs crossing. Elizabeth had waited her entire adult life for sight of the effort of his pen; now she shrank away.

"And Qunneke? My sister-wife? How has she fared?"

Moses reached for her arm not to support her so much as to feel her living self. His hand slipped under her naked wrist and he guided her to sit.

She allowed herself to look into eyes she had made laugh when they were new.

Moses could not stand so far above her. He went down on one knee beside her. "I am sorry to tell you she has passed away! May I call you what you are? Nokace! My mother!"

With an outcry rich with pleasure and pain, she slipped forward, her face full against his coat. His arms closed over her back and his fingers lost themselves in her plaited hair. That caress, those hands, that physical candor, so similar to the touch she had forgone for so many years, birthed sighs in her and the letter fell through their embrace. Elizabeth moved her cheek against his cheek. "My child!"

Moses drew back surprised.

Stephen and Cecil went quietly mad with the lack of noise from the Gray Room. The doors flapped open. Poore and Worth stood in the opening gawking like a pair of geese.

Moses shot to his feet. Behind him the doors closed with a snap.

Elizabeth reached ineffectually for the letter. She gave it up and searched Moses' face instead.

From that yearning look, Moses drank in keener pleasure than he had known or had ever manufactured in fantasy. Elizabeth was looking at him. Him only. She had let Wakwa's letter wait. He reoffered the letter. "Mother!"

Elizabeth grasped his sleeves instead. "Qunneke is gone?"
"Yes!"

His suffering on the point was so sharply clear that she let it lie. She said feebly, "Thomas Kirke is gone?"

Moses sat with her. "He is...gone. Grandly." Moses' voice broke. "Shall I read for you?"

The seal made from red wax bore no imprint from a ring; it carried Wakwa's old mark, two pointed fox's ears with a line scratched across for silence. Moses tried to break the seal with his thumb but Elizabeth pulled a pin from her hair and carefully slit the diagonal line breaking the silence of a decade and a half. Elizabeth could not see. She only passed her hand across the single page as if the terrible truth would enter her mind through her skin.

Moses began at the opening, her name. "'*Elizabeth*!'"

As the story of Kirke's passing swept over her, she gave out the rough sounds of voiding, of the confinement couch, of birth. Her sorrow sought egress because the womb where it lodged was crowded with her crimes against the man who had loved her above his life. With pain, a twisted child whose invisible face was a dead ringer for hers parted her flesh.

Moses' arms were around the waist once large with the waters that had floated him in her. She bowed into his humane embrace. He felt the *Merriweather* guided into port in the mist, drew in London's cool breath, saw the mysterious white arms and the bosom of white that had dissolved at Locke's summons.

As if she read his mind, Elizabeth pulled back and asked in a voice ruined by grief, "Do you remember me?"

"I remember...something...." he left it at that and began to love her when she did not press him for details. Moses stood on shaking legs, somewhat shy of her now the news was broken. "Unless Kirke had died for right, God knows how long it would have taken my father to write to you on any subject or how long for me to deliver his message!"

Elizabeth looked with fascination at the seemly letter of condolence that bore no invitation to return.

CHAPTER SIXTY

January 1765

Incense woke Elizabeth. The smoke rose fragrantly to her. She came up on her arms in her narrow bed and looked toward the little window, expecting in her demi-sleep to see a censor from St. Mark's blessing the canal bordering the Asolo.

Pine trees, black in the dawn, fringed the morning beyond the sill. Elizabeth pulled herself out of her cocoon of blankets and shivered slipperless to the small window overlooking the woods, which had been her view of the world from her infancy. She pushed the transom open and set the brass prop. For the first time she realized the windows in her room matched the windows on a ship.

Elizabeth knelt on the cold floor-planks so that her face was even with the window's open angle. She breathed in sweet smoke. Nowhere else she had travelled offered scent from simple kindling like Sippicon. There was no more apt name for her natal village than Sweetwood.

She and Moses had floated into Buzzards Bay the day before in a brilliant January noon. Elizabeth denied herself the thrill of her first sight of Massachusetts in over fifteen years staying below decks with portholes obscured; she shrank from the morbid prospect of surveying the waters covering *New Psyche II*. Moses pushed her mercilessly to view the harbor haunted by Kirke's martyrdom. A length of mast like a defiant finger pointed out of the ship's shallow grave. Their captain had blasted the scene with a respectful volley of cannon.

The sweet smoke intrigued Elizabeth. She puzzled over a fire so close to the young pines, the aromatic wall she had planted. She had met Qunneke's son, Lightfoot, the evening before. As the apprentice manager of Dowland Farm, would he have built such a fire? She dismissed the notion as irrational and dashed back to the bed of her innocent days.

Her eyes resisted closing. After so many years lived in Italy surrounded by stone and gold and glittering things, she could not relinquish the wholesome sight of plain, waxed wood. She stroked the parti-colored quilt whose stitches had been poked into existence by the knarled fingers of local matrons who once peopled her family's life and wove stories at the Dowland fire.

Elizabeth was amazed that she had slept at all with the great steadiness of land under her, with the sight of Kirke's underwater grave burned into her mind's eye, with the pressure of the Worths' welcoming embraces still warm against her body, with Moses close at Worth Farm, with Augusta and Michael Beckett under the Dowland roof. She breathed deeply of the wispy smoke and pondered how she could have slept when word was that Silent Fox would pay his respects at tea on this the first full day of her return.

Certainly, this formal visit was not the swift run together across the lawn she had girlishly pictured seventeen, ten, even five years before. Wakwa's sedate house call presaged nothing more than his following in his official capacity the etiquette of the locale.

Out of bed a second time, she watched the now pink sky for a trace of the smoke and was rewarded with a rush of gray upward. The fire had just been dashed. Its scent livened her imagination. Would Wakwa Manunnappu, the Black Fox Who-waits, desert his name, which was his soul? Yes, he was one who waited; he had done that. He was also the black fox, invisible at night, and seen only against the light of dawn.

Excited by the sudden delivery of a truth, Elizabeth opened the lid of the small trunk she had packed with necessaries for her first hours on the farm. She lifted out a nightrail, her brushes, her soaps, her creams, her portfolio, two changes of linen and a woolen dress. She seized a pair of skin trousers and a jacket lined with seal. She stood naked, convulsing from cold, dipped her hands into the cold water in her washing bowl and splashed herself clean. Dressed, she pulled on low fur boots. She left her hair in last night's braid and took the stairs like a boy.

Roused by the muffled racket in Elizabeth's room, Augusta struggled up and onto the gallery just in time to see a youth disappear below into the kitchen. Horace Beckett's wife stole across to Elizabeth's door expecting to see her lying murdered. Finding no one, she crossed the empty room to close the window. Augusta reached it just in time to see Elizabeth, mannishly dressed, enter the pines.

Maddened with curiosity, with heart-bursting, baseless joy, Elizabeth made her way among the conifers. The after-scent of the sweet wood smoke led her to the smothered fire as if by a chain. She regarded it as one might regard a mine of diamonds or of gold. Elizabeth pressed ahead for Twisting River. She moved boldly over open ground but stopped on a hilltop. Dense forest of many species flourished at her right hand. Ahead, a wild hedge screened the farmland from a large pond. A man bare above his waist knelt there twisting a floss of reeds. Her heart sliced her as it beat. The man was Wakwa.

His ritual above the water, cleaning his teeth first with the fine string and then with clay from the border of the pond occupied him for long minutes. Her muscles gave and she found support against an arm-thick vine. Wakwa's methodical regimen, even aware she was housed not a quarter mile away, struck Elizabeth like a blunt object. Yet, he was there, as tall, as unhurried, as full of grace as when she had first held him in her sight when she had run from Hudson's dog. Wakwa's face was averted, denying her any hint of his state of mind. His hair in a queue looked less black than the ebony she remembered. Was it the distance, the misty morning that quieted its color; was his hair gray?

She became convinced that he had kept a vigil behind the evergreens. She grew soft at the idea that he had kept watch over her, over Dowland House. Then her stomach turned to stone as she recalled that Wakwa's vigil after her exile from the tribe had not climaxed in his coming to comfort her or to take her back.

Elizabeth knew from old experience of him that Wakwa Manunnappu would prepare his person well for the diplomatic chore ahead. He would go to pesuponk, steam the fear, the fatigue out of himself in the hut and then dash into the river. After a swim, he would light his pipe and smoke. He would plan the words he would say as if polishing an arrowhead. He would think of her as she had been. When he finally entered Dowland House what would he make of the slight slippage of her cheeks to sorrow? Would he detect the effect of the years on her? Her self-concern disgusted her.

Wakwa retrieved a skin shirt from his blanket roll and put it on. He tossed the strowd over his shoulders. He began climbing the slope, moving straight toward her. He veered north to gain the trees.

Elizabeth leaned forward as if to touch him. She strained against an imbecilic showing of herself. When the forest had swallowed him she abandoned her hiding place to find him.

The pines whistled, bare branches clacked. Wakwa stopped. He listened. He walked again, north and east. Having mandated privacy for his preparations, there should be, could be, no trespasser in his sector.

Elizabeth slowed when he slowed, stopped when he stopped.

Wakwa sensed he was not alone for the swifts started up from their nests as he approached and did not resettle after he passed by. Porcupines scuttled out of his path and did not close behind him. The hair at the back of his neck bristled. Distraught at the prospect of that afternoon's remeeting Elizabeth with all his plans dust, he half-hoped the man-hunter close behind him stalked to kill. Assassins were accomplished, silent. His ears taught him that he was the prey of a careful, imperfect, persistent invader. His heart pounded. Wakwa played with pace. He moved fast, took the upgrade fast, for fifty yards he ran the old deer path toward the hunting lodge. He stopped in his tracks. His hunter did not. He heard her unmistakable tread.

Elizabeth stymied a cry when his hands hid his face.

Stiff from the effort of not turning toward her, Wakwa limped away along the deer path.

Elizabeth used a tree for a spine. She turned her head denying herself the solace of tears. She turned back. Wakwa was gone.

Wakwa fell back on the ancient way. He did not want to be wrong. He lost himself in the trees, made his circle, doubled back behind her to be sure it was she. No one had a step like Elizabeth's, her run a lion's, straight to her target, no movement extraneous.

He saw her. A woman thirty-seven, surprisingly the same, slender, her hair still bright chestnut and shining, her skin paler than the paleness he had once caressed. Her eyes looked even larger than in the memories he had cherished of them, their greatness amplified by a face winnowed by experience. Like the Elizabeth he had once known, she pulled the leaves off her masculine clothes, thought, lifted her chin, then walked north at her own pace.

He saw she anticipated his destination as if without a break in their relation. The invisible rope binding him to reason, to his long-held plans, jerked him to his knees. Here was a chance to take refuge in the otan, to withhold sight of his defeated self from her till the tiny winter sun was on the wane, some mask for his failures, but he refused to slink away like small game. He rose like an ox bent to the yoke and chose another way to the lodge.

The hunting lodge, not built as a dwelling, had been their first real home. The door she had asked for in place of the woven curtain still hung on its wooden hinges. The roof shingles were still broken by the glass skylight Wakwa had made to bring the sun to her. Tall pines still circled it like sentries and dropped a carpet of spent needles making footsteps soft and fragrant. To this structure Wakwa had carried her from her lying-in in the woods, their newborn in Qunneke's arms.

Her advance on that hallowed place in this haphazard way culminated in a wild cry. Elizabeth called Wakwa out. She was sure he was inside without even the sign of fire from the smokehole. Her voice was an eruption of the foul mix of her suffering at his hands, of her addiction to him, of all that she had swallowed for years for the sake of intractable love. *WAKWA!*

As the embittered sound of his name cut through the wood, the last wall between them, he was laying a fire. His voluntary muscles shook him as if they had brains of their own. He noisily stacked peachwood from trees planted accidentally in the wilderness by the stones of the fruit cast out of Englishmen's orchards. The journey of the seeds, so like Elizabeth's, made him feel the sacrilege of burning those particular branches. With nothing else at hand, he piled them on. His head sank into his hands as her roar diminished to a moan. He reached into his pack for a punk shell with its live embers.

The door creaked open. Wakwa, like the condemned before his executioner, turned toward Elizabeth from his low position.

She saw a little something of his face in the thin light of the nearly windowless lodge.

Half-crouched like a runner in a race, he came to his feet.

"Forgive me!" She stood humbly, her eyes downcast.

"Woman!" Wakwa, the spokesman, groped for words. He sank down to sitting, the heels of his hands pressing his eyes into his skull.

Elizabeth cried out, "Look at me!"

He looked at her. He came to his knees and faced her. Then his beautiful voice broke. "I am not...clean!"

She understood him and asked simply as she closed the door behind her, "How clean am I?"

Something in her statement brought the Sachim smartly to his feet. "*I* was to bring you home! I am covered in shame like a slave is covered in soot at the fire! In every design of my life I have *failed*!" Signs of duress cut into his face.

She dug in near the threshold scolding, "I love you yet, and you say you have failed!!!"

Something akin to happiness pervaded him, easing the lines, lightening the shadows. He permitted himself a few steps forward.

She waited.

Wakwa approached her. He stood just out of her reach. He reeked of smoke and of sweat brought out by his agitation. "You always have had such a way of speaking!" His eyes glittered in half-belief as if she might be a ghost he could pass his hand through. "You are here!"

"I am."

Then he was sure. He pulled back.

She took the few steps to him and captured his hands in hers. A cry boiled out of her. His great, strong, long hands were in hers. She brought them to her eyes to block the sight of his turmoil. She touched his broken nails with her fingertips.

He carefully pulled himself from her grasp.

Her voice went to mud. She retreated. "Wakwa, shall I leave you?"

He looked with static fascination at her, her hand on the latch as his had been when, before he had known her in her flesh, for honor's sake he had proposed to give her up to her father and make the case against her bond to Hudson.

He moved not at all.

She turned and pulled the latch, her hand wrapping the edge of the door he had built. She hunched like a crone, waste, tearless. She gave herself over to the death of hope she had foiled for nearly two decades.

"Stay!" He said, "Elizabeth!"

Wakwa reeled her in and, crushing her body against his, somehow brought her close to the struggling, untended fire. Together they sank to the rude wood floor and lay heaped bone on bone hurting terribly. They felt their bones so heavy, heavy with the years, years shouldering other loves, duty, pain, their bones rang against one another's like metal pipes tossed to the ground. They lay like people dead. Desire for the presence of the other impacted for so long like marrow diseased, choked motion. Time lay crushed under their static bodies. Had breath ceased, they would have been found like that, like driftwood.

The flesh lifted their burden the way peachwood slowly catches fire, throwing sparks, the red cascade igniting the branches into steady, hot, bright flames, a clear and beautiful light. With his fingers, his legs, his chest, his throat, Wakwa perceived that Elizabeth actually lay in his grasp. "You are with me!" He breathed amazed. She made a single weeping cry and took his hands against her breast so that he could feel the pumping of her heart. "For this moment I have kept alive!"

The native man accepted the homage in silence.

"My sin!" She confessed.

He turned her face up to his. He probed her eyes for her condition. He said not without pride, "*I* caused your sin. Your sin is mine!" His tongue on her lips savored the sweetness of their fault.

Nothing slow now, the trappings of human modesty slipped. Her fingers, as fast as insects' wings, untied the fur closures of her jacket. His shirt melted away. They gloried in the kiss of skin.

"Forgive me this!" Wakwa kept Elizabeth close.

Elizabeth acknowledged their momentous loss groaning, settling her cheek under the masterly bone of his cheek. The pleasure so long missed stabbed her with lost youth, failure of soul. Again she made her searing call.

He prepared their way. His presence of mind awakened memories in her. He reached into purple shadows and pulled a batting toward the fire. "I have hurt you enough!" He lifted her to the softer place. His face went young. He slipped far into her interior, not artlessly but without artifice, like a boat into its cove.

Moses rode ahead of Gil. Hanna and her new maid, recently bought from a slaver and expensively freed, followed in Matthew Freeman's wagon close behind. They passed Lightfoot at the smokehouse collecting the breakfast meat.

Tapping at the kitchen door, Worth made his way in first. "Don't get that look in your eye, Millie. We've eaten. Where is everyone?"

They found Michael Beckett and Augusta in the sitting room, dressed for day, although Beckett's head sported an ice pack.

Gil chose to overlook it. "Lady Augusta! *Lord* Beckett."

Beckett mumbled, "Really annoys you doesn't it, Worth? For that reason alone, I'll regret dropping the title when Horace kicks the military in the balls while scorching the King's earth in some sedition or other."

"Careful!" Gil warned. "In present company."

Unhappily hung over, Beckett regarded Augusta Brite. "My daughter-in-law should know better than anyone what I'm talking about."

Hanna slipped into the room between the sunbeams, the freedwoman, Zenobia, in tow. Making her good-mornings, Hanna said, "I hope you were both comfortable last night. Lady Augusta, things are simple here! Elizabeth not down?" Hanna's color was high, her step quick, her breath snapped like a sail. "On such a day?"

Augusta found herself face to face with Moses who was solemn, intent.

Beckett swung out of his chair as the sunlight found him.

Gil scolded him quietly, "If I've mentioned it once, I've done so a thousand times, this is a dry house. I must be able to trust you will not use alcohol here. Stay at Worth Farm if you're intent on destroying yourself."

"I will remember the kindness of your invitation."

"Beckett...!"

Beckett raised a forefinger. "*Lord* Beckett to you!"

Hanna ignored their banter and made for the stairs. "She's not hesitant? Not having second thoughts?"

With mighty effort Beckett turned. The bag of ice fell to the floor and split. "On the contrary, Hanna, Elizabeth Dowland has but one thought. And hesitant she is not."

Together Gil and Hanna asked, "What is that supposed to mean!"

Beckett looked seriously troubled. "I shall have a devil of a time on the bench if my most obvious declarations confound my hearers. I defer to Lady Augusta!"

With a dignity so quiet it cast blueness about her, Augusta announced, "While in this fresh, naturally noble place, I am no longer a duke's daughter, nor Lady Augusta Brite Beckett, wife of a baronet. I am Mrs. Horace Beckett. I should like to be called by my familiars by my name, Augusta, and I even would prefer Gus. I miss being called that. As to Elizabeth, I saw her leave at dawn. She went into the pine wood."

Moses struggled with the notion. "My mother? In the forest? Alone?"

Beckett reacted, "There is a falling off in apprehension among us that I take quite seriously. We are speaking the same language after all. At least, the same words! Can you people take nothing at face value? Elizabeth Dowland without taking the least notice of my counsel has slipped away into the trees once again. It is the idea fixee that has led us all by the nose for years. Really, I have quite enough to do getting the Admiralty Court not to hang Locke and Dray, and riding herd on Gilbert's everlasting architectural revisions, let alone wringing my hands over his niece's perambulations without having to repeat every sentence twelve times!"

Hanna and Gil were already caught in conference. Zenobia, without instruction was attending to the debacle on the floor.

Moses sought out Augusta. "You are sure? She went so many hours ago? You told us not?"

Augusta looked at him surprised. "You did not take exception when you found me in my garden. Elizabeth Dowland is freeborn. Should she not have the freedom of her ground?"

As if Augusta had never been his passion Moses responded coolly, "This is not her ground. It is mine. Conveyed by Elizabeth Dowland to me and administered by my uncle till I am twenty-one. My mother has crossed from ground not hers onto ground not hers! You should have called me. You and your *father-in-law*. Anything could happen!"

Beckett barged in, "And I submit that it already has. Any leverage we need with the Sachim is dashed. Why do you think I uncorked my medicinal whiskey in the ante-meridian?"

Moses turned his back on them and joined Gil and Hanna.

Gil said, "I'll take the north quarter. You'll want to go into the otan. Take your aunt."

"Take me too!" Augusta leaped at such a possibility.

"This is no shooting party!" Moses set her back. "I want you to meet the People, Augusta. But they must *invite* you."

"Aren't you one of them?"

Worth hardly heard their squabble. "If we find her she may be quite unsettled. In her mind."

Holding his temples, Beckett shouted in place, hobbled by the African maid sweeping chips of ice into her apron, "Her mind is quite settled on one thing and one thing only! Her recent widowing notwithstanding! Although, I cannot grudge her pluck. More, I do not know how I can advise her if she remains incorrigible."

Worth stepped up. "What advice is necessary? You have secured her land to her son. Move on!"

"You are just a farmer after all." Beckett showed his disappointment. "Do you think the Parliament will stop at a tax on stamps? Do you think the Crown will stop at snuffing out an initiative here, a voice of reason there, a riot somewhere else? Kirke's violent passing is a terrible omen opening a floodgate of royal abuses that I cannot yet imagine. The King, my benefactor, is a known madman. Ha!" Beckett laughed at himself. "If his brain is squeezed by the wrong manipulator do you think the conveyance will stand? Do you think the Indian town will stand? Do you think the legal standing of the native Peoples will not be abridged and in one easy wipe of the board all the carefully laid pieces won't be brushed to the floor? Think you not, the very Stamp Tax is to pay for killing off Indians in the war just won?" He danced out of Zenobia's way. "Do you think?"

With one eye on Beckett, Worth asked his wife, "What is your feeling, Ana? She has been gone a long time."

Hanna looked at her shoes at that. "A long time. Yes. I think she knows her way. I just do not want to see her hurt again."

Moses strained to separate their meanings. "You think my father would hurt her?"

Hanna Dowland Worth held him close. "Find Awepu. Surely he will know what we should do."

Wakwa dealt wood to the famished flames and they grew. He built the fire dangerously high. He rejoined Elizabeth under the blood-red strowd and whispered, "We are like children!"

She cast an arm across her eyes.

Wakwa held that long, white arm, sparer than when she was half her age. "Woman! Woman!"

She rose against him on her side. "We are *not* like children!"

Wakwa had forgotten the precision of her mind, her lack of humor if humor touched a sore part. He hesitated then plunged ahead, "Was there no joy...?"

She laid her finger against his lips. "In the marriage *you* arranged for me with Thomas?"

His face altered and he looked more the guilty youth than the man of fifty.

"I strove. Not hard. Poor man."

He hushed her. Covered her eyes and nose and mouth and chin and let his hand slide to her throat. Bearing no resemblance to the uninitiated young, he lifted her scars away, his face, his hands, his teeth, his tongue, as his scalpels. He backed against the wall, her fragrance high as if she were an apple split open in the cold.

The big room lit by the single window revealed him to her. His skin around his ribs shone with subtle scars - four on each side. She placed her fingers on each of them and was thrown by how exactly her hands suited the closed wounds. She found no way to question him.

He said only, "Your marks. When they pulled you away. I was told to keep them open and I did."

She rocked him like a baby.

He soothed her upset with his knuckles against her cheek. A smile of perverse joy spread. "I did not tell them it was a way to keep you next to me."

In that insubordination she took untellable pleasure. She sought his eyes and stopped at his hollowed cheeks, their engraved lines smoothed by fresh experience of love. As she had when she proposed long ago that he take her as his second wife of two, she set her hand on his thigh, no victim to the years. His eyes, bent on her, he remembered.

"What will we do?"

He sighed, "We should bathe!"

She laughed.

A puckish smile fought his middle age. He looked at her, delighted at her joy returning. But he threw the mood aside and groaned, "I want to sleep. I want to take you away with me to sleep for at least as many years as we have been apart."

"Sleep! There is much to do! We must save Dire. There are people to see to. Wakwa! It is as if I have been asleep all these years!"

"If we do not linger we can arrive at Dowland House by dark." She looked at him in panic.

"Unless you wish to arrive alone."

"I wish for us to arrive on time!"

At four, the appointed hour, the sinking sun cast light upward through the naked trees lighting the tribal guests' arrival. Awepu, the master of this event, advised the English family waiting, "The Sachim and Elizabeth are coming. Together."

The order Awepu chose was to send first Wakwa's father, Tame Deer's mother, the council of elders, and his own wife, Meadow-in-the-Night, with their three unmarried sons. They mingled with their hosts in an easy arc at the perimeter of the Dowland sitting room. Awepu had timed a slightly later entrance for his second son, Tamoccon, with his bride, Sequan, Wakwa's daughter. Lightfoot, dressed cleanly in simple English clothes, arrived alone from his cabin in the pine glade.

Gil whispered to Hanna, "I was not half this nervous waiting for Silent Fox the first time!"

Hanna squeezed his hand and watched Augusta watch the Ninnuock.

Beckett watched the clock. "Lateness after the rigors of their day will make quite a bad impression." He peeled away toward the kitchen windows. "Worth! He shouted. Do not miss this!"

"There is no need to bellow! *Michael Lord Beckett*!"

"Worth, you are such a stiff from time to time, I wonder *you* haven't got a title!" Beckett blasted back.

Augusta boldly followed Gil to the humblest quarter of the house.

Out of the luminous backdrop of trees, ten guards advanced. These were young men, brave ones, in buckskin.

Beckett's brows spoke to Augusta about such showiness.

The path went empty. A tall figure grew larger from the vanishing point.

"At last! In the flesh!" Beckett announced. "This Silent Fox. This Black Fox Who-waits. The Grand Mufti of Massachusetts! Once a statesman recognized, reduced now to trafficking in overbred nags! He prevails in all situations by sheer stubbornness. He outlasts all claims on him notwithstanding civilization, progress, or force. Time and adversaries are to him as eggshells. If he isn't the magnificent humbug!" Beckett carried on.

Augusta, shoulder to shoulder with Gil, stood transfixed.

Elizabeth walked briskly. Close to her, Moses. Behind them, their guards.

Beckett dashed reverence. "His crown's askew, his hunting's done, his ways and means of living shot, his voice reduced to a peep in the wilderness, the decorated hero of the French War marching to the jeers of his beneficiaries."

"Look!" Gil remarked to Augusta. "Look at Beth's face! Just a day with him!"

But Augusta looked at Moses.

Beckett could not resist saying, "You, Lady Augusta, the daughter of dukes, are observing at rare close-range the Great Huckster himself. He survives by adapting and adopting the

English way, not to mention possessing, or more properly, repossessing, the reluctant heiress, the long-suffering and eternally useful daughter of Charles Dowland."

Augusta's sight was filled with Silent Fox, with his carriage, his color, his form, his pride, his ascendant affection for the grown son whose hand he now held, his soft step near the woman he loved. Augusta could not move her eyes from him. "Father-in-law, the Sachim is no humbug nor huckster, neither. He, *Lord Beckett*, of Princeton, is a prince *born*!" She swept away from Beckett's vantage point to wait in her place in the sitting room.

CHAPTER SIXTY-ONE

January 1765

Wakwa and Elizabeth shared the settle. Wakwa wore the clothes of state: his dark green coat from the war, a shirt of cream-colored wool closed at the throat with the Governor's Medal awarded him after Quebec. His legs were covered in skin trousers. His footgear was a pair of tall mockussinchass, their fur linings turned out to form cuffs just below his knees. His wild majesty, simply and deliberately created, was augmented by a sash of black money aslant his chest and back. In a gesture to the imposing headdresses of the past, a single green feather ornamented his loose black hair.

Elizabeth, too, was attired with attention to the significance of the occasion. She had sent to the house for the dense wool gown from her trunk. Its fitted bodice ending in a point from the waist to her crux, its soft gathers at the hips and long flowing sleeves tight at the wrists made it eminently comfortable in a woodland setting. A small ruff of the same teal-colored wool edged in pale green Venice satin protected her throat and hinted of a life exotic and supremely civilized. Her boots were of pale ostrich skin. In place of a sedate cap, she wore a crown of braids.

Michael Beckett sat opposite, indignant at their display. Hanna and Gilbert Worth, in a state of fluctuating joy, kept the Stirlings and the Lows company in side chairs. The Ninnuock, calm, almost smug with rewarded expectation, placed themselves behind their British family close to the proscenium fire.

Moses stood on the periphery next to Augusta. She clutched the back of a ladder-back chair and watched the native company as if viewing rare plantings through a garden gate. Moses concentrated on the sight of his father indivisible from a woman not Qunneke. Their nearly desperate attachment snared his imagination. He saw them holding to one another as a parent holds a child lately lost - each a parent to the other, each visibly aching with the pain of separation and rediscovery.

Augusta touched Moses' hand. "She shines like a star against him!"

Moses saw it. His voice was raw. "He has been moving toward that light since I can remember and gotten nowhere. She had to come to him."

Augusta swallowed as if feeding on something sharp. "Your father is gloriously beautiful!" Blushing fiercely, she tried to correct any misimpression, "Not only his person."

Moses witnessed her spinning and drowning as if she were a lovely insect.

Nor did she aid her recovery with, "I want to kneel before him!"

Moses took some pity. "'*Manittoo*!' That is what we say of such a phenomenon. It means, '*he-is-like-a-god*!'" Then Moses delivered the coup de maitre, "My veins run with his blood. Am I not Manittoo? Do you want to kneel before *me*, Augusta?"

"You?" She faced him fully and paid him roundly. "You, the lone Wolf?"

Wounded, he looked to his parents, small comfort when their romantic tie was so evident, their differences endemic to their appeal; his sire, primeval, the woman who had conceived, carried, and borne him, ethereal. For the first time, Moses gave thought to his Grandfather Dowland, to his quandary and his suffering when the fact of the bond had been made plain to him.

Augusta made a frail attempt at civility. "What has she got that holds him so?"

Moses savaged her. "Is it what she has got or what she gives?"

A country buffet went forward. Gourds, bottom-levelled, warming the palms cupped around them, held a delicate soup of squash and cinnamon. A roast of beef, breads of wheat and corn, pickled peppers and soquttahhsh made the main course. Numerous pies of fruit served with tea of borage satisfied most. But the principles showed little interest in their plates. After a short while forks ceased clattering and voices were muted.

Beckett took the lead. "Silent Fox! Elizabeth Dowland Kirke! I have on the table at my side the papers necessary in a civil marriage. Avail yourselves of your advantage, for the Stamp Tax will overtake these colonies soon and legal documents be prohibitively expensive. More than that, as a judge, I can perform the rite here and now, for once in Princeton with the load of work the jurisdiction carries I do not know when I can be pried loose to help you."

Wakwa looked sweetly at Elizabeth, "My Great Lord Michael Beckett...."

"Lord Beckett is sufficient." Beckett cleared his throat.

"Lord Beckett! Elizabeth and I have not discussed such a step."

Beckett rolled his eyes. "Discussion of your remarriage is moot. From what I see, Mrs. Kirke has wasted no time on the Widow's Walk."

The entire company jumped.

Worth fought the lawyer. "No matter what the Crown calls you these days, you caustic bastard, you have no right!"

Beckett swatted at Worth's flagrant disrespect. He continued, "Sachim, I advise you to observe the formalities. Much rides on your despatch."

Elizabeth arched her back. "Lord Michael...."

"Do not think to charm me by flattery, madam. Raising me to duke is yet out of turn. *Lord Beckett* is the way to go. As to this business, although we now sit comfortably, so to speak," he looked balefully at Dowland's uncompromising furniture, "the designation of the Dowland estate as your son's is become tentative. Change is in the air."

Elizabeth said in complete disregard of his contention, "I was about to say, I never agreed to a divorce from the Sachim. I have never ceased to be married to him!"

Wakwa's eyes sparkled.

Beckett found no merit in Elizabeth's fractiousness. "Let's gloss over your personal opinion of your status. The legal fact is, if you were not divorced in '49, and I was present for the breaking of your marriage reeds and the rest of it, and I have your hot-head of an uncle, and sensible Awepu and Pequawus here among others as my witnesses, if you were not divorced, madam, you were married to two men simultaneously. And bigamy does not go down well in estate law. Ah! I see you understand that!"

Wakwa grasped more of Elizabeth's hand and even her forearm. "Again, if that is how you would have it, Michaelbeckettlord...."

"Lord Beckett is enough!" Beckett's exasperated smile deceived no one. "Grasp this, please! It is not how I would have it; it is as it must be! A little of this realization in your private life and public doings would save old Uncle Gilbert a bundle in legal fees."

In shame Wakwa admitted, "Lord Beckett! As I have always done, except on occasion when I held the good of the People above Elizabeth's good, as if...she were not one of the People...I will take no step that will harm her."

Beckett looked dubious. "With all due respect to your attainment, Sachim, in the eyes of most you have harmed her from the first and continue to do so by virtue of your skin."

Consternation rolled with a rumble from white to red, red to white.

Wakwa was not flustered. "If that be so, it were better we just fade together into the forest...."

Beckett seized the bridge of his nose in defense against migraine. "Fade you must!"

"Lord and Justice...."

Beckett's temples throbbed visibly. He hissed, "Lord Beckett!"

I am so sorry, Lord! This was made clear to you by my Elizabeth a long time ago. You opposed her point of view. Now you espouse it. Very well. If we withdraw from public view, all can be settled on Moses as decreed."

"My dear Sachim! First, Moses Bluehill is not yet twenty-one! Second, the times are changed. *Then* is when you should have been the aggressors and taken the Boston Court, let alone Whitehall, by storm! Not done it halfway, got snarled in the Treaty of Submission, and, as a result, beat it into the mountains without her, for God's sake! Now is when you must *disappear* to survive. As a pair."

Worth exploded, "Then what difference if they remarry or do not!!"

"Watch you do not induce stroke on yourself, *Mister* Worth, especially now it is too late to do me any good!"

Hanna asked frigidly, "What can you mean by that, *Lord* Beckett!"

Beckett fidgeted, "Mock me? There is thinking to be done!"

Pequawus intoned from his corner, "Reason then, Englishman."

Beckett bowed his head in actual gratitude. "Silent Fox, Elizabeth Dowland Kirke! *Remarry*! I tell you, the conveyance is more securely your son's with this marriage certificate signed than not. Not to mention a vast improvement in your general status which is diminishing in direct ratio with the swelling of the proprietary attitude of your Colonial allies in the French War. That agreed, what difference can it make to you whether you are reconnected under English law or by the common law of your folk or by a holy man with banns or one with bear's teeth round his neck? You daily adjust your living to the vagaries of British ways. What possibly could prevent you from doing so when the stakes are so high?"

Wakwa placed his hand on Elizabeth's shoulder. "This conveyance of land to the People was too heavy for our marriage reeds. Elizabeth and I have the same trouble now as before."

"Then would you like a minute to yourselves so you can *pop the question* and be married with an instrument of more tensile strength?"

"Lord Mr. Beckett...."

Beckett raged. "Why can't anyone get that straight? Oh, just call me what you've always called me."

Gilbert Worth ventured, "Aloud?"

Again, Beckett flicked his derision away.

Wakwa's sable eyes sparked. "Then, Michaelbeckett, we need no minute to ourselves. I say you have 'popped the question' for me. For King George is evidently to sleep with Elizabeth and me and eat with us and be a part in all our thoughts and all our actions no matter how we try to shake him off. Without discussion, we accept your proposal!"

"God in heaven!" Beckett praised and threw his hands high in thanks.

Elizabeth asked timorously, "Would it hurt you, Lord Beckett, if...."

Beckett groused, "You know, I'm beginning to miss my given name. Call me Michael. Please. Just Michael. Everybody, call me Michael!" His razor glance located Worth in the suddenly jovial group. "Almost everybody."

Elizabeth paused peculiarly long, remembering Kirke's despite of titles. Finally, she rose, a little flushed, and resumed her question, "Would it be all the same to you if we went to Newport to have Pere Claude perform the rite?"

Beckett sputtered. "A religious marriage, especially a Catholic one, will certainly *not* be all the same to me *or* to the law, especially concerning estates. Tut! You know that very well as Hudson's surviving spouse."

Worth, abhorring the sound of the dead minister's name in Dowland House, blocked the reference. "Can't you see she's having you on, Mike?"

Beet red, Beckett kept doggedly on, "I see a woman deadly serious. Once and for all, a civil ceremony is what the law requires. And, considering the difference in race between you and the Sachim, I am not sure even that will suffice!"

Worth chirped, "We have the precedent of Pocahontas and John Rolfe."

Beckett slapped him down, "Who asked you?" He turned back to Elizabeth and Wakwa. "Respice finem! Bear in mind the end! Think of your son. His legitimacy looked good to that great judge and friend of humanity, Jeremy Lord Duhmmer. However, Lord Duhmmer is currently dead!"

Elizabeth returned to the settle and crumpled against its wooden wing.

"Come, come! A little cheer from the bride?" Beckett was not kind.

The onlookers, especially Moses, could not fathom her trouble, having within her grasp all she had lived for.

Wakwa continued for her, "Since you cannot be sure an English marriage will aid our situation you...presume such."

"Well...." Beckett thought about it. "Yes." Beckett rose to his nicely shod feet. "Shall we get on with it?"

Disregarding Beckett's rush, Wakwa added, "Therefore, I wonder why it is that Dire Locke remains the captive of the Admiralty Court in the matter of the sinking of Great-Kirke's ship?"

Blank on the connection between these subjects, Beckett used the back of his straight chair as a podium. "The Admiralty has jurisdiction."

"It is not to Dire's advantage that you see the matter in that light."

"What other light is there but the light of the law? The incident took place on the wave, so to speak. Between two Crown revenue cutters and a licensed, independent merchantman, captained and manned by subjects of the Crown, subject to its laws, the ship factored by Locke and owned by a knight of the realm who was, moreover, on board!"

Cautious of Elizabeth's feelings, Wakwa took a different tack. "Before I was named a sachim, I saw Elizabeth as a simple man sees a woman he would love. I saw to it that the elders on both sides of us approved our union. Then I lived like a god. But when I kissed my uncle's shoulders and accepted the headdress of a sachim, I saw the whole People instead of my wives and my children...." Wakwa found each child with his gaze and then looking at Elizabeth bore on, "and they suffered as they must." His attention turned back to Beckett. "You are now a judge and see like a judge. How can you counsel Kirke Company unless you see wholly from its vantage point?"

Beckett's head snapped up like a colt's first feel of the bit.

Wakwa progressed, "As a judge you are bound strictly by the law. English law. But this is not England. It is a place of many kinds of law." He counted, "Ninnuock law, unwritten though it is. The laws written down by the Assembly in Boston...."

"The civil law...." Beckett drew on Wakwa's train of thought.

"And then there is the looking-back law, the law of precedent, as you say."

"The common law." Beckett defined it for him.

Gil let slip, "John Rolfe and Pocahontas."

Beckett ignored him and concentrated with some excitement on Silent Fox. "And you are saying that I might say, considering the Constitutional problems endemic to the American Revenue Act, to wit, the Sugar Act, the law by which Kirke...Sir Thomas...I beg pardon, met his untimely end, that there is no precedent in English law for prosecuting such a matter as the attack on the *New Psyche II*."

"There is not. And so you *must* say it."

Beckett narrowed his eyes. "According to you, Sachim, if the jurisdiction is in question we should just pick the one most advantageous to us."

"I say more than that."

"Eh?" Beckett prided himself on quick comprehension and minded this correction.

"I say, Michaelbeckett, you should find a man of law born here, raised in Massachusetts, who worries over the things that worry us in this room, and, for a time, let him be counsellor to Kirke Company."

"You are sacking me!"

Wakwa denied, "I am in no position to do that."

"You would be if you married Elizabeth Kirke!"

"The widow of Thomas Kirke needs not a husband to do that."

Gil followed their volley. "Good shot!"

Beckett curled his lip.

"How shall I say?" Wakwa sought to avoid further offense. He spoke as an image opened to him. "Hanna Worth boils a jelly out of the horns of the deer I bring her or of the stomach of a calf, or of a calf's hoof. As the clear, liquid extracted of these parts sets, Hanna floats in it violets or bits of fruit or meat...."

"I see. I am what now? A rennet salad? I am a tongue suspended?"

"Just so!" Wakwa half-stood in delight at Beckett's quickness. "If it will help Dire out of that cold jail, yes. Suspend your tongue. It is winter."

Beckett blew warm breath over the knuckles of one hand and queried enviously, disapprovingly, "How is it you can think so clearly holding the hand of a woman?"

Wakwa answered although no answer was desired. "It was when I let this hand go that my mind turned to ice." He held Elizabeth's hand to his forehead for all to see. "Now thought flows like a stream."

Beckett was silenced.

Wakwa said from pity, "I do hope you can know this quickening in your new life at Princeton."

Beckett gave vent to his utter frustration. "Why is it in this group of people am I considered something of a jackass?"

Wakwa played on Beckett's words. "I consider you a great advocate. You over any other one can move the case out of the naval court!"

Beckett relented, "Even I?" Then slowly, ever so slowly, a grin began. "It could be attempted. But the grounds for moving must be solid as granite."

The Reverend Mayhew Low gripped the arms of his chair and spoke his mind. "The crime against Kirke was a paid assassination. Everyone knows that!" He kept on although Dolly tried to quiet him in sympathy for Elizabeth and fear of Augusta. "The problem is the payer will forever go unchecked for it is a regal payer with plenty of practice and no one will witness against it."

Beckett remarked, "Reverend Low, with all respect, we have no legal evidence the Crown was involved."

Elizabeth lost color.

Tamoccon, Wakwa's son-in-law, spoke up. "Proof lies at the bottom of the Bay. There was no contraband! I will dive for the cargo. In front of witnesses. Winter or no winter."

"Well. That's very energetic." Beckett reacted acidly. "Your efforts would only bring on questions about exactly how Thomas Kirke came to be fastened by ropes to his underwater bed. The

Sachim by his gallant gesture has yet again placed his neck in a noose. We shall all feel fortunate if the *Eocha* incident is dismissed by the court as sloppy work done by overzealous agents of the King. Nothing more."

Worth bit out, "Except for two rank and cold-blooded murders."

Beckett spun toward him. "Of course *your* experience would appertain to that."

Hanna seethed, "Michael!"

Beckett began stalking the shadows. At last he spoke. "I do admit, Worth, every now and then you say something of value."

"Was it very valuable?"

Beckett tapped his temple. "Follow along. There are a couple of firebrands in Boston, young lawyers who could use the experience and the fee...."

Moses stepped forward. "I could assist them! Thomas Kirke was a father to me and to the Ninnuock."

Wakwa sought Elizabeth's hand again to share his pride in their son.

Beckett carped, "Such a public case, too."

"Lord Beckett!" Moses chastised Beckett for the insult. "You know I read well." Then, as if at swordplay, he jabbed, "I studied under Blackstone."

Beckett ground him, "Briefly! And he's not Moses on the Mount with his tablets writ by the hand of God! I have an advance copy of Sir William Blackstone's compilation newly published. Signed! It makes interesting reference but, as your prescient father intimates, there is no precedent for suing parties for negligence. Blackstone doesn't apply! If you want to continue in law in this land, Bluehill, come clerk for me. I'll arrange this other thing for you if it amuses you."

Moses would not vie with him so sealed the bargain with, "It does!"

Beckett ignored him and paced, and spirits lifted because his pacing had for decades been known to produce the desired result. "Now. Back to cases. We will overlook the revenue cutter's relation to the Royal Navy entirely. We save the face of the Admiralty by lifting the filthy mess off their blotter and plunking it down in front of the Supreme Court Magistrate of Massachusetts Bay as simple aggravated murder on two counts," he stated with a nod to Gil, "for, after all, the captains of the cutters, in particular the cutter's commander who ordered the fatal shots, never boarded *Psyche* as required by law, never looked for contraband, never acted in the Crown's behalf. Overtly."

"He was probably drunk." Worth tossed a bomb.

Beckett let it skid by. "My brief will portray this revenue captain as nothing more than a pirate."

Hanna chimed in, "Wouldn't piracy be covered by naval law?"

Beckett fairly shouted a refinement, "In the name of Elizabeth Dowland Kirke, I will file suit against him for *reckless homicide*! Which suit will force the Admiralty to give the case over even temporarily. I will have Tamoccon dive till he's blue! No evidence excepting against the revenue cutter can be recovered and the thing just - blow away. Crazy King George will be much pleased."

Wakwa added, "As will all of us! Dire Locke helps. He must be helped."

Elizabeth stood abruptly. Wandered a few steps.

Beckett enquired, "The matter, Widow Kirke?"

Bitterly, "This - *thing* - should *not* blow away. I want the King in the dock!"

Beckett soothed, "The Fox's principle must rule."

"Must it?" A woman formed of stark experience, Elizabeth fought for her idea. "It seems Thomas Kirke was the only man I've ever known with the courage to stand up to His Majesty!"

Beckett was at no loss. "Thomas Kirke was a man purposely unsaddled by ground. As are you! What had he to lose but his life nearly lived out?"

Elizabeth roared.

"He planned it all, madam! No debts. All paid! And having myself arranged those matters at his request, I know that what's left of The Company's cash, mainly the gold in your uncle's cellar, is tied up in Kirke's New York bank. Nothing to lose but you! His loss evidently the Fox's gain. Don't you think that was factored into his dissent! You'll be doing Thomas Kirke a favor if you comply! It was his dying wish that Dire Locke live to bait the King in London!"

She cried out, "I object to protecting the guilty to gain some other good!"

"Ha! Count the corpses littering the field of your objection!"

"Brute!" From Worth.

Beckett, the Maestro of such situations, changed his tone. "Browneyes! We are standing in a place where a jar of cold cream is considered to be a work of the Devil. With all respect for your revolutionary bent, I will now collar your infamous uncle...." Beckett interrupted himself, "Worth! Are you ready? Once more into the breach...who has a ring? Oh, a very nice ring!" Beckett approved the one Augusta sacrificed. "Pen! Pen! Fox, what's your occupation? Hunter would be stretching veracity a bit."

Wakwa lifted the plume adroitly from Beckett's grasp, found the line and wrote, *farmer*.

Beckett could only hoot softly. "Lightfoot may be managing Charles Dowland's acreage, and while you are his father and Moses' father, and while Moses will also one day possess this farm and Worth Farm, I cannot, in truth, agree that *you* are a farmer!"

Wakwa's hands dropped to his sides. His chin rose. He reasserted the notion that once would have been noxious to him. "I am a farmer."

"Your crop?!"

"Tobacco."

"Pfff! That's a pastime."

"It is not a pastime!"

"Oh? As a former Virginian, I seriously doubt your contention. Where is your market?"

"In England."

"Is that so?! And with Kirke Company Ltd. defunct and Dire Locke in jail, who is your factor?"

"Dire Locke."

Beckett crossed his arms and whistled a clear, glassy whistle. "You are not called Fox for nothing! Moses, are you attending the Sachim? Of his proficiency is history directed. We are come full circle. Of course Locke's freedom is part and parcel of the Sachim's marriage plans! Elizabeth Dowland, marry this man! He is at least as skilled as the late Thomas Kirke in matters of business. And I? I continue useful." Beckett placed his graceful signature at the bottom of the document.

Lifting Elizabeth's left hand into Gil's and her right one into Wakwa's, Michael Beckett droned, "I, take thee, Silent Fox, to my wedded husband to have and to hold from this day forward, for better, for worse, for richer, for poorer, in sickness and in health, to love and to cherish, till death do us part and thereto I plight thee my troth!"

The business was accomplished.

The haunted stillness that had reigned in Dowland House for nearly twenty years was rent with the cries and cheers of Wakwa's and Elizabeth's folk when the marriage form was completed. The house lost its coldness. Rather than depart, its ghosts struck against love like flints. The fires and fibres of Dowland House cast light and fragrance to the corners. Lightfoot and Tamoccon dragged the cider barrel from the cellar. Red and white mixed, animated. Only Moses noticed Wakwa's withdrawal to the dimmed dining room, saw Wakwa pull the head chair to the corner of the laden table, watched Elizabeth find him and sit close to him. Their arms rested among the decimated platters and half-empty pitchers. Wakwa's head lowered irresistibly as if the brain within could not withstand any further assault. Warily, Elizabeth stroked his hair. Wakwa seized her hand and pulled it around to his mouth and he gnawed her wrist like an old, blind dog who by some lucky chance has unearthed his favorite bone.

The Ninnuock were housed for the night at the Meetinghouse Hospital. Hanna and Gil took Moses home with them. But Wakwa and Elizabeth walked by torchlight from the farms through the dank breath of January toward the frame house where Qunneke had never slept.

Elizabeth suffered the sight of pitched roofs and silvered shingles in place of roundhouses and bark walls. The new otan, its houses strung along the river or thrown back off the path among the trees, seemed no otan at all but an artificial Sweetwood. But the tribe was there, Elizabeth knew. The scent of chimney smoke hovered and the fires in Wakwa's house were high although no serving girls appeared. She tasted in her mouth this embrace of all for all - the milk and honey long denied her.

They lay in the loft under the weight of trade blankets. The simple fact of her presence made stone of his face, the days eternally lost for them killing him from inside. His glittering black eyes made her see the half-frozen ocean under the moon for thousands of miles. Wakwa cast about for something to say. "I have no gift for you, Elizabeth, to celebrate that we are wed once more - you so used to precious things of great beauty."

She touched his face in the flickering light. "None such as you!"

Stricken at her unconscious reference to her exile, Wakwa demanded, "Name something I can present you!"

Her sigh was soft, like laughter. "Present me with - SNOW."

It fell while they slept and made velvet and diamonds under her webbed shoes when they walked the next day in the sun.

CHAPTER SIXTY-TWO

January 1765

"Strange bedfellows, you two!" Dire Locke wheezed from the corner of his cell. Green-and-blue-speckled from cold, and with his eyes bugged-out from starvation, his head shaved to solve the scourge of lice, his corroded coat rent at the seams and clinging like seaweed, Locke looked like a lobster in the trap. "Beckett and Bluehill! Sounds like a law firm."

Moses hooked the factor under the armpits and by strength of forearm, thigh, and back, pulled him to his feet. "Dire! You are not dulled by prison! I read with Lord Beckett now."

Locke's facial muscles were too moribund from cold to allow a smile; nevertheless a smile curled its way around his heart at the sound of the sturdy title. "Lord Beckett!"

Michael Beckett held back from Locke and Dray, the sour smell of human bodies unwashed, meagrely warmed, poorly fed, and the clothes, out and in, worn to rags causing his revulsion.

Locke wobbled toward the wall. Summoning the shreds of his mental resources he croaked, "You've made out quite well, Judge Beckett!" Locke forestalled fainting by pressing his temples against the cold, slimy stone. He gasped, "Congratulations on such a daughter-in-law." Locke staggered toward Beckett to shake his hand.

Beckett gave Locke the narrow eye and a wide berth. He did not like the factor's tone or his stench. But out of fairness he admitted, "It turned out as you said, Locke. To think, I'd imagined you'd gotten the better of me."

Locke backed toward the wall remarking with some grace, "It is nice to be right. I do not like the hair shirt is all."

Beckett's cautious heart opened. "Here is a matter for the Court!" He indicated Locke's abysmal confinement with a wave of his hand. "I will instruct your lawyers to see to it. Your interview with them earlier this week apparently being mutually satisfactory. Reparations are due! You don't have sores of any kind?"

Even in his scurfy, depleted condition Locke speared the lawyer with eyes of steel. Without switching his glance, he called to his cellmate, "Dray! You don't have sores of any kind?" Weakened by his efforts, Locke slid down the wall like a drunkard.

Moses propped him up and put a flask to his lips. "Dire, he meant nothing by it. He is only discovering what facts your lawyers may bring before the Court."

"Oh." Dire remarked with no apparent interest. "What Cognac is this?"

Beckett looked up from his notetaking. "Bluehill! Did you have to use *my* flask?!!"

Locke smiled his inscrutable smile. "In days gone by, Lord Beckett, I might have said, 'Never mind my infectious lips upon your silver bottle! I'll replace it with one of gold.' But your patron, King George, has decreed otherwise." Locke lost himself to the flask as if he were an infant at his milk. Catching his breath, he quipped, "Your elevation has improved your cellar!"

Beckett snapped, "The flask is mine. The Cognac, Worth's."

"Ah!" Dire's eyes glittered. "Now that makes sense!" He passed the flask to Dray with Moses' aid. Liquor-loosened, Dire observed, "I'd've thought Gilbert would spring me from my prison, he and the Fox. Wakwa's polishing his statement for the Court, what?"

"Don't be ridiculous." Beckett's humane instincts did not extend to the legal arena. "Like his rich crony, Worth, Silent Fox forced himself out of the picture. Can't possibly be of use to any of us. The man tied Kirke to his damned deathbed! Kirke drowned of it!" The Sachim'll be up for murder if he makes a peep on your behalf. And you can't be serious wanting the word of an Indian to save you!"

Moses flared, at last, "Judge! Was it not an Indian, more, that very Indian, enlightened you how to free his factor from his dungeon? Inspired you how to move the venue out of the Admiralty Court? Grounds of negligence the key which a lowly Indian snatched from Kirke's sinking ship?"

Locke would have sworn in a court of law he heard the grinding of the baronial teeth.

Avoiding the risks of new entanglements with English patrol boats, the four journeyed overland to Sweetwood. The fifty miles were worn away inch by inch, revolution-by-revolution of the wheels.

Beckett denied his strong inclination to ride horseback to avoid the odor of the freed prisoners.

Moses volunteered as they rolled down the Post Road, "My father used to run to Boston in four hours, conclude his business, and be back in the otan before the People lay down for the night."

The recollection fell flat or, better, fell like a cannon ball among them ripping open any illusion that the future could resemble the past.

Moses turned from the constantly changing scene to Locke and added, "The Sachim is remarried to my mother."

Dire amazed them all by bursting into tears.

Two hours after mid-night, the vigil of the Worths, Wakwa and Elizabeth, the Lows, and Augusta, was rewarded. Locke and Dray were closetted at the hospital, scrubbed and lightly fed under Israel's direction. Beckett was packed off to Dowland House with his daughter-in-law in spite of the ungodly hour. Matthew Freeman managed the removal, never too spent to separate the lawyer from Hanna Worth.

Moses retired last. The darkness of the country night, alleviated only by embers in the public rooms, not at all where doors were closed, pictured for Moses his isolation. He left the sitting room and climbed toward the oblivion of his bed. Firelight was flung like a rug across the open threshold of the half-storey room. Moses nestled on the last dark step just below the fluctuating, bright patch. Words from inside the room grew distinct.

Elizabeth spoke over Wakwa's dry, unwilling weeping, a tearless scrooping. She pleaded, "Don't, don't cry!"

Moses' surprise yielded to criticism. His father held in his arms the person he loved apparently above all others. *Now what was the matter?*

"I cannot believe...!" Wakwa left his thought unfinished.

"I said that to you once! Remember? I was innocent! I could not believe...when first I felt you in me!"

Moses stopped his ears with his forearms but they went lead-heavy and descended to his chest as if for armor.

"Elizabeth, I cannot believe you should be here!"

Moses squirmed in place. *This was the man irresistible to women?*

"Manit!" Wakwa cried out for his god.

Moses sent a prayer Manit's way himself; that he would strike the Massachuseuck spokesman dumb.

"Shhh! Shhh!"

Moses agreed with the woman. Wakwa had said quite enough. He had said too much.

"Hold me!" Elizabeth demanded.

"You begged that of me once and I did not do it!"

Moses pressed his head against the wall.

"I held my arms away. With my will! How could you come back to me!"

Moses nearly broke for their door to tell his father to stop. What mistakes the Sachim made with women! Why would a man stoke the ashes of the worst blunder of his life?

Wakwa's strained voice came again. "Should you be here?"

Moses began to think his father a born fool or his mind a secret casualty of the French War.

Elizabeth poured ice water over Wakwa's plaint. "I am assured by Judge Beckett it is quite legal."

Moses' opinion of his alien mother shot high.

Wakwa droned on, "I am a poison to everyone. My own kind choke on me the way I used to choke on Waban! Michaelbeckett is right! I hurt you from the first. I deprived you of your father, your son. I forced you to change and to change back. I stole your youth! I bargained you like a blanket to another mate!"

Now Elizabeth was crying.

Little wonder, Moses thought. Moses' forehead struck his knees.

The ticking of clocks.

Elizabeth asked in a wavery voice, "Did you not do to yourself what you did to me? Every last thing?" She moved. "Were you satisfied here?"

Wakwa uttered a surprised cry.

Moses' brows and head rose. His birth-mother was no frigid Calvinist. He crowed over the fact.

Wakwa's voice fell down a well inside him. "You know all my failings."

"I have had ample time to meditate upon them."

Moses stood with raised fist.

"Elizabeth!"

"And there is more! You decline joy. You are sinfully proud. Stubborn. You think you are right about everything...and what is worse...you usually are."

And Wakwa, the spokesman, the Sachim, the leader of men, the hero of war, the sage with a juridical turn of mind, choked audibly on this estimation of his character.

"And now that I am here, you wish Tame Deer were back with you!"

Moses shrank down, shocked. *Refute her*!

But Wakwa agreed. "Yes!" His relief at her saying it was grand.

Moses gave up on his sire. He was wracked by Wakwa's mistakes.

"We never were without her." Elizabeth mourned.

Moses supplied mutely for his father, "'*She was never between us. When we were alone it was you and I*!'"

But Wakwa said, "Not for a moment!"

Moses stifled a cry.

"From the first time you spoke to me in English, you spoke of her."

"Now, Elizabeth...."

Moses' soul rang. *At last*! Then he cupped his hand around his ear to hear Elizabeth.

"Aye! She was always with us, Wakwa. She made our connection. She made it what it was. No! What it became! Her suffering me with you made a tension like a harp string. Anytime we plucked it - what happiness! How wild we were!"

Moses, flushed and hot as their fire, put his hands together as in prayer. *Stop now! Say no more. Either of you*!

Wakwa breached the silence. "And now. The old cord lies broken."

Moses mouthed, "*Idiot*!"

"Unmendable." Elizabeth's voice was dry, constricted.

Moses jammed his fists against his mouth. He waited a long time for some resumption, his young gut hard with the horror that all the years, all the dirt of suffering, of yearning, of laboring to leap over the void of their separation, even their reunion, meant absolutely nothing. In those moments on the stairs, Moses decided to leave them, to lean upon The Company for money, to escape them for Oxford to live with Gordon. He could make the Trinity Term by end of April. True, L.66 had been expended in advance on three years' tuition, and his caution-money and admission and matriculation fees were safely in the bursar's coffers, but there were the washing, the kitchen, the buttery fees, L.19 right there, and he must eat and he might as well eat well, and that would be at least three shillings a meal and, by God, there would be the wine club at L.10 for he would not have his gaming club to depend on for entertainment and funds as he had done in the Michaelmas term as a freshman. He would need at least L.20 ready cash and what with the tailor and firewood, room rent, examination fees, the gate bill, messengers, the bookseller, the chemist, the perfumer, the boot-maker, not to mention the care and feeding of a new horse, let alone its purchase, he could see in a minute that to live quietly as a studious gentleman he could not get away with less than L.200 per annum.

There was gold in Worth's cellars. A great deal of gold. Moses readily saw that if he dared to be more of a sport, join every club, row every bucket, deflower every virgin, and go for honors, he could breeze through L.300 a year. Oh yes! They would pay the piper for his honors degree and then he, Moses Bluehill, Muckquashim-ouwan Noh-annoosu, the son of a farmer's daughter and an Indian chief, could court the vicious King and be approved the bloody prime minister from which lofty office he could demolish and reorder the universe!

"We have that." Wakwa summarized. "That same - break. That is what we have now."

Elizabeth agreed. "That loss. Lost touch. Lost time. Our separate griefs...."

"And you are here...."

"My being here makes Qunneke walk before your eyes, and you make me see Thomas beneath the water and creatures with scales and fins that we eat eating his flesh...."

"Stop!"

Moses could hear Wakwa holding her, the bed linens telling tales.

"And the water eating him and undermining his substance and the brine washing and polishing his very bones...."

"No more!"

"For me he ended like this!" Elizabeth screamed lightly. "How can you care for me?! Oh, God!" Like Wakwa she called upon the Deity.

Moses revolved on the stairs. Onto his belly.

"Elizabeth! Wife! My only wife!" Wakwa's voice made its way beyond their bed to the son he did not know was there.

The sound of it, gruff with passion, rich with intent, a complex food, force-fed, forced Moses to soundless laughter. This was his father's politic voice; Elizabeth must recognize it. This was his persuasive voice, his council-room voice, his selling and telling voice. This was the voice that wound governors around his finger. This was the voice that had made a savage of a Puritan woman.

"My *dearest* wife, this is what we have! Our difference. Our break. Our dead!"

The suspension of sound astounded the son. His mother was either stone cold from despair or being pressed by a kiss. He became convinced of the latter. These ancestors found the slenderest provocation!

Wakwa's voice poured out again, this time, honey. "Did we not have pains and pangs when we met so young? Was I not from an unknown and unlettered tribe of men? And you from a cruel and resourceful people? A people whose best soul is writ in rhyme on paper! And yet we started with each other. We lived anew. We lived as if we were our own race, our own tribe, our own story!"

She wept for the days lost to them.

Moses disapproved of her mood as ill-timed.

"Shhh. Shhh." Wakwa said now as at first she had done. "Listen thou to me!" He spoke through her hard-dying sobs, "You put me in mind of a passage from your sacred book, this Jesus saying a wise thing of what is torn. It concerns a piece of clothes, an old garment, and a new garment. Remember it? Something such as, *'One does not....'* no. *'One tears not....'* no! *'No one tears a piece from a new mantle...and sews it on an old one.'*"

Elizabeth continued to cry.

"Now, Elizabeth, you with your needles know this best of all. *'No one tears...'* how doth it go...?"

Moses began to hear the passage in his own head, a thing from John, no, from Luke. He mimed Wakwa's struggling recollection.

Wakwa concentrated. "'*No one tears a piece from a new mantle and sews it on an old one, or...if he does, he will both tear the new one and...and...the piece from the new one will not match the old.*' See you, Elizabeth? Our only hope is to lay the old garment gently down. And weave and wear the new. We know it can be done. We did it once. Come! Come! Put on new life with me?"

Moses heard the sheets again, suddenly taut, stretched beyond the weave by movement uninhibited, like the ropes of sails full with God-given wind. One never heard such commotion from the soft coverings in an Indian house. But where maids smoothed linens with heat, the human tale was told better than with the voice. He slipped upstairs beyond the melding of male and female, beyond the sort of light that could not be seen.

Elizabeth stepped into Moses' room. She bent to the cold hearth. She touched her candleflame to the kindling ready-laid and blew a small blaze into existence. Turning to view Moses asleep, she jumped at seeing his eyes open. "I am sorry to wake you!"

"Don't be." He was sincere.

She saw his nightclothes untouched where Matthew had laid them but passed that over for, "You used to watch me that way when you were a baby."

Moses smiled vaguely. Wondering.

She smiled shyly, "Things come back to me. A little at a time."

Moses rose up on one elbow. "May they come to me!"

Elizabeth's breath was suspended by gratitude. She drew his blankets to his chin. "This room is ice."

"I am recently to bed." His golden look bored into her.

She stayed quiet, did not enquire about the obvious. Then, "I have been wanting to tell you something. Something that...came to me." She looked at his face, orange leaping over it from the fire behind her. She leaned toward him, her woolen nightgown, the ribbons of her cap, her shawl, softly grazing the quilt.

He knew she knew he felt the light touch of her wrappings.

She kissed him, his cheek and the cheekbone. "I needed to kiss you before...for I do not know if you can love me or speak to me in the days to come after what I shall tell you!"

Moses curled into fetal posture under the down, "Then, tell me not!"

Elizabeth looked at him straight. "You are a gentleman."

"I like you, Mother. More and more. Very much more than I thought I would. Or should." He sat up, threw off his covers, his stockinged feet on the floor, his long legs miles long in the distorted light from the hearth.

She removed from his bedside to the coldest part of the room. She broke the curtains to view the starlit January fields. Quaking, body and voice, she said, "I think I failed you. In England. With Augusta's father."

Moses snapped, "What can you mean?!"

She answered slowly from shame, "Asked, I could not assure him there was hope for Augusta with you. I could not speak! My voice would not come! My pain over myself overcame me. I said nothing! I could not reply! I begin to see...I should have found some voice...should have... seen beyond my...dread for her...my experience...even of you...I did not know you!"

Moses grabbed the quilt to his face and hid in its softness. At last he gasped, "You would not be sane or honest if you had denied for convenience sake your feelings of a lifetime!"

"Moses!"

He raised a hand to stop her protest. "If there is blame, it is mine. No matter what you said or did not say, I would be married to her this day if I had reversed myself. William Leed was…as was she…well disposed toward me."

Elizabeth groaned.

"Mother, Mother! Was it possible? Politically? And I would have tired of it. Lady Augusta, for all her nobility of soul, reveals herself very…English."

Elizabeth came near to him and looked sadly into him.

"I have proven to be my father's son. But Augusta has not proven to be you!"

Elizabeth dropped to the floor and buried her face against his knees. Moses bent over her, smelling the cleanness of her scalp through her cap and something else - a fragrance of leaves - leaves felled by rain – he guessed it as his father's scent.

Moses raised her up and sat her next to him. His arm slipped around her. "I will fail any idea you have of me as a worthy human being if I tell you a dream that keeps coming in the nights since I have been home. My most loved friend, Ho Beckett, dies gloriously in battle like his hero General Wolfe. Then Augusta falls to me!"

Elizabeth gasped.

"We'd better sleep!" He spoke with no little irony.

She lingered. A smile preceded her next words. And as she spoke, Moses realized for the first time that Elizabeth Dowland was capable of charm. "Bring me back to my room, dear son. How shall I rest thinking of you here, so close, yet divided from us by a bit of plaster?"

"Gil! Come see!" Hanna hurried him out of their room in the bright morning as he was tying his neckcloth. "Moses is gone. He did not even go to bed! His night-rail is untouched!"

Gil observed, "The bed's rumpled. Fire's been lit."

"He's not here! He's not downstairs. Cooke has not seen him."

"He's taking breakfast with the Becketts." Gil's face twitched with worry.

"Matthew's checked."

"We are an open book!"

Hannna let the complex topic drift. "Moses has not been there. Nor is he with Dire at the Hospital."

"Could he not have traipsed off to the otan?"

"His horse is in our barn. Would he walk there between midnight and dawn?"

"You are right."

Hanna looked at her husband. "I just want some calm."

"We'll have to get them up. We'll have to tell them. Wakwa will find him. Damn!"

Hanna made the sound of raindrops with her nails on the guestroom door. Gil leaned toward it with her. They heard breathing, heavy breaths of heavy sleep. Gil carefully opened. The Worths took a moment to interpret what they saw. They made out three people in the bed. Three adults at rest. A woman and two men. Elizabeth bordered by her son and his father. A wife at her husband's side with the son they had conceived lying next to her, his arm circling hers. Gil and Hanna stayed for some time in the doorway.

The eastern sun turned the room bright and hot.

CHAPTER SIXTY-THREE

Spring 1765

Spring in Sippicon burst its bonds like a wildcat. Its fangs tore at the Cape Cod coast and came away with chunks of it. Raw March rain marked the days inland.

The gloom over Wareham was garish with the glow of fires never totally extinguished after *New Psyche II* with Thomas Kirke aboard was attacked, run aground, and sunk. Blood-red skies showed for miles, for months.

Locke said the violence *at* the horizon meant violence *on* the horizon. Worth saw the eerie light as a glimpse into the forge of rebellion, kindling courtesy the Crown.

A parade of cripples, once strapping members of Kirke's ship's crew, splashed its way to the harbor's meetinghouse, doubling as courthouse, and huddled against the wooden walls. Each man waited with the patience of debility to witness to events fresh in memory although six months had passed by the calendar.

Israel Stirling escorted Dire into the chamber through the door behind the Bench. Kirke's ubiquitous and best factor appeared fragile, gaunt, pallid, aged, and, in the odd wheeled-chair, invalid. Hanna and Gilbert Worth attended, their oilskins, hoods, muffs and steaming cider mugs in full array and use. They sat ready to be called.

Gil asked his wife, "How is it I could not design such a chair for your brother? This was simple enough. Bigger wheels."

"Dearheart?"

"It wanted bigger wheels for a steadier ride. Little wheels! Silly! With bigger wheels Locke, if he were stronger, would propel himself! This idea needs to go into general manufacture! With riot and rebellions all around us better wheel chairs will be all the rage! I need someone who can draw!"

"You draw." The wife supported him.

Lines crosshatched Worth's cheeks as he smiled. "Someone who can draw in three dimensions."

"If Henry had lived...."

Gil sighed. "Beth's little brother would be hanging his offhand sketches in Whitehall not penning mechanical drawings for farm implements and surgery furniture."

Hanna rose to bring Locke a warm drink. "Horace Beckett draws, doesn't he?"

Horace Beckett was intrigued by the motley and literally colorful society of New York. Christian and Jew, Dutch and English, German and Irish, a smattering of exotics from southern Europe and Eastern places and Africa and their servants and slaves made a populace as restless as the sea and as rich of element.

What seized his vitals was the fact that, no matter their variety, New Yorkers possessed one voice. The New York voice was impatient, unphilosophical, a gut-cry for survival. Syrupy sentiment excusing the appetites of the Mother country, a step-mother at best, was not part of the city's vocabulary. Theirs was a blood-dripping outcry against the rapaciousness of the English monarchy; their rights as English subjects, as free men, were defiled by recent statute.

The New York plaint was other than that taxes levied on them without representation in Parliament or consent thereto rendered the colonies less protected by recognized natural rights than a conquered people. It was simply that New Yorkers would not brook financial ruin by pen-stroke.

New York bought from and through England one-fourth of all goods imported by all thirteen of the American colonies: L. 500,000, yearly. Under the Sugar Act and the Currency Act and, shortly, the Stamp Tax, the Crown was sucking the bones out of the entire colonial import trade.

The loss of the judicial tenure debate, i.e., that judges would serve *at the King's pleasure*, the Siamese twin of these fiscal monsters, was more than the city-folk could bear. To the mind of a New Yorker, judges serving *at the King's pleasure* were no judges at all but executioners on strings. Watchful of information falling into the wrong hands, Horace Beckett was silent about his father's new occupation.

New Yorkers of the common classes took to the streets. They braved unremittingly the men in red coats who beat them back from the steps of the Imperial offices. Horace Beckett was one of those red coats and without surprise or shame received swift promotion to the rank of first lieutenant.

New Yorkers of the upper caste, in committee, wrote to every other colonial assembly and correspondence committee about the problems they had in common. In the month when Horace made his vows to Augusta, the gentlemen of New York, by hard-gutted formal resolution, funnelled petitions for redress from injustice through their London agent to no less an authority than King George III himself!

Five committeemen, all of New York, four from the city, resurrected the plan of colonial union born in New York at Albany and abandoned in '54 at the doorstep of history.

Ho persuaded himself that order must rule, that government property must not be damaged, that statecraft not anarchy must resolve the problems of state, that the Crown was sacred, if flawed. He worked at ascribing to tragic human error the death of Thomas Kirke. Ho's truncheon came back to barracks matted with blood and hair. And the warrior's name, given him by Qunneke, fit. They began to call him Hawk in the officer's club; his subordinates knew no other name for him.

It took the irrepressible mob, blood sport for most of his garrison, to mature Horace Beckett. Each time he swung his club, Ho's sympathy with the plight of the subject increased. Each time he swung his club, he mourned the plight of the despot. Young as he was, youth slipped. Wanting and needing to forfeit his commission, Ho thought of Augusta and dutifully took up pistol and sword and ordered his horse brought. He fought against loving Augusta less.

His superiors took note of his performance. Horace Beckett's connections made impeccable credentials; his soldiering added to them. Counting heads cracked, prisoners taken, plots foiled, they promoted him to major and drew orders for Hawk Beckett to put down a rebellious mob in Sippicon at Wareham before going west to fight Pontiac.

Bluehill had warned him.

The jury members, chosen with care and difficulty, slipped into the Wareham courthouse discreetly, one at a time. Two crusty fishermen, a chandler, a grocer, a teacher, a wheel-right, a flax farmer, an apothecary, a scrivener, a retired sea captain, a scion of merchants who had no occupation save exploiting his passion for the piano-forte, and a pressman who published a bi-monthly newssheet, appeared punctually to listen to the lawyers expound and the witnesses testify. The twelve had nothing in common but a keen interest in rendering their verdict and getting back to the business of making money before the Stamp Tax could sock them in.

The young partners in the Boston firm of Badgett, Babcock, & Greene were not without ideas in the case against the cutter-captains, which was fraught with personal risk. But it was Michael Beckett who masterminded the brief. The lion's share of it. He thrilled himself by not softening his position on the charge of premeditated murder.

The newly minted peer first dismissed the co-defendants' potential argument of legal or even of justifiable homicide. In his judgment, the cutter-captains, in their brutal commutation of their orders, engaged in provocation so dangerous as to exhibit the requisite depraved disregard for human life overriding the lesser charge. Notwithstanding, that passive line of reasoning leaned too heavily on the cutter-captains' official role to justify the change of venue that had been granted and, moreover, Beckett would not have Locke bounced like a ball from court to court. Beckett returned to premeditation, the captain of the foremost boat having warned Kirke of his intent to fire on deck. Safer it might be to settle for a conviction on murder in the second degree (not to mention the manslaughter of Ifan William); proof of premeditation requiring the testimony of the principals, controversial witnesses all.

The matter of corpus dilecti haunted the suit.

Badgett, Babcock & Greene saw no problem. *Dredge up the body!*

"Dredge away! Produce a skeleton wound like a tennis racquet then extricate yourselves from that coil, pun intended! Gentlemen! Kirke's bones would prove there was a death not a homicide, and who could say definitively that the bones were Kirke's even if they could be brought up! Identifying a corpse requires witness concerning the decedent's disposition near the time of death and Silent Fox is the last person to have seen Thomas Kirke alive. We will not open that Pandora's box!" Beckett warned his colleagues off calling Wakwa. "Place yourselves in the jury box conjuring the scene - the victim of the attack, to wit, Sir Thomas Kirke, bleeding to death and bound like a mummy in quarters by a local Sachim as the sea water pours over decks!

"And that is only one problem! Rip open the record, and what do you find? Silent Fox, his blatant disregard of the Treaty of Submission, an Informatus Non Sum against him and his cohorts placed before the court at Boston, suspicions scudding about him in the unsolved murder of a man of the cloth, his rival for a woman, a wife, the very man who prepared the Information against him, not to mention the Sachim's recent remarriage to the widow of Vaughan Thomas Kirke by virtue of his having tied the old geezer to his bed in a sinking ship! Another homicide, justifiable perhaps - code of the sea - granting the last wish of the dying, the death-bed wish witnessed by no less than three respectable people, but a case in itself."

The young lawyers took issue with Michael Beckett, ready to rely on rhetorical dash to win the hearts of the jury and the populace, the press, and most important, the judge.

Beckett trounced them with rhetorical bluntness. "Thomas Kirke drowned before he could die of his wound. Silent Fox is useless to us!" With uncharacteristic reverence, Beckett lowered his head remembering how useful Wakwa had been to the Crown in the war and before in arbitration of far-reaching and picayune kind, and, more, as a sort of gold standard among men.

It was then to be as if not one Indian had been present on shore or ship the September afternoon when Kirke was martyred.

"No! The Indians are out and the case hangs on Dire Locke like a millstone and clever he must be under cross-examination for the defense may press for a reduction of the charge to manslaughter, claiming that passion stirred by Kirke's truculence about the matter of contraband lead the cutter-captain to order force which inadvertently caused one death and lead to a second." Hardly taking breath he countered himself, "Of course, one could argue the inadmissibility of such a defense because of the change of venue. "Choppy waters!"

What about Elizabeth? Messers. Badgett, Babcock and Greene wanted to know.

Beckett's black boots ceased their march. "The plaintiff!" Slowly he began to tread the threadbare Sarouk of the neophyte firm. "As signing partner in the House and a board member of the newly chartered merchant bank, she might be of use in proving the absence of the dead man." Then Beckett dug in his heels with a vengeance.

The partners winced for their carpet.

"Note bene! The *conveyance*. Toward its preservation, I enjoined Elizabeth to remarry her first husband, the Indian who for all intents and purposes did Kirke in!" The flat of Beckett's hand massaged his brow where headache had just been spawned. "Motive and intent. *I* handed it to the defense who would have to be gagged not to argue us into the ground or to the gallows with that! We are hamstrung!" And then, "With all respect to the deceased."

THE IDEA. What of her son? Moses Bluehill? Student of law, to wit, their law-devil. A passenger, survivor, step-son to Kirke, in fact, the lifelong subject of his benefices. Use him!

Beckett liked it, yet he jotted an improvement in his notebook. "TAMOCCON!"

Here the young law partners dug in. *No Indians, you say! Then Tammocon must be but an agent of the prosecution recovering the cargo of Kirke's molested ship. It is not Tamoccon but the cargo in evidence that is the most eloquent witness. And what good a pile of gears and shafts and springs if they do not have meaning at their intended port? Those persons the weaving machines were intended to employ, have been cheated of their livelihood by the defendants, have they not? The murders are part of a larger crime. The people of Sippicon have been thwarted and impoverished by the death of Sir Thomas. We must have them in the streets making a hullaballoo! The judge will want to quiet that. For to cut down Kirke and his sub-factor without provocation, under the Acts for excuse, makes the Crown an accessory of the crime. We can't have that, can we?*

The trial went forward against the pair of cutter-captains but not a soul above the age of eight in the port-town was fooled. As Elizabeth hotly desired, George Three was in the dock.

It was as if a war had come to the town. Wareham smouldered. The ruins of the merchant ships littered the harbor. Bonfires fed on precious documents, reducing their threat to ashes. The educated, the people of position, wielding axes as effectively as humble folk, ransacked the offices of merchants stubborn about importing British goods, scorched the stamp agent's quarters - the Act not yet in force.

Added to that unrest was a rowdy crowd from Sweetwood, under Mayhew Low's leadership, screaming at the courthouse door about getting robbed by the cutter captains; something about a new invention that was to save their skins in light of the tariffs and the Stamp Tax and the damage done to their boats in the harbor.

To the tune of the riot outside, Judge Plumb, presiding in the murder trial of the cutter-captains, viewed his courtroom floor studded with metal machine parts arranged according to diagram. It appeared to him that the rich and the poor had complaints against the Crown. Their taking to the streets to demonstrate their dissatisfaction, more, their righteous indignation, presaged a full-tilt insurrection. The judge was alive to the prevailing civil outcry and admitted to his mirror as he shaved in the mornings that revolution was not a far-fetched possibility. He ruled pragmatically, and not a litte cannily, suspending the trial until such time as peace could be restored in the town. He sensed it would take a long while for peace to be restored; possibly the cutter captains would die of pox or scurvy or pneumonia, or liver by then and the judgment be moot. General Gage in New York satisfied Plumb's request for troops. Justice Plumb was quite sure he would have retired from the Bench long before order prevailed and the case was resuscitated. In any case, George Three was off the hook for the time being at least.

Horace Beckett's company left the safety of the frigate for the lighter. As it parted from ship's tow and skidded into shore over the tide, sight of them from the charred little port was peculiar; a detachment of red-coated cavalry massed like tin soldiers on the flat-bottomed boat. Suspicious of the lack of courtesies as they came in, Ho shocked his command, dictating, "No man is to mount till I give orders. Ride splashing up the beach off the barge and end in the brig! We are here to pacify hearts not to gall them!" Hawk Beckett had made sure to make his reputation for strictness. No one refuted him. Except for a pair of heralds trailing him, Hawk Beckett rode alone over the lip of the beachhead to judge conditions with his own eyes. That is what he told his officers.

Ho ate of the view. His memory was of symmetry, simplicity, dove gray and brown and white and pine green. Of an ordered pulse. Of cheer. And the smells - a godly soup of seaweed and salt water and waste shellfish and baking biscuits and foam from beer and the tide.

Now Wareham was disfigured by fire. A drab drizzle cooled the black stumps of incinerated buildings. The damp was as putrid as a cold sweat. A lawless mumble replaced sailors' chants. No Massachusetts men in rippling skins stood silently expectant of his arrival. The young Major Sir Horace Beckett instructed his heralds in enquiring after the sheriff and presenting to the civil authorities his orders from Gage.

Before that order could be carried out, horrific sound erupted near Wareham's center. Hawk Beckett rode toward it. Inured to brawling mobs, he and his company set about breaking up the skirmish. The Americans tore him from his horse. Ho drew his sword and sent their blood flying. They laughed at him. Kicked his boots out from under him. Stabbed him through the white breeches. Screaming, and screaming orders, he took blows, insults. He knew he was kneeling in the street and covering the soft spot of his skull, less to protect his cranium than to create seclusion. He might just as well have been in his father's stone study battered by drunken, demeaning words. Ho covered his head to gain privacy in which to feel the men of Wareham kicking. Kicking back.

Their spirit robbed his joy at quelling the riot, which, in spite of his wound, he did.

CHAPTER SIXTY-FOUR

July 1765

Summer's zenith marked the season of Wakwa's birth. Invisible in the white-hot sun, his bark canoe sat the water of Long Pond. He and Elizabeth kept silence in still waters that glowed like the element of Mercury. They could not see beyond the sun's eye what lay outside in the green wood, what lay waiting. They rested in perfect silence shielded by the glare, embraced by bright blindness. The metallic tongues of the pond water gave no information beyond their own music.

Silver took on importance at the height of that same summer. Piles of silver coins like gamblers' chips stood on kitchen tables, were counted hopelessly against the demands of the King's treasury and, as furtively as moonlight, were returned to the till. The silver waters of Twisting River flowed through the new Dowland textile mill to the sea. At the ocean's edge, silver was sand. Silver marked the normal passage of time; human coloration, even the northeastern seasons gave way to it. Silver's cool shine illuminated the temporal and the eternal. In the serene Sippicon summer one would never guess that anywhere there was fighting to bloody red death over hopes the Massachuseuck had ceased to entertain for a century. Their belief in the Earth never changed. Causes changed. As did the silver standard.

Will Cooper, the tithing man, dusty from his rounds on foot, shambled up the Worths' gravel coach lane and onto their front path. Here, he observed, were the flowers of the rich in riot - Chinese roses, pink spilling over white, violet, red, trembling upright in the afternoon breeze, leaping low stone walls and trailing the lawns like princesses' gowns. Not that he had ever seen a princess's gown but Cooper was not wholly without imagination. Everyday, Sweet Williams did him down his own path. Those and a tuft or two of blue Canterbury bells under the apple tree. Nasturtiums stood the wife for bright color over the dull earth and for salads. That and a fish he might catch in a moment stolen from the business of the village was good enough for him. Nothing like this foam of regal vanities at Worth Farm: roses spread shamelessly to the sun, foxglove swaying behind boxwood, lilies throwing scent enough to provoke a man's privates without his permission or desire.

The message of Hanna's flowers prompted Cooper into action. Cooper knocked. Zenobia opened the top portion of the door. She listened to the official's request to talk to her master and, leaving the top half of the door ajar, let him fry on the stone step.

Cooper called after her, "Miss Brown Betty, if I wasn't on official business, I'd've gone round the back and Cooke would've given me of brown betty worth the eatin'!"

Matthew Freeman answered the summons.

At the sight of Worth's black houseman, Cooper's store of ill-will sprang open. "Could I talk to someone not an African?"

Matthew knew the man, knew his moods, knew his inconsistency and his habit concerning the bottle. "Sir, depending on your business, there is a long list of people not African to speak to on this farm."

"Oh, I see. Your master is lightin' out the back while you detain me with cheeky conversation in the front of the house."

"This, sir, is not a conversation."

Cooper put his hand on the inward side of the door's closed lower portion to hasten his entry.

"Kindly state your business." From the freedman.

But Worth, disturbed at his harp-practice by the long contest in the hallway called out, "Is that you, Coop? Come in but take off your shoes. They've just spanked the rugs."

Matthew commandeered the door latch. Cooper sighed and complained of the difficulty of getting his shoes on again over swollen feet but unlaced his thick, clout-studded brogues. Matthew took them from him through the open section. "I will clean these."

"High and mighty!"

Matthew seized victory with, "And drive you home in the cart."

Cooper squared his shoulders, preened his hempen-cloth suit, and strutted in in his darned hose. "I won't sit, Mr. Worth."

Gil, still behind his harp, grinned, "Shall you drink your lemonade standing?"

"Well, that does sound good."

"Standing or drinking?"

"Mr. Worth! I'm here on serious business."

Gil rang for Cooke, rose, shook Cooper's hand. He ordered refreshments and complimented the tither. "No one can say, Cooper, that you take your duties lightly. The other night when we ran our newly appointed stamp agent out of his rooms and up the Plymouth road, one might have thought he was a stray hog for all the mercy you showed him. Manfully done, Coop!"

A troubled smile pushed at Cooper's mouth but he mastered it. "I'm not long for this job."

"You are weary, Cooper."

"That I am."

Worth disliked the work of talking to Cooper because the tither's narrative game led unfailingly to prosaic ends. "Will you retire?"

"I will sit."

Worth laughed and indicated the settee.

"I hope I won't damage your dainty furniture."

"As does Zenobia. Here, put the shawl under you if it will make you easy."

The lemonade was produced, Zenobia glowering and showing the tither her back. Worth took note.

"You mentioned our preying on the stamp-man the other night."

"Indeed." Worth tried to follow the vacuous labyrinth of the man's mind. "There have been several such nights. I expect more. We back the same cause." Then carefully, Worth added, "Loyal subjects of the Crown, nonetheless, if not of its every policy."

"Now we're gettin' somewhere."

"Oh, Cooper, you may think so." Worth was lost.

"That business of loyalty to His Highness." A clear chard of ice dove out of Cooper's glass and struck the edge of the settee like a knife.

Worth watched the little pool it formed on the rug.

"It was voted last night at the Sons o' Liberty meetin' you did not attend, that I run you in for questioning on the topic of the soldiers quartering at Dowland House."

"Run me...? You are drunk aren't you?"

"I told you I hate this job. I don't care about the stipend anymore. I've got two cows and a patch of ground. I'll survive without the extra money and the aggravation."

"Well, if you're going to quit, quit before you do anything foolish! Surely I saved Sweetwood from riot by gaining the protection of a company of Gage's army, headed, I might add, by a very intelligent and brave and, what's more, sympathetic officer known to the village from the age of six."

"Seven."

"Seven what?'

"Seven years, beggin' your pardon, sir."

"A little punctilious in this heat, aren't we?"

"I tell you it's the Sons o' Liberty! The law reads only so far as the quartering must be done in fit buildings for a barracks."

"We've had this discussion! You agreed to Dowland House, as it is only a few miles from Wareham. And you agreed to Lady Augusta's staying on."

"You intimidated me into that decision and that makes a problem for you, and I'm that sorry over a mess I've helped to cause. It appears to the meetin' you've got *houseguests* for which the village's footin' the bill."

"What a joke!" Worth seethed. "They're sticklers on the law when it's convenient to their purses! I feed the damn army. I send them their grog from my cellar. I haven't seen a penny from Sweetwood, although they were good enough to vote some money for provisions. Their hearts are in the right place but I'm feeling the pinch! What will they do when the law changes for the worse, which it surely will and soon, and more British soldiers come and live in their attics? It costs money to feed a company by day and support one's penchant for dissent by night. I'm not a bottomless pit and there are serious times ahead. Any fool can plainly see that. I'm even willing to pay with my life, but I will not be kicked in the chin for doing the dirty work of Sweetwood's village fathers!"

"Well, Mr. Worth, sir, you've stated the problem exactly. It's some, not all, but some Sweetwooders who feel hung out to dry. They're wondering what your generosity with your silver's gonta get them. What with an English lady, the wife of the major livin' at Dowland House, and blue blood on your side, and sirs and lords and Injuns flyin' all over the place, the village wonders if you would be asked to pay with your life for your acts against the present King or would it be just them poor lot swingin' in the orchard?"

Worth sat dumb.

"In like manner," Cooper reached for eloquence, "there might be no need for quartering soldiers at all if Wareham weren't rioting on account of a member, excuse the expression, of your family."

Gil's lashes flicked with his agitation. "That collection of simps in the undercroft talk of members to me!"

"Now, sir! Careful of your speech. Of the tenor of your speech...."

"My family *member* as you call Thomas Kirke, one of the greatest merchants the world has known and, not incidentally, a benefactor of this community, was gunned down sang froid above decks by a revenue cutter's captain, an agent of the King's! The crime is against us all! For if you can cut down the wheat of this world without reprisal, it would be child's play to cut down the chaff!"

Cooper sighed. "You're very convincing. That's why you're to come with me to answer to the meeting."

"Not under duress!"

Hanna's wide gown of lawn filled the doorway with light. "What's all the fuss? Hello, Mr. Cooper! Oh good, I see you've gotten your lemonade. What meeting?"

Cooper tilted his rear off the seat in respect but shrank back down. "Will you tell her, sir?"

"I? I know I have the member but you have the stipend, Will Cooper. You give it a try!"

Cooper struggled, then he drained his glass. He chewed the delicious ice.

"Very well." Gil faced Hanna. "Sweetwood think I'm a traitor to the cause."

Hanna looked confused.

"They think I'm protecting myself not them. They can't imagine my spending my own money on the troops for their benefit. The little misers!"

"It is for *all* our benefit." Hanna pronounced the obvious.

Cooper stood, perspiring as if his cool drink had had an ill effect. "Ma'am. I'm here to arrest your husband for suspicious activities against the security of the village in times of...a dangerous time."

"ARREST him?!"

"Ma'am I shouldn't be troublin' your graceful, womanly self with such things but there is in the quartering question implications as to a coziness with the Crown just when we Liberty Boys's fightin' to repeal the Stamp Tax. It is also rumored Mr. Worth holds the late Sir Thomas' contraband in his cellar. Guns and money. Chests and chests of it. The Indian dove for it and the Sons think it was transported here with the machine parts."

Tendrils of Hanna's coif shook.

Cooper looked helplessly into her pretty face. "They're sure you're hoarding silver. They say you Worths' got a stockpile and you'll be fine when the Stamp Act descends on 'em 1 November and they'll be in the poor house and lose their farms for they've got a little paper money is all and are used to barter and Dowland Mills is just up and runnin' and ain't turned a profit yet."

Hanna's laugh jingled like bells of precious metal. Her look settled sweetly on Gil. "Mr. Cooper, you've found me out."

Gil was more confused by his wife than by the tithing man. He cautioned, "Hanna. I think Cooper's serious."

"As am I."

Both men stared at her.

"But there is no Kirke silver in the cellar." She demurred to say there was gold. "Yet, I have been naughty. I have not told my husband a certain secret."

Cooper scrambled his hair as if trying to card his brains. "Say no more! I think I should not hear this."

"I think I should!" Gil said in mock outrage, delighted with Hanna's inventiveness.

"Well then, I confess."

"Careful, Goodwife." Worth watched Cooper.

"Goody Worth, I came here over matters, over men's business, over contraband...."

Hanna threw back her shoulders necessarily emphasizing her bosom not much veiled in the summer heat. "Would you like to come to the cellar to see it Mr. Cooper?"

Dry-mouthed as if he had never heard of lemonade in July, Cooper asked, "See what?"

"The Sherry. I have a stock of Spanish Sherry."

Cooper looked at her as if she were an apparition from a better world. "Is that all? Sherry? Sherry?"

"Sherry. I suppose I should be ashamed."

"My dear!" Worth tried to temper the conceit she was weaving. "There is nothing to be ashamed of."

"You do not drink it, do you?" Cooper sounded official.

"Mr. Cooper! Really. I am a Dowland. Before the boycott, the odd glass for medicinal purposes. Nothing more."

"And yet you stock in your cellar smuggled Sherry?"

"Of course not! 'Twas bought legally and stored before the boycott. But I should have broken the bottles!"

Cooper shook a finger at her in panic at the mere idea.

"Mr. Cooper, would you like to...view it?"

Worth ticked his tongue warning her against taking too flagrant liberties with a lesser mind.

Hanna pressed. "Shall we do it now? My husband need never see a thing of it. You and I could go down there together...just we two...."

"Oh, God!" Cooper flushed as red as wine.

Gil twitted him, "Honestly, Coop, blasphemy in the house in front of a lady!"

"We could break every last bottle if it would make it better."

Cooper's composure reinstated itself. "Spanish Sherry?"

"An Oloroso." Hanna sent him a smile as closed as a rosebud.

Worth made his way to the fireplace and reached for his gun. "You are ever the frugal wife, my dear. How nice in you to save the wine for better times." Worth prepared the fowling piece to fire. An operation of eight seconds, rivetted the tither's attention. When Worth rammed the cartridge home and returned the rammer to position he was quite sure Cooper had his message.

Hanna delivered one of her own. "Shall I go with you then, Mr. Cooper, to the meeting to explain? Shall we have the Liberty council here to obtain satisfaction?"

Gil took playful aim at Cooper's frontal anatomy.

Cooper gasped, "No! That is, I'll take your word. What use in having your nice, clean house all tracked up over nothing?"

"Then we'll forget the whole thing. I'm going to put your name on one of the cases for after the boycott and when all the trouble with dear King George is over. Now stay for tea."

Cooper, studying Gilbert with his gun, snapped alert at this last invitation. "Tea? Another luxury?"

"Peppermint tea."

Cooper breathed relief. "I don't know, Ma'am. I do not know. When the villagers get a hold of this here it'll open a tin of worms...."

"Why not say, a Pandora's box?" Worth recoiled at the tither's imagery.

"They've been doin' without and trustin' you both...."

"Not much." Worth interjected. "This interview is ended." Worth cocked his rifle.

Hanna said, "Hush, dear! Mr. Cooper, they are angry. And when we are angry we need to strike out at the nearest annoyance. Arrest *me*. Immediately. For the crates of Sherry. And then the villagers can feel better about life and go about their business which I believe is farming," her geniality went dark and strict, "when they are not terrorizing agents of the King."

Worth was robbed of breath.

Cooper was swept by the boldness of her design. "Steal their thunder as it were! They come to me and say, 'Coop! Do something about them Worths!' and I say, 'Mr. Worth may be an ornery blood but no one can say he's not generous nor not partakin' wholehearted in the activities of the Sons o' Liberty. As much as it rankles to take his jibin', the man'll never let ye down, ye need somethin' big or small. He may be rich but he's careful with his spendin', savin' always for when you and I crawl up his path hat in hand!"

"Is this whole drama an elaborate request for a loan, Cooper?" Gil queried.

With a proud sniff, Cooper trained his mind on the subject at hand. "To go on, sir and madam, pardon for the divulgation...."

"Divulgation!" Worth was blown back by Will Cooper's wealth of words.

"To go on..." Cooper sent Gil a sour look, "I'll say to them, Mrs. Worth is in custody, sirs. And look you do not get discovered in the same offense as hers. She's in jail for a night to pay for a secret store of ante-boycott Sherry which I have seen with my own eyes, dust-covered bottles by the crate," the thither lingered over the vision of one crate with his name scrawled on it in that dust, "in the cellar. And no silver! By my office!"

Matthew Freeman drove the cart empty from the jail, which was actually in the cellar of the tavern. He had left his master and mistress in the dank dirt room which stank of humus and tubers and kegs and sweat and human waste, for although prisoners were let upstairs at their leisure to use the outhouse and a chamber pot for the nights, fright and the overriding effects of too much ale or rum risked accidents and upheavals. The prisoners themselves were compelled to scrub after their own messes but their methods were imperfect.

The cart, driven at unnatural speed, clattered through the neighborhood, causing Ho to raise his voice to Moses in the Dowland kitchen.

"September! My resignation's to be in General Gage's hands by September for my decommissioning in the tenth month. Marking exactly one year of service. An honorable discharge before the first of November will suit me fine. And, surely, I'll get one." Ho slapped his left leg and pounded his stick on the floor. "Gage surely won't commission me to fight Pontiac, my being permanently injured in the line of duty. Surely not."

"Then what will you do?"

Ho sued for time with, "Take the other side of the street. As it were." Air passed through Ho's teeth. "With what I know of how these red-coated chaps go about things, I could be very helpful in any effort against the blows coming America's way. Father says the assemblies will be disbanded. He'll be out of a job, for the courts won't hear cases till the Tax is lifted. And there'll be reprisals, do not doubt it!"

"But what will you do? To feed yourself. You haven't any money I know about."

Slightly offended, Ho said proudly, "I have a small allowance now father's a bigwig. And I might get a pension."

"And you have a duke's daughter for a wife." Moses glanced at the ceiling as if seeing Augusta where she lay napping in Elizabeth's old room.

Ho flushed. It made him handsome.

"Having any woman for a wife means you must have more than a small allowance and a possible pittance of a pension. I doubt you or your lady would be content for long if you must rely for your living on her trust monies."

The friends stayed quiet with the problem.

Moses added, "That may be why it is called a trust." He cuffed Ho's arm.

The clattering stopped outside.

"Isn't there anything you want to do?" Moses dropped his voice in the sudden quiet.

"I might take up manufacturing surgery furniture with your uncle."

Moses made no sense of this ambition.

Then with much hesitation, Ho whispered, "I've been wanting to talk you about something."

Moses guessed, "You want to live *here*? Keep on at Dowland House?"

Ho reached for Moses' wrist and held it hard. "More! I want to do it good. I want to farm it. Develop it. Like your grandfather used to do! Till you get it, of course. Then could we husband it together!"

Moses spun away from his guileless friend. "The two of us? And Augusta? And if you haven't noticed, my half-brother is farming it just fine without us. Shall we move him off? Or move him in?"

Ho looked down. "It was just an idea. My best idea. The fixed idea I've had since I was a kid." He stroked the old pine table tenderly. "With my one good leg and Coney's one good arm we'd make two good farmers!"

Moses laughed with his friend. "Beckett, you would do better to emulate my Uncle Gil. You would make a gentleman farmer quite easily. I do not see you behind a plow. You might also do quite well as an ambassador."

"For what country?"

"Hmnn. We'll think of something."

While Ho and Moses chatted, Lightfoot watched Matthew fighting the hill. He spurred his horse to the houseman's side. He listened to Freeman's tale of events in the village. Lightfoot rode toward the soldier-riddled house to discreetly call out his brother and Horace Beckett.

Ho limped through the door, strapping on his sword; Moses carried Ho's walking stick. Augusta woke at the slight commotion. She reached for her parasol and slipped outside.

In the pine grove where his grandfather had died in Awepu's arms, Moses argued, "There is no statute, law, policy, or decree which states that a person cannot stock wine in her basement! In fact, the locals' non-importation is the act of rebellion. For which they could be jailed. Cooper's action is civil disorder in the extreme!"

"You talk like my father." Ho complained. With military practicality, he explained. "Ani wants it this way. Don't you see? She's successfully kept the hoi ploi away from the gold stores...."

"They're in a sub-cellar of the hospital. I doubt they could be found. Anyway, they'll be out of there any day! Stephen Poore and that Venetian banker are in New York and making ready!"

Matthew Freeman despaired of these boys. "Shall we not tell the Sachim?"

Moses' face twisted. "He might have an idea, but what can he do? They've put Hanna Dowland Worth in jail for a night but they'll *hang* him! All my uncle and aunt need now is a bunch of Indians swooping down on the jail with hatchets high and we've got the riot the quartering was to prevent! Ho will have to kill my father!"

Ho chaffed, "That is not the only problem! I'm an Englishman with the King's men behind me and I can't dig Ani out of jail without causing irreparable harm to her political reputation and my own, even if there came no riot!"

Her unwigged hair a little frowzy from sleep, her speech slightly slurred, Augusta traced events. "I see. Hanna has moved the Town's Eye, as that Cooper-person is called, away from her cellar to the terrible jail." A light laugh rose out of her. "A Dowland in jail!"

"A joke?" Moses reprimanded.

"A disgrace!" Ho looked sullenly toward the village.

"A distraction." Augusta countermanded. "Brilliant!" She sharpened. "A stratagem. The gold is soon to be moved. Mr. Poore and Signor Falier have prepared the vault in New York. Horace, don't you see? Your soldiers are lying idle all over the sitting room floor spoiling for tea. Put them to work! Have them carry the gold out and transport it to New York. What if it takes till September? You can put your resignation in General Gage's hands in person!"

Horace buttoned the throat of his tunic, saying nothing.

Moses murmured, "Do nothing till we talk to Father."

Ho seemed not to hear him. "The gold must be gotten out, now. But the modus operandus...."

Moses and Augusta contested in whispers about the ways and means.

Ho retrieved his stick from Moses and stood firmly. "Under the guise of keeping the peace, I will protect the Worths with my life and the lives of my men. British soldiers will be set about the jail and about Sweetwood. Rifles cocked. I will cordon off Worth Farm, Dowland Farm, and the manse, straight across the road! Every eye will be trained on us and to south, away from Worth Farm. But the Sachim and his men...."

"Beck! No dirt clods for you! You have political genius!" Moses wrested the theme from him. "Lightfoot! Find Father and Sequan. They must somehow take the gold tonight on the river to Dire Locke." Moses' tongue passed over his very white teeth, "*That* the Sachim can do. His silent work. With the help of Sequan's well-trained warriors."

Augusta said blandly, "Two armies. Better than one."

Moses bowed to her, as he would have if he had been dressed in high style, the plume of his phantom hat trailing through the pine needles.

"Hill!" Ho clipped the gesture to ask, "What'll your job be?"

Moses answered benignly, "I...have legal stuff to attend to."

Ho marched away with the benefit of his stick to give orders to his men.

Matthew caught a look too long between Moses and the young Mrs. Beckett.

Gil saw Hanna from the top of the steep wooden staircase. She lay facing the wall on her side on a palette fit only, he thought, for wretches like monks or felons. He edged his way down not to disturb her, sorry that her sheer summer gown was unavoidably touching the odd stuff of underground storerooms, shavings of no particular color, dun piles of soft matter, lumps of what seemed like soil but were probably not and which rolled away from the broom. Hanna had rejected the jailer's moth-eaten blanket. Gilbert saw her shiver.

From the second step to the bottom, he sent his sonorous voice her way. "If Cecil could see you now he would rightfully say I am an ass. That America is an ass. That we should take the next ship for West Sussex and end this experiment."

Hanna half-turned and held out an arm to him.

Gratefully, he fled to her. "Good thing we are not of fulsome habit."

"Oh, Gil. I could be less so." She stroked his shaven cheek. "I cause you much trouble."

"No!"

"I apologize. Remember, if I die."

"Die! One night in this hotel will simply make us appreciate our own bed. You shall not die!" He placed the Jaeger with its silver fleur-de-lis between her and the wall so that he could wrap her in his arms yet retain a grasp on the rifle's trigger. "Your greatest threat here is being kept awake by a choir of mice."

The door above slammed open and red light from the setting sun glared down the stairs. "Now, Mr. Worth, they told me you pushed past the guard. That's not fair! It doesn't count if you're here."

"Does it not!"

The door creaked closed then opened quickly again. "Nothin' lewd down there. No touchin' the prisoner."

Gil's chin lowered to his chest and then it rose. "I will, Mr. Cooper, behave as a good husband to his wife. And if that means shooting your balls off, I shall!"

When they were again at peace, Gil whispered, "I am sorry. These circumstances make us profane."

"Gil! You are always profane. And so I love you."

The Jaeger was forgotten. Gil made himself her cover. Kept her warm. "Breathe near my neckcloth. There's cologne on it."

Their skin touched only hand to hand, forehead to throat. They listened in their entombment to the blood flow in the other, heard the heart of the other beating the same martial music. Hanna's growling stomach sounded like a beast in the dark.

The summer night was cool and underground, cold. They convulsed and woke out of exhausted sleep. Staccato footsteps above and an occasional shout seemed the residue of slumber.

"The world is passing us by overhead." Hanna spoke.

"They cannot do without us." Worth responded. "Without people like us. Remember that!"

CHAPTER SIXTY-FIVE

July 1765

Half a moon and a sky full of stars shyly lit their way. The mishoonash, the word for canoe a whisper, lead the travellers to think that such graceful boats had first been launched at midnight. By means of cedar slings secured around their chests and their foreheads, the Massachuseuck, men and women, toted the dead weight of gold bars up the grueling grade of the sub-cellar's tunnel making egress beyond the tree line.

Each canoe weighed half what a woman weighs; each one was capable of carrying a thousand pounds. Two crates of gold bars, four paddlers, male and female, two abreast in the beam, one fore, one aft, made full burden. Only the very old and the very young were left in the otan.

It took nerve to glide down the dark water without a word, to pass successfully through narrows, feeling the aggressions of the foliage lining the bank. The skin trembled constantly from the kiss of insects. The woods at the river's edge palpitated with the distress of waterfowl wakened by the fleet of many canoes and by branches bent back by the shadow-guard on foot. The relentless voice of sylvan night deadened the ear to actual threats.

⌒♏︎⌒

Dire Locke passed to and fro in his lamp-lit rooms above the warehouse at the wharf. The rude wood walls showed as amber when viewed from Wareham's beach. Locke's slender figure cast a gargantuan image of black against the glow. His silhouette bent and disappeared, then stretched up the wall again, overlapping the ceiling.

A small stone chittered down the thin window-glass, struck the sill and bounced onto the floor. Locke stopped work abruptly. His heart pumped. He picked up the stone, turned it over in his hand then stuck it in his breeches pocket. He leaned far out to see what he could see.

He spied them on the sand, two tall men and a slight woman of elegant posture. Their clothes played the night wind. Dire had desired such a vision for so long that only the smooth stone in his coin-pocket convinced him that it was real. The black water was spotted with fifty canoes low with cargo. It hurt Dire to break the spell with a wave but he did and left the window to allay any misgivings of the night watchman.

⌒♏︎⌒

Elizabeth and Moses crossed the field from Dowland House to Worth Farm in the fury of noon heat on the next-to-last day of July. From under their broad straw hats they witnessed twelve-year-old Annie Beth Stirling carrying a tray firmly toward Lightfoot, who was mounted and trotting to her. The girl's white garb brushing the hissing grass caused Elizabeth to smile.

"I used to carry my father's lunch to him just that way."

Moses shaded his eyes against the glare. "I doubt it was *just* that way. From what I observe, my father's sons are doing not much for the purity of the race."

Elizabeth's full laughter caught and hung on the humid air. "Your father did not do much for it either!"

Moses seized her hand without thought or hesitation.

They progressed toward Worth Farm, Moses releasing Elizabeth to change from his right hand to his left, a square of parchment sealed in blue.

"Nokace. Shall you explain this to Uncle Gil? Should I?"

She struggled with her answer. "It may take both of us."

Without disturbing him, they passed Matthew Freeman nodding on the meadow as he always did at this time of day in this season of the year.

Matthew heard Elizabeth's thin shoes pressing the unmown grass. Making slits of his eyes he watched her as he had watched her escape into the woods nearly nineteen years before. Through the narrow aperture, Elizabeth Dowland, older, looked the same. She moved the same. He closed his eyes, enjoying his steeping in the steaming field, assured that she was, at core, the same. Like the ground he lay on, or the four seasons which rode above it, she did not change her habit: it was her habit that changed the rest of them. He grabbed at light sleep, sensing interruption soon.

They slipped unannounced into the Worth's sitting room through the tall doors open onto the west lawn. By Hanna's familiar salute, Gil knew who was there, although, working over his harp, he faced the front hall away from them.

Not stopping his fingerwork, he received Elizabeth's kiss on his cheek and Moses' tribute on his shoulders. "There is something awful creeping into the folk tunes of our locale. I make bold to say I do not like the direction of the popular melodies nor," he finished with a daring glissando, "will I play the French music. I detect a self-righteous strain in the one and a subjugated strain in the other. Why will the Americans strut so, when they have, as yet, so little to strut about? And why will not the French unchain their notes! It seems they are forever dressing for a dinner party they do not wish to attend." Gil fanned himself with his sheet music. "I sense it is going to be a long while till we strike a true cord."

Moses shared a cogent look with Elizabeth.

Hanna rang a crystal bell. "Beth! What drove you both out under such a sun! Sit!" Hanna called her niece away from the hot south window.

Worth noted that she had taken up the position Wakwa and Dire Locke usually occupied in the room. "Are we to expect the Sachim? I could use a voice of reason just now."

Elizabeth sat at Gil's feet on the needlepoint stool, her old place. Moses cleared his throat and perused the spines of the volumes on Worth's bookshelves his absorption so similar to Pequawus' whenever the elder man was in the room.

They all gratefully received their lemonade from Cooke.

Elizabeth drank deeply. "I've good news, Cooke! Someone's coming to give you a holiday."

Cooke looked from her mistress to her master. "My lemon water is not good enough? I am being replaced?"

Gil tried to speak with a mouthful. He could only choke.

Hanna leaped to reassure, "Don't say that! You know we couldn't live without you!" Then sharply, "Beth?"

Elizabeth explained, laughing lightly, "It is only that Asunta, my cook from Venice is in New York with Stephen Poore. They'll visit!" Elizabeth slipped an arm around Cooke's waist. "You could put your feet up and let someone else produce a meal."

"Not in my kitchen! Dearie, I am sure that woman has never heard of butter nor of onions!" Cooke puffed her apron-bow and made her exit.

Worth sipped his drink more cautiously, eyeing mother and son.

Moses came for his glass, throwing out casually, "We watched Annie Beth bring my brother his lunch. I give that situation three years at best. Want to lay the odds as to the date?"

Gil spewed his drink again. "Damn! There will be sugar all over the rug!"

Hanna's dimples showed, as they had not done for a long while. "I thought I'd noticed some hero-worship. And not discouraged."

Worth said, "Devil time! Am I to understand that Lightfoot will be approaching Israel Stirling soon for the right to court his daughter as once Israel Stirling approached me on Priscilla's account!"

Moses let the question settle.

Gil set his drink firmly down. "I am right in trusting Lightfoot's sobriety and patience?"

"Rabbits move quickly, Uncle! Not patiently."

"What!"

"Lightfoot moves swiftly but wisely." Moses nudged Gil toward good spirits. "As does the Wolf."

Gil rolled down his flowing shirtsleeves. He walked to the window bowed into the gentle vista. Not turning, he enquired, "Does that mean you're engaged, too?"

Elizabeth covered her eyes.

Moses' face darkened, then snatched at opportunity. "In my way!"

Gil turned his back to the green grass. "Let me hear this!"

Moses stood and faced him. "You and my mother slipped the ring on my finger when I was just a pup. This is a family knows all there is to know about arranged marriages...!"

"Careful, nephew!" Gil's look took in Elizabeth.

Elizabeth stood holding her heart.

Hanna interjected, "This abominable heat!"

Moses paced, "Any wife of mine will have to understand that she is really my mistress and the land my wife. As it was, and is, and always will be with Father and, I might add with you!"

"Funny! I've always been accused of romancing music."

Moses let that pass. He lunged at the truth. "My blood is thick with four thousand acres of Massachusetts soil. Not to mention my father's territory! My father! Think what he is! Then think what he is to the English now their war is over. I'll be damned to hell before I gamble one hand's-breadth of Charles Dowland's land on any current appreciation of my legitimacy! Granted the conveyance was more soundly conceived than I was...."

Elizabeth took the blow.

Gil enquired what Moses might be talking about.

Moses showed the parchment square but retained it. "The Throne has, with the infernal Stamp Tax, just blown apart a subject's right to trial by jury! A right in existence since the dawn of England's legal life!"

"Going to school has worried you overmuch." Worth tried to mollify.

"Overmuch! If the Throne can overturn the English legal system over a few farthings spent in a war my father won for them, how difficult will it be for them to overturn a conveyance of land granted on the witness of a man called *Awepu* most would ridicule as a savage!"

The adults stood stunned.

Drenched, as if his pores had released a lifetime of fear, Moses threw aside his linen coat. He stopped close to Gil. "I do not think these things because I am half red! White men of the South and of these parts are writing tracts and speaking in public against the Stamp Tax, not because it will break their purses or bury them in paper, or because they have no representative in the Parliament! *Their argument with the Tax is that the Parliament has no right to tax them at all!*"

"What do you mean?" Gil's thin cheeks went scarlet from excitement.

"They say English settlers cannot be taxed by the English government, because red men had original possession of this Continent and the English King did not! Because English settlers bought lands from the original possessors or stripped lands away from those original possessors. Because the King's jurisdiction over those English settlers extended just so far as chartering them to govern themselves, and through those engagements secured to them the freedoms and other benefits of the British Constitution. I ask you, Uncle Gil, if the settlers of this country are taxed by any authority other than their own representatives, whom they themselves have chosen to run their own governments, how can the Royal promises to me be fulfilled? The Stamp Tax being levied by the Parliament, all the charters granted by the Crown become a sham and the Crown dishonored!"

Gil spoke over him, "Then rest easy!"

"Uncle, when the Sons of Liberty get hold of that, the conveyance is defunct! English law, English estate law, entail itself will be wiped away like beads of sweat! I am named He-hopes. I have hopes. I hope that all will be well. That somehow in my lifetime I will be considered the son of two rational and worthy human beings. Two people whose ancestors possessed the land and the rights to the land and the right to dispose of it according to their lights. But hope is not enough when it comes to risking thousands of acres of fertile farmland to the predations of a mad King and his fawning counsellors who impress me as not *so* stupid as to let fat parcels of land slip back into the stewardship of my father's People, a People eternally opposed to the designs of the English upon it." His stopping to pull in air made no cause for any of them to interrupt.

Low voiced, dark of brow, Moses interrupted himself. "Among these counsellors, Whig though he may be, is William Brite Lord Leed whose daughter already lives at Dowland House and loves it. The house and land could, in these volatile times, with very little maneuvering fall to that family without a penny paid, and a golf links where the corn now grows."

Gilbert Worth's eyes saw less of the room where he was than the spectre raised by the eighteen-year-old.

Moses reached for Gilbert's able hands. "I, as your heir, as Charles Dowland's heir, as the son of my father, and the hope of my mother, ask you, beg you, to execute the lease agreement I have drawn myself and will have Michael Beckett review and certify, passing Dowland House and the land to Horace."

Silence walloped them until Gil mused, "The thing amiss with music today that I hear is a lack of emotion. Even in counterpoint, especially so, the heart is reached! How shall we go forward?"

Hanna shrank against her chair. Her voice wobbling as if she were underwater, she said, "You do not know what you are doing to him!"

Moses turned to his blood-aunt. "I know. Everybody has figured it out but Ho."

Her handkerchief slid up to hide her face.

Worth spoke. "You cannot do this thing. Look at Hanna! She sacrificed...so much...for you!"

"I know!" Moses soothed his own face, his hands passing and passing over his mouth.

Gil allowed Elizabeth to guide him to the settee and take him in her arms.

Moses persisted, "I have squirmed my whole life under the fear that all your effort, all the agony, all the litigation, all your expense of money and soul were for nothing!"

"The land is yours! Beckett has seen to it!"

"Uncle Gil! All the elegance of his brief notwithstanding, Michael Beckett does not control revolution!"

Like soldiers strewn on a battlefield, Gil and Hanna and Elizabeth waited for cannon.

"I cannot own land."

"What are you talking about?" Worth stood him off.

"The right to land, to own land, is over for Indians. At least for an indeterminate time. I cannot own land."

Gil separated himself from Elizabeth. "The boy is raving. Why don't you do something?"

Elizabeth looked to Moses, her face radiant with pride and sorrow.

Moses drank directly from the pitcher and drained it. Speaking exclusively to Gilbert Worth, he said, "It cannot have escaped you!

In '63, Massachusetts Bay incorporated the Mashpee for their own protection as a self-governing town."

"What is wrong with that?"

"Nothing! Except of the five overseers, two must be Englishmen. How long before it is three and then complete outside control? The Mashpee are two-fifths of the way to being government wards! As things stand today, my white side can own land. Can inherit land. My red side may soon be prevented from doing so. I cannot sit idly by and let the land slip out from under us!"

"You are the legitimate heir male of Charles Dowland!"

"I will not deny half of who I am! There is the matter of my paternity. It's on the books! You paid dear to put it there!"

"Beckett saw to it!"

Moses strutted away.

"It was a great thing he did!"

"Was! It is no longer great. For you or me."

"What has his lordship done now?" Gil's face was frozen with contempt in advance of knowledge.

"Not he. The Americans."

Gil snapped alert. A cord in him was plucked as he might pluck a harp string. Turning on Moses, "They have no power. I should say *we*. I am counted among their number. Unlawful parties cannot countermand conveyances or obviate a man's rights!"

Very quietly Moses offered, "A *man's* rights. But an Indian's? A legal case is now being made that red men are not quite men. For if they were, what a sticky business when the Liberty Boys want to draw maps and battle lines and muster troops on Indian lands. The fight has begun, is beginning, and there will be no time or patience to negotiate or forge alliances with crafty, pipe-smoking sachimmaoug wrapped in moth-eaten trade blankets! In their way, the Americans are, with their blind efficiency, showing some consideration in moving native folk aside. Our numbers and variety make a complication too costly to resolve in the teeth of insurrection. And so 'though I am half white, my red half turns out to be problematical as to species and, therefore, that half will, I contend, be herded behind a fence like a farm animal and my white half with it!"

Worth was on his feet. "Beckett brought this news?"

Moses struck his benefactor down with the bludgeon of veracity. "My father has it from your minister, Mayhew Low."

Gil fell back into his chair.

"Think of the strongest treaty my father ever made!"

Gil rifled his memory.

Moses supplied the answer. "The alliance between the northern tribes and Kirke Company. The leasing of that island off the Maine and The Company's training the tribes to build ships. Survival! For both! A living! For both! And peace! And then in a hundred summers - a return of the island should the Indians desire it!"

"A hundred year lease? To Hawk Beckett? All shiny from a year at Oxford you have scribbled this concession on the back of an envelope?"

This provocation channelled Moses' passion and he said as coolly as a seasoned counsellor, "I wrote it with due deliberation while the gold was being carted from your cellars."

Set back, Gil asked hoarsely, "And what are you getting for a century of dispossession?"

"Ho has not much money." Moses informed but did not persuade. "I will not have his wealthy wife, the Duke's daughter, rent it. Not for a million pounds! Her kind do never let go!" Moses' eyes ignited for an instant. Then, "I asked Hawk Beckett for the coins in his pocket."

Gil erupted with a cry much like a woman's.

"Listen to the terms! First and foremost, the land cannot, can never be sold by the lessee, namely Horace, nor transferred to his wife's family. Second! Lightfoot manages the farm for his lifetime. Third, the harvest is shared with the Ninnuock in equal measure, crop by crop! And fourth, the lease must be renewed by me or by my heirs or my legal agent every ten years. Ten times can we take it back in the life of the lease!"

"A colossal presumption that yet unconceived Becketts will play a fair hand with you!"

Wickedly, Moses responded, "Horace Beckett must be trusted to accomplish something!"

"A noble plan. Fit for a king." Gil's eyes pierced Moses on emerald pikes. "And what of your own wife?"

For the first time Moses faltered. He took refuge in the window now. He expelled some air as if at a joke. "I must be about my father's business."

"Eh?" Gil grew keen.

"I shall read law with Mr. Beckett as a start."

"Lord Beckett..." Gil ground his teeth. "Always wanted that house."

"Not Lord, Uncle! He's thrown over the title for Ho's sake. New Jersey has closed down the courts in any wise. He will be solicitor for the merchant bank, so I shall live with him in New York."

"Winner takes all!" Worth seemed to be holding his skull together with the pressure of his hands.

"When I've passed the bar, I shall be taken into the bank. I'll be travelling far and wide to build its coffers. You know full well the cost of backing one's political ideas." Moses returned to Gil, and stood behind him, easing his shoulders with strong hands. "Good Uncle, the Sons of Liberty will come knocking and I will grant them loans." Moses looked far away across the fields and above the encroaching mist as if to his star. "Loans at no interest never to be repaid. It will be my work to cajole these means in excess from the very pockets of the King's men!" Moses appeared at peace with the wonder of a great circle closing.

Gil caught the largeness of Moses' dream. "And in this way you shall keep your debtors on the books!" Gil stood in place, commanding his room. "I see it! You are apprenticed not to Beckett but to Dire Locke! Will the bank be named after Kirke?"

"It's to be *Bluehill Merchant*." And Moses' tongue passed over the edge of his teeth.

As at a wake for the dead or a lying-in before a birth, the afternoon passed in murmurs. The merciful mist tumbled in off the Bay. In the cool that attended it, Gilbert Worth walked to his writing table and wrote his name on the lease with a steady hand. "I knew we'd lose it." Gil's eyes were ringed red like a cuckoo's. "Just not while I was alive."

Moses insisted, "Not lost! Secured according to the times!"

Hanna stood. "Do excuse us. Dinner is at eight. Your uncle and I are going up to rest."

Elizabeth barred the door. "You mustn't do that!"

"What!" Gil and Hanna said together.

"You must pack your things. Wakwa is preparing for you to come to us."

"Oh?" Worth showed his wounds. "The Sachim shaking out the rugs and setting out the silver is he?"

Elizabeth's face switched with feeling. "He is waiting."

Worth said not unkindly, "That is his nature."

"That is his name." Slowly, Elizabeth smiled. "He waits."

They roused Matthew from his meadow and packed in a flurry for a long stay in the wilderness.

Finis

Author's Note

Some scientists of language may hold another opinion but I maintain that one can know a culture through its language. Use of the Narragansett language in *SIPPICON* and its two preceding companion novels, *THE MISTS OF MANITTOO* and *TORN COVENANTS*, (a language without an orthorgraphy but using English orthography credit Roger Williams, *A Key into the Language of America*, 1643, and James Hammond Trumbull, *Natick Dictionary*, 1903) works like a transfusion of blood into the veins of fact and imagination. In Roger Williams' phrase, "A little key may open a box, where lies a *bunch of keyes*." A language's building of syllables into expanded concepts is for the poet an infererence of thought patterns, of the appreciation of and response to circumstance, and a subtle illumination of a People's nerve center that inlays the historical facts of its tenure on Earth. To sound out the words is to hear a People breathe.

Glossary

All Native American words used in this book are of Algonquian stock, represented mainly in the Narragansett dialect. All spellings are taken from *A Key into the Language of America*, by Roger Williams, 1643, and *Natick Dictionary*, by James Hammond Trumbull, 1903, using English orthography, approximating actual Indian pronunciation. The asterisks mark proto-Algonquian words found in *Contributions to Anthropology, Linguistics I*, National Museum of Canada, Bulletn 214, Series No.78, Ottawa, 1967.

Abnaki. A nation or tribe native to Maine
abockquosinash. The mats that cover the house
Agiocochook. The White Mountains of New Hampshire
Algonkin. Algonquian. Natives and language of the Eastern woodlands
Annoosuonk. Hope, expectation of good
askug. A snake
atauskowauog. Lords, rulers
awepu. A calm

cowammaunsh. I love you
cowaw. A pine tree
Cautantowwit. The great Southwest God

Eatch keen anawayean. Your will shall be law

hawunshech. Farewell

Iroquois. The Native American Confederacy of Five then Six Nations
Indianne unnontoowaonk. The Native American language

juhetteke. Fight ye

*kayaskwa. The herring gull
kehtoh. The ocean, sea
kenoonuenuog. Counsellors
koowahush. I know thee

Manit. He who exceeds the normal; God
manittoo. Apprehension of excellency in any being; it is a god
Manittowock. Gods
manunnappu. He has himself, is in possession, remains quiet, sits patiently
Massachuseuck. A small nation or tribe of Massachusetts
matta. No, not
mehtugquash. Trees, woods
miawene. A court, a meeting
mishoonash. Boats
moce-nanippeeam. I will come bye and bye

mockussinchass. Shoes
Mohawk. A tribe of the Iroquois Confederacy
Mohican. A Native American nation or tribe east and west of the Hudson River
Mohicannituck. The Hudson River
mosq. The bear
Muckquashim-ouwan Noh-annoosu. Wolf-of-the-mist He-hopes

Narragansett. A nation or trbe native to Rhode Island
Nauset. A nation or tribe native to Cape Cod
natoncks. My cousin
neechippog. The dew
nickommo. A solemn feast
Ninnuock. The People; the natives of America
nippisse. Little water, a pond or pool
nissese. My uncle
noh pasoo. Bring him
nokace. My mother
noowahik. He (she) knows me
noowahteouum. I know
noowan-anumukquog. They forget me
nosh. My father
nunnaumon. My son.
nunnowa. Harvest time
nuppohwunau. He who hath wings

ohomous. The owl
okasu. A mother
otan. A town

Passamoquoddy. A nation or tribe native to Maine
pequawus. A gray fox
pesuponk. A sweat hut

qunneke. A doe

sachim. "He prevails, has mastery"; one who governs
sachimmaacommock. A prince's house
sachimmauog. Leaders, governors
sagamore. Governor
saunks. "She prevails, has mastery"; mistress, wife of the sachim
sequan. The spring
Sipppicon. Crescent of land curving around Buzzards Bay
soquttahhsh. Boiled kernels of corn
suckauhock. Black shell money
sucki. Black, dark colored, purple
summagunum-wunnutcheg. He holds out his hand
sunnamatta. Is it not?

tamoccon. A flood
taquonk. Fall-of-leaf, autumn
taubotneanawayean. I thank you
taubotne aunanamean. I thank you for your love
taupowaw. A wise speaker

waban. The wind
wadchau. Saviour
*wakwa. Fox
Wampanoag. A nation native to Massachusetts, east of
    Narragansett Bay

waututckques. The coney, rabbit
wenygh. Woman
wetomp. Dear friend
wetu. A house
wosketomp. A man
wushowunan. The hawk
wuttah mao. His heart weeps

Bibiographical Note

Following is a selection from the numerous works which helped to model the historical features of this tale:

A Key into the Language of America, Roger Williams, 1643, fifth edition, 1936.
Natick Dictionary, James Hammond Trumbull, 1903.
The Emancipation of Massachusetts, Brooks Adams. 1887, third edition, 1919.
History of American Costume, Elisabeth McClellan, 1904, fourth edition, 1969.
A History of Venice, John Julius Norwich, 1982.
Oxford, Felix Markham, 1967.
Who's the Savage?, ed. by David R. Wrone and Russell S. Nelson Jr., 1973.

CPSIA information can be obtained
at www.ICGtesting.com
Printed in the USA
BVHW032117060219
539678BV00001B/1/P